Evil for Evil

THE ENGINEER TRILOGY
Book Two

by K. J. Parker

www.orbitbooks.net

New York   London

Orbit
Hachette Book Group USA
237 Park Avenue, New York, NY 10017
Visit our Web site at www.HachetteBookGroupUSA.com

First American Edition, November 2007
First published in Great Britain by Little, Brown and Company, 2006

Orbit is a trademark of Little, Brown Book Group Ltd.

Library of Congress Cataloging-in-Publication Data

Parker, K. J.
  Evil for evil / K. J. Parker. — 1st ed.
    p. cm. — (The engineer trilogy ; bk. 2)
  ISBN-13: 978-0-316-00339-1
  ISBN-10: 0-316-00339-5
  I. Title.
  PR6116.A745E95 2007
  823'.92 — dc22   2007013107

10 9 8 7 6 5 4 3 2 1

Q-MART

Printed in the United States of America

He went back to the tower, changed out of his pretty clothes, and put on something comfortable. Another thing his father had always told him: *If you cheat, sooner or later you'll be punished for it.* That was no lie. Of course, to begin with they were just letters. It was only when he'd become dependent on them that the dishonesty began. It was perfectly simple. She was married—to Orsea, of all people, Duke of Eremia, his people's traditional enemy. But because he knew they could never be together, there could never be anything except letters between them, he'd carried on writing and reading them, until he'd reached the point where he was little more than a foreign correspondent reporting back on his own life to a readership living far away, in a country he could never go to.

And—of course—now she was here, never more than a hundred yards away from him, and he couldn't write to her anymore, let alone speak to her. He'd taken his country to war in order to rescue her, and thereby lost her forever.

He grinned. And Orsea thought *he* was stupid.

Praise for
K. J. Parker

"A richly textured and emotionally complex fantasy.... Highly recommended."

—*Library Journal* (starred review)

"When so many fantasy sagas are tired, warmed-over affairs, a writer like K. J. Parker is more of a hurricane than a breath of fresh air."

—*Dreamwatch*

By K. J. Parker

THE FENCER TRILOGY

Colours in the Steel

The Belly of the Bow

The Proof House

THE SCAVENGER TRILOGY

Shadow

Pattern

Memory

THE ENGINEER TRILOGY

Devices and Desires

Evil for Evil

The Escapement

People are all right as far as they go, but sometimes only places will do. This one's for Century and Stickledown, Langport, Whitestaunton and Middle Room: the pacifist's Valhalla.

Evil for Evil

1

"The way to a man's heart," Valens quoted, drawing the rapier from its scabbard, "is proverbially through his stomach, but if you want to get into his brain, I recommend the eye socket."

He moved his right arm into the third guard, concentrated for a moment on the small gold ring that hung by a thread from the center rafter of the stable, frowned and relaxed. Lifting the sword again, he tapped the ring gently on its side, setting it swinging like a pendulum. As it reached the upper limit of its swing and hung for a fraction of a second in the air, he moved fluently into the lunge. The tip of the rapier passed exactly through the middle of the ring without touching the sides. Valens grinned and stepped back. Not bad, he congratulated himself, after seven years of not practicing; and his poor ignorant student wasn't to know that he'd cheated.

"There you go," he said, handing Vaatzes the rapier. "Now you try."

Vaatzes wasn't to know it was cheating; but Valens knew. The exercise he'd just demonstrated wasn't the one he'd so grudgingly learned, in this same stable, as a boy of fifteen. The correct form was piercing the stationary ring, passing the sword through the middle without making it move. He'd never been able to get it right, for all the sullen effort he'd lavished on it, so he'd cheated by turning it into a moving target, and he was cheating again now.

The fact that he'd subverted the exercise by making it harder was beside the point.

"You made it look easy," Vaatzes said mildly. "It's not, is it?"

Valens smiled. "No," he said.

Vaatzes wrapped his hand around the sword-hilt, precisely as he'd been shown; a quick study, evidently. It had taken Valens a month to master the grip when he was learning. The difference was, he reflected, that Vaatzes wanted to learn. That, he realized, was what was so very strange about the Mezentine. He wanted to learn *everything*.

"Is that right?"

"More or less," Valens replied. "Go on."

Vaatzes lifted the rapier and tapped the ring to set it swinging. He watched as it swung backward and forward, then made his lunge. He only missed by a hair, and the ring tinkled as the sword-point grazed it on the outside.

"Not bad," Valens said. "And again."

Even closer this time; the point hit the edge of the ring, making it jump wildly on its thread. Vaatzes was scowling, though. "What'm I doing wrong?" he asked.

"Nothing, really. It's just a matter of practice," Valens replied. "Try again."

But Vaatzes didn't move; he was thinking. He looked stupid when he thought, like a peasant trying to do mental arithmetic. It was fortunate that Valens knew better than to go by appearances.

"Mind if I try something?" Vaatzes said.

Valens shrugged. "Go ahead."

Vaatzes stepped forward, reached up with his left hand and steadied the ring until it was completely motionless. He stepped back, slipped into third guard like a man putting on his favorite jacket, and lunged. The rapier-point passed exactly through the middle of the ring, which didn't move.

"Very good," Valens said.

"Yes." Vaatzes shrugged. "But it's not what you told me to do."

"No."

"I was thinking," Vaatzes said, "if I practice that for a bit, I can gradually work up to the moving target. Would that be all right?"

Valens had stopped smiling. "You do what you like," he said, "if you think it'd help."

For six days now it had rained; a heavy shower just before dawn, followed by weak sunshine mixed with drizzle, followed by a downpour at mid-morning and usually another at noon. No earthly point trying to fly the hawks in this weather, even though it was the start of the season, and Valens had spent all winter looking forward to it. Today was supposed to be a hunting day; he'd cleared his schedule for it weeks in advance, spent hours deciding which drives to work, considering the countless variables likely to affect the outcome — the wind direction, the falcons' fitness at the start of the season, the quality of the grass in the upland meadows, which would draw the hares up out of the newly mown valley. Carefully and logically, he'd worked through all the facts and possibilities and reached a decision; and it was raining. Bored and frustrated to the point of cold fury, Valens had remembered his offhand promise to the funny little Mezentine refugee who, for reasons Valens couldn't begin to fathom, seemed to want to learn how to fence.

"I think that's enough for today," Vaatzes said, laying the rapier carefully down on the bench, stopping it with his hands before it rolled off. "The meeting's in an hour, isn't it? I don't want to make you late."

Valens nodded. "Same time tomorrow," he said, "if it's still raining."

"Thank you," Vaatzes said. "It's very kind of you. Really, I never expected that you —"

Valens shrugged. "I offered," he said. "I don't say things unless I mean them." He yawned, and slid the rapier back into its scabbard. "See you at the meeting, then. You know where it is?"

Vaatzes grinned. "No," he said. "You did tell me, but . . ."

"I know," Valens said, "this place is a bugger to find your way around unless you've lived here twenty years. Just ask someone, they'll show you."

After Vaatzes had gone, Valens drew the rapier once again and studied the ring for a long time. Then he lunged, and the soft jangle it made as the sword grazed it made him wince. He caught it in his left hand, pulled gently until the thread snapped, and put it back on his finger. *All my life, he thought, I've cheated by making things harder. It's a habit I need to get out of, before I do some real damage.*

He glanced out of the window; still raining. He could see pockmarks of rain in the flat puddles in the stable yard, and slanting two-dimensional lines of motion made visible against the dark backdrop of the yard gate. He'd loved rain in late spring when he was a boy; partly because he'd loathed hunting when he was young and rain meant his father wouldn't force him to go out with the hounds or the hawks, partly because the smell of it was so clean and sweet. Now, seven years after his father's death, he was probably the most ardent and skillful huntsman in the world, but the smell of rain was still a wonderful thing, almost too beautiful to bear. He put on his coat and pulled the collar up round his ears.

From the stable yard to the side door of the long hall; hardly any distance at all, but he was soaked to the skin by the time he shut the door behind him, and the smell was now the rich, heavy stench of wet cloth. Well; it was his meeting so they'd have to wait for him. He climbed the narrow spiral staircase to the top of the middle tower.

Clothes. Not something that interested him particularly. Perhaps that explained why he was so good at them. Slipping off the wet coat, shirt and trousers, he swung open the chest and chose a dark blue brocade gown suitable for formal occasions. He took a minute or so to towel the worst of the damp out of his hair, couldn't be bothered to look in a mirror. One more glance through the window. Still raining. But he'd be dry, and everybody else at the meeting would be wet and uncomfortable, which would be to his advantage. That thought made him frown. Why was he allowing himself to think of his own advisers as the enemy?

He sighed. Today should have been a hunting day; or, if it was raining, it should've been a day for writing her a letter, or revising a first or second draft, or doing research for the reply to the next letter he received from her. But there weren't any letters anymore; she was here now, under the same roof as him, with her husband. On a whim he changed his shoes, substituting courtly long-toed poulaines for comfortable but sodden riding shoes. He hesitated, then looked in the mirror after all. It showed him a pale, thin young man expertly disguised as the Duke of the Vadani; a disguise so perfect, in fact, that only his father would've been able to see through it. Oh well, he thought, and went downstairs to face his loyal councillors.

As he ran down the stairs, he put words together in his mind; the question he'd have asked her in a letter, if they'd still been able to write letters to each other. Force of habit; but it was a habit he'd been dependent on for a very long time, until he'd reached the point where it was hard to think without it. *Suppose there was a conjuror, a professional sleight-of-hand artist, who hurt his wrist and couldn't do tricks anymore. Suppose he learned how to make things disappear and pull rabbits out of hats by using real magic. Would that be cheating?*

As he'd anticipated, the councillors were all wet, and acting ashamed, as though getting rained on was a wicked and deliberate act. They stood up as he came in. Even now, it still surprised him rather when people did that.

He gave them a moment or so to settle down, looking round to see if anybody was missing. They looked nervous, which he found faintly amusing. He counted to five under his breath.

"First," he said, "my apologies for dragging you all up here in this foul weather. I'll try not to keep you any longer than necessary. We all know what the issues are, and I dare say we've all got our own opinions about what we should do. However," he went on, shifting his weight onto both feet like a fencer taking up a middle guard, "I've already reached my decision; so, really, it's not a case of what we're going to do so much as how we're going to do it."

He paused, looking for reactions, but they knew him well enough not to give anything away. He took a little breath and continued.

"I've decided," he said, "to evacuate Civitas Vadanis. For what they're worth, you may as well hear my reasons. First, the war isn't going well. The latest reports I've seen — Varro, you may have better figures than me on this — put the Mezentine army at not far off thirty thousand men, not counting engineers, sappers and the baggage train. Now, we can match them for numbers, but we'd be kidding ourselves if we said we stood any sort of a chance in a pitched battle. So far we've avoided anything more than a few skirmishes; basically, we've been able to annoy them with cavalry raids and routine harassment, and that's all. It's fair to say we've got the better of them in cavalry and archers, but when it comes to the quality of heavy infantry needed to win a pitched battle, we're not in the same league; and that's not taking any account of their field artillery, which we all know is their greatest asset."

He paused to glance down at Orsea, and saw that he was looking down at his feet, too ashamed to lift his head. As well he might be. Someone else who had trouble thinking straight. He wondered: before they were married, had Orsea ever written her a letter? He doubted it.

"That rules out a decisive battle in the open field," Valens went on. "By the same token, I don't like the idea of staying here and trying to sit out either an assault or a siege. We still don't really know what happened at Civitas Eremiae" — here he looked quickly across at Vaatzes, but as usual there was nothing to see in his face — "and I know some of you reckon it must have been treachery rather than any stroke of tactical or engineering genius on the Mezentines' part. The fact remains that the Mezentines won that round, and Eremiae was supposed to be the best-defended city in the world. We haven't got anything like the position or the defenses that Orsea's people had, so the only way we could hope to win would be through overwhelming superiority in artillery. At Eremiae, Vaatzes here had to work miracles just to give Orsea parity. I imagine I'm right in assuming you couldn't do the same for us."

Vaatzes considered for a moment before answering.

"I don't think so," he said. "With respect, there's nothing here for me to work with. There were just about enough smiths and armorers and carpenters at Eremiae to give me a pool of competent skilled workers to draw on; all I had to do was train them, improvise the plant and machinery and teach them how to build the existing designs. You simply don't have enough skilled men here; you don't have the materials or the tools. You've got plenty of money to buy them with, of course, but there's not enough time. Also, it's a safe bet that the Mezentines have been busy improving all their artillery designs since the siege of Eremiae. I'm a clever man, but I can't hope to match the joint expertise of the Mezentine ordnance factory. Anything I could build for you would already be obsolete before the first bolt was loosed." He shook his head. "I'm sorry," he said, "but I don't think I can be much help to you."

Valens nodded. He knew all that already. "In that case," he said, "if we can't chase them away before they get here, and we can't hold them off when they come here, I believe our only option is to leave here and go somewhere else. In which case, the only question we're left with is, where do we go?"

He paused and looked round, but he knew that nobody was going to say anything; which was what he wanted, of course.

"As I see it," he went on, "the Mezentines are maintaining a large and very expensive mercenary army in hostile territory. Thanks to the efforts of Orsea's people, their lines of supply are painfully long and brittle, and living off the land isn't a realistic option. They need to finish this war quickly, before their own political situation gets out of hand. We know we can't fight them and win. Seems to me, then, that our best chance lies in not fighting; and the best way of doing that, I think, would be to keep moving. They can have the city and do what they like with it. We evacuate to the mountains, where we know the terrain and where their artillery train can't go. We dodge about, making them follow us until they get careless and give us a chance to bottle them up in a pass or a river valley. Meanwhile, our cavalry stays on the plains and makes life difficult for their supply wagons. Possibly we could also make trouble for the army of occupation in Eremia, just to give them something else to think about. It comes down to this. We can't beat the Mezentines; neither can Orsea's people or anybody else. The only people who can beat the Mezentines are the Mezentines themselves, by losing the will to carry on with this war. For them, it's a balance sheet. The point will come where the certain losses will outweigh the potential gains, and the political opposition will have gained enough strength to overthrow the current government. Our only hope is to hang on till that point is reached. I think evacuating, avoiding them, making life difficult and costing them money is the best and safest way of going about it. Furthermore, I don't think we have an alternative strategy worth serious consideration. If I'm wrong and I've missed something obvious, though, I'd love to hear about it. Anybody?"

He sat down and waited. He had a pretty shrewd idea who'd be first. Sure enough, Orsea got to his feet. As usual, he looked nervous, as though he wasn't quite sure whether he was allowed to speak, or whether he needed to ask for permission.

"For what it's worth," he said, "I agree with Valens. I think I can honestly say I know the Mezentines better than any of you. I ought to, after all. It was my stupidity that got us all into this situation in the first place, and as a direct result of what I did, I've had to watch them invade my country, burn my city and massacre my people. If it wasn't for Valens here, I'd be dead. Now, because Valens rescued us, you're facing the same danger. It's my fault that you've got to make this decision, and all I can say is, I'm sorry. That's no help, obviously." He hesitated, and Valens looked away. It pained him to see a grown man making a fool of himself, particularly someone who was his responsibility. "The point is," Orsea went on, "we mustn't let what happened at Civitas Eremiae happen again here. It's bad enough having to live with the destruction of my own people. If it happened to you as well —"

"Orsea," Valens said quietly, "it's all right. Sit down."

Orsea hesitated, then did as he was told. The room was suddenly, completely quiet. I'd better do something, Valens thought. He looked round the room and picked a face at random.

"Carausius," he said, "how soon do you think we could be ready?"

Was Carausius smirking slightly? Probably not. He stood up. "It depends on what we want to take with us, obviously," he replied. "Assuming you only want the bare minimum — food, clothes, essential military supplies — we could be on the road inside a week."

Valens smiled. "I don't think the situation's as desperate as all that," he replied. "Let's say a fortnight."

Carausius nodded. "In that case," he said, "the real limitation on what we can take is transport. I had a quick inventory made of all the available carts, wagons and horses, I'll see to it you get a copy before the end of today. In a nutshell, a fortnight's plenty of time to load up all our available transport capacity. Tell me when you want to leave, and what the priorities are."

Valens nodded. "Another thing," he said, and he fixed his eyes on the back wall, just above head height. "We're agreed that one of the best ways of stopping the Mezentines is by being as expensive to kill as we possibly can. We aren't going to get very far with that strategy if we let them get their hands on the silver mines." He felt it as he spoke; a faint shiver, as though he'd brushed an open cut with his fingertips. "I'm prepared to bet that the war faction in the Guild assembly is selling this war to the skeptics on the basis that getting control of the mines will not only pay for slaughtering us, it'll go a long way toward wiping out the losses incurred in conquering and occupying Eremia. As long as the mines are there and capable of being worked, they've got an incentive. Take that away . . ." He shrugged. "We need to give the opposition in the Assembly as much help as we can. So really, we haven't got any choice in the matter. We've got to put the mines out of action, and we've got to do it in such a way that, if they finish the job on us, it won't be worth their while financially to stick around and get them up and running again."

He paused, to give them time to be suitably horrified and angry. To their credit, they hid it well. What he needed now, of course, was someone to stand up and disagree with him. He waited, but nobody obliged. He had them too well trained.

"Let's think about it for a moment," he went on. "It's a question of the degree of sabotage, and the fundamental difference between them and us. They're businessmen. They can only afford to do a thing if it makes money. If the cost of repairing the damage to the mines is too high, they won't bother. We don't have to live by those rules. The silver's all we've got. And if we wreck the mines, the silver will still be there, until such time as we can rebuild and start mining again. If it takes us ten years and all our available manpower, so what? We can afford the time and effort, because our time and our work come cheap. They can't. But if we leave the mines there for them to take — and let's face it, we couldn't defend them against an assault or a siege, any more than we could defend the city — it's giving them a reason to keep going, even if we do manage to hurt them. It's harsh, I know, but . . ." He paused again, shook his head and sat down.

This time he got what he'd been hoping for. Licinius, senior partner of the Blue Crown mine, and the nephew of the first man Valens had ever had put to death. He was frowning as he stood up, as though he was in two minds about raising a matter of marginal interest.

"I take your point," he said. "And in principle, I agree. What I'm a bit concerned about is the practicalities. With respect; it's all very well to say we should sabotage the mines to the point where the Mezentines can't get them running again. The fact is, though, I don't think it'd be physically possible — not in the time available, with the men and resources we could spare. We build our mines to last, after all."

Valens relaxed a little. He couldn't have asked for a better objection. "You're the expert, Licinius," he said, "so obviously I'm happy to listen to what you've got to say. But I think you may be worrying unduly. I've read up on this a bit, and I've talked to some engineers who know far more about this stuff than I do." He noticed Vaatzes out of the corner of his eye, completely expressionless, like a stone goblin. "As I understand it, what you do is fill the ventilation chambers at the ends of the primary access tunnels — am I getting the technical terms right? I'm sure you know what I mean — you fill them with nice dry logs soaked in lamp oil, set a fuse, light it and run. The fire draws its own draft down the ventilation shafts, so you get a really good heat very quickly; more than enough, at any rate, to burn out all the props in the gallery and cave in not just the chamber but the tunnels as well. Once that lot's come down, it'd be quicker to start all over again with new shafts rather than trying to dig out the mess in the old ones. Which, of course, is what we'll have to do, when the war's over and the Mezentines have all gone home. But we've already been into that. As far as what you were saying goes, Licinius, I don't see that there's an insuperable problem."

All Licinius could do was nod politely to concede the point. Valens nodded back, to show that all was forgiven. He'd been bluffing, of course. All he knew about the subject was what he'd read in a standard textbook on siege techniques, and the method he'd described was how they undermined the walls of cities, not the roofs of silver mines. Licinius had just confirmed that the method would work equally well in the mines, which was good of him, even if he didn't know he'd done it. Valens made a mental note to look into the matter in proper detail, when he had the time.

"Right," he said, "I think we're all agreed, then. I'm going to have to ask all of you to help out with the planning; I'll let you know what I need from you over the next couple of days. Orsea, if you could spare me a moment."

That was the cue for the rest of them to leave. He could feel their relief, and also their resignation. But it was his job to make decisions; and if he didn't, who would?

Orsea stood up. The rest of them left without looking at him, as though he was some kind of monstrosity. Years ago, hadn't people believed that if you looked a leper in the eyes, you could catch the disease that way? Maybe they still had the same belief about humiliation.

"I'm sorry," Orsea said. "That didn't come out the way I meant it to."

Valens shrugged, and perched on the edge of the table. "It's all right," he said, "you didn't do anybody else any harm."

He could feel the jab go home. It had only been slight, but Orsea felt the least touch these days. Understandably. He had a lot to feel vulnerable about. "I wanted to explain," Valens said, in as gentle a voice as he could manage, "why I don't want you to come to the council meetings anymore."

Orsea turned his head and looked at him. The expression on his face was familiar: the deer at bay, with nowhere left to run to. The difference was, Valens hunted deer because he wanted them; the meat, the hide, the trophy. Hunting was about reducing a wild thing into possession. He'd never wanted Orsea for anything at all.

"Because I make a fool of myself," Orsea said. "Understood."

"No." Valens sighed. "I was thinking of you, actually. And Veatriz." He paused. He hadn't meant to come so close to the truth. "Look, it's obvious. It's tearing you apart, even hearing news about the war. There's no need for you to put yourself through that. I'll see to it you're kept in the loop, and anything you've got to say, about policy, you can say to me direct." He stood up and walked across, until he was within arm's length. "If you want to keep coming to the meetings, then fine. I just thought you'd prefer not to."

Orsea stayed where he was. The hunted animal runs away. The fencer steps back as his opponent advances, to maintain the safe distance between them. "Thanks," he said. "To be honest, there's nothing useful I could contribute anyway. I mean, it's not like I made a particularly good job of defending my country against the Mezentines, so I'm hardly likely to do any better with yours."

Valens looked away. "You can believe that if you want to," he said. "It's not true, of course. You beat off a direct assault, which nobody's ever done before —"

"That was Vaatzes," Orsea interrupted, "not me."

"Yes, but you chose him. That's what leaders do, they choose the right people."

"Like Miel Ducas." Orsea laughed. "He was very good indeed. But of course, I relieved him of command and had him locked up, just when we needed him most."

Valens froze, as though he'd just put his foot in a snare. "That's beside the point."

"Yes, I suppose it is." Orsea sat down. "None of it's important. What matters is that I started the war in the first place. Nobody else but me. And now it's come here. You know what? I think the war follows me around, like a butcher's dog."

Valens stifled a yawn. This was mere pointless activity, but it was his duty as a good host to carry on to the end. "You didn't start my war, Orsea," he said. "I did that."

"Because of me."

"It seemed like a good idea at the time."

(In his mind, he was phrasing another question for a letter: *Suppose you were fencing with a man who wanted to get killed, but if you kill him, you lose the game. How would you go about it?*)

"Valens." Orsea was looking at him. "Can I ask you something?"

"Of course."

Orsea turned his head. Valens had seen people do something similar before; squeamish men who had to put a wounded animal out of its misery. "You know why I had Miel Ducas arrested?"

"I heard something about it."

"What happened was," Orsea said slowly, "I found out that he had a letter. It was something he shouldn't have had. What I mean is, as soon as it came into his possession he should've brought it to me, but he didn't." He lifted his head; he was looking into the corner of the room. "Apparently that's treason," he said. "I looked it up."

"You couldn't trust him anymore. Well, that's fair enough."

"Trust," Orsea repeated. "That old thing. You know," he went on, "I've been thinking a lot about trust recently."

"Understandably," Valens murmured. "Someone betrayed your city to the enemy."

"Several people, actually," Orsea replied briskly, "including me. But that's not what's been bothering me. I've been thinking — look, can you spare the time for all this? Listening to me rambling on, I mean. It's really self-indulgent of me, and you're a busy man."

"It's raining," Valens said. "I've got plenty of time."

"Trust." Orsea jumped up, still looking away. "Trust's important, because if you can't trust someone, there's a risk he'll do something to hurt you. So you take steps, if you're a prudent man. You take steps to make sure he can't hurt you, assuming he wants to. Isn't that right?"

"Yes."

"Well, there you go. But it's not as simple as that." He seemed to be nerving himself to do something, and failing. "It's not something you can predict, like the workings of a machine. I mean, it's not simple cause and effect. Sometimes, someone you thought was your friend does something to breach your trust, but he's still your friend really, in things that matter. And sometimes your enemy, the man you've never trusted, pops up out of nowhere and saves your life." Now he turned, and looked Valens in the eye. "Stuff like that," he said, "it sort of makes nonsense out of it all, doesn't it?"

Valens found that he'd taken a step back. Force of habit again. "I've always found," he said quietly, "that if I can't understand something, it's because I don't know all the facts."

"Ah well." Orsea suddenly smiled. "That's the difference between us, I guess. When I can't understand something, it's generally because I'm too stupid to get my head round it."

"You can believe that," Valens replied, "if you want to."

Orsea nodded. "Did you know?" he said. "About Miel Ducas, and the letter?"

"I knew there was a letter involved in it," Valens said. "But not the details."

"Not all the facts, then."

Valens shrugged. "It was none of my business," he said, "so I didn't bother finding out."

(Valens thought: my father always told me that what's wrong with lying is that it's an admission of weakness. If you're the strongest, you can afford to tell the truth.)

"Good attitude," Orsea said. "Wouldn't you like to hear the inside story?"

"Not particularly."

"Well." Orsea relaxed a little, as if a fight he'd been expecting had been called off. "Like I said, you're a busy man. No time for things that don't concern you."

"Quite."

Orsea sighed. "And you're right, of course," he said. "There's no point in me coming to meetings anymore, and you're right, they do upset me. I felt I ought to keep coming along, just in case I could be useful. But since I can't, there's no point."

"No."

"Thanks." Orsea took a few steps toward the door. "For what it's worth," he said, "I really am very grateful for everything you've done for me."

Valens let him go without saying anything else. When he'd gone, he sat down, took a deep breath and let it out slowly. Unearned gratitude, he thought, just what I always wanted. More cheating, of course. I wonder: do I like the hunt so much because it's the one thing I do where it isn't possible to cheat?

He went back to the tower, changed out of his pretty clothes and put on something comfortable. Another thing his father had always told him: *If you cheat, sooner or later you'll be punished for it.* That was no lie. Of course, to begin with they were just letters. It was only when he'd become dependent on them that the dishonesty began. It was perfectly simple. She was married — to Orsea, of all people, Duke of Eremia, his people's traditional enemy. But because he knew they could never be together, there could never be anything except letters between them, he'd carried on writing and reading them, until he'd reached the point where he was little more than a foreign correspondent reporting back on his own life to a readership living far away, in a country he could never go to. And — of course — now she was here, never more than a hundred yards away from him, and he couldn't write to her anymore, let alone speak to her. He'd taken his country to war in order to rescue her, and thereby lost her forever.

He grinned. And Orsea thought *he* was stupid.

She'd be at dinner tonight. By way of exquisitely honed masochism, Valens had ordered the seating plan so that she always sat in the same place she'd been in the first time he'd seen her, seven years ago, when she'd come here as a hostage during the final peace negotiations. That reminded him of something Orsea had said about the war. Orsea had been wrong about that, but the phrase he'd used was nicely appropriate. Irony, Valens thought; irony follows me everywhere. When I was seventeen and she was here the first time, I wanted the negotiations to fail and the war to carry on, because as soon as there was peace I knew she'd go away and I'd never see her again. Now, war has brought her back to me again, like a cynical go-between. Pleasant thought: war wants us to be together so much, it'll do anything to make it happen. I never knew war and love were so close.

If my mind were a falcon, he thought, this is the point where there'd be the biggest risk of it not coming back to the lure. He pulled his shoes on and went back down the stairs to the library. It was time for the day's reports; at least he still got some letters, but these days they were all from spies and traitors.

Anser, reporting on the Eremian resistance. He frowned as he broke the seal. He'd sent Anser out of guilt, mostly. The purpose of the mission was to infiltrate the resistance and report back on its activities, but while he was there he'd undoubtedly be making himself useful, if only to help pass the time, and when it came to violence, Anser could be very useful indeed.

Anser to Duke Valens, greetings.

Things aren't going well, but they could be worse. Yesterday we attacked the supply convoy for the main expeditionary force. We did a good job. It was the fifth convoy in a row that we stopped from getting through, which by my calculations means that fairly soon they'll have to turn around and go back to the city or starve. Unfortunately, we got beaten up pretty badly in the process; over a hundred killed, half as many driven off and scattered, quite possibly caught by the cavalry patrols. The Mezentines have hired some new light cavalry; I haven't a clue who they are or where they're from, but they're obviously used to operating in the mountains, and they're proving to be a real nuisance. The bad news is, Miel Ducas is missing. If he was dead and they'd found the body, I think we'd have heard about it by now, it'd be the break the Mezentines have been waiting for. We've been trying to keep the fact that he's missing quiet, but it won't be long before it gets out. When that happens, it'll probably be the end of effective resistance. It's annoying, because we were holding our own, if not making any real progress. Meanwhile, I'm not sure who's in charge here, though I have an unpleasant feeling it's probably me.

This is only a suggestion; but I understand you've got another Ducas there with you in the city, Jarac or Jarnac or some such. If it turns out we really have lost Miel, would you consider sending him here? The Ducas name means a lot to these people, and I guess your specimen's now the head of the family.

Things we need: food, of course, and boots and blankets; a few barrels of arrows would be nice, but I imagine you'd rather keep them for yourself. A good surveyor would have made a hell of a difference a week ago. If you can spare a couple of field surgeons, we could probably find something for them to do.

According to some people who came in last week, the Mezentine seventh infantry have left the city, headed north. If it's true I can't account for it. I don't trust the people who told me this, but I have no reason to believe they're lying.

Trust again. As Orsea had said, that old thing. Valens reached across the table for the ink bottle and wrote a requisition for food, boots, blankets; he hesitated, then added ten barrels of arrows and two surgeons. Wasteful, because if Miel Ducas really was dead, quite soon there'd be no resistance to feed or arm, Anser was quite right about that. Even so; he sealed the requisition and put it on the pile for the clerks to collect. He wondered if he ought to have Anser's letter copied to Orsea, but decided against it.

He picked up another sheet of paper, and wrote on it:

Valens to Anser, greetings.

Make finding out about the Ducas your first priority. I can't send you Jarnac Ducas, he's too useful to me here; at last I've found an Eremian who's good for something other than causing me problems. I'm sending you what you asked for, but there won't be any more. I think it's time to cut our losses, even if the Ducas is still alive. Once you've found out about that, disentangle yourself and come home; we've had a change of plans here, and I need you to do something for me. I'm sorry for wasting your time . . .

Valens hesitated, then picked up the pumice and rubbed out the last line. He wrote instead:

I hope you've enjoyed your holiday (I know how much you like travel and meeting new people). One last thing; if any of your people there have heard any rumors — anything at all — about who sold out Civitas Eremiae to the Mezentines, I want to know about it. Until I know the answer to that question, I'm wasting my time here trying to plan any kind of strategy.

He lifted his head and looked out of the window. It had stopped raining. Too late now, of course. As far as he was concerned, the day was a dead loss.

Well, he was in the library, he might as well read a book. There were plenty to choose from. His father (his father used to say that reading was like taking a bath; sometimes you had to do it) had bought a hundredweight of books (various) from a trader. He had had the books unpacked, and shelves put up in the old game larder to store them on. When Valens was fifteen, he'd told him he could choose five books for his own; the rest would be burned. Valens had read them all, desperately, in a hurry, and made his choice. Varro's *On Statecraft*, Yonec's *Art of War*, the Suda *Encyclopedia*, Statianus on revenues and currency, and the *Standard Digest of Laws & Statutes;* five books, Valens reckoned, that between them contained the bare minimum of knowledge and wisdom a prince needed in order to do his job properly. When he announced that he'd made his choice, his father had had the five books burned and spared the rest; books should be a man's servant, he declared, not his master. Valens wasn't quite sure he saw the point, but he'd learned the lesson, though not perhaps the one his father had intended to convey: that to value anything is to give it an unacceptable degree of power over you, and to choose a thing is to lose it.

Most of what survived the bonfire was garbage: inaccurate books with pretty pictures, elegant and insipid belles-lettres, genteel pornography. When his father died, Valens sold most of them back to the same trader and started building a real library. There were three sections: technical and reference, literature, and the finest collection of hunting manuals in the world.

He stood up, faced the shelves like a general addressing his troops on the eve of battle, and made a choice.

Regentius' *Calendar of Hawks and Ladies* had been one of the original hundredweight. It was a big, fat book with lurid pictures of birds of prey and couples having sex, apparently drawn by a scribe who'd never seen either, but there was one chapter that justified keeping it. The woman is a heron who feeds alone on the marshes; the man is the wild falcon who hunts her and is himself hunted by the austringers, who wish to break him and sell him to the king. To catch the hawk, the austringers first snare the heron with lime and stake her out under a cage-trap. The falcon knows something is wrong, because no heron ever stood still for so long under a tree; but although he knows it's a trap, he can't deny his nature and eventually he swoops to the kill and triggers the snare; the cage drops down around him and he is caught. An allegory, the sort of thing that was considered the height of sophistication two hundred years ago; just in case the reader fails to make the obvious interpretation, there are brightly colored vignettes of men and women in the margin to point him in the right direction.

The point being: the falcon cannot deny its nature, even though it can see the cage hanging from the branches on a rope. The poet is too busy with his stylish double entendres to develop the theme properly, but it's there nevertheless, like a large rock in the middle of a road.

Valens read it (he knew it by heart already), and found that he'd picked up a sheet of paper and his pen without knowing it. He frowned, then began to write.

Suppose that, as the cage fell, it broke the falcon's wing. It'd be worthless then, and if the austringers were humane men, they'd break its neck. The heron is of value because it can be eaten, but a dead falcon is just bones and feathers. The hunters want to catch it so that it can hunt; it needs to hunt (and therefore destroys itself in their trap, and becomes worthless) because that is its nature. Since the heron is the only element in the story that is valuable in itself, wouldn't it have been more sensible to catch and eat the heron and leave the falcon in peace?

Besides, the falcon wouldn't stoop to a tethered bird. It'd be invisible. A falcon can't strike a stationary target, they can only see movement.

He closed the book, folded the paper and dropped it in the pile of spills beside the fireplace (because when you come to rely on the written word, it's time to light the fire with it). He glanced out of the window again, and pulled his collar up round his ears before leaving the room. It had started raining again.

2

He opened his eyes expecting to see the kingdom of Heaven, but instead it was a dirty, gray-haired man with a big mustache, who frowned.

"Live one here," the man said. Miel assumed the man wasn't talking to him. Still, it was reassuring to have an impartial opinion on the subject, even though the man's tone of voice suggested that it was a largely academic issue.

Miel tried to remember where his sword had fallen, but he couldn't. The man was kneeling down, and there was a knife in his hand. Oh well, Miel thought.

"Easy," the man said. "Where's it hurt?"

He put the knife away in a sheath on his belt. Next to him, Miel noticed a large sack on the ground. It was full of boots. There was one particularly fine specimen sticking out of the top. Miel recognized it. That explained why his feet were cold.

"Well?" the man said. "Can't you talk?"

"I don't know," Miel said. His head was splitting, which made it hard to sort out awkward, uncooperative things like words. "What's wrong with me, I mean."

"Can't hurt too bad, then," the man said. "Try getting up."

Behind the man, Miel could see more like him. They were plodding slowly up and down, heads bent, like workers in a cabbage field. Some of them had sacks too; others held swords, spears, bows, bundled up with string like faggots of wood, or sheaves of corn. Harvesters, he thought. Of a kind.

"I can't," he discovered. "Knee doesn't work."

"Right." The man bent over him and unbuckled the straps of his chausse. "No bloody wonder," he said. "Swelled up like a puffball. Got a right old scat on it, didn't you?"

He made it sound like deliberate mischief, and Miel felt an urge to apologize. "I can't remember," he said. "I was in the fighting . . ." He paused. Something had just occurred to him. "Did we win?"

The man shrugged. "Search me," he said. "Get a hold of my arm, come on."

The man hoisted him up and caught him before he could fall down again. "This way," he said. "Get you on a cart, you'll be all right."

"Thank you," Miel said. The man grinned.

It was only a dozen yards or so to the cart, which was heavily laden with more stuffed sacks and sheaves of weapons. The man helped Miel to sit up on the tailgate. "You bide there," he said. "Don't go anywhere."

Miel watched him walk away; the slow, measured stride of a man at work. After a while he couldn't tell him apart from the others.

He knew that this sort of thing happened, of course, but he'd never actually seen it before. Once a battle was over, he left; pursuing in victory, withdrawing in defeat. What became of the battlefield after that had never really been any business of his. He knew that people like this existed, companies of men who went round stripping the dead. As a member of the ruling classes, he understood why they were tolerated. There was a convention, unwritten but mostly observed, that in return for the harvest they buried the dead, tidied up, made good generally. They put the badly wounded out of their misery, and — that would explain it — salvaged those likely to recover and returned them to their own people in exchange for money. It was, he'd heard, strictly a commercial decision as to who they recovered and who they didn't bother with. Apparently, a damaged knee meant he was still viable. So that was all right.

He made an effort, told himself to stay still. Before he closed his eyes (how long ago was that? He sniffed; not too long, the dead hadn't started to smell yet), everything had mattered so much. The battle; the desperate, ferocious last stand. If they'd won, the Mezentine Fifth Light Cavalry presumably no longer existed. If they'd lost, there was nothing standing between the enemy and the four defenseless villages of the Rosh valley. Last time he'd looked, it was important enough to kill and die for; but the man with the mustache didn't know and didn't seem to care, so perhaps it hadn't mattered so very much after all.

An unsettling thought occurred to him. If they'd lost, the resistance was over and done with. In that case, they wouldn't be there anymore to redeem their wounded. But the Mezentines would pay good money for him, if these people found out who he was. On balance, it was just as well the man with the mustache had appropriated his expensive boots. The armor wasn't a problem, since it was captured Mezentine. Jewelry; it took him a moment to remember. All his life, as the head of the Ducas, he'd been festooned with rings and brooches and things on chains round his neck, till he no longer noticed they were there. Luckily (he remembered) he'd sold them all to raise money for the cause. There was still his accent, of course, and the outside chance that someone might recognize him, but he knew he was a lousy actor. Trying to pretend to be a poor but honest peasant lad would just draw attention.

Still, it would have been nice to find out what had happened. It had always struck him as unfair that the men who died in a battle never got to know the result; whether they died for a victory or a defeat. If anything mattered at the point of their death, surely that would. He reassured himself that he'd find out eventually, and in the meantime there was nothing he could do. Well, there was something. He could take his armor off, and save his preservers a job.

Force of habit made him stack it neatly. Not too much damage; he was glad about that, in a way. They had, after all, saved him from dying painfully of hunger and exposure on a hillside covered with dead bodies, so he felt obligated to them, and the Ducas feels uncomfortable while in another's debt. He balanced a vambrace on top of the pile. He hadn't really looked at it before. The clips, he noticed, were brass, and the rivets holding them on were neatly and uniformly peened over. Say what you like about the Mezentines, they made nice things. And at a sensible price, too.

He looked up at the sky. Still an hour or so to go before sunset. He frowned; should've thought of it before. The battle had started just before dawn, and he'd left it and gone to sleep about an hour and a half later, so he'd been out for quite a while. His head still hurt, but it was getting better quickly. It wasn't the first time he'd been knocked out in a battle, but on those previous occasions he'd always woken up in a tent, with clean pillows and people leaning over him looking worried, because the Ducas, even unconscious, isn't someone you leave lying about for just anybody to find. On the other hand, the headache had been worse, all those other times. On balance, things weren't as bad as they could be.

The men were heading back to the cart, leaning forward against the weight of the burdens they were carrying. He remembered when he was a boy, and they'd ridden out to the fields to watch the hay-making; he'd sat under the awning and seen the laborers trudging backward and forward to and from the wains with impossibly big balls of hay spiked on their pitchforks, and thought how splendid they were, how noble, like fine horses steadily drawing a heavy carriage in a procession. Men at work.

Someone was saying to the others: "Right, let's call it a day. Have to come back in the morning to do the burying." A short, thin, bald man walked past him without looking at him, but said, "Best get on the cart, son, we're going now." Not an order or a threat. Miel leaned back and hauled his damaged leg in after him, and the thin man closed the tailgate and dropped the latches.

The sacks of clothing made an adequate nest. Miel put a sack under the crook of his bad knee, which helped reduce the pain whenever the cart rolled over a pothole. The driver seemed to have forgotten about him, or maybe he wasn't in the habit of talking to the stock-in-trade. Miel leaned back and watched the light drain out of the sky.

He wouldn't have thought it was possible to go to sleep in an unsprung cart on those roads; but he woke up with a cricked neck to see darkness, torchlight and human shapes moving backward and forward around him. "Come on," someone was saying, "out you get." It was the tone of voice shepherds used at roundup; fair enough. He edged along the floor of the cart and put his good leg to the ground.

"Need a hand?"

"Yes," he replied into the darkness, and someone put an arm round him and took his weight. He hobbled for a bit and was put down carefully next to a fire. "You stay there," said the voice that came with the arm; so he did.

It wasn't much of a fire — peat, by the smell — and the circle of light it threw showed him his own bare feet and not much else. Well, they hadn't tied him up, but of course they wouldn't need to. He had nowhere to go, and only one functioning leg. If they were going to kill him they'd have done it by now. Miel realized that, for once in his life, he didn't have to take thought, look ahead, make plans for other people or even himself. His place was to sit still and quiet until called for, and leave the decisions to someone else. To his surprise, he found that thought comforting. He sat, and let his mind drift.

He supposed he ought to be worrying about the resistance, but the concept of it seemed to be thinning and dissipating, like the smoke from the fire. He considered it from his new perspective. He had been using every resource of body and mind left to him to fight the Mezentine occupation; what about that? Until today, he'd managed to make himself believe that he was doing a reasonable job. He'd won his battles; he counted them: seventeen. At least, looking at each encounter as a contest, he'd done better than the enemy. His ratio of men lost to enemies killed was more than acceptable. He'd disrupted their supply lines, wrecked carts and slaughtered carthorses and oxen, broken down bridges, blocked narrow passes. For every village they'd burned, he'd made them pay an uneconomic price in men, time and materiel. A panel of impartial referees, called in to judge who had made a better job of it, him or his opponent, would show him significantly ahead on points. But winning . . . Winning, now he came to think of it, meant driving the Mezentine armies out of Eremia, and he understood (remarkably, for the first time) that that was never going to be possible. He might be winning, but his people weren't. They didn't stand a chance.

But they weren't alone, of course. Silly of him to have forgotten that: the Vadani were helping him, or rather the other way about. His job (the Vadani agent had explained all this) was to keep up the pressure, make a nuisance of himself, cost the enemy money. The purpose of this was to undermine the enemy's political will, to give the Mezentine opposition a chance to bring down the government. Excellent strategy, and the only way to beat the Perpetual Republic. So, you see, we can still do it, and it doesn't really matter how many villages get burned or how many people get killed; we're just one part of someone else's greater design . . .

He frowned. The smoke was stinging his eyes. That morning, he'd been able to see the design quite clearly, as though it was a blueprint unrolled on a table. Since then, he'd been bashed on the knee and left for dead, and somehow that had made a difference. It was almost as though a ship had sailed away and left him behind. He'd heard stories about men who'd been stranded on islands or remote headlands. A simple thing, the unfurling of sails, the raising of an anchor; a few minutes either way, the difference between boarding a ship and not making it. In his case, a bash on the knee and another one on the head. In the stories, the castaways accepted that the world had suddenly changed; they'd built huts on the beach, hunted wild goats and cured their hides for clothing, until the world happened to come by again, pick them up and take them home. Those were the ones you heard about, of course. The ones who were never rescued by passing ships, or who simply lay on the beach and waited to die, were never heard from again and therefore ceased to exist.

Miel thought: I've lost everything. I was the Ducas, the head of the family, the Duke's principal adviser, Orsea's best friend. I had land and houses and money, hawks and hounds, clothes and weapons. Thousands of people depended on me. They lived their lives through me, I was the one who made their decisions for them, decided what they should be doing. I wasn't just one man, I was thousands; I was Eremia. Now I can't even walk on my own, and I've got nothing, not even a pair of boots.

I was . . .

Perhaps it was just the sting of the smoke. He rubbed his eyes, and thought about it some more.

Well, he thought, I suppose it's because I was born to it. Orsea wasn't, and that's probably why he did so very badly. All my life I've been aware of it, the responsibility for other people, the knowledge that I can't just do what I want, because so many people depend on me. I could argue that that makes me a good man — except that I had the houses and the land, the hawks and hounds, and I never had to lean on plow-handles in the baking sun or stoop over all day hoeing onions. But I never chose anything, not for myself. I have always tried to do the right thing, because people depended on me.

Someone was standing over him; he looked up. He couldn't make out a face, only a shape. Someone leaning forward a little, holding out a bowl.

"Thanks," he said, and took it. The man walked away.

Well, it was porridge, or maybe very thick soup; something cheap you could boil up in bulk; something that someone had had to work for, and which he'd done nothing to earn. He scooped a wodge of the stuff onto his fingers and poked it into his mouth. It didn't taste of anything much, which was probably just as well. There are different sorts of dependence. There's the social contract between the lord and his people, and there's the man who feeds barley mash to his pig. He thought about that too, while he was at it. Without the farmer, the pig would starve; without him, the pig would never have been born. The pig owes the farmer its life, and in due course the debt is called in, just as my bailiffs collect the rents from my tenants.

He finished the whatever-it-was, put down the bowl and looked round. A few people were still moving about, but mostly there was the stillness of rest after hard work; of men whose only resource was their strength, saving it up for another day. If I could walk, Miel thought, I could offer to help them tomorrow with digging the graves. I can't even do that. I can't do anything.

He lay back. There was a stone or something just under his shoulder blade; he wriggled about to avoid it. Nothing to do; he'd have expected to be bored, since all his life the one thing he could never abide was doing nothing. It wasn't like that, though. It was dark, so it was time to sleep; or, if sleep didn't happen to pass by his way, he would be content to lie still and wait for the dawn. Gradually, awareness of time slipped away from him, and then he slept.

When he woke up, there was someone standing over him again. He recognized the boots.

"On the cart," the man with the mustache said. "Here, I'll give you a hand up."

Miel nodded, and let himself be lifted. "Are we going back to the battlefield?" he asked.

The man frowned, as though he hadn't expected to be asked a question, and wasn't quite sure it wasn't against the rules. "You go back to the camp," he said. "They'll look after you there."

The tailgate closed behind him, and he snuggled back among the sacks. Fine resistance leader I turned out to be, he thought. By now I should've overpowered a dozen guards, stolen a sword and a fast horse and be galloping home. Instead, they put me on a cart. About the best thing anybody could say about me right now is that I'm reasonably portable.

But that'd be silly, he thought. You can't overpower guards if there's nobody guarding you, and I expect if I asked them nicely they'd sell me a sword and a horse, assuming they haven't stolen all my money. (He checked; they hadn't. On the other hand, all he had left was six copper turners and a twopenny bit.)

It was a long ride. The cart had to go slowly over the sad excuse for a track. (Weren't we supposed to have built a new road up here, Miel wondered, or did we never get round to it?) Shortly after noon he saw a small cluster of wooden buildings in the distance. As he got closer they grew into five thatched sheds surrounded by a stockade. That suggested a degree of effort; there weren't any woods for miles, so someone had thought it was worth all the trouble of putting up some kind of fortification. There was no smoke rising, and he couldn't see any people about. Barns, then, rather than houses.

"Is that where we're going?" he called out, and wondered if the driver would reply. He hadn't said a word all day; but then, Miel hadn't either.

"Yes."

There was a ditch as well as a stockade. The driver stopped the cart, jumped down and whistled. A gate in the stockade opened; apparently it doubled as a drawbridge. The cart rumbled over it, jarring Miel's knee. The drawbridge went back up again as soon as they were across.

"Hold on, I'll help you down." The driver, now that he looked at him, was a short, stocky man with a fringe of sandy hair round a bald citadel of a head. Miel thanked him — the Ducas always acknowledges help — and leaned on his shoulder as they crossed the yard to one of the barns.

"Live one for you," the bald man called out as they crossed the threshold into the darkness inside. He put Miel down carefully and walked away.

He'd called out to someone, so presumably there was someone there; but it was too dark for Miel to see, so he stayed where he was, leaned up against a wall, like a hoe or a shovel. He was getting used to being property, he decided, and so far it hadn't been so bad. That could change, of course. He decided to resume some responsibility.

"Hello," he called out. "Anybody there?"

"Just a minute, I'll come down." A woman's voice, which made a change. Not a pleasant voice, though. The best you could say for it was that it sounded like it meant what it said. You knew where you were with a voice like that, even if it wasn't anywhere you'd ever want to be.

There was a hayloft, and a ladder. She came down slowly; a tall, red-haired woman in a plain, clean gown, tied at the waist with plaited straw rope. She was much younger than her voice, maybe his own age, a year or two older; nice-looking, too — no, revise that.

The Ducas is trained in good manners from infancy, like a soldier is trained to obey orders. He's almost incapable of inappropriate or boorish behavior. He instinctively knows how to put people at their ease, and he never, ever reacts to physical ugliness or deformity. He keeps a straight face, and he never stares.

Which was just as well. At some point in the last year or so, the woman had lost her left eye. The scar started an inch above the middle of her eyebrow and reached down to the corner of her mouth. If he'd had to give an opinion, Miel would have said it was probably a sword-cut. It hadn't been stitched at the time, and had grown out broad. Her eye socket was empty. In order to learn that aspect of his trade, Miel had been taken when he was twelve years old to see the lepers at Northwood. For the first time, he felt grateful for having had such a thorough education.

"What's the matter with you?" she said.

It took Miel a second to realize what she meant. "My knee," he said. "I got hit there in . . ." He hesitated. Presumably she was part of the business: doctor, nurse, jailer, all three? "In the fighting," he said. "I don't know if —"

"Hold still." She knelt down and prodded his knee sharply with her index finger. Miel yowled like a cat and nearly fell over. "That seems all right," she said. "The swelling and stiffness won't last long, a few days. You'll have to stay here till it's right again, we can't spare transport to take you back to your outfit. Have you got any money?"

"Excuse me?"

"Have you got any money?"

"Yes. I mean, not very much."

She frowned at him. "How much?"

"Eighteen turners, I think."

"Oh." She sighed. "It's six turners a day for food and shelter, so you'll just have to mend quickly. Not much chance of you working for your keep, is there? What do you do, anyway?"

Now there was a good question. "I'm a falconer," Miel said.

"Are you really?" She looked at him. "Which family?"

"The Ducas."

"Oh, them." She shrugged. "Well, try and keep out of my way." She frowned, creasing and stretching the scar. "What did that to you? One of your birds?"

For a moment he couldn't think what she was talking about. Then he remembered that he had a scar of his own; not as flamboyant as hers, because skillful men with needles had done something about it while there was still time. It had been so long since anybody had appeared to notice it that he'd forgotten it was there.

"A goshawk in a bate," he replied. "I unhooded it too early. My own fault."

She turned away, the set of her shoulders telling him he no longer mattered, and picked up a sack of boots. Then she stopped.

"My brother used to say you should keep them hooded for three days before you start manning them," she said, not turning round.

"Was he a falconer?"

"No." She paused, as though weighing up the issues for an important decision. "You can sew, then."

Of course he couldn't; but a falconer could. "Yes," he said.

"Fine. Something useful you can do. Stay there."

She went out, and came back a little later with a sack full of clothes. Miel had rested his head on it during the cart-ride. From the pocket of her gown she took a thread-bobbin; there was a bone needle stuck into the thread. "Darn the holes as best you can," she said. "Anything that's past repair you can tear up for patches. Don't break the needle."

Bloody hell, Miel thought; then, Well, how hard can it be? "All right," he said.

Apparently, unloading the cart was her job. She came and went with the sacks and the bundled-up weapons, sorting them and stacking them against the walls; no sign of the carter. He tried not to watch her. Instead, he tried desperately to figure out how you were supposed to get the thread to go through the hole in the needle.

As far as he could judge, it was physically impossible. The end, where it had been cut off, was frayed and tufty, not to mention fiendishly hard to see in the poor light, and the hole in the needle was ridiculously small. It was like trying to pull a turnip through a buttonhole. He tried to think; he'd seen women sewing before, you couldn't turn round at home without seeing some woman or other sitting placidly in a corner, her arm moving gracefully up and down. He concentrated, trying to refine a memory. Every so often they'd stop sewing and do something; but they did it quickly and easily — the bobbin would just appear in their hands, they'd run off about a forearm's length of thread, they'd hold the needle steady, and then they'd do something, if only he could remember what it was.

(Come on, he thought; if they could do it, it couldn't be all that hard.)

He tried to squeeze the picture up into his mind. The head would go forward, he remembered that. Something to do with the hand and the mouth. But of course the Ducas is trained not to stare at people, which is another way of saying, trained not to notice things that don't concern him; things and people.

They licked it. That was it; they licked the end of the thread. Presumably, if you got the tufty bit wet, you could sort of mat it down and stop it being all fluffy and hard to manipulate. He tried it, and found he could twist the strands tightly together into a point that would just about go through the needle-hole (there was a word for it, wasn't there? The eye of a needle). He tried that. At first he thought it was going to work. The tip of the point went through easily, and he tried to pinch hold of it with his fingernails as it came out the other side. But clearly it wasn't as simple as that. He'd got most of the strands through, but not all of them, so that when he pulled, the thread started to unravel and jammed. He felt his arms and neck clench with frustration, but he daren't let her see. He tried again, carefully rolling the tip of the thread between his lips; it didn't do to hurry when you were trying something new and complicated. Still no joy; one or two strands stubbornly evaded the eye, like sheep who are too scared to go back into the pen. He was confident that he'd got the technique, but evidently it took both skill and practice to execute. For crying out loud, he thought; human beings are supposed to be resourceful, why can't somebody invent a tool to do this quickly and easily? Or make needles with bigger holes in them, come to that.

The fourth time; he didn't quite know what he'd done differently. It just seemed to go, as if it had given up the struggle. Victory; now what? He went back to his memories. They threaded it, right, and then they cut or broke off a foot or two of thread. He scowled. It stood to reason that if you stuck the needle in and pulled it through, the thread would simply pass through the cloth and come out the other side, and you'd be sitting there with the cloth in one hand and a threaded needle in the other. There had to be some way of anchoring the end of the thread in the cloth; did you tie it to something, or stick it down with glue, or what? All his life, all those hundreds of sewing women, all he'd have had to do was stop and ask and one of them would've been happy to explain it to him. As it was . . .

They tied a knot in the end of the thread. He remembered now, he could picture it. The knot was thicker than the hole the needle made in the cloth, so it stuck. Excellent. He laid the needle carefully down on his knee — the last thing he needed was for the thread to slip out of the eye after all that performance getting it in there — and found the other end. Was there a special kind of knot you had to use, like sailors or carters? The women in his memory hadn't used any special procedure that he could recall, however, so he'd just have to take his chances on that. He dropped the knot and retrieved the needle. Now, he imagined, came the difficult part.

Think about it, he ordered himself. Sewing is basically just tying two sheets of material together with string. Surreptitiously, he turned over his wrist and unbuttoned his cuff.

The Ducas, of course, has nothing but the best, and this rule applies especially to clothes. He had no idea who'd made his shirts — they tended to appear overnight, like mushrooms — but whoever they were, it went without saying that they were the best in the business. Obviously, therefore, they didn't leave exposed seams, not even on the inside, where it didn't show, and their stitches were small enough to be practically invisible. He cursed himself for being stupid; looking in the wrong place. He put his hand into the sack and pulled out a shirt; a proper, honest-to-goodness, contractor-made army shirt, Mezentine, made down to a price and with nice exposed seams on the inside that even the Ducas could copy. He studied them. Apparently the drill was, you stacked the edges of the two bits of cloth one on top of the other; you left about three-sixteenths of an inch as a sort of headland (why couldn't it have been farm work instead of sewing? he asked himself; at least I know something about farm work), and then you ran a seam along to join them together. But even the army-issue stitches were too small to be self-explanatory; he stared at them, but he couldn't begin to figure out how on earth they'd ever got that way. It was a mystery, like the corn or the phases of the moon.

Fine. If I can't work out how a load of stupid women do it, I'll just have to invent a method of my own. Think; think about the ways in which one bit of something can be joined to another. There's nails, or rivets; or how about a bolt on a door? You push a bolt through a sort of cut-about tube into a hole that keeps it — Or a net. Now he was onto something he actually knew a bit about. Think how the drawstring runs through the mouth of a purse-net, weaving in and out through the mesh; then, when you pull on it, it draws the net together. If you do something similar with the thread, weave it in and out through both layers of cloth, that'll hold them together. Brilliant. I've invented sewing. I'd be a genius if only someone hadn't thought of it before me.

He took another look at the shirt-seam. It hadn't been done like that. But if he went up it once, then turned it round and went down again, he could fill in the gaps and it'd look just like the real thing. Was that the proper technique? he wondered. Like I care, he thought.

Now for something to sew. He was looking for damage; a hole, cut or tear. He examined the shirt in his hands, but there didn't seem to be anything wrong with it, so he put it on the floor and took another one from the sack. This time he was in luck. There was a big, obvious tear in the sleeve, just the sort of thing for an enthusiastic novice to cut his teeth on. He looked for the needle, couldn't find it, panicked, found it, picked it up carefully, carried it across to the sleeve and drove it home like a boar-spear. It passed through the cloth as though it wasn't there and came out the other side, but with an empty eye and without the thread.

He looked up. She was standing over him, looking down.

"So," she said, "which one are you?"

His mind emptied, like grain through a hole in a jar. "What?"

"Which one are you," she said, "Miel or Jarnac?"

Oh. "I'm sorry," he said, "I don't know what you're —"

"Jarnac's the falconry nut," she went on matter-of-factly, "but he's supposed to be big and good-looking. I met Miel once, but it was years ago and we were both children, so I wouldn't recognize him again. I could probably guess, but it's easier if you tell me, isn't it? Well?"

He sagged. "I'm Miel," he said.

She nodded. "Actually, I'm impressed," she said. "I've been watching you. It's clever, how you figured it all out. But you need to fold back a couple of inches when you thread the needle," she added. "Otherwise it just pulls out."

"Is that right?" Miel said. "Well, now I know." He sighed, and let the shirt drop from his hands. "So what are you going to do?" he said.

She shrugged. "Obviously," she said, "either I teach you how to sew properly, or I'll have to do all those clothes myself. Why did you pretend to be someone else?"

"I was afraid that if you knew who I was, you'd sell me to the Mezentines," he said. "Isn't that what you do?"

She didn't move or say anything for a moment. "No," she said. "They're the enemy. If it wasn't for them, we'd still be at home on our farms." She frowned. "We don't do this out of choice."

"I'm sorry." He wasn't sure he believed her, but he still felt ashamed. "Do you know what happened in the battle?" he asked (but now it was just a way of changing the subject).

"No. I expect we'll hear sooner or later. Why, don't you?"

"I got knocked out halfway through," he explained.

"Ah." She smiled, crushing the scar up like crumpled paper. "I can see that'd be frustrating for you. Not that it matters. You're bound to lose eventually. You never stood a chance, and at your best you were nothing but a nuisance."

"I suppose so," Miel said quietly.

"Aren't you going to argue with me?" She was grinning at him. "You're supposed to be the leader of the resistance."

"Yes." He knew he was telling the truth, but it felt like lying. "So I'm in a good position to know, I suppose."

"Well." She frowned. "All right, you can't sew. Is there anything you *can* do? Anything useful, I mean."

He smiled. "No."

"And you're hardly ornamental. Do you think the Mezentines really would give us money for you?"

She walked away and came back with a cloth bag that clinked and jingled. As he took it from her, it felt heavy in his hand. "Tools," she said. "Two pairs of pliers, wirecutters, rings, rivets, two small hammers. Do you know what they're for?"

He thought for a moment, then nodded. "I think so," he said.

"I thought it'd be more likely to be in your line than sewing, and it's easier. It must be, men can do it. Figure it out as you go along, like you did with the sewing. When you're ready to start . . ." she nodded into the corner of the barn, "I'll help you over there."

"Might as well be now," he said.

She bent down and he put his arm round her neck. Not the first time he'd done that, of course; not the first time with a redhead. The most he could claim was, she was the first one-eyed woman he'd ever been cheek to cheek with. Her hair brushed his face and he moved his head away.

"You're standing on my foot," she said.

He apologized, perhaps a little more vehemently than necessary. Her hair smelled of stale cooking oil, and her skin was very pale. When they reached the corner, he let go and slithered to the floor, catching his knee on the way down. That took his mind off other things quite effectively.

"It's all right," he gasped (she hadn't actually asked). "I just . . ."

"Be more careful," she said. "Right, I'll leave you to it. I've got work to do."

When she'd gone, he pulled open the nearest sack and peered inside. It looked like a sack full of small steel rings, as though they were a crop you grew, harvested, threshed and put in store to see you through the winter. He dipped his hands in, took hold and lifted. At once, the tendons of his elbows protested. A full-length, heavy-duty mail shirt weighs forty pounds, and it's unwise to try and lift it from a sitting position.

He hauled it out nevertheless, spread it out on the floor and

examined it. Mezentine, not a top-of-the-range pattern. The links
were flat-sectioned, about three-eighths of an inch in diameter,
each one closed with a single rivet. A good-quality shirt, like the
ones he was used to wearing, would have smaller, lighter links,
weigh less and protect better. This one had a hole in the back, just
below where the shoulder blade would be, and the area round it
was shiny and sticky with jellying blood. The puncture had burst
the rivets on five of the links; must've been a cavalryman's lance,
with the full impetus of a charging horse behind it, to have done
that. He looked a little closer, contemplating the twisted ends of
the damaged links. So much force, applied in such a small space.
He'd seen wounds before, felt them himself; but there was more
violence in the silent witness of the twisted metal than his own
actual experiences. That's no way to behave, he thought.

She'd been right; it was much easier to understand than sewing,
though it was harder work. He needed both hands on the ends of
the wirecutter handles to snip through the damaged links, and
after he'd bent a few replacement links to fit (one twist to open
them, one to close them up again), the plier handles had started
blisters at the base of both his thumbs. The only really awkward
part was closing up the rivet. For an anvil he used the face of one
of his two hammers. The only way he could think of to hold it
was to sit cross-legged and grip it between his feet, face up, his
calf jamming the handle into the floor. He tried it, but the pain
from his injured knee quickly persuaded him to try a different
approach; he ended up sitting on the hammer handle and leaning sideways to work, which probably wasn't the way they did it
in the ordnance factory at Mezentia. Hauling the shirt into position over the hammer was bad enough; lining up the tiny holes in
the ends of the links and getting the rivet in without dropping it
was torture. He remembered someone telling him once that there
were fifty thousand links in a really high-class mail shirt. He also
remembered what he'd paid for such an item. It didn't seem quite
so expensive, somehow.

"Is that all you've done?"

He looked up at her. "Yes," he said.

"You're very slow."

"I'll get quicker," he replied. "I expect you get into a rhythm after a bit." He picked up a rivet and promptly dropped it. It vanished forever among the heaped-up links on his lap. "What happens to all this stuff, then?"

"We sell it," she said. "Juifrez'll pick it up on the cart and take it up the mountain to the Stringer pass. That's where he meets the buyers. Of course," she added, "we've got you to thank."

"For what?"

"For our living," she said gravely. "For fighting your war. We've been tidying up after you ever since you started it. If it wasn't for you and your friends, I don't know what we'd have done."

"Oh," Miel said.

"It was Juifrez's idea," she went on. "Our village was one of the first to be burned out, it was soon after you attacked the supply train for the first time. Aigel; don't suppose you've ever heard of it. We ran away as soon as we saw the dust from the cavalry column, and when we came back . . ." She shrugged. "The idea was to walk down to Rax — that's the next village along the valley — and see if they'd take us in. But on the way we came across the place where you'd done the ambush. Nobody had been back there; well, I suppose a few scouts, to find out what had happened, but nobody'd buried the bodies or cleared away the mess. You'd burned all the food and the supplies, of course, but we found one cart we could patch up, and we reckoned that'd be better than walking. Then Juifrez said, 'Surely all this stuff's got to be worth some money to someone,' and that was that. Ever since then, we've been following you around, living off your leftovers. You're very popular with us, actually. Juifrez says you provide for us, like a good lord should. The founder of the feast, he calls you." She laughed. "I hope you've got someone to take your place while you're away," she said. "If the resistance packs up, we're really in trouble."

While you're away; the implication being that sooner or later he'd go back. "He's your leader, then," he said, "this Juifrez?"

"I suppose so," she replied. "Actually, he's my husband. And while I think of it, it'd probably be just as well if you didn't let him find out who you are. Like I said, he thinks very highly of you, but all the same . . ." She clicked her tongue. "I suppose he'd argue that the lord's job is to provide for his people, and the best way he could do that is fetching a high price from the Mezentines. He's not an insensitive man, but he's very conscious of his duty to his people. The greatest good for the greatest number, and so forth."

"Juifrez Stratiotes," Miel said suddenly.

"You've heard of him." She sounded genuinely surprised. "Fancy that. He'd be so flattered. After all, he's just a little local squire, not a proper gentleman. You've met him, of course, when he goes to the city to pay the rents. But I assumed he'd just be one face in a line."

"He breeds sparrowhawks," Miel remembered. "I bought one from him once. Quick little thing, with rather narrow wings."

She was grinning again. "I expect you remember the hawk," she said. "Don't let me keep you from your work."

She was walking away. "When will he be back?" Miel asked. "I mean, the rest of them."

"Tonight, after they've buried the bodies." She stopped. "Of course," she said slowly, "there's a very good chance he might recognize you, even all scruffy and dirty. And you're the only live one they found this time, so he'll probably want to see you."

"Probably," Miel said.

She took a few more steps, then hesitated. "Can you think of anybody else who might want you?" she said. "For money, I mean."

"No."

"What about the Vadani? They've been helping you, haven't they?"

"Yes," Miel said, "but the Mezentines would pay more."

"And they're closer." She hadn't turned round. "But you're good friends with Duke Orsea, aren't you? And he's with the Vadani now. Juifrez isn't a greedy man. If he could get enough for our people . . . Or better still, if you could arrange for us to go there. The Vadani aren't allowing any of us across the border, they're afraid it'll make the Mezentines more determined to carry on with the war. If you could get Duke Orsea to persuade the Vadani, we'd be safe. Juifrez would see the sense in that. Well?"

Miel shook his head, though of course she wasn't looking at him. He wasn't quite sure when or why, but the balance between them had changed. "Orsea doesn't like me much anymore," he said. "And I don't know Duke Valens, there's no reason why he'd put himself out for me."

"Don't you care?" She sounded angry, almost. "You sound like you aren't really interested."

"I'm not," he heard himself say. He'd pinpointed the shift; it had been the moment when he'd remembered her husband's name. "At least . . ." He sighed. "The best thing would be if your husband didn't see me," he said. "But I can't ask you to lie to him, or anything like that."

"No, you can't." Snapped back at him, as if she was afraid of the very thought. "I've never lied to Juifrez."

No, he thought; but you probably would, if I worked on you a little. But I'm not going to do that. I'm in enough trouble already on account of another man's wife. "Good," he said. "Look, if you think it's worth trying to get help from the Vadani, I'm hardly going to argue. I'm just not sure it'll come to anything, that's all."

"You sound like you want us to sell you to the Mezentines."

"No, not really."

The air felt brittle; he felt as though he could ball his fist and smash it, and the inside of the barn would split into hundreds of facets, like a splintered mirror. Just the effect he had on people, he assumed. "I'm not in any position to tell you what to do, am I?" he said, and it came out sounding peevish and bitter, which wasn't what he'd intended. "I'm sorry," he added quickly, but she didn't seem to have heard. "If it wasn't for your people, I'd probably have died on the battlefield, or been picked up by the enemy, which amounts to the same thing."

She sighed. "You're the Ducas," she said. "You can't help being

valuable, to someone or other. Finding you was like finding someone else's purse in the street. We aren't thieves, but we do need
the money." She turned, finally, and looked at him. Exasperation?
Maybe. "It'd be easier if you weren't so damned accommodating.
Aristocratic good manners, I suppose." She shrugged. "And for
pity's sake stop fiddling with that stuff. You're no good at it, and
the Ducas isn't supposed to be able to work for his living. Leave it.
One of the men can do it tonight, when they get back."

She walked away and left him; nothing decided, and he wasn't
even allowed to try and make himself useful. He thought: she
doesn't love her husband, or not particularly, but that's not an important issue in her life. It's probably a good thing to be beyond
the reach of love. And then he thought of Ziani Vaatzes, and the
things he'd done for love, and the things he'd done with love, and
with lovers. Ziani Vaatzes could mend chainmail, and nobody
would think twice about it; he could probably sew, too. He could
certainly bring down cities, and ruin the lives of other people; and
all for love, and with it, using it as a tool, as was fitting for a skilled
artisan.

Use or be used, he thought. These people can use me, as Ziani
used me; it's the Ducas' function in society to be useful. (He wondered: if Vaatzes were standing in front of me right now, would I
try to kill him? Answer, yes; instinctively, without thinking, like a
dog with a bird.)

Nobody likes being bored, especially when their life is also
hanging in the balance. But the Ducas learns boredom, just as he
learns the rapier, the lute and the management of horse, hound
and falcon. Miel leaned back against the wall and put his hands
behind his head.

3

Partly because he was bored and had nothing better to do, Ziani Vaatzes crossed the yard, left the castle by the middle gate, and walked slowly down the slight hill toward the huddle of buildings that snuggled against the outside of the curtain wall like chicks under the wings of a broody hen. He was looking for smoke; not just the wisps of an ordinary household fire, but the intermittent gusts of gray cloud from a well-worked bellows. Once he'd found what he was looking for, he followed it until he heard the ring of a hammer, and then he followed that.

Inevitably, there was a small crowd in the doorway of the smithy. There always is: a customer waiting for his job to be finished, poor and frugal types who'd rather keep warm by someone else's fire, old men wanting to be listened to, chancers waiting for a good moment to ask a favor. One of the old men was talking when he got there. Nobody could hear a word he said over the sound of the hammer, but he didn't seem to care, or to have noticed. One or two heads turned to look as Ziani joined the back of the group. A month or so ago they'd all have stared at him, but the Duke's pet black-faced Mezentine had stopped being news some time back. Now he was just one more straggler from the castle, an aristocrat by association, a somebody but nobody important. They probably all knew that he was an engineer, which would in itself explain why he was hanging round the forge; an assumption, and perfectly true.

He watched the smith drawing down a round bar into a ta-pered square section, and allowed his mind to drift; the chime of the hammer and the rasping breath of the bellows soothed him like the most expensive music, and the warmth of the fire made him yawn. None of these people would have heard the news yet; they didn't know about the plan to abandon the city and strike out into the plains. Probably just as well, or there'd be panic, anger, moaning, reluctance. Valens wouldn't break the news until all the arrangements for the evacuation had been made, right down to what each of them would be allowed to take with him and which cart it'd be stowed in. There'd be an announcement, and just enough time for the evacuation to be carried out smoothly and efficiently, not enough time for anybody to have a chance to think about it. The Vadani didn't strike him as the sort of people who worried too much about the decisions their duke made on their behalf, such as abandoning their home, or starting a war with the Perpetual Republic. He wondered about that. You could evacuate Mezentia in a day; everybody would do as he was told, because that was what they'd been brought up to do. The Vadani would do it because they believed that Valens knew best. In this case, of course, he did. The policy was irreproachably sensible and practi-cal. Ziani smiled at the thought, as a god might smile at the en-lightened self-interest of his creation.

The smith paused to quench the top half of his work and swill down a mug of water before leaning into the bellows handle. The old man was still talking. Someone else cut across him to ask the smith a question, which was answered with a shrug and a shake of the head. Reasonable enough; why bother with words when you know nobody can ever hear what you say. The bellows wheezed like a giant snoring, as though the old man's interminable droning had put it to sleep.

He's working the steel too cold, Ziani thought; but of course it wasn't his place to say so, not in someone else's shop, when his opinion hadn't been asked for. The slovenliness annoyed him a little, just enough to spoil the pleasure of watching metal being worked. As unobtrusively as possible, he disengaged and left the forge. I must find myself some work to do, he told himself, I need to be busy. I wash my hands three times a day here, but they never get dirty.

Back through the gate in the curtain wall; as he walked through it, he felt someone following him. He frowned. Duke Valens was far too well-mannered to have his guests shadowed, and far too sensible to waste an employee's time on such a pointless exercise. He quickened his step a little. There were plenty of people about, no reason to be concerned.

"Excuse me."

He hesitated, then carried on, walking a little faster. "Excuse me," the voice said again; then a shadow fell across his face, and someone was standing in front of him, blocking his path.

Not the strangest-looking human being Ziani had ever seen, but not far off it. He was absurdly tall, not much under seven feet, and his sleeveless jerkin and plain hose did nothing to disguise how extraordinarily thin he was. Probably not starvation, because the clothes themselves looked new and fairly expensive, and he didn't have the concave cheeks and sunken eyes of a starving man. Instead, his face was almost perfectly flat — minute stump for a nose, stupid little slit for a mouth, and tiny ears — though the rest of his head was round and slightly pointed, like an onion. He had a little crest of black hair on the very top (at first glance Ziani had taken it for a cap) and small, round eyes. The best guess Ziani could make at his age was somewhere between twenty-five and fifty.

"Sorry if I startled you," he said. "Are you Ziani Vaatzes, the Mezentine?"

"That's me," Ziani replied. "Who're you?"

The thin man smiled, and his face changed completely. He looked like an allegorical representation of Joy, painted by an enthusiastic but half-trained apprentice. "My name is Gace Raimbaut Elemosyn Daurenja," he replied. "May I say what a pleasure and an honor it is to meet you."

Oh, Ziani thought. He made a sort of half-polite grunting noise.

"Allow me to introduce myself," the thin man went on, and Ziani noticed that there were dark red scars on both his earlobes. "Like yourself I am an engineer and student of natural philosophy and the physical world. I have been an admirer of your work for some time, and feel that there's a great deal I could learn from you."

He's learned that speech by heart, Ziani thought; but why bother? "I see," he said. "Well, that's very . . ." He ran out of words, and couldn't be bothered to look for any more.

The thin man shifted a little, and Ziani could just about have squeezed through the gap between him and the wall without committing an assault. But he stayed where he was.

"I must apologize for accosting you like this," the thin man went on. "It is, of course, a deplorable breach of good manners, and not the sort of thing I would normally dream of doing. However . . ." He hesitated, but Ziani was fairly sure the pause was part of the script. Stage direction; look thoughtful. "We move in rather different social circles," the thin man went on, and Ziani wished he knew a little bit more about Vadani accents. He was fairly sure the man had one, but he couldn't place it well enough to grasp its significance. "You enjoy the well-deserved favor of the Duke. I am only a poor student. It's hardly likely our paths would have crossed in the normal course of events."

"Student," Ziani said, repeating the only word in the speech he'd been able to get any sort of grip on. "At a university, you mean?"

"Indeed." The thin man's smile widened like sunrise on the open plains. "I have honors degrees in philosophy, music, literature, astronomy, law, medicine and architecture. I have also completed apprenticeships in many crafts and trades, including carpentry, gold, silver, copper, foundry and blacksmith work, building and masonry, coopering, tanning, farriery and charcoal-burning. I am qualified to act as a public scrivener and notary in four jurisdictions, and I can play the lute, the rebec and the re-corder. People have asked me from time to time if there's anything I can't do; usually I answer that only time will tell." The smile was beginning to slop over into a smirk; he restrained it and pulled it back into a look of modest pride. "I was wondering," he went on, "if you would care to give me a job."

Ziani's imagination had been busy while the thin man was talking, but even so he hadn't been expecting that. "A job," he repeated.

"That's right. Terms and conditions fully negotiable."

Ziani made an effort and pulled himself together. "Sorry," he said. "I don't have any jobs that need doing."

A tiny wisp of a frown floated across the thin man's face, but not for long. "Please don't get the idea that I'm too delicate and refined for hard manual labor," he went on. "Quite the contrary. At various times I've worked in the fields and the mines. I can dig ditches and lay a straight hedge. I can also cook, sew and clean; in fact, I was for five months senior footman to the Diomenes house in Eremia."

Try as he might, Ziani couldn't think of anything to say to that; so he said, "I see. So why did you leave?"

Every trace of expression drained out of the thin man's face. "There was a misunderstanding," he said. "However, we parted on good terms in the end, and I have references."

Ziani almost had to shake himself to break the spell. "Look," he said, "that's all very impressive, but I'm not hiring right now, and if I did give you a job, I couldn't pay you. I'm just . . ." He ran out of words again. "I'm just a guest here, not much better than a refugee. God only knows why the Duke lets me hang around, but he does. I'm very sorry, and it's very flattering to be asked, but I haven't got anything for you."

"I'm sorry to hear that," the thin man said. "Very sorry indeed. I'm afraid I'd allowed myself to hope." He seemed to fold inwards, then almost immediately reflated. "If you'd like to see my certifi-cates and references, I have them here, in this bag." He pulled a small goatskin satchel off his shoulder and began undoing the buckles. "Some of them may be a little creased, but —"

"No," Ziani said, rather more forcefully than he'd intended. "Thank you," he added. "But there's no need, really. I don't need any workers, and that's all there is to it."

"A private secretary," the thin man said. "I can take dictation and copy letters in formal, cursive and demotic script . . ."

Ziani took a step forward. The thin man didn't move. Ziani stopped. "No," he said.

"A valet, maybe," the thin man said. "As a gentleman of the court —"

Because he was so thin, he'd be no problem to push aside. But Ziani felt an overwhelming reluctance to touch him, the sort of instinctive loathing he'd had for spiders when he was a boy. He retraced the step he'd just taken and folded his arms. "I'm not a courtier," he said, "and I haven't got any money, and I'm not hiring. You don't seem able to understand that."

"Payment wouldn't be essential." The thin man was watching him closely, as if inspecting him for cracks and flaws. "At least, not until something presented itself in which I might be of use. I have . . ." This time the hesitation was genuine. "I have certain resources," the thin man said warily, "enough to provide for my needs, for a while. In the meantime, perhaps you might care to set me some task, by way of a trial. It would be foolish of me to expect you to take me on trust without a demonstration of my abilities."

Too easy, Ziani thought. It must be some kind of trap. On the other hand . . . "All right," he said. "Here's what I'll do. I'll give you a test-piece to make, and if it's up to scratch, if ever I do need anybody, I'll bear you in mind. Will that do?"

The thin man nodded, prompt and responsive as a mechanism. "What more could I ask?" he said.

Ziani nodded, and applied his mind. To be sure of getting rid of him it'd have to be something unusual in these parts, not something he could just go out and buy, or get someone to make for him and then pass off as his own. "Fine," he said. "Do you know what a ratchet is?"

The thin man's eyebrows rose. "Of course."

"All right, then," Ziani said. "At the factory where I used to work, we had a small portable winch for lifting heavy sections of steel bar, things like that. It hung by a chain off a hook bolted into a rafter, and you could lift a quarter-ton with it, just working the handle backward and forward with two fingers. Do you think you could make me something like that?"

"I guarantee it," the thin man said. "Will six weeks be soon enough?"

Ziani grinned. "Take as long as you like," he said.

"Six weeks." The thin man nodded decisively. "As soon as it's finished, I'll send word to you at the Duke's palace. I promise you won't be disappointed."

Ziani nodded; then he asked, "All those degrees and things you mentioned. Where did you say they were from?"

"The city university at Lonazep," the thin man replied. "I have the charters right here . . ."

"No, that's fine." Was there a university at Lonazep? Now he came to think of it, he had a feeling there was, unless he was thinking of some other place beginning with L. Not that it mattered in the slightest. "Well, I'll be hearing from you, then."

"You most certainly will." The thin man beamed at him again, bowed, then started to walk away backward up the hill. "And thank you, very much indeed, for your time. I absolutely guarantee that you won't be disappointed."

Whatever other gifts and skills the thin man had, he could walk backward without looking or bumping into things. Just when Ziani was convinced he was going to keep on bowing and smiling all the way up to the citadel, he backed round a corner and vanished. Ziani counted to ten under his breath, then headed back down the hill toward the town, making an effort not to break into a run.

Back where he'd started from, more or less. This time, he

walked past the smithy and down an alleyway he'd noticed in passing a day or so earlier. It looked just like all the others, but he'd recognized the name painted on the blue tile: Seventeenth Street. Past the Temperance and Tolerance, he recalled, second door on the left. He found it — a plain wooden door, weathered gray, with a wooden latch. You'll have to knock quite hard, they'd told him, she's rather deaf.

He knocked, counted fifty under his breath, and knocked again. Nothing doing. He shrugged and was about to walk away when the latch rattled, the door opened and an enormously fat woman in a faded red dress came out into the street.

"Was that you making all the noise?" she said.

"Sorry." Ziani frowned. "Are you Henida Zeuxis?"

"That's right."

He wanted to ask, *Are you sure?*, but he managed not to. "My name's Ziani Vaatzes. I'd like to talk to you for a moment, if you can spare the time."

"Been expecting you," the fat woman replied. "Marcellinus at the Poverty said you'd been asking round after me." She looked at him as if she was thinking of buying him, then added, "Come in if you want."

He followed her through the door into a small paved court-yard. There was a porch on one side, its timbers bowed under the weight of an enormous overgrown vine, in front of which stood two plain wooden chairs and a round table, with two cups and a wine bottle on it.

"Drink," she said; not a suggestion or an offer, just a statement of fact. She tilted the bottle, pushed one cup across the table at him, and sat down.

"Thanks," he said, leaving the cup where it was. "Did — what did you say his name was?"

"Marcellinus. And no, he didn't say what you wanted to see me about. I can guess, though."

Vaatzes nodded. "Go on, then," he said.

"You're an engineer, aren't you?" she said, wiping her mouth on her left forefinger. "Blacksmith, metalworker, whatever. You need materials. Someone told you I used to be in business, trading east with the Cure Doce." She shook her head. "Whoever told you that's way behind the times. I retired. Bad knee," she added, squeezing her right kneecap. "So, sorry, can't help you."

"Actually," Vaatzes smiled, "the man at the Poverty and Justice did tell me you'd retired, but it wasn't business I wanted to talk to you about. At least," he added, "not directly."

"Oh." She looked at him as though he'd just slithered out of check and taken her queen. "Well, in that case, what can I do for you?"

Vaatzes edged a little closer. "Your late husband," he said.

"Oh. Him."

"Yes." He picked up the wine cup but didn't drink anything. "I understand that he used to lead a mule-train out along the southern border occasionally. Is that right?"

She pulled a face, as though trying to remember something unimportant from a long time ago. It was a reasonable performance, but she held it just a fraction too long. "Salt," she said. "There's some place in the desert where they dig it out of the ground. A couple of times he went down there to the market, where they take the stuff to sell it off. Thought he could make a profit but the margins were too tight. Mind you," she added, "that's got to be, what, twenty years ago, and we weren't living here then, it was while we were still in Chora. Lost a fair bit of money, one way and another."

Vaatzes nodded. "That's more or less what I'd heard," he said.

She looked up at him. "Why?" she asked. "You thinking of going into the salt business?"

"It had crossed my mind."

"Forget it." She waved her hand, as though swatting a fat, blind fly. "The salt trade's all tied up, has been for years. Your lot, mostly, the Mezentines. They run everything now."

"But not twenty years ago," Vaatzes said quietly, and that made her look at him again. "And besides, even now they mostly buy through intermediaries. Cure Doce, as I understand."

"Could be." She yawned, revealing an unexpectedly pristine set of teeth. "I never got into that particular venture very much. Knew from the outset it was a dead end. If he'd listened to me, maybe things'd be very different now." She tilted the bottle over her cup, but Vaatzes could see it was already three-quarters full. "When we were living in Chora —"

"I expect you had something to do with it," he said mildly. "Presumably you were buying the stock he took with him to trade for the salt."

"Could be. Can't remember." She yawned again, but she was picking at a loose thread on her sleeve. "That was my side of the business back then, yes. I'd buy the stuff in Chora, he'd take it out to wherever he was trading that year. Never worked out. Any margin I managed to make at home, he'd blow it all out in the wilderness somewhere. That's what made me throw him out, eventually."

"I can see it must've been frustrating for you," Vaatzes said. "But to get back to the salt. Can you remember who it was he used to buy it from? The miners, I mean, the people who dug it out of the ground."

She looked at him, and she most certainly wasn't drunk or rambling. "I don't think he ever mentioned it," she said. "Just salt-miners, that's all."

"Are you sure?" Vaatzes raised his eyebrows. "I'd have thought that if you were trading with them, you'd have known a bit about them. So as to know what they'd be likely to want, in exchange for the salt."

"You'd have thought." She shrugged. "I guess that's how come we lost so much money."

Vaatzes smiled. "I see," he said. "Well, that explains that. It's a shame, though."

He leaned back in his chair and sipped a little of the wine. It was actually quite good. She waited for rather a long time, then scowled.

"Are you really thinking about going into the salt business?"

He nodded. "And of course," he went on, "I wouldn't expect an experienced businesswoman to go around giving valuable trade secrets away for nothing." She nodded, very slightly. He went on, "Unfortunately, until I've got finance of my own, backers, I haven't got anything to offer up front, in exchange for valuable information."

"Ah."

"But." He waited for a moment, then continued. "It occurred to me, however, that you might be interested in a partnership. Of sorts," he added quickly, as she looked up at him sharply. "I'm sure you know far more about this sort of thing than I do; but the way I see it is, I can't get any serious funding for the idea unless I've got something hard to convince a potential backer with. Once I've got the money, of course . . ."

"I see," she said, with a sour little smile. "I tell you what I know, you take that and get your funding with it, and we settle up afterward, when the business is up and running." She sighed. "No disrespect, but what are you bringing to the deal?"

He smiled. "Energy," he said. "Youth. Boundless enthusiasm. And the information isn't doing you any good as it is," he added. "It's just cluttering up your mind, like inherited furniture."

Her scowl deepened. "There'd have to be a contract," she said.

"Of course," Vaatzes said, smiling. "All properly written up and sealed and everything."

"Ten percent."

"Five."

She made a vague grunting noise, shook her head. "Fair enough," she said. "It's a waste of your time and effort, mind, there never was a margin in it."

"Times have changed," Vaatzes said. "The war, for one thing."

"What's the war got to do with it?"

He gave her a fancy-you-not-guessing look. "All those soldiers," he said, "on both sides, living off field rations. You know the sort of thing: salt beef, salt pork, bacon . . ."

She blinked. "That's true," she said. She hesitated, then added, "The Mezentines always used to buy off the Cure Doce, at Mundus Vergens. Don't suppose the Cure Doce go there much anymore, what with the guerrillas and all." She scratched her nose; the first unselfconscious gesture he'd seen her make. "I wonder how they're getting salt nowadays," she said.

"From Lonazep," Vaatzes said briskly. "I have done a little bit of research, you see. It's coming in there from somewhere, but nobody's sure where. But it's rock salt; Valens' men have found enough of it in the ration bags of dead Mezentines to know that. So it must ultimately be coming from the desert; and no army can keep going without salt, not if they're far from home, at the long end of their supply line. So if someone could find the producers and buy up the entire supply — well, that'd be a worthwhile contribution to the war effort, in my opinion. What do you think?"

She was scowling at him again. "I should've known you'd be political," she said.

"Me?" He shook his head. "Not in my nature. But I think that if I had solid information to go on, I could get some money out of the Duke. I've got a living to earn, after all. It looks like I'm going to be stuck here for a long time, maybe the rest of my life. It's about time I settled down and got a job."

She breathed out slowly. "Like I said," she replied, "there'd have to be a written agreement. You come back with that and I might have something for you."

Vaatzes tried not to be too obvious about taking a breath. "A map?"

"Who said anything about a map?"

"The Duke would want there to be a map," Vaatzes said. "A genuine one," he added sternly, "not one that smudges as soon as he opens it."

"There might be one," she said slowly. "I'd have to look. There's loads of his old junk up in the roof. Maybe not a map, but there could be a journal. Bearings, number of days traveled, names of places and people. Better than a map, really."

Vaatzes dipped his head. "As you say." He stood up. "If you happen to come across it, don't throw it away."

She looked up at him, like a dog at table. "You'll see about a contract?"

"Straightaway."

She thought for a moment, then smiled. It wasn't much, but it was the only smile she had. "Sorry if I came across as a bit distant," she said. "But you've got to be careful."

"Of course. Thank you for the wine."

She looked at his cup. "You hardly touched it."

"I don't drink."

He left her without looking round and closed the door behind him. As he walked up the hill, he tried to think about money. He didn't have any, of course, and he had no way of getting any, except by asking for it. Were he to do so, assuming he asked the right people, he was sure he could have as much as he wanted; but that would be missing the point. Obviously Valens was the one man he couldn't ask (later, of course; but not now); that still left him a wide range of choices. Better, though, if he could get money from somewhere else. Under other circumstances, that wouldn't be a problem. But with time pressing . . .

He stopped. He hadn't seen her (hadn't been expecting to see her, so hadn't been on his guard) and now they were face to face, only a yard or so apart. She was coming out of a linen-draper's shop, flanked on either side by a maid and an equerry. She'd seen him, and there was no chance of her not recognizing him, or taking him for someone else.

"Hello," she said.

He couldn't think what to say. For one thing, there was the horrendous business of protocol and the proper form of address. How do you reply to a greeting from the duchess of a duchy that no longer exists (but whose destruction has not been officially recognized by the regime whose hospitality you are enjoying)? There was probably a page and a half on the subject in one of Duke Valens' comprehensive books of manners, but so far he hadn't managed to stay awake long enough to get past the prefaces and dedications. Other protocols, too: how do you address the wife of a man you betrayed by telling him half the truth about his wife and his best friend? How do you respond to a friendly greeting from someone whose city gates you opened to the enemy? There was bound to be a proper formula, and if only he knew it there wouldn't be any awkwardness or embarrassment at this meeting. As it was, he was going to have to figure something out for himself, from first principles.

"Hello," he replied, and bowed; a small, clumsy, comic nod, faulty in execution but clear enough in its meaning. Cheating, of course.

"I haven't seen you for a long time," she said. "How are you settling in here?"

He smiled. "It's one of the advantages of being an exile," he said. "Everywhere you go is strange to you, so getting used to somewhere new isn't such a problem."

She frowned very slightly. There were people behind her in the shop, wanting to leave but too polite to push past her, her ladies-in-waiting and her armed guard. "In that case, it ought to be like that for me too, surely."

He shook his head. "Not really," he said. "You're not an exile, you're a refugee."

"Same thing, surely."

"No." Should he have qualified that, or toned it down? No, my lady? "There's quite a difference. You left because your country was taken away from you. I left because my country wanted rid of me. I suppose it's like the difference between a widow and someone whose husband leaves her for somebody else." He shrugged. "It's not so much of a difference after all, really. Are you going back to the palace?"

She pulled a face. "I've only just managed to escape," she replied. "It's a wonderful building and everybody's very kind, but . . ." She nodded at the basket one of the maids was carrying. "Embroidery silk. Vitally important that I choose it for myself."

"I can see that," Vaatzes replied. "Hence the cavalry escort. Which way are you going?"

She thought for a moment. "Downhill," she said. "So far I haven't managed to get more than six hundred yards from the palace gates, but I'm taking it slowly, by degrees."

The shopkeeper was standing behind her, looking respectfully tense, with her bottled-up customers shifting from foot to foot all round her. "In that case," Vaatzes said, "might I recommend the fabric stall in the little square off Twenty-Ninth Street? I seem to remember seeing a couple of rolls of genuine Mezentine silk brocade which might interest you."

She raised an eyebrow. "Twenty-Ninth Street?"

"At the bottom of Eighth Street and turn left. I know," he added, "I tried to work it out too. I tried prime numbers, square roots and dividing by Conselher's Constant, but I still can't make any sense of how the numbers run."

"And you an engineer," she said. "I'd have thought you'd have worked it out by now."

"Too deep for me. There must be a logical sequence, though. You'll have to ask Duke Valens. He must know, if anyone does."

"I'm sure." Not the slightest flicker of an eyelid, and the voice perfectly controlled, like a guardsman's horse in a parade. "I gather it's just the sort of thing that would interest him."

She nodded very slightly to the maid on her left, and she and her escort began to move at precisely the same moment, down the hill, toward the Eighth Street gate. At a guess, the little square off Twenty-Ninth Street was a good eight hundred and fifty yards from the palace. It reminded him of the section in *King Fashion*, the unspeakably dull hunting manual that everybody was so keen on in these parts, about the early stages of training a falcon; how much further you let it fly each day, when you're training it to come back to the lure.

They didn't speak to each other all the way down Eighth Street; but at the narrow turning off the main thoroughfare she looked at him and asked, "So what are you doing? Are you managing to keep yourself occupied?"

As he answered her (he was politely and unobtrusively evasive, and told her nothing), he thought: between any other two people, this could easily sound like flirtation, or at the very least a preliminary engagement of skirmishers as two armies converge. But I don't suppose she's ever flirted in her life, and (he had to make an effort not to smile) of course, I'm the Mezentine, so different I'm not quite human. Flirting with me would be like trying to burn water; couldn't be done even if anyone wanted to. I think she's got nobody to talk to; nobody at all.

"You should set up in business," she was saying. "I'm sure you'd do very well. After all, you got that factory going in Eremia very quickly, and if it hadn't been for the war . . ."

"The thought had crossed my mind," he replied gravely. "But I get the feeling that manufacturing isn't the Vadani's strongest suit, and I haven't got the patience to spend a year training anybody to saw a straight line. Besides, I quite like a change of direction. I was thinking about setting up as a trader."

She laughed. "You think you'd look good in red?"

"I forgot," he said, as lightly as he could manage. "Your sister's a Merchant Adventurer, isn't she?"

"That's right." Just a trace of chill in her voice.

"I wonder if she'd be prepared to help me," he said, increasing the level of enthusiasm but not piling it on too thick. "A bit of advice, really. I imagine she knows pretty well everybody in the trade. It seems like a fairly small world, after all."

"You want to meet her so she can teach you how to be her business rival? I'm not sure it works like that."

An adversarial side to her nature he hadn't noticed or appreciated before. She liked verbal fencing. He hadn't thought it was in her nature; perhaps she'd picked the habit up somewhere, from someone. "I was thinking more in terms of a partnership," he said.

"Oh." She blinked. Arch didn't suit her. "And what would you bring to it, I wonder?"

"I heard about a business opportunity the other day," he replied. "It sounds promising, but I'm not a trader."

She nodded. "Well," she said, "I owe you a favor, don't I?" She paused. Something about her body language put her maids and equerries on notice that they'd suddenly been struck blind and dumb. Impressive how she could do that. "I haven't had a chance to thank you," she went on, somewhat awkwardly.

"What for?"

She frowned. "For getting me out of Civitas Eremiae alive," she said.

He nodded. "What you mean is, why did I do that?"

"I had wondered."

He looked away. It could quite easily have been embarrassment, the logical reaction of a reticent man faced with unexpected gratitude. "Chance," he said. "Pure chance. Oh, I knew who you were, of course. But I happened to run into you as I was making my own escape. It was just instinct, really."

"I see." She was frowning. "So if you'd happened to run into someone else first . . ."

"I didn't, though," he said. "So that's all right."

"I'm sorry," she said. "I think I made it sound like I was afraid — I don't know, that you were calling in a debt or something."

"It's all right," he said. "Let's talk about something else."

"Fine." She lifted her head, like a horse sniffing for rain. "Such as?"

"Oh, I don't know. How are *you* settling in?"

"What?"

"Well, you asked me."

She hesitated, then shrugged. "There are days when I forget where I am," she said. "I wake up, and it's a sunny morning, and I sit in the window-seat and pick up my embroidery; and the view from the window is different, and I remember, we're not in

Eremia, we're in Civitas Vadanis. So I guess you could say I've settled in quite well. I mean," she added, "one place is very much like another when you stay in your room embroidering cushion covers. It's a very nice room," she went on. "They always have been. I suppose I've been very lucky, all my life."

The unfair question would be, *So you enjoy embroidery, then?* If he asked it, either she'd have to lie to him, or else put herself in his power, forever. "What are you making at the moment?" he asked.

"A saddle-cloth," she answered brightly. "For Orsea, for special occasions. You see, all the other things I made for him, everything I ever made . . ." She stopped. Burned in the sack of Civitas Eremiae, or else looted by the Mezentines, rejected as inferior, amateur work, and dumped. He thought of a piece of tapestry he'd seen in Orsea's palace before it was destroyed; he had no idea whether she'd made it, or some other noblewoman with time to fill. It hardly mattered; ten to one, her work was no better and no worse. The difference between her and me, Vaatzes thought, is that she's not a particularly good artisan. I don't suppose they'd let her work in Mezentia.

"It must take hours to do something like that," he said.

She looked past him. "Yes," she said.

"Let me guess." (He didn't want to be cruel, but it was necessary.) "Hunting scenes."

She actually laughed. "Well, of course. Falconry on the left, deer-hunting on the right. I've been trying really hard to make the huntsman look like Orsea, but I don't know; all the men in my embroideries always end up looking exactly the same. Sort of square-faced, with straight mouths. And my horses are always walking forward, with their front near leg raised."

He nodded. "You could take up music instead."

"Certainly not." She gave him a mock scowl. "Stringed instruments chafe the fingers, and no gentlewoman would ever play something she had to blow down. Which just leaves the triangle, and —"

"Quite." He looked up. "Here we are," he said. "Twenty-Ninth Street. The square's just under that archway there."

She nodded. "Thank you for showing me the way," she said.

"I hope you find what you're looking for."

"Vermilion," she replied. "And some very pale green, for doing light-and-shade effects on grass and leaves."

"Best of luck, then." He stood aside to let her pass.

"I expect I'll see you at the palace," she said. "And yes, I'll write to my sister."

He shook his head. "Don't go to any trouble."

"I won't. But I write to her once a week anyway."

She walked on, and he lost sight of her behind the shoulders of her maids. Once she was out of sight, he leaned against the wall and breathed out, as though he'd just been doing something strenuous and delicate. There goes a very dangerous woman, he thought. She could be just what I need, or she could spoil everything. I'll have to think quite carefully about using her again.

Money. He straightened up. A few heads were turning (what's the matter? Never seen a Mezentine before? Probably they hadn't). Almost certainly, some of the people who'd passed them by on the way here would have recognized the exiled Eremian duchess, and of course he himself was unmistakable. Just by walking down the hill with her, he'd made a good start.

He started to walk west, parallel to the curtain wall. Obviously she's not stupid, he thought, or naive. Either she's got an agenda of her own — I don't know; making Valens jealous, maybe? — or else she simply doesn't care anymore. In either case, not an instrument of precision. A hammer, rather than a milling cutter or a fine drill-bit. The biggest headache, though, is still getting the timing right. It'd be so much easier if I had enough money.

A thought occurred to him, and he stopped in his tracks. The strange, weird, crazy man; him with all those funny names. What was it he'd said? *I have certain resources, enough to provide for my needs, for a while.* Well, he'd asked to be taken on as an apprentice, and in most places outside the Republic, it was traditional for an apprentice to pay a premium for his indentures.

He shook the thought away, as though it was a wisp of straw on his sleeve. Money or not, he didn't need freaks like that getting under his feet. For one thing, how could anyone possibly predict what someone like that would be likely to do at any given moment?

Embroidery, he thought; the women of the Mezentine Clothiers' Guild made the best tapestries in the world; all exactly the same, down to the last stitch. A lot of their work was hunting scenes, and it didn't matter at all that none of them had ever seen a deer or a boar, or a heron dragged down by a goshawk.

He smiled. Hunting made him think of Jarnac Ducas, who'd never had a chance to pay him for the fine set of boiled leather hunting armor he'd made. Of course that armor was now ashes, or spoils of war (much more valuable than the Duchess' cushions and samplers); but Jarnac had struck him as the sort of nobleman who took pride in paying all his bills promptly and without question. Where was Jarnac Ducas at the moment? Now he came to think of it, he hadn't seen his barrel chest or broad, annoying smile about the palace for what, days, weeks. The important question, of course, was whether he had any money. No, forget that. He was a nobleman; they always had money, their own or someone else's. They had the knack of finding it without even looking, like a tree's blind roots groping in the earth for water. With luck, though it wasn't of the essence, he'd run into Jarnac well before the city was packed up on carts and moved into the wilderness; in which case he'd be able to establish his foothold in the salt business, and everything would lead on neatly from that. Besides, he reflected, it would be appropriate to build Jarnac into the design at this stage; good engineering practice, economy of materials and moving parts.

He sighed. Time to get back to the palace for another of those interminable meals. Why they couldn't just eat their food and be done with it, he couldn't begin to guess. It wouldn't be so bad if the food was anything special, but it wasn't: nauseating quantities of roast meat, nearly always game of some description, garnished with heaps of boiled cabbage, turnips and carrots. They were going to have to do better than that if they were planning on seducing him from his purpose with decadence and rich living.

Jarnac Ducas, though. He smiled, though there was an element of self-reproach as well. So ideally suited for the purpose; he remembered a glimpse of him on the night when the Eremian capital was stormed, a huge man flailing down his enemies with a long-handled poleaxe, an enthralling display of skill, grace and brute strength. A good man to have on your side in a tight spot. Well, yes.

(Another thing, he asked himself as he climbed the steps to the palace yard gate; why so many courses? Soup first, then an entrée: minced meat, main meat, cold meat, preserved meat in a paste on biscuits, fiddly dried raw meat in little thin strips, followed by the grand finale, seven different kinds of dead bird stuffed up inside each other in ascending order of size. There were times when he'd have traded all his rights and entitlements in the future for four slices of rye bread and a chunk of Mezentine white cheese.)

They were ringing a bell, which meant you had to go and change your clothes. Another thing they had in excess. He'd counted fifteen tailors' shops in the lower town that day, but nobody in the whole city knew how to make a kettle. He thought about the Vadani, instinctively comparing them with his own people and finding them wanting on pretty well every score. Their deaths would be no great loss. When their culture and society had been wiped out and forgotten, the world would be poorer by a few idiosyncratic methods of trapping and killing animals and a fairly commonplace recipe for applesauce. Of course, that didn't make it right.

4

The worst words a general can utter, his father had told him once, were, *I never expected that.*

He didn't say them aloud, but that was cheating and didn't absolve him. He pulled his horse out of the pursuit and trotted a few yards up the slope, out of the way of a charge he could no longer check in time. They'd set a trap for him, and he'd obliged them.

Who were these people, anyway? They all looked very much the same to him, with their pigs'-belly faces and unnatural, straw-colored hair. Not that it mattered particularly much at the moment; it'd only make a difference if he lived long enough to make his report. If the observation died with him, it was worthless. Still, he wasn't sure why he knew it, but these weren't Eremians. They handled their horses too well, and their clothes were too clean. In which case, they could only be Vadani.

All he could do now was watch. The counterattack came in perfectly on time, slicing into his column of charging heavy cavalry rather than chopping at it, parting the front three squadrons from the ten behind. The front section carried on with their now fatuous charge; quite possibly they didn't even know yet that they'd sprung a trap and were about to be rolled up and wiped out. The back section had been stopped in their tracks, as though they'd ridden into a stone wall. From where he was he couldn't actually see the heavy infantry who'd been positioned to take them in flanks and rear, but he knew they'd be there. Instead, he watched the front three squadrons press home their onslaught on an enemy that had faded away into the rocky outcrops. He wanted to shout a warning, but they were far too distant to hear him. Instead, he watched the ambushing party come up at a neat, restrained canter. No need to hurry, waste energy unnecessarily, risk breaking their own irreproachable order. He couldn't see the details of the fighting, but he could track its progress by the litter of dead men and horses left behind. Well, he thought, that was that. Time to think about getting away from here.

Uphill, he decided. Of course, there might be further enemy reserves waiting just over the skyline, but he doubted it. No need; and his opponent didn't seem the sort to waste resources on redundant safeguards. If he could get over the crest of the hill, he'd be on the wrong side of the battle, with his conquerors between himself and the road home, but he was just one more fugitive. The enemy would have better things to do than chase him. Ride as far as the river, double back, take it steady. He'd be starving hungry by the time he reached the camp in the ruins of Civitas Eremiae, but that would be the least of his problems.

His horse was far too tired to gallop uphill, and speed would just draw unwelcome attention. He booted the wretched animal into a sullen sitting trot.

The Vadani, he thought; well, that would make sense. He knew next to nothing about them — he'd been recruited to fight the Eremians, and his research time before leaving home had been limited — but he did know that their aristocracy had a long tradition of hunting. That cleared up one small mystery; it explained why the tactic that had defeated him (taken him completely by surprise and off guard) seemed in retrospect so infuriatingly familiar. It wasn't a military stratagem at all; it was simply a commonplace of the hunt adapted for use against men. Cornered, the boar will charge the dogs. While they pull his head down, the huntsman steps forward and stabs him in the flank. Stupid, he rebuked himself; no Mezentine would have seen it coming, of course, but we should've. Father —

I might not ever see him again, he thought; and all because of a stupid mistake.

Well, it wouldn't come to that; and when he got back to camp, he'd make a point of telling General Mesemphytes to get hold of all the hunting manuals and textbooks he could find. If only we'd known we weren't fighting proper soldiers, we wouldn't have got in this mess.

Over the crest of the hill, looking down; below him, two full squadrons of heavy cavalry. They stood still and calm, here and there a horse swishing away flies with its tail. They knew that they probably weren't going to have a part to play in the battle, but they were quietly ready, just in case; eyes front, concentrating on the standards, which would give them the sign to move into action if they were needed after all. No call for them, therefore, to look up the hill, because nothing of any relevance would be coming from that direction. All he had to do was turn round, nice and easy, and go back the way he'd just come.

Someone whistled. Heads began to turn in his direction. Suddenly terrified, hurt and angry at his stupid bad luck, he dragged his horse's head over and dug his spurs in viciously, as though it was all the animal's fault. A jolt from the cantel of the saddle, and now at least he was a moving target, not a sitter. He looked over his shoulder as he approached the skyline. They didn't seem to be following him, so that was all right.

Before he could turn his head back, he felt the horse swerve. Not the best time to lose a stirrup. Without thinking, he grabbed for the pommel of the saddle with both hands, dropping his sword and the reins (panic reaction; haven't done that for twenty years, since I was first learning to ride). It would probably have been all right if someone hadn't hit him.

He felt no pain from the blow itself, but the ground hitting his shoulder was another matter. Bad, he thought, in the split second before the horse's back hoofs kicked him in the head.

When he woke up, he was flat on his back. He remembered that he was in danger and tried to get up, but found he couldn't. Ropes; no ropes. No need for ropes. Very bad indeed.

He could move his head, though; and he saw dead bodies, men and horses; spears sticking in the ground like vine-props blown over in a high wind. Plenty of dead people (nearly all his men, he realized, and was surprised at how little that affected him), but nobody alive that he could see.

His neck was tired and getting cramped, and on balance he'd rather look at the sky than the consequences of his own negligence. He rested his head on the turf, but that turned out to be a bad idea. He let it flop sideways instead. The picture in front of his eyes was blurring up. Well, he thought.

Some time later he felt a shadow on his face, and something nudged him; he couldn't feel it, but he deduced it from the fact that he moved a little.

"Live one," someone said.

He thought about the words, because they didn't seem to mean anything, but after a while he figured it out. Inaccurate, in any case.

Whoever it was said something else, but it didn't have proper words in it, just bulving and roaring, like livestock far away. He decided he couldn't be bothered with people talking anymore. If he just lay still they'd go away and leave him in peace.

"I said, can you hear me?"

No, he thought; but instead he forced his mouth open and said something. It came out as meaningless noise. A very slight increase in the warmth of the sun on his cheek suggested that the shadow-caster had gone away. Good riddance.

So, I won't be going back to camp to tell them about the Vadani, or hunting manuals. I suppose I'll just have to write them a letter. Can you write letters when you're . . . (what's the word? Begins with D), and will there be someone to carry it for me once I've written it?

Suddenly there were two faces directly above him; the ugliest, scariest faces he'd ever seen. He wanted to kick, fight and scream, but apparently that wasn't possible. Then everything hurt at the same time, and while it was hurting he left the ground and was raised up into the air. Angels, he thought; no, not angels, I think we can be quite definite about that. Demons. They come and rip your soul out of your body at the moment of the thing that begins with D, except that we don't believe in demons and all that superstitious nonsense in our family.

Wrong about that, apparently. Shame.

The demons were carrying him; and he thought, I must have led a very evil life, to have deserved this. He couldn't see them anymore because his head was lolling back. All he could see was a cart — plain old farm cart; apparently there're no fine social distinctions in the place where you go when you've been bad, and the fiends that torment you forever have pale skin, like the Eremians — and he was being loaded onto it, like any old junk.

"Get a move on," someone was saying. "Jarnac's men'll be back any time."

He thought about that, but it didn't make any sense. Technical demon talk, he assumed; and then it occurred to him that he hadn't died after all. Now that was unsettling.

He was alive, then; alive, paralyzed and lying in a dirty old cart along with weapons, boots, soldiers' clothes, belts, ration bags and water bottles. He thought of the phrase they used at country auctions back home, when a farm was being sold up: the live and dead stock. From where he was lying, there didn't seem to be much in it, but such subtle distinctions define the world.

Fine, he told the universe. If it's all the same to you, I'd prefer to die now, please. Apparently the universe wasn't listening.

He'd often ridden in carts, of course. As a boy he'd loved haymaking, riding in the wain as the men pitched the hay up. His job had been to compress it by trampling it down; he could remember how it yielded and bounced under his feet like a flexing muscle, as if it was trying to trick him into falling over. He'd loved the view, the fact that for two weeks a year he could be taller than the grownups and see further. He'd imagined himself in a chariot, not a cart, bringing home the spoils of war in a grand procession.

He flicked his eyes sideways and saw the junk heaped up all round him; spoils of war. An ambition fulfilled, he thought, and passed out.

He woke up because something hurt; in fact, he came out of sleep trying very hard to scream, but he didn't seem able to make any sound. Very bad indeed.

"Splint," someone said. He tried to remember what a splint was, but there were holes in his memory large enough for words to fall through. Anyway, whoever it was didn't seem to be talking to him. It hurt, though, and he clenched his hands to work out the pain.

Oh, he thought. Maybe not so bad after all.

"He's awake," someone said, and a face appeared above him; huge and round, like an ugly brick-red sun. Its eyes, round and watery blue, looked at him as if he was a thing rather than a human being; then the head lifted and looked away. "He'll keep," the voice said.

He cleared his throat, but he couldn't think of the right words; he felt awkward, because this was a social situation his upbringing hadn't prepared him for. "Excuse me," he said.

The eyes narrowed a little, as if seeing a man inside the body for the first time. "It's all right," the man said. "You'll be fine. You had a bash on the head, and your arm's busted. Nothing as won't mend."

"Thanks," he replied. "Where is this?"

The man hadn't heard him, or wasn't prepared to acknowledge his question. "You got a name, then?"

Yes, but it's slipped my mind. "Gyges," he heard himself say. It took him a moment to realize he was telling the truth.

"Gyges," the man repeated. "What unit were you with?"

"Fourteenth Cavalry." Also true. Fancy me knowing that.

"Rank." A different voice; someone talking over the man's shoulder.

Oh well, he thought. "Lieutenant colonel," he said.

The man's left eyebrow raised. "Well now," he said — he was talking to his friend, the man behind him. "Not so bad after all."

"Excuse me," he said — that ridiculous phrase again, like a small boy in school asking permission to go to the toilet. "Who are you?"

The man smiled. "Nobody important. Don't worry, we'll get you back to your people, soon as you're fit to be moved."

That didn't make sense; they were Eremians, he was an officer in the Mezentine army, so surely he was a prisoner of war. "Thank you," he said, nevertheless.

The man made a tiny effort at a laugh. "No bother," he said. "Lie still, get some rest."

"What happened in the battle?" he asked, but the man had gone. Besides, he realized, he wasn't all that interested in the narrative. He knew the gist of it already.

Lieutenant Colonel Phrastus Gyges, formerly of the Seventeenth Mercenary Division, currently on detached service with the Fourteenth Cavalry. He remembered it now — not clearly, not yet; it was like thinking what to say in a foreign language. But at least he had a name now, and a body to feel pain with, and possibly even a future; there was a remote chance that, sooner or later, he'd once again be the man whose name he'd just remembered, rather than an item of damaged stock in the back of a wagon. Well; he'd come a long way in a short time.

They had apparently tied a thickish stick to his left forearm. Splint, he remembered; and the man had said his arm was broken. Also a bash on the head. The battle; and he'd taken his helmet off so as to be able to hear the reports of his subordinate officers. Bloody stupid thing to do. It occurred to him that this Lieutenant Colonel Gyges couldn't be all that bright.

He lay back, and saw rafters. He was in a barn. For some reason, he felt absurdly cheerful; he was alive, no worse damage than a broken arm, and all he had to do was lie peacefully for a while until someone took him home. Meanwhile, he'd been granted leave of absence from his life. A holiday. Nothing wrong with being in a barn. He'd been in barns a lot when he was a kid. Better than work, that was for sure.

More sleep. This time, he felt himself slide into it, like the crisp sheets on a newly made bed. When he woke up, there was a different face looking down at him. It was just as pink and ugly as the other faces, and it had a large, three-sides-of-a-square scar on the left cheek, just below the eye. A smile crinkled the scar's shiny red skin.

"Hello," the man said. "So you're Phrastus Gyges."

A different kind of voice. The accent was still horrible. He hadn't been able to get used to the way people spoke his language on this side of the sea. The Mezentines were bad enough, with their flat, whining drawl; the savages (the Eremians, at least; he hadn't heard a Vadani yet) did unspeakable things to all the vowels, and didn't seem able to tell the difference between Ts and Ds. This man was an Eremian, but he didn't sound like the men who'd found him.

"That's right," Gyges replied.

The man nodded. "It's good to be able to put a face to the name at last. I'm Miel Ducas."

Not good.

"You've heard of me, then?" the man went on.

Gyges nodded. He hadn't been expecting anything like this.

"I hope you don't mind me introducing myself like this," Ducas said, "but we've been fighting each other long enough that I feel I've known you for ages. Ironic, isn't it, that we should both end up here."

Gyges breathed out slowly. "Where's here, exactly?" he said.

Ducas grinned. "Haven't you figured that out yet? These people — our hosts, I should say — are the hard-working souls who clear up our messes. They bury the dead, salvage clothing and equipment, and ransom the survivors. We owe them our lives, by the way, so don't go getting judgmental. In my case . . ." He shrugged. "Well, why not? A little melodrama won't hurt. Your showing up here's probably signed my death warrant." He frowned. "I could've put that better, I suppose, but not to worry. You see, they've been trying to decide what to do with me: ransom me back to the resistance or sell me to the Mezentines. As far as I can tell, there can't have been much in it either way, but now you've appeared on the scene they've come to a decision. Since they're going to have to take you back to your camp anyway, they may as well send me along with you. Simple economy of effort, really; saves them having to make two journeys, and they've only got the one cart. While it's away ferrying the likes of you and me around, they can't make collections or deliveries. It's perfectly rational once you see the thinking behind it. Are you thirsty? I can fetch you some water if you like."

Gyges looked at him. Miel Ducas, his enemy. "Thank you," he said; and Ducas stood up and went away.

But that's absurd, he thought. These people are Eremians; he's the rebel leader. They wouldn't hand him over to us. He thought about that some more. People who made their living by robbing the dead might not be able to afford finer feelings. Besides, the Eremians were a treacherous people. Hadn't one of them opened the gates of Civitas Eremiae? Presumably money had changed hands over that; he hadn't heard the details, or not a reliable version, at any rate. Besides, money wasn't the only currency. The Mezentines' stated objective was the obliteration of the Eremian nation, and large-scale treachery could well be the price of a blind eye turned to a few survivors. The thought made him uncomfortable; it was something he hadn't really considered before. Wiping out an entire people; it must be strange to have a mind that could process ideas like that. Meanwhile, the last vain hope of the Eremians had just gone to fetch him a drink of water.

"There you are," Ducas said, handing him a short horn cup. "There won't be anything to eat until the rest of the men get back. Probably a sort of sticky soup with barley in it. It's an acquired taste, and I haven't, yet. Am I annoying you, by the way, or are you usually this quiet? The thing is, there's not many people about here to talk to."

Both hands around the cup; he managed to get two mouthfuls, and spilled the rest. "I'm sorry," he said. "I'm not really up to talking much. But you go ahead."

Ducas laughed. "It's all right," he said. "I'll buzz off and leave you in peace, let you get some rest. They said you'd had a nasty bump on the head. Maybe later, if you feel like a chat. We could talk about some of the battles you lost. I'd like that."

The water tasted of something nasty he couldn't quite place. "If you're here," he said, "who's in charge of your army?"

"Who finally beat you, you mean." Ducas' smile widened. "I don't know," he said. "Wish I did. Whoever it is seems to be doing a good job; better than me, anyhow. It comforts me to know that the war is in better hands than mine." He frowned. "I never really expected to be a soldier," he said. "Oh, I was trained for it, of course, because it was one of the things a man in my position needs to know how to do. War, administration, good manners and chasing animals, and it doesn't hurt if you can play a musical instrument. On balance, I'm a slightly better rebec player than I am a general, but I wouldn't want to have to earn a living doing either; not if I had to compete with professionals." He shrugged. "You'd better get some rest now," he said. "The men will be back soon, and they'll have spent the hottest part of the day burying the dead, they may not be in the best of moods. It's been a pleasure talking to you."

So, Miel thought, as he turned his back and walked away, that's Phrastus Gyges. Younger than I'd expected; otherwise, pretty much like I'd imagined he'd be. And now, I suppose, I'd better think about leaving. I guess that means stealing the horse.

Standing against the middle of the wall was a big old wooden feed bin. He'd noticed it earlier, and what was inside it. Presumably such things were so familiar to them that they no longer noticed them; careless but understandable. Casually, he lifted the lid and peered inside.

Mostly it was sidearms, assorted various; he could see the scabbard chape of a Mezentine Type Fifteen, the scent-bottle pommel and wire-bound grip of a good-quality Eremian double-fullered backsword, the brass stirrup-guard and horn scales of a village-

made hunting hanger. Any of them would do, since he wasn't
proposing to use it; just something to wave in the face of anybody
who tried to stop him. He was pretty sure they wouldn't fight him
to keep him from getting away, just in case he managed to hurt
someone — that'd mean a man off work, possibly for a long time
or even permanently, and they couldn't afford to carry the loss.
The horse, on the other hand; horses, he knew from eavesdropping and his own experience, were a serious problem in this war.
Not enough of them to go round; if, after a battle, you had to
choose between rounding up the spare horses and seeing to your
immobilized wounded, you had to go for the horses whether you
liked it or not. They might well fight him for the horse. Unfortunately, he needed the head start. If he tried to get away on foot,
with his recent injuries and vague knowledge of the local geography, he wouldn't really stand a chance. He wished that, at the
very least, he had some money, so he could leave them enough to
buy another horse. Come to think of it, he'd never stolen anything
before. Never needed to, of course.

The stupid thing is, he thought, I don't really want to leave. I'd
be happier staying here, learning to patch up chainmail and bury
corpses. Now there's an interesting comment on my life so far.

Nobody seemed to be watching; just in case, though, he turned
his back so as to mask what he was doing, and slid his arm in
under the lid of the bin until his fingers connected with something.
By the feel of it, the stirrup-guard hanger — not his first choice,
but he was hardly in a position to be picky. He fished it out, got
it over the edge of the bin, nearly dropped it, point downwards,
on his foot, and shut the lid as quietly as he could. He didn't look
down at the short sword dangling by its guard from his little finger; instead, he drew it flat against his stomach and walked slowly
away, waiting for someone to yell at him. No yell. His first act of
theft — his first crime — successfully carried out.

The idea was to steal a weapon now, while the place was empty
and there was nobody about to see. He couldn't leave until much
later, because the men hadn't brought the horse back yet. Once

they'd come home he was going to have to wait a couple of hours, at least, until they'd finished their work for the day; also, the horse would be tired too, and not in the mood for further strenuous exercise. What he needed now, therefore, was somewhere to hide the sword until it was time to make his move. He hadn't realized how complicated a life of crime could be.

He looked round. His pretext for leaving the barn would be going outside for a leak. Nearly everybody went round the south side of the barn, simply because it was sheltered from the wind. If you went round the east side, you ran a substantial risk of coming back in wearing what you'd gone out to dispose of. Fair enough. He wandered over to the door, doing his very best to look like a man with a mildly full bladder. He had no illusions about his abilities as an actor, but nobody seemed interested in him anyway, so that was fine. Once outside, he turned left, round the corner, and looked carefully about. When he was sure nobody could see him, he reached up and shoved the sword into the loose, ragged thatch of the eaves, until only the little rectangular knob of a pommel was showing. It'd be dark when he came out to retrieve it, but he'd be able to find it by touch.

He paused and frowned, noticing how he'd been feeling ever since he lifted the lid of the feed bin. I'm afraid, he thought, and that surprised him. It had been quite a while since he'd been afraid of anything — haven't had the time or the attention to spare, he realized. When he'd been leading his men into an ambush there was simply too much else to think about. Now, with nobody to consider but himself, he could afford to be self-indulgent. Stupid, he thought; all I'm doing is stealing a twenty-shilling horse, not cutting up a column of Mezentine cavalry at odds of three to one. Maybe, if I manage to get away with this, I can find the time to develop a sense of perspective. It'd be nice to have one of those for a change.

Perspective, he thought, as he went back inside the barn (it was pleasantly cool indoors; nice to be back). Perspective is mostly about value; what things are really worth, in context. Not so long ago (he sat in the corner nearest the door and stretched his legs out), I was a wealthy nobleman. If someone had come up to me and asked me how many swords and how many horses I owned, I'd have had to ask the steward; and he wouldn't have known off-hand, he'd have had to check the house books. Now, when I actually need them, I'm reduced to stealing them from men who have next to nothing.

(Outside, heavy wheels were grinding on stones; the cart was coming home.)

So, Miel thought, I've come down in the world. So what? When I was a boy, I used to worry about that all the time. What'd become of me if we suddenly lost all our land and our money? I used to have nightmares about it; I'd be in my room and nasty men would come bursting in to take away the furniture; they'd throw me out into the street, and all the poor people and ugly beggars and cripples would jeer at me and try and take my shoes. Apparently I used to wake up screaming sometimes; the servants used to ask what on earth the matter was, and of course I refused to tell them.

Any moment now, the door would open and the men would come in. Once they did that, everything would become irrevocable. Someone would tell Juifrez Stratiotes about their latest acquisition, and Juifrez (a pleasant enough man, and painfully shy when talking to his ex-landlord) would make the inevitable business decision, based on cost-efficiency and the availability of the horse. Miel thought about that. If he was Juifrez, he'd tell a couple of his men to keep an eye on the Ducas, just in case he'd put two and two together; don't be obvious about it, he'd say, but don't let him too far out of your sight. He considered the practical implications of that for a moment, decided on a plan of action and put it out of his mind. I wish I didn't have to go, he thought. But it's not up to me. That made him smile. The pleasure, the release, had been in not being in control of his own destiny for a while; but because he was the Ducas, as soon as he stopped being his own master he turned into valuable property, with potentially lethal consequences. He therefore had no choice. His holiday was over, and the best he could hope for was getting away from this place in one piece, preferably without having to hurt anybody. Beyond that, he didn't want to speculate; didn't care.

The door opened. In came the men; silent, too tired to talk. The woman, Juifrez's wife, had gone with them. It occurred to him that he'd have liked to say goodbye to her, but clearly that was out of the question. Now she'd remember him as the man who'd stolen their horse.

If he hadn't already known what they'd been doing all day, he'd have had no trouble at all figuring it out from the smell they brought in on their clothes and boots. He'd done many things in his time, but no digging. He'd always drawn the line at it, even in the kind of military crisis where rank and status were unaffordable luxuries, and even the Ducas was no more than another pair of hands. Digging, in his mind, was about as low as you could sink; miserable hard work, exhausting, tedious, repetitive, the epitome of his old morbid fears of poverty and destitution. Digging graves for strangers in the thin, stony soil of the northeastern hillsides would, by that reasoning, have to be the worst job in the world, and he was fairly sure he wouldn't be able to do it. Half an hour at the most and his soft, aristocratic hands would be a squishy mess of blisters, his back would be agony, and everybody would be jeering at him. He'd rather face a platoon of Mezentine heavy cavalry on his own than dig a hole. He watched them sitting, slowly unlacing boots, resting their forearms on their knees and their backs against the barn wall, their minds empty, their bodies finally at rest. If they had cares and troubles beyond aches and fatigue, they gave no sign of it. Whatever else they might be, they were firmly anchored in the present, with nothing more or less than the people and possessions within easy reach of their seats. It would be so very easy to envy them, Miel realized.

Food and drink went round: cheese, an old store apple each,

half a dense, gritty loaf. Miel knew all about that kind of bread. It was made from flour ground from the last of the previous year's grain, the two or three inches left over in the bottom of the bins when they had to be cleared out to make way for this year's newly threshed corn. Perfectly wholesome, of course; but because it was dredged off the bin floor, it was inevitably full of dust, grit, shreds of stalk and husk. Sensible estate managers bought it cheap for poultry feed and to make bread for the seasonal casual workers. You could break a tooth on it; the old joke said it was better than a stone for sharpening scythe-blades. The Ducas, of course, had outlawed its use on his estate, and made a point of giving away the bin-end grain to the poor (outcasts, beggars, men who dug for a living). The silly thing was that, apart from the grit, it didn't taste too bad at all.

He glanced across at Phrastus Gyges. Stratiotes was there talking to him, keeping his voice down, like a man at market buying his neighbor's sheep. They're talking about me, Miel thought. Half an hour and I'll have to make a move. A pity, but what can you do?

When he got up, he stood for a moment or so and yawned. Nobody was looking at him; he wasn't important enough to merit anybody's limited reserves of attention. He stretched. No need to fake the cramp in his legs. He walked slowly toward the door, the very picture of a man reluctantly compelled to make the effort to stagger outside for a piss. It was only as he smelled the night air outside that he realized there were two men behind him.

Oh well, he thought.

He followed the outside of the barn, past the usual place. Someone called out: "Where do you think you're going?"

He paused, didn't turn his head as he replied, "Need a leak."

"What's wrong with here?"

"I don't like the smell."

"Is that right?"

He carried on until his way was blocked. One man behind him, following; the other had gone round the other way to cut him off. He looked at the man in front of him, trying to feign irritation. "Do you mind?" he said.

"You carry on," the man replied. "Never seen a toff piss before."

Miel laughed. "You haven't lived," he said. "Pay close attention, you might learn something."

He could just make out the frown on the man's face as he turned to face the wall, his left hand reaching for his fly, his right hand apparently resting on the eaves just above his head. Not there; and the horrible thought crossed his mind that someone might have found it and guessed why it had been put there. Then his finger traced something cold and smooth. He explored a little further and found the junction of the grip and the stirrup-guard. He straightened up, the way you do, and used the movement to pull the hilt of the sword out far enough to get his hand round the grip.

Maybe it was moonlight glinting on the blade as it pulled out of the thatch, or it could have been some slight carelessness in the way he lifted his arm that sent a danger signal. "Just a minute," the man to his right said. Miel took a long step back to give himself the right distance, and held the sword out in front of him in a loose approximation to the middle guard.

"Sorry," he said.

The man on his left got the message. The other one didn't. Either he hadn't seen the sword or else he had the mistaken idea that toffs couldn't fight worth spit; he took a stride forward and reached for Miel's arm, quickly and confidently, like a stockman roping a steer.

The middle guard is a good, solid basis for defense, but it lacks flexibility. Against a threat coming in front and high, it can only be developed into a thrust in straight time.

Miel didn't see the point go in. No need; he knew what the inevitable outcome would be, and he needed to give all his attention to the other vector of threat. The other man, the one on his left who'd stopped dead in his tracks, had time and distance on him, making him an intolerable risk. Without hesitating to look at him, Miel took a half-step back and sideways, using the pivoting movement to power the cut. The technique uses only the first half-inch of the sword-blade to cut the jugular vein. Miel had been practicing it once a week for twenty-five years, but this was the first time he'd ever used it in live play. It worked just fine.

The second man was dead before the first man hit the ground, and Miel was still moving (a half-turn and step away, to avoid the thick spray of blood from the severed artery). When he stopped, he found his right arm had swung up into a high hanging guard, to ward off a possible counterattack in second. He froze, thinking, What do I do now, I've forgotten; then he remembered. The fight was over, he'd won. Marvelous.

They lay perfectly still, one on his face, the other twisted half sideways, like clothes dropped on the floor by a drunk undressing. Miel closed his eyes, opened them again, and lowered the sword, keeping the blade well away from him, as if it was some disgusting thing he'd just found. Just marvelous, he thought; and a voice in the back of his head was yelling at him for standing like an idiot when he should be stealing the horse and getting away from there. It was their fault, he tried to tell the voice (which wasn't listening and didn't care); they should have let me go, they should have realized, they were *stupid*. The voice replied: Well, what can you expect from people like that? No, Miel told the voice, but he couldn't get it to listen. There was no point even trying to make it understand. Get the fucking horse, it kept on saying, and Miel knew it wouldn't shut up until he did as he was told. He stepped backward, knowing that once he took his eye off them it'd be over and everything would change. You fool, the voice explained to him; any moment now they'll wonder what's taking so long, more of them'll come out, do you want to have to kill the whole bloody lot of them? That made him angry, but he knew he couldn't fault the logic. He turned his back on them and stumbled (don't run, you bloody fool; tripping and turning your ankle at this point would be the supreme humiliation) toward the stable.

He knew, of course, how to put a bridle on a horse. The stupid animal lifted its head and scowled at him, ears back. He put down the sword, lifted the bridle off its hook and stepped forward. The horse backed away. It can smell the blood, Miel thought, they're sensitive to things like that. He swore at it, then clicked his tongue and chirruped, "Wooze, horse," the way all the grooms he'd ever known had always done. It lifted its head and kept still as he guided the bit into its mouth and fumbled its ears through the headband. Noseband and throat-lash — the straps were swollen and greasy with saddle soap and wouldn't fit through the loops. Saddle; no, you clown, don't stop to check the girths or shorten the stirrups. What with the shouting of the voice and the blur behind his eyes, he could hardly think; just as well this sort of thing was second nature, or he'd be screwed. He mounted awkwardly, dropped the reins and had to lean forward to gather them. He'd forgotten the sword; well, he'd just have to do without. No, couldn't risk it. He dismounted, grabbed the stupid thing in his left hand, nearly cut himself to the bone on it as he remounted. Finally ready, like a woman going to a dance. He kicked the horse much harder than he needed to, and nearly forgot to duck as they went sailing out through the stable door.

Warm night air; he had to work hard to remember where the path was. Light was spilling out of the barn doorway, he heard a voice but not what it was saying. He kicked the horse again, then smacked it spitefully with the flat of the sword. That got its attention. He made no effort to steer; it knew the area far better than he did. He realized that he didn't have a clue where he was heading for; not that it mattered. The horse was too tired to do anything more than a grudging trot. Its back was uncomfortably wide and the stirrups far too short. All in all, Miel thought, I've had better days.

He made the horse keep up its pace for as long as he could, then slumped into the saddle and let it amble. He noticed that he was still holding the sword; its weight was hurting his elbow, so he tucked it between his left thigh and the saddle. The voice was telling him to use the stars to find north. He ignored it. For the first time in his life, he felt totally, abjectly ashamed.

Well, he told himself, at least now you can say you've met the common people. A decent enough bunch, in their way, and they certainly hadn't done anything to deserve the likes of you.

5

"Vegetarians?" Valens frowned. "Are you sure?"

Orsea nodded. "We found out the hard way," he said. "We assumed they'd be complete and utter carnivores, so we got in every kind of meat and poultry and game we could think of, as well as most of the booze in the duchy —"

"Hold it." Valens' frown deepened into a scowl. "You aren't about to tell me they don't drink alcohol either."

Orsea looked away. "It was embarrassing," he said. "Not the high point of my diplomatic career." He stood up and walked to the window. "Though how I was supposed to have known about it . . ." He sighed. "Serves me right for jumping to conclusions. I thought that, just because they're savages, they must eat flesh and drink themselves stupid three times a day. Apparently not."

"Well," Valens said, "thanks for the warning. Nothing about it in any of the reports, and I confess, I'd made the same assumptions as you did." He thought for a moment. "Presumably they must eat cheese and drink milk, or what do they keep cattle for?"

Orsea didn't seem inclined to offer an opinion on that. "When will they be arriving?" he asked.

"Five days' time," Valens answered. "Assuming they aren't held up in the mountains or anything like that. It's odd," he went on. "I've been fighting the Cure Hardy on and off for most of my adult life — raiding parties, that sort of thing; nothing big or political, just plain, unsophisticated robbery — and never in all that time have they ever wanted to come and talk to us. Now, just as we're about to pack up and leave, they turn up on our doorstep asking for a meeting."

"You think they know something? About the evacuation, I mean."

"I doubt it," Valens said, leaning back a little in his chair. "We've kept a pretty tight lid on our plans; besides, why would it interest them, one way or another? As far as they're concerned, we're just people to steal from when they're tired of life. Still, if they want to talk to me, they're welcome. I'll talk to anybody, within reason." He picked up a sheet of paper he'd put on the table earlier. "Talking of which," he went on, "an off-relation of yours, Jarnac Ducas, wants to see me. Wrote me a memo asking for an appointment, which strikes me as a bit formal and businesslike. Any idea what he wants?"

Orsea shrugged. "No idea, sorry."

"Ah well." Valens nodded. He knew the answer, of course, because it was in the letter. "Jarnac Ducas," he said. "Relation of the Miel Ducas who was your chief of staff."

Orsea didn't turn round. "Cousin," he replied.

"Ah yes. He put up quite a show at Civitas Eremiae, didn't he?"

"Jarnac? Yes." Orsea nodded. "I put him in charge of the defenses, at the end. He did a good job in a hopeless situation."

Obviously Orsea didn't want to talk about the Ducas family. Still, it had to be done. "I've been meaning to ask you," Valens went on. "Why did you dismiss Miel Ducas? From what I've gathered, he was perfectly competent."

"I made a mistake," Orsea said.

"Ah. Well, we all do that. Many thanks for the tip about the Cure Hardy," he added, in his best polite you-can-go-away-now voice. "It'll be interesting to find out what they want."

Orsea drifted away; not a moment too soon, as far as Valens was concerned. He was finding him increasingly difficult to tolerate, and the harder he found it, the harder he resolved to try.

In order to give Orsea plenty of time to leave the North Tower before he sent for his next appointment, he picked up the dossier on Jarnac Ducas and read it through one more time. Head of the cadet branch of the powerful Ducas family; presently head of the family as a result of the disgrace of Miel Ducas; a competent, efficient and conscientious soldier, and the finest huntsman in Eremia before the war (Valens smiled at that); given the honorary rank of colonel in the heavy cavalry, currently on detached service with the Eremian guerrillas, commanding the Vadani volunteers fighting the Mezentine occupation. Fine; he knew all that. The reason for the interview was rather more intriguing. He rang the bell, and sent a page to fetch him.

He'd seen him before, of course, and remembered him clearly. Jarnac Ducas wasn't easily forgotten. Valens' first impression had been that there was far too much of him. He loomed, and there was always the danger that he might tread on you by accident. Today, however, he was practically subdued. Valens told him to sit down, and asked him what was on his mind.

"I have a favor to ask," Jarnac replied. He was sitting — no, perching, like a falcon on the wrist of a novice, awkward and unsteady. It was as though he was trying to act normal-sized.

"You want two squadrons of light cavalry for a raid into northern Eremia," Valens said. "I know, it was in your letter." He put on his stern expression. "There's no reason why you should've heard, but I've decided to scale down our involvement with the guerrillas. The plain fact is, they're doing a good job, but I can't afford the manpower. Any day now, you'll be getting recall orders telling you to get your men out of Eremia. Obviously you're entirely at liberty to go back if you want to; after all, you're an Eremian, I've got no right to tell you to stop fighting for your country. But the Vadani troops under your command are a different matter entirely."

When he'd finished, Jarnac waited for a moment or so, then said: "Understood. But if I can just explain . . ."

"Go on."

Jarnac opened and closed his left hand. "When I filed the request for the two squadrons," he said, "I didn't mean I wanted them as general reinforcements for the resistance. The fact is, I want them for one specific operation."

He seemed to have run out of words, but Valens decided not to prompt him. Eventually, Jarnac went on: "It's quite simple, actually. I've heard reports that my cousin Miel's been taken prisoner, and I want to get him out of there."

Valens nodded. "That's different," he said. "What's the position?"

Jarnac closed his eyes, just for a second. He was afraid I'd say no, Valens thought, and I don't suppose fear is something he's had much experience with. He doesn't handle it well.

"As far as I can make out," Jarnac said, "he was picked up by a party of looters. Apparently they're Eremian renegades, I'm sorry to say. They go round robbing the dead after battles, stealing equipment, that sort of thing; and if they find survivors, they hold them to ransom. When Miel went missing after a skirmish a few days ago, I had my people try and find out what had become of him. One of my men knows a trader who buys from these people, and he told me they've got Miel and they're about to open negotiations with the Mezentines. Obviously, we can't have that. Quite apart from the strategic implications — I mean, Miel knows everything there is to know about how the resistance is set up —"

Valens nodded. "Fine," he said. "Go ahead. Will two squadrons be enough?"

"Oh, plenty," Jarnac said quickly. "I don't think these characters are fighters, it'll be more about speed and surprise than weight of numbers."

"Go ahead then, by all means." Valens frowned. "There's just one thing," he added. "I don't know much about the background, but I get the impression there's bad blood between your cousin and Duke Orsea. Presumably once you've rescued him, you'll be bringing him back here. Is there anything I should know about, or is it strictly a private matter?"

Jarnac kept perfectly still for a moment, but his eyes were wide open. "I'm sorry," he said. "I assumed . . ."

"That doesn't sound very good," Valens said. "Perhaps you ought to tell me about it."

Jarnac wriggled a little, and Valens felt a moment of anxiety for the chair he was sitting in. "I assumed you'd have known," he said. "Orsea had Miel arrested for treason."

"I see," Valens said. "I'm assuming he was wrong about that."

It was almost painful to watch. "I suppose it depends on how you define treason," Jarnac said. "You see, Orsea found out that Miel had got hold of a letter he shouldn't have had."

Valens didn't move, not even to breathe. "A letter."

"Yes." Jarnac was looking at him. He had bright blue eyes. "I can't remember offhand whether it was a letter from you to Duchess Veatriz or the other way about . . ."

"I see."

"Anyway," Jarnac went on, speaking quickly, practically mumbling, "Orsea seemed to feel that as soon as Miel got hold of the letter, he should've given it to him straightaway, and hanging on to it like that was an unforgivable breach of trust. Which, I suppose, it was, in a way; but Miel's been crazy about Veatriz ever since they were both kids, it was always sort of understood that they'd marry each other, but then Veatriz became the heiress to the duchy, which nobody had been expecting, and everyone thought it'd be quite wrong politically for the Ducas to succeed to the duchy, because it'd mess up the balance of power." He froze for a moment; Valens nodded, very slightly. "Anyhow," Jarnac went on, "Miel couldn't bring himself to give her away, partly for her sake, partly because he knew how upset Orsea would be if he knew . . ." Jarnac shut his eyes. Not his forte, this sort of thing. "So yes, I suppose it was treason, strictly speaking, and I understand why Orsea had to do what he did. But in my opinion, for what it's worth, I don't think Miel did anything wrong. Frankly, if only Orsea hadn't found out it would probably all have blown over." He looked up. There was a kicked-spaniel look on his face that made Valens want to burst out laughing. "That's it," he said, "more or less. So yes, it might be awkward if Miel came here. Does that change anything?"

Valens sighed and shook his head. "For what it's worth," he said, "the one and only time I met Veatriz — before the fall of Civitas Eremiae, I mean — was years ago, when I was a sixteen-year-old kid. Yes, we wrote letters to each other. It had been going on for about eighteen months. Did you happen to see the letter that your cousin intercepted?"

Jarnac shook his head.

"Fine," Valens said. "Well, you'll have to take my word for it. They were all . . ." He paused. Even talking about it felt like a grotesque breach of trust. "They were all perfectly innocent; just chat, I guess. What we'd been reading, things we'd seen that happened to snag our interest." He sighed again. "I'm sorry," he said, "you really don't want to know anything about it, and I don't blame you. The fact remains that the blame for your cousin's disgrace ultimately rests with me, and it's because of it that he was out there in the first place, so naturally I have an obligation to do whatever's necessary to rescue him. The one thing I can't do is let the Mezentines get hold of him just because having him here would be embarrassing, either to Duke Orsea or myself. However," he went on, "if there's any way of keeping him out of Orsea's way once you've rescued him, I'd take it as a personal favor. Is that clear?"

Jarnac nodded. "Perfectly," he said. "Thank you."

Valens smiled thinly. "My pleasure," he said. "You have complete discretion over the details, and your choice of whatever forces and materiel you might need. I'll have a warrant ready for you by morning; you can pick it up from the clerk's office. Was there anything else?"

Jarnac stood up, back straight as a spear-shaft. "No," he said. "And thank you for your time."

"That's all right." Valens turned his head just a little so he wasn't looking straight at him anymore. "When you get back," he said, "perhaps you'd care to join me for a day with the falcons. I seem to remember hearing somewhere that you used to keep a few birds yourself."

A split second, before Jarnac realized it was meant as a joke. "One or two," he said. "Thank you, I'd be delighted. I haven't had a day out in the field — well, since the war started."

"I know," Valens replied. "That's the rotten thing about a war, it cuts into your free time."

Pause; then Jarnac laughed. "Till then," he said. "And thank you."

He left, and once he'd gone the room felt much bigger. Valens took a series of deep breaths, as if he'd been running. Well, he thought, after all that I know something I didn't know before, so it can't have been a complete disaster. He let his hands drop open and his forearms flop onto his knees. Irony, he thought. First I rescue her husband, and now her childhood sweetheart.

At the back of his mind a couple of unexplained details were nagging at him like the first faint twinges of toothache. He acknowledged their existence but resolved to ignore them for the time being. For the time being, he had other things to think about.

Obviously, then, Orsea knew about the letters. That explained a great deal about the way he'd been behaving ever since he'd arrived in Civitas Vadanis. Methodically Valens drew down the implications, the alternative courses of action open to him and their consequences. Logically — logically, it was perfectly straightforward, one move on a chessboard that would resolve everything. If Orsea was taken by the Mezentines . . .

He allowed himself the luxury of developing the idea. The Mezentines are sick and tired of the war in Eremia, which has dragged on long after the supposedly quick, clean victory at Civitas Eremiae. By the same token, they don't want to have to fight us, but I can't be allowed to get away with interfering as I did. A simple note, therefore, to the Mezentine commander, suggesting that he demand the surrender of Duke Orsea as the price of peace. He makes the demand; I refuse, naturally; Orsea immediately offers himself as a sacrifice — no, too melodramatic. Of course; as soon as he hears about the demand, Orsea quietly slips out of the palace and hands himself over to the enemy. Outcome: Orsea finds redemption from his intolerable guilt; my people are saved from a war we can't win; she becomes a widow.

He smiled. The frustrating thing about it was that if he sent for Orsea and asked his permission to do it, Orsea would almost certainly give it.

Instead, he was going to have to think of something else; annoying and difficult, because it's always harder to find a satisfactory answer to a problem when you already know the right answer but aren't allowed to use it. And it was the right answer; he could see that quite clearly. Further irony, that the right answer should also be cheating.

Instead . . .

Instead, he would have to go the long way round, and nobody would be happy, and thousands of innocent people would have to die. Query (hypothetical, therefore fatuous; another indulgence): would the answer have been different if Orsea hadn't known about the letters? He thought about that for a moment, but failed to reach a clear decision.

He pulled a sheet of paper toward him across the table, picked up his pen and wrote out Jarnac Ducas' warrant: *afford him all possible cooperation,* one of those nice old-fashioned phrases you only ever get to use in official documents. He frowned, tore it up, and started again.

Valens Valentinianus to Ulpianus Macer, greetings.
     An Eremian called Jarnac Ducas will show up in the front office tomorrow morning asking for soldiers and supplies. Give him everything he wants.

He folded the paper and added it to the pile. His knees ached from too much sitting. Somewhere in the building, she was . . . He frowned, trying to think where she was likely to be and what she'd be doing. Needlework, probably. She hated needlework; a pointless, fatuous, demeaning exercise, a waste of her mind, her life and good linen. She was tolerably competent at it, but not good enough to earn a living as a seamstress. There had been five — no, six references in the letters to how much she despised it. In her mother's room, she'd told him, there was a huge oak chest, with massive iron hinges. As soon as she finished a piece of work — an embroidered cushion, a sampler, a pair of gloves with the Sirupati arms on the back — it was put away in the chest and never taken out again; the day after her mother died, the chest was taken away and put somewhere, and she had no idea what had become of it. In his reply, Valens had told her about how he'd loathed hunting, right up to the day his father died. It's different for you, she'd written back, you're a man. It was one of the few times she'd missed the point completely.

Needlework, he thought. When we abandon the city and take to the wagons, I guess we'll have to take her work boxes and embroidery frames and her spinning-wheel and God only knows what else with us. And Orsea, of course, and my falcons and my hounds and the boar spears.

Suddenly he couldn't bear sitting down any longer. He jumped up, scowled, hesitated for a moment and walked quickly out of the library, down the stairs and across the hall to the ascham. He grabbed the first bow that came to hand and the quiver of odds-and-ends arrows, the ones that wouldn't matter if he lost them, and took the back passageway out into the lists. The sally port was still unlocked, and he scrambled down the rampart (he was still wearing his stupid poulaines, he realized, but he couldn't be bothered to go back and change into boots) and ran across the port-meadow into the wood. As he crept and stumbled down the path he could hear ducks squabbling down on the river at the bottom of the hill. It was still three weeks until the start of the season, but the ducks didn't seem to know that. They'd come in early; he'd watched them arrive one evening, a week or so back. It would be cheating, but for once he didn't care. Besides, nobody would be about at this time of day, so the guilt would be his alone. The wet leaves were soft and treacherous under his smooth-soled feet; wild garlic, long since gone over.

As soon as he could see the river through the trees he stopped and made himself calm down. His best chance of a shot would be a drake right on the edge of the water; they liked to sit out after feeding at this time of day, to catch the last warmth of the evening sun. The problem, as usual, would be getting close enough. Twenty yards would be pushing it; fifteen for a proper job. The screen of coppiced willow that edged the bank would cover him, but it would most likely obstruct the shot as well. He ran the odds, and decided that the best bet would be to assume that there'd be at least one pair of ducks on the shingle spit that stuck out into the water a few yards on from where the main path came down to the water's edge. If he left the path and worked his way down to the point where the big oak leaned out from the bank, he could use it as cover and get a clear sight across to the spit; closer to twenty yards than fifteen, but just about in range.

A splash of water, and the unmistakable *quack*-quack-quack-quack of a drake sounding the general alarm. Valens tensed with anger, because he hadn't made any noise; if the ducks had taken fright and launched out onto the river, they were cheating. He scowled, and realized how ridiculous his reaction was, but that didn't really make it any better. He leaned round the tree trunk and saw a solitary drake, head up, floating on the calm, deep water of the river-bend. Bastard, he thought, and nocked an arrow. The drake looked at him smugly, as if he knew he was a sitting target and therefore safe. Valens whistled, then shouted, but the drake stayed where he was. Fine, Valens thought; he pushed the bow handle away with his left hand and drew the string back with his right until his shoulder blades were jammed together and his right thumbnail brushed against the corner of his mouth. He glanced along the arrow shaft until he could see the duck on the point of the blade, then dropped his aim a hand's span. At that point, the three fingers of his right hand against which the bowstring pressed should have relaxed (you don't let go of the string, they'd told him when he was a boy, you drop it); but nothing seemed to be happening. The countdown was running in his mind: three, four, five, and then it was too late. Still restraining the string, he let it jerk his arm forward; the jolt hurt his shoulder and his elbow, and he dropped the arrow onto the ground. The drake made a rude noise, unfolded its wings and lifted off the water in a flailing haze of spray.

He stooped and picked up the arrow. Obviously not my day for killing things, he thought. He lifted his foot to step into the bow and unstring it, then changed his mind. Nocking the arrow once again, he walked slowly and steadily along the bank, trying to persuade himself that it didn't really matter whether he put up anything to shoot at or not. No sign of any ducks; but that was just as well, since they weren't in season yet. At the point where the coppice was too thick to pass through, he turned away from the river and started to walk back uphill. He'd taken no more than five steps when a young pricket buck stepped out of nowhere, stopped, turned its head and looked at him.

He felt the breath go solid in his throat. Ten yards away, no more, and broadside on; but if he moved at all, he'd lose it; there'd be a flash of motion and the buck would be gone. He forced himself to keep still, as the deer studied him, trying to reconcile the lack of movement with the presentiment of danger. To take his mind off the pressure building in his lungs, he made a dispassionate assessment of the quarry. One stud horn, he noticed, the other broken off about half an inch above the crown; a fairly miserable animal all round, thin and spindly-legged, with a narrow chest and too much neck; a weakling, no use to the herd, no prize for a hunter. It watched him, eyes wide, ears forward. I was you once, Valens thought, but not anymore. Nevertheless, I shall ask your permission. I'll make a mistake, and if you run, so be it. As slowly as he could, he lifted the bow, watching the deer's neck all the time over the arrow tip. When he'd put the point on the spot just above the front shoulder, he dropped his aim to allow for the arrow's jump and trusted his fingers to know what to do. He felt the string pull out, dragging against the pads of his fingertips. For a fraction of a second, he closed his eyes.

The sound was right; both shearing and sucking, as the sharp edges of the arrowhead slit open their channel. He opened his eyes and saw the buck stagger a little against the shove of the penetrating arrow. Inch-perfect in the heart. He saw the moment of death, and watched the fall of the carcass, like an empty sack flopping.

He let go the breath he'd been holding for as long as he could remember, and in his mind he was carefully phrasing a paradox for a letter he'd never write; about how a living animal is a pig, a cow, a sheep or a deer, but a dead one is pork, beef, mutton, venison; the two are so completely different that the same word can no longer be applied. The thing lying on the leaf mold in front of him was venison now, so completely changed that it was almost impossible to believe it had ever been alive. He thought of the battlefields he'd seen — all Jarnac Ducas' fault, for mentioning the corpse-robbers he was planning to deal with; if anybody had a word for it, a trade or technical term, it'd be them. Maybe there was one, but he doubted it; the difference being that the dead meat of human beings is no use to anybody.

He went forward, knelt beside the carcass and forked the fingers of his left hand round the shaft of the arrow at the point where it entered the wound. Drawing slowly with his right hand, he pulled the arrow out, and winced as a spot of blood hopped off the blade onto his cheek. I could still prevent the war, he thought. It would be the right thing to do, and I'd do it, if only . . .

If only Orsea wasn't her husband. But he is; which means there'll have to be a war, and killing, a wholesale conversion of life into waste, and one of those lives will quite probably be mine. He looked up sharply, as if expecting to see the hunter watching him, surprised in mid-breath, over the blade of his arrow. Nothing to see, of course; but just because he's not visible doesn't mean he's not there, and now it's his turn to ask my permission.

He wiped the arrow and put it back in the quiver, then stood up and unstrung the bow. Ask away, he thought, I've already made that decision; nor do I begrudge you your shot.

He paused, listening. He could hear the river, the creaking of the tall, spindly birches behind him on the slope, the distant miserable voices of crows. Nothing unusual or disturbing, nothing to put him on his guard. Maybe he couldn't see the hunter for the same reason the deer hadn't been able to see him; not that it mattered. So, he told himself, now I know: there'll have to be a war, and I won't survive it. Query, though: if I'd cheated and shot the drake sitting on the water, thereby scaring off the buck, would that have made a difference?

It was only a pricket, no more than thirty-five pounds dressed-out weight, but lugging it back up the hill on his shoulders left him aching and breathless. The warmth of its blood, trickling down under his collar and mixing with his own sweat, made his skin itch, and he had to stop halfway to adjust his grip, to stop the carcass sliding off his back. He startled the life out of the sentry at the sally port, now closed for the night, as he staggered out of the wood covered in blood.

He left the carcass for the guards to carry the rest of the way, and hurried up the back stairs to his tower room for a wash and a clean shirt. Unfortunately, there was someone lying in wait for him on the landing, hidden in the shadows. He was about to tell whoever it was to go away when he recognized the voice saying his name.

"Oh," he said, "it's you."

Ziani Vaatzes; staring at him as though he was some sort of extraordinary monster. "I'm sorry," Vaatzes said, "it's obviously a bad time. I'll come back later."

Valens grinned. He was exhausted, bloody all over and visibly in no fit state to conduct official business; but Vaatzes was an outsider and didn't count. "Don't worry about it," he said. "Come in and talk to me while I get cleaned up."

By the time Valens had pulled off his sodden, sticky shirt, three middle-aged women had appeared out of nowhere with hot water and towels. Valens knew who they were — he knew everybody in the castle, naturally — but he had no idea how they'd got there, and it wouldn't have occurred to him to ask. He dipped a towel in the water jug and scrubbed the back of his neck.

"So," he said, "what's on your mind?"

Vaatzes was looking away. "You wrote me a note asking for suggestions about how to block up the silver mines," he said. "I've been thinking about it."

"What? Oh, yes. Excellent. What've you come up with?"

"That depends," Vaatzes said to the opposite wall, as Valens poured the rest of the water over his head. "Really, it's a case of how thoroughly you want the job done."

"I see." Valens nodded. "Well, you know the reasoning behind it. First priority's got to be making sure the Mezentines can't open the mines up again in a hurry. If they got hold of them and got them back into production, they'd have all the money they need to pay for the war against us. On the other hand, if and when the war's over and the Mezentines have gone away, we'll need to get the mines going again as soon as we can. Basically, it comes down to cost-effectiveness. Our labor won't cost us anything, because we can use the army or conscripted workers. They've got to pay labor costs and make a profit. Is that any help? It's all right," he added, toweling his hair and pulling on his fresh shirt, "you can look round now and it won't be high treason."

Vaatzes nodded. "Seems to me," he said, "you want to make it look like the mines have been sabotaged beyond economic repair, enough to fool the Mezentine engineers, but really you've only damaged them a little."

"Exactly." Valens sat down on the bed and dragged off his muddy, ruined shoes. "Not much to ask, but presumably you're going to tell me it's not possible."

"Oh, it's possible," Vaatzes replied. "Everything's possible in engineering; it's just that some things take more time and money than they're worth."

Valens shrugged. "Go on," he said.

"Well." Vaatzes hovered for a moment, then rested his back awkwardly against one of the bed pillars. Not someone, Valens decided, who thinks well standing up. "Everybody knows how you collapse a mine. You stuff the weight-bearing gallery full of brushwood and charcoal, soak it down with gallons of lamp oil, set light to it and run like hell. You might need to set up a few big double-action bellows at the outlets of the ventilation shafts, but in most cases the fire'll draw enough air on its own to do the job. Anyhow, you light your big fire, which burns out the prop shafts, and down comes the roof. Entirely effective, but if you want to open the mine up again, it'd be easier to dig new shafts than try and clear out the old ones."

Valens nodded. "Everybody knows that, do they? That's encouraging. Sorry, carry on."

Vaatzes shifted his back a little. "My idea," he went on, "is to build a reinforced chamber, sort of like a cage, about a hundred yards down the main gallery. Instead of wooden props, you use iron, and you have a big, thick iron fire door to close it off. You burn out the first hundred yards in the usual way, but because the reinforced chamber's got iron props, they won't burn out, and the fire door'll stop the fire spreading past the chamber and damaging the gallery beyond. So long as the enemy don't know about it, they'll assume you caved in the gallery and the mine's useless. Once they've gone home, you'll have to excavate the first hundred yards, but the rest of the mine ought to be intact." He paused, then went on, "It's fairly simple and straightforward, but it'd have to be done right. The ironwork needs to be pretty massive, and it'll have to be prefabricated above ground, carried down the mine and assembled down there in the dark, so you'd need precise measurements and close, fine work." He hesitated, though Valens was fairly sure it was mostly for effect. "To be honest," he went on, "I'm not entirely sure you've got enough skilled workers available to do the job."

Valens smiled at him. "Except, of course," he said, "I've got you."

"Me." Vaatzes smiled. "I'm flattered, but I don't think I'd be quite enough, somehow. I've done a few rough calculations, and I reckon you'd need a dozen good blacksmiths, plus strikers and men to work the bellows, so that's three dozen; then you'll need carpenters, masons, carters . . ."

"Fine." Valens shrugged. "I'll have them recruited. We do have skilled artisans in this country, you know."

"Actually," Vaatzes frowned, "you don't. Not what I'd call skilled, anyhow. No disrespect intended, it's simply a fact. You've got men who can make horseshoes and door hinges, but that's not the same thing."

Valens looked up at him. "Is that right?" he said.

"I'm afraid so. I've been wandering around the city over the last few weeks," Vaatzes went on, "poking my nose in, that sort of thing. I've visited pretty well every smithy in town, but I haven't seen anybody I'd give a job to. It's perfectly simple," he added. "The Vadani are a nation of shepherds who suddenly came into money about a century ago, when the silver mines were opened. Since then, you haven't needed home-grown craftsmen; you've got the money, so it's easier to buy stuff from abroad than make it here. You go into any barn or workshop and look around, you'll find most of the tools that aren't a hundred years old were made in Mezentia. Mass-produced good-quality hardware, everything from nails to scythes and plowshares. The Republic trades with your merchants, finished goods for silver; the merchants sell the stuff to the pedlars, who go round the villages and farms and take payment for what they sell in wool, cheese, flour, whatever. It's actually a pretty advanced way of running an economy — you concentrate on doing what you do best, and leave manufacturing to specialists. The problem comes when you're cut off from your supplier — or when you suddenly need home-grown craftsmen, as you do now. Has it occurred to you that every time one of your archers shoots an arrow, you can't replace the arrowhead? All imported, from the people you're currently at war with. Same goes for armor; I've been taking a professional interest, so to speak, and all your guards' kit was made in the Republic. Best-quality munitions-grade equipment, but there's no more where that came from. I'm sorry," he added, "I'd have thought you'd have been aware of that."

Valens was quiet for a moment. "Apparently not," he said. "You know," he went on, "it's a bit hard. I've never had many illusions about myself, but I've always kidded myself that I'm not a complete idiot. Oh well. I guess it's better to find out now rather than later." He sighed, and stood up. "I don't suppose there's anything I can do about it, is there?"

Vaatzes smiled. "As a matter of fact," he said, "there is."

"Really?" Valens turned and looked at him. "Oh, sit down, for crying out loud, instead of hopping about on one foot like a jackdaw. Go on then. Tell me."

Vaatzes looked round, found a chair and sat on it. "The Eremians," he said. "Because they've never had the advantages your people have had, they're used to making the things they need. Not to Mezentine standards, obviously, but their craftsmen know the basics, and they can be taught. I found that out when I was working for Duke Orsea. Now, thanks to the war, there's a fair number of Eremian refugees who've been forced out of their villages by the Mezentines. As I understand it, you've been cautious — understandably — about letting them cross the border. Fair enough; you've got enough problems as it is without several thousand extra hungry mouths to feed. But as I understand it, every Eremian village had its own smith, carpenter and so on. You don't need that many; a couple of hundred, that's all. They'll do your skilled work for you, and they'll train up your own artisans while they're at it. It's not going to happen overnight, particularly since we're evacuating, so everything'll have to be done in tents or off the backs of carts. Fortunately, making arrowheads isn't all that difficult, your people can learn it quickly enough."

Valens nodded. "All right," he said. "What about armor? Can you teach them to make that?"

Vaatzes shook his head. "That takes time," he said. "Also,

there's more to it. You don't just need armorers, you've got to have furnaces to smelt iron ore; mills, preferably, for rolling pig iron into sheet, but that's rather a big leap forward; in the meanwhile, you need a lot of strong men with big hammers. In the short term, I'd recommend killing as many Mezentines as you can and robbing their corpses."

"Funny you should mention that." Valens shook his head. "All right," he went on. "Point taken. Congratulations on your appointment as controller of ordnance. Make a list of everything you need and I'll see you get it as a priority." He paused. "That's why you came to see me, I take it."

"Yes."

"Then I'm obliged to you," Valens said briskly. "My father always used to say, it doesn't matter if you're ignorant so long as you can find people to know stuff for you. Stupidity is staying ignorant when you don't have to. He said a lot of sensible things, my father; it's a shame he never acted on them." He looked up and grinned. "Why are you still here? Suddenly you're the busiest man in the duchy, you'd better get a move on."

"The mine project," Vaatzes said gently. "My idea about using reinforced sections. Do you want me to make a start on that?"

"Yes, if you can. Can you?"

"I expect so," Vaatzes said. "I'll need to get accurate measurements of the shafts of the mines you want blocked off. Who should I see about that?"

"They'll come and see you," Valens replied. "You're too busy to go traipsing about visiting people. Oh," he added, "while I think about it. Presumably if you're going to be doing all this important work, you'll want paying for it."

Vaatzes raised his eyebrows. "That'd be nice," he said mildly. "I hadn't given it any thought, to be honest with you."

Valens frowned. "You know what," he said, "I believe you haven't. That's curious. Is it a burning desire to help the beleaguered Vadani people, or are you just bored with sitting around all day with nothing to do?"

"Something like that," Vaatzes said. "But I'm happy to leave all that up to you."

"Really?" Valens said. "Well, the way things are at the moment, money wouldn't be a lot of use to you; there won't be an awful lot you can buy with it, and when we're all living out of wagons and wheelbarrows, carting it around with you is likely to be a nuisance. You'll just have to trust me to make it up to you if and when life gets back to normal."

Vaatzes shrugged. "Fine," he said. "Right, I'll go and make the list of things I need. When I've done that, who should I see?"

"A man called Ulpianus Macer," Valens replied. "He's my private secretary, practically runs the country. He'll be round to talk to you this evening, after dinner. Will that give you enough time?"

"Yes."

"Excellent." Valens thought for a moment. "You've already done the list, haven't you?"

"I haven't written it out yet."

Valens looked at him for a moment. "Interesting," he said, with a slight frown. "Tell me, are all Mezentines as scary as you, or is that why they threw you out in the first place?"

Vaatzes' expression didn't change. "I'm not exactly a typical Mezentine," he said. "Not for want of trying, but nobody's perfect. Is there anything else, or should I go now?"

Valens raised his hand. "Go," he said. "Leave me to reflect on my own ignorance. It's one of the few indulgences I have left these days. And thank you," he added. "I have no idea what you're really up to, but I appear to be considerably in your debt. That always makes me uncomfortable, so I hope you'll forgive me if I sound a bit ungracious."

Vaatzes grinned. "We don't have graciousness where I come from," he said.

After he'd gone, Valens sat down on the linen press and stared out of the window for a while. He had an uncomfortable feeling that he'd just done something momentous and important, but whether it was a great leap forward or a bad mistake, he couldn't tell. So far, he believed, he'd coped reasonably well with having the Mezentines as his enemies. Having one as an ally, he felt, was likely to be rather more complicated. He thought about what Orsea had said about Vaatzes, how tirelessly he'd worked, his determination, his resourcefulness, his exceptional knowledge and skill. Thanks to Vaatzes, Orsea had said, for a while they'd honestly believed they had a chance of beating the Perpetual Republic and saving Eremia. Orsea liked him and respected him (he'd try not to hold that against him), and the man definitely had a knack for staying alive. There was also the fact that, nominally at least, he was the cause of the war.

Valens frowned. For a moment, earlier that day, he'd seriously considered turning Orsea over to the Mezentines as a way of saving his people. If the Mezentines were serious about why they'd started the war, perhaps there was someone else he could betray instead of Orsea. The same reasoning applied. If the Mezentines were sick of the waste and loss of prestige and would be prepared to go home in exchange for a way of saving face . . .

He got up and lay on the bed, staring at the tapestries on the opposite wall: the boar at bay, crowded in by the hounds, the hunters bearing down on him. He understood perfectly why he couldn't hand Orsea over to the enemy. Vaatzes, on the other hand, was a stranger, a foreigner, an outsider; in the estimation of his own people (and, apparently, himself) a criminal. It was Vaatzes, not Orsea, who had brought about the slaughter of thousands of Mezentine troops, and inflicted on the Republic the worst defeat in its history. Valens was by no means sure what the Republic's real reason for going to war had been. He most certainly didn't care, so long as the war could be persuaded to go away and leave him and his people alone. A lot had changed, however, since the Mezentines invaded Eremia. He understood that wars grew and mutated, finding ways to stay alive; they hung on with the grim tenacity of a weed growing in a crack in a wall, feeding on whatever nutrients their roots and tendrils could find. The war might have started because one faction in the Mezentine government wanted the popularity of a quick, easy victory; that possibility had been extinguished, but the war had not only survived but put on a tremendous spurt of growth; its original sponsors didn't dare end it without a redeeming victory, and other factions with other agendas were undoubtedly considering the opportunities it offered, one of which was surely the Vadani silver mines. Very well; he considered the implications. In all likelihood, the Mezentine opposition was making as much capital as it could out of the administration's misfortunes, but it would be political suicide for them to propose out loud that the Republic should cut its losses and admit defeat. Instead, they would be eager to change the war, redefine its objectives, so that when they overthrew their opponents they'd be able to win a quick victory, make good the financial losses, and if possible turn a profit. The original stated objective — the extermination of the Eremian nation — had proved to be too awkward and expensive, but a loving and generous Providence had intervened by taking away the wits of the Vadani duke, prompting him to interfere in a quarrel that was none of his business. If the war stopped being about wiping out the Eremians and turned into a punitive crusade against the Vadani, all their troubles would be over. They could have their victory simply by killing the stupid arrogant duke and slaughtering his army and a substantial number of his people, and they would have the silver mines. Perfect.

In which case, Valens concluded, it was essential that the current Mezentine government didn't fall; because they must be well aware that their only chance of survival lay in achieving something that could be made to look like the accomplishment of their original objective in the brief space of time remaining to them before their political enemies brought them down. The pretext for the war had been Vaatzes' defection; if they had Vaatzes, and could point to the blackened ruins of Civitas Eremiae, they stood a chance of persuading their constituents that they had done what they had set out to do. Handing over Orsea might just achieve the same result; giving them Orsea *and* Vaatzes would almost certainly do the trick. Vaatzes on his own — well, what mattered to Valens wasn't saving the Mezentine government but striking a deal that would satisfy them. What mattered wasn't whether Vaatzes' head would be enough to rescue them, but persuading them that it might be. Could he do that? He considered his own abilities, and decided that he probably could. At the very least, it was worth a try.

Well, then; problem solved.

He poured himself a glass of wine, looked at it and poured it back into the jug. Wherever you went in the castle, there were jugs and decanters, glasses, cups and mugs; wine, both domestic and imported, mead, cider, perry; the simple fact was that he didn't like the stuff and never had. He didn't like the way it tasted, and he hated the way it fogged up his mind. His father had always said he couldn't think without a few drinks inside him, and that was probably true.

Problem solved, indeed. He sat down again and thought about Vaatzes' visit. Sealing up the mines would deprive the Mezentine opposition of their motive for taking over the war (assuming that they knew about it, and of course they would, if their spies were earning their pay). Understandable, therefore, that Vaatzes should want to see to it that the job was done properly, which meant doing it himself. Vadani engineers, given the job of half sealing the mines, might well err on the side of caution, with the result that the resourceful Mezentines would be able to get past their attempts at sabotage. On that level, Vaatzes' offer of help was reasonable enough. It was, of course, also just a pretext. It had been enough to get him an audience with the gullible Vadani duke (a clever fellow, but not nearly as clever as he thought he was) and an opportunity to make himself indispensable by pointing out the inadequacy of the duchy's materiel resources and taking responsibility for putting matters in order. Basically the same as he'd done in Eremia: giving the Republic's enemies the technological secrets they'd gone to war to keep control of. Once the Vadani accepted Vaatzes' help, simply handing Vaatzes back would no longer be good enough, since the damage would've been done. Clever man; problem not solved.

In which case, it was just as well that Valens had figured out what Vaatzes was up to before it was too late. All the more reason, therefore, to make a deal and hand him over now, while there was still time.

He thought about his reaction to that. Long ago, one of his father's huntsmen had taught him that the one thing a hunter should never do is get angry with the quarry. It would be inexcusable to blame a living thing for doing anything it possibly could to avoid being caught and killed. Feeling angry, or hurt or betrayed, because Vaatzes was trying to manipulate him was therefore out of the question. Instead, when you recognize the trick the quarry is playing on you, the proper reaction is to be glad of the insight you've gained into the way its mind works, because of course you can't hope to hunt something successfully unless you understand it first; and understanding comes from forgiveness, just as forgiveness comes from love.

Problem, then, still solved. What he should do now was write two letters: one to the Mezentines, proposing the deal, one to the guard captain, ordering Vaatzes' immediate arrest. Two letters to save his people from the consequences of his own stupidity. He ought to do it. He ought to do it right away.

Instead, he refilled the wine glass, pulled a face and drank the sour, dusty-tasting stuff down like medicine. It didn't make him feel any better, but he acknowledged the slight fuzziness it produced in his mind. Lots of things wrong with alcohol, but it has one redeeming virtue; it makes you stupid, and there are times when you need to be too stupid to do the intelligent thing.

He looked at the empty glass, then reached for an apple to take the taste away. In five days' time he'd be up to his eyes in savages; pleasant thought. The Cure Hardy; last time he'd had any dealings with them, he'd spent a certain degree of time and effort trying to understand them a little better. He'd ground a few insights out of them before having them killed, which he'd had to do because they were raiding his territory and harming his people. Now, here they were again. He had no idea what they wanted. He yawned.

Someone knocked at the door, and he groaned. He had the option, of course, of simply not being there. Let them knock until their knuckles started to ache, and then they'd go away again.

"Come in," he said.

As it turned out, it was only Macer, with some letters for him to sign. He nodded, and Macer put them down in front of him. The tradition was that letters needing a signature came in on a half-inch-thick sheet of glass; something flat to rest on in an uncertain world. "Do I need to read any of these?" he asked.

Macer shook his head. "Requisitions, mostly," he said. "And you're authorizing payments to a couple of merchants — hay, oats, stuff for the carthorses — and there's a warrant for some character called Jarnac Ducas."

"Oh, him." Valens nodded. "Wasn't life so much simpler when the Eremians were our enemies? You'd think that now there're so many fewer of them, they'd be less of a nuisance. Other way about, apparently." He signed a letter and Macer took it from him for sanding and blotting. "While I think of it," he went on, "the Mezentine, Ziani Vaatzes. I want you to go and see him, directly after dinner."

"Right," Macer said. "What about?"

Suddenly, Valens grinned. "Good question," he replied. "You're either going to make sure he gets anything he wants in the whole wide world, or you're going to have him arrested. Maybe both, and in no particular order, I haven't decided yet." He noticed Macer noticing the used wine glass; that obvious, then. He pulled himself together a little. "Vaatzes will hand you a list," he said. "All sorts of expensive things we haven't got; most of them you won't even have heard of, probably. Find out what they are, where you get them from and how much they cost. Then see me. If Vaatzes tells you to do anything for him, tell him yes, you'll see to it right away, then report back to me. Also, I want details of everywhere he goes and everyone he talks to."

"Understood," Macer said. "Actually, I've been doing that for the last couple of weeks. I've got a list right here, if it's of any use to you."

"Really?" Valens frowned. "Well done. All right, let's see it."

Macer never went anywhere without a battered pigskin folder stuffed with tatty scraps of paper. He opened it, leafed through, took out a scruffy little corner of four-times-erased parchment. Macer's family had been government clerks for six generations.

"Thanks," Valens said, as he glanced at the list. "Who the hell is Henida Eiconodoulus?"

"Merchant Adventurer," Macer replied immediately. "Big woman, wears a red dress. Used to be in the salt business. There's nothing against her."

Valens shrugged. "Maybe he just likes big women," he replied. "This is quite a list. Macer, you annoying bastard, why do you have to write everything so bloody small?"

"Saves on paper."

"Of course." Valens squinted. "Let me guess," he said. "Milo Calceus and Naeus Faber are blacksmiths, right?"

"He's been to see all the blacksmiths in the city," Macer replied. "Most of them before I started making the list."

"Figures. Hello." Valens' frown deepened. "Some familiar names here."

"Quite. And before you ask, he met with them outside the castle, on their own time. Of course, he could just have been finding out about protocol and etiquette and so forth; which knife to use for which course, and who you're supposed to stand up for when they walk into a room."

"That's possible, certainly." Valens stopped. "This one here," he said. "You sure?"

"Yes," Macer said, his tone of voice perfectly neutral. "Actually, that's why I started keeping the list."

Valens put the paper down. "It says here he's met her several times."

"That's right. First time was in the street, about six weeks ago;

he walked with her across town, apparently showing her the way to a draper's shop. After that, twice in the castle, the other time in the park."

"You thought I ought to know about that?"

"Yes."

Valens sighed. "Macer," he said, "you're a clever man. Also very brave."

"Do you want me to pour you another drink?"

"Actually, that's the last thing I want. Does Orsea know?"

"I don't think so, no."

"Try and see to it that it stays that way." He scowled. "Is there anything in it?"

"My opinion?" Macer shook his head. "I don't think so," he said. "I think she's bored and he's an interesting man. She seems to like the company of interesting people."

Valens looked at him in silence for a long time. "I think that's everything for now," he said.

6

Ziani had, of course, lied to the Duke. He'd written out the list of things and people he needed a long time ago; just after he'd first met the salt-dealer's widow, in fact. The four closely written sides of charter paper curled into a roll and hidden in the sleeve of the gown hanging up behind his bedroom door was in fact the third revision of that particular document. Accordingly, he was in no particular hurry as he left the Duke's tower. He walked slowly down the stairs into the east cloister, and sat down on a bench opposite the arch that led to the mews. After a minute or so, he stood up again and retraced his steps as far as the rather splendid marble memorial to Valentius IV, Valens' great-grandfather. Needless to say, the seventeenth duke was commemorated with a fine equestrian statue, about two-thirds lifesize, showing him in the act of leveling his spear against an enormous boar. Ziani knelt down beside the boar's flank and coughed politely.

"Breathing," he said.

Slowly, a man uncoiled himself from the small nook between the boar and the horse's legs.

"I could hear you from right over there," Ziani explained. "Worse than my uncle Ziepe's snoring."

The man stood up straight and scowled at him. "Right," he said. "I'll know better next time."

Ziani shook his head. "There won't be a next time," he said.

"Because if I see you skulking about after me again, I'll assume you're an assassin hired by the Republic to kill me. I'll feel really bad when I find out you were actually one of the Duke's men, but that won't help you very much. Or I may never find out," he added with a mild grin. "I don't suppose the Duke'll be in any hurry to admit he set one of his men to spy on a guest under his roof."

The man took a step back, but the marble flank of Valentius' horse was blocking his retreat. "Just doing my job," he said.

"Of course." Ziani nodded. "You carry on. Just stay in plain sight, where I can see you. Understood?"

"Understood." The man looked at him, then turned his head away. "No problem," he said.

"Splendid." Ziani smiled. "Now," he went on, "I'm just going to sit here peacefully for a while. I promise I won't wander off or do anything treasonable. And since I'll be staying put for a bit, it seems to me you might well want to take this opportunity to get something to eat or take a leak. Come back in half an hour and I'll know it's you, not a Mezentine spy."

The man hesitated for a moment, then turned and walked quickly away. Ziani watched him leave the cloister by the west door, then marched briskly to the arch that led to the mews. Instead of carrying on as far as the mews green, however, he turned right down the tiny snicket that led to the steps that came out on top of the inner keep wall. His luck was in: no sentry, so he was able to slip into the guardhouse and use its staircase to come out in the far corner of the middle keep yard, next to the back door of the kennels. For a man with a generally poor sense of direction, he told himself, he'd got the geography of the place pretty well fixed in his mind.

From the middle keep to the guest wing, where his room was, piece of cake. He ran up the last staircase two steps at a time, wondering how long it would take his shadow to figure out where he'd gone and resume his miserable task. He was, therefore, more than a little disconcerted when he opened his bedroom door and found someone sitting in the chair in front of the fireplace.

It wasn't his shadow, however. Instead, it was a thin man, with a flat face and a slightly pointed head, like an onion.

"You again," Ziani said.

The thin man smiled. "Yes indeed," he said.

"How the hell did you get in here?"

The thin man's smile didn't fade at all. "I told the porter I had an appointment to see you, and it was secret government business. He didn't believe me to begin with," the man added with a frown, "but when I showed him this, he changed his tune pretty quickly."

This was a plain wooden box, slightly larger than a man's head. "Oh," Ziani said. "You made it, then."

"Of course. And I knew you'd want to see it right away; hence my rather unorthodox approach to getting an appointment with you."

Ziani smiled. "It's a good approach," he said. "I use it myself." He sat down on the bed, breathed in slowly and out again. "All right," he said, "let's see it."

The thin man rose and put the box down beside him, rather in the manner of a midwife introducing a mother to her newborn child. "The box is lemonwood," he said, "with brass hinges and a six-lever lock."

Ziani knew that tone of voice. "All made by you, of course."

"I'd finished the main job and I had some time on my hands," the thin man replied, wearing his modesty as a knight wears full plate armor. "Did I mention that cabinet-making —"

"Yes." Ziani held out his hand for the key. He had to admit, it was a beautiful piece of work in itself; stoned and buffed to a deep gloss, and decorated with neatly filed curlicues. He opened the box, trying to remember what it was he'd set the thin man to make for him.

"A small portable winch," the thin man said, right on cue. "To be suspended from a hook in a rafter, capable of lifting heavy sections of material, operated by the pressure of two fingers on the reciprocating crank here."

Ziani reached into the box and lifted it out. For a moment, he was confused; stunned, even. He'd spent his life making machines, designing them to do the jobs they were meant for as efficiently as possible. He understood function as well as a human being can understand anything. Beauty, however, tended to unsettle him. It was something he could recognize; he could even create it, if he had to. But he'd never understood it, maybe because he'd never been quite sure how it worked, and he'd never been able to bring himself to trust it, except once.

The machine he took out of the box was beautiful. That was an absolute fact, not a matter of opinion or taste. The struts that held together the top and bottom plates of the frame had been turned to the most graceful contours imaginable. Each component was immaculately finished and decorated with restrained, elegant file-carving or shallow-relief engraving. The whole thing had been fire-colored a deep sea blue, from which a few twists of perfectly chaste gold inlay shone like watch-fires in the dark. Almost afraid to touch it, Ziani rested a finger on the crank and pressed, until he heard the smooth, soft, crisp click of the sear engaging the ratchet.

"You made this?" he said.

"Yes."

He closed his eyes and opened them again; it was still there. "Does it work?"

"Yes."

He didn't know what to do with it. The heads of the screws and pins, he noticed, were engraved with floral designs, alternating roses and cardoons, each pin-hole and slot surrounded by a border of acanthus-and-scroll work. He didn't want to let go of it, not until he'd examined every component, figured out how it had been made and what it did, but somehow touching it made his flesh crawl. "You made this," he repeated.

"Most certainly," he heard the thin man's voice say. "With respect, it's not the sort of thing I could simply have bought in the market; not even in Mezentia. And you specified the work yourself, so it can't be something I bought somewhere else a long time ago. I also took the precaution of having a notary watch me file the ratchet teeth; I have a duly signed and sworn deposition to that effect here, which of course you are most welcome to have authenticated."

He couldn't resist it; he had to lift it up to the light, so he could see the detail of the spindle bushes. "All right," he said. "So where did you find a lathe in this godforsaken place?"

"I didn't. So I made one."

"You made one. And the milling?"

"No milling. All hand work."

"All —" Ziani had to think how to breathe for a moment. "What, the flats on the spindles and everything? The dividing of the teeth on the main gear?"

"Well . . ." The thin man sounded as though he was making a shameful confession. "I had to build a jig for that; a simple pair of centers, with a handle. But the flat work was just done by eye, checked against a square. I hadn't got a square, so I —"

"Made one." It was as though he'd turned a corner in a busy street in broad daylight and met a unicorn, or a basilisk or a chimera, some mythical animal that quite definitely didn't exist. He could just about believe that work like this — *hand* work, for crying out loud — was theoretically possible. But that this strange, bizarre clown could have made it . . .

"I don't know what you want from me, then," he said. "I couldn't do anything like this."

"I know." The thin man's voice cut him like a jagged edge. "But," he went on, his voice reverting to its usual tone, "when all is said and done, it's just drilling and filing, primitive stuff. The Perpetual Republic knows better ways of doing things that make hand work irrelevant; better techniques, *secrets*." He made the word sound obscene. "That's what you can teach me; and in return, if my poor services . . ." He paused, obviously waiting for some expected reply. Ziani wasn't in the mood.

"All right," he said; and as soon as he'd said it, he felt the little spurt of anger that comes with knowing you've walked into an

obvious trap or fallen for the oldest trick in the book. But the machine in his hands was perfect.

"Thank you," the thin man said. "I promise you, you won't
regret it. Anything I can do for you, anything at all."

"Fine," Ziani snapped. Talking to him was like stroking the
fine hairs on the legs of a spider. "As it happens, I can use someone
like you. I still can't really see what you expect to get out of it, but
if you really want a job, I can give you one." He hesitated; the thin
man either wasn't listening, or else he wasn't interested, to the extent that what he was saying was glancing off him, like arrows off
fluted armor. "Obviously we need to discuss money —"

"With respect." The thin man cut him off. "As I think I may
have mentioned at our first meeting, I have my own resources,
and my position is tolerably comfortable. What I want . . ." He'd
raised his voice, and immediately regretted it. "If and when you
have the time to consider it," he continued smoothly, "I'd be most
grateful for any advice you may care to give me about a small
project of my own. However," he added quickly, "there is absolutely no hurry in that regard, it can wait for as long as necessary,
until it's entirely convenient."

"Really?" Ziani pulled a face. "You may have a pretty long wait,
in that case, because the job the Duke's given me is going to take
up all my time; yours too, if you're serious about wanting to work
for me. If you've got a project of your own and the money to develop it with, you'd be far better off just getting on with it yourself.
Still, it's up to you. Don't say I didn't warn you."

If that was supposed to get rid of the thin man, it had failed.
He was still there, tense and eager as a dog watching its master,
so that Ziani felt an overpowering urge to throw a stick for him to
fetch. He made an effort and resolved not to worry about him anymore. If he wanted to work for nothing, that was his problem.

"Your first assignment," Ziani said briskly, as he stood up
and crossed to the door, where his coat hung from the coathook.
He felt in the sleeve and pulled out a roll of paper. "This is a list
of everything I think we'll need to recruit and train fifty exiled

Eremian craftsmen to do work to an acceptable standard. I want you to read it through, let me know if you think there's anything I've missed out, then copy it out neatly and give it to the Duke's secretary after dinner tonight." He paused. "Where do you live?"

"I have rooms in the ropewalk," the thin man replied instantly. "A workshop; I sleep and eat there as well. I can be ready to move in less than an hour, if —"

"No, that's fine, I just need to know where to find you."

For some reason, the thin man frowned. "The best way is to leave a message for me with the innkeeper at the Patient Virtue. I have an arrangement with him," he added awkwardly. "Any message you leave there will reach me within minutes."

"All right." Ziani shrugged. "Meet me here in the morning, two hours after dawn."

"Certainly. I can get here earlier if you wish."

Ziani couldn't be bothered to reply to that.

The attack came during the salad course, and it took Valens completely by surprise. Thinking about it later, he could only assume it was because he was still preoccupied with what Vaatzes had said to him earlier. That didn't make it any better.

"Oh for crying out loud," he complained hopelessly. "We've been into all this already."

"With respect." There was no respect at all in Chancellor Carausius' face; fear, yes, because all the high officers of state were afraid of him, with good reason. "We haven't actually discussed the matter properly, as you well know. Not," he added with feeling, "for want of trying. But you either change the subject or lose your temper; your prerogative, it goes without saying, but no substitute for a rational discussion." Carausius paused and wiped butter off his chin. "If you have a good, reasoned argument against it, naturally I'll be delighted to hear it."

Valens sighed. "Well," he said, "for one thing, this is hardly the time. We're at war with the Mezentines, we're about to evacuate the city and go lumbering round the countryside in wagons, we're going to collapse all the silver mines, so we won't have any money at all for the foreseeable future. Be reasonable, will you? This really isn't the best moment to be thinking about weddings."

Carausius shook his head slowly, and the napkin tucked into his collar billowed a little as he moved. "On the contrary," he said. "At a time of national emergency such as this, what could possibly be more important than the succession? I mean it," he added, with a faint quaver in his voice that caught Valens' attention. "Face the facts. As you say, we're at war. You have no heir. If you die, if you're killed in the fighting or — I don't know, if you're swept away while crossing a river with the wagons, or if you fall off your horse when you're out hunting and break your stubborn neck, nobody knows who's to be the next duke. You don't need to be told why this is an unacceptable state of affairs."

Valens looked at him. It wasn't like Carausius to be brave unless he was in severe danger of being found out about something, and for once he had every right to a clear conscience. The only explanation, therefore, was that he was sincere. "All right," he said gently, "maybe you've got a point. But you know the reason as well as I do. There's no suitable candidates. I can't just go marrying some girl with a nice smile. We've got to find someone who's got something we need. Right now, that's either money or high-quality heavy infantry. If you can give me three names right now, I promise I'll listen."

A split second of silence, and Valens knew he'd walked into a snare.

"Not three," Carausius said; he'd taken the risk and won, and he was enjoying the moment. "Just one, I'm afraid. But, given the urgency . . ."

Valens put down his knife and folded his arms. "I'm listening," he said.

Carausius composed himself. "Her name," he said, then he smiled. It wasn't something he did very often, sensibly enough. "Actually," he said, "I can't pronounce her name. However, I understand that it translates as White Falcon Soaring."

Just as well Valens had put his knife down, or he'd have stabbed himself in the knee. "You're joking," he said. "No, really, you can't be serious."

"I think it's a charming name."

"You know perfectly well . . ." Valens breathed out slowly. He was determined he wouldn't play the straight man to Carausius, even if he had walked into a painfully obvious trap. "A name like that's obviously Cure Hardy," he said. "Presumably this female of yours is something to do with the delegation we're meeting. And no, not even if it means we win the war and conquer Mezentia and ascend bodily to heaven on the backs of eagles. Not Cure Hardy."

Carausius took a moment to butter a scone. "In your own words," he said, "money or soldiers. The Cure Hardy have both."

"I said heavy infantry," Valens pointed out. It was a bit like trying to sink a warship with a slingshot, but he was determined to fight to the last. "And the Cure Hardy don't even use money."

"They have gold and silver, which amounts to the same thing. Also, I don't agree that we necessarily need heavy infantry. Light cavalry, which is the Cure Hardy's traditional strength —"

"We've got the best cavalry in the world."

"Acknowledged," Carausius said through his scone. "Heavy cavalry, and not nearly enough. The Cure Hardy are faster, more mobile, better suited for informal and irregular campaigning; most of all," he added, "they're one thing our men most certainly aren't. They're expendable."

Valens sighed. What he really wanted to do was run away. "For pity's sake," he said peevishly. "They don't even live in proper houses. Do you really see me with a wife who insists on camping out in a tent in the pear orchard?"

Another smile. Carausius was indulging himself. "The princess — her name, I believe, begins with an A — has spent the last four years being educated in Tannasep; I believe she's been studying music, astronomy, poetry, needlework and constitutional and civil law. Presumably while she was there, she slept in a bed

and learned how to use a knife and spoon. I gather she's also interested in —"

"I couldn't care less what the bloody woman does in her spare
time," Valens snapped. "I don't want to get married, and I most
definitely don't want to get married to a savage, thank you all the
same. Maybe when the war's over, or at least once we're settled
somewhere . . ."

Carausius teased his napkin out of his collar and folded it
precisely. "Logically," he said, "given our immediate plans, a
wife who's used to living under canvas has to be a most suitable
choice."

Valens closed his eyes. When Carausius started making jokes,
it was time to assert his authority. "Thank you for raising the
issue with me," he said, "and I shall give it careful thought. Meanwhile, if that's the only reason why these Cure Hardy are coming
here, maybe it'd be better if you saw them instead of me. I'm sure
you can handle the diplomatic stuff, and I have rather a lot of
work to do."

"That would be unfortunate," Carausius said smugly. "Perhaps
I forgot to mention it, but among the gifts they're bringing with
them are four hundred mounted archers. Not a loan," he added
firmly. "To keep, for our very own. Just for meeting you. I imagine
that if they're fobbed off with a substitute, they may think better of
their generosity."

Valens opened his eyes wide. "They're serious, then," he said.

"I believe so." Carausius had had his moment of revenge. His
voice was back to normal, soft, businesslike and anxious to please.
"My understanding is that they're very keen indeed to make an
alliance with a settled nation. Their chieftain is something of a
visionary. He believes that the nomadic life is all very well, but it's
time his people bettered themselves. In the long term, I imagine
he wants to cross the desert and settle on this side; the tragic fate
of the Eremians means that there's now empty land for the taking.
Naturally he needs an ally, but his choices are clearly limited. Not
the Mezentines, for obvious reasons; similarly, not the Eremians.

That means the Cure Doce — but they're too far away from the land he's got his eye on — or us. If you care to consider what that could mean to us: a powerful, friendly neighbor with practically unlimited manpower . . ."

Valens nodded. "All right," he said. "And thank you, you've done well. But all the same; marrying one . . ."

"It's their principal means of securing alliances," Carausius said firmly. "Without a marriage, as far as they're concerned it's not a proper treaty; once it's done, it means we can rely on them absolutely. They take it very seriously. It's not like the po- litical alliances we're used to. I'm not sure they even have politics where they come from, or at least not in any sense we'd under- stand." He leaned forward a little, lowered his voice. "They aren't complete barbarians," he went on, "they understand that strate- gic and dynastic marriages aren't necessarily the perfect union of heart and mind. If you hate the girl that much, you won't have to see her more than absolutely necessary, she'll understand that. If that's the reason —"

Valens frowned. "I hope you know me better than that," he said. "I understand how things are. I'm just a bit concerned about ending up with a wife who dresses in animal bones and feathers. Which," he added quickly, before Carausius could say anything, "I'd be perfectly prepared to do if I was sure it'd help the war or put our economy straight. But I'm not; so either come up with some better arguments or drop the whole thing."

Carausius looked at him. He knows me too well, Valens re- flected. "There's something else," Carausius said.

"Yes."

"I see." Carausius frowned. "Can I ask what it is?"

"No." As soon as he said the word, he knew he'd lost. "But I will meet these savages of yours, and yes, I'll be civil to them, so don't nag." He shrugged, rather more floridly than usual. "Four hundred cavalry, just for being hospitable. I think I can handle that. Tell me, did the offer come from them, or did you have to haggle?"

"Their idea," Carausius said. "I don't think the Cure Hardy understand bargaining in quite the same way as we do. I don't know if it's true, but someone told me once that their word for trade literally means 'to steal by purchase.' I gather they're a fascinating people, once you get to know them."

"I'm sure," Valens said. "Now, by rights I ought to threaten you with awful retribution if you ever ambush me with something like that again. But I don't need to do that, do I?"

"Certainly not."

"Splendid. I'm a strong supporter of the old tradition that every dog's allowed one bite. I hope it was worth it."

For the rest of the meal they talked about barrel-staves, canvas, salt and rope. Carausius said he was sure they'd be able to get what they needed for the evacuation from the merchants; he'd sounded out the likeliest suppliers, in very general terms so as not to raise suspicions, and the consensus was that it was a buyers' market at the moment; supply wouldn't be a problem, and an acceptable price could easily be agreed as soon as they were in a position to discuss firm orders. "Which means," Carausius went on, "they don't yet know where to lay their hands on what we want, in the quantities we want it in, but they're happy to go away and find out. Luckily, none of the supplies we're after has ever been a Mezentine monopoly, so we should be all right." He paused, just for a moment, then went on, "Have you decided on a date yet? Or are we still working on the basis of six to nine weeks?"

Valens pulled a face. "If you'd asked me that question this time yesterday, I'd have given you a definite answer," he said. "Six weeks, I'd have said, and no messing. Unfortunately, it's not going to be quite as straightforward as I thought, so you'll have to leave it with me."

"Longer than nine weeks?"

"No." The second time in one evening that he'd been backed into saying that. "Work on that assumption, if you like. You won't be far out."

There was music after dinner. Harp, rebec, flute, oboe, pipes, guitar and a singer. It went without saying that they'd been practicing day and night for weeks to be ready for their big chance, playing to the Duke and his court. Everywhere he went, in everything he did, he saw people doing their best, because it was him. He left before the music started.

There was a meeting of Necessary Evil that night. The defense committee had taken to gathering at strange hours — eleven at night or four in the morning — and nobody seemed to know why, though most people assumed it was something to do with their legendary and indefinable flair. The agenda had arrived on his desk shortly after noon; he'd read it through a dozen times, but all his political skill and experience couldn't tease a single shred of significance out of it.

1. Minutes of previous meeting
2. Chairman's report
3. Any other business

Psellus raised his eyebrows, rolled up the paper and slotted it neatly back into the thin brass tube it had come in. All committee correspondence came in message tubes these days, sealed at both ends, never the same seal twice. If he didn't know better, he could well believe that someone on the committee had a sense of humor.

The same messenger had brought him the latest dispatches from Eremia. Two rolls, one brass and one silver; the brass tube was for the official report, the silver one was the truth. He opened the silver one first, which said something about him. He was pretty sure he was the only man on Necessary Evil who read dispatches in that order.

Not good, apparently. There had been successes: villages burned, six; isolated farms and crofts burned, twenty-seven; civilians confirmed killed, a hundred and nine; material seized, various, to include thirteen mail shirts, nine bascinets, three sallets with bevor, five sallets without bevor, nine leg harnesses (nine; an odd number. Had they managed to kill a one-legged man, maybe?), four spears, nine swords, two bows, thirty-two arrows, eight knives, fourteen lengths of wood capable of being used as bludgeons . . .

(Psellus smiled, as an image drifted into his mind of soldiers sent into the forest to cut poles in order to bulk out the captured-material schedule. He wouldn't put it past them, assuming anybody on the expeditionary staff had that much imagination.)

There had also been failures. Dead, forty-six; wounded and unfit for duty in the medium to long term, thirty-eight; horses killed, seven; horses lost, nineteen; wagons lost or damaged beyond repair, eight; issued equipment lost or damaged, see separate schedule. The most serious reverse was an ambush by insurgents at some place he hadn't heard of. While attempting to pursue a small body of insurgent cavalry apparently in retreat, Fifteenth Squadron had come under attack from insurgent archers concealed in a spinney. Casualties . . .

Psellus marked the place with his finger and looked back up the page. That explained where they'd got the thirty-two enemy arrows from. Whether pulling them out of the bodies of the dead counted as capturing, he wasn't sure.

Not that it mattered. There were plenty of men, both in and outside Necessary Evil, who stoutly maintained that every soldier lost was a mercenary who wouldn't need to be paid. Psellus felt there was a flaw in that line of reasoning; nevertheless, reports from the recruiting stations back in the old country assured him that they were still queuing up for a chance to sign on. What bothered him more was the double column of figures at the bottom of the page, the monthly payment and expenditure account. He glanced down at the total and winced.

The news in the brass tube was much better. The forces of the Republic had destroyed six major rebel strongholds, raided a further twenty-seven installations, and killed over a hundred rebel fighters, as well as recovering a substantial quantity of weapons. Losses remained within acceptable parameters, and the war was coming in under budget. In his monthly briefing, Field Marshal Megastreuthes stressed that —

He rolled up both versions and stuffed them back in their tubes. None of it really mattered, not even the ruinous cost. According to the figures, all the exporting Guilds had stepped up both production and sales to meet the demands of the war budget. Prices had necessarily been lowered to ensure that strategically important markets were retained in the face of local competition, but the losses thereby incurred were amply covered by the increased volume. He paused, and looked at the finance report. It had come, he noticed, in a brass tube.

It still didn't matter. The Perpetual Republic could keep on waging war on this scale forever. The key had been lowering prices. Demand in the export markets had been wavering for some time, simply because Mezentine goods had gradually come to cost more than the locals could afford. Cutting prices, however, had been seen as an unacceptable loss of face, a move that would give the buyers more leverage than was good for them and lead inevitably to lower standards, debased specifications, ruin, abomination and death. The war had been the excuse the Republic needed, and the increase in volume had fully justified Necessary Evil's hard-line stand on the issue. Politically, more production meant a slight shift in the balance of power between the leading Guilds. War work had given the Foundrymen a temporary edge over their rivals; now, the need for export sales meant that the Weavers and Drapers were clawing ahead, with the Potters and Cutlers coming up close behind. The Cutlers were still unaligned, though their traditional allegiance had always been to the Foundrymen; the Potters were making a show of resisting the Weavers' attempts to negotiate a rapprochement, but it was generally believed that they were simply holding out for a better deal, which would inevitably involve the fall of Dandola Phrantzes, chairman of the Joint Transport Executive . . .

The war, Psellus realized, was like a tree. Its branches grew and were lopped, but it drew its life from its roots, widespread, tangled and hidden. The plain fact was that what happened in Eremia didn't matter very much. Men died, buildings were burned, endless columns of wagons stirred up the dust as they carried thousands of tons of freight into the deserted mountains, but the real battle was being fought here, a close grapple in the dark between politicians, for whom victory and defeat had very little to do with the deaths of soldiers. That was something he could accept; ever since he was old enough to understand how things worked, he'd known that in Mezentia, nothing mattered except politics, and everything was political. The part he couldn't make out, however, was how he fitted into it; in particular, how he'd come to be co-opted into Necessary Evil in the first place. Until he got to the bottom of that, he was effectively blind, deaf and dumb.

He heard a footstep in the passage outside; somebody who didn't feel he had to knock or announce his presence. A colleague, in that case. He frowned. He wasn't in the mood for the society of his own kind.

It turned out to be as bad as he'd thought: Maris Boioannes himself, condescending to visit him. Such a display of solidarity had to mean complications, at the very least.

"There you are," Boioannes said, dropping easily into the other chair and steepling his fingers. He'd had his hair cut, Psellus noticed. "Have you got a moment?"

Fatuous question. On the desk between them, half a dozen messenger tubes, a few sheets of blank paper, the inkwell. "Always," Psellus replied with a mild smile. "What can I do for you?"

"It's nothing too serious." Boioannes was looking at the wall behind his head, and Psellus suddenly couldn't remember if there was anything on that wall: a picture, a chart, a map of the war. He very much hoped there wasn't anything. The fewer insights into his mind that he conceded to any of his colleagues, the better. "It's just something that's been itching away for a while now, and I was wondering if you could possibly shed some light."

"If I can."

"Splendid." Boioannes frowned slightly, concentrating his mind the way anybody else would sharpen a pen. "As you know, we only managed to take Civitas Eremiae because a traitor opened the gates for us." He paused and smiled bleakly. "Thinking about it, I really feel that *traitor* is far too small a word for Ziani Vaatzes. It's like calling a continent an island."

"He seems to be quite an interesting man," Psellus said.

"Putting it mildly." Boioannes moved his head slightly to one side, scratched the bridge of his nose lightly, and put his head back exactly where it had been. "First he betrays core military secrets to the enemy. Then he betrays the enemy to us." He shrugged, precisely and elegantly. "He causes the war, then ends it — well, not quite, but let's not let a few trivial details get in the way of symmetry. It's tempting to dismiss his motivations as irrelevant, but he's still at large — our best intelligence puts him at the court of Duke Valens, so he's still very much in the center of the action — and I find it irksome not being able to understand him." Boioannes bent forward very slightly from the waist, bringing his formidable head a few inches closer to Psellus. "When you were investigating him at Compliance, I imagine you found out pretty much everything there is to know about the man. I'd value your opinion."

A tiny gleam of light broke through in Psellus' mind, and he answered almost eagerly. "Yes, I conducted an investigation," he said, "and I believe I have most of the pertinent facts. As to whether I've got enough information to base a valid opinion on, I really couldn't say. I'm sure I must have missed something, because it doesn't really make any sense, but I don't know where to look for the missing clue, because I don't know what it is I'm looking for. Quite possibly I have the data but I haven't figured out its significance yet. On the other hand, I could be like a sailor trailing along an established trade-route, oblivious to the fact that just over the horizon there's an undiscovered country. I don't know." He raised his eyebrows. "That's not much help, is it?"

Boioannes pursed his lips. Most of his gestures seemed to constitute self-sharpening, in one form or another. "He's only a human being," he said, "not a paradox of algebra; you should be able to do the equations and solve him, if you try." He leaned back a little. He had the rare knack of looking comfortable on other people's furniture. "Let's start with the obvious. Why do you think he told us how to get into Civitas Eremiae?"

Psellus nodded. "There's the obvious motives," he said. "Remorse: he saw the horrific consequences of his betrayal of military secrets, and felt he had to make amends."

"Discounting that," Boioannes prompted.

"Hope," Psellus continued. "He hopes that, since he gave us Civitas Eremiae, we might be persuaded to pardon him and let him come home. Or, if he's a realist, he understands that we have his wife and daughter."

Boioannes shook his head. "Only a fool would carry out his side of the bargain before negotiating the terms. And he knows we're not savages. We don't take out our anger on innocent women and children."

"Indeed." Psellus twitched; nerves, probably. "It could be some subsequent development we don't know about. For instance, he may have fallen out very badly with the Eremians while he was there, and betrayed them to get his revenge."

"Possible." Boioannes dipped his head in acknowledgment. "Doesn't feel right, though. Oh, it could well be the right explanation, but in order to find it convincing, we'd have to presuppose that his mind had been affected: paranoia, psychotic tendencies. Does he seem to you to be that sort of man?"

"No," Psellus admitted. "But after what he's been through . . ."

"Let's assume it's not that. What else?"

That was as far as Psellus had got in his own speculations. "The other extreme," he said. "He's a desperate man, we can agree on that. We aren't the Eremians' only enemies. Bear in mind that he's now with the Vadani, and they were at war with Eremia for a long time before the Sirupati Truce. He realizes that the Eremians are likely to lose the war sooner or later, so he does a deal with the Vadani; he betrays the Eremians to us in return for asylum in Civitas Vadanis."

The Boioannes thoughtful smile; a rare commodity, flattering but dangerous. "I could believe that," he said, "were it not for the fact that Duke Valens made a last-minute attempt to relieve the siege, and in so doing effectively declared war on us. If your theory's correct, you'll have to make some fairly large assumptions about Valens' motives, too."

Psellus clicked his tongue. "And that, of course," he said, "is the other great mystery: why did Valens attack us, at the precise moment when he had the least to gain from so doing? I can't help thinking that where you have two great mysteries in the space of one transaction, logic suggests that they're probably linked. But, of course, I'm not our leading expert on Duke Valens."

"You're not." The Boioannes smile darkened a little. "I am. And there aren't two mysteries, there're three. Why did Orsea dismiss and imprison his chief adviser — the only competent man in his government — just when he needed him most?" He shook his head. "Two enigmas might be a coincidence. Three . . . But now it's getting unrealistic, isn't it? What on earth could connect Orsea, Valens and our erstwhile Foreman of Ordnance? At the risk of overburdening the equation, I think that counts as a fourth enigma." He sighed; it sounded almost like genuine frustration. "It's ridiculous," he said. "We have sixty-five thousand men in arms and complete materiel superiority. The motivations of three individuals should be totally irrelevant. But apparently they matter, so we have to do something about them."

Psellus nodded. He should have seen it coming; but if he had, what could he have done? "You want me to investigate?"

This time, Boioannes grinned from the heart. "Why not? It's not as though you've got anything else to do."

"Quite." Pause; the question had to be asked, and Boioannes would be expecting it. "In return, would you tell me something?"

"Perhaps."

"What am I doing on this committee?"

Boioannes' grin opened as if for laughter, but there was no sound, just a showing of teeth. "There are various reasons," he said. "First, we need your expertise, wisdom and lively intellect. Second, we needed someone who would do as he was told and not make trouble. Third, there was a vacancy and we already had as many intelligent men as we could accommodate; a committee needs men like you, just as music needs rests or mosaics need blank tiles. Would you like me to continue?"

"Yes. I'd like the real reason, please."

"Very well." Boioannes frowned. "In fact, it's quite complicated and not in the least profound. We wanted . . ." He smiled. "*I* wanted someone inert and pragmatic who would stay peacefully in his office until he was given something to do. Naturally, the Foundrymen on the committee wanted another Foundryman. The other Guilds, in particular the Joiners, were prepared to allow another Foundryman only on the understanding that he was — excuse me — a nonentity. Staurachus felt that taking you out of Compliance would create a vacancy that could usefully be filled by a Tailor or a Draper; since Compliance was likely to be taking the main force of the fallout from the Vaatzes scandal, he felt that the Foundrymen should reduce their representation there and pass the poisoned cup, so to speak, to their natural enemies. If you want my opinion, your name came up because half the obvious candidates for the vacancy were too stupid, and the other half were too intelligent. You were — again, excuse me — a name more or less chosen at random from a shortlist of available Foundrymen. Nobody outside the Guild or Compliance had ever heard of you, but the Foundrymen believed you'd be safe, sensible and properly timid. Finally, it was you who got us into this war. There were other reasons — scraps of reasons — but most of them have slipped my mind."

Psellus dipped his head gracefully. "Thank you," he said. "I'd been wondering."

"Understandably."

"It was kind of you to set my mind at rest. I can stop fretting about that and concentrate on this job you've given me."

"Excellent." Boioannes stood up. "As I understand it, you've already . . ." He frowned again. "*Immersed* yourself in Ziani Vaatzes, so you have the relevant data. His books, for example." The way in which he reached out and picked the book off the shelf told Psellus that he already knew exactly where to find it. "A sensible place to start. Why should a machine shop foreman go to all the trouble of making himself a book out of scrounged materials, and then fill it with low-grade, homemade love poetry?" He opened the book, stared at the pages as if they were an apple he'd bitten into and found a wormhole, shut it with a snap and put it back. "You may find this an interesting comparison," he went on, taking a familiar-looking brass tube from his sleeve. "This is a copy of a letter from Duke Valens to the wife of Duke Orsea, written two months before Orsea's ill-fated attack on the Republic. Fortuitously, it was sent by the hand of a merchant who does business with us, and who had the wit to make a copy before passing it on. There's no poetry in it, apart from a few quotations, but there are distinct parallels which you may find illuminating." He dropped the tube on the desk. It rolled, and came to rest against the inkwell. "Thank you for your time, Commissioner. I look forward to seeing what you come up with."

After he'd gone, Psellus realized that he was shaking slightly. This surprised him. He hoped it hadn't been visible enough for Boioannes to notice.

He got up, with a vague idea of going down to the buttery and getting something strong to drink, but once he was on his feet the idea ceased to appeal. He went back carefully over the interview, assessing it in the way a judge at a fencing match awards points to the contestants, and came to the surprising conclusion that it had either been a draw or else he'd come out of it with a very slight lead. True, Boioannes had beaten him up pretty conclusively, but he hadn't heard anything about his own shortcomings that he hadn't already known for some time. On the positive side, he'd finally been given something to do, which made a pleasant change, and he'd forced Boioannes to tell him an unplanned and largely unprepared lie. A lie, he'd learned long ago, is often the mirror image of the truth; by examining it carefully, you can reconstruct the fact that lie was designed to conceal. That was a step forward, but not necessarily one he'd been anxious to take . . .

(He sat down again. He'd seen a lion once, in a cage in a traveling circus. He'd watched it with a mixture of awe and compassion, as it roared and lashed its tail; absolute ruler of five paces.)

Because the step Boioannes had practically shoved him into taking led to a question that he had no way of answering, but which had quietly tormented him ever since he first read Vaatzes' dossier. Previously he'd assumed that the answer wasn't worth finding because Vaatzes' motivation, soul and very essence didn't really matter very much to the future well-being of the Republic. Now, however, it appeared that Maris Boioannes himself felt that it might have some deeper significance. In which case, he had no option. Until he'd made some kind of headway with the problem, he couldn't get anywhere; it was a locked gate he had to get through, or over.

So. (He tilted the small jug on his desk, just in case an invisible goodwill fairy had refilled it in the last ten minutes.)

Ziani Vaatzes was condemned for abomination because he'd made a clockwork toy for his daughter that contained forbidden mechanical innovations and modifications. Fair enough; but how on earth had he been found out in the first place?

Like a donkey turning a grindstone, he followed the familiar, weary circle. By its very nature, the abomination, the toy, was a private thing, not something liable even to be seen by strangers, let alone dismantled and examined with calipers. Neither the wife nor the daughter could have known about the transgression, since they didn't have the mechanical knowledge to recognize it. Surely Vaatzes hadn't talked about it to his fellow workers, or left notes and drawings lying about. Unlikely that he'd made himself conspicuous by stealing or scrounging materials liable to betray his illicit intentions; as shop foreman, he could requisition pretty much anything without exciting suspicion; besides, none of the materials used had been rare or unusual. An unexpected visitor, calling at the house late one evening and seeing components carelessly left lying about on the kitchen table; no, because the deviations from Specification wouldn't have been obvious out of context, and even if the visitor somehow knew they were meant for use in a clockwork toy, he'd have needed calipers to detect the irregularity. It was, in essence, the perfect crime.

The answer should, of course, have been right there in the dossier, in the investigators' report. But it wasn't. No account of the course of the investigation, because Vaatzes had immediately pleaded guilty.

Not that it mattered, because all he had to do was ask the men who'd brought the prosecution in the first place. Which was exactly what he'd done. He'd written to Sphrantzes, the prosecutor, and Manin, the investigating officer. No reply from either of them; he'd written again, and also to their immediate superiors, their departmental supervisors, their heads of department and the permanent secretaries of their division. He'd had plenty of replies from the upper echelons, all promising to look into the matter and get him his answer. Before giving up and resolving to forget about the whole thing, Psellus had even tried to find the two men and talk to them personally. He'd planned it all like an explorer seeking a lost city in the desert: he'd obtained floor plans of the east wing with Sphrantzes' and Manin's offices clearly marked in red, he'd contrived to get hold of copies of their work schedules so he'd be reasonably certain of finding them at home when he called. In the event, he found their offices empty; neighbors had told him in both cases that they'd been relocated to new offices in the north wing extension, but the corridor and staircase coordinates they gave him turned out not to have been built yet. None of that was particularly sinister. The geography of the Guildhall was a notoriously imprecise science, and every new arrival was treated to the ancient stories of men who nipped out of their offices for a drink of water, never to be seen again until their shriveled carcasses were found somewhere in the attics or the archive stacks. The likeliest explanation was that the internal mail service couldn't find them either, which was why none of Psellus' letters had ever been answered. Manin and Sphrantzes, he knew, were both very much alive and active. They wrote and delivered reports, addressed subcommittees, gave evidence at tribunals and courts corporate and mercantile. Psellus was sure he'd seen Sphrantzes not so very long ago, crossing the main quadrangle one afternoon. The truth was that he'd been glad of an excuse to let the matter lie.

Now, apparently, that excuse had been taken from him. In which case, since he was an officer of the War Commission and therefore a person of consequence and standing (he couldn't help grinning as he thought that), he might as well use his seniority and make sure he got an answer. He flipped up the lid of his inkwell, dipped the tip of his pen and wrote a memo.

To: Maris Boioannes
From: Lucao Psellus
I need to speak to Investigator Manin of Internal Intelligence, and Prosecutor Sphrantzes of the judicial office. I've written to them myself, and to their superiors, but so far I have not received a reply. There's bound to be a rational explanation for this. However, it would be very helpful to me in carrying out the request you made of me today if I could meet both of these men as soon as conveniently possible. Do you think you could ask one of your people to see to it? I'm sorry to bother you with such a tiresome business, but I know how efficient your staff is.

He blotted the page and smiled. He was fairly sure his memo wasn't going to flush Manin and Sphrantzes out of their lairs, but the outcome, whatever it turned out to be, would almost certainly leave him better informed than he had been before; and if he had to have someone like Boioannes in his life, he might as well make use of him. If he'd got nothing else out of the war, it had taught him one thing. Spears and arrows and siege engines and field artillery are all very well in their way, but people are the best weapons.

He walked to the window and looked out. In the courtyard, the scale of the great bronze water-clock ordained that it was a quarter to seven; four hours to go before the meeting started. It was a well-kept secret, which he'd been let into only once he'd joined Necessary Evil, that the water-clock, on which all time throughout the Republic was ultimately based, was running slow. Tiny traces of limescale in the water were gradually furring up the outlet pipes — it was something to do with mining works in the Suivance Hills, which meant the river that supplied the aqueduct that brought the water that fed the conduit that filled the clock was beginning to cut into the limestone bedrock of the hills, hardening the water supply ever so slightly — which meant that the clock's outflow rate was down from nine gallons a day to eight-point-nine-nine-seven-something. Far too small to notice, of course (unless you were the sort of man who carried calipers in your pocket when you paid social calls on your friends); but the plain fact was that time throughout the Republic was gradually slowing down. Every hour was a tenth of a second longer this year than it had been last year; in ten years' time, given the exponential rate of the distortion, an hour would last an hour and five seconds. Eventually, on that basis, there would finally come an hour that would never end. Of course, the problem could be solved in a couple of minutes by a careful apprentice with a bow-drill and a fine bit, but that could only happen if the existence of the problem could be admitted. No chance whatsoever of that.

On his desk lay the messenger tube Boioannes had brought for him; something to do with Duke Valens, he remembered, and somebody else's wife. He picked it up with the tips of his index fingers, one at each end. People are the best weapons. He pushed in gently at one end, and the roll of paper slid out, like an animal flushed from cover.

7

Just because you own a place, it doesn't necessarily follow that you've ever been there.

Miel Ducas leaned forward in the saddle and rubbed dust out of his eyes, leaving behind a silt of dirt and tears. If that big gray thing over there was Sharra Top (and there wasn't much else it could be) and the river he'd just crossed was the Finewater, he was quite definitely on Ducas land. The Ducas owned everything from the Longstone, two combes beyond Sharra, to the Finewater. It was, of course, only an insignificant part of their possessions, always referred to as (he laughed out loud at the thought) that miserable little northeastern strip that's no good for anything.

Miserable, yes. Not so bloody little.

He'd never been north of the Peace and Benevolence at Watershead in his life; possibly he'd seen this land, from the Watershead beacon perhaps, or the watchtower of his hunting lodge at Caput Finitis. If so, it would have been a gray smudge, a vague blurring of the definition of the border of sky and land. Nobody lived here; a few of his more desperate tenants drove sheep up here occasionally to nibble round the clumps of couch grass, but he couldn't see any sheep, or anything living at all. He'd lost count of the days and nights since he'd escaped from the scavengers.

Nice irony: to get this far, just so he could starve to death on his own property. It would spoil the delicacy of it all to bear in mind that, properly speaking, it all belonged to the Mezentines now, by unequivocal right of conquest.

The horse didn't seem unduly worried about anything; the horse could eat grass.

Miel made an effort and tried to think sensibly. If that really was Sharra Top, the Unswerving Loyalty at Cotton Cross was two and a bit days' ride (in his condition, make that three full days) northwest. He was starving. Theoretically, he could kill the horse and eat it, but then he'd have to walk to the Loyalty, and in the state he was in, that was out of the question. If he made it to Cotton Cross and got something to eat (no money, of course) and then carried on toward the ruins of Civitas Eremiae, he'd have the problem of being in regularly patrolled enemy territory, in a place where someone would be bound to recognize him, assuming the Mezentines had left anybody alive up there . . .

Pointless, the whole thing. Particularly galling was the fact that he'd slaughtered two men in order to make his escape, and absolutely nothing to show for it. That wasn't a tragedy, that was *stupid*. The death of the Ducas could quite legitimately be tragic, but stupidity was an unforgivable crime against the family's good name. Nobody would know. *He* would know; and the opinion of the Ducas is the only one that matters.

In the end, the factor that decided the issue for him was the thought of how much energy he'd have to scrounge up from somewhere just to get off the horse. If he carried on riding until he was too weary and famished to stay in the saddle, presumably he'd just keel over and flop down among the grass tussocks and die. No effort needed. Let's do that, then.

As a last gesture of Ducas steadfastness, he pointed the horse's head toward Sharra before closing his eyes. Then he yawned hugely and let his chin sink forward. Every step the horse took jolted his neck.

After a while, it seemed reasonable enough that Death should be riding beside him. No hurry (Death was an urbane, considerate fellow), take your time, if you'll excuse the pun. This is all perfectly natural. Everybody dies.

He lifted his head (he knew his eyes were shut and his chin was resting awkwardly on the junction of his collarbones) and glanced round for one last look at his country; this part of his country, or a part of this part.

I've served Eremia all my life, he said, and now it's killing me. That's nice.

Death didn't approve. Instead of wallowing in self-pity, you should be thankful that you had the opportunity to devote your life to the common good. Come along, now, this is a solemn moment, you'd do well to act accordingly. More gratitude and less attitude, so to speak.

Miel sighed. Oh, absolutely, he said. And look where it's got me.

Now then, said Death. You've lived a life of luxury and privilege, not like those two poor devils you murdered. You've had everything.

No, Miel replied. Most things. Everything that money can buy.

Death clicked his tongue. The mere fact that you're making that distinction proves how privileged you've been. How many people in this world can say they own the land they die on?

Miel laughed, though he couldn't hear himself. You know, he said, I don't think anybody can own land; not great big slices of geography like this. It's a bit like when you see a small man getting dragged along behind a great big dog. Who's walking who?

Death sighed. I'd love to stay here and chat, but you clearly aren't thinking straight. Shall we go?

Not yet. Miel narrowed his eyebrows, as though he was doing long multiplication. I'll tell you something I never had. And it's something that nearly everybody else gets.

Oh, you mean love, Death said. Don't worry about that.

That's easy for you to say, Miel replied irritably. But it's important, it's one of the really important things that matter a lot. You can't just wave a hand and say don't worry about it.

Really?

Yes, really. I missed out on it, and it's not fair. I can hardly remember my parents, so I missed out on that sort of love. No wife, no kids —

You were in love with Veatriz Sirupati, Death pointed out, until she married your friend Orsea.

Doesn't count. She never loved me back.

True, Death replied. Well, maybe when you were both kids, and everybody thought she was going to marry you, for sound political and dynastic reasons.

You can't call persuading yourself to make the best of a bad job love. I'm sorry, but you won't budge me on that one. Love is really, really important, and I missed out entirely. Unfair.

No big deal, Death insisted. Love is a confidence trick, that's all. It's Nature's way of suckering a mammal with a brain and a long, vulnerable gestation period into reproducing. Humans can think, so ordinary animal-grade maternal instinct wouldn't be enough to make human women go through all that, not if they stopped and thought about what's involved. So you have love. It's a substitute for rational thought; look at it that way, it's the complete antithesis of what being human's all about. Humans can make choices, it's what makes them unique. Love takes all your choices away, and there you suddenly are. Worse still, love inevitably leads to the worst pain of all, when you lose the people you love. You might as well be getting all uptight with me because you've never had diphtheria.

I'm not listening, Miel said.

You are, you know. Think how utterly lucky you are. You'll die, and nobody will suffer unspeakable pain because you're not around anymore. Nobody loves you, even your best friend had you thrown in jail. You can die knowing you won't be hurting anybody. Now that's a real privilege.

I don't think I'll die after all, Miel answered, and opened his eyes.

It was getting dark. He considered stopping for the night, in case the horse stumbled and fell, but decided against it. If he was going to reach Cotton Cross before the last dregs of nutrient drained out of his blood, he needed to keep going. I have decided to go on living, he realized, out of pique, just to be difficult. Well.

He could have been lucky, or perhaps the horse was really a fire-dragon or the spirit of one of his ancestors, briefly assuming equine shape in order to keep him alive. In any event, it didn't trip and stumble in the dark, and when the sun rose he was appreciably closer to Sharra Top. Not nearly close enough, though.

In a dip of dead ground was a pool. The water was brown, so dark it was almost black (peat water, seeping up out of the saturated ground at this time of year). The horse put its head down to drink, and he couldn't be bothered to pull it up. He quite fancied a drink himself, in fact he was desperate for one; but that would mean dismounting, and he knew that if he did that, he'd never be able to get back on the horse. The point was academic because he was going to die, but his stubborn streak had worn through onto the surface, like cheap silver plating on a copper dish. I shall die of thirst instead of hunger, he decided, and then all of you who betted on starvation will lose your money. Serves you right. Ghouls.

The horse was still noisily sucking up water. He pulled on the reins to drag its head up, but it jerked back, snatching them out of his hands. He swore, leaned forward to retrieve them, and felt himself slipping, forward and sideways, out of the saddle. He writhed, trying to pull himself back, but it was too late. He'd passed the balance point.

Hell of a stupid way to die, he thought, as he fell. It seemed to take him a very long time to travel the few feet, long enough for him to feel disgust at the ridiculously trivial way his life was ending, and then for the disgust to melt into amusement. If he fell in the water in his state, he probably wouldn't have the strength to swim. Drowning, now; nobody would've bet on that.

The water wasn't deep, but the pool bottom was spongy and soft. He tried to put his weight on his feet, but instead they sank down; he felt peat mud fill his boots, squidging between his toes. He was up to his waist before he stopped sinking. He laughed.

Would being swallowed up in a bog count as drowning, or was it something rarer and unlikelier still? Typical Ducas, got to be different from everyone else. Thorough, too. When the Ducas resolves to die, he's privileged to be provided with a redundancy of alternative causes. Surplus and excess in all things.

"Hold on, don't move." It was a voice, faint on the edge of his awareness. "No, you clown, I said don't move, you'll just go further in." Move? Come to think of it, the voice was right. He was still trampling aimlessly up and down, and each thrashing kick dragged him further into the mud. But a voice . . .

"Now listen to me." The voice was calm but urgent. He liked it. The voice of a good man. "I'm going to throw you a rope, and I want you to grab hold of it and hang on. Can you hear me?"

"Yes," Miel heard himself say. "Where are you? I can't see you."

"Directly behind you." Ah, that'd account for it. Of course, he couldn't turn round to look. He felt something flop against his neck, looked down at his chest and saw the knotted end of a thin, scruffy hemp rope drooping over his shoulder like a scarf. "Got it?"

Miel nodded. He carefully wrapped his right hand round the rope's end, so that the heel of his hand was jammed against the knot. He had no strength to hold on with, but he might be able to keep his hand gripped shut. As an afterthought he folded his left hand round the rope as well.

"Good boy. Don't let go, for crying out loud."

A second or two; nothing happened. Then the rope tried to pull away. He felt its fibers rasping into the soft skin of his neck. He was being hauled backward; he couldn't balance and his knees hinged. He was sure he was going to fall back, but remembered he couldn't. The rope jerked his hands up until his clenched fists bashed the underside of his chin. It was like being punched by a very strong man; he swayed, his eyes suddenly cloudy, nearly let go of the rope — would've let go, except that the knot was jammed against his hand. He could feel himself being gradually, unnaturally pulled, like a bad tooth being drawn. It didn't feel right at all. At the last moment, he tried to save his boots by curling his toes upwards, but he was wasting his time. His feet were yanked out of the boots like onions being uprooted. Now he fell; his backside and thighs were in the muddy water. He twisted round a half-turn, and a big stone gouged his hip painfully. He realized he was lying on his side on the grass. The rope's end was still gripped in his right hand; he'd let go with his left when the rope burned it.

Not drowning or smothering in mud, then. The thought crossed his mind, vivid and shocking as forked lightning, that maybe he wasn't going to die after all.

"It's all right," the voice was saying, "stay there, I'm coming." Miel grinned for pure joy and, quite unexpectedly, sneezed. The whole thing reminded him, for some reason, of a time when he'd seen a calf being born, hauled out of its wretched mother's arse on the end of a rope. So maybe I did die after all, he thought; maybe I died, and was reborn. As a cow.

The rope was tugging at him again. "Let go," the voice said, "it's all right." Miel wondered about that, realized that the owner of the voice wanted his rope back. Well, indeed; what with the price of rope and everything, why not? He let go.

"Right, let's have a look at you." He'd closed his eyes; he opened them, and saw a pair of boots. Old, fine quality, carefully waxed. He turned his head and looked up.

The voice's owner, his savior, was not quite as tall as his cousin Jarnac and not nearly as broad across the shoulders and chest. He was somewhere between forty and fifty years old, if the proportion of gray in his hair was anything to go by; his face was long, intelligent and somehow weak-looking. His hands were small and slender, and there was a big, shiny red scar running the length of his left forefinger; a civilian scar, Miel's instincts told him, rather than a military one. That came as something of a surprise. As well as the fine boots, he was wearing a short riding-coat (shiny and worn around the shoulders, suggesting that the man was in the habit of carrying heavy loads), breeches to match and long leather gaiters. The clothes could have come from Miel's own wardrobe. Correction; they were the sort of clothes he used to give to his grooms and his falconers, old but still perfectly good.

"I'm Tropea Framain," the man said. "Who're you?"

Miel hesitated before speaking. "Thanks," he said. "You saved my life there."

"I know. What did you say your name was?"

"I'm trying to get to Cotton Cross, but I lost my way. Do you think you could possibly . . . ?"

"What?" Framain looked like he'd just remembered something important and obvious. "Oh, right. When did you last have anything to eat and drink?"

Miel shrugged. "Not sure."

"That bad. It's all right," Framain went on, "my place isn't far. If I help you up, do you think you could stay on your horse for half an hour?"

Framain's own horse turned out to be a fine-looking bay mare. The other end of the miraculous rope was tied to its girth, which explained how Miel had been pulled from the bog. For some reason he felt painfully guilty about not telling Framain his name when asked to do so. It was a perfectly civil request, and Framain had done the proper thing by disclosing his own identity first. For the Ducas, bad manners are one of the few unforgivable crimes.

They rode for a little less than the half-hour Framain had specified across an open, stony moor, with no trace of a building of any sort to be seen. The house appeared as though by magic; quite suddenly it was there, as if it had been lying down in the heather and had stood up when it heard its master approaching. In fact, it was concealed in a deceptively shallow saucer of dead ground. There was a big farmhouse, a long barn, a clump of stables, byres and other outbuildings, including one that looked like a giant beehive with a tall brick chimney; a covered well and a sheep-fold, large and empty. No sign of any livestock, unless you counted half a dozen thin-necked chickens pecking about in the yard. This man, Miel realized, isn't a farmer. In which case, what is he? He noticed that the thatch on the farmhouse roof was gray with age and neglect, but the barn roof was bright gold with new, unweathered reed.

"You'll have to excuse the state the place is in," Framain said (he hadn't spoken since they'd started to ride). "I'm on my own here, and there's a lot to do."

Miel muttered something polite. They rode down into the yard, which was open and unfenced. Framain dismounted, tied his horse to the fold rail, and helped Miel down. To his shame, Miel found he didn't have any strength left in his legs; he slithered off his horse, and Framain had to catch him.

"In here," Framain said, and helped him to the farmhouse door. It was open. Miel remembered that when they'd passed it, the barn door was shut; he'd noticed three heavy iron bars and padlocks.

The house was a mess: one long room, mostly filled with an enormous oak table, thick with dust. The windows were unshuttered and empty — no glass or parchment — and as they came in, two crows erupted from the middle of the table, where they'd been picking over a carcass on a broad pewter plate. They flew up and pitched in the rafters for a moment, cawing and shrieking angrily, then swooped low and sailed out through the nearest window. Framain didn't seem to have noticed them. The walls were paneled in the old style, but the wood was gray and open-grained, and in places the damp had warped and split it away from the masonry, leaving behind nails rusted into the stone like arrowheads snapped off in a wound. The floor was dusty and crunched as they walked on it. There were rat and mouse droppings on practically every surface, and the smell was a confused blend of every imaginable kind of decay. Ashes and clinker from the blackened fireplace had spread onto the floor like lava from a volcano, but a thin, straight plume of gray smoke rose up out of an extravagant heap of charcoal in the middle, and there was a full charcoal bucket nearby, next to a small table on which stood a fat, fresh loaf and a grimy earthenware jug. So somebody baked here, and kept the fire banked up, and fetched in the water.

"Like I said," Framain muttered, "it's just me. Sit down, I'll get you something to eat."

He hacked a massive plank of bread off the loaf with an edged tool that Miel couldn't identify but which was never meant for the purpose; then he stood for a moment, frowning and indecisive, before reaching up into the rafters and pulling down the dustiest side of bacon Miel had ever seen. He wiped it with his sleeve before slicing off a chunk the size of his hand. Putting it on top of the bread, he handed it to Miel. "There's water," he said, "or wine." He picked up the jug and peered into it, then poured some into a horn mug he found on the floor. "Better start with water if you're parched," he said. The water was gray and muddy with dust. Miel didn't mind that, or the muddy taste of the bacon, although it was as tough as saddle-leather and he hardly had enough strength in his jaws to chew it. The bread was fine.

Framain let him eat for a while; then he cleared his throat and said, "You're Miel Ducas."

Miel nodded. "You know me from somewhere."

Framain shook his head. "I've never seen you before," he said, "but it's not hard to figure out. You said you were heading for Cotton Cross when you got lost, but you'd never have heard the name unless you knew the area, and if you knew the area you wouldn't have got lost. I can tell from your voice that you're an Eremian of good family. When I asked you who you were you didn't answer, and you looked sheepish, so you're anxious to keep your identity a secret but you haven't had much practice at telling lies or pretending to be someone else. All this area used to be Ducas land, and it's common knowledge that the Ducas himself is leading the resistance. It wasn't terribly difficult to put it together."

Miel thought about the sword; the hanger he'd stolen from the scavengers and used to kill the two men with. He didn't have it with him, so either it was hanging by its hilt-bow from his saddle-hook or he must have dropped it somewhere; in any case, even if he had the strength to fight, it was too far away to be any use to him. He couldn't see any weapons in the room, apart from the cutting thing (a thatcher's spar-hook, he realized) that Framain had sliced the bread and bacon with. Forget it, he told himself; if Framain wanted to hand him over to the Eremians, there was precious little he could do about it until he'd got his strength back.

"That's me, then," he said. "I'm sorry I didn't answer you earlier, it was very bad manners."

"Understandable." Framain wasn't eating or drinking. "In case you're worried, I'm not — let's say, I'm not political. I like to stay out of everybody's way myself."

"I see," Miel said.

Framain laughed. "It's not what you're thinking," he said. "I'm not a criminal or anything, I just like a little privacy. Especially these days, with the Mezentines charging about, and refugees, not to mention your lot, the resistance. No offense, but I tend to regard the whole human race as just a lot of different subspecies of pest."

Miel smiled cautiously. "In that case," he said, "I apologize for intruding. And of course I'm really grateful —"

Apparently Framain wasn't interested in gratitude. "Anyway," he interrupted briskly, "you can stay here and feed yourself up until you're ready to move on, no problem there. You can call it repayment for arrears of rent, I suppose, since technically I'm a trespasser on your property. If you've finished your water, you might like a drop of the wine. You'll like it, it comes out of sealed bottles."

Miel laughed awkwardly, and Framain knelt down and scrabbled about under the table for a while, finally emerging with a glass bottle wound round with swathes of filthy black cobweb. It turned out to be very good wine indeed.

"Wasted on me," Framain said. "Actually, it's stuff my father laid down, about forty years ago. There were a dozen cases or so left when I came here, and I brought them with me. I don't tend to drink the stuff myself. I don't like the taste much, and it gives me heartburn."

Miel smiled politely, wondering how Framain's clothes came to be clean and respectable when he lived in such squalor. Then he remembered the barn, newly thatched and carefully locked.

"Can I ask what you do here?" he said.

"Can you ask?" Framain laughed. "No, you can't. Here, have some more of this stuff. They tell me it doesn't keep once it's been opened."

"I'm sorry," Miel said. "I didn't mean to cause offense."

"Of course you didn't, and you haven't." He stood up. "Now, if you'll excuse me, time's getting on and I'd better get started. Help yourself to anything you want," he added, gesturing vaguely at the surrounding squalor. "Feel free to roam around the place if you want to stretch your legs. I'd stay put here for a day or so if I were you, but if you're in a desperate hurry to get somewhere, carry on. I'll see you this evening, if you're still here."

Miel nodded. "Thank you again," he said. "If you hadn't come along when you did —"

"Well, there you go," Framain snapped, "generous impulses and so forth. Tell you what: when the Mezentines have been driven out and you get your land and your money back, you can make it up to me. All right?"

He left, and a little later Miel caught sight of him through the window that looked out onto the yard; he was standing at the top of the barn steps, opening the massive padlocks with keys he carried on a chain round his neck. Miel looked away, in case Framain noticed him watching. The Ducas does his best to avoid information that he shouldn't have, and forgets it straightaway if he stumbles across it accidentally.

The food and the wine (he finished off the bottle, as instructed) made him feel sleepy, and he woke up with his head cradled on his arms on the table. As he stirred, he startled a rat, which scuttled away into a castle of abandoned, heaped-up sacks and boxes. To his mild surprise, he felt a little stronger, though his neck hurt and his knees were cramped. Feel free to roam about the place; well, it might ease the cramp.

He stood up, wobbled and grabbed the edge of the table. When he released it again, his hands were grimy with black dust, which didn't brush off easily. He made an effort and went exploring.

In the far corner of the room was a staircase, narrow and twisted into a tight spiral, so that Miel had to climb part of the way on his hands and knees. Upstairs there was only one small room, about the size of a hayloft. Apart from dust, and a carpet of crisp brown beech leaves, it was empty. The only other room in the house was back downstairs, at the opposite end of the main room: a pantry with a stone-flagged sunken floor, presumably used for storing root vegetables in the cool. It was empty too; there was a small pool of black water at the far end, where the floor wasn't level. Evidently, then, Framain didn't sleep in the house, unless he curled up under the table like a dog, and Miel couldn't picture him doing that.

A mystery, then; but the world is full of mysteries. Generous impulses, Framain had said; someone who pulled strangers out of quagmires and gave them food and water (albeit mixed with dust) couldn't be a total misanthropist. True, he'd figured out who Miel was with depressing ease, but he wouldn't have known that when he made the decision to rescue him, so it was unlikely that his actions had been prompted by hope of ransom, as the scavengers' had been. The bottom line was that Miel was probably safe, for now, provided that he kept to the rules and didn't go poking about and annoying his host. Small price to pay. That said, he found the place depressing and vaguely revolting. It would be nice to leave and go somewhere else.

That reminded him; he dragged himself out into the fresh air. It was just starting to get dark. The barn door was shut up and locked again, all three padlocks in place in their hasps. Beyond it, he saw a thick column of black smoke rising from the chimney of the overgrown-beehive building he'd noticed earlier. Conceivably it could be a smokehouse, for curing hams and bacon and sausage. Perhaps that was what Framain did for a living. Perhaps.

His horse wasn't where he'd left it; after a rather draining search (still a very long way from a full recovery, then) he found it in a stable, along with the horse Framain had been riding and two others. The stable was much cleaner and tidier than the house: fresh straw, full mangers, clean water in the drinking troughs. His saddle and bridle had been hung neatly on a rack at the far end. The hanger was there too.

That was a comfort; he still had transport and defense, which implied that Framain was sincere about letting him go if and when he wanted to. Not, he realized, that he'd be likely to get very far if he saddled up and left immediately. Quite apart from his sad lack of strength, he had no food and nothing to carry water in. Maybe Framain would provide them, too, but that remained to be seen. Until the issue was resolved, their absence would keep him here just as effectively as a shackle and chain.

Suddenly realizing how weak he was feeling, he stumbled back into the house and flopped awkwardly onto the bench, banging his knee hard on the edge of the table in the process. It took him a while to recover from the strain of his excursion, and when he was alert enough to take an interest in his surroundings, he saw that the light was fading fast. He hadn't seen anything in the way of lamps, candles or tapers, but more or less anything could be buried in among the trash on the table. Gritting his teeth, he reached out and explored, mostly by feel. To his relief, he found a candle, or at least the stub of one; then he looked at the fireplace and saw that at some point the fire had gone out, so he had no means of lighting it. He sighed wearily, and realized that his right hand was resting on something flat and rectangular that felt as though it could almost be a book.

It *was* a book. Miel felt almost absurdly pleased; something to read — not tonight, obviously, but tomorrow, when he'd be spending the whole day in this horrible room. He turned in his seat and held the book up, so that the last rays of the sun glowed on its spine. Nothing to see there, however, so he opened it at random.

It was written in a proper clerk's hand, so it wasn't just some homemade effort, but the letters were painfully, frustratingly small. He wriggled round a little further, screwed his eyes up, and read:

To make green. Take thin sheet copper, soak in warm vinegar in an oak box, allow to stand for two weeks, remove and scrape when dry. To make vermilion . . .

Oh well, Miel thought, and decided that on balance it could wait until the morning, when he could steep himself in it without torturing his eyes. Vermilion, he thought; wasn't that some kind of fancy word for red? Maybe the reclusive and mysterious Framain would turn out to be nothing but a painter, a churner-out of court scenes and hunting scenes on limewood panels or a prettifier of manuscripts. He heard himself laugh; it took him a moment to identify the sound.

Maybe he closed his eyes, just for a moment. When he opened them again, it was broad daylight. No sign of Framain, but someone had left another bottle of the good wine and a plate of bread and rawhide-pretending-to-be-bacon next to him on the table. Thankfully, no birds or rodents this time. He yawned and stretched. He was feeling much better. Good.

He ate his breakfast. Chewing up the bacon should've counted as a full day's work for a healthy man, but Miel managed to do it with only three breaks for rest. That, he reckoned, was a sign that he was well on the road to recovery; in which case, he was fit enough to get out of this strange place and be on his way, wherever that was. There remained, however, the matter of provisions for his journey, and containers to carry them in. He looked round. Yesterday's empty wine bottle was still where he'd left it, and there was a full one to go with it. The remains of the loaf stood on the small table. The bacon was presumably back up in the rafters, but as far as he was concerned it could stay there. He rummaged for a while through the trash on the table, but about the only thing he didn't find there was anything capable of holding water. He took another look at the room and decided to risk it. He didn't feel comfortable here.

Manners demanded that he say thank you and goodbye to his host, but he'd got the impression that his host really wouldn't mind if he neglected that duty. He picked up the empty bottle and walked out into the blissfully clean, fresh air, heading for the well.

Bright morning; the damp grass and the smell of wet foliage told him it had rained earlier, while he was still asleep. He found the well easily enough. It hadn't been there very long, if the color of the mortar between the stones was anything to go by. He wound down the bucket; it took a long time for it to reach the water.

"Who the hell are you?" A woman's voice, right behind him. He turned and saw a tall, slim woman wearing man's clothes (linen shirt, cord breeches, gaiters; almost identical to those Framain had been wearing). She had dark hair, pulled back tight into a bun. He guessed she was his own age or a few years younger, but it was hard to tell because her face was so dirty.

Soot, he realized; there were pale rings round her eyes, and white patches on her cheeks and the tip of her nose. The rest was dull matt black, like a well-leaded stove. Her hands were filthy too, though the cuffs of her shirt were merely grimy. She was scowling at him, as though he was a servant she'd caught stealing cheese from the larder.

"I'm sorry," he said quickly, before he'd had time to figure out what he was apologizing for. "My name's Miel Ducas." Obviously that didn't mean anything to her. "The, um . . ." (Couldn't remember the wretched man's name.) "Tropea Framain let me stay here last night. Actually, he saved my life; I'd got stuck in a quagmire up on the —"

Clearly she wasn't interested in anything like that. "He didn't say anything about guests," she said.

"Oh." Come on, Miel chided himself, you're a trained diplomat, you've negotiated trade agreements with the Cure Doce and extradition treaties with the Vadani, you can do better than *oh*. "Well, I'm sure if you were to ask him . . ."

"He's busy." Statements didn't come more absolute than that. "What're you doing?"

He held out the bottle. "I was just getting some water from the well."

"What for?"

"Well, my journey," he said. "Actually, I'm just leaving."

Her scowl deepened. "What're you doing round here?"

"I got lost," he said. "I was heading for the inn at Cotton Cross, but I must've —"

"Where were you coming from?"

Now that, he had to concede, was a very good question. He had no idea, beyond the fact that the scavengers lived there.

"Merebarton," he said, in desperation. (It had been the name of one of the fields behind the house when he was growing up at the Ducas country seat at Staeca. Why it should've been the first name to come into his head, he had no idea.)

"Never heard of it."

"Small place," Miel said casually. "Just a farmhouse and a few outbuildings in the middle of nowhere, really. About a day and a half's ride the other side of the Finewater."

"You were heading from the Finewater toward Cotton Cross and you got lost?"

"Lousy sense of direction."

"You just head straight for Sharra Top. It's the only mountain on the moor. You'd have to be blind —"

"My mother always said I wasn't fit to be let out on my own," he said wearily. "But it's all right, Framain's given me clear directions. Just head straight for the mountain, like you said."

She was still frowning at him. "You won't get much water in there," she said.

"It was all I could find."

"You should've asked Father. He'd have given you a water-bottle or a jug."

"He went out before I woke up," Miel said. "And I didn't want to bother him."

She thought about that; weighed it and found it didn't balance. "What were you doing in — what was that place you said?"

"Merebarton." He trawled his brains, even toyed with telling her the whole truth. "Visiting relatives," he said.

"I see." Without thinking or not caring, she dragged the back of her hand across her forehead, plowing white furrows in the soot. Miel (trained diplomat) kept a straight face. "Well, if you're leaving, don't let me stop you."

Miel dipped his head in a formal bow, cursory-polite. Someone familiar with Eremian court protocol would have recognized it at once as the proper way to acknowledge a statement or reply from a person of considerably inferior social standing. It was (he trusted) completely lost on her, but it just about constituted honorable revenge. "Nice to have met you," he said, and he concentrated his mind on the job of filling the wine bottle from the bucket. But the edge of the well surround was narrow, and he obviously wasn't concentrating enough, because the bucket toppled out of control and slopped nearly all its contents down the front of his trousers.

There was a snigger somewhere behind him, but he didn't turn round. Still enough water in the bucket to fill the bottle, provided he could just balance . . .

He swore. It was at least a second and a half before he heard the splash that told him his bottle was now at the bottom of the well.

"Don't you hate it when that happens?" said the voice he was rapidly coming to loathe.

He considered the feasibility of crossing the moor with nothing to drink except one bottle of fine vintage red wine, and reluctantly dismissed it. "Do you think your father would let me have a bottle or a jug?" he said plaintively.

"I expect so."

"Could you possibly tell me where he is, so I can ask him?"

"He's busy."

"Then maybe you could be terribly kind and ask him for me."

"All right. Or I expect I could find you something."

"Thanks," Miel said. "I'd really appreciate that."

She'd turned, and was walking back toward the house. "What did you say your name was?" she asked over her shoulder.

"Miel Ducas."

The back of her head nodded. "Anything to do with the big landowning family?"

"Yes."

"Nice for you." Her shoulders expressed a total and overriding disdain for the Ducas and all their works. "And you were out in the middle of nowhere at — sorry, it's gone again, the place you just came from . . ."

"Merebarton."

"Merebarton," she repeated carefully, "visiting relatives. Big family."

"Very big, yes."

She spun round, with the deliberate poise of a fencer performing the volte. "Miel Ducas is the leader of the resistance," she said, and all the melodrama didn't alter the fact that she was very angry. "If the Mezentines come here, or your people, or the Vadani — *anyone* — it'll ruin everything. My father's given everything for this, I've been here helping him my entire life. How *dare* you come here and jeopardize everything we've worked for?"

Miel took a step back, but only from force of habit. Nobody in a furious rage uses words like *jeopardize*. He looked her in the eyes, ignoring the pink smudges on her cheeks and nose; it was like facing down a merchant over a big deal. "You want something from me," he said pleasantly. "Why don't you just tell me what it is?"

He'd watched men working in a foundry once, and seen them draw the plug from the bottom of the cupola, when the furnace had reached full heat and the melt was ready to pour. The whitehot iron had flooded out, dazzling bright, rushed toward him like a tide, so that he'd jumped back; but as it surged it slowed, and he could see it take the cold, fading from white to yellow. Her eyes were cold like the cooling iron as it grew solid in the bloom.

"What makes you think —" she started to say, but he frowned and cut her off.

"If it's something I'm physically capable of doing," he said, "I'll do it. I owe your father my life. Just tell me what it is."

She frowned. "I don't trust you," she said.

"Oh well." He shrugged. "We'll just have to go slowly, then. Right now, all I want out of life is an empty bottle. This makes me an unusually straightforward person. How about you? What do you want?"

She looked at him for a long time. "Sulfur," she said.

It wasn't what he'd been expecting her to say. "Sulfur," he repeated.

"That's right. You do know what sulfur is, don't you?"

Miel raised his eyebrows. "I think so," he said. "It's a sort of yellow powdery stuff you find in cracks in the rocks sometimes. People use it to fumigate their houses during the plague, and I think you can mix it with other stuff to make slow-burning torches. Is that right, or am I thinking of something completely different?"

"That's sulfur," she said. "We need some. Can you get it for us?"

Miel frowned. "I really don't know," he said. "I mean, yes, before the war; I expect the housekeeper or the head gardener would've had some, somewhere. Now, though, I haven't a clue. Is it hard to come by?"

"Not in a city, where there're traders," she replied quickly. "You'd be able to get it in Civitas Vadanis."

"But I'm not —" He stopped; he'd said the wrong thing. "Anywhere else?"

"Well, the Mezentines've probably got barrels of it, but I don't like the idea of asking them."

"I mean," he said patiently, "is there anywhere you can go and dig it out for yourself, rather than buying it?"

She laughed. "Good question," she said. "There used to be a deposit on the east side of Sharra. That's where Father had been, I suppose, when he came across you. But it's all gone now. Used up. We need to find another supply. You're the bloody Ducas," she said, with a sudden, unexpected spurt of anger, "you've got soldiers and horses and God knows what else, you could arrange for a couple of wagonloads of sulfur, if you wanted to."

He sighed. "I said I'd do anything you wanted, if I can. How urgently . . . ?"

"Now. As soon as possible."

He thought for a moment. "Well," he said, "it'll take me, what, three days to reach Cotton Cross; then, if I take the main road, assuming I don't get caught by the Mezentines or run into some other kind of trouble, I should reach Merveilh inside a week. Would they have any there, do you think?"

"Merveilh? No. Tried that. It's just a stupid little frontier post, and the merchants don't go that way because they don't like paying border tolls."

"Fine. Merveilh to Civitas Vadanis — I don't know how long that'd take," he confessed. "I've never gone there that way. Five days?"

"Something like that."

"Then allow a full day to get the sulfur, and however long it takes to get back again." He smiled. "That's my best offer," he said. "Any use to you?"

She looked at him. "That wasn't what I had in mind," she said.

"Oh. What . . . ?"

"I thought you could go back to your army and send some of your men."

He grinned, like a crack in a beam or a tear in cloth. "No good," he said. "I don't even know if there is a resistance anymore, and if there is, I'm through with it."

(And all because his hand had slipped on a bottle, and it had fallen into a well. If he'd managed to keep hold of the stupid thing, he'd be on his way by now, free and clear and heading for a life entirely without purpose or meaning.)

"You don't expect me to believe that."

"Why not?"

"You're a patriot. You fight for the freedom of Eremia. You couldn't just turn your back on it and walk away."

"I was rather hoping to try."

She shook her head. "Someone like you," she said, "if you're not leading people or in charge of something, you'd just sort of fade away. You'd be like the air inside a bag without the bag."

For some reason, he didn't like her saying that. "Do you want your sulfur, or don't you?"

"Of course I want it, or I wouldn't have mentioned it." She grinned sardonically at him through her covering of soot. "But the chances of you getting it for me . . ." She shrugged. "Like I said," she went on, "we keep ourselves to ourselves here, we don't want anybody dropping in. Go away, don't come back, and forget us completely, and that'll do fine. Wait here, I'll get you your bottle."

She came back a few minutes later, holding a two-gallon earthenware jar in a snug wicker jacket. It was corked, and from the way she leaned against its weight as she carried it, full. "Keep it," she said, reaching in her pocket, "don't bother bringing it back, even if you just happen to be passing. And in here there's a pound of cheese and some oatcakes, they'll be better than bread, they won't go stale. You know where the stable is, presumably."

As soon as he'd taken the water and the cloth bag containing the food she walked away. He saw her go into the house, and knew she'd gone there because he'd be watching, not because she had any business there. He shook his head. Sulfur, he thought. It would've been something to do.

Later, he couldn't remember saddling the horse and riding out of the hidden combe. He was thinking about itineraries, carters, women in red dresses who could get things you wanted if you had the money, which of course he didn't, not anymore. When it was too dark to see his way, he dismounted and sat on the ground, holding the horse's reins, still thinking, but not about sulfur or trade routes or who he knew in Civitas Vadanis who might lend him some money. The daylight woke him and he carried on, making excellent time; he'd abandoned the road and was cutting straight up the side of the hill. The horse wheezed and resented the exercise, but he kept a tight rein; not really his horse, after all, so it didn't matter what state it was in when he got there, just so long as he made it quickly. When night fell a second time he curled up behind an outcrop, out of the wind, and waited for dawn without falling asleep. Shortly after noon the next day, he saw smoke rising from the double chimneys of the Unswerving Loyalty and realized — the thought startled him — that somehow he'd made it and he was still alive.

No money, of course. He grinned. He'd have to sell the horse, and then what?

As he came close enough to hear, he could make out voices, a great many of them. He wondered about that. Mezentines; no, they'd have burned the place to the ground. His men, perhaps; unlikely. All right, then, who else would be roaming about this godforsaken moor in a large party? All he could think of was a big caravan of merchants; possible, if they were being forced to go all round the houses these days to avoid the war.

But it wasn't merchants. The horses he saw as he rode into the yard were too big and too fine, and there were bows and quivers hanging from their saddles, and boots to rest spear-butts attached to the stirrups. Very fine horses indeed; and the Loyalty's ostlers and grooms were looking after them with a degree of enthusiasm he wouldn't have expected to see if they belonged to the invaders. Besides, he knew enough about horses to recognize the coveted, valuable Vadani bloodline. He grinned as he passed under the fold gate. Can't go anywhere in Eremia these days without bumping into the Vadani cavalry.

There were two dozen or so men milling about in the yard, but the one he noticed straightaway had his back to him. He was talking to a short man in a leather apron — a farrier, quite possibly, not that he cared worth a damn. The man with his back to him was extremely tall and broad-shouldered, and there was something achingly familiar about the way the presumed farrier was edging away backward, uncomfortable about being loomed over in such an intrusive way.

The troopers stooped talking and stared at him as he rode past them; maybe some of them knew who he was. One of them called out a name as he passed. The tall, broad man looked round and stared at him, and his face exploded into a huge, happy grin.

Miel reined in his horse, dismounted, reached the ground clumsily, nearly fell over. He smiled at the tall man.

"Hello, Jarnac," he said.

Miel Ducas had never really cared much for beer: too sweet, too full of itself, and the taste stayed with you for hours afterward. After Framain's vintage wine and dusty water, it tasted heavenly.

"We'd given up on you," Jarnac said for the fifth time, tilting the jug in spite of Miel's protests. "No trace of you at the scavengers' camp; they swore blind they'd never seen you, we knew they were lying, we assumed they'd cut your throat or sold you to the Mezentines. Anyhow, they won't be bothering anybody anymore." He opened his face and filled it with beer, best part of a mugful. Alcohol had never affected Jarnac at all, except to magnify him still further. "Should've known you'd be able to take care of yourself, of course. Bunch of thieves and corpse-robbers weren't going to keep hold of you for long."

Miel made a point of not asking what had happened to the scavengers. Instead, "Jarnac," he said.

"Yes?"

"Do you think you could lay your hands on three wagonloads of sulfur?"

Jarnac lowered his mug and put it down on the table, like a chess-player executing a perfect endgame. "Sulfur," he repeated. "What the hell do you want with that?"

"I need some to give to somebody."

Jarnac shrugged. You could practically see doubt and confusion being shaken away, like a horse bucking a troublesome rider. "Should be able to get some from somewhere," he said. "Merchants sell it, don't they? Or we could probably requisition some from Valens' lot. Theoretically, I've still got an open ticket with the Vadani quartermaster's office."

Miel frowned. "It'd probably be better if we bought it," he said. "Talking of which, have you got any money?"

Big, Jarnac-sized laugh. "I'll be honest with you," he said, "I really don't know. Ever since I've been with Valens' lot, I haven't actually needed any. But I'm a serving officer in the Vadani cavalry, so I guess they're paying me. Not a problem," he went on, before Miel could interrupt. "Three wagonloads of sulfur, as soon as we get back to headquarters. Anyhow," he went on, "the war. Well, I'm not quite sure where to start. Strikes me, the more battles we win, the further we retreat, which I suppose is probably sensible since it's strictly a hiding to nothing, but it makes it a bit hard to keep score, if you know what I mean. To cut a long story short, though; no easy way to say this, Valens is cutting you loose. No more support for the resistance — which is short-sighted of him if you ask me, because . . ."

Miel kept nodding, but he wasn't interested. He was thinking, not for the first time, about the book he'd found on Framain's table, and a beehive-shaped building with a chimney, a woman with soot all over her face, and sulfur. It was a strange mash of thoughts to have crammed inside his head, but as he turned it over and over again, he realized that it had grown to fill all the available space, driving out everything else — the war, Eremia, the Ducas, honor, duty, loyalty, Orsea, Veatriz . . .

He looked up. Jarnac was wiping beer foam out of his mustache and talking earnestly about the weaknesses in the Mezentine supply lines. Behind his head, the paneling was gray and open-grained, and smoke curled into the room from a clogged fireplace.

Surely not, Miel thought; not in the middle of all this, with the world coming to an end.

8

"They're here, for crying out loud," Carausius snapped, hanging in the doorway. "Valens, this is ridiculous. You're acting like a child who's too shy to come down to the party."

Valens kept his back turned. "Nonsense," he replied sternly. "I just can't decide on which shoes to wear, that's all."

"Now you sound like my wife." Carausius clicked his tongue, loud as a bone breaking. "I'm not going to plead with you. Come down or stay up here hiding, it's your bloody dukedom."

"All right." Valens grabbed a shoe, stuffed his foot into it, stumbled and grabbed the side of the wardrobe. "Wrong shoe," he explained, taking it off and transferring it to his other foot. "That kind of day, really. Hardly auspicious for meeting my future bride."

"Two more minutes and it'll constitute a diplomatic incident."

"I'm coming." Valens pulled on the other shoe, fumbled the buckle and stood up. "So, lamb to the slaughter. I feel like I'm about to lead a cavalry charge against overwhelming odds."

"No you don't, actually," Carausius said with a grin. "You'd be a damn sight more cheerful if you were."

"True. Dying only takes a moment or so and then it's over, but marriage is forever. Promise me she isn't wearing feathers."

"Promise."

"Animal bones?"

"Do you include ivory in that category?"

"Shrunken organs taken from the bodies of men she's personally killed in battle?"

"Valens."

He sighed, let his shoulders slump, like a boy on his way to a music lesson. "Coming," he said.

Vadani court protocol was unambiguously clear about the manner in which the Duke should receive representatives of a richer, more powerful but less civilized and enlightened nation. It was a matter of carefully balancing gravity, recognition and affable condescension. The only possible venue was the Great Hall; however, instead of being in position when they arrived and rising politely to greet them, Valens was required to time his entrance so that it coincided precisely with theirs. That way, assuming he didn't run or dawdle, he'd meet them in the exact center of the room, and the issue of precedence could be neatly sidestepped. They would then withdraw from the Great Hall into the formal solar; he would graciously ask them to sit first, and the ambassadors would then introduce them to him, it being permissible to assume that they already knew who he was. It was the sort of performance that tended to give him a headache; but, as with most things he hated doing, he was very good at it.

He'd chosen the wrong shoes, after all. They pinched, and after a couple of dozen steps he could feel a blister growing on the back of his left heel.

As the footman opened the hall door and stood aside to let him pass, he tried to clear his mind. He'd been reading about the Cure Hardy, of course, everything up to and including the reports he'd had compiled after Skeddanlothi's raid. He knew that there were at least seventeen different nations in the loose confederacy of tribes, each of them radically different from the others in several important respects. He knew that the Aram Chantat — this lot — drove immense herds of cattle from summer to winter pasture in a complex nine-year transhumance cycle, but ate only cheese, butter, yogurt, cream, wild fruit and berries and the occasional green vegetable bartered with more settled neighbors; that they believed that human life was a dream dreamed by one's equivalent in the higher world, and death was the equivalent's waking from sleep, and that birds, quadrupeds and some species of lizard were real, but all snakes, fish and insects were illusory shapes assumed by spirits of violence when they chose to wander the earth; that Aram Chantat carpets, knitwear and leatherwork (they were stroppy about eating their cattle but perfectly happy wearing them) were of high quality and widely exported, but that they were backward in the use of both wood and metal, and relied on imported goods obtained through a complex chain of intermediaries from the Mezentines. He knew that Aram Chantat women who wore their hair long were either unmarried or widowed, whereas if a man was clean-shaven, he was either disgraced or had sworn an oath as yet unfulfilled; that seven, blue and three ravens were unlucky, five, white and an eagle with something in its talons were good omens; that the women held their horses' reins in both hands but the men held theirs with the left hand only. About the only thing he didn't know was why they were there and what they really wanted from him.

The door was open. He took a deep breath and advanced, like a fencer gaining his enemy's distance.

Four of them; easy enough to recognize, because they stood a head taller than his own people. There were two men in early middle age, bearded, wearing long quilted red gowns trimmed with black fur; an old man, bald, with a mustache but no beard (what the hell did that signify?), dressed in a plain brown robe tied at the waist with a rope belt, barefoot; a girl.

Well, he thought. No animal bones.

She was wearing a variant of the quilted gown; red, with puffed sleeves, edged with white Mezentine lace. Her hair was straight, black, glossy, and reached almost to her waist; she wore a net cap of gold thread and seed-pearls, also Mezentine. Her face was triangular, sharp; not pretty, he'd have to think about whether it was beautiful or not. Her hands were clasped in front of her waist-

high, and on her left wrist she carried a hooded goshawk. Her
mouth . . .

(As he walked toward her, he caught sight of Orsea in the left-
hand reception line, and next to him Veatriz. She was watching
him, but looked away.)

Her mouth was thin, very red against her pale complexion — at
this range he couldn't tell if it was powder or natural; the Aram
Chantat prized pale women, on the grounds that pallor comes
from staying in the shade, therefore not having to work. She had
long hands, and, he noticed, big feet. He realized that he'd been
holding his breath for rather longer than was good for him, and
he had to make an effort to let it out slowly and not gasp or pant.
She was . . .

They were now the proper distance apart; if they both reached
out their hands, their fingers would touch. Protocol demanded a
bow; apparently she knew that. He lost sight of her for a moment,
caught a fleeting glimpse of his ludicrous shoes before lifting his
head again. She wasn't smiling, or frowning, but she was looking at him. Suddenly he wanted to laugh. She was looking at him
as though committing the salient points to memory, so she could
describe them to someone in a letter. Realizing that, he knew immediately what he must look like himself, because already in his
mind he was phrasing descriptions, comparisons, all the main
points of interest, for a letter he would never be able to write. For
him, that was sheer force of habit. To see the same look in someone else's face was remarkable. He felt (he hesitated, checked and
confirmed) — he felt like a stranger walking in a foreign town
who sees a fellow-craftsman, a practitioner of his own trade, easily
recognized by his stained hands or his leather apron, or a folding
rule sticking out of his jacket pocket.

"Shall we withdraw?" Someone was talking, and he wanted
to yell at him to be quiet; but it was Carausius, saying the words
needed to get them out of there and into the next room. He saw
the bald man nod, and they took a step forward; for a moment, he
couldn't think what to do with his feet — should he retreat, still

facing them, or turn his back on them and lead the way, or what the hell was he meant to do now? By the time he'd thought all that, she was next to him, and he could see that it was powder, and the red of her mouth was something put on with a brush, and her eyes were small and dark, set with a perpetual slight frown, like a hawk's. It occurred to him that he was now supposed to half turn and walk beside her to the formal solar (he had no idea why it was called that, so she'd better not ask). She looked at him now, and dipped her head in a small, private nod, as if acknowledging the presence of someone she already knew.

It felt like a long walk to the side door of the hall. He made a point of keeping his head up slightly, looking just over the tops of the heads of the people lined up on either side. There were eyes he didn't want to catch; guilt, a little, such as you might feel remembering a small promise forgotten, or a letter neglected and overdue.

As they walked together through the doorway, the goshawk shifted its wings a little. He couldn't remember offhand if that was supposed to be an omen of any sort.

In the solar; he'd forgotten that the tapestries on the walls were all scenes of the kill and the unmaking, the deer paunched, skinned and jointed; not, therefore, really suitable for a race of vegetarians. She stopped. He remembered that he had to take a few steps more, then turn and face her (but no salute or assumption of a guard).

"Duke Valens." He wondered who was talking, realized it was the bald old man. Perfect Mezentine accent, made his own sound positively rustic. "May I introduce the Princess —" And then he made some sort of uncouth noise, which went on for some time and contained sounds Valens was sure he'd never heard a human being make before. Her name, presumably. "And these are —" More noises; the two bearded men, who turned out to be her maternal uncles; and the bald man had a name too.

He remembered, just in time. "Please," he said, and waved airily at the chairs, as though he'd only just noticed them. They sat; his people sat; he sat. That was as far as protocol was going to take him. From now on, he was on his own.

He tried to think of something to say; fortunately, Carausius was better prepared, or more articulate, than he was. "I trust you had a reasonable journey." The bald man assured him that they had. A brief silence; Carausius appeared to have forgotten his lines, or was waiting for a cue that hadn't come. "The roads are generally quiet at this time of year. I hope the desert crossing wasn't too arduous."

Valens was expecting a reply, a polite reassurance. Instead, there was dead silence, as though someone had just said something indiscreet or vulgar. Then the bald man (beautiful speaking voice) said, "The Princess hopes that this gift will be acceptable to you."

He means the goshawk, Valens realized with a slight flare of shock. She was holding it impeccably; King Fashion would've clapped his hands and called people over to see. It was an outstanding bird; a hen, not a tiercel, with its full second-season plumage; bigger and darker than the passagers the merchants brought from northern Eremia. It stood perfectly still on her wrist, and her fingers were lightly closed over the ends of the jesses.

People were looking at him. "Thank you," he said. That wasn't going to be enough. What he wanted to say was, *How come you've got such good taste in hawks when you don't even eat meat?* but he was here to agree a marriage, not start a war. "It's a magnificent specimen," he said.

"The Princess chose it herself," the bald man said. "She also . . ." He hesitated, leaned across to one of the uncles, who whispered something in his ear that made him frown. "Excuse me," he said. "I believe the term is manning a hawk, meaning to train it."

"Quite correct," Carausius said.

"The Princess manned it herself," the bald man went on. "She is a highly accomplished falconer; I believe it is an interest you also share."

"Yes, very much so," Valens heard himself say. All lies, of course; she couldn't have trained a hawk, it took days and nights of agonizing patience and fatigue. *I couldn't do it, so obviously she couldn't, she'd mess up her hair or break a fingernail —*

(He noticed that her fingernails were all cut short.)

"Perhaps, if time permits, we might find an opportunity to fly the bird," the bald man was saying. He looked as though he'd expected rather more enthusiasm for the gift — *I know why,* Valens realized; *they've been told that the only thing I'm interested in is hunting, which is why this poor girl's been forced to take a crash course in advanced falconry.*

"I'm sure that can be arranged," Carausius was saying.

Valens was embarrassed; they're like parents who've taken their children to play with each other, but the children have taken an instant dislike to each other, and are sulking and refusing to make friends. In which case, what he really ought to say now was, *Don't want the stupid hawk.*

Instead, he took a deep breath. "There's a particularly fine heron down on the marshes," he said. "I've been watching it for the past week. Perhaps —"

"Heron?" It was the first word she'd said. Her voice was as sharp as her face.

"A pair of them, actually," Valens said (he could always find something to say about hunting, even when all the other words had dried up), "but the hen's not up to much. I was planning to leave her and go after the cock-bird."

"Do you hunt herons?" She frowned. "I suppose they steal fish," she added.

Diplomatic nightmare. He couldn't very well say that roast heron was a delicacy; and weren't fish supposed to be incarnations of the Evil One, in which case a bird that killed them might well be sacred. Carausius was staring at something on the opposite wall. Valens couldn't remember who else from his side was in the room.

"Herons are very rare in our country." One of the uncles was speaking. "I'm told they taste a little like partridge, only a bit stronger. Is that right?"

Fine, Valens thought; the hell with diplomacy, and if it means starting a war, so be it. "Please forgive me if this is an awkward question," he said, "but aren't you people vegetarians?"

The bald man, the girl and one of the uncles looked at him blankly; the other uncle whispered a translation. The bald man looked mildly surprised. The girl raised both eyebrows.

"No," the bald man said, "certainly not. Whatever gave you that idea?"

For a moment, all Valens could think about was the huge amount of cheese, yogurt, sour cream, curds, watercress and biscuits currently stockpiled in the kitchens. Bloody hell, what are we going to give them to eat? He also wished very much that he could remember who'd told him these people didn't eat meat, so he could console himself by planning a sufficiently elaborate form of retribution. "Fine," he said, "that's all right, then. Some fool told me you eat nothing but cheese."

"Cheese." The girl was frowning.

"But you don't," Valens said quickly, "so that's — Carausius, you'd better . . ."

Carausius already had; one of the minor courtiers was halfway to the door, moving well.

"I take it dinner will be late," said one of the uncles. "Pity. We missed breakfast."

"I'm sure we can find something," Carausius said, his voice brittle, as if he could already feel the rasp of hemp fiber on his neck.

"We're not fussy," the other uncle said. "Something cold will do fine."

The girl laughed, and Valens realized he wanted to laugh too. "I know where there's a rack of smoked venison," he said, "if anybody's interested. I sent it for curing about a week ago, so it ought to be just right."

"Perfect," said an uncle, with the sort of heartfelt sincerity

Valens had never expected to hear in a diplomatic exchange. "There wouldn't happen to be any pickled cabbage to go with that, would there?"

"Don't be silly, Uncle." She was looking straight at him; in fencing it would be the imbrocata, the thrust angled down from a high guard. "These people aren't savages, of course there's pickled cabbage. Please excuse him," she went on, "he forgets his manners when he's hungry."

"Carausius," Valens said, and another courtier took off for the doorway. "Well," he went on, "so far we don't seem to have covered ourselves in glory."

The bald man shrugged. "It's understandable that we know so little about each other," he said. "Fortunately, ignorance is easily cured."

"In that case," Valens said, steepling his fingers in front of him, "is it really true that you believe fish are the devil incarnate?"

One thing the intelligence reports had got right. It wasn't the business about long hair and beards (that, the bald man explained, was the Rosinholet) or the stuff about being someone else's dream (a minority belief among the Flos Glaia, the girl explained, who also believed that the earth orbited the sun, rather than the other way about) or the carpets — the Aram Chantat bought all their carpets from the Lauzeta, during rare truces in their otherwise incessant wars — or ravens being unlucky or women holding their reins in both hands. But it was absolutely true that the Aram Chantat weren't much good at metalwork or carpentry, and that in consequence they had to buy anything made of metal or wood from the Perpetual Republic.

"It wouldn't be so bad," one of the uncles was saying, "if we could trade with them direct, but we can't, none of their traders will come out that far, obviously, because of the impossibility of crossing the desert with wagons. So we have to get what we need from the Flos Glaia, who get it from the Rosinholet, who get it from someone else; it all comes through Lonazep, and we think that some of it's carried by sea at some point, because we're sick of opening barrels and finding everything inside's been spoiled by soaking in salt water. Anyhow, the whole thing's ridiculous, and of course by the time it reaches us, the price . . ." He sighed passionately. "It's lucky we've got something that people want," he said, "or I don't know how we'd manage."

"Salt," the other uncle explained, before Valens could ask. "Which we dig out of the ground every fourth year when we cross the salt flats on our way back from summer pasture. Unfortunately, though, the Lauzeta have taken to mining the same deposits; there're a lot more of them than there are of us, and they've got more transport, so the surface deposits are pretty well all worked out. Obviously, that means we're going to have to go down deeper, but if we do that, it'll change everything; it'd mean leaving a permanent presence there, not to mention fighting off the Lauzeta when they go by that way every third year. And it goes without saying, we don't know the first thing about underground mining."

"*We* do," Valens said crisply. "In fact, we're very good at it." Someone he didn't recognize was standing next to him, pouring wine into a glass. "But I'm sure you know all about that."

"The silver mines, yes," the bald man said. "And we would, of course, be grateful for any advice or help you may care to offer us." He paused, and Valens guessed he was trying to judge whether the time was right to ask for something else; something, presumably, that he wanted rather more. Maybe he decided against it, because he shrugged his shoulders and went on, "But we're getting ahead of ourselves. We haven't decided yet whether increasing our salt production and continuing to depend on trading with the Republic is the right course for us to follow. There are other options we could explore."

"Like leaving where you are now and settling somewhere else." Valens nodded. "Which is why you're here, I suppose."

The bald man and the uncles exchanged glances. "Indeed," the bald man said. "Though I should stress that we're still keeping an open mind about it. But yes, Eremia would suit us very well."

"I've been thinking about that," Valens said, "ever since Carausius told me what you had in mind, and there are a couple of things — I'm sure you've already considered them, but . . ."

The bald man nodded slightly. "Go on, please."

"All right. First, if you occupy Eremia, you risk starting a fight with the Mezentines; second, will Eremia be big enough? Moving around all the time as you do —"

"You're right," the girl interrupted him. The bald man lifted his head but said nothing. One of the uncles looked away. "We have considered both of them," she went on, "and we don't see a problem. If the Mezentines want to mess with us, let them try. And yes; Eremia on its own would be too small. But there's plenty of empty space here, in your country, where nobody lives. And then there's the plain that separates you from the Mezentines —"

Sharp intake of breath; Valens couldn't tell whether it came from the bald man or an uncle. She frowned. "Anyway," she said, "there are possibilities. And we're planning for the long term, after all."

Valens leaned back a little in his chair. "You do realize," he said, "that my country is at war with the Republic. If you're dependent on them for all your manufactured goods, like you say, maybe you ought to be a bit circumspect about forming an alliance with us."

"We don't trade with them, though," she replied crisply. "Not directly. In fact, I wouldn't be surprised if they only had a very sketchy idea of who we are or where we live. The impression I get is that they can't be bothered to differentiate between savages."

The word made Valens want to smile. Time, he decided, to change the subject. "At any rate," he said, "I'm glad we managed to sort out the business about the fish. Talking of which, it's about time we had something to eat. Carausius, can you possibly find out what's taking them so long?"

During the meal (smoked venison, cold roast lamb; acceptable) he sat between the bald man and an uncle. The bald man wanted to talk about Mezentine Guild politics, and the uncle seemed fascinated by the technicalities of deep-level mine-working.

"I'm not the man you should be asking," Valens said, during a brief lull in the barrage of artfully phrased questions. "It just so happens we've got a topflight Mezentine engineer with us, he'd know all about that sort of thing. Carausius," he said, leaning across the table, "where's Ziani Vaatzes? I haven't seen him for a day or so."

"He's not here," Carausius replied with his mouth full (and him a diplomat; for shame). "If you remember, he's away at the mines, looking into that thing we were discussing."

"Ah." Valens caught himself before he frowned. Probably not a good idea to let their guests know that the celebrated Vadani mines, in which they were clearly deeply interested, were just about to be sabotaged to stop them falling into Mezentine hands. "Any idea when he'll be back?"

So much for showing off his rare and valuable possessions; he wondered whether he should keep Vaatzes in a glass cabinet, mounted on a little rosewood stand, for visitors to admire.

"Excuse me," the uncle said. "If you're at war with the Mezentines, why have they sent you a mining engineer? I hadn't realized they were so altruistic."

"Defector," Carausius explained.

"The only specimen in captivity," Valens added, realizing as he said it that the joke wasn't very good. "He came to us after the fall of Civitas Eremiae."

The bald man was very interested in that. "I wasn't aware that the Mezentines allowed defection," he said. "In fact —"

"They don't," Carausius said. "It was the Eremians' decision to grant this Vaatzes asylum that led to the war."

"And you've allowed this man to come here." It was the first thing she'd said for some time. She was wedged in between Carausius and a fat soldier whose name Valens could never remember, and she'd been eating with a single-minded ferocity that Valens couldn't help finding impressive. "Not a good idea, surely."

"We'd already declared war by the time we picked him up," Valens explained, "so we had nothing to lose by it. He's worth

having, I'm sure of it. He organized the defense of Civitas Eremiae, made one hell of a good job of it. For a while, it looked like
they were going to win."

"*You* declared war." She was looking at him past Carausius'
arm and shoulder. "I thought they attacked you."

Valens froze. The unspoken question wasn't one he wanted to
answer to anybody, but her least of all. "It was only a matter of
time," he said briskly. "A preemptive strike seemed worth trying;
they were weak after the losses they took during the siege, the political will seemed to be failing. I miscalculated. I don't think it
made much difference, one way or another."

That was a cue for the bald man to resume his interrogation
about Guild politics, and this time Valens was only too happy to
talk. She carried on looking at him for some time, then went back
to savaging the smoked venison.

She eats like a dog, she thought. She holds the meat still with her
claws, grips it with her teeth and tears it.

It was hard to see the top table from where she was sitting;
harder still to observe her in a proper, scientific fashion without
being caught staring. Orsea's head was in the way, and the man
next to her, some buffoon, kept trying to talk to her about music.
Watching out of the corner of her eye was giving her a headache.

Stupid, she thought. "Orsea," she said, "is there any bread?"

He looked round, moving his head just enough so that she could
see. "It's migrated up the other end of the table," he said. "Hang
on, I'll try and catch someone's eye."

It was stupid, of course, because she wasn't the one who should
be making these observations. He was up there with the subject;
it should be his job to observe, and report back to her in a long,
detailed letter. Instead, she was down here, among the other ornamental courtiers, having to crane her neck and grab fleeting
glimpses. Not scientific.

At least she wasn't wearing authentic tribal costume. Actually, they'd done a pretty good job of dressing her up as a human

being, and to her credit she carried off the imposture well. Training, probably, hours of patient coaching, like the manning of a hawk; teaching her to sit still, to keep quiet, not to jump up and run about the room. Someone had told her that they'd sent her away to somewhere quite grand and exotic to be schooled in civilized behavior — reasonable enough, when you thought about it, and considering what they had to gain from the deal. But they hadn't managed to stop her ripping up her food like an animal.

Veatriz smiled at that, and made a point of cutting the last of her cold roast lamb with the utmost precision; thumb and two fingers only on the back of the knife, just as she'd been taught when she was little. *A young lady doesn't saw, your grace, she slices.* Not that perfect table manners had done her much good in the long run.

Orsea had shifted in his seat again, and now all she could see was the wretched woman's shoulder. Red; the color suited her fishbelly complexion, but hadn't anybody thought to tell her what a red dress meant in these parts? She smiled, thinking of women in red dresses; women in red dresses who brought letters, once upon a time. *I would give good money,* she said deliberately to herself, *to know if that face came out of a pot.* Must have, she decided. If it was her natural color, they must've been keeping her in a dark cellar for the last six months, like blanching chicory. Nice metaphor, if only she had a use for it; the forcing, blanching and bringing on of vegetables for the table.

She frowned, and the boring man sitting next to her must've wondered what he'd said wrong. All very unfair, of course. Probably she was a very nice person, if you got to know her. Someone had told her (she could never remember people's names at these stupid receptions) that she'd been carrying that big hawk when they first arrived. How much would a bird like that weigh? You'd need forearms like a farrier to support that much weight. No; cousin Jarnac had told her once (at just such a reception, sitting next to her and being boring when she really didn't want to listen) that hawks were surprisingly light, something to do with aerodynamics and hollow bones. She'd had to carry hawks herself, of course, on formal days, but she hadn't really noticed how heavy they were. She'd been too busy worrying about whether they were going to huff their wings unexpectedly in her face or bite her.

All politics, of course. They'd dressed her in the hawk, just as they'd dressed her in the red outfit, and the polite conversation and the musical appreciation and the civil and mercantile law, until she was practically an artifact rather than a human being; a mechanical toy, like the clockwork dolls the Mezentines make, but instead of a spring to make her go, deep inside there was a little sharp-clawed predator who tore at her food . . .

She was standing up. Veatriz couldn't see, because of Orsea's stupid chin, but she and the other savages were on their feet; now Valens and his fat chancellor were standing too (rules of precedence to be observed in everything); they were leaving. She lost sight of them behind a thicket of heads, and then there was a tantalizing glimpse of them in the gap between the end of the table and the door; the pack had fallen behind, and she was walking next to Valens as the door opened and they escaped.

Well. It was high time the young couple spent some time together, to get to know each other. They'd probably go for a walk round the knot garden, while the diplomats and the representatives and the whole Vadani government lurked discreetly in the covered cloister, penned in like sheep waiting to be dipped. They would walk round the knot garden, and she would go through her paces like a well-trained four-year-old jennet at a horse fair, and the fate of nations would be decided by how well she made small talk. Meanwhile (everybody else was getting up now) the Duchess Veatriz Sirupati would go back to her room and embroider something.

"Can someone explain to me," Orsea was saying — to her, presumably — "what all that was in aid of?"

He could be so infuriating; but she kept her temper. "Oh come on," she said. "Don't you know who those people are?"

Orsea shrugged. "Someone told me they're ambassadors from

the Cure Hardy, but that's got to be wrong. The Cure Hardy
are —"

"Savages." She nodded. "That's them," she said. "And the
female is going to marry Valens."

It was a moment before Orsea spoke. "Nobody tells me anything," he said.

"Yes they do, but you don't listen." She sighed, as though the
whole thing was quite tedious. "It's all to do with trade agreements
and cavalry," she said. "And it's high time he got married and
churned out an heir. Presumably they haven't got around to telling the savages that they're marrying into a war; that'll be a nice
surprise on their wedding night. Probably they'll be delighted, I
gather the Cure Hardy enjoy a nice war."

"It'd be a stroke of luck for us," Orsea said seriously. "Have you
any idea how *many* of those people there are? Millions of them.
We found that out when —"

"Orsea, what are you talking about?"

"Manpower," Orsea replied, frowning slightly, his mind elsewhere. "What we call the Cure Hardy is actually loads of different tribes; nomads, always on the move. And there's a *lot* of
them; hundreds of thousands. If Valens is going to stand a chance
against the Republic, what he needs most is a very large army,
because as far as I can tell, where the Mezentines hire their mercenaries from, the supply is practically unlimited. If he can tap
into the Cure Hardy for reinforcements, he may actually have a
chance of making a game of it."

A game of it. There had been a time when she'd loved him for
a reason, rather than merely from force of habit, merely because
they'd grown into each other, like briars growing into a tangle.
She could still remember it, though: the belief that he was a good
man, determined to do the best he could in the impossible situation he'd been thrust into. The trouble was, he'd always done his
best and every time he'd failed, his failures leading to disaster and
misery on a scale that mere malice could never have achieved.
Deep inside somewhere, overgrown by tangled briars, he was still

there; but recently she'd begun to feel that reaching him was more effort than it was worth. All sorts of other things had grown up through her love, especially since Eremia fell and they'd come here; there was pity, guilt, a sense of duty; there was Valens . . .

"And how would that help us exactly?" she said, eager to find something to disagree with him about. "It'd just mean the war going on forever and ever, wouldn't it?"

Orsea frowned. "On the contrary," he said. "If the Mezentines see that Valens has got powerful allies —"

"You're blocking the way," she pointed out. "People are trying to get past."

"What? Oh." He hesitated, trying to decide whether to shrink back and let them pass or to head for the exit. She decided for him by walking away. He followed her; she could hear his voice close behind her saying, "If Valens makes an alliance with these people —"

"You really think the Mezentines see things that way?" she said without looking round. "Don't you realize, if they gave up because Valens made friends with the Cure Hardy, that'd be admitting they were afraid, they'd never ever do that. Really, after all you've been through with them, I'd have thought you'd understand them a little better than that."

He'd caught up with her, bobbing along beside her like a friendly dog, or a small boy in the market trying to sell her baskets. He could be so irritating sometimes, she wanted to shoo him away with a whisk of her mane. "I don't think it's like that anymore," he was bleating, "I really do believe things have changed, with the balance of power in the Guilds shifting toward the Foundrymen again and —"

"Orsea." She stopped, making him stop too. "Don't talk rubbish. You don't know anything about Guild politics, so please don't pretend you're the world's greatest authority —" She broke off, wondering why on earth she was talking to him like this. "Let's drop it, all right?" she said. "It's not a subject I like thinking about, the war and what's going to happen to us."

"All right." At least he hadn't apologized, this time. He seemed to have the idea that an apology fixed everything, as though she wanted a husband who was always in the wrong. He'd apologize for sunset if he thought darkness offended her. "So," he was saying, "what do you think? About them, I mean, the Cure Hardy? They aren't anything like the ones who came to see us."

"Aren't they? I didn't meet them."

"Not a bit like," he said. "For a start, they eat proper food. When they came to Eremia, they were all vegetarians, and they didn't drink booze, either."

"Different tribe, presumably," she said.

"Obviously. But I wouldn't have thought one lot would be so different from the others. Still, Valens seems to be handling them pretty well. There's a man who always does his homework."

"He reads a lot," Veatriz said.

"Really? Well, that'd account for it. Anyhow, I'm assuming it's pretty well done and dusted. It's about time he got married, after all."

When she'd stopped she hadn't really been aware of where she was. Now she looked round; they were in the top lobby of the Great Hall, directly under a huge, slightly faded tapestry (hunting scene, needless to say). "Never met the right girl, presumably," she said.

He laughed. "I don't suppose that's got anything to do with it. I've always assumed it was a case of keeping his options open, politically."

"Fine. I'm going back to our room now, if that's all right with you."

(She called it *their room*, as if it was just a bed and a chair and a small mirror on the wall; in fact it was a whole floor of the North Tower, not much smaller than their apartments back in the palace at Civitas Eremiae. Too much space, not too little.)

"Oh." He stood there, directly under the flat, snarling dogs and the bustling huntsmen; cluelessness personified. "Right. I'll see you later, then."

She left him. Too busy, she thought, as she trudged across the courtyard toward the North Tower, far too busy; too much impor- tant needlework screaming out for my attention. Presumably the savage girl had been taught needlework, along with all the other civilized accomplishments. In which case, she decided, there was some justice in the world, after all.

The room was pretty much as she'd left it. Someone had come in and tidied up, and the curtains were drawn neatly and tied back with those loops of tasseled rope which she hated so much. She sat down in her chair; there, on the window-ledge in front of her, was her embroidery frame, with the silks laid out ready in a row, and her red velvet pincushion. She looked at them in blank confusion, as if she couldn't remember what they were for. Then she stood up again and crossed to the big linen press at the foot of the bed. She lifted the lid and several layers of sheets, pillowcases; hidden — why had she hidden it? — was a rectangular rosewood box, her writing case. She lifted it out and hesitated, as a maid might do if she was thinking about stealing it from her mistress. Then she took it over to the window, brushed the embroidery silks onto the floor, opened the box and picked up a sheet of paper.

The silence had lasted a very long time; long enough for a cook to chop an onion, or a smith to peen over the head of a rivet. Much longer and it'd constitute an act of war. So . . .

"Well," Valens said, straightening his back a little, "how was your journey?"

She looked up at him. She was sitting on the stone bench in the middle of the knot garden. She'd been examining the rosemary bush as though she was planning to write a report on it.

"Not bad," she said.

"A bit of an ordeal, I imagine."

"I'm used to traveling about." She frowned. "Can we go to your mews, please? I'd like to make sure my hawk's being properly looked after."

Her hawk, then; not a present after all. "Certainly," he said;

then he thought of something. "Tell you what," he said. "If we go back through there, the way we came, we're going to have to wade through all your people and all my people, and they'll be staring politely at us to see how it's going, and it'll take forever and be extremely tiresome. But if we go through that doorway over there, we can take a short cut through the back scullery into the kitchens, round the back of the charcoal store and out into the mews. Saves time; also, it'll puzzle that lot out there half to death. Would that be all right, or would you rather go the long way round?"

She frowned. "Why wouldn't I want my uncles to know where I've gone?" she said.

A slow smile crept over Valens' face, like evening shadows climbing a hillside. "Why indeed?" he said. "We'll go and see how your hawk's settling in, shall we?"

Carausius, he noticed with mild amusement, was visibly disconcerted to see him back so soon. The bald man just bowed. The uncles were talking to some people, and didn't seem to have noticed. Valens led the way; she kept pace with him, as though it was a secret race and she was pacing herself for the final sprint. They went the long way round, and Valens kept himself amused by pointing out various features of interest: the long gallery, the avenue of sweet chestnuts, the fountain, the equestrian statue of his grandfather —

"Sculpted by Ambrosianus Bessus," she interrupted, "and cast in only three sections, using a lost-wax technique previously unknown outside the Republic." She nodded, as though awarding herself bonus marks.

"I never knew that," Valens said. "Well, there you go. Can't say I like it much myself. He's sitting too far back in the saddle, and if you ask me, that horse's got colic. Still . . ."

She frowned. "It's the greatest achievement of classical Vadani sculpture," she said reprovingly. "I went to a lecture about it while I was at the university."

"Did you? Good heavens." Valens shrugged. "When I was twelve, my friend Jovian and I snuck out one night when everybody was at a banquet and painted it bright green. It took half a dozen men a week to scrub all the paint off, and they never did figure out who'd done it."

Her frown tightened into a bewildered scowl. "Why did you do that?" she said.

Valens blinked. "Do you know, I'm not sure after all this time. Maybe we thought it'd look better green."

"The action of verdigris on bronze statues produces a green patina," she said hopefully. "Presumably —"

"That's right, I remember now." He looked away and pointed. "That squat, ugly thing over there is the clock tower. At noon every day two little men come out, they're part of the mechanism, and one of them belts the other one over the head with a poleaxe. The Mezentines gave it to my father shortly after I was born. Unfortunately it keeps perfect time, so we've never had an excuse to get rid of it."

The frown had settled in to stay on her forehead, and she made no comment, not even when Valens pointed out the obscene weather-vane on top of the East Tower. It's a gag, he told himself, a practical joke or something; and if I ever find out who's responsible, I solemnly undertake to decorate the Great Hall with their entrails come midsummer festival. "That's the kennels over there," he heard himself say, "and the stables next to it, and that gateway there leads to the mews." She was looking ahead; seen from the side, her neck was long, slender and delicate, her shoulders slim. "Did you really train that goshawk yourself?" he asked.

"Yes."

He nodded. "I tried it myself once, but I failed. I kept it awake for three days and nights, and then I fell asleep. I knew it was going to beat me in the end. Then I turned it over to the austringer, and he had it coming in to the lure in less than a week. I think they can tell if you've got the strength of will or not."

"I followed the directions in a book," she replied. "I didn't find it particularly difficult."

Plausible, Valens thought. Perhaps the hawk was stupid enough to try telling a joke, and she looked at it. Fifty years of this, or let the Mezentines have the duchy. Too close to call, really.

They'd put her wretched bird in the dark room at the end of the mews. She approved; after the trauma of the journey, a day in complete darkness and silence would settle it down. It should not be fed until midday tomorrow, she said; then it should be flown to the lure for no more than five minutes, and after that it should be given two-thirds of its usual ration. She would feed it herself tomorrow evening. Now, perhaps he'd be kind enough to show her the other hawks.

Even so; as they walked back to the main building, he couldn't help wondering how she'd felt, when they came to her and told her she'd be marrying the Vadani duke. Unless it had been her idea in the first place, of course; but assuming it hadn't. (Come to that, how had Veatriz felt when they told her she was to marry Orsea? But she loved him, so it was quite different.) Had she frowned and asked, who? Had she made a scene, or just nodded her head? Had she asked questions, or waited for the briefing? She must have known she was going to marry someone foreign and strange, or else why had they sent her away to be educated and refined? Had she complained about that, or welcomed it? *As part of your training, you will be required to tame a hawk.* He thought of himself, shuffling and stretching up and down the chalk line in the stables, learning to fence like a gentleman, his fingertips still raw after an hour's rebec practice. His education had taught him to excel at those things he hated most; at some point, he'd struck the balance between detesting them for their own sake and taking pleasure in his hard-won skill and accomplishments, to the point where what he did no longer mattered, so long as he did it well. They'd trained him, and then been surprised because he'd never fallen in love.

(Or that was what they thought. Likewise, they'd never found out that, all the time he was learning to fence elegantly with the rapier, the smallsword and the estock, he was paying a guardsman with his own money to teach him how to fight properly with a Type Fourteen infantry sword. When they'd sent her away to the university, had she asked, *How will learning civil and mercantile law help me make the Vadani duke fall in love with me?* She could probably fence, too. At least, he wouldn't put it past her. The question was, had someone had to sit up with her three days and nights in a row before she mastered the basics of the high, low and hanging guards?)

For want of anywhere else to go, Valens led them back to the formal solar. As he opened the door, he surprised half a dozen servants busy cleaning. They froze and stared at him for a moment, like crows taken unaware on carrion, or thieves caught robbing the dead; then they retreated backward, clinging fiercely to their brooms and dusters, and let themselves out through the side door.

"If it's convenient," the bald man said, "now might be a good time to discuss exchange rates."

9

The first thing he saw was smoke. It rose in the air like a feather stuck in the ground, a black plume fraying at the edges, a marker pointing down at the exact spot. Ziani had grown up with smoke, of course. In Mezentia, every morning at six sharp, fifteen thousand fires were laid in and lit in forges, furnaces, kilns, ovens, mills and factories in every street in the city; by half past six, the sky was a gray canopy and the alleys and yards stank of charcoal and ash. Every sill and step had its own soft blanket of black dust, every well and sewer had a gray skin, and everybody spat and sneezed black silt. The smell of smoke was something he'd missed without even realizing.

There had to be a river, of course. He saw it eventually, a thin green line dividing the mountains from the flat brown plain. A little further on, he could make out towers, which were probably no more than planked-in scaffolding, and the spoil heaps. He'd never seen a mine before in his life.

Before long, he began to see tree stumps; hundreds of them, thousands. A few wore sad garlands of coppice shoots, their leaves grimy with black dust. Others had died long ago, and were smothered in grotesque balls and shelves of bloated white fungus. Deprived of the shelter of the canopy of branches, the leaf mold that had once carpeted the floor of the lost forest had dried out into powdery dust, which the wind was diligently scouring away. Soon it would be down to bare rock, like a carpenter stripping off old varnish. Nothing much seemed able to take root in it, apart from a few wisps of yellow-white grass and the occasional sprawl of bramble.

"All this was cleared years ago." Carnufex, the man Valens had sent along to look after him, had obviously noticed him gawping at the tree stumps and figured out his train of thought. "I can't remember offhand exactly how much charcoal they get through every day, but it's a lot. Something of a problem, actually. We aren't marvelously well off for trees in this country at the best of times. In the old days, of course, they could supply all the charcoal we needed just from coppicing, but when Valens' father made us double our production, the only way we could keep up with our quotas was clear-felling. I think they're carting the stuff in from Framea now — which is also a problem, since it's only a few hours from the Eremian border, and if the Mezentines wanted to come and cause trouble . . ." He shrugged. "Not that it matters much anymore," he added.

"All I was thinking," Ziani lied, "was where we're going to get our timber from; for building the frames, and the firewood for burning out the props."

"Ah." Carnufex nodded. "All taken care of. It'll be along in a day or so; twelve cartloads, and there's more if you need it. The only problem was getting hold of a dozen carts. Anything with wheels on is a problem right now, for obvious reasons."

Considering what he was and who'd sent him, Carnufex could have been a lot worse. He was a short, stocky man, about fifty-five years old, with a great beak of a nose, a soft and cultured voice, small bright eyes and snow-white hair. He was never tired, hungry, frightened or angry (come to think of it, during their three-day journey Ziani had never once noticed him fall out of line for a piss, or take a drink of water from his canteen). Most of the time he hung back with the escort cavalrymen (he had been a soldier himself before he was transferred to the mines) and kept up an unremitting torrent of the filthiest jokes Ziani had ever heard, including some he couldn't begin to understand, even with an engineer's instinct for intricate mechanisms. He was, of course, there to watch Ziani as much as to help him, but that was understandable enough.

"We won't need that much in the way of lumber," Ziani replied. "How about the steel I asked for? I know that's likely to be difficult."

Carnufex smiled. "Not likely. By a strange coincidence, my wife's kid brother's the superintendent of the steel depot at Colla Silvestris. At least," he added innocently, "he is now; used to be a clerk in the procurement office, but he got a surprise promotion about two hours after I got this commission. A buffoon, but he does as he's told. With any luck, your steel should be there waiting for you when we arrive."

Ziani was impressed. When he'd talked to the previous superintendent, he'd been told there wasn't that much steel in the whole duchy. "That's handy," he said.

"I always knew young Phormio'd come in useful for something eventually," Carnufex replied. "I could never begin to imagine what it might be, but I had the feeling. Oh, while I think of it," he added, "you were asking about skilled carpenters. I've found you some."

"That's wonderful," Ziani said. "How did you manage that?"

The smile again. "I had a dozen seconded from the Office of Works, thanks to the new chief clerk there. My brother-in-law, actually."

Ziani nodded. "Your wife has a large family."

"Bloody enormous."

An hour later, Ziani could see gray patches standing out against the sandy brown of the mountain; also he could hear faint tapping noises, like an army of thrushes knocking snail-shells against stones. The closer to the mountain they came, the louder the noise grew, and before long he could see them, hundreds of tiny moving dots swarming up and down the side of the slope. "How many men work here?" he asked.

"Between eight and nine hundred, usually," Carnufex replied. "Just over two hundred underground, the rest breaking up, cleaning and smelting ore, maintenance, supply, that sort of thing. In fact, we're short-handed, we could do with half as many again. It's a pity nobody pointed out to Valens' father that if you want to double output, it might be a good idea to take on a few extra hands. But there," he added, with a mildly stoical shrug, "we have a curious idea in this country that anything can be achieved provided you shout loud enough at the man in charge."

"I see," Ziani said. "Does it work?"

"Oddly enough, yes."

The tapping was getting steadily louder. It seemed to be coming from every direction (the sound, Ziani rationalized, was echoing off the mountainside) and he wondered if it was like that all the time. "What are those big timber frames?" he asked, pointing.

"They're the drop-hammers," Carnufex replied. "You see where the streams come down off the mountain? They're banked up into races, and they turn those big waterwheels you can just see there, behind those sheds. The wheel trips a cam which lifts and drops a bloody great beam with an iron shoe on the end, which smashes the ore up into bits; then it gets carried down onto the flat — you can see the big heaps of the stuff there, look — and it gets broken up even finer by a lot of men with big hammers. Then it's got to be washed, of course, so it's carted back *up* the hillside and shoveled into the strakes — look, do you see the lines of conduits coming down the slope? They're open-topped, made of planks, and they carry the millstreams downhill to turn the wheels and eventually join up with the river. You can see they're dammed up at various stages; the dams are called strakes, and as the ore's washed down by the stream, each one filters out different grades of rubbish, so that when it reaches the bottom it's mostly clean enough to go in the furnace. That's the trouble with this seam; there's plenty of it, but it's full of all kinds of shit that's got to be cleaned out. Biggest part of the operation, in fact, preparing the ore." He grinned. "I expect this all looks a bit primitive to you, after what you're used to."

Ziani shrugged. "We don't do anything like this where I come from," he said. "The materials I used to use came in rounds or square bars or flat sections, we didn't mess about breaking up rocks. This could be the state of the art for all I know."

Carnufex looked mildly disappointed. "Ah well," he said. "I was hoping you could give us a pointer or two about improving the way we go about things before you show us how to pull it all down."

Closer still, and the tapping was starting to get on Ziani's nerves. He was accustomed to noise, of course; but this was different from the thumps and clangs of the ordnance factory, where the trip-hammers pecked incessantly and the strikers hammered hot iron into swages. It was sharper, more brittle, a constant shrill chipping, and he doubted whether it was something he could get used to and stop hearing after a while. The men swinging hammers stopped work to stare at the newcomers; the leather sleeves and leggings they wore to protect them from flying splinters of rock were caked with dust, their hair was gray with it and their eyes peered out from matt white masks, so that they looked like actors playing demons in a miracle play. Eventually someone yelled something and they went back to work, bashing on the chunks of rock as if they hated them. No, Ziani thought, this isn't like the factory at all. There's no grace here, no patient striving with tolerances in the quiet war against error. This is a violent place.

"The actual workings are over there a bit," Carnufex was saying, as calm and matter-of-fact as if he was showing someone round his garden. "I don't suppose you'll need to bother with anything above ground. I mean, no point sabotaging it; anybody who wanted to could replace the whole lot from scratch in a month or so."

Ziani nodded. He didn't want to open his mouth here if he could help it.

"You can see where the shaft runs underground by the line of wheels," Carnufex went on. He was pointing at a row of wooden towers, each one directly under a branch of the millrace, which gushed in a carefully directed jet to turn the blades of a tall overshot waterwheel. Each wheel's spindle turned a toothed pulley which drew a chain up out of what looked like a well. Piles of ore were heaped up beside each well-head; men were loading it into wheelbarrows and carrying it away to be smashed. As well as the clacking of the wheel and the ticking of the chain, he could hear a wheezing noise, like an overweight giant climbing stairs. "Bellows," Carnufex explained, "inside the tower, they're powered by cams run off the wheel-shaft. They suck the bad air out of the galleries and blow clean air back in."

Bellows, Ziani thought; they'll come in handy. He nodded, careful not to exhibit undue interest or enthusiasm. "Where's the actual entrance?" he asked.

"This way. We might as well dismount and walk from here," Carnufex added. "It can be a bit tricksy underfoot, what with all this rubble and stuff."

The entrance was just a hole in the hillside, five feet or so high and wide, with heavy oak trunks for pillars and lintel. There were steps down, and a lantern on either side, flickering in the draft that Ziani guessed came from the constant pumping of the bellows. Their light showed him two plank-lined walls vanishing into a dark hole. He let Carnufex lead the way.

For what seemed like a very long time, the shaft ran straight and gently downhill. Carnufex had taken down one of the lanterns, but all Ziani could see by it was his own feet and the back of Carnufex's head, his white hair positively glowing in the pale yellow light. To his surprise it was cool and airy, delightfully quiet after the hammering outside. Even the smell — wet timber and something sweet he couldn't identify — was mildly pleasant. But his neck and back ached from walking in a low crouch; he felt like a spring under tension.

"This is the main gallery." Carnufex's voice boomed as it echoed back at him. "Spurs run off it to the faces, where the ore's dug out. We're always having to open up new ones, of course."

"What's holding the roof up?" Ziani asked, trying not to sound more than mildly curious.

"Props," Carnufex answered crisply. "Thousands and thousands of them; it's a real problem getting enough straight, uniform-thickness timber. Without them, of course, this whole lot'd be round your ears in a flash."

"Right." Ziani knew that already. "So if it's the props that keep it from collapsing, how do you dig the tunnels to start off with; before you have a chance to put the props in, I mean?"

"Slowly," Carnufex replied, "and very, very carefully. Ah," he added, stopping short, so that Ziani nearly trod on his heels. "We've reached the first spur. Do you want to go and have a look?"

"No thanks," Ziani replied quickly. "I think I've seen enough to be going on with, thanks."

"Really?" Carnufex sounded disappointed, like a musician who hasn't been asked for an encore. "Suit yourself. Do you want to go back now?"

Yes, Ziani thought, very much. "Not yet," he said. "I need to take measurements first."

With Carnufex holding the end of the tape for him, he measured the height and width of the shaft at ten-inch intervals, starting at the point where the spur joined the gallery and going back about a dozen feet toward the entrance. As Carnufex called them out, he jotted down each set of figures with a nail on a wax tablet, unable to see what he was writing in the vague light from the lantern. "All done," he said, when they'd taken the last measurement. "Now can we go back, please?"

As they headed back the way they'd come, Ziani asked Carnufex how long it'd take to dig out the gallery, if it collapsed.

"Not sure," Carnufex replied. "Let's see: ten feet a day, double that for two shifts, so let's say a month. No big deal, if we can get timber for the props."

Ziani nodded, not that the other man could see him do it. "And the ventilation shafts?"

"Trickier. They're lined with brick, you see."

"That's all right," Ziani replied. "With luck I should be able to brace them the same way I'm planning on doing the gallery." Of course, he reflected, that would mean they'd have to be measured too; someone would have to go down each shaft, presumably lowered down in the ore bucket. All in all, not a job he wanted to do himself; but it would have to be done properly, by someone who knew how to take an accurate measurement. Fortunately, though, he knew just the man for the job.

"Certainly." His face hadn't changed at all.

Ziani looked at him, but the dead-fish eyes simply looked back, expressionless except for the permanent, faintly hungry look that made Ziani think uncomfortably of a patient predator.

"You sure?" he asked. "It won't be much fun hanging down there in a bucket."

Gace Daurenja, his absurdly thin, ludicrously tall, appallingly flat-faced self-appointed apprentice and general assistant, shrugged. "I've done worse things in my time," he said. "And confined spaces don't bother me, if that's what you were thinking. I was a chimney-sweep for a time, and a chargehand in a furnace. And this won't be the first time I've worked in a mine, either."

Ziani tried not to frown. He believed him; ever since he'd turned up in Ziani's room with the marvelous winch he'd made to his order, he was prepared to believe anything the thin man told him, though he wasn't quite sure why. Possibly, he'd thought, it was because it was such a huge leap of faith to believe that this extraordinary creature could exist at all. If you could accept that, anything else was easy in comparison.

"Fine," Ziani said. He reached out and pulled a sheet of paper across the table. Immediately, Daurenja's attention was focused on it, to the exclusion of everything else. "Here's the general idea; it's the same for the vent shafts as well as the gallery."

Daurenja nodded slowly. His expression showed that the diagram was the most wonderful thing he'd ever seen in his entire life.

"Steel girders," Ziani said, trying not to let Daurenja's manner bother him. "Really, it's just a steel cage. We build it where we want the cave-in to stop, if you follow me —"

"Perfectly."

Ziani ignored the interruption. "So we stuff the shaft with trash wood, charcoal, old rags soaked in lamp oil, set light to it — those bellows are a stroke of luck, we can get a nice burn going with a bit of air — and that'll burn out the timber props but leave the steel cage intact; it'll look like we've caved in the whole lot, of course, and then when the war's over, they'll only have to dig out as far as the cages; beyond that, the props should be unharmed. Quite simple, really, assuming it works."

"Brilliant."

Ziani ignored that, too. "The problems I can foresee are with what the heat might do to the cage. If it gets too hot we could warp the girders or even melt them, so we'll have to be careful not to get carried away. I'm hoping, though, that as soon as the props are charred halfway or three parts through they'll give way, and the falling rock'll snuff out the fire, or at the very least act as a heat-sink. The cage in the gallery ought to be straightforward enough, but I haven't made up my mind yet how best to anchor them in the vent shafts. They'll have a huge weight bearing directly on them from overhead, even if they're only ten feet or so down the shafts. We'll have to drive pins into the brickwork to take the weight; that'll be a fun job, swinging a sledge in such a tight place."

"I'll have a go if you like," Daurenja said immediately. "Back when I was working in the slate quarries —"

"They're miners," Ziani said, "let them do it. I'll want you with me in the fabrication shop, setting rivets. Not the most exciting job in the world, but it'll have to be done right. Then more rivet-ing, of course, once we've got the bloody things into position."

"Not a problem," Daurenja said, as full of confidence as a lion roaring. "I did a great deal of riveting when I was working in the foundry, and —"

When Ziani had eventually managed to get rid of him, he put on his coat, drew a scarf over his face to filter out the worst of the dust, and went for a walk. He had pictured this place in his mind as long ago as his conversation with Miel Ducas, back in the Butter Pass, but back then it had been nothing but a geometrical design of wheels and levers. It was the ferocity of it that bothered him, the sheer brutality of falling iron-shod beams pounding rock into rubble. He wondered; he'd never seen a flour mill, even. He could feel the cracking and grinding and splintering in his bones, every time the cams tripped and the beams fell. It reminded him too much of things he'd only considered so far in the abstract, rather than in practice. Even the slaughter of the Mezentines, shot down in their thousands by the scorpion-bolts he'd made, hadn't affected him as much as this place did. There was a ruthlessness about it that he was reluctant to come to terms with. On the other hand, he was very close to resolving a number of issues that had been bothering him for some time, areas he'd left blank in the design, knowing they were possible but lacking the precise knowledge of detailed procedure and method. Not a comfortable place, but enlightening.

Daurenja, he thought, and he could feel his skin crawl. With any luck, the rope might break while he was dangling down a vent shaft in a bucket, and that'd be one fewer set of calculations to bother about. He tasted dust in his mouth, in spite of the scarf, and spat.

He walked toward the mine entrance, pausing to look up at one of the wheel towers. Crude, compared to a Mezentine waterwheel. There were no bearings to ease the turning of the spindle, and a significant amount of the water slopped past or over the blades, wasted. But he was here to sabotage the mines, not improve them. He shrugged. Fine by him.

A miner passed him, struggling with a wheelbarrow loaded with too much ore. As he went by he must've caught a glimpse of Ziani's face; he hesitated, the barrow wobbled and ran off line, making him stop. Ziani made an effort not to grin. He was getting used to being stared at, the only dark-skinned Mezentine in the duchy. It usually saved him the bother of having to explain who he was; everybody knew that already.

"Hang on a second," he called after the miner. "Can I ask you something?"

The man let go of the barrow handles and straightened up. "You're him, right?" he said. "The Mezentine."

Something else he was getting used to. Curious, to be known only for a quality he was no longer authorized to have, the thing that still defined him but had been taken away. "That's me," he said. "Ziani Vaatzes. Who're you?" he added.

The miner frowned, as if dubious about answering. "Corvus Vasa," he said. "I'm not anybody," he added quickly.

Ziani smiled. "It's all right," he said. "I just wanted to ask something, if you're not too busy."

Vasa shrugged. "Go ahead."

Ziani sat on the edge of the barrow. "I was talking to Superintendent Carnufex," he said, stressing the name and rank only very slightly, "and he was saying a man can dig ten feet of tunnel a day, average. Is that right?"

"Dig and prop, yes. I mean, usually there's at least four of you to a face, two digging and two propping, and four blokes'll usually do twenty foot a shift, two shifts a day, forty foot. So we say ten foot a man a day, as a rule of thumb, like. That's in earth," he added, "a bit less in clay. Plus, of course, you've got another two blokes coming up behind you to load the spoil, and another bloke to carry it. Teams of seven's the rule."

Ziani nodded. "Fine," he said. "What if you're cutting through rock?"

Vasa grinned sourly. "We don't," he said, "not if we can help it. You hit rock, best thing you can do is go back and work round it. Plus, you give the surveyor a right bollocking afterward."

"All right," Ziani said, "but supposing there's no way round and you've just got to cut through. That happens sometimes, doesn't it?"

Vasa nodded. "Sometimes," he said. "And it's a bastard. Then it's a man on the drill and another man to strike for him, cutting slots to fit wedges in. Two or three foot a day, depending on what sort of rock it is."

Ziani clicked his tongue. "What about granite?"

"Wouldn't know," Vasa replied, "never had to find out, luckily. I heard tell once that you can shift hard rock by lighting a bloody great big fire, get it really hot, then chuck water on it to split it." He grinned. "Sounds fine when you say it, but I wouldn't like doing it myself."

"I bet." Ziani smiled. "No granite in these parts, then."

"Never come across any. What d'you want to know about that stuff for, anyhow?"

"Oh, just another job I've got to do, sooner or later. Thanks, you've been a great help."

Vasa hesitated for a moment, then said, "They're saying you're here to block up the mine, because of the war. Is that right?"

"Afraid so. Means you'll be out of a job for a while, but think about it. If the Mezentines got hold of the mine intact they'd be wanting men to work it for them, and I don't suppose they'd be planning on paying any wages."

He could see the point sinking in, like water soaking away into peat. Then Vasa shrugged. "Let's hope the war's over soon, then," he said. "It's not a bucket of fun, this job, but it pays good money. I'd rather be here than on wall-building, like my brother-in-law. That's bloody hard work, and the money's a joke."

Ziani dipped his head in acknowledgment. "Vasa, did you say your name was?"

"Corvus Vasa. And there's my brother Bous, he works down on the faces, if ever you're looking for men for this other job of yours."

"I might well be, later on," Ziani said. "So if your brother works on the faces, he must know a thing or two about cutting rock."

"Him? Yeah, I should think so. I mean, that stuff's not hard like granite, but you don't just scoop it out with a spoon."

"Thanks," Ziani said, smiling. "I'll bear you both in mind."

"No problem." Vasa picked up his wheelbarrow, nodded over his shoulder and went on his way.

(And why not? Ziani thought. I will be needing skilled miners,

when the time comes. Assuming I can figure out the last details . . .
He shook his head, like a wet dog drying itself.)

Two days, and he was so sick of the place he'd have given anything just to walk away. Simply staying was like trying to hold his
breath, an intolerable pressure inside him. Two days did nothing
to acclimatize him to the noise and the dust; if anything, their
effect was cumulative, so that he noticed them more, not less.

Unfortunately, the job wasn't going well. The steel turned up
exactly on time, as Carnufex had guaranteed, but not the anvils,
the tools or the ten Eremian blacksmiths he'd been promised
faithfully before he left Civitas Vadanis. Even Carnufex had no
luck trying to track them down, and without them, nothing could
be done. On the evening of the second day, Carnufex told him the
adjutant would be arriving tomorrow and maybe he'd be able to
get it sorted out; he seemed uncharacteristically vague and tentative, which Ziani reckoned was a very bad sign.

There'd been some progress, however; mostly due, it had to be
said, to Gace Daurenja. He'd taken measurements in nine of the
twelve ventilation shafts, hanging out of the winch bucket with a
lantern gripped in his teeth, with seventy feet of sheer drop waiting to catch him if he happened to slip. Ziani could hardly bear
to think about it, but Daurenja didn't seem bothered in the least,
while the plans he produced (working on them at night after an
eighteen-hour day in the bucket) were masterpieces of clear, elegant draftsmanship, and annotated in the most beautiful lettering
Ziani had ever seen (when he asked about that, Daurenja attrib-
uted it to the time he'd spent copying manuscripts for a society
bookseller). The only thing he seemed bothered about was how
long the job was taking him, and Ziani had to tell him to stop
apologizing for being so slow.

He'd drawn up the plans for the cages himself, taking his time
for want of anything else to do. Carnufex had let him use his office
as a drawing room; he could still hear the noise, and the dust
managed to get in somehow, in spite of shutters on the windows

and curtains on the doors, but at least it was tolerable, and the slow, familiar work helped take his mind off the misery of it all. If he tried really hard, he could almost fool himself into thinking that he was back in the city at the ordnance factory, and that the hammering was the slow, constant heartbeat of the trip-hammers, and the dust was foundry soot, and the men who came when he shouted were his own kind, not barbarians.

On the third day he decided he'd had enough. The adjutant had arrived and spent a thoroughly unpleasant evening being quietly shouted at by Carnufex, but there was still no clue as to the whereabouts of the anvils or the tools, let alone the blacksmiths. That, as far as Ziani was concerned, wasn't good enough. He called Daurenja and gave him a letter.

"I want you to ride back to the city," he said, "and give this to Duke Valens personally. Wait for a reply."

Daurenja nodded sharply, a picture of grim determination. "Right away," he said. "Leave it to me." He was out of the office before Ziani had a chance to tell him where to find a horse or collect his conduct letters, which he'd have to produce before he'd be allowed past the sentries at the palace gate. Presumably he didn't feel the need, or thought that that'd be cheating; Ziani pictured him scaling the palace wall with a grappling hook and crawling down a chimney into the Duke's bedroom. Wouldn't put it past him, at that.

He'd finished the last of the plans, and cramp made going outside an unpleasant necessity. This time he walked up to the sluices where the ore was washed. He wasn't particularly interested in that stage of the operation, but he'd already looked at everything else. The foreman seemed happy enough to explain the procedures to him.

"That other bloke was up here yesterday, asking," the foreman added, after a long and rather confusing account of how the crushed ore was washed through the strakes. "But I don't think he was taking much of it in. Kept interrupting and asking questions; didn't make much sense to me."

"The other bloke?" Ziani asked.

"The long, thin bloke. You know, him who's been measuring the vents."

"Oh," Ziani said, "him. What did he want to know?"

The foreman shook his head. "Not sure. I was telling him how we get all the shit out, calamine and pyrites and sulfur. But I think he must've lost the thread, because he kept asking what we did with the stuff we took out; and I told him, it's just washed away, it's garbage, we don't want it. He got a bit excited about that, like I was doing something wrong; then he said *thank you for your time,* all stiff and uptight, and went storming off in a right old state." The foreman shrugged, expressing a broad but reluctant tolerance of lunatics. "I told him, if the stuff's any good to him he's welcome to it, if he can figure out a way of collecting it, but I think he thought I was trying to be funny."

Ziani scowled. "Calamine," he said.

"And pyrites, sulfur, red lead, all that shit. I suppose there's people who can find a use for anything."

"I'll ask him when he gets back," Ziani replied. "But that won't be for at least a week."

Wrong. Daurenja came back two days later, in a thunderstorm, riding on the box of a large, broad-wheeled cart. There were four other carts behind him, carrying crates covered with tarpaulins, anvils sticking out from under heavy waxed covers, and half a dozen wet, bemused-looking men who proved to be the first installment of the promised blacksmiths.

"They didn't want to let me in to see the Duke," Daurenja said, standing bare-headed in the yard with the rain running down his spiked hair like millraces and puddling around his feet. "They said I needed a pass or a certificate or something. But I got through all right. I'm afraid I'm rather used to getting my own way."

Ziani pulled his collar round his ears. He was having to shout to make himself heard above the splashing. "How did you manage that?" he said.

Daurenja frowned. "To be honest, I lost my temper a little; and one of the guards shoved me — at least, he was just about to, but I beat him to it. There was a bit of a scuffle, and that brought the duty officer out, and I said I had an urgent message for the Duke, from you. The adjutant had the common sense to take me straight to the Duke. He was just sitting down to dinner, but he agreed to see me right away. I gave him the letter, and I could see he was absolutely livid. He sent for the Chancellor and gave him quite a talking-to, with me standing right next to him able to hear every word. The poor man went bright red in the face, and then a footman or something of the sort took me to one of the guest rooms. Everything was ready by dawn the next day, all signed for and loaded on the carts. We were on the road by mid-morning, and well, here we are."

Ziani frowned. "And he was all right, was he? About you hitting one of the guards?"

"He didn't mention it," Daurenja said, and Ziani couldn't tell whether he was lying or telling the truth. "There's some sort of diplomatic thing going on, important foreign guests. I think the Duke's planning to get married or something. Anyhow, as soon as he realized I was there on your behalf, he dropped everything and saw to it that we got our supplies straightaway. That's a good sign, isn't it?"

Ziani shrugged. "Business before pleasure," he replied, "though from what I've seen of Valens, I don't suppose state receptions are his idea of fun. Maybe he was just glad of an excuse to get away from all the socializing. Look, can we get in out of this bloody rain, please?"

The storms faded away as quickly as they'd come; in the morning it was bright and dry, perfect conditions for open-air iron-working. As well as the things Ziani had asked for in his list, the carts had brought a genuine Mezentine-made reciprocating saw, complete with a drive belt and spare pulleys; Ziani had told the Duke in passing how helpful such a thing would be for cutting the iron bar-stock to length, but he'd never imagined he'd ever see one again. He had no idea where Valens or his agents had contrived to get it from, but that didn't matter. It was like meeting an old friend in the middle of the desert, and he'd had it carried over to one of the wheel towers and connected up to the spindle while the rest of the carts were still being unloaded.

"You're in love," Carnufex said, as Ziani put in the drive and watched the flywheel spin. Ziani shook his head.

"This is better than love," he said. "This is home."

Carnufex laughed. "I can't figure you out," he said. "Ever since I've known you, all you've done is witter on about how wonderful everything Mezentine is, and how much better they do things there. If I'd been shafted by my country as badly as you have, I'd snarl like a wolf every time somebody mentioned the place. I certainly wouldn't keep telling everybody how splendid it all is. Or is it just the people in charge you don't like?"

Ziani straightened up. The power feed was running perfectly. "Would you really?" he said. "Hate your country, I mean, if you had to leave it?"

"Of course not," Carnufex said. "But if they tried to put me to death for something I didn't do —"

"Oh, I did it." Ziani smiled.

"But it was stupid. You made some kind of clockwork doll for your kid."

"That's right."

Carnufex thought for a moment. "Fine," he said. "Apparently, you seem to think that making kids toys ought to be a capital offense. I don't quite see how you can believe that, but never mind. If you thought it was wrong, really, really bad, why the hell did you do it?"

Ziani looked at him as though he thought the answer might be hidden somewhere in his face. "That," he said, "is a very good question. Because I thought I could get away with it, I suppose. Why does anybody ever do something wicked?"

"You're strange," Carnufex said.

"Not in the least," Ziani replied. "It's no different from robbing people in the street. You know it's wrong. It's against the law, if you get caught, you'll be punished. You know it's wrong; you wouldn't like it if someone did it to you. But people still do it, because they need money, because they're just lazy and greedy. In my case, I suppose it must have been arrogance."

"You suppose. You don't know."

Ziani furrowed his brow. "No, actually, I don't, now you come to mention it. At least, I haven't thought about it very much since. Maybe I ought to, I don't know."

Carnufex looked as though he wanted to end the conversation and walk away before he was moved to say something undiplomatic, but after a moment's indecision he took a step closer. "Maybe you should," he said. "It might help you figure out where your loyalties lie, right now."

"Oh, no question about that," Ziani said. "And in case you're having doubts, you might care to consider what I did for the Eremians. If you could've seen what the scorpions I made did to the Mezentines, I don't think you'd be worrying about whose side I'm on." He shook his head. "You can love someone and want to hurt them as much as possible," he said, "that's perfectly normal behavior."

"Normal," Carnufex repeated. "All right, but that's not what we were talking about. You were saying you did this thing, making the clockwork doll, that you knew was wicked and bad, but you can't remember offhand why you did it. That's . . ." He shrugged, as if to say there weren't any words for what that was.

"You're right," Ziani said, "it's strange. I'll have to think about that. Meanwhile, perhaps we ought to be getting some work done. Have you seen Daurenja this morning?"

"Daurenja." Carnufex scowled. "I meant to have a word with you about him. He's been annoying my foremen."

"Annoying?"

"Wasting their time. Getting under their feet. Asking them all sorts of bloody stupid questions and then insulting them when they say they don't know the answer. Look, I know he reports directly to you, but can't you talk to him? If he carries on like that, someone's going to lose their temper and damage him; presumably he's useful to you, so it'd be as well if you spoke to him about it."

"He's . . ." Ziani shrugged. "Fine, yes, I'll deal with it. Now, I want the long steel sections fetched over here so we can start cutting, and I want the anvils carried over to the small ore furnace, we can use it as a forge without any major modifications. Can you get the ore shed cleared out? I want to set up the small portable forges there for riveting."

Carnufex had the grace to know when he was beaten. He nodded submissively as Ziani reeled off his list of jobs to be done, and withdrew in good order, leaving his opponent in possession of the field. Nevertheless, it wasn't a victory as far as Ziani was concerned; he'd been forced into a lie, which he resented, especially since it was essentially self-deception.

On the other hand, the mechanical saw made up for a lot. He watched it gliding through six-inch square section bar, smoke curling up out of the cut as one of the men dribbled oil into it, a drop at a time. The sheer joy of seeing something done properly, after so long among the savages . . .

"Is that what I think it is?" Daurenja, peering over his shoulder; he wanted to shudder and pull away, as though a spider had run across his face. "Mezentine?"

"I never realized they exported them," Ziani replied, and there was a hint of doubt in his voice. Surely it was wrong to sell something like this to the barbarians, in case they tried to copy it for themselves. A right-thinking man, a patriot, might feel betrayed. "Apparently they do. Well, it's the basic model."

"It'll do," Daurenja said, with a degree of relish verging on hunger. Stupid, Ziani thought, he's making me feel jealous. "This ought to save us two days' work, easily."

"Not far off that." Ziani looked away. Somehow, Daurenja had spoiled the moment. "I guess Valens wants this job done quickly. I'll write and thank him tonight, when I've got a moment."

"Good idea. While you're at it, you could ask if he could send us a trip-hammer."

The next stage, punching the rivet-holes, was long, tedious and difficult. Each newly cut section had to be heated red in the forge and held over the hardy-hole on the back of the anvil while one of the six blacksmiths hammered a half-inch punch through it. If the hole was an eighth of an inch out of true, the section wouldn't line up with the others and would therefore be useless, and there wasn't exactly a wealth of spare material left over to make replacements from. The work went painfully slowly, even after both Ziani and Daurenja each took an anvil and joined in.

Even so; it was better to be working again. Ziani was shocked by the sense of release he felt as he rested the punch on the mark and swung his hammer. He was at a loss to explain it, but it refused to be denied. It made him think of the frantic pace of work in the weeks before the assault on Civitas Eremiae; how, for a short while, he'd managed to give himself the slip as he plunged into the endless, sprawling, choking detail of building the scorpions. He thought about them, too. If he'd been classified as an artist, like a painter or a sculptor, they would have been acclaimed as his finest creation, the masterpiece he'd achieved at the height of his powers. That would be wrong, of course. Judged objectively, as though by a panel of his fellow engineers, the best thing he'd ever done had been the mechanical toy he'd made for his daughter, a long time ago in a place he was forbidden to go back to.

(What had become of it, he wondered; had it been completely destroyed, smashed up and melted down, the metal once cool buried or sunk to the bottom of the sea; or did it still exist somewhere, locked away in a warehouse, or the cellars under the Guildhall? He could picture it still in his mind's eye; every detail, every brazed joint and polished keyway, every departure from Specification. He grinned; when they came to inspect it, they hadn't found all his modifications. Some of his best, variations too subtle and delicate for the naked eye, or even gauges and calipers, hadn't been mentioned in the list of charges read out at his trial. There were tiny but significant alterations to the pitch of the threads that fed the worm-drive. On the inside of the crank-case, he'd replaced a flush-set rivet with a setscrew. The teeth of the middle cog in the main gear train were beveled on top rather than plain. If the mechanism still existed somewhere, it bristled with unpurged abominations, which only he knew about and which they'd been too careless to notice. It was a slight victory, but an important one.)

The punching took a day. When it was finally finished (Ziani had insisted on working into the night; that hadn't made him popular), all he wanted to do was crawl away to his lodgings and go to sleep. He'd walked half the distance when he realized that Daurenja was still with him, talking at him, like a long, thin, yapping dog.

"It'd mean cutting the slot with a chisel," Daurenja was saying, "because you couldn't get in there with a milling cutter, not even a long-series end-mill, but if you went at it nice and slow, and finished it up afterward with a four-square file . . . After all, the dimensions wouldn't be critical, it's just got to guide the slider into the mortice . . ."

Ziani blinked, as if he'd just woken up. "Fine," he said. "You do it that way."

"You sound like you think there'd be a problem."

"What? No, really. I think it'd work. In fact, I'm certain of it."

"Excellent." Daurenja was beaming at him. Even though his back was to him, Ziani could feel the glare from his smile on the back of his neck. "Which really only leaves the question of how to make the receiver head. And what I was thinking was, how about making it in two parts? Dovetailed together, then brazed or even soft-soldered, it's not a load-bearing component . . ."

Ziani sighed, and stopped in his tracks. "Would it be all right if we talked about this tomorrow?" he said. "Only it's been a long day, I can't really think straight."

"Oh." Disappointment; the yapping dog finding out it wasn't being taken for a walk after all. "Of course, I understand. But if you're at a loose end and you felt like turning it over in your mind, I'm sure you could figure out a much better way of doing it."

"I'll see what I can do. Meanwhile —"

"Yes, right. Thanks, and see you tomorrow. We're making a start on assembling the frames on site, are we? Or are we going to do a trial run first, just to make sure everything fits before we lug the whole lot underground?"

Ziani hadn't thought of that, and it was a valid point. It'd be a nightmare if they dragged the components down the tunnels only to find that they wouldn't fit together. "Well of course," he snapped. "I'm not stupid, you know."

"Sorry. I didn't mean —"

"That's all right." Ziani drew on his last scratchings of patience and stamina. "Yes, we'll do a dry run up here first thing, and if all goes well we can shift the bits and pieces down the mine say around mid-morning. See to it that everybody's there on time, will you?"

"Of course." Ziani was struck by the total absence of fatigue in Daurenja's voice. They'd both done more than a full day's work, but Daurenja sounded as fresh and insufferably bouncy as ever. "Well, if you don't need me for anything else tonight, I'll turn in. I can get a couple of hours' work done on my designs." Short pause. "It's very good of you to agree to take a look at them. I really appreciate that."

"No problem," Ziani yawned. He had no recollection whatsoever of agreeing to anything, but presumably he'd made some kind of grunting noise while Daurenja had been yapping at him and he hadn't been listening. In any event, too late now to go back on his word. Sliders, he thought, and hadn't there been something about a two-piece receiver head? He thought for a moment, but he couldn't begin to imagine what Daurenja's pet project could possibly be. "See you tomorrow."

"Later today, actually," Daurenja chirped. "It's past midnight already. Time flies, doesn't it?"

No, Ziani thought, and went to bed.

Needless to say, he was by this point far too tired to sleep. Instead, he lay on his back with his hands behind his head, his eyes shut, contemplating a design of his own. He'd reached the point now when it was there every time he closed his eyes, like the afterburn of looking directly at the sun. Too weary to think constructively, he contented himself with tracing the main lines, ignoring the details: the beginning, parts already made, fitted and in operation, beginning with his escape from the Guildhall, his infiltration of the Eremian court, the making of the scorpions, the betrayal and sack of Civitas Eremiae, the dual use he'd made of Duchess Veatriz. In his mind's eye, those parts of the design were dull gray, the remaining mechanisms in that section that had already been built but which weren't yet in service standing out in black or red. He considered them, as he'd done so many times before, and conceded that they were satisfactory. Next he contemplated the middle: not much gray here, plenty of black and red, and a few hazy clusters of dotted lines here and there where he knew a sub-mechanism was needed but where he hadn't yet attended to the details of their design. As always, he picked up one or two slight errors, minor infringements of tolerance, parts that had moved or distorted slightly under load. There was Miel Ducas, for example; also the salt-trader's widow, Duke Valens, possibly the Mezentines. Fortunately the divergences were slight and he could take up the play easily by tightening the jibs.

As for the final section: thinking about it for too long was uncomfortable, because it was so hard to see past the tangles of dotted lines to the firm, strong black and red beyond. In particular, there was the huge gap just before the end. Having talked to the miners, he knew that the expedient he'd been relying on to plug that gap wasn't going to be up to the job; but as yet he hadn't been able to think of anything to take its place. There was something, he knew; he remembered hearing something, or reading it, a very long time ago, but he'd taken no notice at the time. Now, for some reason, whenever he contemplated the deficiency, his thoughts had a strange tendency to turn to Daurenja, as though he could possibly have something to do with it. But that was unlikely. When he'd outlined the final part of the movement, he hadn't even known that Daurenja existed.

Thinking about him made his head ache. The trouble was, he

was infuriatingly useful; competent, more than competent, at anything he was asked to do. The more Ziani used him, however, the less comfortable he felt. What was it that Carnufex had been complaining about? Hanging round while people were working, asking strange and irritating questions. Well, that sounded plausible enough. Something about calamine, or pyrites, wasn't it? What the hell would any rational man want with garbage like that?

I could get rid of him, he thought, and then I wouldn't find myself relying on him anymore, and that'd be a good thing in itself. He felt the tug of that idea, but fought it. Appalling enough that he'd reached the point where he could comfortably think in disgraceful euphemisms: *get rid of* for *send to his death*. The simple truth was, he didn't like Daurenja, a man who apparently worshipped him as some kind of god of engineering, and who was working like a slave day and night to help him. Was that the difference, he wondered; because he'd liked Miel Ducas and Duke Orsea, and Duchess Veatriz and Cantacusene the blacksmith's wife; Duke Valens had started teaching him how to fence; come to that, he didn't even mind Carnufex the mine superintendent. All of them he'd taken to, as human beings; all of them he'd used, slotting them into the mechanism where they could do a job or two. Daurenja rubbed him up the wrong way, but he wasn't useful, not yet, to anything like the same extent. It'd be wrong to make him a sacrificial component; it'd be a waste of material, and murder.

Maybe, he thought, I shouldn't be doing this.

He sat up, suddenly wide awake. Before, whenever that thought had come to call, he'd summoned up the faces of his wife and daughter, like setting the dogs on a trespasser. Now, he could only see her hair, the curl as it touched her shoulder, the faint redness of its shine under lamplight. Her face had turned away into shadow, as though she couldn't bear to look at the thing he was making on her behalf, the abomination . . .

On her behalf.

His chest felt tight, and there was cold sweat on his forehead and neck. She hadn't asked him to build this machine; not this one.

Something Carnufex had said. The design faded from his mind like a reflection in water shattered into broken rings by a stone. Something he'd said in passing, and I told him I'd have to think about it; but he was getting on my nerves, pressing on them like an arrowhead broken off and healed over, and I made the thought go away. He made me tell a lie, to him and myself.

He scowled into the darkness, following the red and black lines of the thought; and then, as suddenly as the flash of inspiration that comes to a genius once in his life, the connection was made. The doll, the mechanical toy, the modifications he'd made that weren't on the list of charges at his trial.

It was like putting something in his mouth and finding it was too hot to swallow; just having the connection inside his head was an unbearable burning, a torment of dotted lines. Somebody else, he felt (the thought burned itself in, like heating the tang of a file to make it fit into a handle), there was somebody else involved. He fought, resisting the sudden understanding like a woman trying to stop herself giving birth. This changes everything.

No; it was a conscious decision. Changes nothing. Not as long as it's just intuition. Besides, it's probably just some stupid stuff — guilt, frustration, a long, hard day, the sort of horrible self-tormenting shit that keeps you awake in the early hours of the morning. And even if there's something there and it's true, it still doesn't change anything. Just one more bit to be fixed, at the very end of the job.

That didn't help him sleep. He'd never felt more wide awake in his whole life.

It didn't bloody well fit. It was hopeless. It was never going to fit. The holes were all in the wrong places, and drilling them out two whole sizes wouldn't be enough to cure it. Neither would any amount of bashing with hammers, bending, drawing out, pissing around . . .

"All right," he heard someone say, "try it now."

He put his weight on the bar, knowing it wouldn't line up

enough for the rivet to go through. It was all hopelessly screwed up, and would have to be done again . . .

"There. Perfect. Piece of cake."

He looked down, stunned. The rivet was in the hole. He relaxed, gradually letting the bar go. It flexed a small amount, then stopped. It was in. It *fitted*.

In which case, the whole ridiculous contraption fitted together, and they'd won, however unlikely that seemed. He could feel his face drawing into a huge, stupid grin.

"Good," he said, very low-key and matter-of-fact, though his heart was bursting with relief and joy. "Now get that last rivet set and we can all go home."

10

"Sulfur," Valens said with a scowl, dropping the paper on his desk and watching it roll itself back up into a scroll. "He'll be lucky. Where the hell am I supposed to get sulfur from in the middle of a war?"

Carausius didn't reply, which was sensible of him, and Valens took his silence in the spirit in which it was intended, as a mild and respectful rebuke. He made an effort and took a long, deep breath. "If by some miracle you can find a few barrels," he said, "get them shipped off, with my compliments. After all, we're stabbing the poor sod in the back, cutting off aid to the resistance. The least we can do is give him a nice retirement present."

"Sulfur," Carausius repeated, his voice carefully neutral. "I wonder if the salt woman might know where to find some. You know," he added, "the merchant Ziani Vaatzes teamed up with a while back."

Valens held still and quiet for a moment. Rather a leap, he thought, from salt to sulfur; not the sort of connection he'd have made himself. But someone who knew rather more about the salt woman's business affairs than he'd disclosed to his duke might be in a position to make that connection. He noted the possibility in his mind and moved on.

"Bad timing, really," Carausius was saying. "A week or so back, he could've had the stuff by the cartload; it's one of the by-products of the silver mines. But now Vaatzes has shut them all down, I guess he's out of luck."

The subject, Valens gathered, had been officially changed. "He's all done, is he?"

Carausius nodded. "The last shaft was sealed up two days ago, apparently, so that's that part of the job done. Whether the other part's come out all right we won't know till we try and open them up again."

Valens pulled a face. "Quite," he said. "Still, on balance I'd rather be remembered as the idiot who trashed his own mines for no reason than the idiot who let them fall into enemy hands. Ziani's on his way home again, presumably."

"Last I heard," Carausius confirmed. "Of course, it'll take him a while, with all that salvaged plant and equipment he's bringing back with him. Practically looted the place before he left, according to Superintendent Carnufex." He smiled. "Are you worried he won't get back in time for the wedding?"

"Absolutely," Valens said. "It wouldn't feel right, getting married without my senior engineering adviser there at my side. Actually, I was thinking about the move. It's not long now before we have to get that under way, and I've got some ideas which I think he might be able to help with. Don't look so sad," he added, "you haven't missed anything, they're just ideas, quite probably completely impractical. If anything comes of them, you'll be the first to know."

"No doubt." Carausius didn't want to talk about the move. "While we're on the subject of the wedding . . ."

Valens made a helpless gesture. "Now what, for crying out loud? Anybody'd think you're my mother."

"Fine, if you're determined not to take an interest. In which case, I'd be grateful if you'll refrain from yelling at me if it doesn't turn out the way you want."

Valens half rose from his chair, then sat down again. "I'm sure you're doing a marvelous job," he said, "and I wouldn't dream of interfering. Just let me know where I've got to be and when. If you could possibly arrange for it to be in the morning, that'd be good, because then I'd have the afternoon free to take the hawks out. Joke," he added quickly. "Honest."

With the baffled air of a predator cheated of its prey, Carausius gathered up his bits of paper and went away. After he'd gone, Valens sat perfectly still for a minute or so; then he opened the ivory casket on his desk and took out a small square of tightly folded parchment.

Well, he thought.

Holding it with the tips of his fingers, he turned it over a couple of times. Duke Orsea's seal, but not his handwriting. He took a closer look. Orsea's seal was a running stag glancing back over its shoulder. This impression had a small bump on the stag's neck, made by a tiny chip in the seal-stone. That bump was the only way you could tell Orsea's second-best seal, the one he used for private correspondence, from the official one he used for state business. Somehow, both of them had survived the fall of Civitas Eremiae; but it was the slightly chipped one that lived in Orsea's own writing desk, which he kept in his private chambers, unlocked. He'd seen that little bump many times before.

Courage was one of those virtues that Valens had but set little store by. As far as he was concerned, he was brave in the same way he was right-handed. By the same token, he treated fear like indigestion or a headache, just another annoyance that had to be overcome. He slid his finger under the flap and pressed gently upwards, until the wax cracked, splitting off the stag's head and crumbling its neck into fine red powder, like blood.

Veatriz Sirupati to Valens Valentinianus, greetings.

Only myself to blame, he thought. Getting engaged to be married to someone else could only be construed as a hostile thing, an act of war. Besides, it's not as though we were ever . . .

Just letters. Nothing more.

And here was a letter, its integrity guaranteed by the flawed stag he'd just snapped in half. He thought, unexpectedly, of Miel Ducas, the sulfur enthusiast, disgraced by another of these small packets of thought and feeling. Our fault; my fault. If Miel Ducas had commanded the defense of Civitas Eremiae . . . Wouldn't have made any difference, since the city fell by treachery, and I'd still have done that one bloody stupid thing, which in turn led inevitably to the war, my desperate need for allies and manpower, a political marriage, this letter.

Courage is a virtue best not taken to excessive extremes; someone brave enough to stick his hand in a fire is an idiot by any criteria. I could leave this letter unread. Wouldn't have to destroy it; just put it back in the ivory box and turn the little silver key.

(She's got no right, in any event. She was the one who got married in the first place, not me. I, on the other hand, am paying the price for saving her life.)

Veatriz Sirupati to Valens Valentinianus, greetings.

I guess congratulations are in order.

It's none of my business, in any case. Orsea explained it all to me; apparently, it's mostly to do with light cavalry, and the Mezentines being scared stiff of the Cure Hardy, because there're so many of them. He feels guilty, by the way, because he says he told you they're all vegetarians, and they turned out not to be. It was, of course, exactly the sort of mistake he would make. The ones he met were, you see, so he was sure that what he told you was true. He was trying to be helpful. He told me once, there's nothing causes more harm in the world than men like him trying to do the right thing. He knows it's true, but he can't understand why. I think that's probably why I still love him.

Sorry; the L word. This is neither the time nor the place. Let's talk about something else. Read any good books?

I haven't. I do a lot of embroidery instead. I know you have a wonderful library full of books I'd give anything to read, but I can't, because they're yours. I used to be really jealous that you had so many books; I resented that, and you writing to me telling me things out of them. I also knew that reading the books for myself wouldn't be the same as having you quote from them in a letter. Maybe at some point I got you and your library mixed up in my mind; what's the word, I identified them with you. A bit like the way you identify a country with its ruler; you say, the Vadani did this and that when you mean the Duke did it, and the other way around. For instance, the Mezentines could say the Vadani declared war on them by attacking, when you came for me.

I have no idea what I'm saying, so excuse me. I think it's just that I'm out of practice. It seems ever such a long time since I wrote a letter.

As well as embroidery, I daydream; which is silly. I have this fantasy about a girl who writes a letter to a prince. It's pointless, because he's married; but it's all right really, they're just letters. She has an idea he doesn't really care much for his wife. The trouble is, she gets to depend on the letters; she sits waiting for them to come — and they do, but she can't help wondering what it'd be like if they stopped coming, and she was stuck out there in the middle of nowhere, stranded in a tower embroidering cushion covers for the rest of her life. Sometimes I try and talk to her; I shout, but she can't hear. I try and tell her it's a very bad idea, and if I were in her shoes I wouldn't do such a dangerously stupid thing.

The other day, I went for a walk. I don't think I'm supposed to, but there's only so much cross-stitch a woman can do before her brain boils out through her ears. I walked down some stairs and across a courtyard and up another flight of stairs and down a passage, and in through an open door. There was a maid in the room, cleaning something; as soon as she saw me, she ran away, which was a bit disconcerting. The point is, I remembered the room. It used to be my room when I first came here; you remember, when I was a hostage, during the peace talks. It was pretty much as I remembered it: same furniture, even the same mirror hanging over the fireplace. I looked in the mirror and you'll never guess who I saw there. At first I was a bit taken aback — I'd heard she was dead, or had gone away. But then it occurred to me that she must've been there all this time.

No offense, but I don't think the barbarian girl is quite right for you. She's got a nice figure if you like them springy, but you could cut yourself on that mouth. Not that I'm feeling catty or anything. Still, who needs love when you can have cavalry?

I'm sorry, that was deliberate, not just an unfortunate slip of the pen. Who needs that thing that starts with L? Not me. You see, I'm married to a dear, good man who used to love me very much, though it's rather slipped his mind lately, because of everything he's had to contend with. You don't; or maybe you do, but you can't have it if it interferes with work. You're identified with your country, remember, and countries can't go around falling in love. Imagine what'd happen if Lonazep suddenly fell madly in love with the Eivar peninsula, and Lower Madeia got jealous and died of a broken heart. There'd be chaos, they'd have to redraw all the maps.

So, there we are. Eremia sends her best wishes, what's left of her.

He took a moment to fold the letter up neatly, like a man putting away a map in a high wind. He dropped it into the ivory box, turned the key and lolled back in his chair. For a little while, he stared at the tapestry on the opposite wall; the usual stag at bay, confronting the usual hounds. It was so familiar that he scarcely ever saw it these days; once it had hung in his father's bedchamber, and he'd come to know it well while he was waiting for his father to die. One of the first things he'd done when he became duke was have it brought up here.

Well, he thought, so there it is. Mind you, if this is being in love, I don't think much of it.

He glanced at the clock — beautiful, huge, Mezentine; the craftsmen of the Republic excelled at clockwork, not just time-pieces but automata, gadgets, mechanical toys. In three-quarters of an hour he had to go and see his future wife. Someone had made an appointment for them to take a stroll in the herb garden. It would be at its best at this time of the evening, stinking of lavender, bay and night-scented stock. At their last encounter they'd talked quite civilly for some considerable time about sparrowhawks; a day's falconry was being arranged, or would be as soon as Jarnac Ducas came back from the wars (sulfur; why?), he being recognized as the finest falconer, apart from Valens himself, in the duchy. It was a treat he was looking forward to intensely; and once it was over, he planned on making a public announcement about leaving the city for the duration of the war.

The Mezentines would burn it to the ground, of course. Presumably they would loot it scrupulously clean first; in which case, his father's tapestry would be taken away and sold, which at least meant it would survive. He'd very nearly made up his mind to take it with him, but space on the carts was going to be very tight indeed and it'd set a bad example. He smiled; he'd seen it in passing for most of his life, but he'd never actually looked at it. That was as bad as continually dipping into a book but never actually sitting down and reading it from beginning to end; or like being in love with someone since he was seventeen but never admitting it, even to himself, until it was finally, definitively, too late to do anything about it.

But so what? You heard all sorts of good, positive things about love; they wanted you to believe that you couldn't be happy without it. That was plain stupid, like saying you could never know true happiness unless you learned to play the flute. In any event, he knew all about love. He'd learned it like a school lesson, irregular verbs or dates of coronations, when he'd sat in his father's room staring at the tapestry because he couldn't bear to look at the man lying on the bed.

So, he thought, the hell with it. He still had forty minutes.

He jumped up, opened the long triangular cupboard in the corner of the room and took out a case of practice rapiers (Mezentine, a little too heavy, with three-ring hilts and bated points). Then he clattered down the stairs into the courtyard, wondering who would be unlucky enough to be the first to meet him.

There was a special pleasure in the irony; Orsea was sitting on the stone bench, watching the sunset.

"Hello," Valens called out cheerfully. "I hoped I might find you. Any good at fencing?"

Orsea turned his head, saw him and stood up. Excellent manners. "What, you mean swordfighting with rapiers?"

"Yes."

Orsea shook his head. "Pretty hopeless, actually. Of course, they tried to teach me when I was a kid, but I never had the —"

"Fine. Catch." Valens threw him one of the foils; he grabbed at it, knocked it up in the air and managed to catch it on the second bounce. "Come over to the old stable with me, we'll have half an hour's sparring."

Orsea frowned. "No, really," he said. "I'm dreadful at it."

"I'll teach you," Valens replied. "I'm a pretty good instructor, though I do say so myself."

By rights they should have worn face-masks, padded jackets and heavy left-hand gloves with the palms reinforced with chain-mail. But it would have taken time to fetch them, and there was no need. Valens was too good a fencer to get hit, or to hit his opponent dangerously. So they fought in shirtsleeves, like men trying to kill one another. Valens demonstrated the lunge, the pass, the stroma-zone (a flick across the enemy's face with the point of your sword, designed to cause painful superficial cuts). Orsea turned out to be every bit as bad as he'd said he was, and Valens poked him in the ribs, slapped him about with the flat, tripped him, knocked the foil out of his hand, drew blood from his ear and lower lip with little wrist-flips, and loosened one of his teeth by punching him in the face with the knuckle-bow of his hilt. There was no reason to it apart from the sheer joy of hurting and humiliating

him, showing him up for the clown he was, goading him into losing his temper and thereby laying himself even more open to attack. In the last objective, Valens failed. The more he was hit, the
more guilty Orsea seemed to get, the more painfully ashamed of
his lack of skill and ability. At last, having knocked his foil out of
his hand and across the stable ("That's called the beat in narrow
measure," he explained helpfully) and kicked his knees out from
under him so that he was left kneeling on precisely the spot where
Valens had had to learn the four wards as a boy — it had to be
that place and no other; it took him a full minute to herd Orsea
onto it — he lowered his foil, held out his other hand and pulled
Orsea to his feet.

"You're getting there," he said encouragingly, "but there's still
quite a way to go. We can make this a regular thing, if you like;
once a week, or twice even, if you'd rather."

"It's very good of you to offer," Orsea said, wiping blood out
of his fringe, "but I know how busy you must be right now with
other —"

He yelped; Valens had just stung the edge of his cheek with another flick. "Steady on," he shouted. "I haven't got my sword."

"So you haven't," Valens replied. "I'd go and fetch it if I were
you."

Orsea backed away a couple of steps, then turned his back as
he crossed the stable and retrieved the sword. I could do it now,
Valens thought; I could put the tip of my sword under my boot
and snap off the button and stab him through the neck. There's
nobody to see, everybody would believe it was a horrible accident.
There'd have to be at least a month of formal mourning; we'd
postpone the wedding, and then maybe there'd be a hitch; and
she'd be a widow . . .

"Ready?" he called out.

Orsea turned to face him. He looked very pale and rather
scared, and he was holding the foil all wrong. "Ready," he said.

"Right. Now," Valens went on, lowering his foil until the tip
rested on the flagstones, "I want you to lunge at me. Straight at

my face'd be best. There's an old saying in fencing; the way to a man's heart —"

Orsea lunged. At least, he took a giant stride forward at the same time as he stuck his arm out in front of him, but his foot caught in a crack where the damp had forced up a flagstone, and he stumbled forward, off balance, all his weight in front, windmilling both arms to keep from going over. Valens took the regulation step back and left, preparing for the volte he'd been planning, but Orsea's wildly swishing foil came out of nowhere, and the tip smacked on the flagstones, knocking off the button, before hitting him in the mouth. Valens felt the jagged edge of the broken foil slice along the length of his bottom lip like a knife.

Orsea, balance regained, was staring at him. "I'm so sorry," he was saying. "I think I tripped on something, I didn't mean . . ."

Valens stepped back a pace — force of habit, to maintain a wide distance — and wiped his mouth on the back of his hand. "Perfectly all right," he muttered. "In fact, I'd have been filled with admiration if you'd done it on purpose." But you couldn't have, he didn't add. "That's the stromazone, by the way, what I was telling you about earlier. Nothing like a bit of pain to break the other man's concentration."

Orsea lowered his sword. "Maybe we should . . ."

"What, when you're just starting to get the hang of it?" Valens lunged; a slow, lazy move, slovenly, better signposted than the main road to Mezentia, but Orsea didn't move or parry or do anything. The button hit him in the hollow between the collarbones, the softest and surest target of all on an unarmored man; the blade, being a foil, bent like a bow. "On the other hand," Valens said, moving the sword away, "that's probably enough for one day. If you fence when you're starting to get tired, accidents can happen."

He sucked his lip until his mouth was full of blood, then spat. It was surprising how much it hurt, a little scratch like that. "Are you all right?" Orsea was saying. He nodded.

"Which isn't to say," he said, "that it won't be awkward, so close to the wedding. Don't suppose I'll be getting much kissing done with a mouth full of stitches."

If a man could die of embarrassment . . . Then Orsea would be dead, and no need to murder him. Valens started to smile, but the pain checked him. Snap off the button and stab him through the neck; well. Accidents can happen.

"I really am sorry," Orsea was bleating. "I did tell you, I'm absolute rubbish at fencing."

"You were," Valens amended. "Now you're slightly better at it." He reached out and pulled the damaged foil from Orsea's hand. "Might as well ditch the pair of them," he said. "This one's not worth mending, and the other one on its own's no good. I never liked them much anyway."

Orsea opened his mouth; he didn't need to speak, it was obvious what he'd been going to say. His first impulse had been to offer to pay for a replacement pair, but then he'd remembered that he hadn't got any money, apart from the allowance Valens made him. Buying a man something with his own money would be a uniquely empty gesture. "It can't be fixed, then?" he said instead.

Valens shook his head. "You'd need to re-temper the whole blade," he said. "Forget about it. One less piece of junk to agonize over leaving behind."

(As he said that, he tried to remember if Orsea knew about the evacuation. But yes, he did; he'd been at the staff meeting. Of course, there was no guarantee that he'd been paying attention.)

"Suppose I'd better go and get cleaned up," he said. "I'm supposed to be meeting the princess in about ten minutes."

He walked out of the stable, not noticing whether Orsea followed him or not. As he crossed the yard, he realized he was still holding his foil. He stuck it point downward in a stone urn full of small pink flowers and made his way into the main hall. Ten minutes; he sent someone to find the surgeon, and sat down on a bench.

"Don't ask," he said, when the surgeon arrived.

"I wasn't going to. Was it clean?"

Valens nodded. "Hurry up," he said, "I've got a date with a girl."

"This is going to hurt a lot," the surgeon said, threading his needle. "Don't bother being brave just for my benefit."

"I won't," Valens said.

He managed not to scream, even so (the Duke is always brave, always for his own exclusive benefit). The surgeon snipped off the end of the thread with a little silver knife. "Taking them out won't be much fun either," he said. "But there shouldn't be much of a scar. Be more careful next time."

His clothes were covered in blood, of course. He dragged himself back up to the tower room, changed and slumped down again. He was late for his appointment (whatever the right word was for half an hour of diplomatically mandated flirtation) and the cut was hurting like buggery. Still, it'd be a good way to get the conversation going.

"You've hurt your mouth," she said, as soon as she saw him. It was practically an accusation.

"Yes," he replied. "My own silly fault."

"What happened?"

He shrugged. "I got careless handling the goshawk you gave me, and she swiped me."

She frowned. "You should bathe the cut in distilled wine," she said, "to stop it getting infected. I'm surprised, though. I had hoped I'd trained her better than that."

"Not her fault," Valens said. "I'm just lucky she didn't strike for the eyes."

"That would have been very bad," she said. "You should have her killed."

"Certainly not," Valens said. "She's a very fine hawk."

"Yes. Even so."

He smiled. It hurt to smile at her, not entirely because of the stitches. "Besides," he said, "that'd be a poor way to treat a wedding present."

She frowned again. She seemed to be finding him rather hard

going. "The hawk isn't my wedding present to you," she said. "My official present is two divisions of light cavalry, and my personal gift will be a suit of lightweight scale armor, a riding sword and a warhorse."

"Oh," Valens said. "You've spoiled the surprise."

She looked at him as though he was talking a language she didn't know. "The gifts are specified in the marriage contract," she said. "I'm sorry, I assumed you'd have read it."

"That's right, I remember now." He could still taste blood in his mouth. It made him feel hungry. "Anyway, let's talk about something else. This is the herb garden."

"I know."

"Of course you do. That one over there's mint; that's rosemary, and oregano."

"Basil."

"Sorry, basil, you're quite right. You know your herbs, then."

She nodded. "I read a book about them. We don't use herbs much at home, they're too hard to get hold of. Most of our meat is salted to preserve it, or smoked or dried. As well as common salt, we use wild honey and saltpeter, both of which are fairly abundant in our territory."

"I see," Valens said. "Interesting," he lied. "You must find the meat here pretty bland, in that case."

"Yes," she said.

"Tell me . . ." He racked his brain for something to ask her about. "Tell me what sort of food you eat in your country."

She raised her thin, long eyebrows. "Well," she said, "we are, as you know, a nomadic society. Accordingly, most of our food is provided by our livestock. We eat beef and mutton, cheese and other dairy products, and game, of course."

"How about bread? Vegetables?"

"We gather a wide variety of fruit," she went on, as though he hadn't interrupted, "and wild honey, which we use for a great many things besides preserving. We get a certain amount of flour from the Mezentines in trade, but it's still very much a luxury; for one thing, it's heavy and bulky to carry in any quantity. Nuts and berries —"

"And what you mostly trade with is salt," he broke in. "That's right, isn't it?"

She paused, as though his interruption had made her lose her place. "Salt, some hides and furs," she said. "But salt mostly."

"That's . . ." Valens couldn't think of a suitable word, so he shook his head. "Changing the subject rather," he went on, "there's one thing I'm a bit curious about. How did you actually find out about us, in the first place, I mean? Because, to be honest, I'd never heard of your people, except as a name."

Disapproval all over her face; clearly not diplomatic. "You'd have to ask my uncles," she said. "Similarly, I'd never heard of the Vadani until I was told I was to marry you. However, I trust I have now made amends for my ignorance. I have put a considerable amount of effort into my studies."

"I can see that," Valens said. "And you've done really well."

"Thank you." She hesitated, then said: "Now there are three things I should like to ask you about, if that would be in order."

Valens shrugged. "Go ahead."

"Very well." The way she paused reminded Valens of several experienced public speakers he'd listened to over the years. "If any of these questions strike you as offensive or impertinent, please say so. First, I should like to know why, at your age and in your position, you are still unmarried. Second, given that you are the absolute ruler of this country, why are you allowing your advisers to pressure you into a marriage that clearly holds little attraction for you. Third, I would be most interested to know your reasons for going to war with the Mezentine Republic."

Valens shut his eyes for a moment. What the hell, he thought.

"Tell you what," he said. "Would you like to hear the truth?"

She looked at him.

"Fine. Look, can we sit down for a moment?"

She nodded. "The pain from your injury is fatiguing you," she said.

"Yes." He sat down on the arm of a stone bench. She settled next to him like a bird pitching on a branch.

"The goshawk didn't attack you, did it?" she said.

He laughed. "No. I made that up, sorry. No disrespect intended to your hawk."

Her mouth tightened a little; if we were already married, he thought, I don't suppose I'd be getting off so lightly. "Very well," she said. "What did happen?"

"I got carved up a little by a jealous husband."

"I see. I take it the man in question will be punished."

"Not necessary."

She scowled. "He drew the blood of his ruler," she said firmly. "There can be no clemency in such a case."

"Let's not talk about it," Valens said.

"If you wish. You were about to answer my questions."

"So I was." He looked away, took a deep breath, let it out slowly. "When I was seventeen, I saw a girl. She was a guest here. I fell in love with her, but not long afterward she married someone else. After that — I don't know, there wasn't anything conscious about it. I stopped thinking about her as soon as I heard about her marriage. My father had just died, I had a lot of other things on my mind. I suppose I was glad of an excuse not to have to concern myself with all that stuff."

"That seems plausible enough," she acknowledged. "My second question . . ."

"Why now, you mean? Well, various reasons, really. Mostly, to be frank, we need this alliance. We've — I'm sorry, *I've* got the country into a pretty awful mess, and it looks as though you're our way out. Also . . ." He shivered. "It's been a long time since I was a seventeen-year-old kid. Everybody grows up eventually."

She was looking at him again. "I don't think I understand what you mean," she said.

"Don't you? Well." He smiled. "Not entirely sure I know myself. Let's just say it's taken me a long time to come to terms with it, but I got there in the end."

She shrugged. "And the war?" she said.

"A mistake," he replied. "A very big, bad, stupid mistake. I thought it'd make the Republic leave us alone, but it had the exact opposite effect. Silly me."

The frown was back. "That seems rather unlikely," she said. "We've been studying your career, and the major decisions you've taken since you became duke. Before your intervention at Civitas Eremiae, your political judgment was flawless. I find it hard to believe that such a wise and resourceful man as yourself would have done something so rash and dangerous without a very good reason."

"There you go," Valens said with a grin (which pulled on the stitches and squeezed out a large drop of blood). "It just goes to show, nobody's perfect. There are times when I surprise myself."

She clicked her tongue. "I gather you're not prepared to answer that question," she said.

"No."

"I see." Her voice was cold; polite anger. "Obviously you're entirely at liberty to keep secrets from me, but I trust you understand the nature of the relationship you're proposing to enter into with my family. A marriage alliance is a very serious business, as far as we're concerned."

"I'll bear that in mind," Valens said gravely. "And you don't need to remind me what a serious business this all is." He sucked the blood and spit into the back of his mouth and spat it out onto the grass, then wiped his mouth gingerly on the back of his hand. "Well, this has been quite delightful, but I think we ought to be getting back to the others, or they'll think we've eloped."

As soon as he'd handed her back to her uncles (the bald man wasn't there; off discussing the minutiae of the contract with Carausius, presumably), he hurried back to his tower room and threw up violently into the washbasin. He felt better for it, but not much. That set his lip bleeding again, which didn't help. He sat down at his desk, staring out of the window, then drew a sheet of paper toward him, dipped a pen in ink and started to write.

Valens Valentinianus to Veatriz Sirupati, greetings.

This is stupid. My whole life has gone septic; everything hurts at the slightest pressure.

Isn't love supposed to be the most wonderful thing that can happen to you? I don't think so. I think it's a nasty, miserable thing that brings out the worst in people; if you don't believe me, ask Orsea how he got all those cuts and bruises.

Losing you to Orsea all those years ago was bad enough. Now, apparently, I've got to lose myself as well. I've got no choice: we need the alliance if we're going to stand any sort of chance of scaring off the Mezentines; otherwise we're all dead. Have you met her? No, I don't suppose you have. She's inhuman. She might as well be one of Ziani Vaatzes' mechanical statues. Her loathsome family have taken her apart and made her into an artifact. I'd be desperately sorry for her if I thought she could still feel anything. Anyway, that's what I've got to marry. Count yourself lucky; you got an idiot who goes around wrecking everything he touches and then tearing himself to bits out of guilt. I'm getting a machine. What the hell did either of us ever do to deserve this?

When my father died, I knew my life was over too. I realized I could never be myself again. To begin with, I tried to be him, but I couldn't do it. Strange how sometimes you only get to know someone once they're not there anymore. I couldn't be him because I can't bring myself to be deliberately stupid. He was a stupid man. Instead, I became what he should have been. The best joke about me is that everything I hate doing I do really well. At least I could be proud of what I'd done for this country. I kept the peace, nobody was starving, people could leave their houses and families in the morning and be fairly sure they'd still be there when they came back at night. Then Orsea started his war, you were in danger and I threw it all away.

I have to have something to live for. It used to be your letters. Now you don't write to me anymore, and I'm going to be married to that thing. I've been thinking about my options. I thought about getting up very early one morning, taking a horse from the stable and riding until I reached somewhere nobody's ever heard of me. I wish it was that simple.

I can't do it, Veatriz. My father used to say, there's no such word as can't. If you can't do it, all it means is you aren't trying hard enough. That used to make me so angry — quiet, speechless-with-resentment anger — that I'd find a way to do any damn thing, just so as not to give him the satisfaction of being disappointed in me — and then he'd nod and say, told you so, I knew you could do it if you just applied yourself. I know that deep down he believed I wasn't up to the job of running this country. I showed him, didn't I? But that doesn't work anymore. I can't make myself do what I've got to do just so I can score points off my stupid, dead father. Maybe he was right all along. Take away the hate I used to feel for him, and what've I got left?

I think love and hate are really the same thing. They're what you feel when someone matters more to you than anything else; more than yourself, even. I know you can love someone and hate them at the same time. My father was always the most important person in my life. I loved him and hated him, and there wasn't room for anybody or anything else. Then he cheated by dying. He left before I could get the better of him, and I've been trapped by his death ever since. I think what's shaped my life is the fact that I lost you and him so close together. Now I think about it, I realize I'm still the seventeen-year-old boy whose father died unexpectedly. I'm pinned to that moment, like a man whose horse has fallen on him.

Well, that's me about finished. For the first time since he died I don't know what to say, I don't know what to do. I shall be very grateful indeed for any suggestions.

He put the pen back in the inkwell, knowing that if he started to read what he'd just written, he'd tear it up and burn the pieces.

Instead, he folded the paper up small into a packet, melted wax and sealed it, tucked it up his sleeve and left the room.

It took him a long time to find the person he needed: a woman in a red dress, who curtseyed very politely, offered him some mead spiced with cinnamon and pepper (he refused) and asked him to sit down.

"It's been quite a while since you needed me," she said. "I was beginning to think —"

"Please," he interrupted, "don't waste my time or try my patience. You're to deliver this to her personally when she's alone. I suggest you do exactly as I say, because if you don't I'll have you killed. You know me well enough to realize I don't make empty threats."

She blinked. "I see," she said. "Can I refuse?"

"I'm afraid not, no."

"Very well then." She took a deep breath, and smiled. "Can we talk about money now, please?"

"A hundred silver thalers when you come back and tell me you've delivered it," Valens said. "All right?"

She thought about that for a moment. "That'll be fine," she said. "Also, I'd quite like a border pass, open, no dates, and there's a silly misunderstanding about an excise license which I'd like sorted out, if that's no trouble."

Valens sighed. "It's a point of honor with you people, isn't it? Taking a mile."

She laughed. "My mother told me, never accept anything you're offered, always insist on one little thing more. Of course, I'm in no position to bargain."

"Deal," Valens said. "If you can get it done today, there'll be an extra fifty thalers."

"So sorry." She shook her head. "Can't be done. Not even for fifty thalers. I have to apply to the senior lady-in-waiting for an appointment. A bribe will get me one, but she always makes me wait a full day. If I insist on seeing the Duchess today, it'd look suspicious, the lady-in-waiting will get frightened and tell Duke Orsea, and — well, I don't need to tell you what that'd lead to."

Valens frowned. "Double the bribe," he suggested. "I'll pay."

"That'd just make things worse," she replied sadly. "There's a very strict protocol about bribing court officers. If you mess about with it, there'll be trouble. And please don't tell me how to conduct my business. I happen to be very good at it."

Valens held up his hands. "Heaven forbid," he said. "Thanks. I'll see myself out."

After leaving her he walked down through the town to the river. People stopped and stared but nobody spoke to him or came near him. It was well known in Civitas Vadanis that when the Duke came into town on his own, without guards or secretaries, he wanted to be left alone. It was, of course, a tribute to the way he ran his country that he could walk about the city on his own whenever he wanted to. Like all the best privileges, of course, it had to be used sparingly.

He stopped at a saddler's stall down by the west gate; a rather fine set of jesses and a hood, in dark tan leather, embossed with ivy leaves. A nice, considerate present for his wife-to-be, whose name he couldn't pronounce even if he could remember it. The stallholder noticed him looking at them and moved across.

"How much?" he asked.

"One thaler the set," the stallholder replied. "Genuine Mezentine."

That was a lie, of course; about the only thing the Mezentines didn't make was falconry accessories. "You mean Cure Doce," Valens said.

"All right, genuine Cure Doce. You want them, or what?"

Valens nodded, looked round for someone who wasn't there. He frowned, and felt in his pockets, which were, of course, empty.

"No money," he said.

The stallholder looked at him. "Is that right?"

"It's all right," Valens said. "Hold on to them for me, I'll send someone."

"Will you now?"

A little spurt of anger fired in Valens' mind. "You don't know who I am."

The corners of the stallholder's mouth tightened a little. "That's very true, I don't."

"Forget it." Valens walked away. He could feel the stallholder's eyes on the back of his head. Of course, in a few weeks that man would be out of business for good, on the decision of his duke, who he hadn't even recognized. There was something wrong with the way the world was run, Valens thought. He had half a mind to write to somebody about it.

Four stalls down from the saddler there was a cutler. As Valens passed, the man looked up and saw him; his eyes seemed to double in size and his mouth dropped open. He gave the boy standing next to him a vicious nudge in the ribs, and pointed with his chin. The boy grunted and carried on polishing something.

Oh well, Valens thought. "Good morning," he said.

The cutler seemed to flicker, like a candle-flame in a draft. "Your majesty," he said. "Yes, what beautiful weather, for the time of year."

Depends on your idea of beauty, Valens thought. Nothing on the man's stall had caught his eye, but he was snared now, as though he'd put his foot in a wire. He stepped up to the cutler's table and looked round for something to admire.

There was a hanger; a plain thing, two feet of curved blade, lightly and crudely fullered, with a brass knuckle-bow and back-strap and a stagshorn grip. Valens picked it up, one hand on the hilt, the other near the tip, and flexed the blade. It felt adequate.

"Nice piece," he exaggerated.

"Thank you," the cutler said. "Genuine Mezentine, of course. You can see the armory mark there on the ricasso."

Sure enough, someone had scratched a little animal on the squared-off section just below the hilt. Unfortunately, the Mezentine stamp was a lion, and the scratched mark was quite definitely a cow. "You're right," Valens said, "so it is." He sighed. It was good, sturdy, munitions-grade stuff, functional enough to cut briars with. One of the assistant huntsmen would be pleased to have it.

"How much will you take for it?" he asked.

The cutler swelled like a bullfrog. "Oh no, I couldn't," he said. "Please, take it. As a mark of . . ."

He didn't seem able to make up his mind what it was a mark of, but the general idea was clear enough. "Don't be silly, man," Valens said, "you're a businessman, not the poor relief." He estimated how much it was really worth, then doubled it. "Two thalers."

"No, really." The man was close to tears. "I'd be honored if you'd take it." He hesitated, then lowered his voice. "My eldest son was at Cynosoura," he said. "It'd be for him."

"Right," Valens said, trying to remember what the hell had happened at Cynosoura. "Well, in that case, I'll be pleased to have it. Thank you."

"Thank *you*," the cutler said. "There's a scabbard with it, of course." He looked round; there were no scabbards of any kind to be seen anywhere. "Thraso, you idiot, where's the scabbard for this hanger, it was here just now . . ." He nudged the boy again, who scowled at Valens and crawled under the table. "I'm really sorry about this," the cutler said, "it's my son, he moves things when my back's turned, and I never know — ah, here we are." He pulled a sad-looking scabbard out of a wooden box by his feet; softwood with thin black leather pasted on, by the look of it. "I'll just find some silk to wrap it in, please bear with me a moment."

"That's fine, really," Valens said, "please don't bother." He smiled as best he could. "I only live just up the hill there, so I haven't got far to go."

The cutler stared at him for a moment, then burst out laughing, as though that was the funniest thing he'd ever heard in his life. "Of course, that's right," he said, and slid the hanger into the scabbard. It stuck, about halfway down, and had to be taken out and put back in again. Valens managed not to notice. "There you are, then, your majesty, and I hope it brings you all the good luck in the world. Thank you," he added, just in case there was still any doubt about the matter.

"Thank *you*," Valens replied, and fled.

All the good luck in the world, he thought, as he walked back up the hill. A fine example of the lesser irony there; because of who he was, he couldn't buy what he wanted but he was obliged to accept a free gift he had no real use for. (That made him think about Veatriz and the other girl, the one whose name escaped him.) He carried the hanger low at his left side, hoping nobody would see him with it.

"Where did you get to?" Carausius demanded, pouncing on him as he crossed the courtyard in front of the Great Hall. "You were supposed to be meeting the uncles to talk about the marriage settlement."

Valens frowned. Not in the mood. "You covered for me."

"Yes, of course, but that's not the point. I could tell they weren't happy."

Valens stopped. "It's obvious, surely. I'm a young man of great sensibility, very much in love. The last thing I want to talk about is crass financial settlements. Right?"

Carausius sighed audibly. "So you went shopping instead."

"What? Oh, this." He glanced down at the object in his left hand, as though wondering how it had got there. "That reminds me. What happened at Cynosoura?"

"Where?"

"Cynosoura. Look it up. I want a detailed account on my desk in half an hour."

Carausius gave him his business nod, meaning that it would, of course, be done. "Where are you going now?" he said. "Only there's a reception . . ."

"I know, in the knot garden," he replied, remembering. "Forty minutes."

"It starts in a quarter of an hour."

"Then I'll be late. Cynosoura," he repeated, and walked away.

To the stables. Nobody about at this time of day. He walked in, shut the door firmly and looked around for something substantial to bash on. Just the thing: there was a solid oak mounting-block. He remembered it from childhood; he'd got in trouble when he was eight for hacking chunks out of it with a billhook he'd liberated from the groom's shed. Offhand he couldn't remember why he'd done that, but no doubt he'd had his reasons.

In the corner was a good, sturdy manger. He lifted the block onto it and tested it with his hand to make sure it wouldn't wobble about or fall down. Then he drew the hanger, took a step forward and slashed at the block as hard as he could. The blade bit in a good inch and vibrated like a hooked fish thrashing on the end of a line. The point where the knuckle-bow met the pommel pinched his little finger. He had to lift the block down again and put his foot on it before he could get the blade out, but when he held it up to the light it was still perfectly straight, and the cutting edge wasn't chipped or curled. Not bad, at that.

He put the block back on the manger, breathed in, and smacked the flat of the blade viciously against the thick oak six times, three smacks on each side. That was the proper way to proof a sword-blade, preferably someone else's. There was now a red blood-blister on the side of his little finger, but the hanger had survived more or less intact; blade still straight, hilt still in one piece, no cracks in the brazed joints, no rattle of loosened parts when he shook it. That was really quite impressive, for cheap local work. Once more for luck; he stepped back and took another almighty heave at the block — no fencing, just the desire to damage something, the block or the sword, not bothered which. The cut went in properly on the slant, gouging out a fat chip of wood from the edge. As the shock ran up his arm and tweaked his tendons, it occurred to him to imagine that the cut had been against bone rather than wood, and he winced. Of course it was a hunting sword, not a weapon of war; even so.

Got myself a bargain there, then, he told himself; also, all the good luck in the world. Genuine Mezentine. Doesn't anybody but me remember we're at war with the fucking Mezentines?

The report was there on his desk when he got back to the tower room, needless to say. Nothing much had happened at Cynosoura, which turned out to be a very small village in the northern mountains. A routine cavalry patrol consisting of a platoon of the Seventeenth Regiment had stumbled across a Cure Hardy raiding party. Recognizing that they were outnumbered and in no fit state to engage, they'd withdrawn and raised the alarm, whereupon Duke Valens and two squadrons of the Nineteenth had ridden out (I remember now), engaged and defeated the enemy and captured their leader, one Skeddanlothi, who provided the Duke with valuable intelligence about the Cure Hardy before dying under interrogation. As for the encounter at Cynosoura, there was only one casualty, a cavalry trooper shot in the back at extreme range as the patrol was withdrawing; he died later, of gangrene.

Valens read the report, nodded, and left it on the side of his desk for filing. He took the hanger out of its scabbard and wiped it on his sleeve — oak sap leaves a blue stain on steel, unless it's cleaned promptly — before sheathing it and propping it up in the corner of the room. Then he went to the reception to be polite to the Cure Hardy.

11

Ziani Vaatzes, returning to Civitas Vadanis at the head of his wagon train after the successful decommissioning of the silver mines, encountered a heavily laden cart going the other way on the northeast road. Because the road was narrow and deeply rutted, with dry-stone walls on either side, the driver of the cart tried to pull into a gateway to let Ziani's convoy pass. In doing so, unfortunately, he ran his offside front into the stone gatepost, knocking off the wheel and swinging his cart through ninety degrees, so that it completely blocked the road.

Ziani sighed. He was tired of sleeping in the bed of a wagon on top of a sharp-cornered packing case, and he wanted to get back to the place that he was starting to think of, in stray unguarded moments, as home. He told his driver to stop, and slid off the box onto the ground, nearly turning his ankle over as he stepped on the ridge of a rut.

"All right," he called out, "hold it there. Leave it to us, we'll have you out of there."

The driver of the wrecked cart looked down at him with a sad expression on his face.

"Fuck it," he said. "I'm on a bonus if I get this lot delivered on time."

"You might still make it if you shut up and leave it to us," Ziani said. "This is your lucky day. I've got sappers, engineers and blacksmiths, with all the kit."

The carter noticed him for the first time, stared, then grinned. "You're the Duke's Mezentine, right?"

"Yes."

"The engineer, right?"

"Yes."

The grin spread. "In that case, you crack on."

It turned out, of course, to be considerably worse than it looked. The cart wasn't just missing a wheel, it was also comprehensively wedged into the gateway. Daurenja, who'd sprung down off his wagon like a panther as soon as the swearing started and crawled right under the damaged cart, re-emerged with the cheerful news that the axle had splintered and two leaves of the spring had snapped. He suggested unshipping the long-handled sledgehammers and smashing the cart up into small pieces; that would get the road clear, and the carter would be able to claim the cost of a new cart from the war department.

"That's no bloody good," the carter snapped. Something about Daurenja seemed to bother him quite a lot. Perhaps it was the ponytail, which Daurenja had adopted while he was working in the mines; probably not. "It's not my cart, it's the Duke's, I can't take responsibility. Besides, this lot is urgent supplies. I got a special through-pass. You can see it if you don't believe me."

"It's all right," Ziani interrupted, "nobody's going to smash up your cart." He glanced round at the mess, looking for inspiration to help him reach a quick decision. "We'll have to take the gatepost down, and the wall," he said. "Meanwhile, Daurenja, I want you to take some of the men, get the busted axle off; see if you can fix it with rawhide or letting in a splice or something; if not, use your imagination and think of something. You," he went on, turning his head, "I can't remember your name offhand. Unload the portable forge, the one with the double-action bellows, get it set up and lay in a fire. Also, I'll want the two-hundredweight anvil and whoever's best at forge-welds."

"Can't weld the busted spring, you'll wreck the temper," someone muttered. Ziani looked to see who it was, but someone else's head was in the way. "You'd have to anneal the whole unit and re-temper it."

"I know," he said. "And that's what we're going to do, so I'll need a water barrel or something like that for a slack tub. I'm assuming there's no oil left, so you'll have to quench in water and go nice and steady. And if anybody wants to show his ignorance by saying you can't butt-weld hardening steel, now's his chance. No? Fine, carry on." He nodded to the carter. "Let's leave them to it," he said. "Let me buy you a drink. So happens we've got a couple of bottles of the good stuff left."

The carter had no objection to that. Ziani retrieved the bottle and led him well away from the noise of the work. "Sorry about all this," he said, sitting on the wall and cutting the bottle's pitch seal with his knife.

"That's all right," the carter said. "Just look where you're going next time."

Ziani passed him the bottle. "So," he said, "what've you got there that's so important?"

The carter glugged five mouthfuls, then passed the bottle back. "Sulfur," he said.

"Sulfur," Ziani repeated. "Seems an odd thing for the government to want shifted in a hurry. Where are you taking it?"

"Me," the carter replied, "as far as the Eremian border. Someone else is taking it on from there, and bloody good luck."

"Quite." Ziani handed the bottle back untasted. "Not my idea of a quiet life, smuggling supplies into occupied territory. Specially if it's something useless, like sulfur. I mean, you'd feel such a fool if the Mezentines got you, wasting your life for something that's no good to anybody."

The carter pulled a face. "I just drive the wagon," he said. "No business of mine what the stuff's for."

"That's right," Ziani agreed. "Trouble is, you've got me curious now. Tell you what; let's have a look at that pass of yours. It might have the name of the bloke this lot's going to."

The carter glowered at him. "Why would I want to show you that?"

Ziani smiled pleasantly. "Because I'm asking you," he said, "and my men have got your cart in bits all over the road. Of course, if you'd like to put it back together again on your own . . ."

The carter must have seen the merit in that line of argument, because he fished down the front of his shirt and pulled out a folded square of paper. Ziani took it and his eye slid down the recitals until a name snagged his attention.

"Miel Ducas," he said aloud. "Small world."

The hardest part, unexpectedly enough, turned out to be getting the cart unjammed. Only once the gatepost and the wall had come down was it possible to see what was really holding it; both nearside wheels, wedged deep in a rut. Because of the angle the cart stood at, there was no chance of using Ziani's wagon teams to pull it free, which meant they had to dig it out. That proved to be no fun at all. Whoever had built the road, a very long time ago, had laid a solid foundation of rubble and stones, over which two feet of mud had built up over the years. The ruts cut through the mud into the stone, and that was what was binding the wheels. Because the cart was in the way, there was no room to swing a sledge to drive in the crowbar. One of the men had his wrist broken by a careless hammer-blow, whereupon the rest of them declared they'd had enough and reminded Ziani of the basically sound idea of smashing the cart up into little bits. He had to shout to make them calm down. After that, nothing got done for a long time. The carter got hold of the other bottle while Ziani's attention was distracted, and went away somewhere. One of those days.

"All right." Ziani pulled himself together. He was, after all, in charge, though he really didn't want to be. "This is what we're going to do. Daurenja, I want you to . . ." He looked round. He'd become so used to the thin man hovering a few inches away that he was surprised to find he wasn't there. Instead, he was on his knees under the cart, peering up at something. "Daurenja," he repeated, "leave that, for crying out loud, I want you to —"

"Sorry." Daurenja seemed to bounce upright, a movement that no ordinary human being should have been capable of making. "I was just wondering, though."

Ziani sighed. "What?"

"This is probably stupid," Daurenja said, "but why did you decide against lifting the cart up out of the ruts, rather than excavating?"

It was one of those questions that makes your head hurt at the best of times. "What are you talking about?"

"Well," Daurenja said, "I was just looking at the cart chassis, and I can't see why we can't just raise it on levers and keep putting stone blocks underneath until we've lifted it up out of the rut. Presumably you considered that and saw why it wouldn't work. I guessed it was because there wasn't anything in the chassis strong enough to take the strain of levering, which was why I was looking at the spring mountings, which I thought looked plenty strong enough, but —"

"Fine," Ziani said, "let's try that."

It worked. They raised the cart on crowbars, piled stones from the broken-up wall under it and floated it over the ruts, which they then filled with gatepost debris. The spliced axle and welded spring went back in without a hitch. It couldn't have gone more smoothly if they'd been practicing it for months.

"There you go," Ziani said to the carter, as he staggered across to inspect his perfectly refurbished cart. "Piece of cake. Sorry for the inconvenience."

"Took your time, didn't you?" the carter replied. It took him several goes to get up onto the box. "If I miss my transfer at the border . . ."

"Drive fast," Ziani advised him. "Don't worry about the road surface, you'll make it. A few bumps and jiggles never hurt anybody."

The carter gathered his reins, whipped on the horses and

set off at a rather wild trot. A minute or so later, once he'd left the Mezentine and his convoy well behind, he began to wonder whether the second bottle had been such a good idea after all. But then he hadn't expected that they'd be able to fix the cart so quickly, or at all. So much, he thought, for the Duke's famous Mezentine engineer. Sure, he was good at shouting and ordering people about, but it hadn't been him who sorted it in the end. It was that long, thin, evil-looking bugger with the flat nose, and he was no Mezentine. He frowned; then a jolt shot him three inches into the air, and when he landed his teeth slammed together, and he whimpered. Maybe it'd be a good idea to slow down a little.

Screw the Mezentine, he thought. And anyway, aren't we supposed to be at war with those buggers? So, really smart, having one of them in the government, or whatever. The Duke was all right, but he was too trusting. The creep was probably a spy, or a saboteur, and he'd seemed very interested in the cargo. The carter thought about that, as his horses slowed to an amble. He wasn't sure who bothered him more, the Mezentine with his black face and his loud mouth, or the thin, snake-faced one with the ponytail. Nasty pieces of work, both of them, and now he was going to be late and lose his bonus.

The providence that looks after honest working men was there for him, however, and brought him to the border with a good hour to spare. They grumbled at him, claiming he'd kept them waiting and cost them money, but he couldn't be bothered to get into an argument about it. They gave him his docket, which was what he needed to get paid, shifted the barrels from his cart to theirs, and trundled away, until the dust swallowed them. He dismissed them from his mind and went for a drink.

The team who'd undertaken to carry the sulfur from the border into Eremia consisted of an old man and his twelve-year-old grandson. Before the war they'd been held in low esteem by the authorities on both sides of the border, who'd accused them of smuggling and all manner of bad things. Now they were patriotic heroes, which they didn't mind, since heroism paid slightly more, and the risks were roughly the same. The work was no different, and they were good at it. The thing to remember, the old man never seemed to tire of saying, is to stay off the skyline and go nice and steady; that way, you get to see the bogies long before they see you. If his grandson had any views on the subject he kept them to himself.

They reached the Unswerving Loyalty at noon on the third day of their journey; exactly on time. As usual, the place was so quiet it appeared to have been abandoned. The old man drove his cart into the stable, untacked the horse, fed and watered it and went to find himself a drink. The boy stayed with the cart as he'd been told. He felt, not for the first time, that this was both unnecessary and unjust. Nobody was going to steal the barrels, because there wasn't anybody here, and if he was old enough to drive the cart and see to the horse, he was old enough to drink beer. He'd argued this case on several occasions with no little passion, but his grandfather never seemed to be listening.

He sat still and quiet on the box for a minute or so, until he was sure the old fool wasn't coming back; then he jumped down, took out his penknife and started carving his initials into one of the doorposts. He was proud of his initials; a Vadani border guard had taught him how to write them, when they'd been arrested and there was nothing to do for hours. The L was easy to carve, just straight lines, but the S was a challenge, and he was never quite sure which way round the curves were meant to go. One of these days he'd meet another educated man and ask him, just to make sure. He was proud of his knife, too; it had a hooked blade and a stagshorn handle, and there was a mark on it that meant it was genuine Mezentine.

He got the L done and was scoring the outlines of the S when he heard a footstep behind him. Quickly he dropped the knife onto the ground and scuffed straw over it with his foot, at the same time leaning against the gatepost to cover up his work.

"It's all right," a man's voice said. "I used to do that when I was your age."

"Do what?" the boy said warily.

"Carve my initials on things." The man was tall; quite old, over thirty; his face was all messed up with a scar. "Trees, mostly. If you cut your initials into a tree, they get wider as the bark grows. Bet you didn't know that."

The boy frowned, suspecting a trap. "No, I didn't," he said. "What do you want?"

The man walked past him. He was looking at the cart, but he didn't look much like the sort of man who usually took an interest in the stuff they carried. "Is that my sulfur you've got there?" he asked.

"Don't know," the boy replied. He bent down, picked up his knife and put it away. A beam of light shone through a hole in the roof, sparkling off specks of floating dust. The man was climbing up into the cart. Duty scuffled with discretion in the boy's mind. "You can't go up there," he said.

The man laughed. "It's all right," he said, "this lot's meant for me, I've been waiting for it. Here," he added, reaching in his pocket and taking out a coin, "have a drink on me, somewhere else."

The coin spun in the air, and the boy caught it one-handed. It was, of course, an obvious bribe, implying that the man had no business being there. On the other hand, it was a silver quarter-thaler. The boy clamped his hand firmly around it and fled.

Miel counted the barrels. Six. He stooped, put his arms around one of them, bent his knees and lifted. Two hundredweight at least. Of course, he had no idea whether it'd be enough, since he didn't know what Framain and his daughter wanted the stuff for. None of his business, anyway. He had owed them a debt, which he could now discharge honorably, as the Ducas should, and that'd be that. Once it was delivered, the rest of his life would be his own.

Sulfur, he thought. No earthly good to anybody, surely.

He looked round for the boy, then remembered he'd paid him to go away. No matter. He got down, left the stable and went back to the tap room.

There he saw an old man, presumably the carter. He was holding a big mug of beer, using both hands. Miel sat down opposite him and waited until he'd taken a drink.

"Is that your wagon outside?" he said.

The old man looked at him. "Who's asking?"

"My name's Miel Ducas," Miel replied, "which is what it says on your delivery note."

The old man grounded his mug, carefully, so as not to spill any. "Ah," he said.

Miel smiled. "Let me buy you another of those," he said.

"No thanks. This'll do me. I got a long drive ahead of me, I need a clear head."

"Talking of which." Miel edged a little closer. "Are you in any hurry to get anywhere? I need someone to deliver that lot for me, and nobody around here seems to have a cart for hire. It's not far," he added, "five days there and back. Ten thalers."

The old man thought about that. "All right," he said. "Give me a couple of hours to catch my breath, mind."

"Fine. I'll go and get my things together. I'll meet you back in the stable."

Just to be on the safe side, he bought provisions for seven days. Finding the inn from Framain's hidden combe hadn't been a problem; all he'd had to do was keep his eyes fixed on the mountain. The return journey, by contrast, called for a higher level of navigational skill than he had any reason to believe he possessed. He'd taken note of landmarks along the way, of course, but by the very nature of the country those were few and far between. No wonder the Mezentines had left this region well alone. The map Jarnac had given him was pure fiction, needless to say. The only halfway accurate maps of these parts had been the old estate plans compiled over the years by the Ducas bailiffs, stored in the map room at the estate office at the Ducas country house. They were all ashes now. As the cart lumbered out of the inn courtyard on a half-remembered bearing into the dust and rocks of his birthright, Miel wondered, not for the first time, what the hell he thought he was playing at.

"Do you know this country at all?" he asked the old man hopefully.

"No," the old man replied. "Not once you're past the Loyalty. Nobody lives there," he explained, reasonably enough. Miel stirred uncomfortably and looked across at the boy. He was cutting bits off a piece of old frayed rope with his knife, and humming something under his breath.

"Not to worry," Miel said. "I know the way."

Two days' ride southeast of Sharra Top; true, but lacking in precision. There had been a road; he remembered that, but of course he'd had to be clever, and he'd abandoned it on the second day of his ride from the hidden combe. Well, it had always been a fool's errand. If he rode southeast for two days into the bleak, featureless moor and then gave up, turned round and headed back to the Unswerving Loyalty, would the Ducas honor be satisfied on the grounds that he'd done his best? No, but never mind.

After a long, silent day they stopped nowhere in particular. The boy jumped down, unharnessed and hobbled the horse. The old man curled up on the box like a dog and went to sleep. The boy crawled under the cart. Miel climbed down, propped his back against a cartwheel, and closed his eyes. He was weary and sore from the incessant jolting of the cart, but he'd dozed off too often during the day to be able to fall asleep. A fox barked once or twice in the distance. He tried to remember all he could about his previous visit to Framain's house, but the most vivid images had no bearing on matters of navigation. So, unwillingly, he thought about other things.

The war: well, as far as he was concerned, it was over. He had no idea how many of his men were still alive, or whether they were still trying to fight the Mezentines. It didn't really matter. According to Jarnac, Duke Valens had withdrawn his support, and without help from the Vadani, it was pointless going on. If the war was effectively over, where did that leave him? Interesting question. Under other circumstances, he'd already be in Civitas Vadanis, with Orsea, doing what little he could as a leader of the Eremian government in exile. But Orsea didn't want him. On that score he'd been left in no doubt whatever. Orsea had known for some time that he was still alive, but he hadn't recalled him, or dropped the charges against him, or written him a single letter. He'd asked Jarnac, back at the inn, if Orsea had said anything about him. Jarnac had looked unhappy and tried to change the subject, until Miel forced him to admit that Orsea hadn't mentioned him once.

That shouldn't have been a surprise. Orsea and his wretched, all-destroying sense of right and wrong, his fatal compulsion to try and do the right thing; and, needless to say, he applied the same rules to those closest to him. Apparently he was convinced that Miel had betrayed him, and therefore he could never forgive him. He'd recognize, of course, that this meant wasting an ally, a valuable one, though he said so himself; it meant that, because Miel was organizing the resistance, Orsea could have nothing to do with it. That hadn't passed unnoticed; why, his men had asked him over and over again, isn't the Duke out here with us; why hasn't he even sent us a message of encouragement? Men who'd asked him that question and received the inevitably vague and unsatisfactory replies he'd managed to cobble together generally deserted a day or so later. Why fight for their country if their country had no use for them? Poor Orsea, he thought, still trying to do the right thing.

Which left him, the Ducas, with no master to serve, no work to do, no purpose . . . That was an extraordinary concept. The Ducas can't exist without duty, just as a flame can't burn without air. Take it away and you're left with a man — thirty-odd, moderately bright but with no skills or abilities relevant to his own survival; thinner, permanently cured of any dependence on his customary affluence and luxury, an adequate rider, swordsman and falconer, just about capable of boiling an egg. Worse specimens of humanity managed to stay alive and make some sort of living, but why would anybody bother to live without a function? The Ducas without duty was no more than a mechanism for turning food into shit and water into piss, and a cow or a pig could do that just as well, if not better.

But here I am, he reflected; here I am, sitting beside a cart in the middle of a desert I used to own, in company with an old man, a boy and a quantity of powdered sulfur, trying to find a man called Framain and his daughter. I owe my life to Framain, who found me and pulled me out of a bog. The sulfur is my way of repaying the debt. But I wouldn't have been alive to contract that debt if the scavengers hadn't found me after the battle, and I repaid them by killing two of them and stealing their only horse. Ah, but they were going to sell me to the Mezentines, so that makes it all right. Except that it doesn't. I was theirs to sell, and I stole myself from them; and now it's too late to make it up to them, because Jarnac slaughtered them for daring to lay violent hands on the Ducas. It's a funny old world.

At one point he slid into a doze; woke up some time later to find it was still dark, and he had a crick in his neck. The problem, however, had managed to solve itself while he'd been asleep. Silly, really; it was as plain as the nose on his face. If he was no longer the Ducas, then nothing he did mattered anymore. There were no more rules. When he'd fallen asleep he'd still been an Eremian nobleman and the slave of duty, but he'd woken up a free man, worthless and burdened by no obligations of any kind.

The first thing he did was feel in his pocket and count his money. Twenty-seven Vadani thalers, not counting what he owed the old man and the boy for the cart-ride. Hardly a fortune, but most people in the world start off their lives with considerably less. He also owned a stolen horse (but that was back at the Unswerving Loyalty; he doubted whether he'd ever see it again), some clothes, two boots and a hanger. Not entirely without value, therefore; not, at least, until someone crept up and robbed him in his sleep.

For no reason, he remembered the book he'd glanced at, back in Framain's house. A technical manual of some kind; lots of different formulae for mixing up paint.

His brief nap might have played hell with his neck, but apparently it had done wonders for his brain. Paint recipes; the locked barn, and other buildings with chimneys, all hidden away in a dip in the ground where nobody would think of looking. Eremia had fallen to the Mezentines, but Framain hardly seemed to have registered the change of management. Miel laughed out loud, and into his mind drifted a memory of the pantry at the Ducas house in Civitas Eremiae, at any time before the siege and sack. Also the table in the main hall, set for a formal dinner, or any of the bedrooms that had a window-seat, which would always be decorated with a vase of fresh flowers. Every morning, someone had got up before dawn with a basket and walked down to the market to buy them — no, not a basket, there were twenty-seven windows facing the inner courtyard, they must've had to take a wheelbarrow, or a small cart, to shift all those flowers. He tried to call to mind the occasions on which he'd noticed the flowers in his house, and managed to think of four. The rest of the time they'd been there — they must have been, because it was a rule of the house — but presumably nobody had noticed them, once the chambermaid had pulled the dead stalks out of the vase and replaced them with the fresh ones. So much duty done, so little notice taken.

Never mind; he was through with all that now, and at least he had an idea what Framain and his daughter were up to in their secret lair, and why they needed sulfur. The only annoyances were that it had taken him so long to figure it out, and that he'd never find the place again and have the satisfaction of knowing he'd been right.

But if he did manage to find them . . . Well, he had power over them, simply by virtue of having guessed their secret. It was a thing of value in itself; quite possibly valuable enough to the Mezentines to buy him his life, if he chose to sell it to them, as the scavengers had proposed selling him. Alternatively . . . Well, he was a tolerably quick learner, and he had nothing better to do.

As he turned the possibility over in his mind, he became aware of someone standing over him. He lifted his head and opened his eyes. Not yet broad daylight, but enough to see the old man by.

"Soon as you're ready," he said.

"I'm ready," Miel replied.

"Fine." The old man didn't move. "Which way?"

Miel grinned. "Look for smoke," he said.

It was as though he'd told the old man to keep a sharp eye out for dragons. "Why?" he said. "Nobody lives here."

Miel shook his head. "Yes they do," he said. "And every morning they light a big furnace. My guess is they burn peat mostly, because it costs them money to bring in charcoal, so they save it for special occasions. I'm guessing that you can't see the smoke from Sharra; that's why they live where they do. But we're a day closer, so we're in with a chance."

The old man looked rather taken aback, and Miel could sympathize; something of a shock to the system to realize that you've been dragged out into the middle of nowhere on the whim of a lunatic. But he was under no obligation to consider their feelings, as the Ducas would have been. He was paying them to do as they were told, and that was all there was to it.

It was the boy who saw the smoke. At first, he muttered the news to the old man, who assumed he was making it up and ignored him. It was probably only pique at not being believed that induced him to mention it out loud. What mattered was that he was right. Just the faintest smeared line, like a woman's smudged eyeliner. Miel looked at it for a moment, then grinned.

"That's the place," he said.

As they got closer, Miel started to recognize things that had imprinted on his mind the first time: a shallow, dusty pit scraped out of the heather by sheep rubbing their necks against a large stone; a thorn tree wrenched sideways by the wind, its roots standing out of the soil on one side like fingers; a brown pool in a dip fringed with bog cotton; a single wooden post, gray with age, leaning at an angle, tufts of wool lodged in the splinters of its gaping grain. For some reason, all these were as familiar as sights he'd seen since childhood but somehow depressing, so that he felt like a man returning to a home he'd been glad to leave, many years earlier.

When they were half a mile from the smoke, it began to rain. It was no more than a few fat wet drops, but the wind slapped them into his face so that his eyes fogged as though he was crying, and he had to keep wiping them with his fingers. The old man pulled his collar round his face and shrank back into his coat — he reminded Miel of an animal in a field, stoically miserable. The boy scrabbled about with some old, bad-smelling sacks and crawled under them. They, of course, would be turning round and going back this way as soon as the barrels had been unloaded. They'd have the rain on their backs, if it settled in, tapping them on the shoulder like an annoying acquaintance you'd prefer to ignore.

Just like last time, the house came as a complete surprise, standing up out of the combe as though the creaking of the wagon had startled it. Miel smiled. This time, he had a fair idea what the man and his daughter were so busy with that strangers could creep up on them without them noticing. He told the old man to pull up outside the barn and wait, then jumped down and ran up the broad stone steps. The door was shut but not padlocked; he thumbed the latch and walked in.

Framain was standing on the other side of a long, massive plank bench, covered with jars, pestles, trays, pots and small metal tools. For a moment he froze, a stunned look on his face, as though Miel had walked straight through the wall instead of the door.

"You again," he said.

"I've brought your sulfur," Miel said quickly.

Framain stared at him. Not anger, or fear, hatred or suspicion. Horror. "What do you know about sulfur?" he said quietly.

"What's he doing here?" Miel hadn't noticed the girl, in the shadows at the back of the barn. She came forward like an animal preparing to defend her young from a predator, and Miel had taken a step back before he realized he'd done it.

"The sulfur you asked for," he said to her. "I brought it, just like I said I would."

Framain didn't say anything, but the silence wasn't hard to interpret. Now it was the girl's turn to look horrified.

"You brought it," she repeated.

"Yes." Miel grinned. Too late now to worry about being popular. "Not the three cartloads you asked for, I'm afraid, because there wasn't that much to be had, but there ought to be enough to be going on with."

"You asked him to get us sulfur?" Framain said.

"I didn't think he'd actually . . ."

Just a slight adjustment of his shoulders, but Framain conveyed with exquisite precision the information that as far as he was concerned, his daughter no longer existed. "That was very kind of you," he said, his eyes fixed, as far as Miel could gather, on his throat. "But really, you shouldn't have gone to so much trouble," he went on, in a voice that made Miel want to get out of there as quickly as possible. "My daughter is inclined to prattle away when we have visitors, says the first thing that comes into her head. People who know us have learned to ignore her. I suppose I should have warned you, but I was hoping you wouldn't run into her."

Miel had to remind himself that in his time he'd faced down charging boar and Mezentine heavy cavalry. "I'm sorry," he said. "I didn't mean to intrude. But I was sure you'd be glad of the sulfur. I assume you need it for making the glaze."

There was a knife on the bench, about eight inches from Framain's hand. It was short, with a blade hooked like an eagle's beak and a plain bone handle. Miel watched Framain look down at it and think for a moment.

"What are you talking about?" he said.

"The glaze," Miel repeated, his eyes fixed on the knife. "I know what it is you're doing here. She didn't tell me," he added quickly, "I figured it out for myself. You're trying to work out the formula for the glaze the Mezentines use on their translucent white pottery, the stuff that sells for twice its weight in silver." As well as the knife, he could see Framain's hand on the bench. It was perfectly still. "I'm guessing that you discovered a deposit of the right kind of china clay somewhere on the lower slopes of Sharra. That's why you stayed here, even when the war came and anybody with any sense cleared out. Nobody anywhere in the world can make that stuff except the Mezentines, because they control the only source of the clay. If you've found another deposit, or something that'll do instead, I can well understand why you wouldn't leave here, no matter what the risk. But of course it's no good being able to make the pottery if you can't glaze it, and that's what you haven't quite figured out yet; which is why you're still tinkering with ingredients rather than churning the stuff out by the cartload from that huge, expensive kiln you had built out the back there."

"Actually, I built it myself." Framain had a crooked smile on his face. "Just me and my son, who's dead now, and the man who used to be my business partner. It took us five years. I don't think there's a better one anywhere, not even in the Republic."

Miel nodded toward the knife. "Are you going to kill me or not?" he asked.

Framain slumped a little against the bench, and sighed. "It crossed my mind," he said. "Actually, it was quite close for a moment. If the knife had been longer or a bit closer to hand, I'd definitely have been tempted. But I weighed up the relevant factors. You're younger than I am, probably quicker and better at fighting; and by then, I realized killing you would undoubtedly cause more problems than it'd solve, because if you managed to get sulfur you must have friends, probably among the Vadani, and . . ." He shrugged. "I contemplate a lot of things I never actually do," he said. "I'm not sure whether it's a strength or a weakness."

Miel could feel the moment draining away, and allowed himself to relax a little. "So I was right, then," he said. "Good. I'd have felt rather stupid if I'd made that speech and it turned out I'd jumped to entirely the wrong conclusion."

The girl took a step forward, but Framain shifted just a little and she stopped, as if the line of his shoulder was a barrier she knew she wasn't allowed to cross. She stepped back, and her father's shadow obscured her face. "Quite right," Framain said. "And you're right about the other thing, too. It's an obsession with me, I admit it. Actually, I'm surprised you didn't recognize my name; I'd have thought the Ducas would know such things."

"Sorry," Miel said.

Framain smiled. "That puts me in my place. We were never nobility, you understand. My father was really just a farmer, though he'd have hated to admit it." He leaned forward until his elbows were resting on the bench, his head hanging down as if in shame. "When he died we lost the farm as well; there was some money left, enough for a reasonable man, but not for me. My father had a Mezentine dinner service; it was about the only decent thing he had left, at the end. When I sold it, I was amazed at how much it was worth; I found out how valuable the stuff was, and I thought, if only I could discover how it was made, I could get some money and buy back our inheritance. Typical muddle-headed thinking, just what you'd expect from a spoiled middle-aged man suddenly taken poor; nothing would've come of it, except that I met a man who told me he'd worked out the formula and found a deposit of the clay." Framain scowled, and waited for a moment, as though he had heartburn. "When he was able to prove he was telling the truth, we became partners; we came here, built this place, everything was going beautifully well. Within a few months we'd fired our first batch. It came out perfect; all we needed was the glaze, and we'd be in business. But . . ." He took a deep breath and let it out slowly. "We gave up trying to find the glaze formula and built the kiln; we were still experimenting, of course, but failure was so frustrating that we felt the need to accomplish something tangible, and building a kiln was hard work but at least we could do it. And then . . ." He stopped. The girl turned away. "My partner and my son quarreled about something; it was trivial, a technical matter to do with our experiments. I'd always known my partner was a vicious man with a murderous temper, but I was sure he'd learned to control it. Apparently not. He killed my son and nearly killed me, and then he went away. Unfortunately . . ." Framain smiled. "Unfortunately, he was the clever one, the scientist.

He taught me a great deal, a very great deal, but probably not enough; either that or I simply don't have the spark of genius that he had, and all the hard work in the world won't make up the deficiency. My daughter, however, shows promise, even if she hasn't learned discretion — for which, of course, I have only myself to blame." Framain yawned, and Miel got the impression that it had been a long time since he'd talked so much; he seemed tired, the sort of fatigue that comes from unaccustomed exertion. "And there you have it," he said. "You can understand why it'd be plain foolishness to kill you, just to preserve a secret that isn't really worth anything."

"And the sulfur," Miel said quietly. "It's one of the ingredients for the glaze."

"Not even that." Framain grinned sourly. "We've been using it as a kind of flux, to draw impurities out of the compound. I found a deposit of the stuff not far away, many years ago, but it's all used up now. I told my daughter; apparently she got the idea that without it we couldn't continue our work, but that's not really true. There are better fluxes. It's quite possible that using sulfur's been holding us back, even." He lifted his head. "But I'm sure you aren't interested in technical details. I have an idea you'd already worked out our secret before you came here. What are you going to do?"

Miel looked at him. "I don't know," he said.

Framain shook his head. "It could well be that the Mezentines would give you safe conduct in return for it," he said. "I confess, I've assumed so, ever since the start of this ridiculous war. I told myself that if the worst came to the worst and they happened to find us, or if we were betrayed, I could save myself and my daughter. To be honest, I'm not so sure. The clay makes good fabric, you need to know what you're looking for in order to tell it apart from the real thing; but I'm sure you know how fussy they are about their precious specifications. It could be that using a different clay would count as a mortal sin, and they'd never countenance it. Or else it'd cost too much to mine it and cart it to make it worth their while; I really don't know."

"I could stay here," Miel said, "and join you."

There was a long silence. Eventually the girl said, "Doing what?"

Framain turned his head and said, "Be quiet."

"But Father," she said, "he'd be no use, he doesn't know anything about it, and we can't spare the time to teach him, he's useless. He'd just get under our feet."

Framain looked Miel in the eye and grinned a rather sardonic apology. "My fault," he said. "I taught her metallurgy when I should have been teaching her manners."

"She's right," Miel said. "I don't know the first thing about making glazes. I don't really know much about anything, apart from how to fight wars and manage an estate. But . . ." He pulled a sad, ridiculous face. "There must be something I can do to help, digging peat or shoveling clay or sweeping the floors. I probably wouldn't do it very well, because I haven't had much experience, but I could try. I'm no use to anybody else, myself included."

"That still doesn't explain —" the girl started to say, but Framain shut her up with a gesture.

"It's entirely up to you," he said. "Stay here, if you want to. There's usually plenty of food, and no doubt you can find somewhere to sleep in the house. In fact, you can have it; we don't use it very much, as you've probably gathered for yourself. And if you really feel that fetching and carrying and cleaning for us is what you want to do, I'm sure we can accommodate you. In fact, you could start by chipping the soot out of the furnace hearth. It needs doing, and I've been putting it off for months."

"Fine," Miel said. "If that'd help."

"Father," the girl said angrily, then fell silent.

"That's settled, then," Framain said. "Though if I were you, I'd have something to eat and drink first, and change into some scruffy old clothes, if you've got any. It's pretty filthy work, chipping soot." He shrugged. "You can borrow some of my things, I'm sure they'll fit you. Mahaud'll find you something."

The girl scowled, then walked quickly past them both and out of the barn, slamming the door behind her. As soon as she was gone, Framain seemed to relax.

"I find her very wearing sometimes," he said, "but there you are. It's natural enough, I'm sure, for fathers and daughters to get on each other's nerves if they're cooped up together for too long." He paused, then looked at something on the opposite wall. "I assume she's why you came back."

Miel didn't reply.

"In which case," Framain went on, "you have my blessing; which, together with a tin cup full of water, is worth the cup. You have friends at Duke Valens' court?"

"Yes," Miel said. "For now, anyway. My cousin Jarnac . . ."

"Lines of supply," Framain said carefully, "have been a concern to me over the years. We always used to buy our food from two local farmers — I believe they thought I was either an outlaw or a lunatic hermit of some kind, but I paid well, in cash. They moved out when the Mezentines took Civitas Eremiae; sensible fellows, I don't blame them at all. Since then, I've bought supplies through the innkeeper at the Unswerving Loyalty, but that's a very dangerous arrangement. If your Vadani friends or your followers in the resistance could supply us, it'd be a great weight off my mind. And then there are certain materials." He straightened his back, like a man lifting a heavy weight. "Over the last month or so I've seriously considered giving up because of the difficulties the war has caused me; none of them insuperable on its own, but taken together . . ." He turned back and looked at Miel, as if trying to decide whether or not to buy him. "In return, you can have pretty much anything you want from me. It's quite simple, really. If I succeed and find the formula, and start producing pottery in quantity, there'll be so much money, we won't know what to do with it. If we fail, what does any of it matter? In any case," he went on, with a slight shrug, "I think I'm past the point where I care about wealth and getting back what I've lost. The life I wanted to recapture has gone forever, thanks to the war. It'd be nice to be a rich man, I'm sure, but all I really want to do is solve the glaze problem, just so I can say I've done it. As I think I told you, I'm quite resigned to the fact that I'm obsessed with this ridiculous business. Lying to yourself just makes everything so dreadfully tiresome, don't you find?"

Miel found looking at him made him feel uncomfortable. "I just want something to do," he said. "And working here, helping you, would make a nice change from the war."

Framain considered him for a moment, then laughed. "Don't be so sure," he said. "When you've known her as long as I have, you'll probably wish you were back in the cavalry."

Framain was right about one thing. Cleaning out the furnace hearth was a filthy job. Miel worked at it until the lamp ran low and started guttering, at which point he realized he was too tired to carry on anyway. He'd been attacking the dense crusts of soot as though they were the enemy of all mankind, chipping and flaking them away with an old blunt chisel Framain had given him, stopping every hour or so to sweep away the spoil. As far as he could tell, the job was going to take the rest of his life in any event; his first savage onslaught had hardly made an impression on it. Like fighting the Mezentines, he thought, as he slumped against the wall and caught his breath; you get rid of a whole sackful, and still there's an infinite quantity left to do. Perhaps it was better that way. Leading the resistance, Framain's fruitless search for the formula, hacking soot out of the hearth; people doing pointless, impossible things because they felt they had to, for reasons that didn't stand up when you looked at them logically. It was pretty clear that Framain believed he was in love with the girl (Mahaud; a grim name, he'd always thought). It was entirely possible that he was right about that, but even then it was only part of the explanation. Somehow, he had no idea why, he felt at home here, in the secret house in the hidden combe in the middle of nowhere. For some reason, he felt it was the right place for him to be. As for Framain and his obsession, that was exactly right, too. Pottery, of all things; tableware. Plates, cups, vases, scent-bottles, little dishes and saucers — perfectly true, in the world he'd left behind (no idea whether it still existed), rich men like the Ducas had paid ludicrous prices for the stuff, not because they liked it or because it did a job better than wood or metal, but simply because of what it was. In the old world, it'd be like finding a vein of silver; just dig it out of the hillside and take it away and suddenly you'd be rich, and all your troubles would be over. A small thing like the world changing behind your back could easily be overlooked; and besides, what harm did fine pottery ever do anybody, compared with war and weapons, Vaatzes' scorpions, politics and diplomacy and the destruction of great cities? A man whose business that sort of thing had been might well do worse than the pottery trade. You could go to sleep at night knowing that even if you succeeded, nobody was going to die as a result (but then he thought of the look on Framain's face as he tried to decide whether or not to reach for the knife. Obsession is just another kind of love, after all).

He picked up the lamp. It flickered alarmingly; he didn't want to be stranded there in the dark all night. He went slowly and carefully, to make sure it didn't go out. It'd be easier, he decided, if he was there because he was in love with Mahaud. There were precedents for that sort of thing, it was like the stories in books, whose heroes and heroines were generally dispossessed princes and princesses anyway, which made it all perfectly acceptable and in keeping with the established rules. If he'd fallen in love with the hermit wizard's daughter, it'd be all right, he'd know why he was there and what he was supposed to be doing. In order to win her heart, he'd purify his soul by honest manual labor, purging himself of the gross and decadent superfluities of his privileged upbringing and still ending up with a suitable wife of good family. In the process, no doubt, he'd help the wizard complete his work, which would be a good thing — maybe they could use the pottery money to hire an army that'd drive the Mezentines out of Eremia; something like that.

He crossed the yard. The door to the house was open. Framain and Mahaud slept in the hayloft above the barn, so as not to waste two minutes every morning getting to work; he had the house to himself. Earlier he'd found a bed, buried under a pile of old, damp sheets that looked and smelled as though they'd been used for straining something. He didn't mind. He'd slept on the bare ground, in mud, among rocks; compared with what he'd been used to lately, this was luxury fit for the Ducas himself. He pinched out the lamp, lay back and tried to empty his mind, but he couldn't help thinking about the scavengers, wondering if Jarnac had left any of them alive, and if so, what had become of them. To them, this place really would be luxury, as remote and incomprehensible as Fairyland.

He forced them out of his mind, like a landlord evicting tenants, and fell asleep listening to the scuttling of mice.

12

"I had a letter from my man at the silver mine," Valens said, making a point of not looking Ziani in the eye. "He says they're finished there now, all sealed up. He says the men have been told the mine's been put out of commission for good. I hope he was lying."

Ziani didn't say anything, and Valens didn't look at him.

"Anyhow," Valens went on, "the idea is, the first thing the Mezentines are likely to do is round up as many of the mineworkers as they can. Our people will tell them the mine's useless, and with luck they'll believe it and give up. Meanwhile, I've sent the men you trained to do the same at the smaller workings. Do you think they'll be able to manage?"

"I expect so," Ziani said. "They seemed perfectly competent."

Valens shrugged; he was fairly sure that Ziani was watching him. "Doesn't matter," he said. "By our calculations, it won't make business sense for the Republic to work the smaller mines, what with the overheads they'd be facing. One good thing about fighting a war against businessmen, we can do the same sums they do, which means we can more or less read their minds."

"The Republic won't bother with them if they can't make a profit," Ziani said.

"Which means the government won't be able to kid the opposition into a full-scale occupation purely on commercial grounds," Valens said. "I believe that surviving this war is very much about not fighting it, if that can be arranged. If there's nothing here for them — no city to sack, no mines to take over, no people around to kill — where'd be the point? Of course," he added, "that's just my guess at how they think. I imagine Guild politics is a bit more complicated than I'm making out."

"I wouldn't know," Ziani said.

Valens leaned forward, planting his elbows on the desk. "You're too modest, I'm sure."

"Really." Out of the corner of his eye, Valens saw Ziani turn his head away. "I believe what you and the others have been telling me about factions among the Guilds and so on, but most of it's news to me. That sort of thing doesn't tend to trickle down to the shop floor."

"Oh." Valens rubbed his eyes. He was tired, and these days he found talking to the Mezentine rather trying. "Well, it's the best intelligence we've got, so let's hope it's accurate. Now then. Moving on; literally, as well as figuratively. My wedding's been brought forward a month, now that the mines have been sorted out. I want to be in a position to start the evacuation as soon as possible after that. You told me you had some ideas on the subject, but you were all coy and secretive about it." Now he turned his head and looked Ziani in the eye. "If it's going to need preparation and materials, I'd better know about it now."

"Fine," Ziani said. His face was blank, and he didn't move at all. "The thing is this. I'm no strategist, but as I understand it, your idea is to keep your people on the move, out of the way of the Mezentine soldiers."

"That's right."

Ziani nodded slowly. "I can quite see the thinking behind it. Show them a clean pair of heels, they'll soon get tired of chasing after you, spending money, with no victories to write dispatches home about. The opposition — that's the term you were using, wasn't it? — they'll make capital out of the fact that nothing much seems to be happening and the bills keep rolling in, and either they'll overthrow the people who are running the war or else force them to back down."

"You're skeptical about that," Valens said.

Ziani smiled. "You've been teaching me things about how my country is run that I never knew before," he said, "so who am I to tell you anything? But while I was involved with the defense of Civitas Eremiae, I did learn a bit about the Mezentine military. Bear in mind: the soldiers and the men commanding them aren't my people. They're foreigners, recruited a long way away across the sea. We have the same color skin, and my people originally came from there, but they're nothing like us at all. They're the ones who are in charge of running the war out here; they report to my people, who pay them, or decide to stop paying them."

"I see," Valens replied. "But it's still not their decision, ultimately."

Ziani shrugged. "If I was the commander of the army," he said, "I'd want to get results, as quickly as possible, to justify my employment and make sure I got paid. I'm not a lawyer, but I bet you the mercenaries' contracts aren't just straightforward. There'll be performance-related bonuses, or targets that have to be met, or financial penalties. We have them in all our other contracts with foreigners, all designed to keep them on their toes and make sure they do their best for us. I imagine it's the same with the soldiers."

"No doubt," Valens said. "What's this got to do with the evacuation?"

"Simple," Ziani replied. "Don't underestimate them; they're motivated by the hope of making a lot of money and the fear of not getting paid. And they have a lot of cavalry."

Valens nodded slowly. "You're saying they'll come after us."

"And a cavalry division can move a hell of a lot faster than a convoy of wagons," Ziani said. "Don't imagine you can lose them in the mountains; they'll track you, or they'll get hold of stragglers or people who decided to take their chances and stay behind, and get what they want to know out of them. They'll find out where you are, and their cavalry will come after you. Now," he went on, frowning, "I know that your cavalry is very good indeed."

"Thank you," Valens replied without expression.

"It's also a fact," Ziani went on, "or at least I believe it is, that there aren't all that many of them. Now I'm sure every Vadani is worth ten Mezentines in a fight, but that's not the point. You're outnumbered; your cavalry can be drawn off by diversions while they attack the wagons. If they do that, they'll have their quick, cheap victory, and you . . ." He shrugged. "I'm sorry, I don't mean to be melodramatic. I'm sure this thought has crossed your mind too."

Valens' turn not to say anything.

"This," Ziani said, and he seemed to grow a little, "is where I think I can help. My people will assume that if they can get past your cavalry, they can dig in to a soft target."

"They'd be right," Valens said.

Ziani smiled. "I borrowed a book from your library," he said, "I hope you don't mind. It was called *The Art of War* or something like that; actually, I think there was a mirror in the title. All the books in your library are called the mirror of something or other. I suppose it's a convention. Anyway, not important. The book said, always attack your enemy's strengths and invite him to attack your weaknesses. I reckoned that sounded pretty stupid until I thought about it. Really, it's just simple common sense. He won't expect you to attack where he's strong, so you attack on your terms. Like-wise, if you know where he's going to attack you, because you've drawn him into it, you can be ready for him, with a few surprises. Now I come to think of it, that's how the Ducas defended Civitas Eremiae."

The name made Valens look up. "Really?" he said.

"Absolutely. Their strength was their artillery; we attacked their artillery with ours. Our weakness was being pinned down in one place, where they could use their machines against us; we let them come right up to the city, exactly what they wanted to do. I still believe we'd have beaten them if someone hadn't betrayed us. We'd beaten them where they were strong, you see; we'd let them do exactly what they wanted, and then turned round and slaugh-tered them."

Valens looked at him for a moment. "You know," he said, "I'm sure I must have read that book, but obviously I didn't get nearly as much out of it as you did. What's your idea?"

Ziani straightened his face until it was completely at rest. "What they'll want to do is attack your wagons. I say, let them. Don't be obvious about it, of course. Send out your cavalry, have them do everything they can to keep my people away from the wagons. But expect them to fail."

Valens breathed out slowly through his nose. "With you so far," he said. "Then what?"

Ziani was getting visibly more animated; Valens could have sworn he was swelling, like a bullfrog. "Ask yourself: if my people were in your position, what would they do? Facing the danger of being engaged out in the open by enemy cavalry?"

"I imagine they'd dream up some ingenious machine or other."

"Exactly. Which is what I've done." Ziani was smiling, pleased with himself. "Not machines as such, because anything too complex would take too long to build, and we haven't got enough plant and machinery, or enough skilled people. No, what I had in mind was this." He reached in his pocket. "Here're some sketches that ought to give you the general idea. Of course they aren't to scale or anything."

Valens frowned, and looked at them. "Carts," he said.

"Ordinary carts, yes. That's an important point, because of the time pressure. We need to be able to modify what we've already got, rather than building from scratch."

"Carts with . . ." Valens paused, looking at the sketches. "This is all a bit far-fetched, isn't it?"

The flicker of annoyance on Ziani's face came and went very quickly. "I don't think so," he said. "What do you do if you want to protect a man from weapons? You put him in armor. Sixteen-gauge wrought-iron sheet; that's about a sixteenth of an inch. You know what level of protection you can expect from it, that's what your helmet and your breastplate and all that are made out of. It'll turn arrows at anything but short range, it'll stop cuts from swords and axes. It's not exactly light, but when you're wearing your armor it's not so heavy you can't move almost as easily as you can without it. Look, we can't carry stone ramparts around with us, or palisades of tree trunks; what we can do is use the wagons themselves as walls. Each wagon has an iron sheet bolted to one side; half of them on the left, the other half on the right. Think of it as each wagon carrying a shield. When the enemy attacks, they do what infantry do: line up, form a shield wall. Instant fortifications. Your cavalry opponents lose all their advantages of mobility and impetus; suddenly they're reduced to being foot soldiers trying to storm a fortress, except they haven't got any siege equipment — no battering rams or scaling ladders or pavises. They can run up and try and climb over, if they're keen enough, but I don't suppose they'll be stupid enough to try it twice. Then, once you've driven them off, you span the horses in again and carry on with your journey as though nothing had happened."

Valens sat and stared at the sketches for a long time. "We're talking about every cart in the duchy," he said at last. "There's not enough sheet iron in the whole world."

Ziani laughed. "Please," he said, "trust me to understand about material procurement. I used to run a factory, remember. That's the real beauty of the whole scheme. Sheet iron is just iron you heat up and bash until it's spread out flat and thin. You don't need trained smiths or engineers, just a lot of strong men with hammers."

"The miners," Valens murmured.

"Strong men used to hammering." Ziani nodded. "And badly in need of something to do. As for iron; well, even simple rustic folk like yourselves use iron for practically everything. You build a dozen big furnaces, say — bricks and clay, nothing complex or time-consuming — and you cook up all the iron tools and furniture and fittings and stuff you don't actually need to take with you on the journey — all the things you were planning on abandoning for the Mezentines to loot, basically; you melt it and pour it into great big puddles, what we call blooms, and then your ex-miners and your soldiers and anybody who can swing a hammer bashes it out into sheets. I'll need a few competent men to cut the sheets and fit them, of course, but that's about it as far as skilled tradesmen go. As for how long it'll take; that'll depend on how many people we can get on it."

Valens said nothing for a long time. "Fuel," he said at last. "You'll need a hell of a lot of coal or charcoal or whatever it is you use."

"All of which you've got," Ziani pointed out, with more than a touch of smugness. "Stockpiled, at the mines. I've taken the liberty of having an inventory made of the supplies you've got available. I think there'll be plenty. Even if the whole idea is a complete failure, at the very least that's one more resource the Mezentines won't be able to load up and take home with them."

That made Valens smile. "Business thinking," he said.

"I'm a Mezentine," Ziani replied. "Cost out everything before you start, know where your supplies are coming from so you aren't taken short halfway through the job, and try not to waste anything. Oddly enough, there's nothing about that sort of thing in your art-of-war book. Maybe that's because you really do think of it as an art, rather than a trade; you expect it to be financed by wealthy amateur patrons, instead of running to a budget."

Valens laughed. As he did so, he realized that the man he was facing was essentially a stranger, someone he hadn't talked to before. Maybe, he thought, it's simply the confidence of an expert in his element; but that wasn't all of it, by any means. The other thing the Mezentines were famous for, he remembered: they were reckoned to be born salesmen.

"All right," he said. "We'll give it a go. Now, you see, I've been learning from you as well. Build me some prototypes, so I can see for myself if any of this'll work. Build me a shielded wagon, and a scrap-iron furnace. If I give you full cooperation, how long will you need?"

Ziani took a deep breath, as if this was the moment he hadn't been looking forward to. "I'll need to build the furnace in order to make the material for the wagon," he said. "Ten days?"

"You're serious? Ten days?"

"We don't have much time before the evacuation, you said," Ziani replied. "While I'm making these prototypes, I can be training the men who'll be my foremen once we're doing it for real. Yes, ten days."

"Fine," Valens said, frowning. "Ten days. You'll be wanting to start right away, so don't let me keep you. I'll have Carausius write you a general commission; that'll authorize you to make all the requisitions you want, men and supplies. Good luck."

"Thank you." Ziani stood up to leave. Valens let him get as far as the door, then said, "One other thing."

"Yes."

"I had a rather strange conversation with Jarnac Ducas a while ago," Valens said. "You know, Miel Ducas' cousin. Presumably you came across him at Civitas Eremiae."

"I know who you mean," Ziani said.

"Thought you might." Valens paused for a moment, leaving Ziani standing in the doorway, his hand on the latch. "Anyway, Jarnac Ducas told me a rather curious story about you." He smiled. "I'm not sure how to phrase this without sounding hopelessly melodramatic. The gist of it was, you're supposed to have cooked up some kind of plot to get Miel Ducas disgraced. Something to do with the Duchess, and a letter."

"Oh, that." Ziani looked at him; it was the way the feeding deer looks up at a slight noise from the hunter; not fear, but more than curiosity. "Well, I can't blame the Ducas for being angry about it, but he only had himself to blame. A man in his position . . ." He shrugged. "What exactly did he say I'd done?"

"I can't remember, to be honest with you," Valens said smoothly. "I prefer not to listen to personal quarrels, unless they're getting in the way. But I'd be interested to hear what it was actually all about."

Ziani's face closed like a door. "The Duchess lost one of your letters," he said, "or it was intercepted, or something like that. The Ducas got hold of it, and kept it instead of taking it to Duke Orsea. I assume he was going to blackmail her with it, or else he had some scheme going on for getting rid of Orsea and taking the throne. I think he was always a bit resentful about Orsea marrying the Sirupati heiress; that's the impression I got from what people were saying, anyhow. They were more or less engaged at one time, I understand."

"I see," Valens replied. "And so when you found out about the letter . . ."

"I wish I hadn't," Ziani said. "The plain fact is, Miel Ducas was a much more competent soldier than Orsea, he'd have made a much better duke. But it wasn't my choice to make; I wasn't even an Eremian citizen, I was Orsea's guest. When I found evidence that pointed to the Ducas plotting against him, I didn't really have any option. Of course," he went on, "there's no hard evidence to prove that the Ducas had anything to do with the city being betrayed to the Mezentines, it's all circumstantial. On the other hand . . ."

"You think the Ducas handed over the city to your people?"

Ziani shook his head. "Really, it's none of my business. Yes, the Ducas seems to be the only man with a strong motive who was actually in a position to do it. That's evidence, but it's not proof. So, if you're asking me if I blame myself for the betrayal of Civitas Eremiae, I'd have to say no. I may have influenced matters to a degree, but at the end of the day I know it wasn't my fault. Why, how do you see it?"

Valens smiled wryly. "Well," he said, "naturally I don't like the thought that the man who opened the gates of Civitas Eremiae could be here, in my city, prepared to do the same again or something similar if he feels his personal agenda requires it. Do you think I ought to do something about Miel Ducas?"

"He's not here, though," Ziani replied. "Isn't he still in Eremia, leading the resistance?"

"So he is. Mind you, the resistance has more or less run out of

steam now. I've stopped supplying them, they're not a good investment. So, presumably, Miel Ducas will be coming here sooner or
later. What do you think I should do with him when he arrives?"

Ziani shook his head. "Not up to me, I'm delighted to say," he
said. "I don't think I could do that; make decisions about other
people's lives, I mean. You'd have to be so very sure you were
doing the right thing, or else how could you live with yourself?"

"Oh, you manage," Valens said casually. "After a while, you
get the knack of being able to forget they're people, and you start
seeing them as pieces in a game, or components in a machine. I'm
not saying it's something to be proud of, but you can train yourself
to do it easily enough."

"I'll take your word for it," Ziani said. "It's not something I'd
like to find out by experience."

Ziani left the Duke's tower and walked quickly across the yard,
as though he was afraid someone would come after him. Valens,
he decided, reminded him of what his old supervisor used to say
about the vertical mill. The most useful machine in the shop is
usually also the most dangerous.

Ten days; had he really said that? Crazy. Even so; if Valens had
brought the wedding date forward, as he'd just said, ten days was
about all the time he had.

He went back to his room. There was a letter waiting for him;
an invitation from the Lord Chamberlain to attend the royal wedding. He read it quickly, looking for the important part. There was
a timetable; early morning reception, the wedding itself, then the
wedding breakfast, another reception, followed by an afternoon's
falconry, in honor of the bride and her guests. By implication he
was invited to that, too. He smiled.

Enough of that. Just enough time, before collecting his commission from the Chancery, to see to the other chores. He put on
his coat and hurried out of the castle, into town.

"I was beginning to wonder about you," the woman said, as
he walked through the door into the back room of the Selfless

Devotion. "We're supposed to be partners; and then you vanish up to the castle for weeks on end, and I don't hear a word out of you."

"Been busy," Ziani replied, trying not to stare. The dress she was wearing this time was the worst yet; a gushing, flowing mess of crimson velvet that made her look as though she was drowning in blood. "I've got the money," he went on, "or at least, I'll have it for you this evening, without fail."

"That's a big *or at least,*" she grumbled, but he knew he was safe. "Cash?"

"Draft," Ziani replied. "*Royal* draft," he added, as her face tightened, "drawn direct on the Chancery, and no questions asked. My man'll bring it down to you before the ink's dry."

"Whatever." She was doing her best not to be impressed; on balance, succeeding. "That'll save me a trip, then. When he brings me the money, I'll give him the map."

"Fine." Ziani dropped into a chair, trying to look casual, his legs suddenly weak. "Now, let's talk about quantities."

"Thought you'd say that." She grinned at him, pleased to have read his mind so easily. "Obviously, given the overheads on each caravan, each consignment's got to be big enough to give us our margin; say a minimum of seven tons a time."

"Oh," Ziani said. "I was thinking a minimum of ten."

She gave him a pitying look. "You got any idea how many mules it takes to shift ten tons of salt?"

"Mules," Ziani repeated. "Why mules? Why not carts?"

She sighed. "It's not just the run from here to the border," she said. "You'll see when you get the map. You avoid the desert, sure, but you've still got to get across the mountains before you reach the salt pans. Which means carts are out; it's all got to go on mules."

Ziani nodded. "I appreciate that," he said. "But you can take a train of carts up as far as the foothills, can't you?"

"Well, yes. But what good's that?"

Panic over; Ziani breathed out slowly. "Well, couldn't you take the stuff down the mountain on mules and then load it onto carts once you're back on the flat?"

She laughed, making her many chins dance. "Shows how much you know about the haulage business. Do that and you'll have to hire one team for the mule-train and another team for the wagons. Double your wage bill for an extra three tons. Not worth it."

"I see," Ziani said, "I hadn't thought of that."

"Obviously. Just as well you've got me to hold your hand for you. No, seven tons is your maximum, each trip. The idea is to get in as many trips as possible while the weather's good. By late autumn you've got the rains in the mountains, the rivers flood, can't be crossed, you're screwed. Ideally you want two mule-teams, one going and one coming back, all the time. But then you run into production difficulties, meaning the bloody idle savages in the mines. Oh, they'll promise you fifteen tons on the nail, swear blind they'll deliver bang on time; but when you get there, it's nine tons if you're lucky, and if you're not, you're stuck out there in the desert waiting for them to get around to doing some work. Honest truth, they don't understand the meaning of time like we do. Today means tomorrow or three weeks or three months, and if you lose your rag and start yelling at them they stare at you like they can't understand what all the fuss is about. Doing business with people like that . . ." She made a wide gesture with her hands, half compassion, half contempt. "And then people whine about salt being expensive. Bloody hard way to earn a living, if you ask me."

Ziani grinned. "You'd better not let the Duke catch you talking like that about his future in-laws," he said.

"Out of his tiny mind," the woman replied sadly. "If he knew those people like I do, he'd steer well clear of them, and I don't care what promises they're making. The thought of one of them as duchess; it's just as well his father's not alive to see it, it'd break his heart."

"Really? I'd sort of got the impression he didn't have one."

She scowled at him. "That's his son you're thinking of," she said. "Actually, it's her I feel sorry for; the savage woman. Of course, I don't believe all the stuff you hear about him not being the marrying kind, if you follow me, but even so . . ."

Back up the hill, as soon as he could get away. The commission was ready for him, the ink still glistening, the seal still warm.

"That," Carausius said, as he handed it over, "makes you the second most powerful man in the duchy."

Ziani frowned. "I hadn't looked at it in that light," he said.

"Of course," Carausius went on, "you'll be keeping detailed accounts."

"Naturally," Ziani replied, without looking up from the document.

"I strongly suggest you take great care over them," Carausius said. "The Duke instructs me that you're accountable directly to him, which means he'll be going over them himself. In other words, you'll have an auditor who can have your head cut off and stuck up on a pike just by giving the order. You may care to reflect on that before you start writing out drafts."

Ziani looked up and smiled pleasantly. "The sad thing is," he said, "that's the least of my worries."

Daurenja was waiting for him when he reached the room he'd been assigned as an office. The day before, it had been a long-disused tack room, and it still reeked of saddle-soap, wet blankets and mold. "Get this place cleaned up, will you?" he snapped without thinking. Daurenja nodded and said, "Of course."

"Fine." Ziani made himself calm down; he didn't like losing his cool while Daurenja was around. "Now, I want you to take a letter for me to a merchant in the town. She'll give you a letter to bring back. It's essential that you don't leave without it. I don't trust her as far as I can spit; so, polite but firm. All right?"

He wrote out the draft. Carausius had given him the appropriate seal, and ten sticks of the special green wax that was reserved for government business. He thought about what the Chancellor had said; second most powerful man in the duchy. Looked at from that perspective, he'd come a long way from the shop floor of the Mezentine ordnance factory. A reasonable man would consider that a great achievement in itself. "When you get back," he said, shaking sand on the address, "we need to talk about materials."

"You persuaded him, then?"

Ziani nodded. "Worse luck, yes. We've got ten days to build prototypes. The cart and the foundry."

Daurenja's mouth dropped open. "Ten days? He's out of his mind."

"My suggestion," Ziani replied. "We need to get moving. We can't start full-scale work until we've got approval on the prototypes; ten days is as long as I can spare. What are you still doing here, by the way? I asked you to do something for me."

Daurenja seemed to vanish instantaneously; not even a blur. Ziani took a deep breath, as though he'd just woken up from an unsettling dream, and reached for a sheet of paper and his calipers. By the time Daurenja came back, he'd finished the design for the drop-valve cupola.

"Did you get it?"

Daurenja nodded. "She wasn't any bother," he said, handing over a fat square of parchment, heavily folded and sealed. "She told me to tell you, she's thought about what you were saying about scheduling, and —"

"Forget about that," Ziani said. "I want you to look at this." He turned the sketch round and pushed it across the table. "I'm concerned about the gate," he said. "It's got to be simple, nice broad tolerances. We can't expect these people to do fine work."

Daurenja bent his implausibly long back and studied the drawing for a while. "You could replace that cam with a simple bolt," he said. "Not as smooth, obviously, but it'd be a forging rather than a machined component. Their forge work isn't so bad."

Ziani was looking at the map: a diagram, a different sort of plan; lines drawn on paper, on which everything now depended. "A bolt's no good," he muttered without looking up, "it'll expand in the heat and jam in its socket."

"Of course." He could hear how angry Daurenja was with himself. "I should have thought of that, I'm sorry."

"You were thinking aloud, it's all right. If we had time, we could make up templates so they could forge the cams, but we haven't, so that's that. I've noticed with these people: give them a model, a bit of carved wood, and they can copy it pretty well, but they can't seem to work from drawings." Ziani traced a line on the map with his finger. Of course, it meant nothing to him; places he'd never been to, mountains conveyed by a few squiggles, a double line for a river. He tried to picture a landscape in his mind, but found he couldn't. He forced his mind back into the present, like a stockman driving an unruly animal into a pen. "Here's a job for you," he said. "Get me a full list of all the competent metalworkers we've got on file, and get the Duke's people to organize the call-up. I want them here, this time tomorrow, with basic tools and six days' rations. You'll have to sort out money with the paymaster's office, and billeting as well. I imagine someone's got a list of the inns somewhere. Can I leave all that to you, while I get on with the drawings?"

"Of course." The answer came back like an echo.

"Fine. When you've done that, get back here, I should be ready to give you a materials list, so you can get on with procurement. It'll save time if you go through the Merchant Adventurers' association; they'll rip us off unmercifully but so what, it's not our money."

"Understood."

"And then . . ." Ziani paused for a protest, but of course none came. "Then I want you to get a requisition made out for all the carts and wagons in the country. I think Valens' people have been quietly making a register for some time, so it shouldn't be a problem finding them. They can sort out compensation and so forth. Oh, and bricklayers. That's another job for the Duke's people. Get me two dozen, any more'll just get under our feet. Got all that?"

"Yes," Daurenja said. "Metalworkers, payment and billeting; materials, and the Merchant Adventurers; carts, and bricklayers. You can leave all that to me."

"Splendid." Ziani was still staring at the map. Just lines on paper; a plan; a plan of action. "You'll need to take the commission with you. Actually, we could do with some more copies. I expect the Chancery clerks can handle that."

When Daurenja had gone (like breath evaporating off glass), Ziani laid the map down and frowned into space. He hadn't felt afraid of anybody for a long time, not since he'd been in the cells under the Guildhall, because the worst anybody could do to him after that was kill him, and in the eyes of the Republic he was already supposed to be dead. Dying would, of course, be an easy way out, practically a let-off, as though the supervisor had told him he could go home early and leave the work to someone else to finish off. Since his escape, the work had been the only thing, far more important than he could ever be. He'd served it, as he'd served the Republic, tirelessly and without any thought for himself. The pain was simply the weight of being in charge, carrying the responsibility of the whole thing being in his mind alone. Now, somehow, here was Daurenja: a man who wanted something, but he didn't know what; a man who served the work with the same single-minded ferocity as he did, but who didn't even know what it was. He was exceptionally competent, exactly what Ziani needed, a safe pair of hands, utterly reliable, a godsend and a lifesaver . . .

(I could ask Valens to have him killed, or deported, or thrown in jail; I expect he'd do it, if I made up some story. It'd be the right thing to do, but he's so useful . . .

It doesn't matter, though. If he doesn't know what the work is — and how could he? — he can't damage it. In which case, whatever it is he wants, he can have; his business. But perhaps it would be wise to share these fears with the Duke, so that when Daurenja finally does turn savage, I can be rid of him without any blame rubbing off on me and the work. Perhaps; when the moment arises.)

He covered up the map with a sheet of paper, to stop himself staring at it.

A proper fire is always a good place to start. He'd requisitioned a disused drill-square behind the cavalry barracks, four hundred yards each side, flat and level, with sheds in one corner. The carpenters had already built a scaffold and plank lean-to in the middle, to shelter the fire-pit for the forge. They'd found him the biggest anvil in Civitas Vadanis; it had come out of a chainmaker's shop, and it had suffered a long, hard life, to judge by the scarred face and rounded edges. Half a dozen smaller anvils were grouped round it, placed so that all of them had easy access to the fire. Simple oak trunks had to do for rollers, to slide the blooms to and from the anvils. The smiths, all there against their will, stood about in small groups, muttering and resentful, while the general laborers lifted and strained on ropes and levers, shifting carts full of baskets of charcoal, limestone, iron scrap. In the far corner of the improvised shed, the nail-makers were already busy, with their own forge, slack-tub, swages, wire plates and blocks. They were slightly happier, since at least they knew what they were supposed to be doing, and could get on with it straightaway. Ziani dismissed them from his mind.

The furnace was a compromise, forced on him by time and lack of materials. The previous day, the bricklayers had built a simple hollow tower, ten feet high and four feet square. In each face, about a foot off the ground, was a hole into which fitted the nozzle of a double-action bellows; above each of these was another hole, shrouded with sheet iron, to serve as an air intake. Through one side, at the very bottom, protruded a thick-walled clay pipe with a four-inch bore, stopped with a clay bung on a length of wire, draining onto a flat bed of sand. They'd lit a fire inside the tower before he arrived; it had caught nicely, fanned by slow, easy strokes of the four bellows, each blowing in turn. The laborers were tipping in bucketfuls of charcoal mixed with limestone rubble. When the tower was half full, Ziani gave the order and the men started loading the iron scrap, smashed up into lumps no bigger than a man's hand. There was only enough room in the prototype for about five hundredweight of iron — Daurenja had had trouble finding that much at a day's notice — before the topping of limestone chunks was tipped in, leaving the chamber about three-quarters full. Ziani told everyone apart from the bellows-workers to stand back, and gave the order to start blowing.

"How's the mortar?" he asked Daurenja, who was standing beside him (no need to look round to see if he was there). "It's only had twelve hours to stand, it must still be pretty soft."

"It's dried out quite well since they lit the fire," Daurenja reassured him. "It'll probably crack up when the furnace cools down, of course, but that's all right. This is just a trial run, after all."

"I hope you're right," Ziani muttered. "It's not going to look too good if the whole lot collapses in on itself when the Duke's watching." He looked round. "Shouldn't he be here by now? When did you tell him . . . ?"

"I said noon," Daurenja replied. "It'll take till then before we're ready to pour. He won't want to be standing round with nothing to see, and if he misses it — well, he can still watch the bloom being hammered out. That ought to be spectacular enough, with all the sparks flying."

The bellows gasped, like a man in a seizure, and puffed, like a fat man running upstairs. Flames were starting to lick the top edge of the tower; still blue. When they turned yellow, the metal would be melted and ready to pour.

"I don't like the steam coming off the brickwork," Ziani said. "That's the damp mortar. The last thing we need is any moisture getting through to the melt, the whole thing could blow up."

"Unlikely," Daurenja said, and Ziani was pleased to allow himself to believe him. "The heat's going outwards, after all."

Ziani shrugged. He knew that, of course, but he wanted to have something to worry about. "How long do you reckon? Ten minutes?"

"With those bellows? About that."

They'd have better bellows for the real thing, of course. Ziani had already designed them: true double-actions, with valves on the Mezentine pattern, that blew on both the up and the down stroke. It was essential that the metal be brought up to heat as quickly as possible, to keep it clean. The melted limestone would flux out most of the garbage, of course, but he had no great faith in the quality of Vadani iron. He was saving the Mezentine scrap to sweeten the full-weight batches later on. There were boys on hand to keep the bellows-workers supplied with wet cloths to wrap round their faces and arms; without them, they'd be scorched raw in minutes.

(There's so much anger in heat, Ziani thought; you can contain it, or protect yourself against it if you're careful, but all the useful work is being done by anger, a furious resentment of all solid things, that'd reduce me to ash if I stood just a little too close to it; and a single drop of water on the hot brick or the molten iron would do more damage in a second than a hundred men with hammers in a year. The forces I have under my control are unimaginable. I've got to keep them that way; just me . . .)

The Duke had arrived, quietly, while Ziani was looking the other way. He looked tired, thinner and slighter than normal. (I thought he was taller and broader across the shoulders; and he's younger than he seems when you're talking to him. If he understood exactly what's going on inside that brick tower, would he be thinking the same as me?) Ziani went over and greeted him. The small knot of courtiers stepped back to let him through.

"How's it going?" Valens asked. "Any setbacks?"

Ziani shook his head. "This is everyday stuff," he said. "That square box there is stuffed with iron and fuel, a bit of sand to stop it chilling and some lime for flux. We've cooked up a good fire, which'll melt the iron; we'll know when it's ready because the flames change color; should be any minute now, I think. Then all we do is nip the plug out of that bit of pipe there, and the liquid iron'll run out onto the sand. It'll be a moment or so before it takes the cold enough to be moved, and then we roll it over those logs, grab it with big tongs, lift it up onto the anvil and start bashing it flat with big hammers. The trick'll be to work it down to the right thickness before all the heat goes out of it. In case we don't, and it's a fair bet we won't manage it all in one pass, we'll have to get it hot again on that forge over there. It's awkward because the blooms are heavy; we've got the rollers to make it a bit easier, but it's still a fair amount of heavy work." He realized he was chattering, and fell silent. Valens nodded, and said nothing. He seemed preoccupied, and he was too far away to feel the heat.

The flames turned yellow. Daurenja was the first to notice. He pointed and yelled, as though he'd seen a miracle — for the Duke's benefit, perhaps. Ziani nodded. It would be as well to let the melt sweat for a while.

"What's that man jumping up and down for?" Valens asked.

"He's letting me know the flames have changed color. That's my assistant, the man we were talking about a while ago."

"Oh, him." Valens frowned. "Excitable sort, isn't he?"

Ziani hesitated. "He's a first-rate craftsman," he replied, "and he certainly knows how to make himself useful."

"Fine. Didn't you say the change in color means it's ready?"

"I'll give it a little longer," Ziani said. "It needs a chance to sweat out the rubbish. If it's not clean, you can get brittle spots that'll crack when you hammer it, and that's a whole plate wasted. Well, that's not strictly true, you can heat it up and weld it, but that's more time and effort." Telling him far more than he wanted to know; a sign of nerves, or maybe he felt an urge to impress, because the Duke was standing so still and quiet. "Right, that's long enough," he said, though it wasn't. "Let's have the gate open and see what we've got."

Someone tugged on the wire, and the clay bung popped out. Half a heartbeat later, a dribble as bright as the sun nuzzled its way out of the pipe, like the nose of a sniffing mouse; it hesitated, then came on with a rush; stopped as if wary, then began to gush. It was impossible to see because of the dazzling white light — like looking at an angel, Ziani thought suddenly, or how he'd heard some people describe the onset of death, when they'd been on the verge of it. Valens winced and looked away.

"There we go," Ziani said.

The sand it flooded out onto crackled and popped, and a thin cloud of steam lifted and hung over it like a canopy. Ziani fancied he could see the heat in it moving about, vague dark flickers inside the searing brightness. It had the oily sheen of the melt. Someone approached it with a long stick, presumably to see if it had started to set cold. Ziani yelled at him to stay away.

"When it's this hot it'll take all the skin off your face if you get too close," he explained. "A puddle that size ought to stay white hot for a good long while."

Valens nodded. "Well, your furnace seems to work," he said. "What happens now?"

"Nothing, for a minute or two. Soon as it's cooled down enough to be moved, the real work starts. Talking of which," he added, and turned round to give the signal to the smiths to light the forge fire. "Shouldn't be long now," he said, and he realized he was making it sound as though the delay was somehow his own fault.

The laborers and most of the smiths were closing in, picking up tools. Daurenja, swathed in wet cloth, sidled forward like a nervous fencer and prodded the shining mass with a long poker.

"Ready," he shouted.

"Here goes," Ziani said, and the laborers stepped forward. They had long poles with hooks on, like boathooks. "They've got to drag the bloom — that's the puddle of hot iron — onto the logs. The awkward part is lifting it off the logs onto the anvil. That thing weighs over three hundred pounds, even after all the waste's been fluxed out in the furnace."

As soon as the bloom hit the rollers they began to smoke, as the dried bark of the logs caught fire. They did their job well enough, nevertheless, and it wasn't long before the bloom lay at the base of the big anvil, glowing like a captive star. Three men on one side drove steel bars under it and levered it up on its edge; three more men laid the ends of longer, heavier bars under it, then stepped back smartly as the levers were drawn out and the process was repeated on the other side. That done, men crowded round to pick up the bars and lift the bloom, like pallbearers raising a coffin. Four smiths with long hooks teased it carefully onto the anvil and jumped out of the way as their colleagues stepped in with sledgehammers.

The first blow shot out a cloud of white sparks — drops of

still-molten metal, Ziani explained, scattered by the force of the hammer. A dozen smiths were striking in turn, timing their blows so that there was no gap between them. The sound was like the pattering of rain, the chiming of bells, the crash of weapons on armor. To begin with, it seemed as though they were having no effect at all. As Valens watched, however, the bloom gradually began to squeeze out at the edges, gradual as the minute-hand of a clock but constantly moving, like the flow of a very thick liquid. With each strike, the target area dimmed a little. The blinding white was starting to stain yellow, like snow made dirty, and the smiths were straining to strike harder. They were working in a spiral, starting at the edges and working inward to the center, then back out again, the same pattern in reverse. Each blow slightly overlapped each other, and as the hammer lifted, a vague blur of shadow appeared in the metal and faded, like a frown. Occasionally there was a crack and a sizzle, as sweat from someone's forehead landed on the surface. All twelve of the smiths were wringing wet, as though they'd been out in the rain.

"We're losing the heat," Ziani said, raising his voice over the incessant pecking clang of the hammers. "Once it drops from orange to red it's not safe to work it. That means it's got to go in the other fire."

Valens was frowning. "You're really going to bash it down to a sixteenth of an inch?" he said.

Ziani nodded, noticing that although Valens had hardly raised his voice at all, he could hear him quite clearly through the hammering. "As it spreads out, we can support the edges on the smaller anvils and work it on them," he shouted. "It'll be awkward, though, keeping the thickness consistent. We'll need to keep shifting it around so the bit we're working on stays directly over the anvil face. At the ordnance factory we had rollers and jigs and derricks to handle the weight, but of course we haven't got the time or the facilities for a setup like that."

Valens yawned. "But it's all going to plan, is it?" he asked. "You're pleased with how it's working out?"

He's had enough, Ziani thought, he wants to go away and do something else. "All fine so far," he said.

"Splendid," Valens said, and yawned again. "In that case, I guess you've proved your point. I'll want to see your accounts, of course, but in principle, yes, you carry on. Let me know from time to time how you're doing; if you need anything, see Carausius. I've told him this project's got priority." He fell silent and stared at the gradually flattening bloom for a moment. "You've done well," he said at last. "I've got no idea whether this'll help us fight off the Mezentines, but you seem to me to be making a good job of it. Sorry, but I've got to go now. That racket's giving me a headache."

That racket, Ziani thought; that racket's the sound of the trial you asked for, the miracle you want me to achieve for you. But it didn't matter. "Thank you for —" he started to say, but Valens nodded, smiled tightly, and walked quickly away, the courtiers scrambling behind him like chicks following a broody hen.

It was dark by the time the first full sheet was finished. It was horrible, no other word for it. Ziani didn't need his calipers to know that the thickness varied wildly, from a sixteenth up to a full eighth in places. But three such sheets, riveted to a frame or simply nailed to boards, would protect a wagon against fire, axes and arrows. Left unsupported at the top, it'd be too flexible to climb over or bear the weight of a ladder. Against cavalry, it'd be as effective as a stone wall. It was an affront to everything he believed in, but it was good enough; and besides, the others would be better. This was simply a demonstration, put on for the benefit of a man who hadn't even stayed to see it, because the ringing of the hammers made his head hurt. That didn't matter either.

"We did it, then." Daurenja's voice in his ear; he didn't bother to look round. There were times when he wondered whether Daurenja was actually there at all, or whether there was just a voice he could hear. "I trust the Duke was impressed."

"Impressed enough," Ziani replied (it was a word he was coming to hate). He took a deep breath, as though about to confess a mortal sin. "Thanks to you, mostly," he said. "You've been a great help."

"Me?" Genuine surprise. "I just did as you told me."

"Yes." Trying to find words to talk to him was getting harder all the time. "Just what I needed. I owe you a favor."

"Please, think nothing of it."

There were stories he'd heard when he was a boy, about the demons who tempted fools. Apparently they were the spirits of foxes — Ziani had never seen a fox until he ran away from Mezentia — who possessed human bodies, and they attached themselves to weak, ambitious men and gave them anything they wanted, in return for some unspecified future favor, which turned out to be the victim's body. When the process was complete, the fox simply drove the poor fool out of his own head and left him to die, like a snail out of its shell.

Ziani turned round sharply. One or two of the men lifted their heads to look. "No, I insist," he said, and his voice wasn't friendly. "You've done all this stuff for me, hard work, tedious chasing around that'd have driven me crazy. There's got to be something you want in return, but so far you haven't told me what it is. I think it's about time I found out what I'm letting myself in for."

Daurenja's face had gone completely blank; it reminded Ziani of dead bodies laid out for a wake, their faces nudged and prodded and molded by skillful fingers into a total lack of expression. "Not at all," he said. "It's a pleasure and an education to work for you. I've learned so much from this project."

"You're lying," Ziani said.

The bewildered look on Daurenja's face was completely false. "I promise you, I'm not. Besides," he went on, with an equally false simper, "even if I have got some weird ulterior motive that you don't approve of, it wouldn't affect you. All you'd have to do is say no."

Ziani breathed out slowly, hoping it would calm him down. It didn't. "That's right," he said. "That's all I'd have to do."

Daurenja smiled. It could have been a beautiful expression; friendly, open, reassuring. "In any case," he said, "you're far too smart to let anybody take advantage of you. Quite the reverse."

Ziani felt something twist in his stomach. "You reckon."

"Absolutely. Anybody who could manipulate Duke Orsea and Duke Valens so adroitly with nothing but a simple letter . . ." He shrugged. "And the salt merchant," he added. "A stroke of genius. Tell me: did you know about the secret road before you met her?"

After such a long time being in charge, making plans, carrying them out, bearing so much weight, it was almost a relief to be paralyzed. "What do you want?" Ziani said.

"Nothing," Daurenja said. "Trust me."

13

"You again," she said.

Psellus nodded, and sat down in the chair across the table from her. Politeness, he told himself. In the face of a resentful, angry witness, good manners are a shield. "Thank you for coming in," he said. "I hope it's not too inconvenient."

Her eyes were bright, and completely out of place in her mild, beautiful, insipid face. "It's not as though I had any choice," she said. "Soldiers on my doorstep at five in the morning . . ."

"They weren't soldiers," Psellus said pleasantly. "Guild security officers. I thought you might appreciate a lift, instead of having to walk."

She folded her thin arms across her chest. "I like walking," she said.

He copied her gesture, except that he kept his back straight in his chair. "That's fortunate," he said, "now that you live so far out of the center of town. Your old house was much more convenient."

She shrugged. She seemed to be trying to look behind her left shoulder. "There's nothing I need to go into town for," she said. "I can get all my shopping in the Eastgate market, and it's cheaper."

Psellus nodded. "That's true," he said. "Personally, though, I don't think I'd like living in the suburbs. I've lived my whole life in the center of the city."

It was intended as a rest, an empty moment. She kept still and let it pass.

"Do you like your new house?" Psellus asked.

"It's all right."

"Just all right?" He smiled indulgently, like a kind old uncle. "It seems a lot of trouble to go to, all the aggravation of moving, if the new place isn't any better than all right."

"I hated living in the old house," she said coldly. "After everything that happened there."

"I can understand that," Psellus said soothingly. "A lot of painful memories, I'm sure."

She turned her head a little. A small chin, rounded, but not weak. "I didn't like living there by grace and favor, either," she said.

"You were allowed to stay there for as long as you needed to," Psellus reminded her. "True, it was a dispensation rather than a right —"

"Grace and favor," she repeated.

"I understand. And how's your daughter liking her new home? Settling in? Making new friends?"

She shrugged, as though she wasn't really interested.

"It must help," Psellus went on, "that she's living in a different neighborhood, where the other children don't necessarily know about what her father did. It must have been very hard on her, at the old house."

"Not really." She was, he conceded, superb in defense, using every aspect of her weakness to the full. Sympathy glided off her, like arrows off the best proof armor. "We never mixed much with the neighbors anyway."

"Apart from your own family, of course." No response to that. "It must be hard on you, living so far from them."

"It's not all that far," she corrected him, almost scornfully. "Half an hour's walk."

"Indeed." Big smile. "Half an hour's walk is a *very* long way for me, but I'm old and fat." Pause; in his head, he counted to four. "All in all, then, things are working out well for you."

"I suppose so, yes."

"You suppose so." He raised an eyebrow, but she wasn't looking at him. "I'd say you've been quite fortunate — no, that's not quite the word, it does rather imply that you don't really deserve your good fortune. In your case, it's more like a just reward, or compensation at the very least."

That made her look at him. "What?"

He smiled broadly. "Finding true love," he said. "And in such difficult circumstances."

Her look should have punctured him like a bubble, but he'd been ready for it; invited it, like a fencer tempting his opponent with a feigned weakness. "That's right," she said.

"Actually, that's why I asked you here," he went on, as smoothly as he could in the presence of such brittleness. "Your application for a dispensation to remarry, even though your husband is still alive."

"Oh," she said. The same maneuver, mirrored; a feigned relaxation of her guard. "Is there a problem?"

He shook his head. "No, I'm pleased to be able to tell you, we've considered all the facts and, in view of the circumstances —"

"I mean," she interrupted, "he's as good as dead, isn't he? In the eyes of the law he's dead, because he was condemned to death. For all anybody knows, he *is* dead. So —"

A cue; deliberate, or fortuitous? "As a matter of fact," he said quietly, "Ziani Vaatzes is still very much alive. We have intelligence that places him at the court of Duke Valens of the Vadani. He's just completed the sabotage of the Vadani silver mines; a very neat piece of work, I should add, thanks to him the mines will be completely useless to us once we've conquered the country."

She shrugged. "He's still making a nuisance of himself, then."

Psellus had read the reports. Dry, needless to say, and doing their best to gloss over the things that had caught his imagination. In his mind's eye, nevertheless, he'd seen them: thousands of dead men, killed as they advanced in perfect formation, without even the time to break rank and start to run. Making a nuisance of himself. "That's none of your concern now," he said. "Just in case you've been worrying, nobody holds you in any way responsible for his actions, either before his escape or since. The findings of the board of inquiry were absolutely explicit on that point."

The words *board of inquiry* made her flinch, as well they might. No bad thing to remind her of how close she'd come to sharing her husband's disaster.

"So that's all right, then," she said. "Falier and I can get married."

"Indeed you can, I'm delighted to say." None of that delight seemed to be reflected in her face. "You'll be able to get on with the arrangements, let your family know the date and so forth. I'm sure there'll be a great deal to do."

"We're keeping it quiet and simple," she said. "We don't want lots of fuss. And besides, we can't afford a big do."

"Really." Careful frown. "Now that your fiancé's the foreman of the ordnance factory, I wouldn't have thought money would be a problem."

"We've got better things to spend our money on."

"I'm sure." She was trying to shake him off, like something nasty stuck to the sole of her shoe. That was a flaw in her guard. He leaned back a little in his chair.

"Is that it, then?" she said. "Can I go now?"

"In just a few minutes," he said firmly. "It's been a while since we had an opportunity to talk."

"What do you need to talk to me about?" she said. "I thought you said you're giving us permission . . ."

Psellus congratulated himself on his timing. Letting her think she was almost free, giving her a sight of the door, so to speak; now she was in a hurry to get away, which meant that the longer he kept her there, the stronger his advantage would be. "Would you like something to eat or drink?" he said. "I usually have a glass of something and a biscuit around now."

"No thank you."

He shrugged. "If you change your mind later on, just say so."

He rang the little silver bell that stood just by his elbow. He'd had all sorts of trouble getting hold of one, but it looked as though the effort would be justified. The door opened, and the clerk (on loan for the day from the records office) nodded a polite little bow, as though he'd been a footman all his life. "Mulled wine with honey and nutmeg for me, and one of those delightful cinnamon cakes," he said. "Are you sure I can't get you anything?"

"Have I done something wrong?"

Psellus raised both eyebrows. "Not that I'm aware of."

"If I haven't done anything wrong, why can't I go home?"

"Of course you can go home, as soon as we've finished."

Her scowl only lasted a very short time, a tiny sliver of a second, before her face reverted to dull, wary vacancy. Psellus picked up a sheet of paper — minutes of some meeting, to which he hadn't been asked — and reflected that, however close the play and however smoothly the participants work together, anticipating each other's thoughts, sharing an intimacy otherwise experienced only by lovers, there must always be a gulf between predator and prey; because if the predator loses, he stays hungry for a day, whereas the prey loses forever. Such a disparity gives the advantage in motivation to the defense, provided it's backed up by sufficient skill. The predator, by contrast, must be more outgoing, more extreme.

The clerk arrived, with a cup and a plate. Psellus took a sip — water, as he'd specified — and nibbled the rim of the biscuit, like a mouse.

"Is that why you're keeping me here," she asked, "to watch you eat?"

He laughed, as though she'd made a good joke. "I'm sorry," he said. "I missed breakfast. Well now," he went on, settling himself comfortably in his chair, "there're just one or two points I'd like to clear up, while you're here."

"About my husband."

"Of course. Why else could anybody possibly be interested in you?"

Her eyes widened, just a little, then closed down again. "Go on, then."

Psellus stroked his chin thoughtfully. "As you know," he said, "I used to be attached to the commission that investigated the circumstances of your husband's offense. That investigation is now complete, overtaken by events, somewhat; the file's closed, to all intents and purposes, I've moved on, and so have you. But in spite of that, I can't help worrying away at loose ends, it's in my nature. The more I try not to think about something, the more it weighs on my mind. When it got to the stage where it was getting in the way of the work I'm supposed to be doing, I decided I'd better deal with it once and for all. For that, I need your help."

He paused and looked at her. Nobody there. Fine.

"Your husband," he went on, making his voice low and even, "built the mechanical doll. So far, we've concentrated — reasonably enough — on *how* he built it. Nobody seems to have stopped to consider *why* he built it. I think that's where my problem lies. It seems," he added with a smile, "such a curious thing for anybody to do."

She shrugged. "He made it for our daughter," she said.

"Quite so, yes. That much was admitted from the outset." Psellus nodded gravely. "That doesn't answer the question. Why a mechanical doll?"

Another shrug. "No idea."

"That's curious too. Did your daughter tell him she wanted one, very much? Had she seen one somewhere and admired it especially?"

"She could have done, I don't know."

"Well, why should you?" Psellus smiled. "Perhaps your daughter told him, but not you. Perhaps it was their secret. Daughters are often closer to their fathers than their mothers, in some respects. Isn't that right?"

"Maybe."

"Well, that's what people keep telling me," Psellus said pleasantly. "I'm not a family man myself. But anyway; he decided to build her the doll, for whatever reason. Now we come to another mystery. Your husband . . ." He paused again. "He's not by nature the rebellious type, is he?"

"I don't understand what you mean."

Psellus dipped his head. "Some people," he said, "have a problem with authority. Breaking rules, to them, is almost an end in itself; doesn't matter what the rule happens to be, the fact that it's a rule makes it fair game, if you follow me. It's a sort of independence of spirit, usually combined with high self-esteem and a low opinion of the system and society in general. But Ziani wasn't like that, was he?"

She shrugged.

"I don't think he was," Psellus said. "I think he understood the merits of the system pretty well. He was ambitious, of course; but his ambition was entirely orthodox, if you see what I mean. He wanted to succeed in the proper manner, by climbing the ladder of promotion. That was what gave success its value, I guess. He'd want to win, but cheating would spoil it for him. He assessed his own value in conventional terms."

"If you say so."

"Quite." He stopped talking and stared at a mark on the ceiling for a moment. "I can understand Ziani wanting to make a toy for his daughter, something she wanted very much that he could make for her. What I have trouble with is the fact that he saw fit to change the specifications. What do you think?"

"It was against the law," she said. "He shouldn't have done it."

Psellus clicked his tongue slightly. "That's not at issue. What I'm asking myself is this. Let's leave the issue of risk out of it for a moment; let's suppose that he firmly believed that he wasn't going to be found out. A reasonable enough belief, by the way," he added, "but we'll come back to that. One thing at a time." He leaned forward a little, crowding her. "At his trial, it was sort of assumed by default that he did it out of arrogance, just because he could; he thought he knew better than Specification, and that's a mortal sin. Now, what kind of man do you reckon would think that way?"

She didn't say anything. He kept quiet, making it clear that she was required to answer.

"I don't know," she said. "Someone cocky."

"That's what I'd have said, too," Psellus replied. "Let's see; someone who sees a better way of doing something — what he believes is a better way of doing something, at any rate — and can't abide to do it the approved way instead, just because of some rule. Is that how you'd see it?"

"I suppose so."

Psellus nodded firmly. "That's not Ziani, though, is it?" he said. "I mean to say, he worked in the factory all those years, and he didn't go around criticizing the way things were done."

"Of course not. It's against the law."

Psellus smiled. "Not in the ordnance factory," he said. "As you well know, it's an exception to the rule. He had the scope, working where he did; and yes, he did propose a number of innovations — quite correctly, through the proper channels — but not in such a way as to rock the boat or put anybody's back up. Most of the time, as far as I can tell, he was perfectly happy to follow Specification, because he acknowledged that it's perfect as it is. Not the behavior, in other words, of the malcontent or the compulsive rebel."

She made a show of stifling a yawn. Psellus couldn't help approving of that.

"Here's our paradox, then," he said. "For some reason, he decides to make the doll. Eccentric, yes, but perfectly legal; he was entirely within his rights, breaking no laws. He'll have gone to the specifications register and copied out the drawings and the commentary, gone home and planned out how he was going to tackle the job — the tools he'd need, the materials; and then he takes it into his head to make changes, improvements. Can you explain that, do you think?"

"No."

"Neither can I," Psellus said, "which is why you're here, and why you can't go home until I have an answer that makes sense.

All right, let's break it down into little bits and see if that helps. Let's start with the sequence of events."

"The what?"

"The order he did things in. Do you think he made the changes while he was reviewing the plans, or did they occur to him once he'd started?"

She shrugged, a very small movement. "I don't know."

Psellus acted as though he hadn't heard her. "I think," he said, "he made them before he actually began to cut metal; I don't see him as the sort of man who improvises in midstream, not unless something goes wrong. If I'm right, do you see the implications?"

She shook her head.

"It means," Psellus said, "that he started out with the view of — I don't know, of making the best mechanical doll he could possibly make, and to hell with rules and laws. That's different, don't you agree, to making a change on the spur of the moment. More deliberate. A stronger intention."

"I suppose so."

"Of course, I'm only guessing," Psellus went on. "Perhaps the changes were spur-of-the-moment decisions after all. But here's another thing." He straightened his legs under the desk. "If I was a very skillful craftsman, as Ziani was —"

"You keep talking like he's dead or something."

"So I am," Psellus said. "As he is, then; if I built something very clever and difficult, like a mechanical doll — well, I'm making it for my daughter, we know that. But I think I'd also want to show it off, just a little: to friends at work, other craftsmen, people who'd know and appreciate the quality of my work. I couldn't resist that, it's only natural, don't you think?"

She said nothing.

"I think so. But by changing Specification, I'm making that impossible. I'm building this very clever machine, and nobody else will ever see it, apart from a kid who won't understand. Now, we're saying that a man who changes Specification must be guilty of the sin of pride; but if he was proud of the work, he'd want to show it off, wouldn't he? There's the paradox. You can see it, can't you?"

Still nothing. She was looking just past his head.

"Maybe now you can see why I'm in such a tangle," Psellus went on sadly. "None of it makes any sense, does it? There's no sense in building it at all — if your daughter had wanted a mechanical doll more than anything in the world, I'm sure you'd have known about it, her mother. She'd have nagged and begged and wheedled and made a pest of herself. And if she didn't want it so desperately, the only other motive for building it would be pride, and we've just agreed it couldn't have been that. What a muddle," he added. "It really doesn't add up."

"I suppose it doesn't," she said quietly. "And I'm sorry if it bothers you, but I can't understand it either. Not when you put it like that."

Psellus smiled. "Ah," he said, "but that's only the little mystery. That's nothing at all compared to the big mystery. You wait till we get onto that, and you'll see why I simply can't leave it alone." He took a deep breath, and sighed. "But we won't bother about that now. Let's talk about something a bit less gloomy. How about true love?"

Her eyes gleamed angrily. "What are you on about now?"

"Falier," he replied, "the man you're going to marry, now that you've got your dispensation. Your true love. At least, I'm assuming . . ." He grinned. "I take it you two *are* in love; why else would you be getting married, after all?"

"Yes," she said, and her voice was like the grating of the two ends of a broken bone. "Yes, we love each other. All right?"

He nodded. "I thought as much," he said. "After all, it's a big step, for both of you. He'll be taking on another man's child, for one thing; not to mention the wife of the Republic's most wanted man. It stands to reason he must love you very much."

"He does. You can ask him, if you like."

"I might, now you suggest it." Psellus nibbled a bit more off the rim of his biscuit. "And then there's you. Intriguing, let's say. A lot of trouble was gone to so that you could stay in your house and get your pension from the Guild — I almost said widow's pension, but of course, Ziani's still alive. Someone really put himself out to arrange all that. You wouldn't happen to know who, would you? I seem to be having a certain amount of difficulty finding out through approved channels."

That got her attention. "Sorry," she said, "no idea."

"Some anonymous benefactor, then," he replied. "My first thought was your father; and yes, he made representations, through his head of chapel. I saw the file; the application was dismissed. The other file — the one that was approved — seems terribly difficult to find, however. I've had archivists scurrying around the records office looking for it, but it doesn't appear to be there. They think the mice may have eaten it, though apparently they didn't manage to get their teeth into the approval certificate. I had a good look at that, and it says quite clearly: by order of the Guild benevolent association, you get to stay in the house and draw the pension for life or until remarriage. All perfectly in order. Not signed, of course. Being a certificate, it's got a seal rather than a signature; which is annoying, because a signature would've given me a name, someone I could've pestered for some background. But a seal simply means it was sent down to the clerks' office with the other approved documents." He shook his head slightly. "Not to worry. We were talking about love, not office procedures. The point I'm making is, thanks to this unknown altruist, you were nicely placed for life: a home and an income — not a fortune, but as much as any Guild widow gets. More, actually, because of Ziani's status. I think that, in your position, most people would've been very grateful for that."

"I was. What are you getting at?"

He waved his hand vaguely. "I'm not getting at anything. I'm just saying: your marriage to Falier can't just be a single mother's entirely understandable desire for security, a roof over her head, food and clothes for the kid. No, you're giving all that up — for life or until remarriage, remember? Yes, I'm sure you do. So you're making sacrifices, just as Falier is. Therefore, logically, you must be in love, or why do it?"

"We're in love," she snapped, "I just told you that."

He nodded. "And I'm explaining why I believe you," he said soothingly. "It's not as if I don't approve of love; on the contrary, I think it's a splendid thing, and so does the Guild. Official policy; love is a benefit to the community at large, and should be encouraged." He chuckled. "They did a study once, did you know? They did a survey, and they found that happily married men, and men who were either engaged or going steady, had a sixteen percent higher productivity rating, adjusted over time, than bachelors and men who didn't get on with their wives. So, you see, love is good for business as well as everything else."

"That's really interesting," she said flatly.

"Isn't it? Of course," he went on, "that's good news for the ordnance factory. When Ziani was foreman, productivity was excellent; if the survey's to be believed, presumably it's because he loved his wife and was happy at home. Since he left and Falier took over, productivity — measured in output per man-hour — has dropped by seven percent. But now Falier's getting married to someone who loves him very much, so with any luck we ought to be able to claw back that seven percent and who knows, maybe even notch up an extra point or two. Coincidence, of course, that he'll be marrying Ziani's wife; but the view the committee took is that if you made Ziani happy, it's likely you'll make Falier happy too. A proven track record, as you might say."

She gave him a poisonous look, and said nothing. He drank the rest of his water. Siege warfare, he thought; the attacking army lines up its siege engines, its catapults and mangonels and trebuchets and onagers, and lets fly a horrendous bombardment against the city walls, until the air is thick with the dust from pounded masonry, but the walls are thick enough to shrug it off. But the bombardment is just a decoy, because while it's going on, the sappers are digging under the walls, laying their camouflets, lighting their fires; and when the walls fail, it's not the direct attack that's done the trick, it's the undermining.

"Anyway," he said, lifting his empty cup. "Here's to love." He mimed a sip and put the cup down. "Now, I think, it's about the right moment to go back to that big mystery I was talking about a while ago. Are you ready for it, do you think?"

She made a soft, disdainful noise in her throat.

"Splendid," he said. "Here goes, then. I told you just now that the mice ate the records of the board's decision on your pension application. Well, it seems we've got quite a serious vermin problem down there in the vaults, because they aren't the only records that appear to have got all chewed up — assuming that's what happened to them, of course. Another batch of papers that seems to be very difficult to get hold of is the early part of the file on Ziani's investigation; you know, the inquiries that led to his arrest. The interesting stuff, not the bits they read out at the trial. The bits that'd tell me how they found him out in the first place."

He looked at her. Blank, sheer, closed, like a city wall.

"Well," he went on, "I couldn't get hold of the papers, but I thought, that's all right, all I need to do is find the investigating officers and ask them; simple as that. And here's where it starts to get a little disturbing, because those officers seem to have become confoundedly elusive. I wrote to them and got no answer; I wrote to their superiors, and all I got was an acknowledgment. I got my superiors to write to their superiors, and they told me my inquiry had been noted and they'd see what they could do about arranging interviews, but I waited and nothing happened. I went to the paymaster's office and checked, just to make sure the officers were still alive and in the service; no worries on that score, they're still on the books and drawing their pay. That set my mind at rest; I was worried they might have got lost down in the archives and eaten by the mice. But I still haven't been able to talk to them, or get a letter from them, or anything resembling answers to my questions. And then I thought of you."

"Me," she repeated.

He shrugged. "It's worth a try, I thought. Maybe you might know. You see," he went on, "logically, there're only a limited number of ways that anybody could've found out about what Ziani was doing. He could have shown the doll to someone and told them; or someone could have visited the house and seen the doll, or drawings and sketches; either that, or someone else must have mentioned it — informed on him direct to the Guild, or told someone who did the actual informing. One of those three possibilities, unless you remember different, or you can think of any other way. No? Fine."

"It came as a complete shock," she said. "They just turned up on the doorstep one day, said they were from the Guild, and where was his workshop? Then they started measuring things with calipers and rules and stuff, and when Ziani came home, they arrested him."

Psellus nodded slowly. "That's interesting," he said. "Interesting, I mean, that they seemed to know what they were looking for. Of course it's all a bit technical — I can explain it for you if you like, or you can take my word for it — but the thing is, the actual changes he made, the abominations; they weren't the sort of thing you'd notice just by looking. You'd need to measure everything very carefully, do all sorts of tests before you found them. You mentioned calipers and rules, by the way; can you remember anything else they used? Any other kinds of equipment?"

"There could have been other things," she said. "I wouldn't know what they were. I don't know about technical stuff."

"Of course not. But they'd have needed resistance gauges — that means gadgets you use to measure the strength of a spring; other tools like that. They're quite bulky, not the sort of thing you can cart around in a pocket or a tool-roll. Were they carrying heavy bags, or cases?"

"I don't remember."

"Ah well." Psellus looked down at his hands for a moment. "Maybe we can get rid of the second alternative — if you remember, that was someone, a visitor, catching sight of the doll while it was being made, and noticing something was wrong. I'd figured out a perfectly plausible way it could've happened; a dinner guest wandering into the wrong room, or going to get a coat he'd left. But this notional visitor would have to be someone who knew that particular specification intimately — rather narrows the field, I'd say — and who just happened to have calipers and a resistance gauge handy at the time . . . And then I thought, perhaps what he saw wasn't the doll itself, but drawings and schematics, and he noticed the changes. But that'd still mean he'd need to be an expert on the specification. No, I think we can sideline that possibility. In which case, we're left with the other two. Either Ziani told someone, or someone else knew what Ziani was up to and informed on him." He looked up and smiled brilliantly. "And, of course, both of those are impossible too. Aren't they?"

She looked past him. "You've lost me," she said.

"Really?" He raised his eyebrows. "It's not exactly difficult to follow. Ziani wouldn't have told anybody, because we agreed, it's not in his nature. And there can't have been anybody else who told on him, because who else would've known about it? Only someone who knew he was making the doll, and who knew he was including the abominations — someone he'd *told* about the changes he was planning on making. And, frankly, who could that possibly have been? Nobody." He looked up, at a spot on the ceiling directly above her head. "Well, you, possibly. Just conceivably he might have told you. But that makes no sense, because why on earth would you betray him to disgrace and death? After all, you stood to lose everything. And," he added, "you loved him, of course. True love."

"That's right," she said, quietly and icily. "I didn't know, and if I'd known I wouldn't have told."

"Of course not," Psellus said. "Of course you wouldn't. But then who does that leave? No one at all. Except . . ." He rubbed the bridge of his nose. "There's Falier, of course. His direct subordinate at the factory, the man you're about to marry. He'd understand the technical stuff. I don't suppose for one minute that he'd be carrying the mechanical doll specification around in his head, but he'd know where to look it up. Even so; that still needs someone to have tipped him off, so he could go and inform on Ziani to the Guild. And who could've done that? Someone who wanted to, and someone who knew about it. That rules you out," Psellus said, smiling, "on at least one count. So, now you understand why I've taken to thinking of this as the big mystery. It's not just big, it's huge, don't you think? Not that it'd matter a damn," he went on, "if Ziani hadn't managed to escape from the Guildhall the way he did. Because, all said and done, it's irrelevant exactly how he was found out. What matters, in the end, is the fact that he did actually commit the crime. He was guilty. We know that, because he said so. No, it's only worth going over all this old stuff because Ziani's still very much alive and on the loose. You know, don't you, that he betrayed Civitas Eremiae to us?"

(There, he thought; the camouflet sprung, the props burned out, the walls undermined.)

She looked at him for three heartbeats. "No," she said, "I didn't know that."

"Perfectly true." Psellus smiled. "Odd thing to do, don't you think, given that he'd built the scorpions that slaughtered our army. Because of him, in fact, we were that close to giving up and going away. Then, after causing us all that trouble, he turns round and hands us the city. Would you care to suggest why he might've done that?"

"No idea."

"Well." Psellus ate the last of the biscuit, brushed crumbs off his chest. "He wrote a letter to a friend; the one man in Mezentia he reckoned he could still trust. I'm surprised, actually, that you don't know. I'd have thought Falier might have told you."

"What's he got to do with it?"

"It was Falier he wrote to."

She couldn't stop her eyes widening; and it was like seeing a crack appearing in masonry. "He didn't tell me, no. I suppose he was ordered not to."

"Oh, quite so. But still; when you're as much in love as he is . . ."
He shrugged. "But that fits in with what we know about Falier; a
very trustworthy man, reliable. Anyway, to go back to what we
were saying. Why would Ziani have done such a thing, do you
think?"

"Didn't he say why? In the letter?"

Psellus smiled. "As a matter of fact, he did. He said it was because he was filled with remorse and wanted to make things right.
Do you think that's likely to be the real reason?"

She shrugged. "I don't know."

"It occurred to me," Psellus went on, "that he was hoping we
might forgive him, and let him come home. Of course, that would
be impossible." She looked up when he said that. "Out of the
question, naturally. First he creates a crisis, by arming the enemy
with scorpions; then he hopes to get his free pardon by solving it.
No, we wouldn't do business under those conditions." He paused,
waited for a moment, then went on: "Actually, we would. In order
to save face, after a disaster like the defeat the Eremians inflicted
on us — if he'd come to us with an offer like that, we'd have listened, for sure. I think we'd probably have agreed. But he wasn't
to know that, of course; certainly, he'd have to be out of his mind
to formulate a plan on the assumption that we'd give in to him.
And anyway, he didn't even try to negotiate. He simply gave us
the information, with no conditions, no demands. Now *that*," he
said wearily, "is a puzzle. On its own, it's enough to give you indigestion. Taken with the other puzzles . . ." He shrugged. "There
now," he said. "Did you realize you're married to such an enigmatic character?"

Something was bothering her; he hadn't had her full attention
for the last moment or so. "Would you really have let him come
home?" she said. "If he'd tried to do a deal?"

Psellus put on a serious face. "Hard to say," he said. "If he'd
been able to convince us beforehand that he could give us a way
into the city, then I'd have to say yes. Or at least, that's what we'd
have told him. I don't think the Guilds believe they'd be bound

by a promise to a convicted abominator. But then," he went on, "I'm not sure how he'd have got us to believe he was sincere; we'd have assumed it was a trap of some sort, leading us into an ambush. It's crossed our minds, of course," he continued, "that giving us Civitas Eremiae could've been by way of a free sample." She looked up at him; now, apparently, she was interested in what he had to say. Quite a change. "What I mean is," he said, "he betrayed the city to us just to prove that he could be trusted, so that next time —" He stopped, as though he'd shocked himself with the implications of what he was saying. "So that," he went on, "if he sent us another message like that on another occasion — offering us Civitas Vadanis, say, but with conditions attached this time — we'd know that he meant it, and could deliver. Of course, that'd imply that he thinks a very long way ahead, and has complete confidence in his own ability to manipulate people. A bit farfetched, now I come to think about it. Also, he'd have had to have some pretty surefire way out of Civitas Eremiae lined up before making us the offer. Otherwise he'd be running a terrible risk of either being recognized and arrested when the city fell, or getting himself killed in the wholesale massacre. Now, we know that he did in fact escape; but only because Duke Valens suddenly turned up at the last minute. Did he know about that? I wonder. Had he actually booked himself a ride with the Vadani before he approached us with the offer? No, impossible; because in order to do that, in order to tip Valens off to come to the rescue at precisely the right time, he'd have had to make it clear to them that he knew exactly when the city was going to fall, and that'd have made it obvious that he was the traitor. Even so," he continued, after a pause for breath, "we've kept that option open by not letting the Vadani know that it was Ziani who sold out the Eremians; just in case he's got it in mind to hand them to us on a plate as well. When I say *we*," he added, "I mean my colleagues on the war commission. I voted to let Valens know straightaway, send him some hard evidence to back the claim up, so he'd have Ziani arrested and strung up. But the rest of the commission disagreed, and . . ." He shook his head. "By the way," he added, "not a word about this to anybody. If Valens finds out what Ziani did and has him killed, it'll be obvious that there's been an unauthorized disclosure, and since I voted against keeping it a secret . . ." He smiled. "I'd make it a point of honor to see to it that my last official act before being thrown off the commission and charged with treason would be having you arrested for complicity in Ziani's crimes. A friendly warning. Understood?"

She dipped her head. "I just want to forget he ever existed," she said.

"Well." Psellus suddenly felt very tired; he wondered if she did too. "You've listened very patiently, and it seems there's not a great deal of light you can shed on any of my problems. I was hoping you might be able to point me in the right direction; but what you don't know you can't tell me, I guess. Pity, but there it is."

He realized that she was looking straight at him. "Do you really think there's a chance he might come home?" she said. "Any chance at all?"

Wonderful how she'd said that; no clue as to which answer she'd prefer to hear. Since he couldn't glean it from context, Psellus decided, why not ask her straight out? "Do you want him back?" he said.

"Me? No, of course not. Not when I'm just about to marry someone else."

"Ah yes, true love. It had slipped my mind for a moment. Well, I don't think you need have any worries on that score. As I think I told you, he's just finished helping Valens to decommission the Vadani silver mines, to keep us from getting them. That means Ziani isn't the most popular man in the world, as far as the Guilds are concerned. They might just be prepared to overlook the deaths of five thousand or so mercenaries, but cheating them of the richest silver deposits in the world — I don't see them deciding to forgive and forget that in a hurry."

She was back to looking past him as though he wasn't there. "Can I go now, please?" she said. Not quite a whine, but with the same level of urgency; like a child on a long journey asking *Are we nearly there yet?* Looking at her, Psellus could quite see how she'd been able to wind Ziani round her little finger. Not for the first time, he thanked providence that he'd never been in love himself.

"Yes, thank you," he said, and she stood up immediately.

"The dispensation," she said.

"What? Oh yes, of course. It'll be issued straightaway. You ought to have it in, I don't know, three weeks. Four at the very most."

"Four weeks? Can't you hurry it up a bit?"

You had to admire her. Single-minded as an arrow, self-centered as a gyroscope, and nice-looking into the bargain. Ziani would never have stood a chance; nor, apparently, Falier. "That depends," he said. "If you happened to remember anything that might help me with my puzzles, any time over the next five weeks . . ."

"You said four."

He made a vague gesture. "You know what the clerks are like. They will insist on that big, flowing, joined-up writing, not to mention taking their time over illuminating all the capital letters. Taking pride in their work, you see, even when it's nothing but a routine dispensation. All it takes is one spelling mistake, and they tear it up and start all over again. It's a wonder anything ever gets done in this city, really."

She was standing in the doorway, right up close to the door, like a goat on a chain straining for a mouthful of grass just out of reach. "We'll just have to be patient, then," she said, "because there isn't anything else I can tell you."

"Of course." He nodded sharply. "Thank you for your time. You can go now."

She went. It was all over in a flicker; door opened, door closed. Anybody who could move that efficiently, Psellus reckoned, must be an excellent dancer. Would there be dancing at the wedding, he wondered, when she married Supervisor Falier? Somehow, he was inclined to doubt it.

He lifted a stack of papers on his desk; under them was the dispensation. He flipped open the lid of his inkwell, dipped a pen and wrote his initials, just underneath the signature of the deputy chief registrar. Ziani, he decided, must've had his reasons, when he gave Civitas Eremiae to the Republic without bargaining first. Although he couldn't understand what those reasons were, he'd come to respect his opponent enough to trust his tactical and strategic abilities. Imitating him, therefore, was probably a good way to proceed. He sprinkled the paper with a little sand, and rang the bell.

"What?" The borrowed clerk wasn't nearly so obsequious now he was alone.

"Could you do me a favor and run this up to the dispatcher's office?" Psellus asked.

"What's your problem, cramp?"

"Bad knee," Psellus said. "Rheumatism."

The clerk frowned. "I'm going that way anyhow," he said, moving forward and taking the paper.

"That's lucky," Psellus said. "Thanks. If they could see to it that it gets there as soon as . . ."

The clerk nodded, and left. Psellus sat back. With luck, it'd be there waiting for her by the time she got home; a pleasant surprise, he hoped, and totally disconcerting.

Left alone, Psellus took a book from his shelf, sat down, put his feet up on the desk and started to read. As a senior member of the executive, he had access to a much richer choice of literature than the ordinary Mezentine; instead, he'd chosen to read garbage. No other word for it. Lately, though, he'd found himself dipping into it over and over again, so that the inept similes and graceless phrases had seeped into his vocabulary, private quotations that served as part of his mental shorthand. Even as a physical object, the book was ludicrous, having been crudely made by an amateur out of scrounged materials — packing-case wood for the covers, sacking thread for the binding. Its fascination lay in the fact that it was a collection of love poetry written by Ziani Vaatzes to his wife; the small, pretty, rat-like woman he'd just been talking to. Throughout their conversation, it had been at the back of his mind to haul the book out and read bits to her — except that she wouldn't have understood the significance, since he was quite certain Ziani had never shown or read her any of his painful compositions. It remained, therefore, a secret that he shared directly and exclusively with his opponent, the arch-abominator and the Republic's deadliest enemy, who had once written:

I saw her walking down the street.
She has such small, such pretty feet.
And when she turns and smiles at me
I'm happy as a man can be.

A puzzle. He turned the page. Here was one he hadn't seen before.

I know she loves me, but she just can't say it.
It's not the sort of thing we talk about.
No words or looks of hers can yet betray it
But still her love for me is not in doubt.

He winced. If Vaatzes had been only twice as good at engineering as he'd been at poetry, he'd never have had to leave the city.

Someone coughed. He looked up sharply, reflexively dragging his feet off the desk before he noticed that it was only another clerk. "Well?" he grunted.

"Message for you," the clerk said, squinting sideways to read what was written on the spine of the book. Psellus closed it and dropped it in his lap. "Let's have it, then."

The clerk handed him a folded piece of paper and went away. It was an ordinary sheet of thin rag paper, universally used for internal memos, but it was folded twice and closed with the official seal of Necessary Evil. That made it important. He sat up to read it.

Boioannes to his colleagues, greetings.

The abominator Vaatzes has contacted the Guild. Herewith a transcript of a letter delivered through intermediaries; Commissioner Psellus to report to me at his earliest convenience to examine the original and verify the handwriting against other documents currently in his keeping.

Text as follows . . .

14

It had been, everybody agreed, an efficient wedding. The necessary steps had been taken in the proper manner, the prescribed forms of words had been used in the presence of the appropriate witnesses, the register had been signed and sealed by all the parties to the transaction, and the young couple were now thoroughly married, fixed together as tightly as a brazed joint.

Unfortunate, perhaps, that neither of them had seemed particularly happy about it. More unfortunate still that both of them had made so little effort to dissemble their feelings. The Vadani people were, on the whole, fond of their duke and didn't like to see him looking miserable. Accordingly, there had been a rather strained, thoughtful atmosphere at the ceremony itself, and the scenes of public joy that greeted the departure from the chapel had been distinctly subdued. Never mind; the mortise doesn't have to love the tenon, just so long as they fit snugly together and accept the dowel.

"It's only politics, after all," someone he didn't know said to Orsea, as they filed in to the wedding breakfast. "Now that's all over they can stay out of each other's way and get on with their lives. Well, not entirely out of each other's way, there's the succession to think of. That aside, it's a pretty civilized arrangement."

Orsea smiled weakly. When he'd married the Countess Sirupati, heiress to the duchy of Eremia, he had only seen her two or three times, in crowds, at functions and the like. On his wedding day, he hadn't recognized her at first — he'd known that he was going to be marrying the girl dressed in the big white gauzy tent thing, but when she lifted back the veil, it hadn't been the face he'd been expecting to see. He'd got her confused in his mind with her second sister, Baute. A few days later, of course, he'd found himself more deeply in love than any man had ever been before or since . . .

"No reason why they shouldn't get along quite amicably," the man was saying. "By all accounts she likes the same sort of thing he does — hawking, hunting, the great outdoors. So long as she's got the common sense not to disagree with him about which hawk to fly or whether to drive the long covert before lunch, they ought at least to be able to be friends; and that matters so much more than love, doesn't it, in a marriage."

Something to do with roads, Orsea thought; deputy commissioner of highways, or something of the kind. Whatever he was, the man was extremely annoying; but the line was tightly packed and slow-moving, and he had no hope of getting away from him without a severe breach of protocol. Even so . . .

"Do you think so?" he said, as mildly as he could manage. "I think love's the only thing that matters in a marriage."

"You're a bachelor, then."

"No."

"Oh." A shrug. "In that case, congratulations and I'm delighted for you. In my case . . ." The annoying man looked sad for a moment. "Pretty straightforward," he said. "My father had the upland grazing but virtually no water, her father had the river valley but no summer pasture. At the time I was head over heels for the local notary's daughter. Carried on seeing her for a bit after the wedding — wife didn't make a fuss, pretended she didn't know, though it was obvious she did really. I don't know what happened after that. I just sort of realized that love is basically for teenagers, and when it comes to real life for grown-ups, you're far better off with someone who's moderately pleased to see you when you're around, but who leaves you in peace when you've got things to do. When you're trying to run a major estate as well as holding down an important government appointment, you simply haven't got time to go for long hand-holding walks in the meadows or look sheepish for an hour while she yells at you for forgetting her aunt's birthday. Nowadays we get on famously: I've got my work, she messes about with tapestries and flowers and stuff, and she's got her own friends; we meet up once a day for breakfast and generally have a good old natter about things . . ."

They reached the table. Mercifully, the annoying man was sitting right down the other end. So, apparently, was Veatriz. He could see the top of her head over a short man's shoulder.

"You're Duke Orsea, aren't you?" There was a female sitting on his left; a nondescript middle-aged woman in green, wearing a massive necklace of rubies.

"That's right," Orsea said, as though confessing to a misdemeanor. "I'm sorry, I —"

"Lollia Caustina," the woman replied promptly. "My husband's the colonel of the household cavalry. So, what did you think?"

About what? Orsea thought; then he realized she must mean the wedding. "Very nice," he mumbled.

She started to laugh, then straightened her face immediately as a hand reached past her shoulder and put down a bowl of soup. "Game broth," she said sadly. "I might have known. Something the Duke killed for us specially, I assume, but as far as I'm concerned he needn't have bothered. I thought it was absolutely fascinating."

"I'm sorry?" Orsea said.

"The wedding. Fascinating. Politically, I mean."

"Oh," Orsea said.

"I mean, take the exchange of rings," the woman went on. "You saw who was carrying the tray with the bride's ring on it. Calvus Falx, of all people. If that's not a smack in the face for the moderates —"

"I see," Orsea lied. A bowl of soup materialized in front of him, and he reached for his spoon. The woman, he noticed, slurped when eating soup.

"And don't get me started on the presents," she was saying. "Talk about making a statement; they might as well have built a stage in the market square and read out speeches. Chancellor Carausius' gift to the bride's uncles; you saw it, of course."

Orsea tried frantically to remember what he'd given to who. "Well, no, I —"

"Hunting knives," the woman said bitterly, "silver inlay, *Mezentine*. I had a good look when nobody was looking, the makers' marks were there plain as anything. Of course, it's pretty obvious what all *that* was about; but if he thinks he's going to convince them that easily, I'd say he's in for a nasty surprise. They may be savages, but they aren't stupid. They know as well as we do, trading at fourth hand through intermediaries for finished manufactured goods is going to cost us an absolute fortune, and with the mines all closed up . . ."

Luckily, she didn't seem to expect anything from him apart from the occasional interested-sounding grunt, and he was good at those. Accordingly he was able to turn his mind out to graze on the implications of something the annoying man had said. *They ought at least to be able to be friends; and that matters so much more than love in a marriage.* He thought about that, and wondered if it was true. Veatriz — he loved her, or he had loved her very much, but they'd never been *friends*, not as he understood the word. He hadn't needed her for that; he'd always had Miel Ducas.

(Who'd always loved her, ever since they were children, and who should have married her, except that that would've meant the Ducas getting the throne, which would have been a disaster politically; and who loved her enough to conceal the letter from Valens, who loved her as a friend, because to him there was no difference; and for that Miel had been disgraced, and Valens had come to save her, thereby bringing down ruin on his people, just as Orsea had ruined Eremia. He imagined a map, with great big areas on it hatched in red: *these regions laid waste for love . . .*)

To his unspeakable relief, as soon as the soup was taken away and replaced with a cured venison salad, the woman turned away sharply, like a well-drilled soldier, and started talking to the man on her other side. Free, Orsea ate some lettuce and a bit of meat (felt and tasted like honey-cured rawhide) until the woman on his right said, "Excuse me, but aren't you Duke Orsea?"

He hadn't even noticed her. She was wearing a dress of deep red velvet, down the front of which she'd spilled at least one full spoon's worth of soup. She was round-faced, steel-haired, with eyes that bulged slightly, like a dead rabbit.

"That's me," Orsea said. "Who're you?"

"Calenda Maea, at your service," she replied, with a short, vigorous nod. "Specializing in heavy materials. Iron ore, lumber, best prices anywhere." She grinned. "So you're the genius who thinks we should all nail sheets of tin to our carts and take to the hills."

Orsea blinked. "I'm sorry," he said. "I haven't the faintest idea what you're talking about."

"It's all right, I know it's supposed to be hush-hush, I won't embarrass you. Let's talk about something else. Your pet Mezentine, the one who's giving all the juicy orders to the Falcata sisters. Is money changing hands somewhere I don't know about, or does he actually enjoy being ripped off?"

Orsea sighed. "I think you may have got me mixed up with someone else," he said. "I haven't got anything to do with Vaatzes these days. In fact, I don't really do anything."

She frowned. "You're on the emergency council, aren't you?"

"That's true," Orsea said. "But they've stopped telling me when the meetings are, so I don't go anymore."

"Oh. So you aren't really involved with purchasing."

"Me? No."

"Ah." She shrugged. "My mistake. So, who should I be talking to about bulk consignments of quality scrap iron?"

Orsea shrugged. "No idea," he said.

"Fine." The woman frowned at him, as if to say that he had no right to be there if he wasn't any use to her. "So what do you make of it all, then?"

"I don't."

"What? Oh, I see. No comment at this time, is that it?"

"If you like."

She nodded. "Sounds like the administration's got something up its sleeve it doesn't want anybody knowing about, in that case," she said. "Playing its cards close to its chest, in case word gets out and sends materials prices rocketing. Fine, we'll find out anyway, we've got other sources of information, you know. No, what I meant was, the marriage. What do you reckon?"

"None of my business," Orsea said.

She laughed. "Politicians," she said. "Well, please yourself. Me, I think it's an absolute disaster. Good for business, of course, because all those soldiers, they're going to need feeding and clothes and boots and tents and all that. We do a lot of business with the Cure Doce — carriage is a nightmare, of course, but we manage; no such word as can't, my mother used to say — so I think we'll be getting our slice sooner or later, even if your chief of procurement is sleeping with the Falcatas. But otherwise . . ." She shrugged, and the contents of her dress rolled like the ocean in fury. "I hope I'm wrong, of course, but I know I'm right. Fair enough, I'm no great authority on happy marriages. You've just got to look at the idiot I ended up with to see that. But I reckon, if you're going to get married at all, it ought to be for the right reason, and well, there's only one reason for getting married, isn't there?"

"Is there?"

"Are you serious? Of course. If you're going to marry, marry for love. Not for money, not to please your family, and certainly not for cavalry. I mean," she went on with a sour expression on her face, "you've just got to look at her. Miserable, sharp-faced bitch. Oh sure, they've done a fantastic job training her, she can sit on a chair and eat with a knife and a spoon and talk just like people, but that doesn't change what she is. Still, that's the price you pay for sitting in the top chair. I guess he's done well to hold out as long as he has done."

Orsea frowned. "Valens, you mean?"

She nodded. "They've been on at him for years to get married, but he's dug his heels in and fought them like crazy, every time. Nice girls, too, some of them. They used to say he was, well, you know, but I never believed that. I mean, if that was true, he'd have married the first one they threw at him, just to get them all off his back, and then got on with his own way of doing things, so to speak, and no bother. Trouble with Valens is, though, he's a romantic."

Orsea couldn't help reacting to that. "You think so? I'd have thought he's the most down-to-earth man I've ever —"

She laughed; genuine laughter, but not kind. "You're kidding, of course," she said. "No, our dashing, moody young duke is a play-actor. He plays at being himself, if you see what I mean. He's like an artist, creating one great masterpiece: himself, of course. He's his life's work. Mostly he sees himself as Valens the Great, best duke the Vadani ever had. Other times, though, he's Valens the dark, driven, passionate lover — and that only works, of course, if you can't have the one you really want. Settle him down with a nice cheerful girl with a sense of humor, he'd pine away and die. That's what all this is about, of course. If he's got to marry someone — grand self-sacrifice to save the duchy in its darkest hour — he picks the most impossible girl anybody could imagine: Cure Hardy, dour, miserable, wouldn't know a joke if it burrowed up her bum. You can't help feeling sorry for him, though. Well," she added thoughtfully, as if she'd just remembered something. "*You'd* be the exception, of course. I expect you're breathing a big sigh of relief, now today's over. Though of course you never had anything to worry about. Not his way."

The temptation to pour the contents of the oil-cruet down the front of her dress was one of the strongest forces Orsea had ever encountered in his life. He resisted it — epic poems should have been composed about that battle — and instead shrugged his shoulders. "I don't know what you mean," he said. "And I don't really want to talk about the Duke's private life, if it's all the same to you."

"All right," she said, with a grin. "Let's talk about niter."

For a moment, Orsea was sure he'd misheard her. "What?"

"Niter." Big smile, revealing many teeth, all different shapes and sizes. "Stuff you get when you boil up a big load of dirt off the floor of a chicken run or a pigsty; when all the water's steamed off, you're left with a sort of white powder. They use it for preserving meat."

Orsea nodded slowly. "And you foresee a demand for preserved meat because of the war. Rations for the soldiers."

"Stands to reason," she said. "They'll be crying out for the stuff, when we evacuate. Not to mention rations for the Duke's dowry; don't suppose they eat bread, or porridge, though I suppose they may prefer their meat raw. Pull it off the bone with their teeth, like as not. Anyhow, I've got a customer who wants all the niter he can get, and I know for a fact the bloody Falcatas have got all the domestic stocks tied up — contrary to the public interest, I call it, cornering the market in essential supplies when there's a war on. So I thought, there must be loads of chicken coops in Eremia, and nobody much left to take an interest in them, if you see what I mean. And my lot, the Merchant Adventurers — well, I'm not saying we've got a relationship with the Mezentines, that'd be a gross overstatement and not very patriotic, of course; but trade's got to go on, hasn't it, or where would we all be? So what I'm saying is, the fact that any possible niter deposits may happen to be in occupied territory wouldn't be the end of the world, so to speak. Not absolutely fatal to a deal, if everything else falls into place."

Orsea shook his head. "Sorry," he said. "We probably had chickens in Eremia; in fact, I'm fairly certain of it. But where they lived and who looked after them —"

"Doesn't have to be chickens," she said. "Could be pigs. Bats, even. You get a cave where bats have been roosting for a good many years, that's a real treasure-trove. Anywhere there's shit, basically, or other sorts of animal stuff rotting down. I heard somewhere you can make niter from the soil of an old graveyard." She smiled at him. "You must've had *them* in Eremia."

Orsea sighed. "I wouldn't be at all surprised," he said. "But the answer's no, I can't help you. Maybe if you got in touch with someone in the resistance —"

"Them? Oh, they're ancient history, now Valens has cut off the money. Thought you'd have known that, it being your duchy."

"So you deal in minerals, then?" Orsea said, polite and brittle as an icicle. "I thought you said you were in lumber and iron ore."

"Bulk commodities," she replied. "All the same to me. Of course," she went on, "the big thing coming up's going to be salt, thanks to the marriage. Beats me, though. Everybody's talking about salt, how these savages have got access to the salt pans and how we're going to get it all and salt's going to be the new silver. What nobody seems to have thought about, however, is the fact that there's a bloody great big desert between them and us, and nobody can get across it with a caravan or even half a dozen carts. Have you heard how many of the princess' entourage died crossing the desert on their way here? Shocking. They just don't value human life the way we do." She wiped her lips on her napkin, and picked up a partridge leg. "I mean, I reckon I'm reasonably smart, I like to think I know what's going on; but if someone's cracked that particular problem, they haven't told me about it. So," she went on, and Orsea took a deep breath, enduring each second as it came and went, "they can have the salt business and much good may it do them. Meanwhile, there's other stuff in the world that wants buying and selling, and if they want to waste their time on salt, that's fine by me. You're *sure* about the niter, are you? All right, how about sulfur? There's been a lot of people talking about it lately, so maybe there's a market coming up . . ."

Thinking back on it later, Orsea couldn't say how he survived the rest of the wedding breakfast; but he managed, somehow. Valens and his new bride got up and left the Great Hall; there was a short pause, and then the rest of the high table filed out; once they were gone, there was a general polite push-and-shove for the exits. The horrible woman in the red dress was still talking at him when the currents parted them. He didn't stop until he was safe, fifty yards down the long cloister. Then he remembered: he was invited to the afternoon hunt, which meant fighting his way back to his rooms to get changed. Praying fervently that he wouldn't bump into the dreadful woman, he turned back and forced his way upstream until he reached the arch that led to the courtyard. Then he picked up his heels and ran.

"Where did you get to?" Veatriz demanded as he burst through the door. "You'd better get ready, we'll be late."

He was already lifting the lid of the clothes press, nosing about for a clean tunic. "You're coming?"

"Well, yes. Had you forgotten?"

He looked at her. She'd changed already, into a plain, straight green gown and low-heeled red shoes. "What? No, sorry." He scowled. "I got trapped at the breakfast talking to this appalling woman, she's jangled my brains so badly I can't think. Yes, of course you're coming too. Where the hell is my suede jerkin?"

She sighed. "You won't want that," she said, "not for hawking. Besides, you'll boil. You want a light linen tunic and a silk damask cotehardie."

"Oh. Have I got . . . ?"

"Yes. In the trunk."

He nodded, slammed the press shut and started digging in the trunk like a rooting pig. "Shoes," he said.

"Boots. You're riding, remember? Wear the ones you had on yesterday."

"They're horrible."

"They were a present from Valens."

"He won't notice if I —"

"He's just the sort who would," she snapped. "When are you going to realize, we've got to be polite to these people?"

He stood up and looked at her. There was a great deal he

wanted to say, more than he'd wanted to say for a very long time. He looked away and pulled off his shirt.

"Come *on*," she said. "Think how it'll look if we keep the whole party waiting."

In the event, they were neither late nor early, and nobody seemed to have noticed that they'd arrived. The main courtyard was filled with horses and grooms (marry for love, not cavalry, the woman had said), falconers and austringers and the hawks themselves on their wrists, bizarre in their tasseled hoods. Orsea realized that he knew hardly anybody there.

"Who's that smiling at us?" he hissed in his wife's ear.

"Pelleus Crux," she whispered back. "Something to do with . . ."

He didn't hear the rest of what she said, because a hawk bated next to him, its wing slapping his face as it shot off the falconer's wrist and stopped abruptly, restrained by the jesses.

"I'm sorry," said a familiar voice. "I'm new at this, and I guess I must have . . ."

Orsea peered round the falcon and saw an unmistakable face; brown. "Hello," he said.

Ziani Vaatzes grinned sheepishly at him. "Would you do me a great favor," he said, "and get this stupid bird off me?"

Veatriz giggled. "Go on," she said. "The poor thing's scared out of its wits."

"The same," Ziani replied gravely, thrusting his wrist in Orsea's direction, "is probably true of the bird. Not," he added, "that I care, so long as somebody else takes it."

Orsea smiled, and nudged his finger under the hawk's claws. It stepped up onto it, and he said, "Untie the jesses, I can't take it otherwise."

"The what?"

"The leather strings round its legs. They're tied to your arm."

"Are they? So they are." Ziani fumbled for a moment, and the jesses dropped. Orsea grabbed them quickly with his left hand and tucked them into his right fist. "I'm very sorry," Ziani was saying. "Some fool came and shoved this thing at me. I got the impression it's meant to be a great honor, but —"

"It is," Orsea said. "What you've got here is a peregrine. Nice one, too."

"Peregrine," Ziani repeated. "Hang on, I know this. The peregrine is for a count —"

"Earl, actually," Orsea said. "A count would have a saker. But you're close." He frowned. "Have you been reading King Fashion?"

Ziani nodded. "Not that it's done me much good," he said. "It's hard memorizing stuff when you haven't got a clue what any of it means." He pulled a face, as though concentrating. "You're a duke, so you ought to have a falcon of the rock, whatever that's supposed to be."

Orsea laughed. "Actually, nobody knows, it's been the subject of learned debate for centuries. Most people reckon it means either a gyrfalcon or a gyrfalcon tiercel, but there's another school of thought that reckons it means a goshawk, even though they're short-winged hawks and not really falcons at all." He clicked his tongue. "I'm sorry," he said. "I'm told that falconry is the second most boring subject in the world, if you don't happen to be up on it. I can't remember what the first most boring is. Hunting, probably."

Ziani shook his head. "Engineering," he said. "Trust me, I've seen the glazed look in people's eyes when I've been talking at them too long."

"Well, I won't contradict you," Orsea said sagely. "Though I reckon fencing's got to be pretty close to the top of the list, and Mannerist poetry, and estate management. All the stuff I actually know something about," he added with a grin, "which says something or other about an aristocratic education." Out of the corner of his eye, he caught sight of Veatriz; she had that fixed smile that meant her attention was elsewhere; the men were talking, her job was to keep still and look respectably decorative. Of course, he told himself, *he* didn't think like that; perish the thought. On the other hand, he could have a fairly animated conversation with a relative stranger, but only ever talked to her in questions — where's my shirt, what time are we supposed to be there, did you remember to bring the keys? Well, he thought, marriage. When you know someone as well as you know your wife, there's not a great deal that needs saying out loud (he didn't believe that, but it sounded comfortably plausible). "Anyhow," he said, a little too loudly, as if he'd just caught himself nodding off to sleep, "I'll look after this beauty for you, if you don't want . . ."

"Please," Ziani said, with a shudder that was only mildly exaggerated for effect. "I'd only hurt it, or lose it or something."

"You don't like the idea of being an honorary earl, then?"

"Me? Not likely. I remember looking at that list in King Fashion, and there doesn't seem to be a species of bird of prey appropriate for a factory supervisor."

Orsea pursed his lips. "No," he said. "Unless a supervisor counts as a clerk, in which case you're entitled to a male sparrowhawk. You wouldn't want one, though, they're useless."

"Orsea." Veatriz tugged very gently at his sleeve. "They've arrived."

"What? Oh." Orsea looked round, and saw a party of five, already mounted, on particularly fine matching dapple-gray palfreys. Valens was in front, looking pale and uncomfortable in gray velvet. Next to him, the savage woman — the Duchess, Orsea corrected himself — also in gray; next to her, the two uncles, overdressed in fringed, slashed buckskin over scarlet satin; bringing up the rear, the head austringer. All five carried hawks on their wrists. The Duchess looked solemn to the point of sourness, Valens looked apprehensive, and Orsea had the feeling that neither of the uncles was completely sober. Jarnac should have been here, he caught himself thinking; then he remembered that Jarnac (the frivolous, irresponsible buffoon who lived only for hunting and hawking) was still in Eremia, fighting what little was left of the war for the survival of his people. The question is, Orsea asked himself, what the hell am I doing here? To that, of course, there was no sensible answer.

Time to mount; he looked round, suddenly realizing that he no longer owned a horse; but there was a groom standing next to him (hadn't been there a second before, he could have sworn) holding the bridle of a tall chestnut gelding; for him, apparently. He handed the hawk to Veatriz, heaved himself into the saddle, kept still while the groom fussed over the stirrup leathers and the girth, then leaned forward and took the hawk back. It settled comfortably on his wrist, as though there was a socket there for it to snap into. Anybody looking at him would be forgiven for thinking he was somebody important: a duke, say.

Veatriz was mounted too; they'd given her a small, rounded bay jennet and a pretty little merlin, with a green velvet hood. He looked past her to see what they'd brought for Ziani, and was amused to see him heaped up (no other word for it) on the back of a huge, chunky black cob, with legs like tree trunks. He looked very sad, and was clearly trying not to think of how far off the ground he was. At once, Orsea thought back to the disastrous hunt that Jarnac Ducas had organized, not long before the siege of Civitas Eremiae; Ziani Vaatzes had contrived to get himself in the way of a wounded and very angry boar, and it had taken some pretty spectacular heroics from Miel Ducas to save his hide . . . But Orsea didn't want to remember Miel Ducas just then.

Movement. He legged his horse round to fall in with the rest of the party, looking for Veatriz; but she'd joined the column further up, and was riding next to a fat man on a huge roan mare, just behind the five dapple-grays. He frowned. He wanted to be closer to her, but it'd be a fearful breach of protocol to jump places, now that the party had set off. He glanced over his shoulder. Ziani was bringing up the rear, on his own, a few yards ahead of the hunt servants and the hawks. "Fine day for it," the man beside Orsea said.

"Not bad," he replied. "I'm sorry, I don't know . . ."

"My name's Daurenja," the man said; and Orsea looked at him properly. Extraordinary creature, he thought, somewhere between a rat, a toad and a spider, with a long ponytail of dank black hair. But he rode very well, with a fine upright seat, head up and shoulders back, and he wore the sparrowhawk on his wrist like some sort of ornament, the way fine ladies wished they could. "I work for Ziani Vaatzes, the engineer."

"I know Ziani," Orsea said. "He's just behind us, if you're looking for him."

"I know," the man replied. "But he's really not used to this sort of thing, and since I'm his assistant, I don't want to make him feel self-conscious. He'd feel I was showing him up."

Fair enough, Orsea thought; and if Valens saw fit to invite this character, that was entirely up to him.

"Mind you," the man went on, "I'm pretty rusty myself. Haven't been out with the hawks for years, not since I was a kid. My father kept a lanner and a couple of merlins, we used to go out quite often at one time, but . . ." He shrugged expressively. "Things got in the way since then, you know how it is. So this is quite a treat for me. I must say, I was surprised when I got the invitation. I'm guessing they only asked me because they assumed I'd refuse."

Orsea smiled bleakly. "Valens has got quite a reputation as a falconer," he said. "Chances are we're in for a good day."

"It's a privilege, I know," the man said. "Ever since I came here, I've been lucky enough to be associated with some exceptional people."

Orsea tried to think of something to say, but couldn't.

They rode down into the valley, along the river, past the lake toward the marshes. "Looks like we're starting with heron," the man said cheerfully. "I hope so," he went on, "that'd give your peregrine a chance to show what she's made of. That's a beautiful bird you've got there, by the way."

"Thanks," Orsea said awkwardly. "Actually, she's not mine. I think she belongs to the Duke."

The man nodded. "Conditions should be just right for her; nice warm day, the air rising. I'm not sure what I'll find for this old thing to fly at, unless we head up through the stubbles later on and put up a partridge or two. I don't think she's done much," he added sadly. "The woman I borrowed her from — merchant,

down in the town — I think she only keeps her as a fashion acces-
sory. I just hope I don't lose her as soon as I let her go. That'd be
embarrassing."

"That's sparrowhawks for you," Orsea heard himself say, in the
cheerful, slightly loud voice he used for being polite to people he'd
taken an early, irrational dislike to. "They're as bad as goshawks
for straying."

"Absolutely," the man said earnestly. "And so damn picky with
their food, die as soon as look at you, out of sheer spite. My father
bought one for my mother, but she couldn't stand the thing, so she
passed it on to my elder brother to catch thrushes with. He'd had
it six months, just starting to think he'd reached an understanding with it, and then suddenly one morning he comes down and
finds it lying on the mews floor, dead as a nail. Put him right off
hawks for life." He sighed, as though reliving the sadness of it all.
"What I always wanted," he went on, "was a saker. Of course,
there wasn't much river work where I grew up: partridges in the
autumn, pheasant and woodcock in winter. A saker's much more
of a moorland hawk, I always feel, though of course the best ones
come from the south; I expect our new best friends favor them, for
desert work."

At least, Orsea told himself, he doesn't seem inclined to talk
about the wedding. Small mercies. Even so, it would be very pleasant to get back to his room later on, and bolt the door.

They were skirting the edge of the marshes, riding slowly, picking their way between tussocks of couch grass along a black, peaty
sheep-trail. The sunlight glared off steel-gray pools, and the stink
of bog mud was very strong. Through a curtain of reeds Orsea was
sure he'd caught sight of ducks, floating in the middle of a broad
pool, but apparently they weren't the quarry Valens had in mind.
Orsea could just see him, well ahead of the rest of the party, riding
with the master falconer at his side; they spoke to each other occasionally, a few low words. Suddenly Valens held up his hand. The
column halted — Orsea had to rein in quite sharply to keep from
barging into the tail of the horse in front — and Valens and the

falconer went on ahead, moving slowly but with obvious purpose, as though looking for something they knew was there.

It proved to be a pair of herons, which burst out of a clump of reeds and soared upwards, pumping their wings as they gained height. Valens and the falconer were unhooding their hawks — the Duchess' goshawk, and a superb white gyrfalcon which the falconer had been carrying. By the time the hoods were off, the herons were black specks smudged by the glare of the sun, but the hawks lifted and followed their line, binding to them straightaway, overtaking them, turning them back and swooping when they were almost directly above Valens' head. The goshawk struck a second or so before the gyrfalcon, at which the Duchess' uncles cheered and clapped loudly; nobody else moved or made a sound. Presumably it was either a political point or a good omen. The falconer dismounted to break up the dead herons; he cut them open, twisted and tugged out the wing-bones, cracked them like a thatcher twisting a spar and teased out the marrow as a reward for the hawks. They ate it off the side of his hand, quickly and disdainfully, as though eating was hardly a proper activity for a well-bred hawk.

"Pretty flight," Daurenja was saying, "though the goshawk was a bit slow to bind, I thought. Still, she made up for it through the air."

Orsea nodded, since it was easier to agree than to think about what he was saying. The falconer was stringing the herons from his saddle by their necks; their heads drooped like wilted flowers. While he was busy, a dozen or so men appeared over the skyline, with four long, thin greyhounds and four spaniels at their heels: beaters, presumably, to drive the reeds.

"This is more like it," Daurenja was saying. "I guess they'd marked that pair of herons beforehand, and Valens wanted to start with them to try out the new goshawk, so he held the beaters and dogs back in case they put the ducks up early."

(There you are, then, Orsea thought. Another of life's mysteries solved.)

Valens, the falconer and the leader of the beating party were deep in conference, each of them pointing in a different direction and looking thoughtful and solemn. Evidently, there had been some unforeseen development that had thrown out their carefully framed strategy. If only we'd taken this much care over our tactical planning during the war, Orsea thought, I'd probably still be in Civitas Eremiae right now; either there or inside Mezentia, interviewing potential garrison commanders. The conference appeared to break up; then Valens must've changed his mind, because he waved the head beater back for a second round of negotiations, while three of the dogs lay down in the heather and went to sleep. The falconer came back and joined in, there was quite a bit more pointing; then Valens nodded his head decisively and everybody started to move at the same time. The dogs jumped up, their heads lifted; the beaters slipped the chokes over their necks and led them off, apparently back the way they'd just come.

"Wind direction," Daurenja commented sagely. "I don't know if you've noticed, but it's changed, coming from the south now, so I guess the beaters are having to sneak round the south edge and come up that way, in case the ducks spook and go back. We've just got to bide here till we get the signal that they're in position. Then he'll spread us out so we're surrounding the pond, and we'll all get a fair crack once the ducks get up."

"More than likely," Orsea muttered. Any pleasure he might have wrung out of the afternoon was being leached out by Daurenja's insufferable commentary. He wished he could think of some perceptive or erudite comment to make, so he could show Daurenja that he knew much more about the subject than he did. Nothing came to mind, however, and the peregrine was starting to shift about on his wrist. He yawned, and wished he was somewhere else.

"You've got to hand it to Valens, though," Daurenja was saying, "he definitely — hello, we're moving." Sure enough, the master falconer was waving his free arm in a circle, and the rest of the column was breaking formation. Orsea realized he hadn't been paying proper attention, and didn't know where he was supposed to go. Of course it'd be just typical if he ruined everything by being out of position . . .

He swallowed his pride. "Excuse me," he asked Daurenja, "but did you happen to notice . . . ?"

"Where he wants us?" Daurenja nodded. "Over there, either side of that scrubby little thorn bush. Not a bad spot; we won't get any action as they're heading out, but we should get a couple when they start coming back in, if we're lucky."

"Thanks," Orsea replied, trying not to resent the *us* part of it. He legged his horse round and followed Daurenja, splashing through a shallow pool of brown water. He looked up; if Daurenja was right about the likely sequence of events, the sun would be in his eyes at the critical moment. Somehow, he wasn't in the least surprised.

He reached what he guessed was his assigned position, settled himself in his saddle and looked round to see what was going on. The hunting party was encircling the pool where he'd seen the ducks, standing off from it about twenty yards. He couldn't see the birds over the curtain of reeds, but he could hear the occasional reassuring quack. The stillness and quiet was familiar, at any rate, and gradually he could feel the excitement build inside him, as suspense and impatience tightened his chest. He found himself anticipating the possible flight lines of ducks leaving the pool, drawing lines and calculating angles in his mind. On these occasions he felt like a component in a machine, some part of a complicated trap, his movements directed and dependent upon the movements of the rest of the mechanism. That made him think of Ziani Vaatzes, who claimed to be able to see complicated designs in his mind; he glanced round for a sight of him, but couldn't pick him out. He looked down at the hawk on his wrist and saw it properly for the first time. His job was simple enough, though with plenty of scope for error. As soon as the ducks got up, he'd unbuckle the hood-straps and the jesses and throw the hawk, so that by the time it struck its first wingbeat, it would already have the necessary speed and be following the right line. On his day, he knew, he was very good at it. If it wasn't his day, he was perfectly capable of messing it up beyond all recovery. He hoped very much that nobody would be watching him. Then it occurred to him that he didn't know where Veatriz was. He looked round for her, and therefore was facing entirely the wrong way when a splash told him that the spaniels were in the water.

He lifted his head, trying to figure out where the angry quacking was coming from. He could hear the slapping of wingtips on water, someone was shouting angrily at a dog, the sun was blinding him and he was trying to undo the peregrine's hood-straps by feel, without looking down. One of the other sort of days, he decided, as the first duck shot directly over his head like an arrow.

Shouting, on all sides. Some of it was anger, some just loud communication. The loop under the buckle of the hood-strap was stuck; he had nothing to lever with, and his carefully trimmed fingernail was too short to pick it out. The falcon was objecting, not unreasonably, to his harsh and clumsy handling of it. Out of the corner of his eye, he saw Daurenja making his cast — a sparrowhawk could never bring down a duck; well, a teal, perhaps, or maybe the spaniels had put up some stupid little birds while they were crashing about among the reeds. Ducks were streaming overhead, most of them directly over him, and he was missing them all . . .

"Orsea, for crying out loud." He recognized Valens' voice; the agonized rage of a man who's planned a perfect treat for other people, and has to watch them waste it. "What's the matter with you? Get that bloody hawk in the air, before they all get away."

The hood came off — for a single, terrifying moment he thought he'd pulled the falcon's head off with it — and he fumbled with the jesses. Fortunately, they were more cooperative. Finding itself suddenly in a world of light and movement, the falcon spread its wings and bated, jerking sharply against the half-released jesses. One last furious fumble and he'd freed them. He started to move his arm for the cast, but the falcon had had enough. It hopped off his wrist into the air, struck a powerful beat and began to climb.

As he watched it disappear into the sky, Orsea felt overwhelming relief, as though he'd just been let out of prison. He looked round, and saw that everybody else was loosing their own hawks. I wasn't the last, then, he consoled himself, until he realized with a feeling of horror that, since he was at least nominally still a duke, protocol demanded that everybody else apart from Valens couldn't fly their hawks until he'd released his. He winced. Two or three ducks were still in the air; the rest were long gone. He'd contrived to spoil it for everyone, yet again.

Moving his head to look away, he caught Valens' eye, and winced again. It wasn't the contempt, so much as the complete lack of surprise. It occurred to him that, when they were assembling in the courtyard, they hadn't brought him a hawk; the peregrine had been entrusted to Ziani, who'd passed it on. Now he could see why.

He heard yelping: the dogs, running in to pick up ducks grounded by the falcons. That suggested that, in spite of his best efforts, it hadn't been a complete washout. He looked up at the sky. One or two ducks were coming back to the water, but he could see precious few hawks. He knew what that meant. Flown after quarry that had already gone too far, the hawks had gone looking for prey on their own account, and were unlikely to come back any time soon. The falconers would be spending the rest of the afternoon looking for them; if they'd killed and roosted, it'd mean someone would have to sit out all night under the roosting-tree, and then climb up at first light to catch the hawk before it woke up. All things considered, he couldn't have ruined Valens' wedding-day hunt more efficiently if he'd planned it all in advance.

Daurenja's sparrowhawk came back, with a thrush in its claws. That, Orsea reckoned, more or less put the seal on the whole sorry business.

No sign of his peregrine. He knew the drill: if his hawk hadn't come back within a certain time, he was obliged to notify the master falconer, who'd organize the search for it. Orsea wasn't looking forward to that. Knowing his luck, the peregrine would turn out to be a bird the master had trained himself, sitting up with it for four days and nights without rest or sleep; he wouldn't say anything, but the look in his eyes would be enough to kill a dragon. There'd be plenty of other people nearby, of course, waiting in line to report their own missing hawks; they'd be looking at him too, and not saying anything. Twenty yards or so away, he saw Veatriz, talking to her majesty, the new duchess. He could guess what they were saying. Excuse me, but do you happen to know who that bloody fool was who ruined everything? Well, yes, actually that's my husband.

Valens had joined them; Veatriz backed up her horse and moved a few steps away. He considered riding over and joining her, but decided that that would be unkind. A duck rocketed low over his head, returning to the water. Its cry sounded just like an ordinary quack, but Orsea knew it was laughing at him, and he could see the joke.

No need for clocks, sundials or counting under his breath. Orsea could feel the moment come and go, marking the time limit for the hawks to have come back before they were officially considered strayed. People were starting to look round for the master falconer. He heard Valens say, in a loud, carrying voice, "Well, I suppose we'd better forget about it for today." People murmured back, and muttered to each other. Yes, Orsea thought, just about perfect.

"That was a bit of a shambles, wasn't it?" Daurenja had materialized next to him, his sparrowhawk hooded and perfectly aligned on his wrist (no sign of the dead thrush; slung, presumably, into some bush). "What went wrong? I wasn't looking."

"It was all —" Orsea stopped. He'd caught sight of a couple of riders coming round the edge of the reeds. At first he assumed that they were the falconer's men, assembling to begin the search for the strayed hawks. Then he noticed that they didn't look right; not dressed for hawking, more like soldiers, in armor, with shiny steel helmets and lances. Also, their faces were very dark; like Ziani's.

"Who the hell are they?" someone said, close by.

Orsea looked over his shoulder, to see if Valens had noticed them, and saw five more just like them, coming up from the opposite direction. Strange, he thought; they're almost dark enough to be Mezentines, except that —

One of them nudged his horse into a slow canter, heading straight for a fat man in dark blue and his wife, who were both looking the other way. Someone shouted to them — Orsea couldn't quite catch the words — but they hadn't heard or took no notice. The dark-faced rider came up between them; the fat man's horse shied sideways, just as the dark-faced stranger lifted a hand with a sword held in it and slashed him across the back of the neck. The fat man slumped forward immediately, as though he'd been held up by a string which the sword had cut; the woman turned her head just as the dark-faced man brought his arm up and backhanded a thrust into her face. She fell sideways; her horse broke into a trot, dragging her by one stirrup, so that her head bounced up and down on the ground like a ball.

A woman screamed. The rest of the dark-faced men — Orsea didn't have time to count them, but at least two dozen — were moving forward too; the ones with lances were couching them, while the others were drawing swords. "What the *hell* do you think you're doing?" a man called out in an outraged voice, as if he'd caught them stealing apples.

Orsea remembered: the war. The one he'd brought here with him.

"Are those men Mezentines?" Daurenja's voice, frankly puzzled, groping for an explanation. For some reason, the sound of it stung Orsea like a wasp. I've got to do something, he thought; but that was stupid. They were soldiers, in armor; he was unarmed, in his pretty clothes, attending a wedding.

One of them crossed in front of him, no more than five yards away, stopped, and turned his head to stare at him. There was no malice in the man's dark eyes, just a flicker as he identified a legitimate quarry. He tugged lightly on his left rein, turning his horse's head.

Coming for me, Orsea thought; and then, Oh well. Then he remembered something, though even as he thought of it he doubted its relevance. He was a nobleman; except on a very few specific occasions, a nobleman doesn't leave his bedchamber without some kind of sidearm, even if it's just something decorative and stupid, such as the mimsy little stagshorn-handled hanger he'd hurriedly threaded on his belt as an afterthought, just before dashing out of the door. He felt for it and found it, as the dark-faced man closed with him. He'd actually managed to draw it halfway when something slammed very hard into the side of his head, squeezing all the light down into a pinprick.

15

Out of their minds, Valens thought, as he dragged his horse's head round. Completely, suicidally insane, to mount an attack three miles from the city gate. They must know that, as soon as the alarm's raised, they'll be surrounded, outnumbered a hundred to one, annihilated in a matter of seconds. Nobody could be that stupid; therefore it can't be happening.

Without needing to look down, he found the hilt of his sword; then remembered that, since this was a hawking expedition in the safest place in the world, all he had with him was a stupid little hanger, adequate for clearing brambles but not a lot of use against armor. They'll all be killed, yes; but by then they'll have slaughtered the entire Vadani government. Maybe not so crazy after all.

He realized he was looking for her; well, of course. Two of them had seen him; they were slowing down, turning toward him, but he couldn't be bothered with them right now. He caught a glimpse of her — alone, separate from the main party, which was being cut down like nettles round a headland. *Stay there,* he begged her, and turned his attention to the immediate threat, because he couldn't do anything to help her if he was dead.

The funny little sword was in his hand. He kicked his horse into a canter and forced it straight at the right-hand Mezentine (a lancer, spear couched, coming in fast). At the last moment, when he felt his horse slow up in order to shy away from a direct collision, he pulled over hard to the right. His horse stumbled — he'd expected that — but recovered its stride with its next pace, as the Mezentine, going too fast to stop or swerve, drew level with his left shoulder. Valens threw himself to the left, almost pulling himself out of the saddle, crossing his right arm over his chest and shoulder, the hanger held as firmly as he could grip it; as the Mezentine rushed past him (neither hand free to fend off with), his neck brushed against the last inch and a half of Valens' sword-blade, and that was all there was to it.

Wrenching himself back up straight in the saddle, Valens hauled his horse through a half-circle, in time to see the dead man topple slowly backward over his horse's tail. Looking past him, he watched the second lancer come around, level up and address him, the look in his eyes confirming that the same ploy wouldn't work twice. Tiresome; but he still had the advantage in defense. A lancer trying to spear one particular target in the open is like a man trying to thread a moving needle. He kicked on, riding straight at the lancer; let him underestimate his enemy's imagination. As the distance between them dwindled into a blur, Valens could see him getting ready to anticipate the coming swerve; he'd make a swerve of his own, and hold his lance wide to sideswipe him out of the saddle. Fine. Valens kicked his poor, inoffensive horse as hard as he could, driving him into the Mezentine like a nail. At the moment when he knew the horse would refuse and pull away right, he jerked the left rein savagely, bringing the horse to a desperate standstill. The force of deceleration threw him forward, but he knew the Mezentine's outstretched lance would be there to stop him flying forward over the horse's ears. As he felt himself slam into the lance-shaft, he let go of the reins and grabbed with his left hand, closing his fingers around the shaft. There was a moment of resistance before the lance came away. *My lance now,* he thought, and sheathed the hanger.

The Mezentine, unarmed and only vaguely aware of what had just happened, was slowing up for his turn, leaving a tiny wedge of opportunity. Valens kicked on; the horse sprang straight into the canter, giving Valens just enough time to grab the reins with his right hand and poke the lance out with his left. The point caught the Mezentine just below the left shoulder blade, shunting him forward onto his horse's neck. Valens let go of the lance just in time, and legged hard right to swerve round him.

That chore out of the way, he reined in and looked to see if she was still where he'd left her. She wasn't. Swearing loudly, Valens stood up in his stirrups, making himself ignore the rich detail of the slaughter going on all around him (people he'd known all his life were being killed everywhere he looked, but he simply hadn't got time to take note of that; it'd have to wait), and eventually caught sight of her. For some reason she was riding straight toward a knot of them, four horsemen or was it five, engaged with some opponent on the ground he couldn't see. Furious because he wasn't being allowed any time to plan ahead, he dropped his painfully won lance, drew the ridiculous hanger and kicked forward. Out of his mind, he thought wryly; must be catching.

By some miracle, the one he reached first hadn't seen or heard him coming. Valens drewcut the back of his neck as he passed him, in the gap between the bottom of his aventail and his shoulders, and hoped he'd done enough, since he had no time to look and make sure. The second one thought he was ready for him, but raised his shield a couple of inches too high in his anxiety to cover his face and chest. Another drawcut, just above the knee; useful arteries there. Even so, he managed to land a cut before Valens was clear of him; he felt the contact, and something like a very severe wasp-sting, which could be anything from a flesh wound to death in a matter of seconds. Nothing he could do about it, so he didn't waste valuable time looking to see where he'd been cut. Ducking low as the third Mezentine swung at him, he punched his sword arm forward as he passed. He felt the point grate and turn on bone, dragged his horse round to address the fourth, and found he wasn't there anymore. Small mercies.

The luxury of a moment to pause and take in the situation. One Mezentine was still in the saddle, but he was leaking blood from

his leg like a holed barrel, and could be safely ignored. Two rider-
less horses; one Mezentine riding away: one man, at least, with a
bit of common sense. She was sitting motionless on her pretty little
horse. Her dress was soaked with blood, but not hers; the Mezentine's. She was staring at the dying man, watching the spurt
and flow ebb as he quickly ran dry. Quite likely the most horrible
thing she's ever seen in her life, Valens reflected; and true love did
that, riding yet again to her rescue.

There was someone else involved, he realized: a man, someone
he recognized. Reasonably enough — once seen, never forgotten,
the bizarre, spider-like character, Vaatzes' assistant. What the hell
was he doing here, anyway?

Answer: he was standing astride a dead horse, holding the front
half of a broken lance, which he'd just pulled out of a dead Mezentine. He too was bloody to the elbows; his eyes were impossibly wide and he was gasping for breath as though he'd just been
dragged out from under the water. That was impossible, because
he had no call to be there, certainly he had no business fighting,
heroically . . . Valens forced him out of his mind and looked round
a second time. Three Mezentines were heading for him, lances
couched. One damn thing after another.

The ugly, spidery man had seen them too; he swung round
from the hip to face them, holding out his half-a-spear as though
bracing himself to receive a charging boar. Immediately, Valens
understood; it was all in King Fashion, after all. He turned his
horse's head and rode away, forcing himself not to look back.

The lancer who detached himself from the pack of three to
come after him hadn't seen the breakaway maneuver he'd used
on the first Mezentine he'd killed, so the ploy was worth risking
again, and succeeded quickly and efficiently. Even so, time was
very tight. Valens wheeled round, almost too scared to look, but
it was all right, just about. One lancer had charged Vaatzes' man,
who'd dropped on one knee, spear-butt braced against his foot
(pure King Fashion), and allowed the lancer's horse to skewer itself
through the chest. That left one Mezentine to be the boar engaged

with the pack. Valens rode in on him from the side and cut half through his neck before he'd figured out what was going on. Then there was just the unhorsed Mezentine on the ground; he was dazed from the fall, and probably never knew what hit him.

But it was all a waste of time, Valens realized, as he looked up again and took in the shape of the engagement. Hardly anybody left alive, apart from a full dozen Mezentines, taking a moment or so to form up and surround them. A little spurt of anger at the unfairness of it flashed through Valens' mind. He'd done his best — done pretty well, in the circumstances — but he was going to lose anyway, in spite of his efforts. If only there'd been time, he'd have complained to somebody about it.

The Mezentines had completed their ring; all they had to do was close it up in good order and they could finish the job without further loss or fuss. Instead, they seemed to be hesitant about something. What, though? One man with a toy sword and a freak with a sharp stick? Maybe he was missing something. He glanced over his shoulder, and saw the most beautiful sight.

(Perhaps, he thought later, that was how she felt, when the Vadani cavalry swooped down through the fire and slaughter at Civitas Eremiae to carry her to safety. He doubted it, somehow. She'd only have seen the disgusting spectacle of killing, too horrible for her to differentiate between heroes and villains. He, on the other hand, could feel ecstatic joy at such a sight, because he knew it meant that his enemies were going to die and he wasn't.)

One platoon of the household cavalry; only thirty men, but enough to make all the difference in the world. They were standing to a furious gallop; Valens sketched it all out in his mind, and found that there would be time for the Mezentines to close in and kill her, and him, but only if they couldn't care less about being slaughtered a moment or so later. The fact that they were hesitating told him what decision they were going to make, whole seconds before they made it. They wheeled and galloped away. All over.

Valens felt the strength empty out of his body as the pain broke through. He struggled to draw a breath; he thought, I've been cut up before now, this is something else, but he couldn't think what. His mind was clogging up, with pain, with repressed fear, shock, all manner of nuisances and all of them the more intense for having been kept waiting, like petitioners left for too long in an anteroom. He looked at her, and the blank horror in her face was too much to bear. She's disgusted just looking at me, he realized, and he could see why. It was not what he'd done, but how he'd done it — quickly, with the smooth efficiency and minimal effort that comes only from long practice. Whenever she saw him now, she'd see the slaughterman.

The hell with that, he thought resentfully — he could feel himself starting to slide off the horse, but it was too much effort to fight for balance. His mind was almost clotted now, but something was nagging at the back of it, shrill, like the pain of toothache. He remembered: his wife. Was she dead or alive? As if it mattered.

A shift in balance, and the ground was rushing up to meet him. It hit his shoulder and hurt him, but it was too big to fight.

Someone was standing over him, telling him something. His eyes hurt.

"Syra Terentia and her two daughters, Lollius Pertinax, Sillius Vacuo and his wife, and they cut off their daughter's arm at the elbow . . ."

He struggled to place the voice. All he could see was light, and a blur. "What's the . . ." he heard himself say, but he didn't know how to finish the question.

"Sir?" Ah, Valens thought, someone who calls me *sir*. Not many of them whose names I know. "Do I know you?" he asked.

"Nolentius Brennus, sir," the voice said. "Captain of the Seventh Company, Household Cavalry." A short, nervous pause. "Sir, do you know what's just happened? Can you remember?"

The temptation, wicked and seductive, was to lie back and pretend to be asleep; but no, he couldn't do that. The young soldier was scared, on the edge of panic and, very probably, in charge.

He needed his duke's help. "Yes, it's all right," Valens muttered, opening his eyes wide and making an effort to resolve the blur into the soldier's face. Never seen him before: a long, thin nose, weak mouth and a round bobble for a chin. *If anybody's having a worse day than me,* Valens thought, *it'll be this poor devil.* "I'm sorry," he said. "I didn't take any of that in. This is the casualty list, yes?"

"Yes, sir." He saw the young man — Brennus, he knew the family but not this particular specimen — take a deep breath, ready to start the whole painful rigmarole over again. He felt sorry for him, but it had to be done.

"First things first," Valens said. "The Duchess. Is she . . . ?"

"She's fine, sir. At least, as well as can be expected."

"Her uncles?"

The fear in Captain Brennus' eyes made the words superfluous. "Both dead," he said. "They died defending the Duchess, but they had nothing to fight with."

"Yes, all right. Who else?"

The cataract of names. He wasn't counting; the list seemed to go on forever. There'd be two he'd never heard of, then three he'd known since he was a boy, then another stranger, then another old friend or cousin. Carausius was dead; that shocked him so much he missed the next five names.

"Orsea?" he interrupted.

"No, sir. Both he and the Duchess survived."

Valens nodded, and the recital continued. Orsea had survived — well, of course he had, it went without saying. The sky could cave in and flatten the earth, mile-wide fissures could open and gobble up the city, but Orsea would survive, somehow or other. "What about Ziani Vaatzes, the engineer? Did they get him?"

Captain Brennus shook his head. "No, sir, he was the one who raised the alarm. If it hadn't been for him . . ."

Valens groaned; he hadn't meant to, but the pain popped up suddenly and ambushed him. "What sort of a state am I in?" he asked.

"Well, sir . . ." Brennus hesitated. "Maybe I should get the doctor, he can tell you more."

Valens felt his chest tighten. "That bad?"

"No, sir. I mean —"

"Oh for crying out loud. Am I going to die, or not?"

It was almost amusing to see Brennus pull himself together. "You got a bad cut to your left arm; they've stitched and dressed it, but there may be some permanent damage. The arrow —"

Valens' eyebrows shot up. "I was hit by an arrow?"

"Yes, sir."

"I never even noticed. Where?"

"In the right thigh," Brennus said, his voice wavering. "The shaft was already snapped off when the surgeons treated you; they had to cut it out, but they don't think there'll be any lasting effect."

Valens smiled. "Is that it?"

"Concussion," Brennus said, "from the fall. They were quite worried, because you were unconscious for so long."

"Was I?" Valens pulled a face. "Well, I wouldn't know about that, I've been asleep." That seemed to bother Brennus a lot; was he supposed to laugh at the Duke's feeble, scrambled-brain jokes, or should he ignore them? Best, Valens decided, if I don't make any more. "So apart from that I'm all right?" he said.

"The doctors said you shouldn't even think about getting up for at least two days," Brennus said apprehensively, obviously anticipating a storm of angry refusal. Valens nodded.

"Suits me," he said. "For one thing, it feels like I've pulled every muscle in my body." He winced, remembering some of the things he'd done. His own worst enemy and all that. "All right, then," he said briskly, "who's in charge? It doesn't sound like there's many of us left."

He didn't like the pause that followed; not one little bit. "It's you, isn't it?" Valens said.

Brennus swallowed something. "I was the duty officer," he said, as though admitting that he'd planned the whole thing, suborned by Mezentine gold. "I've sent messages to the divisional commanders, someone ought to be here before sunset, but until then I suppose, theoretically . . ."

Valens smiled. "You carry on," he said. "You appear to be doing a fine job." He paused, then added, "Is anybody at all left out of the civil administration? Anybody higher up than, say, a permanent secretary?"

It was meant as one of those jokes he'd resolved he wouldn't make, but then there was another pause. Valens frowned. That wasn't good.

"I see," he said. "In that case, I'm putting the military in charge until we can get everything sorted out. You're it, in other words."

Brennus looked as though he'd just been sentenced to death by bastinado. "Like I said, sir, I've notified the divisional commanders, I'm sure one of them'll be here very soon, and then . . ." Pause, while he pulled himself together again. "I've given orders to close the gates, and I've sent out patrols; there's no sign of the enemy in a ten-mile radius of the city. What else should I be . . . ?"

Valens closed his eyes. "If I were you," he said, "I'd leave it at that. Just concentrate on keeping everybody calm and quiet until the army gets here. I'm sure you can manage — every confidence."

He could feel himself sliding away into sleep; no reason why he shouldn't. "The Duchess, sir," Brennus was saying. "Should I — I mean, would you like to see her now?"

Valens opened his eyes and smiled. "No," he said, and went back to sleep.

The next time he opened his eyes, it wasn't thin, pale Captain Brennus.

"Mezentius? Is that you?"

The familiar face of his chief of staff grinned down at him: the point of a nose and two small, pale eyes in a shrubbery of beard. "This is a right mess," he said.

Valens tried to raise himself on one elbow. Not his brightest idea ever. "When did you get here? What time is it?"

"About ten o'clock in the morning, and around midnight," Mezentius replied. "Since when I've been chasing round looking for something to do, apart from inspecting dead bodies. That young Guards captain's done a good job, by the way. I'll have him for the Seventh when you've finished with him."

Valens nodded. "Everything's under control, then."

"In the circumstances." Mezentius was frowning. "I told the Seventh and the Fifth to get here as soon as possible, but we've had patrols out, no sign of any more of them. It's looking like a single raiding party who knew exactly who they were after and where to find them. Which," he added quietly, "is rather more disturbing than a full-scale assault, if you care to look at it that way. You've heard the casualty list?"

Valens nodded. "It hasn't really sunk in," he said. "But the impression I got was, nobody's left except me."

"More or less," Mezentius replied, and the way he said it made Valens wince. "I've talked to all the survivors who're up to answering questions; basically, nobody on our side made a fight of it except you and that weird engineer, the one who looks like some kind of insect."

Valens had forgotten about him. "That's right," he said. "Did he make it?"

"A few cuts and bruises," Mezentius replied. "Twisted ankle. Fought like a maniac, so I gather. Amazing, really. He didn't strike me as the type, the one time I met him."

"Go on," Valens said.

"Well," Mezentius continued, "apparently he came charging up just as one of the bad guys was about to take out Duke Orsea; he jumped up, dragged Orsea off his horse at the last moment, grabbed the lance out of the bad guy's hands and stuck him with it; then Orsea's wife came rushing over, apparently she'd seen Orsea go down; four of them close in on her, but this Daurenja holds them off single-handed, does for two of them — did one of them with his teeth, apparently, bit his throat out like a dog. Then more of them join in, and then you showed up, and you know the rest. No, it sounds like the engineering department pretty well saved the day, one way and another. Oh, and the uncles as well, I expect you've heard about that. The rest of the embassy's kicking up one hell of a fuss, as you'd expect."

Valens kept his sigh to himself. "What are they saying?"

"Well, they're still on our side," Mezentius said, with a crooked grin. "The old chap was the one I spoke to. Basically, he wants to wipe the Mezentines off the face of the earth. Man after my own heart, really."

"That's good," Valens said. "It's always good to have something in common with your in-laws. I suppose I'd better see him."

Mezentius shook his head. "I've told him you're fragile as an egg and not to be disturbed for at least a week," he said. "Only way I could keep him from bursting in here and waking you up."

Valens nodded. "Who is he, by the way? I've been talking to him all this time, but nobody's actually told me where he fits in."

"Oh." Mezentius frowned. "He's sort of the grand vizier, prime minister, the head man's chief adviser. He reckons he pretty much runs the show, though I don't know whether the rest of them would agree. Anyway, he's pretty high-powered; and he's really pissed off about the uncles getting killed. Probably some background there I wasn't briefed on."

"It'll keep, I expect," Valens said with a yawn.

They discussed other things — a new civil authority, which posts could be filled by co-option and which would have to wait for formal elections; suitable candidates for offices, the balance of power between the old families and the mining companies; the effect recent events (Valens smiled to himself; call them *recent events* and you cauterize the wound?) would have on the marriage alliance, plans for the evacuation, the war. Exhaustion came up on him suddenly, like an ambush. He stopped Mezentius in the middle of a sentence and said, "You'd better go now, I'm tired." Mezentius nodded.

"I'll send the doctor in," he said.

"No, I just want to get some sleep," Valens mumbled. His eyes were already closing. He heard the sounds of movement, someone standing up, the legs of a chair grating on a stone floor. He felt cold, but couldn't be bothered to do anything about it. He listened to his own breathing for a moment or so, and realized that he was back on the edge of the marsh, watching the ducks flying in. It had been a disaster, a wretched mess, all because of that fool Orsea. Standing next to him, King Fashion and Queen Reason were talking about the day's hawking. He was surprised to hear the King say that it hadn't been too bad after all: three dozen mallard, a few teal, three brace of moorhens, but it was a shame they hadn't managed to pull down the heron. Perhaps they should have flown lanners instead of sakers. As they talked, they were watching the sky, waiting for the hawks to come back. They didn't seem worried, but Valens knew that the hawks were gone for good; dead or scattered, not that it mattered a great deal. After a long silence, the King shrugged, and called to his master falconer to make up the bag. They were laying them out on the ground, in pairs, a male and a female; Sillius Vacuo and his wife, Lollius Pertinax and Syra Terentia, Carausius and the eldest Fabella girl, a hen to every cock-bird. He counted them: eighteen brace, just as the King had said. He almost expected to see himself among them as the falconers passed loops round their necks and hung them in their pairings from the top rail of the fence; but of course, he wasn't there, the heron had got away.

Queen Reason was talking to him. She was asking him if he was awake.

"Don't be silly," he said. "I'm dreaming, of course I'm not awake."

He realized that he'd spoken the words aloud, and that he wasn't asleep anymore. He opened his eyes.

"Oh," she said. "I'm sorry, did I wake you?"

He blinked, just in case. She was still there.

"I was just dozing," he said. He was struggling to remember which one she was; whose duchess, his or Orsea's. But then it all came back to him; he remembered now. There had been some sort of ghastly mix-up, and he'd married the wrong one, and this was the fool's wife he was talking to: Veatriz, who used to write him letters.

"Are you all right?" he said.

She nodded. "How about you?"

"Oh, I'm fine," he said. "Just skiving, so someone else has got to clear up the mess. Soon as everything's been sorted out, I'll make a miraculous recovery."

She smiled: thin, like lines scribed on brass with a needle. "I thought I ought to thank you," she said. "It's becoming a habit with you."

Something about the way she'd said that. "You wrote to me," he said. "You wanted to talk."

"Yes, but that was before the wedding." She hesitated. Not fair to bully a sick man. "It was very brave of you . . ." she started to say. She made it sound like an accusation. He didn't want to hear the rest of it.

"It sort of rounded off a perfect day," he grunted.

"Not quite the honeymoon you'd have chosen?"

"I hadn't thought of it like that," he said. "But, since you mention it, better than the one I had planned."

She frowned. "I should go," she said. "Shall I let your wife know you're awake and receiving visitors?"

"I'd rather you didn't," he sighed. The pillow was suddenly uncomfortable, and his arm itched. "I heard about Daurenja," he said.

"Who?"

"The man who saved your life. And Orsea's too," he added maliciously. "How is he, by the way?"

"In bed. They were worried about the bang he got on his head, but they think he'll be all right now."

"Ah. So that's all right, then." He looked away, up at the ceiling. "Daurenja's the long, spindly man with the ponytail who rescued both of you. Maybe you should look in on him too."

"I will. He was very brave." He wasn't looking at her, so he couldn't see the expression on her face. "Isn't he something to do with Vaatzes, the engineer?"

"That's right." His head was starting to hurt, making it a painful effort to think. Nothing came to mind: no bright, interesting observations to found a conversation on. He'd prefer it, in fact, if she went away. (Interesting, he thought; does this mean love is dead? He couldn't decide.)

"I'm sorry Orsea spoiled your hunt," she was saying. "He didn't want to come. I think he was afraid he'd show himself up, one way or another. But he reckoned it'd have been rude to refuse the invitation."

"Oh well," Valens replied. "As things turned out, it wasn't the end of the world."

"The people who were killed." She sounded as though every word was an effort, like lifting heavy blocks of stone. "Were they . . . ?"

"Most of the government," he said. "My friends. People I grew up with. It's going to be very strange getting used to the idea that they won't be around anymore. I mean, so many of them, and so sudden." He paused, reflecting. "But you'd know all about that, of course," he said. "At least they didn't burn down my home."

She laughed, brittle as ice. "I never liked it much anyway," she said.

"Is it better here?"

"No, not much." A pause. It seemed to go on for a ridiculously long time. "The thing is," she said, "I've been shunted about like a chess piece ever since I was fourteen years old; you know, move to this square here, then back, then sideways to cover the white knight. After a while, places just don't matter very much anymore. And it's not like I've ever done anything. At least," she added, "I've caused a lot of trouble for thousands of people, but I never asked anybody to do any of that. Unless you count writing letters about poetry and things I could see from my window."

Valens shrugged. "I think if I'd had to live your life, I'd have gone mad, or run away. Haven't you got a sister who's a merchant?"

"Yes. She's a horrible cow and I haven't seen her for years. Why?"

"Oh, nothing. I never had any brothers or sisters. What's it like?"

"Noisy. There's always someone slamming doors in a huff. Why the sudden interest?"

"I was just making conversation. It's something we never got around to discussing, and it was always on my mind to ask you about it."

She stood up. "Some other time, maybe," she said. "I really ought to go. You look tired."

He yawned. "I was born tired," he said. "Rest just spoils my concentration." She turned and walked away; reached the door and hesitated.

"Should I ask the doctor to come in?" she said.

"I'd rather you didn't."

"Goodbye, then."

"Goodbye. I'm sorry," he added.

"Are you? What for?"

He closed his eyes, just to make her go away.

"Everybody's dead," the woman in the red dress complained bitterly. "Which is hell for business. I've got a hundred yards of silk damask, beautiful sort of bluey-green, and I can't shift it. No customers. All the money in the duchy's tied up in probate, and what there is has all gone on estate sales, all the heirs selling up at the same time. It's a bugger for luxury goods. I should've stuck to bulk commodities, like my old mother told me to. You could kill off every bloody aristocrat this side of the mountains, and people'll still want quality lumber."

Ziani nodded. "For coffins," he said, "if nothing else."

She sighed; not in the mood for comedy. "And what's going to become of the marriage alliance, that's what I'd like to know. If that goes out the window, that's our venture in the salt trade well and truly stuffed." She tilted the jug, but it was empty. "Bastard thing," she said, a trifle unfairly in Ziani's opinion, since she'd been the one who'd emptied it. "And I don't know what you're being so fucking calm and superior about. It's your money as well, remember."

Ziani shook his head. "It's not going to muck up the alliance," he said soothingly. "Quite the opposite. From what I can gather, the Cure Hardy are fighting mad, because of the uncles getting killed. Blood vengeance is a big thing with them, so I've heard."

She shook her head. "You're getting them confused with the Flos Gaia," she told him. "They're the ones who carry on blood feuds for sixteen generations. In fact, it's a miracle there's any of the buggers left. This lot are pretty sensible about that sort of thing, for savages."

"Not where royalty's concerned," Ziani replied. "And don't forget, there's a whole lot of young braves back home who'd love a chance to have a crack at the Republic, as a change from cattle-raiding against the other tribes. It'll be fine, you'll see. Blessing in disguise, even."

She scowled, tried to get up to fetch a bottle from the cupboard, gave that up as too much effort. "That's not going to help me get shot of my silk damask, though, is it? Genuine Mezentine, cost me two thalers a yard and I had to fight like a lunatic to beat them down to that. I'd been hoping to shift it for clothes for the wedding, but it didn't get here in time, what with having to come the long way round to stay out of trouble. This bloody war'll be the ruin of us all, you'll see."

Ziani smiled. "You want to hang on to that cloth," he said. "Take the long-term view. Once the savages are coming here all the time, money in their pockets from the salt deals, there'll be a demand for prestige goods, and who else is going to be carrying any stock to sell them?"

She opened her mouth to say something, then closed it again and thought for a moment; slow but sure, like a cart drawn by oxen. "That's a thought," she said. "All the rest of 'em will be getting out of luxuries and buying into staples; and you're right about the savages, they won't want to go home empty-handed."

Ziani stood up. "You've got the idea," he said. "If I were you, once your colleagues start selling out their fine ware at sacrifice, you want to be in there buying. After all," he added, "you know something they don't. Only," he added, "for crying out loud be a bit discreet about it. We don't want anybody putting two and two together."

He left her to her long thoughts and the unopened bottle, and walked back up the hill. People were staring at him as he went by; not just because of the color of his skin, now that he was the hero of the hour, the man who'd raised the alarm and saved the Duke's life. The thought made him smile.

He heard the foundry half a mile before he reached it. There were all sorts of rumors about what was going on there. The favorite, for the time being, was that all that steel sheet was for making armor, to equip the thousands of cavalrymen the Cure Hardy would be sending to help avenge the massacre. The proponents of this theory weren't having it all their own way; they couldn't explain to those awkward-minded cynics who wanted to argue the point how all these notional soldiers were going to get from the Cure Hardy homelands to Civitas Vadanis, given that there was a huge, impassable desert in the way. That uncomfortable fact was very much in people's minds; had been ever since the news of the marriage alliance had broken. It was all very well making friends with a nation that had endless resources of warlike manpower, but what help was that likely to be if it was going to take them six months to get here? (Six months was the figure usually quoted; pure conjecture, since nobody really knew how big the desert was or how you got round it.) The same point had exercised the minds of most of the Duke's court; but Carausius had been quite adamant that the problem was by no means insoluble, and since he hadn't been prepared to discuss the matter, his assurance had been generally taken on trust. Hooray for autocratic government.

That thought made Ziani smile too, as he banged on the massive gates of the foundry and waited for the porter to let him in. It had cost him a good deal of effort and ingenuity to find a way of sharing the secret of the salt road across the desert with Carausius, since the late Chancellor had taken a dislike to him from the start. In the end, he'd had to plant in his business partner's mind the idea of selling Carausius' wife twenty yards of best hard linen at practically cost, and hanging around to chat after the deal had been made. He'd explained that if the marriage alliance went ahead, there'd be a need for regular traffic between the Cure Hardy and the Vadani; which meant convoys of troops, which meant free escorts for the shipments of salt they'd be taking across the desert, and quite possibly free fodder for the horses, someone else to carry the water, all sorts of fringe benefits. Thanks to his gentle, patient suggestions, Carausius had learned about the secret road across the desert, firmly believing he'd found out about it by happy chance rather than being force-fed it by someone he regarded as a threat to national security. In his apparent monopoly of the secret, he'd seen a wonderful opportunity to consolidate and maintain his grip on power. As far as Ziani could find out, he hadn't even shared it with Valens himself; and now, of course, Carausius was dead. The Cure Hardy still believed that in order to get to Civitas Vadanis, they had to struggle across the desert the hard way, and that way was very hard indeed: the bride's escort had consisted of the wedding party, fifty horses to carry water and supplies and their drivers. Twenty men and thirty-seven horses had died in the crossing, quietly and without complaint; these losses were rather lower than had been anticipated when the party set out. The Cure Hardy were serious about the alliance. How pleased they would be, therefore, when they saw the map Ziani had hidden under a floorboard in the cramped back room at the foundry that he used as an office.

"They'll be pleased to see you," the porter told him mournfully as he swung open the gate. "They're having problems with the drop-hammers."

Ziani closed his eyes, but only for a moment. There had been a short, happy interval when he'd actually come to believe that Vadani workmen could be trusted with mechanisms more complicated than a pair of tongs, but that was some time ago. "Where's

Daurenja?" he heard himself say. "Couldn't he have sorted it out?"

"They were looking for him," the porter replied, "but he's off somewhere. They're having to do the blooms by hand."

Patience, Ziani ordered himself. The idiots'll be beating the sheets out to any old thickness, and quite probably cracking and splitting them as well; a day's production, only fit to go back in the melt. "Wonderful," he said, and he quickened his pace. He always seemed to be rushing about these days; not good for someone who didn't really like walking, let alone running.

Nothing wrong with the drop-hammers that a blindfolded idiot couldn't have fixed in five minutes; but the Vadani foundrymen were standing around looking sad, still and patient as horses in a paddock. He put the problem right — a chain had jumped a pulley and mangled a couple of gear-wheels, but there were spares in the box — shouted at the men whose names he could remember, and scampered off to get on with some real work.

He was building a punch, to cut mounting holes in the plates, to save having to drill each one. It was nothing more complicated than a long lever bearing on cams, bolted down for stability to a massive oak log, but he was having a little trouble with the alignment of the bottom plate, and the sheets were coming out distorted after the holes had been punched. All it needed was shims, but that meant laboriously hacksawing, drilling and filing each one by hand, since such basic necessities of life as a lathe and a mill were unknown in this godforsaken country. He clamped a stub of two-inch-round bar in the vise, picked up the saw and set to work, pausing after every fifty strokes to spit into the slot for lubrication. He was three-quarters of the way through when he heard footsteps behind him, a pattern he recognized without having to turn and look.

"Daurenja?" he called out.

Immediately he was there: long, tense, attentive, unsatisfactory in every way. Today he had his ponytail tied back with a twist of packing wire, and there was something yellow under his fingernails.

"Where the hell did you wander off to?" Ziani asked.

"I had some errands to run," Daurenja answered. "I'm very sorry. I gather there was some bother with the —"

"Yes. Two hours lost. You should've been here to deal with it."

Being angry with Daurenja was like pouring water into sand; he absorbed it, stifling the healthy flow of emotion.

"You know we're in a hurry," Ziani went on. The default had been trivial enough; two hours' lost production wasn't the end of the world, or even a serious inconvenience. If it hadn't been for Daurenja's energy, initiative and enthusiasm, the whole project would probably have stalled by now and be in jeopardy. "You know you can't leave these clowns on their own for ten minutes, but you bugger off somewhere without a word to me; they could have trashed the place, wrecked all the machinery, blown the furnace . . ."

"I'm sorry. It won't happen again."

Ziani put the hacksaw down on the bench and wiped sweat and filings from his hands. "It's not bloody well good enough, Daurenja," he said, and the thin man's pale eyes seemed to glow at him as Ziani took a step forward, balling his right fist. "I never asked you for help; you came to me, remember. You came begging me for a job."

"I know. And I'm grateful, believe me."

"Yes, you are." Ziani grabbed the front of Daurenja's shirt with his left hand and pulled, forcing Daurenja to come close. "You're always so very grateful, and then when my back's turned . . ."

He'd learned how to punch in the ordnance factory; not a scientific philosophy of personal combat, like the rapier fencing Duke Valens had tried to teach him, more a sense of timing refined by desperation into an instinct. You don't have to teach a dog or a bull how to fight; it comes by light of nature and works out through practice. He jabbed his fist into Daurenja's solar plexus, making him fold like a hinge; as his head came down, he let go with his left hand and bashed him on the side of the jaw. It felt hard and thin, like hammering on a closed door. Daurenja staggered sideways, and as his balance faltered, Ziani kicked him hard on the left kneecap, dropping him on the ground in a heap.

"Get up," he said. "Oh come on," he added, "you're a fighting man, you held off the entire Mezentine army the other day, armed with nothing but a bit of stick."

Daurenja struggled to his knees; Ziani kicked him in the ribs and put his foot on his throat.

"Fine," he said. "Don't fight if you don't want to. I'll break your ribs one at a time."

There was something about the way he lay there; it took Ziani a moment to recognize what it was. Practice, because this wasn't the first time, not by a long way. He was enduring the beating the way a chronic invalid endures some painful but necessary treatment he's been subjected to many times, holding still so as not to inconvenience the doctor as he goes about his work, tilting his head sideways or holding out his arm when he's told to. To test the hypothesis, Ziani lifted his foot off Daurenja's throat and swung it back for a kick; sure enough, Daurenja moved his head a little to the side, anticipating the attack, not trying to avoid it but seeking to minimize the damage it would cause without being too obvious about it. Ziani stepped back. "Stand up," he said. "Beating's over."

He held out his hand, caught hold of Daurenja's bony wrist and pulled him to his feet; Daurenja swayed a little and rested his back against the bench. He hadn't even tried to ask what the attack had been for.

"Now we've got that out of the way," Ziani said pleasantly, "maybe you could tell me what it is you want."

"I don't —"

Ziani frowned, and punched him on the side of the head, just above the ear. His skull was just as bony as he'd imagined it would be. "Yes you do," he said. "You understand perfectly well. You want something from me, something really valuable and important, and there's nobody else you can get it from." He took a step back, a unilateral declaration of ceasefire. "I'm not saying you can't have it," he said, reasonably. "I just want to know what it is, that's all."

Daurenja looked at him. "Do you mind if I sit down?"

"Be my guest."

"Thanks." Daurenja slid one buttock onto the top of the bench; he seemed to hang as well as perch.

"Something," Ziani hazarded, "to do with sulfur."

"In a way." Daurenja sighed. It was, Ziani realized, the first indication of weariness he'd ever seen from him. "I'd better begin at the beginning, hadn't I?"

Ziani shrugged. "If it's a long story."

"It is." Daurenja paused for a moment, as if composing himself before giving a performance. "Some years ago," he said, "I met a man who was trying to set up a pottery business. He'd found a seam of a special kind of clay, the sort you need to make the fine wares that people pay a lot of money for. It's always been a Mezentine monopoly, and everybody's always believed they controlled the only sources of this special clay. Well, he convinced me, and it turned out he was right. The stuff he'd got hold of was the right sort of clay, or at least it turned out the same way when you fired it. We thought we'd got it made. After all, making pottery's no big deal, peasants do it in villages. All we needed to do was find out how you decorate it — make the pretty colors you get on the genuine article. We thought that'd be the easy bit."

"But it wasn't."

Daurenja nodded slowly. "We could produce colors all right, reds and greens and blues. You can find out how to do that from books, anybody can do it. But they weren't quite the right colors — very close, but not quite. It was pretty frustrating, you can see that. We worked at it for a long time, experimenting, fine-tuning the mixes, trying everything we could think of, but we could never quite get there. Anyhow, I'll skip all that, it's not relevant. One day, I was messing about with some of the ingredients, grinding some stuff up together in a mortar, and there was an accident." He rolled up his sleeve to reveal a scar, a handspan of smooth, melted skin. "That's where this comes from," he said, with a wry grin. "There's another one like it right across my chest. Burns. The stuff I was mixing suddenly caught fire and went up; it was like when you let a drop of water fall onto molten metal. The mortar I was using — big stone thing the size of a bucket — smashed into a dozen pieces, and the heat was amazing, just like leaning over a forge at welding temperature. All from a few spoonfuls of this stuff I was grinding."

Ziani realized he'd forgotten to breathe for a while. "What stuff would that be?" he asked.

Maybe Daurenja hadn't heard him. "Obviously," he said, "that got me thinking. As soon as I was on my feet again — I told my partner I'd tripped and fallen into the furnace, and that's how I got all burned up; I don't think he believed me, but that couldn't be helped — I set about trying to do it again, on purpose, as it were. It took me a while. Where I went wrong to start with was assuming that it was the pounding that set it off. In fact, it must've been a spark or something, that first time. What actually gets it going is plain ordinary fire; a taper or a spill. Once I'd figured that out, it was just a matter of getting the proportions right. And keeping it to myself, of course."

"You didn't want your partner to find out."

"Well, of course not." Daurenja frowned. "I'd come to realize he wasn't to be trusted. All my life people have cheated me, taken advantage. Once I'd worked out the proportions of the mix, I left him; I didn't need his workshop anymore, and in any case, he was getting on my nerves. I think he believed I'd found the formula for the colors we'd been looking for, and I was keeping it to myself. There were other problems too, but I won't bore you with them. Personal stuff."

He was silent for a moment. "So you left," Ziani prompted.

Daurenja nodded. "I set up a little workshop of my own," he said. "I had money, so it wasn't a problem. What you've got to understand about the mixture I discovered," he went on, "is the extraordinary power it produces when it flares up. The first time it happened, one chunk of the stone mortar was driven an inch deep into a cob wall. It's like a volcano; a little volcano you can set off whenever you want, and if you could only contain it . . ." He stopped; his voice had risen, and his hands were clenched. "If you could contain it," he said, "in a pot, or a bell, so that all the force went in one direction only . . ." He looked up; his eyes seemed very wide and round. "You worked in the ordnance factory," he said, "you know about the scorpions and mangonels and torsion engines that can throw a five-hundredweight stone a quarter-mile. If only I could contain this — this thing that happens when the mixture flares up; if I could build a sort of portable volcano, something you could carry about and point at a wall or a tower, it'd make all your Mezentine engines seem like toys. You could crack open cities like walnuts."

Ziani breathed out long and slow. "You've tried, of course," he said.

Daurenja laughed, like a dog barking. "I've tried all right," he said. "I tried stone mortars, but they shatter like glass. I tried casting a mortar shape, only in metal. I used brass first, then bronze, then iron. I think the problem is something to do with the way the metal cools down." His words were coming out in a rush now, a fast, smooth flow like lava. "Because it's got to be thick, to contain the force, I think that by the time the metal on the outside has taken the cold, the inside's still hot, and this causes little flaws and fractures; either that, or there's air bubbles, I don't know. All I do know is that I've tried everything, and every time it either cracks or shatters. I've lost count of how many times it's nearly killed me. In the end, I reached the point where I couldn't think what to do next. Everything I know about casting in metal, everything I could find out, none of it was any good. I tried casting a solid trunk and boring out a hole in the middle; I built a lathe ten feet long, with a three-inch cutting bar. Still no good. I nearly gave up."

He looked away. It was as though he'd just said, *I died.*

"And then you heard of me," Ziani said.

"*Yes.*" Suddenly Daurenja stood up; and Ziani wondered what on earth had possessed him to attack this man, because he was as full of strength and speed and anger as a wolf or a boar. "I heard about you: a Mezentine, foreman of the ordnance factory — if anybody knew how to do it, you would. It was like a miracle, like something out of a story, when the gods came down from heaven. I knew I had to have you." He stopped. "I knew I had to have you help me, because the Mezentines do the most amazing castings, great big bells and statues, the frames of machines; you've got ways of blowing a furnace so you can pour iron as easy as bronze. I'd even thought of going to the Guilds myself, except I knew they'd take it away from me and make it their own, and I can't have that. But I can trust you; you're an outsider too, like me, you've been thrown out of your home and persecuted."

(He didn't say, *Just like I was;* he didn't have to.)

"I'm sorry," he went on — Ziani could see the effort that went into calming himself down. "I thought, first I'd prove to you that I'm not just some lunatic who thinks he's figured out how to do magic. I'd prove that I'm what I say I am, an engineer, a craftsman, so you'd take me seriously. I heard all about what you did in the defense of Civitas Eremiae; how you built the scorpions, practically from nothing. I knew you'd need an assistant, someone you could rely on — an apprentice, really. And then, when we'd come to know and trust one another . . ."

Ziani looked at him. For a moment, he was afraid that it would be like looking into a mirror.

"I know," Daurenja went on. "I'm good with brass and iron, but I've never got the hang of dealing with people. I never seem to be able to make them understand me, and then problems develop. I suppose it's been the same with you, and these people here. I thought when I saved that woman, during the hunt, when the Mezentines attacked . . . It seemed like such a wonderful opportunity, to get the Duke on my side; and then, when we need to ask him for help — money and materials; and he's got a war to fight, it couldn't be better from that point of view. I don't know; if I'd told you earlier, maybe. But I wanted to make sure."

Ziani was quiet for a long time. He knew Daurenja was hiding something, and that no amount of violence or manipulation would get it out of him; the question was whether it was important, or whether it was just slag on the top of the melt. He wondered too about the serendipity of it all. To crack open cities like walnuts; he already knew how to do that, even if this strange and unpleasant man could show him a more efficient way. He was a refinement, an improvement, but an unnecessary one — a departure from Specification, and in orthodox doctrine, wasn't an unnecessary improvement inevitably an abomination?

On the other hand, he needed a good foreman.

"Casting's not the answer," he said eventually. "All castings are brittle, you'll never get round that." In the corner of the shop, he caught sight of the slack-tub; just an old stave barrel, half full of black, oily water. "You don't want a mortar," he said, "or a bell. You want a barrel."

16

"It was a success, I grant you," Boioannes was saying, in that loud, carrying voice of his. "Twenty-seven confirmed dead, including the Chancellor. I concede that it was well planned and efficiently executed. What I'm asking, however, is whether it was a good idea or a bad one."

The meeting had already overrun by an hour. By the look of it, someone else had booked the cloister garden for a meeting or a reception; Psellus had seen a man's head bobbing round a pillar with a look of desperate impatience on his face — the establishments clerk, probably, too timid to dare interrupt Necessary Evil, but petrified that he'd be blamed for double-booking. The Republic's bureaucracy ran on the principle of symmetry; for every blunder, one responsible official. He sympathized, but found it hard to spare much compassion for someone else. Never wise to be too liberal with a scarce commodity you may well need for yourself.

"In order to assess success or failure," Boioannes went on, "it's always helpful to know what the object of the exercise actually was. Fortuitous incidental benefits are all very well, but it's my experience that every time you stoop to pick up a quarter in the street, a thaler falls out of your pocket. Bearing in mind what we stand to lose by this action, I feel we have a right to know what the precise objective was. If the intention was to assassinate Duke Valens, for example, we failed."

"That wasn't the primary target," someone said; Psellus couldn't see who, because Steuthes, the loaf-headed director of resources, was blocking his view. "The purpose of the mission was to kill the abominator, Vaatzes."

Boioannes hesitated, just for a moment. It was like watching a waterfall freeze for a split second. "Now we're getting somewhere," he went on. "And did we get him?"

"The reports are inconclusive." Whoever the speaker was, he didn't sound in the least intimidated by the full force of Boioannes' personality. Probably he could juggle white-hot ingots with his bare hands, too. "We're investigating, naturally, but our lines of communication are necessarily quite fragile, it doesn't do to push too hard. As soon as we get an answer, I promise you'll be the first to know."

Psellus frowned. He knew for a fact that that hadn't been the reason for the cavalry raid, because he'd been told about it, well in advance. It was inconceivable that he knew something Maris Boioannes didn't. And if he did, then why? The answer to that, he was sure, wouldn't be anything good.

"In any event," the hidden speaker continued, "as you said yourself just now, the exercise has fully justified the expenditure of resources. Just as we're about to launch a major offensive, the Vadani are confused, terrified, practically leaderless. They know we can strike them at will, in the very heart of their territory. They know that they have no friends. Thanks to their own acts of sabotage, they've lost their principal source of funding. The fact is, we're poised to win a victory that will end this war, quickly, cheaply, ostentatiously. Caviling over details is a pretty sterile exercise, in the circumstances."

Smelling politics, Psellus allowed his attention to drift. Had they really managed to kill Ziani Vaatzes? He doubted it, somehow. Something told him that if Vaatzes was dead, he'd have felt it by now. Or maybe that was just wishful thinking; because, he realized, he didn't want Vaatzes to die in a distant country, with all the answers to all the questions locked inside his head.

The thought made him want to smile, though long practice froze the muscles of his face. Here in the middle of the great affairs of the Republic — war, peace, increased prosperity or ruinous expense — all he was concerned about was scratching his own intellectual itches; and all because he was superfluous, a makeweight in Necessary Evil of whom nothing was demanded or expected. If I dropped dead tomorrow, he thought, it wouldn't make any difference to anybody. Which, in a very real sense, is true freedom.

"Assuming Vaatzes is still alive . . ." The phrase snagged his attention like a fisherman's lure, but he was too late to catch the rest of the sentence. Someone else's voice, but nobody he knew. Nearly a year now as a member of this committee, and still he only knew a handful of the members by sight. Each time he attended a meeting, most of the people were strangers.

"It's quite true to say that Vaatzes was the cause of the war," yet another unknown voice was saying; Psellus managed to locate its source, an improbably old man with thin, wispy white hair. "To say that he is still the reason for it, or even a significant factor, would be hopelessly oversimplistic. The war has moved on, as all living, growing things do. What's it about now? Well, the answer to that is: many things. It's about regaining the prestige and respect we squandered when our forces were slaughtered at Civitas Eremiae. It's about the silver deposits in Vadani territory; it's about finding some sort of exit from the miserable, draining occupation of Eremia; it's about the delicate balance between outgoings from Consolidated Fund and increased income for the Foundrymen and the other Guilds engaged in war work, as against those struggling to maintain productivity and output in general commerce. I put it to you that the main effect of this war is to exalt the Foundrymen at the expense of all the other Guilds, regardless of the overall effect on the well-being of the Republic; and unless this short-sighted, selfish agenda is abandoned at the earliest possible . . ."

More politics. It was almost disconcerting to listen to so much truth presented with so little conviction. Extraordinary, when you stopped to think about it. All these people knew the truth about the war; but, instead of trying to find some way to reverse or at least mitigate the disaster, they were cheerfully serving it, like keepers put in charge of some captive wild animal. There were good reasons for that, of course. To abandon the war, or even suggest that it should be abandoned, would be political suicide — because everybody in politics had to maintain at all costs the notion that the Republic was invincible, its resources inexhaustible, its doctrines irreproachable, even though they all knew (everybody knew) that none of these was true. It was a bit like the doctrine of Specification itself; the denial of any possibility of improvement, even though everybody knew that any design, however good, can always be bettered; even though the Guilds themselves made an explicit exception where armaments were concerned. What a wonderful magic politics is, Psellus thought; it can recognize the truth and still override it, providing you can get consensus among the people who matter.

Lofty stuff; way above his head. Instead, he went back to thinking about Falier, the foreman of the ordnance factory. The new foreman; except that he wasn't all that new anymore. By now, he'd be married to Vaatzes' wife. Would it advance the war effort, he wondered, to write to Ziani and let him know? By all accounts, by the evidence of the homemade book, Vaatzes had loved her very much. They had so few weapons that could reach him; love was one they hadn't tried yet, but it would be relatively easy, relatively cheap. Why send a squadron of cavalry if you can send a letter instead? For a moment, he pictured a tightly folded square of parchment being loaded onto the slider of a scorpion and aimed at the walls of Civitas Vadanis.

Careful; he'd almost allowed himself to smile.

"Councillor Psellus." Nightmare: someone was talking to him, and he hadn't been listening.

"I'm sorry," he said, jerking his head up and looking round. "Could you repeat that, please?"

It was Boioannes, and he was smiling. Nobody else he knew

had ever reminded him more forcefully that the smile is fundamentally a baring of teeth. "I hadn't actually asked you anything yet," Boioannes said. "I can say it and then repeat it, if that would help."

Psellus bowed his head like a submissive dog.

"We were wondering," Boioannes went on. "You're our resident expert on Ziani Vaatzes; you've made quite a study of him, I believe."

"That's right, yes."

"Your diligence is noted. Such attention to detail; for example, your repeated visits to his wife." Short pause, to allow time for dutiful snickering. "I trust your examinations there have been productive."

Psellus looked straight ahead, eyes fixed on a chip on the edge of the ornamental fountain. "I do believe I've made some progress, yes. However, I've run into some unexpected obstacles, which you might be able to help me with, since you've raised the subject. For instance, the prosecutor —"

"Write to me," Boioannes snapped; unusual flare of petulance, almost a minor victory. "To return to the topic we're currently discussing. Do you believe that Vaatzes would be prepared to negotiate for a free pardon, in return for helping us?"

The things I miss by not paying attention, Psellus thought bitterly. "I don't know," he said. "I think it would depend on what guarantees we're able to offer."

Someone laughed. "Obviously, nothing substantial," Boioannes replied, "since we naturally have no intention of honoring them. However; we must consider the fact that Vaatzes has already helped us, unasked, requesting no reward; presumably he's given us this help as an earnest of good faith, to persuade us to open negotiations. The implication must be that he is prepared to trust us, under certain circumstances and conditions. If we can use him, he could potentially be of service to us. Do you agree?"

Psellus nodded.

"Excellent." Boioannes beamed; all those strong white teeth

simultaneously. "In that case, who better to conduct the negotiations than yourself? Assuming the committee agrees . . ."

Of course they did.

Later, back in his cold, safe office, Psellus read (for the fifth or sixth time) the dense, concise summary of instructions he'd received from Boioannes' clerks. Most of it was a tangled thicket of things he wasn't allowed to offer or agree to, not even on the strict understanding that he'd be lying through his teeth; there was always the risk that the letters might be intercepted, by the enemy or (even worse) by friends, and some maneuvers would be too painful to have to explain away. Most of the rest of the brief consisted of what the Republic wanted from its stray lamb — the Vadani, for instance; the heads of Duke Valens, Duke Orsea, their heirs, counselors, ministers, families, friends, acquaintances . . .

Well, that was the job he'd been given, the first real work he'd had since he joined Necessary Evil. Better than spending all day staring at the wall, or reading Vaatzes' atrocious poetry for the umpteenth time. More to the point, here was a beautiful kind of serendipity, such sweet timing. He picked up his pen, suddenly inspired, and started to write.

Lucao Psellus to Ziani Vaatzes, greetings.

What a bizarre thing to be doing; writing a letter to the abominator, the arch-enemy, the man who'd slaughtered the Republic's army at Civitas Eremiae. It was like writing a letter to Death, or Evil; it was also, he felt with a stab of guilt, a bit like scraping acquaintance with someone you've always wanted to meet.

Allow me to introduce myself. I represent the standing committee on defense of the Perpetual Republic of Mezentia [*inelegantly phrased; he was writing too fast in his enthusiasm*] and I am authorized . . .

Pause. Nibble end of pen. Another sheet of paper.

Lucao Psellus to Ziani Vaatzes, greetings.

I have never met you, although I suspect I know you better than anybody outside your immediate family — better, quite probably, than most of them. I work for the Guilds. That's all you need to know about me.

First, you ought to know that your wife — I mean your ex-wife — has married someone else. I'm sure you know the lucky man: Falier, your successor at the ordnance factory. Well, of course you do. Wasn't he your best friend?

I enclose a notarized copy of the marriage certificate. You know as well as I do that a Mezentine notary wouldn't falsify a certificate for anybody, not even the Guilds in supreme convocation. But if that's not good enough for you, ask for whatever proof you need and I'll try and get it for you.

So much for personal affairs: to business. I represent the standing committee on defense [*there; that particular stylistic bear-trap neatly avoided*] and they have authorized me to offer you a free pardon, in return for your help with the war. Of course, it's not quite as straightforward as that. We need to be able to trust you — rather a difficult proviso, in the circumstances. Likewise, you need to be able to trust us.

This is what I have in mind . . .

Yes, Psellus thought; but what do I have in mind, precisely? He frowned, as though trying to squeeze inspiration out of his forehead by sheer clenching of the brow muscles. When it came, it was little short of horrifying.

This is what I have in mind. I will come and meet you. I should make it clear straightaway that I am a person of no importance whatsoever. I don't know anything that would be helpful to the Vadani, so capturing and torturing me would be a waste of effort. Nor would the Guilds pay a ransom for me, or exchange prisoners for me. Ask anybody, assuming you can find someone who's heard of me.

I will meet you, face to face, at some place convenient to you within easy reach of the Eremian border. If you like, I'll bring with me any further proof you want of Ariessa's remarriage. When we meet, we can figure out between us what it'll take for us to trust each other. I'll come alone, of course. You'll know as soon as you see me that you're in no danger whatsoever of assassination or abduction. I couldn't hurt a fly if I wanted to; not a big fly, anyway.

If you decide you don't want anything to do with us, that's fine. If that's your decision we will, of course, have you killed, sooner or later. If we can reach some sort of agreement, on the other hand — think about that. Think about what you've already lost, permanently and beyond hope of recovery, and what you may still be able to salvage from the wreckage. I feel it's very important that we should be completely honest with each other right from the very start; talking of which, I really like your poetry. It's got a very basic simplicity which I found quite moving.

Use the same courier to reply. I look forward very much to meeting you.

He had to try hard before he could get the pen back in the ink-well; his hand was shaking. But now he'd written it, there was no way back. Of course, Vaatzes might not reply . . .

He shut his eyes. Dying wouldn't be so terribly bad; but if they tortured him . . . He reached out for the letter, but stopped before his fingertips touched it. Of course, Boioannes might well forbid him to do it; a member of Necessary Evil, strolling alone and un-armed into Vadani territory. Boioannes would do no such thing. No risk whatsoever; you can't betray what you don't know. His orders would be: *If they capture and torture you, here's the misinformation you're to feed to them, and make sure they believe you.* Best not to put that idea into his mind.

Talking of minds, I must be out of . . .

Yes, he thought. Yes; but I really don't have any control over it, not now the letter's actually been written, not now that it exists, separate from me. It's a fixation, a compulsion, a need that overrides everything, even fear of pain and death. Quite possibly, being in love must be something like this; in which case, all the irrational, plain stupid things I've heard of lovers doing suddenly make sense. I want . . . No, I don't want, I need to meet him, to see his face and hear his voice, to share a space with him, to understand.

(He stood up; far too restless to sit down.)

And it'll be out of the office; that'll be a pleasant change. I'll be staying in inns, always wondered what that'd be like, and eating food that hasn't come from the Buttery. All kinds of fascinating new experiences, that I don't actually want, that I've spent my whole life avoiding.

He folded the letter, sealed it; it'd be safe now, because nobody would dare open a letter sealed by Necessary Evil. Not even Lucao Psellus; especially him.

Lucao who? Oh, him. That clerk.

He shoved through the door, scuttled down the corridor and stopped the first clerk he met. As he gave the instructions — so fussy about the details, repeating them over and over again — he realized that his voice was high and squeaky with excitement, wondered if the clerk had noticed it too. He wished he'd made a copy of the letter, so he could read it again; he couldn't seem to remember what he'd written, but he was sure it was vilely phrased, clumsy, possibly illegible. Should've got a clerk to copy it out in fair hand. Too late now; it's sealed, and the clerk's taken it, it's gone.

The thought of going back to his office was hateful. How long would it take the courier to reach Civitas Vadanis? She would be under orders to disguise her true intentions; presumably she'd go to Lonazep first, then up along the Cure Doce border, doing her stupid little business deals as normal, haggling a little extra small change out of provincial drapers and cutlers for run-of-the-mill Mezentine worsteds, brass buttons and table knives. Only then would she slip across the border into Eremia (with her safe conduct carefully hidden in the luggage, for use only in the direst of emergencies); buying now rather than selling, because the huddled pockets of Eremian refugees had no money. Gradually she'd work her way down the frontier, crossing into Vadani territory through one of the mountain passes, after which she could head straight to the capital without arousing suspicion. Two weeks? More likely three, and the same for the return trip. I can't wait that long, he told himself urgently, I'll fret myself to death in that time. Six *weeks* . . .

The hell with it. He bolted down the stairs, across Little Cloister, short-cut through the mosaic portico, up the main stairs, arriving breathless and racked by stitches in the anteroom of Boioannes' suite of offices.

No chance whatsoever of getting in to see the man himself; not without an appointment, and you had to have had your name put down at birth for one of those. But eventually he talked his way into the presence of Boioannes' chief assistant deputy clerk, a godlike man with a perfectly spherical head.

"Lucao Psellus," the clerk told him, and coming from such an authority, it had to be true. "How can I help?"

Psellus explained. Urgent Guild business, a direct commission, approved by a unanimous vote of Necessary Evil . . . At this point the clerk stopped him with one upraised forefinger, and leafed through a bound folio of manuscript until he came to the minutes of the relevant meeting.

"As you say," he said, one eyebrow slightly raised. "Level seven authorization, no less. What can we do for you?"

The letter, written, entrusted to a courier; on reflection, the usual channels far too slow; could the courier be stopped or called back, and the letter sent by express messenger instead?

The clerk frowned. "Express messenger?"

"Somebody fast," Psellus explained. "Instead of going all round the houses. Like the way you send orders and dispatches to the front line."

The frown deepened. Set foot in that frown and you'd be sucked down into it; all they'd ever find of you would be your hat, floating on the top. "You mean the military post." Long, thoughtful pause, as if the clerk was doing long division in his head. "Strictly speaking," he said eventually, "your authorization does allow you to make use of the military post. That said, I can't see how it'd help, in the circumstances. It would get your letter to Civitas Eremiae, say, in forty-eight hours. It couldn't get it across the border, let alone into the hands of the enemy." A sigh, full of sadness for the contrariness of the world. "No, they'd have to find you a covert messenger at Civitas Eremiae — one of those merchant women, they're really the only line of communication we've got for cross-border work. In all honesty, I think it'd be quicker to use the normal channels."

Psellus could feel his jaw getting tense. "All right, then," he said. "What about a diplomatic courier? A herald, or whatever you call them."

The clerk actually smiled; more than a hint of the Boioannes grin there. True what they say: after a while, dogs start to look like their masters. "First," he said, "you don't have authorization. Second, we aren't sending any diplomatic representations to the Vadani for the foreseeable future."

Psellus took a deep breath. "Then arrange one," he said. "Make something up. Pretend. Write to the Duke and tell him he's got one last chance to surrender. Any pretext, so long as you can send a courier with my letter sewn inside his trouser leg, or whatever it is your people do." He stopped, feeling ridiculous. It wasn't appropriate for a member of Necessary Evil to beg a clerk to send a letter. "If you'd rather, we could go and ask Councillor Boioannes. I'm sure he wouldn't mind being interrupted."

War, fiercer than anything that had taken place in Eremia, was raging behind the clerk's eyes. Not hard to figure out what he was thinking. Just possibly, Psellus the forgotten man, the Republic's leading nonentity, wasn't bluffing and genuinely had authorization from Boioannes himself; in which case, hindering him would be a very dangerous course of action. "We can send your message," the clerk said. "We're a resourceful lot, we'll think of something."

A terrified man rode through the main gate of Civitas Vadanis. He was unarmed, dressed from head to foot in dusty white, and four heavy cavalrymen flanked him at the four cardinal points, as though shielding their fellow countrymen from all possibility of contagion.

Needless to say, everybody had stopped what they were doing to stare at him. Some, mostly mothers with young children, backed away; others pressed forward as if they were going to attack, and the four outriders had to guide their horses to shove them back into the crowd. A few objects, some stones but mostly fruit, were thrown, but with poor accuracy. A flying cordon of guards advanced in reverse chevron formation from the palace door, enveloping the five riders and whisking them inside.

The terrified man, who hadn't said a word since he rode up to the official border post at Perrhagia, looked round. He wasn't used to places like this: fountains, statues on plinths, cobbled yards glimpsed through archways. The nearest thing he'd ever seen was the Guildhall, but that was bigger but plainer. This place was small, busy and almost deliberately arrogant, as if making no secret of the fact that, in spite of its ornate extravagance, it was the house of just one man, and everybody else here was some degree of servant. The thought appalled him; he hadn't realized that people could actually live like that.

They stopped in front of a pair of tall wrought-iron gates; gilded but disappointingly crude by Mezentine standards. The escort dismounted — nobody spoke to him, but he guessed he was supposed to dismount too — and the gates opened. He didn't look round, because he'd seen enough Vadani soldiers already for one day.

"Is this him?" A young man with a meager, thin face and hair the color of rust was talking to the escort leader, who must have nodded, because rust-head turned and walked into the building. The four escorts edged toward him, like drovers crowding a pig into a pen. He did his best to ignore them, and followed rust-head through the doorway, across a covered way and into a cloister garden. It was pretty enough, if you liked flowers and that sort of thing. In the middle was a small round walnut table — again, shoddy work once you got close enough to see — behind which sat a single man.

He'd been briefed before he left Mezentia, needless to say. They'd told him that Valens, the Vadani duke, was a young man, slightly built, shorter than most Vadani, with hair the color of dead leaves. The description fitted the man behind the table, just about. He looked tired, worried, angry about something. "This him?" he said.

"We searched him at the border," the escort leader said.

"He doesn't look particularly murderous," the man who might be Valens replied. "You're Mezentine, aren't you?" he added, without shifting his head, so that it took the terrified man a moment to realize he was being spoken to. "I mean, a real Mezentine, not one of the overseas mercenaries."

"Yes," the terrified man said, wondering whether he was supposed to add *sir* or *your highness*. Too late to do that now, so he'd better work on the assumption that a citizen of the Republic refuses to acknowledge the superiority of any man, even by way of formal greeting. "My name is Lexao Cannanus, permanent secretary to the —"

"I'm Valens. Sit down." Valens frowned. "No, don't do that, wait till someone fetches a chair. I do apologize for my household's inexcusable lack of manners. If I've told them once, I've told them a thousand times: accredited diplomats are not to be expected to sit on the grass."

All this humor, Cannanus assumed, was for the servants' benefit rather than his, though he could see it would have the additional benefit of making him feel uncomfortable. An efficient man, then, the Vadani duke; capable of making one operation do two jobs. If he was Mezentine, he'd probably be a Foundryman. Someone brought a chair — a silly thing, too fussily carved and not very sturdy — and he sat on it. The four soldiers were looming over his shoulder, but he did his best to pretend they weren't there.

"Apparently you've got a message for me," Valens said. "Or would you like something to eat or drink first? Now I'm the one forgetting his manners."

"No, that's fine," Cannanus said stiffly. "I'm sure you're a busy man, and I'd like to do my job and go home as soon as possible."

"Of course." Just a hint of a grin on Valens' face? He's making me think I'm sounding pompous and stupid, Cannanus realized. Clever man. "Well in your own time, then."

For a horrible moment, Cannanus couldn't remember what he was supposed to say . . .

"Greetings," he recited, in a flat, dead voice, "from the convocation of Guilds of the Mezentine Republic. This is to inform you that unless you accede forthwith to the Republic's legitimate demands, a state of war will exist between yourself and —"

"Just a moment," Valens interrupted. "What demands?"

Cannanus blinked. "I'm sorry?"

"What demands? I don't know what you're referring to. We haven't had any demands, have we, Mezentius?"

The rusty-haired man, who'd joined them at some point, shrugged. "Not that I'm aware of."

Valens sighed. "Which isn't to say there haven't been any," he said. "The trouble is, this sort of thing's the province of my chancellor, and unfortunately he was killed only a few days ago. As a result we're still in a bit of a tangle, not quite back up to speed. Would you be very kind and just run through them for me? The demands," he added, as Cannanus goggled at him. "Just to jog my memory, really. For all I know, we might be able to clear all this business up here and now."

Nightmare, Cannanus thought. There'll be a war that could have been avoided, and it'll all be my fault. "I'm sorry," he said. "I don't know. I'm just a messenger."

"Oh." Big frown. "That's a nuisance. Mezentius, do you think you could quickly go and scout through the papers on Carausius' desk, just in case they're there?" The rusty-haired man nodded and stomped away. "Won't be long," Valens said coolly. "Now, would you like a drink while you're waiting? I'm having one."

Infuriating. "Yes, thank you." If he can be polite, so can I; we'll see who crumbles first.

"Splendid." Valens nodded, and someone appeared at once with a tall, plain earthenware jug and two silver mugs. They at least were Mezentine, though ordinary trade quality. "Well, what shall we talk about? It's not often I get a chance to talk to a real Mezentine these days."

A cue, if ever there was one. "Is that right? I was under the impression you had a Mezentine living here at your court."

"A real Mezentine, I said." Valens grinned. "If you're thinking of my friend Ziani Vaatzes, I tend to think of him as one of us now, rather than one of you."

"Talking of him." Too good to be true, surely. The Duke was suspicious, hence the slightly forced lead. It wasn't fair, he reflected bitterly, to send a clerk to play at top-level diplomacy. A trained diplomat would be able to interpret all these subtleties. Instead, he had the feeling he usually only felt in dreams: playing chess against a master, and suddenly realizing he didn't know the rules of the game. Nevertheless, he was here now and there was nobody else. "I take it you can confirm he's still alive."

Valens tilted his head slightly on one side, like a dog. "So that's what the ambush was all about, was it? To kill poor old Ziani. In which case, yes, you wasted your time. Pity, really. A bit of a disaster all round."

"I wouldn't know," Cannanus replied. "I'm afraid the standing committee doesn't discuss policy with the likes of me."

"But they want to know the answer," Valens said, smiling. "It was one of the instructions you were given: find out if Vaatzes is still alive."

That question clearly didn't need an answer. "I wonder," Cannanus said, "if it'd be possible for me to talk to him. Just for a moment."

At least he'd contrived to take Valens by surprise. There was a short pause before he said, "Now why would you want to do that? I assume," he went on, recovering a little of his previous assurance, "that you aren't going to try and murder the poor chap."

"I have a message for him from the council."

Valens raised both eyebrows, then laughed. If Cannanus didn't know better, he'd have believed the amusement was genuine. "I'm very sorry," Valens said, "but I really don't think that'd be a terribly good idea. Will it spoil your trip terribly if I refuse?"

Cannanus shrugged. "To be honest with you," he said, "it wasn't part of my mission at all. I was just curious."

"Curious?"

"I wanted to see what he looks like."

"Oh." It was clear from his face that the very perversity of the idea appealed to Valens on some level Cannanus probably wouldn't be able to understand. "No, sorry. The wretched fellow's got enough on his plate without becoming a tourist attraction."

"I understand." He tried to put just the right hint of resentment into his reply, while keeping it diplomatically polite. "I'm sorry if the request was out of line."

"Think nothing of it," Valens answered. "Now, if it'd been me you'd wanted to see, I'd have had no problem with it. Probably have charged you two quarters for admission, but that's all. Now, where's Mezentius got to with those documents? He's a fine soldier, but not at his best with paperwork."

As if he'd been waiting behind a pillar for his cue, the rust-haired man came back, scowling and slightly short of breath. "I couldn't see anything on his desk," he said. "It could be anywhere in the files, of course, but it'd take days to go through all that lot."

Valens shrugged. "Well," he said, "since the alternative is war with the Republic, what's a few days scrabbling about in the dust? Get some clerks to help you." He turned and frowned politely at Cannanus. "You're not in a tearing hurry to get back, are you? Or will they dispatch a million cavalry if you're not home by this time tomorrow?"

"I don't think so," Cannanus replied. He didn't like the thought of hanging around in the Vadani capital for a moment longer than necessary. It made his flesh crawl; not fear, in fact, but disapproval. "But I think it'd be better if I went back and explained that the previous correspondence has been . . ." He scrabbled for the right word. "Mislaid. Otherwise," he added, with what he was sure was overdone ingenuousness, "they might just assume you're playing for time."

"Of course." Valens nodded firmly. "You do that, then. If you could possibly do your best to persuade them not to invade us till the copies have arrived, that'd be really kind." Valens stood up, an unambiguous indication that his ordeal was over. "Mezentius, would you mind showing our guest out? Unless he'd like to stay to dinner? No? Well, maybe next time, when you come back with the copy of the terms, I'll look forward to it. You'd better get a fresh horse for him," Valens went on. "Find him a good one, nothing but the best for our friends in the Republic."

The rusty-haired man started to walk away, and Cannanus hurried to follow him. The four guards came forward, as though to follow, but rust-head waved them away; the dreaded Mezentine apparently wasn't such a threat after all.

They walked about ten yards down the cloister, rust-head leading at a brisk pace that Cannanus found it irksome to match. Then he stopped dead and dropped a couple of documents. Looking down, Cannanus saw they were blank sheets of paper.

"I thought you hadn't seen my signal," Cannanus said.

"Quiet," rust-head snapped, not looking up. "Keep your voice down. Quick, look like you're helping me with these papers."

Cannanus knelt down beside him and picked up one of the blank sheets. "Sorry about not giving you any notice," he said quietly. "But it's an emergency, no time to warn you in advance."

"I'd gathered. And yes, I saw your signal, thank you very much. It's supposed to be a subtle hand-gesture. The way you were carrying on, you could've put someone's eye out."

Just stress and irritation talking; besides, there wasn't time.

"I've got a letter," Cannanus said. "For the abominator, Vaatzes. Make sure he's alone when he gets it, all right?"

"I'm not completely stupid. Well, where is it, then?"

"In my shoe."

"Oh for crying out loud."

"Well," Cannanus muttered, fumbling with his shoe-buckle, "I knew I'd be searched at the frontier. You want to upgrade your security procedures. If it'd been a Mezentine checkpoint, inside the shoe's the first place we'd have looked."

"What minds you people must have." Rust-head took the small, square packet from him and tucked it firmly into his sleeve. "Now let's get you out of here before anything goes wrong," he said. "And next time . . ."

"I know. We're sorry."

Rust-head sighed and stood up. "It's going to be much harder for me from now on," he said. "Chances are I'm going to be promoted, now that there's so many jobs that need filling, so I'll have to be that much more careful. Whose idea was that, by the way? The sneak attack, I mean."

Cannanus shrugged. "They don't tell me stuff like that."

"No, I suppose not. Anyway, you tell them from me. Next time I want plenty of advance warning, or the deal's off. Can you do that? They know I'm far too valuable to piss off."

"I'll be sure to mention it," Cannanus said.

"Do that." Rust-head glanced up and down the cloister. "And while you're at it, you can tell them that the evacuation's been brought forward again, in spite of the attack. And your abominator's been keeping very busy indeed, bashing out great big iron sheets. Nobody knows what it's all in aid of; rumor has it they're mass-producing armor, since they can't buy ready-made off your lot anymore, but it's not true. I'll try and find out from Valens what's going on, ready for when you come back."

"It probably won't be me on the return trip . . ." Cannanus tried to tell him, but he'd started walking again. Meeting over.

The horse they'd given him was beautiful, a Vadani mountain thoroughbred, intended to make him feel guilty and in their debt. He felt the guilt in spite of himself, but not the gratitude; it'd be impounded by the messengers' office as soon as he got back and given to some colonel in the mercenary cavalry. Just as well; it wouldn't be right to keep something the enemy had given him.

The fine, handsome, morally questionable thoroughbred cast a shoe almost as soon as he crossed the Eremian border, a few miles after his Vadani escort had turned back and left him on his own. That, he couldn't help thinking, was probably a judgment on him for his ingratitude, or else for being tempted to keep the horse. It gave him a certain amount to think about as he walked, leading the gift-horse by its reins, along the dusty, stony track that passed for the main road to Civitas Eremiae.

Other concerns, too; less high-minded and abstruse, rather more immediate. One of them was the fact that he'd forgotten to fill his water bottle back at Valens' palace; rather, he'd assumed that one of the Duke's countless servants would have done it for him while he was busy with the meeting. Another was the emptiness of his ration sack: the scrag end of a Mezentine munitions loaf, turned stale by the dry mountain air, a bit of cheese-rind and a single small onion.

He could, of course, ride the horse; but that would lame it, maybe cripple it for good on these horrible stony roads, and it was such a very fine horse, with its small, graceful head, arched neck and slim, brittle legs . . . Walking it lame would be as bad as damaging government property, for which he was personally responsible. That, he reckoned, was the Vadani for you: they bred exquisite horses, but their farriers couldn't nail a shoe on properly.

As if on purpose, the track started to climb steeply. Being a highly trained courier, Cannanus wasn't used to walking, and it wasn't long before he felt an ominous tightness in the back of his calves. He tried to picture in his mind the maps of the Eremian border country that he'd glanced at before he started out. The big stony thing he was struggling up was tall enough to count as a mountain, worth marking on a map and giving a name to; but there were so many mountains in Eremia that that was no great help. He gave up and started looking about him, but all he could see on the plain below was empty, patchy green blemished here and there with outcrops and bogs. Not a comfortable environment for a city boy at the best of times.

The thought that he could die out there, stupidly, through carelessness, took a while to form in his mind, but once he'd acknowledged it, he found it hard to silence. People died, lost in the mountains (but he wasn't lost, he was on the main road), particularly if they had no water and only a few crumbs of food (but Eremia was Mezentine territory now; there'd be patrols, hunting down the resistance or keeping out insurgents). He remembered passing an inn at some point. He'd only caught a glimpse of it as he galloped past (he'd been making up time after being held up crossing some river — a whole river full of water, unimaginable excess). He could remember the name from the map — the Unswerving Loyalty at Sharra Top — but he couldn't place it in this disorganized mess of landscape; could be an hour away, or a day's march on foot. Nothing for it; he was going to have to ride the stupid horse. After all, deliberately allowing a courier of the Republic to die of thirst in the desert was surely a worse crime against the state than crippling some overbred animal. Reluctantly, almost trembling with guilt, he ran down the stirrup, put his foot in it and lifted himself into the saddle.

The horse reared.

High-strung, temperamental thoroughbred, he thought, as his nose hit the horse's neck and his balance shifted just too far. He hung in the air for a moment, realizing objectively that he wasn't going to be able to sit this one out, and watched the sky as he fell.

Not as bad, actually, as some of the falls he'd had in the past; he'd been expecting worse, he told himself, as the pain subsided enough to allow his mind to clear. He opened his eyes, tried to move, found out that everything still worked. Stupid bloody horse, he thought, and dragged himself up, feeling the inevitable embarrassment of the seasoned rider decked by a mere animal; won't let it get away with that, or it'll think it's the boss. He looked round for it. Not there.

The rush of panic blotted out thought for a moment. He recovered, hobbled a little way to a tall rock, scrambled up and looked round. There was the horse; off the track, heading down the steep, rocky slope at a determined canter, obviously unaware of the desperate risk to its fragile, expensive legs. Served it right if it broke them all.

It took at least two heartbeats before he realized that it had gone too far — just too far, but enough — for him to have any hope of catching it, unless it stopped of its own accord, to rest or graze (graze? Graze on what?). No horse, no transport; and, needless to say, his few crumbs of food were in the ration sack, just behind the saddle roll.

Fear came next. He felt its onset, recognized it from a distance, as it were; but when it overtook him, there was nothing he could do about it. He was going to die; he was going to die very slowly, his throat and mouth completely dried out, like beans hung in the sun; it was all his own fault that he was going to die so unpleasantly, and there was no hope at all. He felt his knees weaken, his stomach tighten, his bladder twitch, he was shaking and sobbing. For crying out loud, he tried to tell himself, this is ridiculous; you haven't broken a leg, you're fit and healthy and it can't be far to that inn, but the forced hopes turned like arrows on proof armor. He dropped to the ground in a huddle, and shook all over like a fever case.

Fear came and went, taking most of him with it. He stood up; he was talking to himself, either out loud or in his head, he couldn't tell. You're not thinking straight, he said, you're going to pieces, that's not going to help; and you're missing something really important.

That stopped him. He looked round, like a man who's just realized he's dropped his keys somewhere. Something important that he'd seen just a few moments ago, before the fear set in and wiped his mind. Something . . .

It came back to him, and he thought, *idiot*. It had been there all the time, he'd probably been looking straight at it while he was crouching there quivering and blubbing. It had been a silvery flash; sunlight on the surface of a bog-pool, down below in the valley.

Some of his intelligence was starting to creep back. He looked for patches of darker, lusher green, and soon enough he caught sight of that flash again. He tried to gauge the distance — hard in such open country, but no more than two miles away, probably less, and all downhill. Now he thought about it, the horse had gone that way; there was a chance he'd find it again, drinking peacefully. Two miles downhill; he could do that, and then he'd have water. Not water to spare — the water bottle was with the ration sack, on the saddle of the stupid fucking horse — but enough to keep him alive, give him a chance to calm down and get a grip. He heard someone laugh, high, braying, almost hysterical; it took him a moment to realize he was listening to himself, but now he thought about it, he could see the joke.

To begin with he tried to hurry, but a couple of trips and sprawls made it clear that haste could kill him, if he fell awkwardly and twisted something. He'd been careless twice already that day. He slackened his pace to an amble, as though he was strolling home from work. All the way, he kept his eye fixed on the spot where he'd seen the silver flash, just in case it turned sneaky on him and crept away.

When he got there . . . It wasn't beautiful, even to a man who'd killed himself with anticipated thirst only an hour earlier. It was a brown hole surrounded by black peaty mud, sprinkled with white stones and fringed with clumps of coarse green reeds, a very few clumps of dry heather, here and there a tuft of bog-cotton. He slowed down as he approached it; wading into the mud and getting stuck would be careless too, and he was through with carelessness for good. From now on, every action he committed himself to would be exquisitely designed, planned and executed with all proper Mezentine precision, a work of art and craft that anybody would be proud to acknowledge.

In accordance with this resolution, he crept forward, taking care to test the ground with his heel before committing his weight. It soon struck him that he was wasting his time; the mud was slimy and stank, but the most his boot sank in it was an inch or so. He quickened his pace; he could see the water now, and smell it too. Nothing to be afraid of . . .

He stopped. In front of him, unmistakable as a Guild hallmark, was the print of a horse's hoof. He frowned. So the horse *had* been this way — the print was fresh, he could tell by the sharpness of the indentation's edge, the deeper pits left by the nail-heads. Maybe it was still somewhere close, in which case at least some of his troubles could well be over. He swung his head, looking round, and saw another print, identical, and then another, at just the right interval. He'd found the wretched animal's tracks, so he could follow it until he caught up with it, and . . .

The fourth print he found was of an unshod hoof. Definitely his horse, then.

He hurried along the trail of prints. As he'd anticipated, it was heading straight for the water. Logical: horses get thirsty too. He wondered how much of a head start it'd have on him by now. Not too much, he hoped. The miserable creature would just be ambling along, grazing as it went, in no particular hurry. And it shouldn't be too hard to spot in this open, flat country.

He stopped. He'd reached the edge of the pond, a black beach of glittering mud, with two hoofprints in it; the water beyond, like a silver inlay in rusted steel. For a moment he forgot about the horse. It was only when he thought, And now I'll be able to fill my water bottle, too, that it occurred to him to wonder where the horse had gone from there. No hoofprints leading back the other way, after all. It looked for all the world as though the stupid animal had swum out into the middle of the pond . . .

Horses do swim, of course; but not unless they're made to. The horse had come this way, arrived here, but not gone back. There was no sign of it to be seen anywhere. Therefore, it had to be here still, somewhere.

Fear again. Not something he wanted to go through a second time in one day, but it swooped and caught him up before he could ward it off with deliberate thought. As he struggled to breathe, he shouted at himself, *It's all right, all you've got to do is go back exactly the way you came, you know that's all firm footing.* The very thought made him lose his balance. He staggered, as though drunk, and when his misplaced foot touched down there was nothing under it to take its weight, nothing at all, like standing in slow, thick water. He jerked his foot back, felt something sucking on his boot, but the seal broke and he wobbled helplessly on one foot, a ludicrous object, hanging in the balance between life and death. For two long seconds he knew he had no control over his body or his destiny; it was all to be decided by subtle and accidental forces of leverage and balance. His foot touched down, sank a heart-stopping two inches, and found a firm place.

At least it explained what had become of the horse. He sucked in air, although his lungs felt sealed; the battering of his heart shook him, as though someone behind him was nudging him repeatedly in the back. The insides of both his legs were wet and warm, and he spared a little attention for the momentary feeling of revulsion.

Well, he thought. I can't move. Under no circumstances am I going to move my feet, ever again.

As if they'd heard him and wanted to tease him, his knees had gone weak, to the point where they were endangering his balance. He knew what he had to do. Very slowly, keeping his back perfectly straight, he folded himself at the waist, bent his knees and squatted, stretching out his left hand as far as it could be forced to go so as to test the mud directly in front of him with his fingertips. Only when he was absolutely sure of it did he finally drop forward and kneel. That, he reckoned, was about the best he'd be able to do.

He looked up. There was the water, a thousand million gallons or so, but impossible to reach under any circumstances. He knelt and stared at it, almost as though he believed he might be able to train it to come when he whistled; but it didn't move, not even a ripple or a spread of circles where a water-fly had landed on its face. He laughed, a sound like his mind grating as its gears slipped their train. He was out of the mud, but he was completely and irrecoverably stuck. Big difference.

A certain amount of time passed. Mezentine precision could calibrate a scale to measure most things, but not time spent in terror, despair and that particular sort of shame. Once or twice he almost managed to nerve himself to move, only to fail when he made the actual attempt. He noticed that the water had a strange, colored sheen to it, and that one of the stones near his hand was crusted with yellow crystals. He thought: I shall spend the rest of my life here, and nobody will ever know what became of me. Maybe the horse had the right idea, after all. What would it feel like, drowning in mud? You'd try and breathe in, but nothing would come, the reverse of holding your breath. There'd be panic and spasm, but surely not for very long. Does pain actually matter if you don't survive it?

Something was different. He was aware of the change long before he realized what it was, probably because it was so mundane, among all the melodrama. Nothing but the light fading (and how long could he hope to survive once it was dark and he couldn't see the danger?). He was tired, he realized, more tired than he'd ever felt in his life, now that the panic had turned to terrified resignation. No chance at all that he'd manage to stay awake. Sleep would come for him, quiet as a poacher; he'd slide or roll into the mud, and . . .

The water turned red as the sky thickened; sunset brought a sharp chill that finally gave him a legitimate reason to tremble. Mosquitoes were buzzing a lullaby all round him. In spite of everything, it was impossible to believe that when the sun came up again, he wouldn't see it. He'd been in a battle, a tangled skirmish at the very end of the Eremian war; his horse had been shot under him and he'd ended up lying on the ground, trapped beneath its dead weight. All around him there'd been dying men, Mezentines and Eremians jumbled together, too damaged or too weak to move. He'd listened to them for three hours, shouting, screaming for help or yelling abuse, groaning, begging, sniveling, praying. He'd heard their voices fade one by one as the long wait came to an end. That he'd been able to understand; this — a healthy, strong man, uninjured, not yet starved or parched enough to be more than inconvenienced — was too arbitrary to be credible, because people don't just die, for no reason. He fought sleep as it laid siege to him; at first ferociously, as the Eremians had fought the investment of their city; then desperately, a scampering withdrawal in bad order to inadequately fortified positions; then aimlessly, because there really wasn't any point, but one has to do one's best. On his knees, supporting his weight with hands flat on the ground and fingers splayed, he let his head wilt forward and closed his eyes, allowing the equity of redemption to drain away. No point in keeping his eyes open when it was dark and there was nothing to see. Could you drown in your sleep, without ever waking up? If so it was a mercy, and it would be churlish to . . .

He was dreaming, and in his dream a man was standing over him, prodding him spitefully with a stick. It was an unusually vivid dream, because the prods hurt almost as much as the real thing would have done, had he been awake. The man began to shout. He dreamed that he opened his eyes and saw thin, gray light, the sort you get just before dawn; he saw the man with the stick, and for some reason he was straw-haired and fishbelly-skinned. Curious, almost perverse. Why, in his last dream before death, should his mind have conjured up an Eremian?

"Fucking wake up," the man yelled, and stabbed him with the stick, catching him on the edge of the collarbone. You can't hurt like that and still be asleep.

He saw the man's face. It was smooth, unlined, but horribly spoiled by a long, shiny pink scar. "If you don't wake up *now*," the man was bawling, "I'm bloody well leaving you here, all right?" He raised the stick again for another jab. Instinctively, Cannanus began to flinch away, remembering just in time not to move.

"I'm awake, for crying out loud," he gabbled; and as he said it, it occurred to him that there was a man, a fellow human being, there with him in the bog. "How did you get here?" he demanded. "It's a bog, you'll be *eaten* . . ."

The man looked startled, as though a friendly dog had snarled at him. "Oh," he said, relaxing a little, "I see what you . . . It's all right," he said, "I know the path, so long as we stay on it we'll be fine." Something must have occurred to him; he asked, "How long have you been there?"

"All night," Cannanus replied. "Can you get me out of this? Please? I'll do anything . . ."

"Just keep still and don't thrash about, or we'll both be in trouble." The man's voice had something about it, unfamiliar yet acting directly on him, as though the words didn't really matter. Authority, he supposed, but not the stern, brutal voice of a man giving orders. Rather, it was someone who naturally and reasonably expected to be obeyed when he told you what to do; it reminded him a lot of Duke Valens, but without the edge.

"It's perfectly simple," the man was saying. "We just go back the way I came. You can see my footprints, look. Easiest thing would be if you followed them exactly, put your feet on them. Oh, and don't let me leave without my sack."

For a moment, Cannanus didn't recognize the word. "Sack?"

"Sack. Come on, you know what a sack is."

Sure enough, there was a sack; two-thirds empty, but the man grunted as he lifted it onto his shoulder. "Mineral samples," he explained, unasked. "Sulfur. That's what I came here for, though it's pretty well picked clean now. One of the few places you can still find clean, pure sulfur crystals; I got some mined stuff the other day, loads of it, but it turned out to be filthy, full of crud, no use at all." He paused to let Cannanus catch up; he was racing ahead, as though there was no danger. "I expect you're wondering," he went on, in a cheerful voice, "why an Eremian should risk his neck to fish a Mezentine out of a bog."

Cannanus hadn't, as it happened. He'd had other things on his mind.

"Well, if you aren't, I certainly am." The man turned back and grinned at him, twisting the scar into a thin, angry line. "I don't know, really. Well, the fact is, it's not long since a passing stranger risked his neck to drag me out of one of these wretched bog-pools — not this one, another one a couple of miles further on. When I saw your tracks, I guessed you might be in trouble. It was only after I'd figured out a safe way in — you can see it, if you've been shown what to look for, it's a certain way the light shines off the mud; pretty metaphysical stuff, though I guess there's a perfectly reasonable explanation. Anyhow, I'd already done all the waiting around for the light to come up so I could see those special reflections, and then the dodgy part, charging in and finding out if I'd read the signs right, before I realized you're actually one of the enemy; and by then it seemed a bit silly, really, to turn round and walk away. The fact is, the bloke who rescued me had every reason to leave me there, but he didn't; so I guess I'm under a sort of obligation to repay the favor vicariously, if you follow me; even if you are a Mezentine. Stupid, really; if we'd met in a battle rather than a bog-pit, I'd have done everything I possibly could to kill you. Just goes to show how arbitrary the rules we make for ourselves really are."

The man certainly liked the sound of his own voice, although Cannanus charitably decided it was part of the rescue, keeping him distracted with cheerful chatter so he wouldn't suddenly panic and trip into the mud; a wise, resourceful man who thought of everything. He prattled about minerals and where to find them, their properties, the difficulties that lay in refining them, the time and labor . . . One thing he said, however, was very interesting. "My name's Miel, by the way. Miel Ducas." Pause. "Quite likely you've heard of me."

Cannanus said nothing, though that in itself constituted a clear admission.

"Fine," Ducas said. "You know who I am. I don't suppose there's any point telling you I'm through with the resistance — well, the resistance is more or less done for anyway, it's just that I chucked it in before it withered away and died, and I don't think that was cause and effect, either. Truth is, I was in one fight too many. Oddly enough, I only realized that was the reason after I'd decided to give up. I got separated from them — well, lost, actually; the irony is, all this used to be my land, though I'd never even been out this far before. Well, I had my chance to hurry back and carry on with the noble struggle, but instead I thought, the hell with it, I'll stay here. Now I'm in business with . . ." Just the slightest hesitation as he considered his choice of words. "With some people, and I'm doing something useful for once. Crazy, really. I spent most of my life ignoring all the good things I was born to, pursuing what I believed to be my duty to my country and my people. Plain fact is, when it really mattered I only ever did them more harm than good. Now I've lost everything, but found something I actually want to do — for myself, I mean, not because it's expected of me. And no, I don't know why I'm telling you all this, except maybe because you're a complete stranger, and sometimes you need to talk to someone."

Suddenly he stopped. Cannanus froze in his tracks, terrified that Ducas had come the wrong way, led them both into horrible danger. Instead, he turned round and said, "Well, here we are. Safe from here on; you can run up and down like an overexcited dog if you want to and you won't suddenly disappear into a bog-pool. Which means," he added, breathing in deeply, "that if you want to carry on going, get back to the Republic and tell your intelligence people you've found where the rebel leader's hiding out, now's as good a time as any. Just keep straight on up that mountain — Sharra, it's called — and you'll come to an inn, about a day and a half's walk from here. Last I heard, your people don't come out to the inn; too far for them to patrol and still be back in camp by nightfall. Even so, you ought to be able to send word to the nearest garrison camp to come and fetch you. If that's what you want to do, I mean."

Cannanus could hear his own breathing. "You won't . . ."

Ducas laughed. "Now that really would be silly," he said. "I risk my life to save you, and then risk it again killing you. No, the hell with it. You're bigger than me, I don't suppose I could subdue you by force and drag you back to our place. If anything, it'd be the other way round, you'd take me to the Mezentines. So, let's avoid the issue, shall we? If you want to go, go."

Cannanus remembered something: practicalities. Not so long ago, he'd been resigned to a miserable death, and that was before he'd wandered into the bog. "I can't," he said. "I've got no water, or food."

"I told you," Ducas replied, with maybe a hint of impatience for feebleness. "Day and a half straight up the mountain, you'll come to the Unswerving Loyalty. Basic home cooking and they won't give you water, you'll have to make do with beer, but it'll keep you alive."

"I'd get lost," Cannanus said wretchedly.

"Probably you wouldn't."

"Possibly I might." As he heard himself say the words, he understood for the first time just how terrified he'd been, ever since the horse threw him and he became aware of how dangerous the world was for a mere pedestrian. In a way, it was a bit like what Ducas had said, about losing all his wealth and power, only in reverse. When he'd still had a horse, he could have done anything. It was all the horse's fault — stupid Vadani thoroughbred — and it had got no less than it deserved.

Ducas scowled. "If I take you back with me," he said, "my partners are going to be so angry."

It hadn't occurred to him that Ducas didn't want him. He'd assumed . . . Unreasonable assumption, that just because someone rescues you, he's prepared to put himself out even further on your behalf. "Straight up the mountain, you say."

"Follow your nose, you can't miss it." Ducas was bending over his sack, taking something from it. "Here," he said, holding up a two-pint leather bottle. "If you're so worried. I'll have to tell them I dropped it somewhere. Hardware doesn't grow on trees, you know." He lobbed the bottle; Cannanus caught it clumsily on the second attempt, terrified it'd fall on the stones and split.

"I can get home without a drink, assuming I don't trip and do my ankle or something stupid. No food, I'm afraid, but you'll last out, you don't look exactly emaciated to me. Of course," he added slowly, "a good man, someone with a bit of something about him, wouldn't tell the authorities where he got that bottle from; who gave it to him, I mean. He'd feel a sort of obligation. At least, he would where I come from. I don't know how duty works in the Republic."

Cannanus didn't say anything.

"Well, anyway." Suddenly Ducas seemed in a hurry. "Straight up the mountain. If you hit a road you've gone too far west, but don't worry, just follow it and go easy on the water, it gets you there eventually. If you go too far east you'll come to a river, so that's all right." He grinned, as if at some private joke. "If I'd known that a few months ago, I'd be in Civitas Vadanis right now, with my cousin, paying off a few old scores of my own. Duty, you see. Horrible thing, but they tell you it's important when you're a kid, and like a fool you believe them. That was the motto of our family, you know: Masters of North Eremia, Slaves of Duty. Fifty generations of idiots, and then came me." He turned and started to walk away.

Cannanus hesitated; Miel Ducas, the rebel leader, his savior. "Thank you," he said.

"My pleasure," Ducas said, without looking back.

17

It was as though a volcano had erupted in the middle of Civitas Vadanis, and was blowing out carts instead of lava and ash. The streets were jammed with them, their tailgates crushed against the necks of the horses behind, their wheel-hubs jammed against gateposts and thresholds. Lines of backed-up carts flowed down the gate turnpikes like frozen rivers, while soldiers and gatekeepers strained to lift, push and drag the stranded and the stuck, to clear the bottlenecks. Under the thin, high-arched promenade bridge, which carried the elevated walkway over the main street, two hay wagons coming from opposite directions had tried to pass each other and had ended up fixed as tight as hammer-wedges; a group of hopeless optimists from the rampart watch were trying to lift one of them up out of the way, using ropes lowered from the bridge boardwalk. A free spirit who'd tried to jump the line by taking a short cut through the yard of the ducal palace was being taken, much against his will, to explain his reasoning to the duty officer.

"We should've told them to muster in the long lists, under the east wall," someone said gloomily, as Valens watched the mess from the top of the North Tower.

"We did," someone else replied. "But that's the public for you, always got to know best."

Valens leaned his elbows on the battlements. "What we should have done," he observed sourly, "is stagger the arrivals, so they didn't all arrive at once; assemble them down in the valley, then send them up in batches of a dozen."

"We did that too," said a young, dough-faced man, with a sheepish grin. "Unfortunately, the steelyard crews seem to have underestimated the time they'd need, so they're way behind and all our careful timetabling's gone out of the window. You can't blame the yard workers, though. I went down to check on progress about an hour ago, never seen men work so hard."

Valens lifted his head. "Who did you get the time estimates from?" he asked.

"That creepy chap, the thin one with the ponytail. He told me, half an hour per cart, start to finish. But it's not all his fault, either. Apparently, they were kept hanging about waiting for a consignment of bolts from the forge."

Valens yawned. "I see," he said. "In that case, we'll hold up on the beheadings until we can be absolutely sure whose fault this is. Meanwhile, would it help if we sent some more men down to the yard, to clear the backlog?"

The young man sighed. "Not really," he said. "I offered earlier, but the creepy bloke said that extra bodies would just be in the way. Apparently, the problem is, they've only got a limited number of those drill things — sorry, I don't know the right word. Curly steel thing like a pig's tail, and you turn a handle like a wheel spoke."

"Augers," Valens said.

"That's them," the young man said cheerfully. "They've only got two dozen of the things, so Mister Creepy told me, and drilling the holes is the bit that takes all the time. Once that's done, offering up the plates and bolting them down is a piece of cake. That Mezentine's rigged up cranes and winches and things to move the plates about, and wooden frame things to show them where to drill the holes —"

"Jigs," Valens said.

"Is that the word? Anyway, all highly ingenious stuff, but I guess he's used to this sort of thing."

Valens shrugged. "We'll get there in the end," he said. "But I want Orchard Street cleared and kept open; we need one way in and out of the town, even if all the rest are blocked solid."

Someone nodded, accepting the commission, and disappeared down the spiral staircase. Valens groped for his name; an Eremian, from one of the leading families. Surprisingly knowledgeable about falconry, for an Eremian. "Who just left?" he asked.

"Jarnac Ducas," someone said. "You put him in charge of the day watch, remember?"

"Did I?" Valens shrugged. "I've lost track of who's doing what these days."

"He volunteered," someone said, and someone else sniggered. "Very keen, the Eremians. Some of them, at any rate."

"I remember him now," Valens said. "Annoying but highly competent. Well, at any rate he'll get the traffic moving again, if he has to kill every carter in the city with his bare hands." He frowned. "I shouldn't joke about that," he added. "I saw him fighting at the siege of Civitas Eremiae. Quite glad he's on our side, really." He looked up at the sky: well past noon. "I suppose I'd better go and do some work," he said sadly. "Does anybody know where Mezentius has got to?"

He found him in the exchequer office, sitting at the great checkered counting table, his head in his hands and a heap of silver counters scattered in front of him. "Bad time?" he asked.

Mezentius looked up. "I've got a confession to make," he said angrily. "I don't know how to work this stupid bloody thing."

Valens frowned. "It's not exactly straightforward," he said. "I spent hours trying to learn when I was a kid, and I still have trouble."

Mezentius spun a counter on its rim, then flicked it across the tabletop. "No you don't," he said. "You can make it come out every time."

"True." Valens picked up the counter and put it back with the rest of the pile. "I have trouble, but I overcome it, slowly and painfully. I find the key to success is not losing my temper."

Mezentius sighed. "Point taken," he said. "But I shouldn't be having to do this, there should be clerks."

"There were. But I had to promote them all, remember? So, for the time being, we all do our own tiresome and menial chores. I'm sorry, but there it is. Duty must be done, and all that."

"Quite. How's married life, by the way?"

"Delightful, thank you," Valens snapped. "Now, when you've finished whatever it is you're doing, I need to talk to you about who's going to command the light cavalry decoy detachments. I did ask you for some names about a week ago, but I'm assuming you've been busy."

"I'll see to it," Mezentius said. "You know, I liked it better when we were soldiers."

"We still are," Valens replied. "Unfortunately." He turned to leave, then remembered something and paused. "While I think of it," he said. "Have we heard back about the demands yet?"

"Nothing."

"Ah well. I thought we could play for time, but obviously they aren't that stupid. Happy figuring."

Crossing the yard, he could hear the forges, the shrill, distant clank and bash of the trip-hammers and sledges beating out hot iron blooms into plate. What it must be like for people in the city, he didn't like to think. They were working three shifts now. He hoped for his fellow citizens' sake that after a while they got so used to it that they stopped noticing it; hoped, but doubted. It wasn't a sound you could ignore.

Next chore: he unlocked the little sally port that gave access through the back wall of the palace into the narrow lane that led down into the flower market. The steep gradient and pinched, winding alleys made it impossible for carts to get this far, and the congestion was keeping the traders from getting through, so the market was deserted. From the corner of the square, a long flight of steps took him down to a derelict block where the big tanners' yard used to be, and from there he followed a spider's web of snickets and entries until he arrived at the side gate of the old covered market where Vaatzes had set up his small-assemblies workshop.

The noise was different there. The screeching and graunching of files was loud enough to blur out the beat of the hammers; it reminded him of grasshoppers, but there was a tension about the place that made him feel uneasy. He was getting used to it, however; he experienced it wherever Vaatzes had made his presence felt, a kind of sad, determined anger.

Where the old market stalls had been, there were now rows of long, narrow benches, to which stout wooden vises were bolted at intervals of six feet or so. Behind each vise stood a man, his neck bent, his feet a shoulder's width apart, his arms reciprocating backward and forward as he guided his file; each man just slightly out of time with his neighbor, so that the movements appeared sequential rather than concerted, like the escapement of a vast mechanism. Valens walked the length of one aisle and came to the drilling benches, set at right angles to the rest of the shop. He vaguely remembered Vaatzes complaining about something or other to do with drilling; there weren't enough proper pedestal drills in the duchy, so he was having to waste valuable time and skilled manpower building them, badly, with wooden frames instead of cast iron. Presumably that was what the men were doing; they worked in teams of three, one man working a treadle, one man feeding a squared beam along a bed of rollers, the third man slowly drawing down a lever to guide a fast-spinning chuck. They stood up to their ankles in yellow dust; it spilled out of the holes they drilled like blood from wounds, and from time to time a spurt would belch up into the air, blinding them and making them cough. There was a clogging smell of dust, sap and burning, and the air was painfully dry. Beyond the drills were more benches, more processes, different shapes but the same shared movement, as though the whole building was powered from one shaft driven by one flywheel, hidden and turning imperceptibly slowly.

A worried-looking man with a bundle of notched tallies cradled in his arms tried to step round him; a supervisor, presumably.

Valens moved just enough to block him, and shouted, "Where's Vaatzes?"

The supervisor frowned, shrugged, said something Valens couldn't make out through the noise.

"Vaatzes," he repeated, louder. The man tried to point, lost his hold on his tallies, and watched them slither out under his elbows onto the floor. It was probably just as well that Valens couldn't make out what he had to say about that, as he stooped to gather them.

"Vaatzes," he said a third time, putting his foot on a tally so the man couldn't retrieve it. That got him a ferocious scowl and a vague indication, somewhere beyond the banks of buffing wheels. "Thank you so much," he said, and walked on.

In the end, he found Vaatzes standing at a bench, cutting a slot in a steel plate with a file. He tapped him on the shoulder; Vaatzes turned, hesitated for a moment and put the file down, saying something Valens couldn't hear.

"Is there somewhere we can hear ourselves think?" Valens shouted.

Vaatzes nodded and led the way, down the aisle to what looked like a square hole in the floor, with the top rungs of a ladder sticking up out of it. "Down here," Vaatzes yelled, and vanished down the hole before Valens could object.

Strange place for the Duke of the Vadani to be; certainly somewhere he'd never been before. After a moment's thought he decided it was probably the market's old meat cellar, somewhere cool to keep the unsold stock overnight. It had the feel of a tomb about it, a stone-faced chamber carefully designed for storing dead flesh. There was a plain, cheap table in the middle of it, on which stood a single lamp, a sheaf of papers and an inkwell.

"My office," Vaatzes explained. "The real one, where I actually do some work. About the only place in this town you can hear yourself think."

True enough; no distant thumping of hammers, even the squeal of files was missing. "Excellent," Valens said. "I might just commandeer it for myself, until all this is over."

Flat joke; so flat you could have played bowls on it. "You wanted to see me," Vaatzes said. "I could have come to the palace."

Valens waved that aside. "You're busier than I am," he said, "your time's worth more. And I was curious, I wanted to take a look for myself. I've never seen anything like it before."

Vaatzes gestured toward the single chair. Valens raised his palm in polite refusal. "It's not a pretty sight, I'm afraid," Vaatzes said. "If you want to see the real thing, go and visit the ordnance factory, or any of the Guild shops in the city. The best you can say for this lot is, we're getting the job done, more or less."

"Not up to the standard you're used to?"

Vaatzes laughed. "Not really."

"Pity," Valens replied. "I'd have liked to think you were making yourself at home. Or at least, as close to home as you can make it. I get the feeling you aren't comfortable out of your proper surroundings."

"Curious thing to say," Vaatzes replied. "I can't say I'd thought of it like that before. You think I'm trying to turn all the places I go to into little replicas of the city, just because I'm homesick."

Valens shrugged. "Something like that. Not that it bothers me if you are. We need your help, simple as that. None of our people could've set up something like this."

"True," Vaatzes said. "It's just as well we aren't trying anything ambitious. It was different in Eremia. Yes, they were primitive by Mezentine standards, but in the event it didn't take long to get the local artisans up to speed. Here . . ." He pulled a sad face. "You've got no real tradition of making things," he said. "Understandable, no need, when you could buy anything you wanted in trade. But we're coping. This time tomorrow, it should all be finished."

"Really?"

Vaatzes nodded. "It may look like a shambles, but actually it's going well. The only problem I'm anticipating is getting the finished carts out of the way, once they've been armored."

"I've got someone taking care of all that," Valens replied. "Anyhow, I'm relieved to hear you say we'll be ready more or less on time, because I've decided to bring the evacuation forward by two days. If we leave early, people won't have time for their last-minute packing, they'll have to grab what they can and run. That way, we can keep the wagons from getting laden down with unnecessary junk." He hesitated. He was finding it hard to concentrate. A conclusion was trying to form in his mind, but as yet he couldn't find the shape of it. "Anyway, that's all I wanted to ask you. I'll let you get back to work."

But Vaatzes was looking at him. "You came a long way just to get a progress report. You could've sent someone."

That was true, but it hadn't occurred to Valens to send a messenger. "I haven't had a chance to talk to you," he said, "not since the attack." He frowned. "I guess I ought to thank you, for raising the alarm."

"Self-interest," Vaatzes replied shortly.

"Maybe, but if you hadn't . . ." The conclusion? Only the leading edge of it. "I'll admit," he said, "it scared me. I don't think I'd realized just how close they are."

"Hence the hurry to get the evacuation under way?"

"Partly." No, he realized. It's not the Mezentines that frighten me. "That man of yours, Daurenja. Where did you get him from? He came in handy."

A slight reaction, as though he'd grazed a sore place. "He just turned up one day, wanting a job," Vaatzes replied. "To be honest with you, I don't know what to make of him either. But he works hard, and he's been very useful."

They were just making conversation; acquaintances spinning out a tenuous discussion to plaster over a silence. "Let me know as soon as the last cart's been done," Valens said briskly. "And I'm obliged to you. It can't have been easy, but you've done a good job."

The praise seemed to glance off, like a file off hardened steel; hardly what you'd expect from a refugee artisan praised by his noble patron. I don't matter particularly to him, Valens realized;

and maybe that's the conclusion, or another of its projections. "I'll let you get on now."

"There's one other thing." The tone of Vaatzes' voice stopped him in his tracks.

"Go on."

Vaatzes was looking straight at him, as though aiming. "Did you ever find out what the object of the attack was?"

"Fairly obvious, surely."

"To get you, you mean?"

It had seemed obvious, not so long ago. "You don't think so."

"I was wondering," Vaatzes said, "if it was me they were after."

"What makes you think that?"

"Well, this whole war's about me, more or less." He said it as though it was something so generally accepted as to be trite and not worth emphasizing. "They invaded Eremia because I was there. Now I'm here. Maybe, if they haven't got the stomach for another full-scale war, they reckoned they could get out of it by going straight to the heart of the problem, so to speak."

Valens decided his other commitments could wait. "I'm not sure I agree," he said. "They're upset with me because I made an unprovoked attack on them, at Civitas Eremiae. Can't say I blame them for that."

"Maybe." Vaatzes was still looking straight at him. "But suppose I'm right. Suppose it's me they really want, and that's what the attack was all about. If you thought that, what would you do?"

"That's easy," Valens said quietly. "I'd let them have you."

"Of course. Has the thought crossed your mind at all?"

"Yes." He hadn't intended to say that. "I consider all the options. I decided against it."

Vaatzes nodded, a mute acknowledgment. "Why?" he asked.

"I don't believe it'd get them off my back," Valens said. "And you're very useful to me. And I don't think the war's about you, or at least, not anymore. It's all about Mezentine internal politics now. Sending you back might get me a truce, but they'd be back again before too long."

"My fault again." Vaatzes smiled. "If I hadn't built the scorpions for Duke Orsea, they'd have had a quick, easy victory in Eremia. Instead they were humiliated, and they've got to get their self-respect back. They need me for that."

"You make it sound like you want to be sent back. Do you like yourself as a martyr or something?"

"Of course not. I just want to know where I stand."

"Reasonable enough." Valens wanted to look away, but that wouldn't be a good idea. "You've got nothing to worry about on that score," he said. "It's against my nature to give up anything I can use as a weapon, when my enemies are breathing down my neck. If they'd asked me politely, at the beginning . . ." He paused, and shook his head. "I wouldn't have trusted them, even then. If the war's anybody's fault, it's mine. I attacked them, it's very straightforward."

(Later, it occurred to Valens that Vaatzes didn't ask him why he'd taken his cavalry to Civitas Eremiae. Perhaps it was diffidence, or simple politeness.)

"Well, that's all right then," Vaatzes said, and Valens felt as though he'd been released, on bail. "You'll excuse me for asking, but you'll understand my concern. Especially after the attack."

After he'd shown the Duke out, Vaatzes came back to his cellar and sat down at his table. For a while he didn't move, almost as though he was bracing himself for something unpleasant. Eventually, he reached for a sheaf of drawings, picked them up and put them neatly on one side. Under them was a small sheet of parchment, marked by fold-lines.

I enclose a notarized copy of the marriage certificate. You know as well as I do that a Mezentine notary wouldn't falsify a certificate . . .

He frowned. Notaries; he'd never given them much thought before, but now their code of professional ethics had suddenly become the most important issue in the world. He cast his mind back, trying to remember everything he could about notaries.

. . . a Mezentine notary wouldn't falsify a certificate for anybody, not even the Guilds in supreme convocation. But if that's not good enough for you, ask for whatever proof you need and I'll try and get it for you.

He had, of course, already sent his reply.

But so what; so what if the certificate was genuine, and she really had married Falier? It didn't necessarily mean anything. If they'd told her he was dead . . . She had their daughter to think of; maybe they'd told her he was dead and they were going to throw her out of the house, she'd need somewhere to go, someone to look after them both. Falier had been taking care of them, he'd have felt the obligation. If she thought he was dead, marrying Falier would be the practical, sensible thing to do; and on his part, no more than the logical extension of his duty to care for his friend's wife and child. There was a raid on the Vadani capital, they'd have told them; we sent a squadron of cavalry to kill him, and we succeeded. Oh, the savages won't admit it, they'll probably make out he's still alive; but you can believe it, he's dead, he's not coming back. So she married Falier; why not? She's got to take care of herself, of them both.

Think about what you've already lost, permanently and beyond hope of recovery, and what you may still be able to salvage from the wreckage.

He smiled at that. Where everybody went wrong was in assuming that he was some kind of complex, unfathomable creature, full of deep, subtle motives and enigmatic desires, when all the time he was the simplest man who ever lived.

But supposing . . . He winced at the thought. Supposing she really had married Falier, and that with him she'd found some sort

of quiet, comfortable resolution. Wife of the foreman of the ordnance factory . . . All he wanted to do was get back what had been
lost; for her, for himself, for the three of them. Supposing she'd
already done that (believing he was dead, of course) — quietly,
without needing to slaughter tens of thousands, throw down cities,
rearrange the whole world just to put back one small piece where
it belonged. Suppose, just suppose, that the mechanism was complete, functional, all except for one component that suddenly was
no longer necessary to its operation . . .

Just suppose.

He picked the letter up. It would, surely, be the height of stupidity not to accept the mechanism simply because it no longer
needed him. If she was all right; if she didn't need him anymore;
to have married Falier — the symmetry couldn't be mere coincidence, could it? And if he carried on with the design, wasn't there
the danger of wrecking the whole machine just to accommodate
the bit left over at the end, after it'd all been put back together? He
laughed, because that was an old joke among engineers.

The question was simple enough. When he'd escaped from the
Guildhall, as soon as he was outside the walls and free again, he'd
known what he had to do. It had been quite obvious, no ambigui-
ties, compromises, no choices at all. Now the question arose: who
was he making the mechanism for? Up till now, that had been
the most obvious part of it: *for us*, because the three of them were
inseparable — the assumption being, she couldn't survive without
him, just as he couldn't exist without her. But that was an equation, the variables susceptible to revaluation; if she could survive
without him — no great effort to calculate — his existence wasn't
necessary anymore. He could simply drop out, and then both sides
would balance.

Drop out. He stood up and listened; the sound of the files was
faint and far away. If there was something he could gain for her
by ending the war, that would be justification enough for having
started it. Give them what they wanted — the Vadani, himself —
any bargain would be a good one, since what he had to give them

had no value other than what it might buy her. He smiled at the thought: *promote Falier to superintendent of works, and I'll betray Valens to you and give myself up.* It doesn't matter how much you pay, if the money's what you've stolen from the buyer in the first place. It would be a relief, as well, if nobody else had to die or have their lives ruined to serve the mechanism. All in all, it was unfortunate that it had proved so demanding, in terms of effort and materials; it had taken on a life of its own, the way great enterprises do. Being rid of it would be no bad thing, in itself.

Assuming she believed that he was dead.

But there were too many assumptions: that one, and the assumption that the certificate was genuine, that she really had married Falier. Maybe, when the Mezentine got here, he could ask to see Falier, hear it straight from him. Could this Psellus arrange that? he wondered. But that could be a mistake, since presumably Falier too believed he was dead, or he'd never have married her. Assuming he had. Assuming.

Bad practice; making the components before you make the frame. How soon could Psellus get here? Nothing quite as frustrating as waiting for parts to arrive from the contractor, before you can get on.

Slowly he pulled open the drawer under his table, and took out a plain rosewood box. It wasn't even his. Daurenja had lent it to him, when he'd been moaning to nobody in particular about not having a decent set of measuring and marking-out instruments. He flicked the two brass hooks that held it shut and leaned back the lid. Inside, the gleam of steel, burnished and mirror-polished, astonished him, as it always had. Silver's too pale; gold and brass distort the light with their sentimental yellow glow. But steel — filed, ground, rubbed patiently on a stone until the last toolmark and burr has vanished, rubbed again for hours on end with a scrap of leather soaked in oilstone slurry, finally buffed on a wheel charged with a soap of the finest pumice dust — shines with a depth and clarity that stuns and shatters, like the sun on still water in winter. The reflection is deep enough to drown in, the image perfect, free from all distortion. A scriber, a square, dividers, straight and dog-leg calipers, a rule, thread gauges, gapping shims, transfer punches, and a three-sided blade, six inches long, tapering to a needle point, for reaming off burrs from the edges of newly drilled holes.

He lifted out the burr reamer and tested its point against the ball of his thumb.

Think three times before cutting once; they'd told him that on his first day. The wisdom of the ages — taking metal off is easy, putting it back is fraught with difficulty, sometimes impossible, and even more so, of course, with blood. A sharp point placed against an artery, gentle but firm pressure to punch a small, neat hole; any fool of a junior apprentice on his first day in the workshop could be trusted to do it. Even a Vadani.

He thought for a moment about the thing he'd built, which would survive him. Too late now, of course, to do anything about it. He'd brought war down on the Eremians, decimated them, moved on to the Vadani, marked them out for cutting, set the feed and speed, engaged the worm-drive and started the spindle running; if he dropped out now, who would he spare? The Cure Hardy — well, who gave a damn about them? — and the Mezentines, of course. A little gentle pressure on the handle of the burr reamer would save the lives of tens of thousands of his fellow Guildsmen, turn away the siege engines and the sappers from the city walls; so much could still be saved, even at this late stage, if he only saw fit to modify the design a little, just enough to take out one process, the evolution that restored one small component to its original place. Surely, if there was a cheaper, quicker, easier way of getting the job done, even if it meant sacrificing one function, it would be good design and good practice.

He grinned. Been here before. If he'd learned one lesson, it was not to try and improve on the specified design. There was a good old-fashioned Mezentine word for that, and only a complete idiot makes the same mistake twice.

He saw his face in the shimmering flat of the burr reamer, with the Mezentine maker's stamp neatly in the middle of his forehead. He wasn't a great one for omens in the usual course of things, but he wasn't completely blind to serendipitous hints. With all proper respect he put the reamer back in the box, straightened the tools so the lid would shut and flipped the catches back. Wait for Psellus, check the assumptions, consider the implications, and then cut.

They sent someone to call him, and he climbed up out of the cellar into extraordinary silence. No screech of files or pounding of trip-hammers, nobody shouting to make themselves heard, no clatter of chains or grinding of winches, and the man they'd sent to fetch him wanted him to be quick, because everybody was waiting. As he hurried through the workshop he saw men standing beside their benches, arms folded or by their sides, nobody working. Outside in the crisp, cold air people stood about in groups, turning to look at him as he passed, as though he was the guest of honor. A cluster of men he didn't know were waiting for him at the gate, like runners in a relay race. They led him through the city to the yard, which was jammed with men and carts; and each cart had a square plate of sheet iron bolted to one side, supported by a frame of wooden battens, loads shifted to the other side to counterbalance the weight. "Is there a problem?" he asked several times, but maybe they were too far ahead of him to hear. They were walking fast, and he had to make an effort to keep up.

He saw the cranes, jigs and fixtures, but nobody was doing anything. There was one cart drawn up in position, one iron sheet dangling from a crane. A man was leaning on the crossbar of an auger; another held a long spanner for tightening the retaining bolts; and standing next to him, Daurenja.

He guessed before Daurenja spoke. "Thought you might like to be here when we finished the last cart," Daurenja said, beaming like an idiot. They'd already drilled the holes, done the alignment, inserted the bolts. Some kind of ceremony, then. Well, presumably it was good for morale, or something like that. He looked round and saw Duke Valens, looking uncomfortably cold in a long gray coat, surrounded by bored-looking officials. He hoped there wouldn't be any speeches.

Daurenja nodded to someone he couldn't see. The crane winch creaked as it took the strain, lifting the iron sheet a few inches. Two men pressed against it, moved it slightly to line up the projecting bolt-ends with the holes in the sheet. The man with the spanner stepped forward; someone passed him the nuts and he wound them on — finger-tight to begin with, then tightening them all in turn with the long wrench. Nobody seemed particularly inspired or overawed, even when the spannerman put his weight on the long handle for the last time, straightened his back and stepped away. The job was finished, successfully and on time. So what?

The Duke stood up and began to speak. Not a speech, any more than his own mumbled, preoccupied words to his workers were speeches; he was giving the order for the evacuation to begin, commands without explanations — schedules, details of who should report where and when, rules and prohibitions. The Vadani listened in complete silence.

". . . utmost importance that we shouldn't take anything with us we won't immediately need; food, clothes, blankets, tools, weapons, and that's it. For security reasons I can't tell you which direction we'll be heading in. You'll find that out soon enough in any case. Don't worry about how long the food's going to last. We've got supply points already in place, plenty for everybody so long as we're careful; don't go loading your wagons down with a year's supply of salt fish and dried plums, you'll only slow yourselves down, and anybody who can't keep up the pace is going to get left behind, as simple as that."

The silence was amazement, fear, a little anger (but not at Valens), but mostly they were listening carefully so they could do exactly as they were told. Remarkable, Ziani thought. Just think about that for a moment. He stands up and says they're going to have to leave their homes, all their things, all the places they know, their work, all the components that make up the mechanisms of their lives. Prospects of ever coming back: uncertain at best, probably none. Some people, of course, couldn't accept something like that. Some people would refuse, or at least they'd go with the full intention of coming back, even if they had to make a bit of trouble along the way.

(He thought of the rosewood box and the burr reamer; there's more than one way of refusing to go along.)

Yet here were the Vadani; careless, inept craftsmen, the sort of people who can't be taught why it's morally wrong to use a chisel as a screwdriver, but so flexible, so trusting that they'll pack up a few scraps of their lives in a steel-plated cart and take to the cold, windy road, just because the Duke thinks it's the best idea in the circumstances. It could only be faith; and hadn't he had faith, in the Guilds, the doctrine of specifications, the assertion that perfection had been found and written down? Could you get the Mezentines to leave their city, pile onto wagons and leave everything behind to be burned, looted, trashed by savages? Of course, the Guilds would never give such an order. They'd prefer to stay in the city and burn with it. In the end, for a Mezentine, it comes down to place: knowing one's place and staying there, if the worst comes to the worst fighting to the death to get back there. For the Vadani, it must be different somehow, presumably because they're primitives, more pack animals than men. That had to be it. No other explanation could account for it.

Silence broke his train of thought. Valens had stopped talking, and the dead quiet that followed had a curious quality about it. In other places his speech would've been received with shouts and cheers, or there'd have been trouble. No such reaction from the Vadani, just as the foreman doesn't get a round of applause after handing out the day's assignments. He'd given them their instructions, and that was all there was to it. No enthusiasm, no grumbling, not even any discussion. People started to walk away. A man clambered up onto the newly plated cart, as the ostlers backed the horses into the traces. He'd go home, load his few permitted possessions, then go to the place where he'd been told to go, pick up his neighbors' things, a few passengers, elderly, sick, babes in arms, and set off to join the convoy. Remarkable; except for one enormous difference, which Ziani cursed himself for only just spotting. They weren't leaving home, because they were taking home with them. To them it wasn't a place; it was people.

He remembered Jarnac Ducas when he saw him: a huge man, far too much material for one human being, like a double-yolked egg. He remembered his annoying manner, his knack of coming too close and talking a little bit too loud; his vast smile, his insufferable good humor.

"Broad Street's clear and moving freely." Boomed into his face, like the blast from a forge. "There's a bottleneck in the Haymarket, of course, only to be expected, but I've got some men down there directing traffic. We'll stagger the departures, naturally, so I'm not expecting any problems there."

"Excellent," Valens said, trying not to meet those ferociously blue, shallow eyes. He wasn't sure why. For all his size, volume and intrusiveness, there wasn't anything intimidating about Jarnac. Maybe it was just fear of bursting out laughing, and giving offense. "You've got it all under control, then. That's good."

Jarnac Ducas soaked up praise like a sponge; it made him grow even bigger. "Just one other thing," he said. "What about you? Your party, I mean. I don't seem to have any details down in the manifest . . ."

"Don't worry about that," Valens replied. "I'll be riding with the rearguard, and we'll be escorting my wife and her people. Tell you what," he added. "You could do me one last favor."

"Of course." Big, expectant eyes, like a dog watching you at mealtimes.

"I'd like you to ride with Orsea and his lot," Valens said. "Unless you've made other arrangements."

Jarnac grinned, as though he'd been given the treat he'd been hoping for. "I'd be happy to," he said. "I'll keep an eye on them for you." As he said it, a thought must've crossed his mind; the frown was there and gone again as fast as a twitch. Valens had a fair idea of what the thought must have been: that it wasn't Orsea he wanted specially guarded . . . Not that it mattered what Jarnac Ducas thought about anything.

"Fine, thanks," Valens said, "carry on." That had the desired shooing effect; Ducas bowed and strode away. It was enough to exhaust you, just watching him walk. There was a man who went through life like someone forcing his way through a tangle of briars, powering through the obstacles by sheer determined energy, not caring too much if the thorns caught and snagged him. A rare breed, fortunately.

There was something he'd forgotten to do. What was it, now? Ah yes. Pack.

The Duke, of course, wasn't bound by his own orders and could therefore take with him whatever the hell he liked, even if it meant filling up half the carts in the convoy with superfluous junk. He could be absolutely certain that nobody would object. They'd naturally assume that whatever the Duke chose to take with him had, by definition, to be essential — velvet gowns, porcelain dinner services, stuffed bears' heads, whatever. With that in mind, Valens rammed two clean shirts, a pair of trousers, two pairs of boots and a scarf into a satchel, and filled another small bag with books. He opened the closet where his armor was stored, and saw that his business harness wasn't there; someone else had packed it for him, so that was all right. He looked round the tower room at his possessions; he knew each of them so well that he could close his eyes and picture them, or describe them in detail from memory, down to the last chip and scratch. Not to worry. The Mezentines could have them, and welcome. As a very last afterthought, he grabbed the cheap and nasty hanger the stallholder in the market had given him, and tucked it under his arm. He supposed it had brought him luck when the Mezentine raiding party had attacked; either the hanger, or something else. Anyway, he took it.

On the threshold, he paused. It was a rule of his life that, every time he packed to go away, he forgot something. He wondered, with a sort of detached interest, what it'd turn out to be this time.

All of it, said a voice in his head, and that was entirely possible. He'd known all his life but never admitted that his claim that he'd never been in love had always been a lie. There were things in this room, possessions, that he loved far more than any human he'd ever known. He loved the silver niello of his Mezentine falchion for its startling beauty; the comfort and loyalty of his favorite hat, the company of his favorite books, every memory he shared with the things that had been his companions when people were too uncertain and dangerous to allow himself to become attached to them. Suddenly he realized that he'd never see or hold or use them again, and the pain staggered him, freezing his legs and loosening his knees. His breath caught and his eyes blurred — you idiot, crying over *things* — and for a moment he didn't dare move, because if he turned his back they'd all be lost, forever. Wasn't there an old story about the man who went down to hell to rescue his girl from death; and the lord of the dead told him he could take her, so long as he never took his eyes off her until they were both safely back in the light? Turning away from them now would be the end of them; just things, wood and metal, cloth, leather, paint, ink, artifacts and manufactures, irreplaceable, precious, inert, dead. I'd give my life for them if it'd help, he realized, with surprise and shame, but unfortunately that option isn't available. For some reason he thought of Vaatzes, the Mezentine. He remembered him telling how he'd escaped by jumping through a window and running, taking nothing with him but the clothes he was wearing. Curious how he'd never appreciated the implications of that before: to leave behind every familiar thing — your shoes, your hat, the spoon you ate with, your belt, your hairbrush, everything. A man gathers a life around him like a hedgehog collecting leaves on its spines; what sticks to you defines you, and without them you're bare, defenseless, a yolk without a shell. To leave home, and take nothing with him except people. I guess that means I've never really liked people very much. Sad to think that that was quite probably true.

He turned and walked away, leaving the door open; no point

in shutting it, the Mezentines could press a thumb on a latch and push. Turning your back on love is the only freedom.

Mezentius was waiting in the courtyard, holding his horse for him, while the escort sat motionless in their saddles. As he reached up for the reins, his horse pushed back its hind legs and arched its back to piss, clearly not aware that this was a solemn and momentous occasion. He stepped back just in time to avoid being splashed, and nobody laughed.

He mounted, checked the girth and the stirrup leathers. The Mezentines would probably burn and raze the palace to rubble; he knew every inch of it by heart, but the day would come, if he lived so long, when he'd find he couldn't picture it anymore in his mind; he'd forget the covered alley that led from the stable yard to the well court, the half-moon balcony at the top of the back stairs, the alcove in the laundry, the attic room where the big spider had scared him half to death when he was five. The pain of love is how slowly it dies. "Well," he said. "We'd better be going."

As evacuations go, it was virtually flawless. Everybody did as they were told, and the plan turned out to have been a good one, efficient and practical as a well-designed machine. By twilight, the last cart had rumbled under the gatehouse, echoing for a couple of seconds. The rearguard of three hundred riders stayed behind, to put the required distance between themselves and the convoy; they left an hour after sunset, making out the road by memory and contrast in the shadows. They left lamps and fires burning, as canny householders do to make thieves think somebody's at home.

The last man to leave Civitas Vadanis was Mezentius. When the evacuation was first planned, he'd made a point of asking to be duty officer, with the task of locking the palace gates at sunset and bringing the Duke the key. Instead of doing that, however, he went to the throne room and left a letter on Valens' chair. It was addressed to a minor Mezentine official by the name of Lucao Psellus. When he rejoined the rearguard, Valens didn't ask him for the key, which saved him the effort of pretending he'd dropped it.

18

The fifth time she asked him, he answered.

He was exhausted, after a morning shifting sacks of charcoal up from the fuel cellar. Each sack weighed close on a hundred-weight, and he'd had to wrestle them one at a time up the winding spiral stairs. He'd asked Framain why he'd chosen such a hope-lessly impractical place to store bulk fuel, and how on earth he'd managed to get it down there. No explanation.

Twenty-six sacks. Sweat had cut white canals through the thick black crust of grime on his forehead and face. Everything smelled and tasted of the stuff; his nose was blocked with it, and his eyes were streaming. So, naturally, she chose that time to come and sit next to him, as he slumped against the wall, too weary to move a yard to get to the water jug.

"Tell me what happened at Civitas Eremiae," she asked.

He sighed; not for effect. "What happened to the city, or—"

"I know what happened to the city. What about you?"

He shook his head. "That's a good question," he said. "I'm not quite sure myself. The short answer is, I was in prison when the city fell."

"Oh."

"Charged with treason," Miel went on. "I think," he added. "Nobody ever got around to telling me; and it's a fair bet that if you're locked up and nobody'll tell you why, it's treason of some sort. It's a pretty vaguely defined term," he added. "It can mean more or less what you want it to."

"I see." Either no emotion, or something kept firmly under control. "What had you done?"

"Ah." Miel smiled. "I concealed evidence of a possible threat to national security. Which probably is treason, when all's said and done. Or if it isn't, it ought to be."

She was frowning at him, as if to say that it wasn't something to make jokes about. Quite right, too.

"It's a long story," he said.

"Go on."

He leaned forward, elbows on knees, to ease the ache in his back. "When I was a boy," he said, "my family sort of arranged that I'd marry this girl, daughter of another noble family. The usual thing: land came into it somewhere, and grazing rights, and equities of redemption on old mortgages. The silly thing was, I really liked her; ever since I could remember. I think she liked me too."

"You think?"

He shrugged. "Didn't seem important," he confessed. "We were going to get married, come what may. I assumed she liked me; the point is, she knew the score as well as I did. We were born to it. In our families, you didn't even think of choosing who you were going to marry. It'd be like trying to choose who you wanted to be your uncle."

"I see. And did you marry her?"

Miel shook his head. "She was in line to succeed to the duchy," he said. "I knew that, of course, but it was all very remote and unlikely. A lot of people had to die in a very precise order before it could be her turn. Unfortunately, that's exactly what happened. Suddenly, she was the heiress to the duchy. Obviously she couldn't be the duke herself, but whoever she married would get the throne. Which is why I couldn't marry her after all. Lots of political stuff; basically, all hell would break loose if a Ducas got to be duke; it'd scare the living daylights out of half a dozen other great houses who we'd been feuding with on and off for centuries. So they married her to the Orseoli family instead — sufficiently noble, but political nonentities, the perfect compromise candidate. Coincidentally, Orsea and I had been friends practically from birth." He grinned. "My family used to ask me why I bothered hanging out with riff-raff like the Orseoli, who'd never amount to anything. They were absolutely livid when Orsea succeeded to the title."

She nodded. "What's this got to do with treason?" she asked.

"Ah." Miel rubbed his forehead, feeling the charcoal dust grinding his skin like cabinet-maker's sand. "I guess you could say I was Orsea's chief minister and closest adviser. The truth is, Orsea's a lovely man but he was a useless duke. Always trying to do the right thing, always getting it wrong and making a ghastly mess. I did my best to straighten things out. When the war came, and the Mezentine showed up and started building the war-engines for us, I was pretty much in charge of the defense of the city. I'm no great shakes as a general, but the Mezentine's catapult things really had given us a sporting chance. I honestly thought we might get away with it."

"And?"

Miel hadn't realized he'd paused. "Then it turned out that Orsea's wife — the girl I was supposed to have married, but didn't — she was . . ." He hesitated. Words were too clumsy, sometimes; treacherous, too, always trying to twist around and mean something slightly different. "I came across a letter," he said, "which proved that she'd been writing to Valens, the Vadani duke, and he'd been writing back; for quite some time, by the look of it. Well, you know our history with the Vadani. There was other stuff in this letter, too; I didn't really know what to make of it, but it was obvious enough that it'd cause a hell of a lot of trouble for her if Orsea ever saw it. And it wasn't just her I was thinking of," he added briskly. "I knew Orsea would be shattered; he really did love her, you see, and he'd never quite believed she loved him — which she did, I'm sure of it, but Orsea's got such a low opinion of himself. Anyhow, it was as much for his sake as hers. I put the letter away somewhere safe, where nobody would ever find it. Why I didn't burn the stupid thing I'll never know, but there you are. My fault, for being an idiot."

"What happened?" she asked quietly.

"This is the bit I'm not sure about," Miel said. "What I think happened is that the Mezentine somehow found out about the letter; what's more, he figured out where I'd hidden it and bribed one of my servants to take it to him. Then he gave it to Orsea, who had me arrested. Anyway, that's what the Mezentine told me he did, and I can't see why he'd make something like that up."

"Oh. Why did he want to get you in trouble?"

Miel shrugged. "You tell me," he said. "Sucking up to Orsea, presumably; though why he should want to do that, I have no idea. He was the national hero and our blessed savior already, because of the war-engines. Not that it did him a lot of good, because not long afterward the city was betrayed and that was the end of Eremia. I got out of prison in the confusion at the end and sort of strolled into the fighting, presumably with some half-witted idea about dying a hero's death just to spite the lot of them. I got a bump on the head and when I woke up it was all over. I wandered away and tried to get up some sort of resistance against the occupation. When that failed — well, here I am." He looked away. "The simple fact is, I like it here better than I ever liked being the Ducas, back in Civitas Eremiae."

She clicked her tongue, as if she'd caught him stealing biscuits from the jar. "That's not true," she said.

"Actually, it is." He was staring at a mark on the wall. "Which isn't to say that this is the earthly paradise, or that all I've ever wanted to do with my life is carry sacks of charcoal up a dark, winding staircase. It's just better than being who I used to be, that's all."

"I don't believe that."

"You have the right not to." He sighed, shifted a little. "Not that it matters a hell of a lot. Actually, I think that's the key to it — to this whole industrial-idyll business, I mean. For the first time in my life, what I do doesn't matter to anybody except me. You can't possibly imagine what a weight that is off my shoulders."

She thought for a moment. "Responsibility makes you feel uncomfortable."

Her tone of voice annoyed him. "Yes," he said. "But putting it like that's like saying an arrow through your forehead can sometimes cause slight discomfort. Back home, I was . . ." He groped for a word. "I was this strange creature called the Ducas. I owned half the country, for pity's sake. When you think about that, you can see just how ridiculous it is. I owned this place, and I'd never even been here. I didn't know it existed. How can a man own a place? It's not possible. It's only since I came here that I realized it was really the other way about. The Ducas owned me. And a lot of other people as well," he added, surprised at his own bitterness. "The truth is, I never liked the Ducas much. Now he's gone away, it's really much more pleasant."

She grunted; a mocking, disapproving noise. "My heart bleeds," she said.

"You asked." He realized he was grinning. "I know, it sounds pretty lame. Maybe it's just something really trite, like everybody wants to be the opposite of what they are."

"That's true," she said. "For example, I'd like to be someone who doesn't live in a hovel and spend her life grinding up bits of rock in a mortar. Unfortunately, I don't think the world's going to turn itself upside down just so I can get out of here and discover my true identity. I think the world only does handstands for you if you're rich and famous."

Miel laughed at that. "You mean I'm just shallow and self-centered; the original human gyroscope, in fact. You could be right, at that. If the city hadn't fallen, and the Mezentines hadn't slaughtered us like sheep, I'd probably still be in my cell in the prison, waiting for some bastard to tell me what I was being charged with."

"You knew what you'd done," she said.

"Yes, but I wanted someone to tell me." Again, the intensity of his feelings took him by surprise. "You're quite right," he said, "shallow and self-centered. It was my own stupid fault; not Vaatzes', or the Perpetual Republic's, or Orsea's. Burning down a city just so I can get out of jail is excessive no matter how you look at it."

"You didn't do that, though."

"No, but . . ." Miel sighed. "If I hadn't got myself locked up in the first place, I'd have been there to conduct the defense of the city, instead of leaving Orsea to make a hash of it, and maybe things would've come out all right, maybe the city wouldn't have fallen after all. I don't know."

"The city was betrayed, wasn't it? Someone opened the gates and let them in. That wasn't your fault."

"No, but that was . . ." He lifted his head. "I was just about to say, that was just lucky; like whoever opened the gates somehow saved me from bearing the guilt of losing us the war. Your case proved by admission, I think."

This time, she laughed. "You're an idiot," she said. "Carrying sacks of charcoal's about all you're fit for."

He smiled. "Thank you," he said politely. "I think so too."

"Good." She tutted again. "But if you think you're some kind of disaster — you know, carrying death and destruction about with you wherever you go, like a snail with its shell — I'm sorry, but I'm not convinced. I think the world can go to rack and ruin quite well enough without you."

"You don't . . ." Again, the right word had strayed from his mind, like the cow that insists on getting out through the gap in the bank. "You don't approve of me, do you?"

That amused her, at any rate. "No, I don't," she said.

"Why?"

Pause. She was giving his question serious thought. "We came here when I was sixteen," she said. "I was just getting ready to have the time of my life — well, you know what upper-class women's lives are like. The first sixteen years are strict training; you're taught to be fascinating, beautiful, accomplished, desirable, like it's a trade. I was good at it. I studied really hard, it's my nature to want to do well at things. Then, after you've learned all that stuff — you know, deportment, accomplishments, literature, singing, playing at least two fashionable musical instruments — you've got three years of being frantically pursued by eligible suitors, like you're the most desirable thing in the world, and they'll die of broken hearts if they can't have you; then you're married, and it's a lifetime of being pregnant and doing needlework, while your husband's out running the estate or hunting or fighting wars. I was all set for my three years. I knew the score. Those three years were going to have to last me the rest of my life, so I was going to do them very well indeed. And then, out of the blue, my father told me we'd lost all our money and my three years were canceled. Or," she added, frowning, "postponed. That was actually worse, I think. He said it'd be all right, because he knew a way to make us rich again, much richer than we'd ever been before. I'd be a great heiress, so it wouldn't matter that I was a year or so older than the other girls in the cattle market. The handsome young lovers make allowances if you're as rich as we were going to be. Meanwhile, he said, there'd be a slight delay, and we were going to have to move to a rather boring place out in the sticks; and he was going to have to work very hard at the project, and I'd have to help him, because he couldn't trust anybody, except his business partner and me." She was still and quiet for a while. "And here I am," she said. "I know more about ceramics and industrial chemistry than any woman in the history of the world, and I can carry one of those hundredweight sacks up those stairs as easily as you can, or easier. I tell myself it's been a better life than embroidering cushion covers and gossiping about the latest scandals; and it has, I suppose. That's the sad thing, if you stop and think about it. But you come here and tell me that the life I used to dream about, all the things we've worked so hard for, isn't worth having anyway, and you're happier here lugging fuel and scraping out furnaces . . . No, I don't approve of you at all. Just think," she added, and her voice was sharp enough to shave with.

"Back then, you're the suitor I'd have dreamed of: the Ducas. I'd have worked so hard . . ." She laughed, a sound like grating steel. "Some people just don't like work, but not me. My father says I can't relax, I haven't got the knack, I've always got to be working, and it's got to be just right or I get miserable. You can imagine what it's been like, getting it wrong year after year, not being able to find the right stuff to make the pots turn exactly the right color." She stood up. "So there you are," she said, her voice a little shriller. "Obviously, this is the place where all our dreams come true. You've found the true peace of menial labor, and Fate has brought me the Ducas. That probably explains why we're all so bloody happy."

He watched her go, wondering what he'd said.

Next morning, they made a start on true vermilion.

Framain had brought the book in from the house. He carried it in both hands, as if it'd shatter if he dropped it. He swept a patch clear of dust and ash with his sleeve and laid it down, like someone carrying an injured child.

"We tried it before," she told Miel, as they waited for Framain to find the right place, "about five years ago, with the bog sulfur. Didn't work. But Father thinks that sulfur you brought us might be different. No reason to think it'll work where the other stuff didn't, but I suppose it's worth trying. Of course," she added, "it was useless for making sweet spirits of vitriol with, so it'll probably be useless for this too. But you never know."

"There are actually three kinds of sulfur," Framain said, not looking up from the book. "As well as the yellow variety, there's the black and the white. Unfortunately," he lifted his head and looked at them, "the wretched book doesn't say how you tell them apart, or which one's suitable for the job. Presumably you're just meant to know, by light of nature. I'll need the scales."

Miel knew where they lived; he darted forward to fetch them, a bit too eagerly. He heard her tutting as he took the rosewood box out of the drawer under the bench. She was bashing something in the big stone mortar; a vicious chipping noise, like a thrush pounding a snail against a stone.

"Quicksilver," Framain said, with distaste. "Have we got any left?"

"Yes," she replied, not stopping her onslaught. "Wear your gloves, it's filthy stuff."

Framain didn't put his gloves on, but he handled the thick-walled glass bottle as though it was a live snake or a huge poisonous spider. "Hold the scales," she told Miel, as she scooped a spoonful of yellow dust out of the mortar into the left-hand scale pan.

"Two parts of quicksilver, by weight." Framain said. "Hold the spoon, would you?"

She held the spoon steady while he tilted the bottle. The stuff that came out was a silvery-gray liquid, the color of polished and burnished steel. Both of them winced a little at the sight of it. He trickled it from the spoon into the right scale pan, a shining silver droplet at a time, until the beam stopped swaying and the little needle above the pivot was dead center. Very carefully, he lifted the right-hand pan, as she hurried to put a clay saucer underneath it; he tipped the pan out, and she put the saucer down on the bench.

"Fine," Framain said. "And the same again."

They repeated the procedure, and Framain emptied the saucer into a different thick-sided glass bottle. "Get that stuff tidied away before we spill it," he said, to nobody in particular. Before Miel could move, she'd stoppered the quicksilver bottle and put it back on the long shelf. "Now we need fresh clay. I dug some this morning, you'll find it in the bucket by the door."

Like a sculptor with an important commission, Framain scooped and molded the wet brown clay all round the bottle — trickles of brown water squeezed back over the webs between his fingers, and down the back of his hands to his wrists — until it was completely covered. "Mustn't let any of the vapor get out," he explained. "The book doesn't say why, but for all I know it could be deadly poison. It's wise to assume that anything with quicksilver in it is out to get you. Blow the fire, would you?"

Miel worked the bellows until Framain said, "Fine, that's enough"; then he put the clay-covered mess down on the steel grille over the fire. "Once the clay's dry, we've got to blow up a good heat. Apparently we've got to listen out for a cracking noise, which means the sulfur's combining with the quicksilver. When the noise stops, it should be ready." He pulled a face. "Let's hope so, anyway."

"The last time we did this, it came out a disgusting brown sludge," she said. "And the bottle cracked."

"We let it get too hot," Framain said mildly.

(Outside, it had started to rain, a tapping on the thatch, blending with the hiss of the fire; every few seconds a soft plink, as a drip from the roof hit a tin plate on the bench. Miel had to make an effort not to wait for the next one.)

"It was the wrong sulfur," she replied. "It says in the book there're three kinds, doesn't it?"

"The book isn't always reliable," Framain said with a sigh. "But it's the only one we've got, so we just soldier on." He bent down to peer at the clay mess. "Open the vent a touch, will you? The fire's starting to run away a bit."

Nothing much could be done while the clay was drying. Framain went back to the bench, leafed through the book, fetched a couple of jars but didn't open them, went back and checked the fire, put one of the jars back and got out two more, looked something else up in the book, scraped rust off a spoon with the back of a chisel. "He's always nervous," she said, as though he wasn't standing only a few yards away, "ever since he let a crucible get too hot and it shattered. Burning pitch everywhere. I got burned — look, you can still see, on the back of my arm here — and some embers got in the underside of the thatch, we nearly lost the roof and —"

"Accidents happen," Framain said to a sealed jar. "Only to be expected, since we don't really have a clue what we're doing. Because, of course, if anybody'd done it before, there'd be no point doing it again. That's what discovery means."

Miel took a step back out of instinct. He had a feeling this conversation, or others just like it, had been going on for many, many years. Two people talking at each other with intent to wound, like overcautious fencers probing each other's flawless guards. Just another manifestation of love, he decided. He'd seen the same sort of thing with married couples. For something to do, he went and looked at the fire.

"If we can produce a true vermilion," Framain told the jar, as if explaining his scheme to a crowd of skeptical investors, "we stand a chance of being able to make the soft white for backgrounds; it's a mix of the white lead tarnish cooked yellow, vermilion and ordinary flake-white, with green-earth to balance out impurities. We need to get the background right before we can start on the colors themselves, of course, because otherwise we won't know how the colors will react with the background. For example, viridian —"

"It's ready," she interrupted.

"Are you sure? If we give it the full heat before it's thoroughly dried —"

"Look for yourself."

And yet, what closer bond of love could there be than between a father and his daughter? Miel had been watching closely for some time now; everything one of them did seemed to irritate the other beyond measure. There'd been days when both of them had talked to him, as if to an interpreter, rather than acknowledge the other one was actually there in the room. He wondered about the mysterious business partner, the one who'd absconded or been thrown out. Had they talked through him this way? If so, no wonder the poor man left.

"Ready." Framain's voice was unusually tense. "Blow up the fire a bit, will you? More coal."

A drip hit the tin plate, making Miel jump. Was it his imagination, or was something about to happen? Probably just the atmosphere between Framain and his daughter, making him nervous. He dug the scoop into the charcoal scuttle.

"We're running low on fuel," she said. "And when that's gone, with the war and everything . . ."

Framain didn't bother to reply; he shushed her. They were

supposed to be listening out for a cracking noise, Miel remembered. He could smell damp, a hint of moldy straw. I'm just in the way here, he thought, they don't need me for anything. For no real reason, he drifted over to the bench and glanced down at the book, remembering the first time he'd seen it.

. . . To make flake-white, place sheets of lead beaten thin in a wooden box, cover with vinegar mixed equally with urine, leave for a month. To convert flake-white to red lead, grind fine and heat in a new pot. To make Mezentine green, place thin copper foil . . .

"The book," he heard himself say. "Where did you get it from?"

"It belonged to my former partner," Framain said, not looking round. "He had quite a library."

"Half the things in that book simply don't work," she put in. "Whoever wrote it must've made them up and stuck them in just to fill it out."

"It's the only book we've got," Framain said wearily. "And some of it —"

"There's a perfectly ridiculous thing in there," she went on, ignoring him, "about hardening chisels by quenching them in the urine of a red-headed boy; or, if you don't happen to have one handy, goats' wee filtered through dry bracken will do almost as well. For all we know, the whole book could be a spoof; you know, a parody, in-jokes for colormen and engineers. And here we are, following it religiously as if it's gospel."

"Quiet." Miel had heard it too, a sharp click, like twigs snapping.

"In fact . . ." She'd raised her voice, and it was higher, too. "In fact, whoever wrote it seems to have had a thing about urine, because he tells you to use it in practically everything, the way the Vadani use parsley in cooking. Makes you wonder what —"

"*Quiet.*" Framain lifted his hand. More cracking, syncopated with the patter of the rain, the growl of the fire and the tap of the drip on the tin plate. It was getting dark; rain-clouds outside,

Miel supposed, covering up the sun. But it was hard, somehow, to believe in the existence of the outside world, as he stood by the bench waiting for the cracking noise to stop. It seemed unnecessary elaboration, like crowded detail in the background of a painting that distracts your attention from what's going on in the foreground; sloppy composition.

"I think it's stopped," Framain said, just before the loudest crack so far.

"Are you sure that's not just the bottle getting too hot?"

Framain was counting under his breath.

"All it'd take would be one drip from the roof onto the bottle, and it'd shatter right in our faces, like that other time." Her voice sounded absurdly loud. "We really ought to do something about the leaks, but he's afraid of ladders."

"It's ready." Framain had a pair of tongs in his hand; he took a long stride forward and closed them around the clay-caked bottle. "Right," he said, in a tight, cramped voice. "Let's open it up and see what we've got. Chisel."

"Let it cool down first. He's always in such a hurry, it leads to mistakes."

At the end of the bench was a two-inch-thick slab of polished slate. Framain put the bottle down on it, carefully opening the tongs with both hands. "Chisel, please," he repeated, and Miel realized he was being spoken to. There was a rack of chisels on the wall, two dozen of them, all different shapes and sizes and contours. He chose one at random, hoping it'd do. At least he had the sense not to ask which one Framain wanted.

"Thank you." Framain took it from him without looking. He had a beech mallet in the other hand, and tapped the chisel lightly against the clay.

"Careful," she said, as he tapped again, flaking off a shard of clay.

He breathed hard through his nose but said nothing. Another tap, and the clay webbed with cracks. He paused to flick off a few loose flakes.

"There's somebody outside," she said.

Framain looked up, frowning.

"There is," she said urgently. "Listen."

Muttering, Framain carefully put the bottle down and stood up, looking round. Miel guessed he was searching for something he could use as a weapon — the adze, perhaps, or the sledgehammer. "Shall I go and take a look?" Miel suggested. Both of them thought about that for a moment, then Framain nodded.

"Are you sure you heard . . . ?" Framain mumbled.

"*Yes.*"

Miel noticed that the door was bolted on the inside. He slid the bolt back, slow and careful; took a step back from the door before opening it, to give himself distance just in case there was trouble outside. Not that there would be . . .

The door swung open. He waited a couple of heartbeats and slid through, not opening it further than he needed to.

Outside the air was sweet with the smell of rain. He stood at the top of the steps and looked up and down the yard. Nobody there, of course. She'd imagined everything . . .

Except the gate at the top was always shut, tied with a bit of old hemp rope because the latch and keeper were no longer on speaking terms; but now it stood a yard open, the rope hanging limp from one of the bars. Of course, old rope half rotted through could easily break of its own accord, if a high wind got behind the gate and pushed. But there'd been no wind, only rain.

Staying exactly where he was, he concentrated furiously on what he could see of the rope. It hadn't been untied, because he could see the knot still in it. More than anything in the world, he wanted to know whether the dangling end of the rope was ragged and frayed or squarely cut through. To find that out, however, he'd have to go down the steps and walk at least ten paces up the yard. The Ducas is no coward, but neither is he recklessly stupid. He stayed where he was, looking for secondary evidence.

"Well?" her voice hissed from behind the door.

Yes, when he'd last looked at it the rope had been rotten and slimy. But it was also thick; if three strands had worn and moldered through, that still left two or three more, plenty to hold the gate shut, particularly in no wind. A stranger wanting to get into the yard might not have the patience to wrestle with the slippery, nail-tearing knot. He'd cut the rope.

"Is there anybody there or isn't —"

"Ssh." The house windows were shuttered tight, as always, but he couldn't see the back door from where he was standing. A stranger would try the house first; a harmless traveler, lost on the moors, desperate for a drink and a bit of food; or someone else. He heard a horse, that unmistakable sound they make by blowing through closed lips. Framain's horses were out in the paddock, weren't they? Or had he brought them in, in case it rained?

One thing he could be absolutely sure of: standing motionless at the top of the barn steps was hardly sound tactics. An archer stooped down behind the pigsty wall, or lurking under the woodshed eaves, would have a beautifully clear shot. Even if there was no archer, he was advertising his position and his apprehension with alarming clarity, and getting no useful information in return. "Stay inside," he hissed, then jumped down off the steps and walked briskly toward the house.

First, see if there was anybody there. If there wasn't, nip inside and get the hunting sword, the one he'd stolen from the looters. Probably not much use, if the place really was under attack, but holding it in his hand would make him feel slightly better.

He'd forgotten that the back door creaked. Inside the house was perfectly still and quiet, but it didn't feel right. Stupid, he told himself, that's just you being nervous. He went straight to the pile of rugs where he'd last seen the sword; there it was, just where he'd left it. He grabbed at it like a drowning man reaching for the hand of a rescuer.

Ridiculous, he thought. There's nobody here.

The house didn't take long to search. Nobody there, no unaccountable marks in the dust, no door open that he'd left shut. Looking out through the front door at the curtain of rain, he felt himself relax. Just possibly, a man, maybe even two, could be hiding in the yard somewhere. But if unwelcome guests had come to visit, they'd have come on horseback; from where he was standing, he had a clear view of everywhere a horse could be tethered. No horse; no intruder. Therefore, the breeze or simple entropy must've broken the gate rope, and there was nothing to be afraid of.

To prove it to himself once and for all, he strode briskly up the yard and inspected the ends of the rope. Cut through.

Well, that cleared things up. No more dithering; he had to get back to the barn, warn them, organize a safe, swift evacuation to a defensible stronghold. By now, stealth was pointless. He ran.

Up the steps, through the door; he drew a breath to deliver his warning. Then something slammed between his shoulder blades. He stumbled, heard the sword go bump on the floor, saw the floorboards rushing up at him. He landed on his elbows, and saw a pair of boots.

"That him?" someone said.

He was grabbed and hauled upright. "Well?" the voice said.

"Yes."

Her voice. He turned his head and saw a dark brown face just behind his shoulder; then his left arm was wrenched behind his back and twisted.

There were two more Mezentines, besides the one holding him. One of them stepped out from the shadows behind the bench. The other was the owner of the boots. He said, "Miel Ducas."

"That's me," Miel said.

The Mezentine didn't seem interested in talking to him. "Bring the other two as well," he said. He was wrapping a bit of rag round a stick. Why would he be doing that?

"All right, you've got your man," Framain was saying. "Now why don't you . . . ?"

The Mezentine shoved his wrapped stick in the furnace fire, waited for it to catch. Framain was saying something, but Miel didn't get a chance to hear it; he was being hauled out of the barn and down the steps. He heard a shriek; possibly a man's voice, probably a woman's. Dutifully he considered trying to fight, but a twist on his forearm excused him.

Two more Mezentines appeared in the yard. One was holding a horse. The other put a loop of rope round his neck, then held his stirrup for him as he mounted. That let him off trying to ride them down and escape; just as well, because he'd have had to come back and try to rescue Framain and the girl, which would almost certainly have been suicide. He saw smoke filtering out in plumes from under the eaves of the barn, but no sign of Framain or his daughter being led out. One of the Mezentines had grabbed his hands and was tying them behind his back. Redundant, since they had the noose round his neck to dissuade him from being annoying. Presumably they'd be left inside the barn while it burned down. Excessively harsh, he thought, until he remembered that that was standard operating procedure when mopping up Eremian settlements. Part of him wanted to feel furiously angry about that; the rest of him felt the shame of no longer being capable of anger, only the quiet acceptance of the unspeakably weary, the dreadful acknowledgment of the truth that it really doesn't matter, at the very end.

(Once he'd seen condemned prisoners digging their own graves; and at the time he'd thought, that's ridiculous, you wouldn't do that, not when you knew they were going to kill you anyway. You'd drop the spade and stand there, tell them, *You dig the bloody hole.* Now, though; if they pulled him off the horse and handed him a shovel, he'd start digging, wouldn't even need to be told. At the very end, nothing matters enough to be worth making a fuss about.)

They hadn't come out; but neither had the other two Mezentines. Suddenly, it mattered a lot.

"What's going on?" he heard himself say. Apparently, nobody heard him.

He started thinking, making calculations. The rope round his neck; if he could grab it with his tied-together hands and keep a hold of it as the horse started forward, might he be able to pull it out of the man's grip before it strangled him? He'd be prepared to risk it if the odds were, say, four to one; but how did you calculate risk in a situation like this?

The thatch was burning on the outside, so inside it must be thick with smoke; still the Mezentines hadn't come out. The others didn't seem concerned. They were standing patiently, like well-trained tethered horses, as though they ceased to exist between orders. Keeping still while the last minute or so wasted away; clearly it was the Ducas' responsibility to do something. It all turned on the timing of catching hold of the rope . . .

The barn door flew open. Framain led the way, his arms full of bottles and jars. She followed him, clutching the book, and the glass bottle still caked in its clay. The Mezentines brought up the rear, not in any particular hurry. One of them carried a large wooden box, familiar; Framain kept it under the bench, got anxious if Miel took too much interest in it.

"Get the horses," the boss Mezentine said. "And two more for these. Stable's round the back."

So that was all right, Miel told himself. No action needed. He let the calculations — timings, angles, distances — slip from his mind. I don't care what happens to me so long as it happens later.

There was just one Mezentine now, standing back from him, holding the rope. The others had gone off to get the horses, presumably. Now that he had the time, he speculated: Framain had told them he had a secret, something that'd be worth a fortune, an opportunity the Mezentines couldn't risk ignoring just for the sake of a quiet life. In which case, it was unlikely that they'd betrayed him, so it had to be the courier, the man he'd pulled out of the bog. That disappointed him, but he couldn't bring himself to feel angry about it. He couldn't have left a man, enemy or not, to sink into the black mud. You could fill a book — someone probably had — with the selflessly heroic deaths of the Ducas. Dying of thirst in the mountains, the Ducas gives the last mouthful of water to the rebel leader he's captured and is taking back to face justice; awestruck by the example, the rebel carries on to the city and meekly surrenders to his executioners. Fighting a duel to the death with the enemy captain, the Ducas gets an unfair advantage when the enemy slips and falls; to forbear to strike is to give the enemy a clear shot, which he's obligated to accept since he too is fighting for the lives of his people; the Ducas holds back and allows himself to be killed, since duty to an enemy overrides his duty to his own kind. In such a book, there'd be pages of notes and commentaries at the end, explaining the complex nuances of the degrees of obligation — nuances which the Ducas understood and calculated in a split second, needless to say. If there had been such a book, it would have curled and turned to ash in the burning of Civitas Eremiae, and nobody would add a supplement recording Miel Ducas and the Mezentine in the quagmire. Did that matter? If not for the paradox, it should have been the perfect exemplar to round off the lesson: the Ducas makes the sacrifice, knowing there will be no page for him in the book . . .

"What're you laughing at?" the Mezentine said.

Miel looked down at him. Even betrayed and captive, the Ducas looks down at his enemies. "Nothing," he said. "Private joke."

The Mezentine stared at him for a full second, then gave the rope a short, sharp tug. The effect wasn't pleasant. No more private jokes from now on.

"Was it the courier?" Miel asked.

"What courier?"

No reason to suppose the soldier knew the background story, or even why he was here. "Doesn't matter," Miel said. "I'll be quiet now."

They brought horses for Framain and the girl; also ropes to tie their hands, and nooses for their necks. Standard operating procedure; clearly it came easily with practice, since the leader didn't need to tell his men what to do. Trained soldiers know their duty, just as well as the Ducas knows his. Duty is obligation, the bastard child of loyalty and the will to serve; when you think about it, just another roundabout way of saying love. No wonder it causes so much pointless damage.

The Mezentines mounted their horses, the leader gave a sign

to get under way. For a short while, Framain rode beside Miel.

"Serves me right," Framain said (more in sorrow). "I should have left you in the quagmire."

"Did it work?" Miel replied.

"What?"

"The vermilion. Did it work?"

Framain didn't answer; a tug on his rope drew him ahead of Miel, too far for a shouted conversation. She was riding behind him somewhere. He fancied he could feel her staring balefully at the back of his head (weren't you supposed to be some sort of hero? You should've rescued us, killed them all with a screwdriver or something, repaid us for our kindness, won my undying love; it was your opportunity, couldn't have been more convenient if we'd all sat down and planned it together; so why didn't you *do* something?). He wished he could explain that to her, at least; that it all turned on his possession of a two-foot-six strip of sharpened metal at the critical moment, and when that moment came, the metal was on the floor, not in his hand. Simple mechanics.

A pity, but there it was. Not that it mattered, with no book. If there'd been a book, there'd have been a reason to die trying, instead of meekly at the hands of an executioner. With no book, it was just pointless activity; if they give you a shovel, might as well dig a hole as not. All the slaves of duty dig their own graves sooner or later.

The ride to the Unswerving Loyalty was long, hot and boring. There were possibilities, of course. A lone peasant could have jumped up from the cover of a pile of rocks and shot the Mezentines dead with a longbow; *your father paid for the medicine that saved my little girl's life,* he'd have explained, as he cut the ropes and set them free, *it was my duty to help the Ducas.* But that didn't happen; neither did the scattered remnants of Miel's resistance army sweep down through a narrow pass. Jarnac failed to arrive with fifty Vadani light cavalry. The innkeeper of the Loyalty didn't sneak out to the stables and cut them loose in recognition of the generous tip Miel had left him the last time he was there. So many splendid opportunities for Fate to indulge itself in satisfying, heart-warming symmetry; all wasted.

But as they were led across the yard to the stables, Miel caught sight of the old carter and his grandson, the pair who'd carried the load of sulfur. They were sitting on the mounting block in the yard, staring. At last, he thought, and for some reason he felt the faint quickening of hope. Odd that it should be them, rather than Jarnac or the rebels or the grateful peasant with his bow, but that just adds piquancy. They can't be here merely by coincidence.

"Who've you got there?" the old man called out.

"Rebel leader," a Mezentine replied. "What's it to you?"

The old man shook his head. "You're welcome to him," he said, "bloody troublemaker."

The Mezentine leaned forward a little in his saddle. "You two Eremians?"

"Not likely. Vadani."

A shrug. "You'll be next, don't you worry."

So much for symmetry; also loyalty, duty and poetic justice. Out of the corner of his eye, Miel caught sight of the scowl on the boy's face as he passed. Just one kick, he thought; right now I'd cheerfully sign over the whole Ducas estate north of the Blackwater just for the privilege of booting that brat's arse.

It was dark in the stables; too dark to see the expression on their faces, once the door slammed shut behind them. Miel sat with his back to the wall, his eyes closed, hoping for sleep with the same degree of pessimistic realism as he'd waited for the peasant sniper, or Jarnac and the cavalry. Outside it had started raining again. Somewhere, there was a leak in the roof. He counted the interval between drips: nine seconds.

19

A tolerably civilized chaise as far as the Lonazep turnpike. A basic but acceptable mail coach from there to the edge of the plain. A night on a plank bed in a rather sparse post-house. A military stage, overcrowded with junior officers, very rudimentary suspension, all day, all night and the next morning with only half a dozen stops up the Butter Pass to the camp in the ruins of Civitas Eremiae. A ride with the quartermaster's clerk on a solid-chassis supply cart as far as the frontier post at Limes Vadanis. Four days away from the Guildhall, Psellus staggered off the box of the cart and stood in a dusty, rutted road under a disturbingly broad sky, staring apprehensively at mountains. If this was the world he'd heard so much about when he was growing up in the suburbs of the city, they could stuff it.

"I don't know," the garrison captain said in reply to his urgent question. "I got a letter this morning to say you were coming, but that's all. Didn't say who you are or what we're supposed to do for you. Always happy to oblige the central administration," this said with a confidence-diminishing grin, "but you can see for yourself, we're just a border post, not a diplomatic mission." He paused, thought, frowned. "I suppose you might be able to hitch a ride with a trader," he suggested. "Strictly speaking it's a closed border, but we turn a blind eye if it's just ordinary commercial traffic.

You may have to wait a week or so, but I expect you could find a corner of the guardhouse to crash in."

It's all right, Psellus urged himself, I'm equipped to handle this. I have the magic letter. He took it from his pocket, observing that it was rather more dog-eared and crumpled than it had been four days ago. Still, what mattered was the blob of red wax at the bottom, into which was impressed the great corporate seal of Necessary Evil. He smoothed the letter out and handed it to the captain.

"If you'd just care to read that," he said.

The captain glanced at it. "Like I told you," he said, "we aren't set up here to do escorts for civilians."

Psellus clicked his tongue; supposed to be authoritative verging on majestic, came out petulant. "You'll notice," he said, "that it's signed personally by Commissioner Boioannes."

"Who?"

In the event, they were quite kind to him; they fed him on bean porridge with bacon and lentils, which was what they ate themselves, and gave him a fairly clean blanket and a reserved-for-officers-only pillow. The guardhouse floor wasn't actually any harder than the bed in the inn at the post-house. He was, he reminded himself, right out on the very edge of the world. If he got up in the night for a pee and wandered a yard too far, he'd be across the frontier and in enemy territory, an accidental one-man invasion. The thought made him cross his legs until morning.

Breakfast — bean porridge with bacon and lentils — and a stroll round the compound. Six troopers in disconcertingly full armor failed to notice him, presumably for some valid military reason. He found an upturned packing case in the shade of the wall, and sat on it for an hour or so, his back resolutely turned on the view. Too many mountains, not enough tall buildings. My beautiful office, he said to himself, my beautiful *small* office.

"Good news." The garrison captain had somehow materialized next to him while he wasn't looking. "Actually, it's something I'd clean forgotten about, until you made me think of it. I've got orders to send a survey team to map the road between here and . . ." He hesitated, scowling. "Some river," he said, "can't remember the name of it offhand. But if you want to go with them, they'll take you most of the way to where you want to go. It means walking, of course — they measure distances by counting footsteps, apparently — but at least you won't be on your own. Mind you, there's always the risk that a party of our lot wandering about in Vadani territory's going to attract unwelcome attention from the locals; you may feel you'd stand a better chance of sneaking in unnoticed on your own."

So that's good news, is it? "Can I think about it?" Psellus asked.

"Sure." The captain smiled. "No rush, they won't be leaving till this evening. Best to cover the first twenty miles under cover of darkness. Just in case."

Psellus agonized over his decision for a full five seconds. "You said something about traders," he ventured.

Another night on the cold, hard floor; but the thought that he could be spending it scampering along mountain tracks in the dark with a company of military surveyors made the stones a little softer. Breakfast next day was a pleasant treat: bean porridge with bacon and lentils. A man could get to like life in a frontier post; as opposed to, say, death a few hundred yards beyond it. The morning passed. Early in the afternoon, one of the soldiers actually spoke to him. Evening ebbed in, trailing its hem across the mountains like a weary child dragging his heels. They hadn't told him what dinner would be, but he was prepared to hazard a guess.

"You're the Mezentine." A woman's voice, somewhere in the shadow of the guardhouse tower. He looked round sharply, but all he could see was a slightly denser patch of darkness. The voice itself was middle-aged, provincial and coarse.

"That's right," he said. "Who . . . ?"

"Lucao Psellus?"

"Yes."

She stepped forward into the torchlight ring; a tall, stout

woman, fishbelly-white face, Eremian or Vadani, dyed copper-beech hair heaped up on top of her head like a lava flow, clashing horribly with her loudly crimson dress. Her bare forearms were both fat and muscular, the muscle quite possibly built up by the effort of lifting so much monolithic gold jewelry.

"Well?" she said.

"I'm sorry," Psellus said cautiously. "I don't think I know you."

"Quite right, you don't." She made it sound as though only sheer all-conquering magnanimity was keeping her from holding it against him. "You wanted a ride into Vadani territory."

Merchants; of course. Among the savages, it was quite usual for women to be merchants. "That's right, yes," he said quickly.

She looked at him, as though she'd bought him sight unseen and was regretting it. "I'm headed for Civitas Vadanis, more or less direct," she said. "Are you carrying diplomatic credentials?"

Psellus smiled. "I've got a letter . . ."

"Let's see."

After a moment's hesitation he took it out and handed it to her; she rubbed her hands on her thighs before taking it. "Boioannes himself," she said, "impressive. So why isn't the military giving you an escort?"

Well, why not? "I've been asking myself that," he said.

She grinned; sympathy and contempt. "Don't take it to heart," she said. "If they weren't completely clueless, they wouldn't have pulled garrison duty. Anyway, isn't the whole big deal about Necessary Evil how shadowy and secret it is? Hardly surprising they've never heard of Boioannes."

"You have," he pointed out.

"Yes, but I've got a living to earn. I don't wait for briefings, I find things out before I need to know them. Talking of which: sixty thalers."

Psellus blinked. "Excuse me?"

"My fee," she explained. "For getting you across the border and all. Practically cost," she added, with a practiced sigh. "Meaning, the donkey you'll be riding could be carrying merchandise that'd earn me that much. Plus extra food and water to keep you alive, taking up more space. Say yes quickly, before I put it up to a hundred."

"A donkey."

"Yes. Well, what do you expect, a carriage and four?"

Psellus looked at her. "I've never ridden a donkey before."

"Easy. You just sit. If you can ride a horse, you can ride a donkey."

"I've never ridden a horse."

"Look, if you're just going to make difficulties . . ." But then she paused, made an effort, got the grin working again. "Put it this way," she said. "You're a Mezentine, right? The superior race, masters of the known world? Well, then. If a poor benighted savage like me can do it, so can you."

Now I understand, Psellus said to himself: she's been sent — and paid — to collect me. If she goes back without me, she'll have to refund the fee. Otherwise, by now she'd have written me off as more trouble than I'm worth and told me to get lost. "A wagon," he said, "or no deal."

She scowled horribly. "Out of the question. The way we go, you can't take wagons. It's a donkey or walk."

He shrugged. There'd been a hint of panic in her voice, implying that as far as wagons were concerned she was telling the truth. "Fair enough," he said. "Sixty thalers; half now, half when we get there. When are you leaving?"

Later, when he thought about that journey, Psellus found it hard to remember it clearly: the sequence of events, the constant terror, the agonizing pain in his backside and thighs. It was, he supposed, the same mental defense mechanism that caused him to forget his worst nightmares as soon as he woke up. The only impressions that lingered were the smell of drenched wool and the sight of the rocks that littered the ground on either side of the miserable tracks they followed, rocks on which he was convinced he would fall and split his head open like a water jug. One thing he knew he would never forget, however, was the first sight of Civitas Vadanis, glimpsed for a moment through a canopy of birch branches as they scrambled up a scree-sided hill. Really, it was nothing more than a gray blur, too big and regular-shaped to be yet another rocky outcrop. To Psellus, however, the mere fact that it was man-made lent it a beauty that no mountain, hillside, combe, gorge or valley could ever aspire to. Buildings; houses; people. It didn't matter that the people were hostile savages, as likely as not to kill him and eat him on sight, and to hell with the fact that he carried universally recognized diplomatic credentials. Two days and a night of spine-jarring across bleak, empty rocks had left him with an overpowering need for human contact, even if it took the form of a lethal assault.

"That's it all right," the woman in red assured him. "Not much to look at from this distance, but when you get up close it's a bit of a dump, really. You'd never think the Vadani were rich as buggery just from looking at their architecture."

Psellus didn't reply. Even from three miles away, he'd noticed something that set his teeth on edge.

"No smoke," he said.

It took her a moment to figure out what he'd meant by that. "There never is," she replied. "Not by your standards, anyhow. I gather your city looks like it's in permanent fog, because of all the forges and kilns and whatever."

He shrugged. "That's all right, then," he said.

But it wasn't. There was more to it than that, and as they got closer the apprehension grew. There should have been specks on the road, carts carrying things to and from the city, riders, people walking; even savages needed to eat, so there should have been constant traffic bringing food to town. On the other hand, plague was a possibility, but surely they'd have heard rumors. Plague aside, how else could a city be empty? The answer was that it couldn't be, and his impressions were false. But the city looked all wrong; it looked dead, like the still, flat corpse of an animal beside the road. While he'd been marooned in the frontier station, had the war come here, been and gone, without anybody bothering to tell him? Possible, he had to acknowledge. After all, he was always the last to know everything.

A mile out, even the woman in red fell silent and looked worried. They were on the main turnpike now, a straight metaled road that looked down at the city like an archer's eye sighting along an arrow, but they had it entirely to themselves. Furthermore, there was no sign of livestock in the small, bare fields, divided up neatly into squares by low, crude dry-stone walls. Plague wouldn't have killed off all the sheep and cows as well as the people; or if it had, surely there'd be bodies lying about, bookmarked by mobs of crows. Eventually, after not saying a word for nearly half an hour, the woman cleared her throat and said, "This is odd."

"There's nobody here," Psellus replied.

She appeared not to have heard him. "I heard your lot sent a cavalry raid not long back," she said. "My guess is, they've cleared everybody out of the outlying villages and farms and barricaded themselves inside the city, to be on the safe side." She made it sound as though Psellus had planned and led the raid himself, and therefore this desolation was all entirely his fault. "Could make it tricky for us getting in. We'll have to play it by ear, that's all."

It turned into something of a farce. The woman in red insisted on acting inconspicuous, even when it was obvious that there was nobody to see. Her idea of inconspicuous shared several key elements with Psellus' definition of low pantomime — talking in a loud voice about deals she was planning, deals she'd recently made; stopping every fifty yards or so to check the loads on the donkeys; bawling out each muleteer in turn for imaginary offenses; retreating demurely behind every third bush for a mimed pee. The city, meanwhile, grew nearer in total silence and deathly stillness. She was giving the performance of her life in an empty theater.

A quarter of a mile from the main gate, Psellus lost his patience.

"Do me a favor," he said, slithering awkwardly off the donkey and wincing as he landed on a stone. "Wait here."

She scowled hideously at him. "Out in the open?" she hissed. "You can't be serious. We'll all be arrested."

"Thank you so much for your help," he said politely, without looking back, and limped painfully on his wrenched ankle up the road to the main gate.

A hundred yards away, he saw that it was open, which finally put paid to her theory about the Vadani barricading themselves inside the city for fear of a repeat of the cavalry raid. Gate open, no guards; but a single chicken pecked busily in the foregate. It scuttled a yard or so as he approached, then carried on feeding.

Through the shadow of the gatehouse, out into the light on the other side. He walked a few yards, then stopped. He had no idea what he was supposed to do next. *He will meet you,* the instructions had said, and Psellus had been too preoccupied with the other prospective horrors of the journey to think too closely about that part of it. Subconsciously, he'd never had much faith in his chances of getting this far, so there hadn't seemed much point.

But now he was here, by the looks of it the only living creature in Civitas Vadanis, apart from the chicken. He drew in a breath to call out "hello" with, but the sheer scale of the silence overawed him and he breathed out again.

Cities don't just empty themselves, like barrels with leaky seams. Either everybody was dead, or there'd been an evacuation. Either way, it looked as though he'd wasted his time. He was struggling to come to terms with that when he saw something move, in an alley on the other side of the square. At first he was convinced it was just a stray dog; but when it came out of the shadows he saw it was a man; a dark-skinned man, like himself.

Well, then, he thought. This must be Ziani Vaatzes.

Shameful to have to admit it to himself, but he was shaking; not with fear, because his city's worst living enemy was striding toward him in an empty place. The last time he'd shaken this way was when he was seventeen, and the girl who'd agreed to come with him to the apprentices' dance had stepped out of the porch of her father's house into the lamplight, and the rush of mingled joy and fear had crippled his knees and crushed his chest.

"Lucao Psellus?"

The voice startled him. He'd been expecting a deep, powerful sound, something like the first low roll of thunder before the first crack of lightning. The voice that called out his name was high, rather tentative; and the embodiment of complicated evil shouldn't have a whining downtown accent.

"That's me," he heard himself say. "Are you Ziani Vaatzes?"

A slight nod. He came to a halt about three yards away; about average height for a Mezentine, stocky, square; thin wrists and small hands, unusual in an engineer; a weaker chin than he'd expected, a rounded nose, hair just starting to thin on the top of his head. Such an ordinary man; the only way to make him stand out was to empty the city. Painfully hard to believe that this was the man who'd caused the war, slaughtered the mercenaries, betrayed Civitas Eremiae, written the atrocious poetry. Had he really come all this way to meet such an ordinary little man?

"Where is everybody?" Psellus asked.

Slight grin. Just a tuck in the corner of the mouth, but quite suddenly Vaatzes' face changed. He said, "There was a general evacuation." The grin said, *I sent them away.* Psellus realized that he had no choice but to believe the grin.

"Why's that?" he asked.

Vaatzes shrugged. "I think it might have something to do with the war," he said. "Anyhow, you can be the first to pass on the news. That on its own ought to be worth a promotion." He adjusted the grin into a small smile. "I'm forgetting my manners," he said. "You've been traveling, I expect you'd like to sit down, have something to eat."

Thanks to a donkey with a backbone like a thin oak pole, the last thing Psellus wanted to do was sit down, ever again. "Thank you," he said, with a formal nod.

"I'm sort of camping out in the gatehouse," Vaatzes said. He raised his hand, and Psellus noticed for the first time that he was carrying a basket, the sort women bring shopping home from market in. "I've been scavenging," he went on. "All the bread's gone stale, of course, but I found some apples and a bit of cheese, stuff like that. There's water inside, and a bottle of the local rotgut."

So many years in politics; Psellus was used to the airy politeness of enemies. Vaatzes, he realized, was talking slightly past him; hadn't looked at him once since the first encounter. That was faintly disturbing. Is he going to kill me, Psellus wondered; is that why he won't meet my eye?

Back into the dark shade of the gatehouse; through a doorway into a bleak stone cell of a room; a plain plank table and two benches; on the table, an earthenware jug, a bottle and two horn cups. With a whole city to plunder, this was the best he could do? Not a man, then, who cared too much about creature comforts. He waited for Psellus to sit down, then slid onto the bench opposite and started cutting the pitch off the neck of the bottle.

"Not for me," Psellus said.

Vaatzes nodded and put the bottle down. "Probably better if we both keep a clear head," he said. "The water's a bit murky and brown, but harmless." He tilted the jug, filled one cup and pushed it across the table before filling the other. Realizing how thirsty he was, Psellus left it where it was.

"The proof," Vaatzes said.

It took Psellus a moment to figure out what he was talking about. "Of course," he said, and reached inside his coat for the tightly sewn parchment packet. "You'll find it's all there," he said. "There's a notarized copy of the register, plus the original applications for dispensation to remarry. I'm sure you'll recognize her handwriting, and your friend Falier's."

Vaatzes looked up sharply, then went back to scowling at the packet. Understandable if he didn't want to open it. "If you'd rather read it in private," Psellus went on, "I'll step outside for a few minutes." So considerate; such manners.

"No, that's fine." Vaatzes put the packet, unopened, on the table. "I don't need to read them, do I?" he said. "I'll take your word everything's in order."

"As you like." Psellus forced himself not to frown. He noticed he'd picked up the horn cup and drunk the water without realizing he'd done it. "I'm supposed to ask you to let me have the applications back," he said. "Because they're the originals, you see, not copies, and strictly speaking I shouldn't have taken them out of the archive."

"I'll keep them, if it's all the same to you."

Psellus nodded. "That won't be a problem." He breathed in; now he was afraid. "I've got something else you might want to have," he said, laying the homemade poetry book gently on the table.

He watched Vaatzes look at it; for several seconds he sat perfectly still. "Thanks," he said eventually. "I assume you've read it."

"In the course of my investigations, yes."

No word or movement, but for a moment Psellus could feel the heat of his anger. "Not up to much," Vaatzes said. "Not my line, I'm afraid." He picked the book up, and it was as though he wasn't sure what to do with it; he held it in his hand, a gentle but firm grip, soft enough not to crush it but secure enough that it wouldn't fall and shatter. "Has anybody else read it?"

Apart from the entire Guild assembly? "No," Psellus said. The lie was sloppy work. He felt ashamed of it.

Vaatzes nodded, unconvinced. "Well, then," he said, and put the book clumsily in his pocket. "We might as well get down to business, don't you think?"

Business. Something scuttled on the floor, making Psellus jump out of his skin. How long had it been since the evacuation, and already the rats and mice were getting bold, or hungry and desperate. No guards in the gatehouse meant no crumbs. Business, he'd said, as if they were there to broker shipments of dried fish and roofing nails. Business.

(It occurred to him that Vaatzes might have poisoned the water; some of which Psellus had drunk, while Vaatzes' horn cup had remained empty. Too late to worry about it now, of course.

Besides, why bother to be sophisticated, in an empty city, against a slow, fat clerk?)

"I expect you already know," Vaatzes was saying to the wall behind his head, "that I gave you Civitas Eremiae. I sent a message telling you how and where to break into the tunnels that serviced the underground cisterns. You know about that?"

Psellus nodded.

"I assumed you knew. And about the cavalry raid, here."

Psellus looked up. "Yes," he said. "Some of it."

Vaatzes nodded. "I sent a letter to your committee," he said, "telling them about Duke Valens' wedding, and the grand celebratory bird hunt; I said that practically the whole Vadani establishment would be riding about in open country, unescorted. I gave them as much notice as I possibly could, so they could get a raiding party up here and in position." He paused. "I'd just like to point out," he went on, "that on both occasions I asked nothing in return, and on both occasions I put myself at risk. True, the second time I was able to plan things a little better. I sort of gatecrashed my way on to the guest list for the hunting party, as an alibi; I was with them when they set off, and then I turned back almost immediately — just as well I'm who I am, really; I'm an embarrassment, they feel uncomfortable around me, so they didn't really notice that I wasn't there. I went straight back and raised the alarm; so far, I don't think anybody's thought about that, me raising the alarm before the attack had actually happened." He paused, smiled thinly. "I think I scheduled it pretty well, time for your men to slaughter the Vadani but not enough time for them to get away. Of course, they only did half a job, but even you must admit that wasn't my fault."

He paused, expecting some comment or reply. Psellus couldn't think of anything intelligent to say.

"Why?" he said.

Vaatzes frowned. "Why did I do it, you mean?"

Psellus nodded. "The first time, I can understand," he said, "I think. My guess was, you were sickened at the slaughter of our army, frightened when you realized we'd never give up; we could never forgive a defeat, we both know that. You thought: if I die in the assault, so what? If I escape, I've given them earnest of good faith; when I make them an offer a second time, they'll know I'm serious. We were expecting you to bargain. Instead . . ."

Vaatzes nodded, as though acknowledging an admission of an elementary mistake. "Instead, I give you the Vadani government, free of charge. You're confused. One free sample is the custom of the trade; two is simply eccentric." He leaned forward, elbows on the table. "Let me guess for a change," he said. "You had a meeting, to discuss the contingency. Yes?"

Psellus nodded.

"It was agreed," Vaatzes went on, "that if I sent an offer, to give you the Vadani, you'd agree. You'd negotiate, make a good show of striking a hard bargain; in the end, you'd give me what I really want — a pardon, permission to come home, my old job back. When you'd got me back to the city, there'd be a show trial, followed by an execution. The moral being: nobody forces a compromise out of the Perpetual Republic, no matter what." He smiled. "Is that what the meeting decided?"

"Yes," Psellus said, "more or less."

"I thought so." Vaatzes leaned back in his chair, laid his hands on the table. They were perfectly still. "Now I'm going to have to extrapolate from pretty thin data," he said. "I'm guessing that there's a great deal of resentment among the committee about the fact that I armed the Eremians, made it possible for them to kill so many of your troops — I keep wanting to say *our* troops; if I forget, please just take it as a slip of the tongue — just so as to raise my own value, if I can put it like that; to get myself into a position where I could bargain with you from a position of strength. Is that right?"

Psellus frowned. "Actually," he said, "that's not how we interpret it. We feel that when you first escaped from the city, you went to our most prominent enemy because it was the only place you felt safe; the Eremians would never hand you over to us, on principle.

Particularly not after you'd shown them you could give them the same weapons that had wiped out their army. We assumed you hadn't thought it through; that giving them the scorpions would make it inevitable that we'd invade and wipe out the Eremians." He paused. "We underestimated you."

Vaatzes smiled. "The way you say it," he said, "I take it you didn't share the majority opinion."

It was like the moment when the girl you love but know you'll never dare talk to comes across and asks you to dance. "I had my doubts," Psellus said. "That's why . . ." All his courage. "That's what led me to talk to people who knew you. Your work colleagues. Your wife."

Vaatzes didn't move, not even a flicker.

"It began as little more than idle curiosity," Psellus went on, trying to keep his voice from cracking. "I was intrigued to know what motivated you; the great abominator, and so on. Then, after a while, I got the reputation of being the leading Vaatzes expert. I moved from Compliance to Necessary Evil as a result. That's what set me thinking."

"Go on," Vaatzes said.

"Well." Now that the moment of moments had come, Psellus found he'd lost the ability to think of words. "It seemed to me," he said, "that there were two explanations for why I'd been promoted like that. The obvious one was that they were expecting you'd be important in the scheme of things, sooner or later; they were expecting that you'd make us an offer, and so they needed to have an expert on you on the staff, so to speak."

"Reasonable," Vaatzes said quietly.

"I thought so," Psellus replied, "until I realized that they'd misunderstood you, the way we were talking about just now. They hadn't realized, or they didn't believe, that you'd got your plan of action more or less worked out from the start. That what you wanted — all you wanted — was to come home." He paused, aware that he'd been talking too fast, tripping over words. "That didn't make sense, of course," he went on. "That view of your motivations didn't fit with the idea that you'd be important, possibly the key to winning the war. Something as crucial as what you actually wanted . . ." He shook his head, and during the pause remarked to himself on the dead silence; here, at the main gate of a capital city. An abomination, if ever there was one. "If they believed you were just a runaway, scared for your own skin, only interested in staying safe, what did they need a Vaatzes expert for? They didn't. So, that explanation didn't work."

Vaatzes nodded slowly; a little genuine respect. As though she'd looked up at you and smiled.

"Which left the alternative," Psellus went on. "Namely, that they promoted me from Compliance up to Necessary Evil simply in order to keep me under control. Which is something I should've figured out long ago," he went on, "after I'd been sitting alone in my office with nothing to do for weeks on end; completely out of the loop, isolated — I might as well have been locked up in a cell somewhere. It was because there was something about you they didn't want me to find out. I was blundering about, talking to your wife, the people at the factory. Sheer aimless curiosity; but they didn't want me doing it. I knew something was funny when I tried to contact the men who'd investigated the case, the prosecutor, the advocate; and for one reason and another, all quite reasonable, I couldn't. They didn't answer my letters, they weren't available, they'd been reassigned. As far as I know, none of them've died or disappeared, but perhaps that's only because I stopped poking around. I wondered why they hadn't just got rid of me; I think that was when I started worrying about what the whole business was doing to me. But it's hard, when you're cooped up in an office all day long with absolutely nothing at all to do."

He stopped. Vaatzes was looking at him.

"Which is all I can tell you, really," he said. "And it's just a theory, I can't prove anything. I believe that there's some unpleasant secret, something about the circumstances of your —" He was about to say *offense*. "Of what you did. I'm more or less certain that you weren't aware of it; at least, not at the time. But now I've reached the dead end, as far as what I can find out on my own, back home. Basically, if I'm going to solve this puzzle, the only one who might be able to tell me anything useful is the source himself: you. And . . ." Deep breath. "And I thought," he went on, his voice shaking just a little in spite of everything, "it also occurred to me that you'd probably be interested in any conclusion I might reach. Which is why I'm here," he added feebly.

Silence; not even rats or chickens. Just the two of them.

"One thing," Vaatzes said, eventually, in a voice so tense it hurt Psellus to listen to it. "Is it true? Really? About . . . ?"

"The wedding?" Psellus nodded. "And no, it's nothing to do with me, not something we arranged. Probably I was the only one in Necessary Evil who even knew about it."

"You told them?"

"Yes. By then I was starting to have my suspicions, about why I was there. On reflection, it didn't seem wise to advertise the fact that I was still — well, taking an interest."

"I think it matters," Vaatzes said. "I think it's really important; if any of them knew, before you told them. Do you agree?"

One expert consulting another. Psellus nodded. "I'm not sure how I can find out," he added. "Obviously. But I'll try."

"Thank you."

Two words that mean so much. "That's all right," Psellus said. "I feel —"

Vaatzes interrupted him. "This is getting strange," he said, with a slight grin. "Not what I expected. I hadn't anticipated you having anything to offer that I might actually want."

"You think I'd come all this way with nothing to sell?" The words came out before Psellus was ready; but they were gone now, too late to worry about it. "I would like to ask you some questions," he said. "But maybe not straightaway. I want . . ." He nerved himself. "I want you to be able to trust me. So I'd like to get the other stuff out of the way. The stuff I was sent to do. If I bring it up afterward, you might think . . ."

"I understand." Vaatzes' eyes were cold, but not hostile. "I take it there's an offer."

"Yes."

"I'd be interested in hearing it."

So Psellus told him. The Vadani, in return for immunity in exile.

"I see," Vaatzes replied, after a long moment. "Is that the opening bid, or the final offer?"

This was the boundary; he could cross it, or hold back. "They feel it's important that you trust them," he said. "They know that you'd be suspicious if they offered you a chance to come home, but that's what they want you to hold out for. My mission isn't supposed to succeed. I'm supposed to make you an offer they know you'll reject. Accordingly, immunity in exile is all I'm authorized to offer you."

"I see."

"Which is where the marriage was useful," Psellus said (bad choice of words; he cringed). "I was supposed to tell you about it — well, it was my idea, they agreed — so you'd realize there's nothing left for you back home; you might as well accept exile, settle down, find a nice girl, get a job. I was supposed to believe there was a good chance you'd see the sense in that and accept."

Vaatzes grinned. "They underestimated you."

"Something I'd have said was impossible," Psellus replied, "but apparently they managed it. So, there's the offer. Take it or leave it."

They looked at each other across the table; two Mezentines in a strange, empty city.

"I accept," Vaatzes said.

After Psellus had asked his questions and Ziani had answered them, they discussed the implications for a while. Then Ziani said, "I think I understand now."

"It's only a theory," Psellus said nervously. "I couldn't prove . . ."

Ziani shook his head. "You don't have to," he said. "Not for my benefit. After all, it's not as though it changes anything."

It amused him to see Psellus shocked. "It doesn't?"

"Not now." To make his point, he rested his hand lightly on the packet of documents lying on the table. "That's changed everything, you see. You do understand, don't you?"

"Yes." No, of course he didn't.

"Are you married?" Ziani asked.

"What? Oh, yes." Psellus frowned. "Well, after a fashion. We're separated. Have been for years. Most of our married life, actually." He said it lightly.

"Why?" Ziani asked.

"We can't stand living in the same house," Psellus replied. "As I recall, it took us a whole month to realize. I haven't set eyes on her for . . ." He frowned.

"As long as that." Ziani nodded. "Why didn't you simply get a divorce?"

"Not an option," Psellus replied, looking away. "I guess you could call it a political marriage. To be honest with you, I can't actually remember the details; it was pretty complicated, and of course everything's changed since then, the whole balance of power between the Guilds. I suppose I could get rid of her now, but where'd be the point? I'm far too set in my ways to bother about such things."

Ziani nodded, as if to say he understood. He didn't, of course. It was as though Psellus had said he was too old and cranky to be interested in breathing. "That's your business," he said, trying to keep the disapproval out of his voice. "It seems a bit of a waste of a life, though."

"The least of my worries," Psellus said.

Strange, Ziani thought. Such a very different attitude to the business of being human. But he said, "I suppose you're lucky, being without love."

Psellus looked uncomfortable. "You know what they say," he replied. "What you've never had . . ."

"I suppose so. I can't pretend I've had any luck with it myself. After all," he added with a humorless chuckle, "if it wasn't for love, I'd still be working in the factory, and the Eremians would still have their city." He decided not to go there. "But that's like saying the cure for death is not being born. I still believe in it, you know. Love."

Just hearing him say the word seemed to embarrass Psellus. "Do you? I'd have thought . . ."

"Yes?"

"In your shoes," Psellus said slowly, "I'd look on it as an escape. Like a runaway slave."

Ziani thought for a moment. "There's a bit of poetry I heard once," he said. "About falling out of love. It's not just escaping from the game, it's taking the dice with you. I used to wonder what that meant."

Psellus pursed his lips. "You mean it, then? About not wanting to come home anymore."

"What is there for me to come home to?"

"Doesn't that mean . . . ?" Psellus was looking at him. "Well, it's admitting that you've lost, isn't it?"

Ziani couldn't help laughing at that. "Who cares?" he said. "As far as I'm concerned, it's as if they'd both died. Nothing left to go home to. I might as well find something to do with the rest of my life." He smiled. "One thing's for sure, I've found out a lot of things about myself I'd never have dreamed of before. The things I've achieved . . ." He paused. "I could make a great deal of money," he said. "I could be a nobleman, a great lord, like all these ridiculous Eremians and Vadani I've been spending so much time with. Great big houses, country estates; I could go hawking and hunting. I could marry a nobleman's beautiful, accomplished daughter, have a whole brood of aristocratic children who'd never have to work for a living. Well? Can you see any reason why not? I've proved what I can do, more or less without trying. If I could make my peace with the Guilds, so I wouldn't have to be looking over my shoulder all the time for a Compliance assassin, there's no reason at all why I shouldn't. And . . ." He shrugged. "It's not as though I've got anything better to do." He raised an eyebrow. "Or are you going to tell me about my duty to my country; my duty not to steal her secrets and hand them over to the savages?"

Psellus shifted in his seat. "None of my business," he said. "I'm not in Compliance anymore."

Ziani laughed. "Nicely put," he said. "Tell me, why did you come here?"

"To negotiate with you."

"Nonsense. You've as good as told me that the Guilds have no intention of honoring any agreement we may make."

"True." Psellus' shoulders slumped a little. "To ask you questions," he said.

"To see if they'd confirm your theory?"

"I guess so, yes."

"Because that'd explain why you were transferred from Compliance to Defense."

"I suppose so."

"Well, then." Ziani yawned. "Did you know that Duke Valens' closest adviser is spying for the Republic?"

Awkward silence. "No," Psellus said, "I didn't know that."

"His name's Mezentius and he reports back directly to Councillor Boioannes," Ziani said. "I take it he hasn't been sharing what he's learned with the rest of the committee."

Psellus didn't answer that. "How do you know?" he asked.

Ziani shrugged. "Luck," he replied. "As you know, I use the women traders to carry messages for me, find things out, that sort of thing. I was talking to one of them a while back, and I must have said something that gave her the impression that I was in on the secret, maybe part of the setup. She told me things that left me in no doubt." He paused to marshal his thoughts before continuing. "You can see why it concerns me," he said. "To put it simply, if Boioannes already has a pet traitor, someone much better placed than me, he doesn't need me as well. He can get this Mezentius to give him the Vadani. So, obviously, any deal he offers me is bound to be a trap." He smiled. "I can also see how it affects you. If Boio-annes could have the Vadani any time he wanted, why's the war still going on? He must be up to something, and his plan must turn on the war carrying on. Well, if he likes the war so much, maybe it's a fair guess that he was the one who started it."

Psellus nodded. "By using you."

"Flattering, I suppose, though I could have done without the honor. Anyway," he added, "something for you to think about on your long ride home. Consider it a thank-you from me." He tapped the packet of papers on the table. "In return for this."

Psellus appeared to think for quite a while. "Do you mean it?" he said, avoiding Ziani's eyes. "About not wanting to come home anymore."

"Of course. Like I've been telling you, there wouldn't be any point."

"Where can you go? To start your new life, I mean."

"Oh, anywhere." He was pretty sure Psellus hadn't been taken in by that. "The Cure Doce seem a reasonable bet. I never realized how huge their territory is. In fact . . ." He stopped and clicked his tongue. "A year ago I'd never heard of them, except as a name. If you'd have asked me then, I wouldn't have been able to tell you if they were real, or something out of a fairy tale."

"You wouldn't like it there," Psellus said. "They're primitives."

"Worse than these people?" Ziani laughed. "And even if they are, they won't be for long, if I go there. I could go right the other side of their country, off the edge of the Guild maps, and in six months I'd be building my first factory. It seems I've got a talent for it. It turns out that the world's a fairly big place, and no matter where they live or what color their skin is or what language they speak, they're going to want nails, plowshares and cheap tin buckets. It's a law of nature."

Psellus nodded slowly. "I'm glad I'm not in Compliance anymore," he said, with feeling. "You're exactly what we used to have nightmares about: the monster . . ."

"If I'm the monster, you made me into it," Ziani replied

casually. "But of course, it all depends on this deal you've come here to arrange."

"Oh," Psellus said. "That."

"Yes. Here's my offer." Ziani paused for a moment. The silence bothered him, as silence always did. Twenty years in machine shops, tenement houses, the streets of the city; he needed noise just as much as air. "Arrange it so that . . ." He'd almost said *my wife.* "So that she'll be all right, so that they won't take it out on her, and Moritsa. In return, I'll go away, and nobody will ever hear my name again. They can say I'm dead; that they've seen my body, hung up on a hook. You can be the witness; they'll trust you, because you're too small to lie. That'll solve their political crisis for them. Oh, and I'll throw in the Vadani, for good measure, if that's what Boioannes really wants. I'll deliver them just like I did with the Eremians; I know how to do it, incidentally. I've arranged it so it'll be a piece of cake. Yes, I know," he added, turning away. "The Guilds don't negotiate with abominators, and any deal they strike won't be binding on them. But I'm lucky; I've got you to sell it to them. You can explain. Will it really matter if I'm dead or not, so long as I'm officially dead, and everybody believes it? We can manufacture some proof. We could get a head, smash its face in so nobody could recognize it; they can nail it to a gateway somewhere, and have a public holiday. If I'm officially dead, and the Vadani have been wiped out, then the Republic has prevailed, the way it always does. Boioannes can stage his discreet coup and be god-on-earth for a bit, until someone gets rid of him. Everything will be all right; and you'll be right on top, of course, because you'll tell them it was all your idea, the result of your incredibly skillful and delicate negotiations, your painstaking research that gave you the insights you needed into the mind of the abominator. Well? Isn't it perfect?"

As he finished his speech — definitely a speech, he admitted to himself, faintly ashamed — he was watching Psellus as though he was some complex mechanism (too complex; overengineered, built arse-about-face, not something he'd ever be proud to admit to, but functional, he hoped). It would be interesting to see whether he'd assessed this contemptible little man accurately, or whether he'd underestimated him, as others had.

"No," Psellus said. "They'll pretend to agree, but they won't let you go."

"You reckon?"

"I know," Psellus replied. "You see, there's nothing in it they couldn't make for themselves. They could fake your death, and dismiss any reports of you as rumors and lies. And if you're right about Boioannes having a spy already, they don't need you to give them the Vadani. There'd have to be something else; and what else have you got to offer?"

Ziani smiled. Nice to be right. "As it happens," he said, "I do have something else. I can give them the silver mines."

20

She hadn't spoken to him for two days; not since they'd climbed to the top of the ridge that overlooked the city. He wondered if he'd offended her, though he couldn't imagine how.

As the coach stumbled over the potholes in the road, he looked sideways at her, considering her as though she was some ornament or work of art he'd bought in a rash moment of enthusiasm. Seen in profile, her nose was long and almost unnaturally straight; in profile, of course, you didn't notice how thin it was. There was a slight upward curve to her top lip that he couldn't help but find appealing. The weakness of her chin, on the other hand . . .

Her eyes flicked sideways and he turned away, embarrassed at having been caught staring. No reason, of course, why a man shouldn't look at his own wife. Even so; he'd got the impression she didn't like it. He concentrated on the road ahead, but that was simply distressing.

Of course, he thought, I could try talking to her, rather than waiting for her to talk to me. A radical enough notion, but it couldn't do any harm. Could it?

"I guess you must be used to this sort of thing," he said.

She turned full-face and looked at him. "Excuse me?"

"Traveling in carts," he explained. "I mean, your people being nomadic."

"I see." She paused, thinking through her answer, like a conscientious witness in court. "Yes, we travel extensively," she said. "However, our vehicles are more comfortable, and much better designed for long journeys. For example, I would normally travel reclining on a three-quarter-length couch, rather than sitting on a bench. Also, because of their superior suspension, our vehicles travel appreciably faster, which gives us scope for longer and more frequent stops for rest and exercise. Our horses have been bred specifically for stamina over many centuries."

"I'm sorry," Valens mumbled.

"What for?"

"The discomfort. The coach not being up to what you're used to. We don't do much of this sort of thing, you see."

"I know. I've made allowances. However, it's — considerate," a slight stumble over the word, "of you to be concerned. Besides, I've traveled in worse."

You could cut shield-leather with those eyes. More than ever she reminded him of a bird of prey; he wished he had a hood he could fasten over her face, to stop her looking at him. "We had to organize all this at very short notice," he went on. "Perhaps, when we're settled again, you could give our coachbuilders a few tips."

She frowned. "I'm not really competent to advise on technical matters," she said. "However, I'm sure I could arrange for some of our coachbuilders to be seconded to you for a while."

Valens nodded, and went back to staring at the road ahead. Sooner or later, he told himself, I'm going to have to sleep with this woman. Won't that be fun.

Try again. "The reason we're going so slowly isn't just be-cause our wagons are a bit primitive," he said. "Bear in mind, we're carrying all this armor plate. We've got to be a bit careful, in case the extra weight busts the axles when we go over holes in the road."

"Our suspension systems would help in that regard," she said. "Instead of steel springs, we use a laminate of horn, wood and sinew, similar to the material we make our bows from. We find that steel tends to fatigue and crack with heavy use; the composite

springs hold up much better. Of course they're costlier and harder
to make, but we find it worth the effort and expense in the long
term. A broken spring can hold up an entire caravan for days."

"Horn and sinew," Valens repeated, trying to sound interested.
"That's clever."

She nodded. "It's an efficient design," she said. "The horn is
ideally suited to absorb shock, while the sinew offers almost unlimited flexibility. The wood is simply a core. The weakest component is, of course, the glue that holds the layers together. We
use a compound made up of equal parts of sinew and rawhide
offcuts . . ."

More about making springs than anybody could possibly want
to know, ever. At another time, in another context, explained
by someone else, it might have been mildly interesting, to somebody who actually gave a damn. Vaatzes? No, he'd have a fit. The
Mezentines made cart-springs from steel, so anything else would
be a (what was the word?) an abomination. He'd probably spend
the rest of the trip trying to convince her steel springs were better.

(Talking of which, where was Vaatzes? Couldn't remember
having seen him for a while.)

She'd stopped talking. "Well," he said, "that's fascinating. We'll
definitely have to give these composite springs a try sometime."

"Advisable," she said. "The best sinew for the purpose is the
back-strap of a cow or horse; ordinary cowhorn suffices for the
inner layer. For wood we prefer maple, though ash makes an acceptable substitute where maple's not available."

"Not much maple in these parts," Valens heard himself say.
"Presumably birch'd be too brittle."

"Yes."

Really, she was like a bear-trap or a pitfall; words just dropped
into her to curl up and starve to death. Tremendously well-
informed, of course; she'd be a real asset, if only he could get past
her unfortunate manner. Regrettably, he found himself passionately not wanting to know anything she could teach him. Not like
him at all — he thought of the hundreds of books, presumably

still on the shelves of his library, waiting patiently for the Mezentines to steal or burn them. Irresponsible to reject a potentially useful resource simply because of a clash of personality.

"How about where you come from? Much maple there?"

"No. We have to trade for it with the Luzir Soleth, who know how much we value it and demand an extortionate price. For that reason, we use it very sparingly."

Another thing he'd heard about these people; they respected truth above all things. The perfect education, they said with pride, consisted of horsemanship, archery and telling the truth. He could believe that. She answered all his questions as though she was on oath.

"I'm hoping we'll reach the Sow's Back by nightfall," he said. "It's the last range of hills before the long plain."

"The Sow's . . . ?"

"It looks like a pig's back," he said. "A bit. The trouble is, it's pretty close to the Eremian border, and the Mezentines have been sending patrols across; just to be annoying, I think, but we don't want to be seen, obviously. After that —"

"Where are we going?" she asked him.

"I just said, the Sow's Back. If we can get clear of that, it ought to be a straight run."

"In the end," she said. "Where are you taking them?"

The truth above all things. "I haven't decided yet," he said. "It's more a case of traveling hopefully; just keeping on the move. The nomadic life, you might say."

"That's . . ." She frowned. "That's a drastic change, for a sedentary people."

He laughed, which annoyed her. "I don't think we've got a choice," he said. "If we go somewhere and stop, unload the carts, build houses, sooner or later the Mezentines will find us and attack. That'd be the end of us. They took Civitas Eremiae, which was the strongest fortified city in the world, apart from Mezentia itself. Nothing we could build would be likely to hold them up for long."

"Eremia fell through treachery, not direct assault."

"Yes." He sighed. He didn't like discussing things he already knew about. "But it was just a matter of time. They'd have modified their siege engines, trebled the size of their army. The problem with them is, beating them just makes them more determined to win."

She raised a thin, high-arched eyebrow. "In that case . . ."

"In that case," he said, "the only way we'll get out of this is not to fight. If we fight, either we'll lose, which'd be bad, or we'll win — unlikely, and just as bad. But if we can avoid fighting for long enough, there's a chance they'll give up and go home. Their internal politics —"

"I've made a study of the subject," she said. "Councillor Mezentius has been most helpful. You're hoping they'll lose the political will to continue, once the cost of the war begins to affect their economy."

"Exactly." If she'd known all along, why had she made him explain? But she hadn't, of course. "So my idea is, we keep going. I haven't worked out a detailed itinerary because it's essential we keep our movements random; if there's a set plan, they might find out about it. It's pretty clear from what happened in Eremia that they've got good spies. No; I've got a list in my head of places where we can get supplies, and the distances between them. That's as organized as it gets, for the time being."

She was still frowning. "And the iron plates?" she said.

"We're going to be attacked, at some point," Valens replied. "So I'm hoping to turn that to our advantage. The only way they'll be able to engage us is by sending out cavalry detachments, to look for us when we have to come down from the mountains for supplies. I'm hoping that they will attack us, and that all this iron-mongery will give us the advantage, against cavalry."

"You want to fight them and win. But you said —"

Irritating bloody woman. "Yes, but beating off cavalry attacks isn't the same thing as beating them in a pitched battle. It's . . ." He searched for an analogy. "Losing a few dozen cavalrymen would come out of income rather than capital. It'd be annoying rather than a dishonor that could only be purged in blood. It's more likely to persuade them we aren't worth the effort and expense."

She nodded, and he felt as though he'd just passed a test.

"Anyway," he went on, "that's the general idea. It's not brilliant, but it's the best we could come up with. Let's just hope it works."

She looked at him. "There is an alternative," she said.

"Really?" He tried not to sound impatient, but he was fairly sure he failed.

"If your people are resigned to a nomadic life, as you put it, you could join with my people."

For a moment, Valens wondered who the hell was sitting next to him. She was all sorts of things, he'd assumed up till now, but definitely not stupid.

"That's a really kind thought," he heard himself say, "but I don't think it'd be practical."

"On the contrary." She was lecturing him; he felt an urge to take notes. "My people are used to life on the move. It's not nearly as simple as you seem to think. There are many hazards and complications which you have probably not considered; understandably, since you have no experience. I can advise you, but it takes more than knowledge. You will need resources which you most likely have made no provision for. If you join with us, we will take care of you." She paused, studied him for a moment. "If you're concerned that I don't have the authority to make this offer, I can reassure you that I do. My family —"

"It's not that," Valens said, a bit too quickly. "Well, for one thing, there's the desert. It can't be crossed, simple as that."

Now she was thinking he was stupid. "We crossed it," she said, "on our way here."

"Yes, but most of your party died," he snapped.

"Some of our party," she said, as though correcting his arithmetic. "And, naturally, some of your people wouldn't survive the crossing. At a guess, I would say between a third and a half. But in the course of three or four generations, you would make up the loss."

"That's —"

"Unacceptable." She sighed. "Whereas you're prepared to risk the decimation or annihilation of your people in the plan you've just outlined to me."

Valens didn't reply. Better not to.

"I should point out," she went on, "based on my experience of migratory life, that even if there were no enemies searching for you, it's quite likely that you will lose at least a third of your people in the first year, given your lack of experience and preparation. Spoiled or stolen food reserves; rivers in flood; mountain roads blocked by landslides or washed away by heavy rain; have you considered these contingencies and made allowances?"

Much better, Valens decided, when she'd just sat there and not said anything. "Of course I have," he exaggerated. "And we've got people who know the country. It's not like we're in hostile territory . . ."

"The presence of the enemy," she went on, as though he hadn't spoken, "greatly increases the risks. You say you're relying on reserves of supplies at specific locations. It's inevitable that the enemy will find out about at least some of these. If just one supply dump turns out not to be there when you reach it, you face disaster. Will you have enough left to get you to the next one? And what if that one's gone too?"

"We can live off the land to a certain extent," he replied, trying to stay reasonable. "There's plenty of game we can hunt."

She smiled. "There speaks an enthusiast," she said, insufferably. "You imagine that your hobby can become a means of survival. Hunting is an essential part of my people's lives, but we know from experience that it's not enough. You'll have to do better than that, I'm afraid. Compared with the risks you face by staying in your own country, the losses from crossing the desert seem moderate, if anything. And fighting the Mezentines . . ." She shook her head. "You should come to us," she said. "It's the only sensible course open to you."

But I'm not going to, because I'm not going to let you turn my people into savages. It took rather more effort not to say that than he'd have thought. "I'll have to think about it," he said

"If you must. It shouldn't take you long to decide."

Back to silent sitting. When Valens realized he couldn't take the silence any longer, he leaned forward and told the driver to stop the coach. An escort trooper rode up to see what the matter was.

"Get my horse," Valens told him. "I'm going to go and inspect something."

"May I ask . . . ?"

"No."

Something at the other end of the column, as far away from her as I can get. As soon as his horse was brought up, he mounted and waved the coach on, then sat still for a while, watching the carts go by. The mountain in the distance, the crown of the Sow's Back, was only vaguely familiar to him. When was the last time he'd been out here? He wasn't sure; quite possibly, when his father was still alive. They'd come up here one summer after mountain goats and chamois — a complete waste of time, they'd misjudged the onset of the breeding season, the she-goats had all been in kid and were therefore out of bounds, and there was no point hunting he-goats in the rut. His father had sulked and picked fights with everybody who got in his way. Not a place with happy memories. So; if that was Maornina, and that spur to the west was the Shepherd's Crook, then the range he could just see on the horizon was Sharra, over in Eremia. Too close, he decided. Not a good idea to hang about here any longer than they could help.

A harassed-looking junior officer cantered up to him, to tell him there was a problem. Six carts in the middle detail were breaking up; the weight of the armor had cracked the front-side frames, and they'd had to pull off the road before the cracks sheared right through. The problem seemed to be a result of the way the armor had been mounted — a three-quarter-inch bolt hole drilled through a load-bearing timber, weakening it and allowing too much weight to rest on an unsupported member. With all the potholes . . .

Valens made an effort not to groan aloud. "It sounds serious," he said. "Are many other carts likely to have the same problem?"

The officer nodded. "It's the half-lock carts and the bow wagons," he said. "The high-sided carts are all right, there's enough strength in the frames to take the stress. But when they were drilling the holes for mounting the armor, they only had the one set of jigs. If we carry on much further without fixing it, there's a danger we'll lose about a fifth of the carts."

"All right." Valens stole another look at the mountains; Sharra peering over their shoulders, like a nosy old woman spying on her neighbors. "Get up to the front and call a general halt; find someone to organize a survey, find all the carts likely to have the problem, have them fallen out so they can be worked on. Get three squadrons of cavalry back here to guard them when the rest of the column moves on. And find Vaatzes, and that sidekick of his, Daurenja; I want a fix for the buggered-up wagons, top priority. I'll be back at my coach."

But Vaatzes, it seemed, was nowhere to be found, and neither was Daurenja. That evening, another equally harassed-looking junior officer reported that he'd made inquiries, and nobody could remember having seen either of them since the column left the city. Meanwhile, an ad hoc committee of carpenters and wainwrights had been considering the problem. Their advice — far from unanimous — was to nail on big slabs of batten across the cracks on the already damaged carts and see what happened. If that worked, they could fix any further casualties the same way. If it didn't work, it was their unanimous considered professional opinion that the whole column was screwed.

Valens had sent Mezentius off to supervise the cavalry screen, and the rest of the general staff had more than enough to do; that just left him. He'd always prided himself on his ability to delegate, but it had one serious disadvantage. It meant he was stuck in the coach, alone with his wife; nobody to talk to.

"Why have we stopped?" she asked.

He explained.

"I warned you," she said. "Your vehicles aren't designed for this kind of work; and the armor just makes things worse. You'd be better off removing it, before it wrecks all your wagons."

The thought had crossed his mind. "We can't do that," he said. "I thought I'd explained all that, about how —"

"Yes. But if the armor is breaking up the wagons, you have to remove it. You have no choice."

Vaatzes, he thought bitterly; I hate the fact that I need him. Of course, if he was the engineering genius he's cracked up to be, he wouldn't have drilled all those holes in the wrong places, and we wouldn't be having this problem. (At the back of his mind he had a vague recollection of a memo from Vaatzes complaining that the short-frame jigs were behind schedule because the jig-makers had buggered them up somehow, and quite possibly they wouldn't be ready on time. He ignored it.) If and when he turned up . . . But perhaps he wasn't going to turn up. Desertion, assassination, or maybe just forgotten about in the rush to leave and left behind; and his odious associate as well, which wasn't promising. The thought that Vaatzes might change sides, betray them all to the Mezentines, hadn't really seemed worth considering before. The Mezentines would never forgive him; his only chance of survival lay in sticking close to the Vadani, making himself indispensable. He'd done that. He should be here, when he was needed.

Odd, then, that he wasn't.

Too big and unsettling a problem to tackle now; better to hide from it behind all the lesser, more immediate problems, and hope it'd go away. He climbed out of the coach, stopped the first officer he saw, and ordered him to round up the carpenters and joiners. Shouting at them would take his mind off the ghastliness of the mess he was in, and might goad them into doing something useful.

No such luck. They looked away, shook their heads, tutted, sighed; can't patch up splintered frames, got to cut out the busted timber and replace it with a new one. Could try letting in a patch, but that'd take time; could try wrapping the split in rawhide, but couldn't promise anything; nailing on battens would be as good as anything; bolting them on would be better; could try it, but it probably wouldn't work. Could've told you this'd happen if you go boring holes in frames. No help at all.

His father would have had them all strung up, as an example to all tradesmen who failed to work miracles on demand. Instead, he thanked them for their time and told them he was sure they'd do their best. Then he went to look for Mezentius.

"We can't stay here," Mezentius told him. "Far too close to the border. They've been sending patrols out along the river valleys below Sharra for some time; quite likely they've got watchers on the Sow's Back by now. Maybe they already know we're here. If we stay put, you can make that a certainty."

Infuriating to hear your own depressing thoughts echoed by someone else. "I don't think it's as bad as all that," Valens lied to himself. "Even if they've seen us already, they've got to report back, gather their forces . . ."

"There's a full squadron stationed at the Unswerving Loyalty, last I heard. Probably double that by now."

"Well, we can handle two squadrons. And it'd take them two days to get here." Mezentius' frown expressed entirely justified skepticism, which Valens ignored. Am I turning into Orsea? He panicked for a moment. "And suppose they do come? I don't know about you, but I'd have no worries at all about fighting off a cavalry attack here, on a rocky hillside. They couldn't ride, they'd have to dismount and fight as infantry. In fact, I've half a mind to stay here and see if they do come. The sooner we start this war . . ."

Mezentius was staring at him. He closed his eyes, as if trying to wash the image out of them.

"That bad?" he asked.

"It's understandable," Mezentius replied; he could hear the restraint in his voice. "The strain's getting to all of us, and now this stupid thing with the carts . . ." He shook his head. "If you want my considered opinion, I would prefer not to engage the enemy right now."

Valens took a deep breath. "Agreed," he said. "Not now, or ever. But certainly not now." He stood up. "I'll go and plead with the carpenters a bit more, see if I can fire up their imaginations. And please, ignore what I said just now. I've been talking to my wife. It's not good for me."

Mezentius laughed, but nervously. "Understood," he said. "Good luck with the carpenters. Did you find out where that bloody Mezentine's got to, by the way?"

When he reached the broken wagons, he found the carpenters standing round looking sad. They explained that they'd thought about it some more, and they were pretty sure that nailing on battens wasn't going to work, so there didn't seem much point in starting.

Valens swallowed his anger. He was getting used to the taste of it. "Try it anyway," he said.

They explained how the damage should be repaired, by removing the entire damaged timber and replacing it. They could more or less guarantee that that would work; however, it would probably take several days, even if they had suitable material, which they didn't. They could go up the mountain and look for ash trees of the right size and width, though ash didn't usually grow well in this soil; that wouldn't really help, however, since green timber would be far too weak, and they'd be wasting their time. But if that was what Valens wanted them to do . . .

He smiled. "Let's try the battens," he said.

They nodded silently. He could tell they were waiting for him to go away, so they could carry on standing about looking miserable. "I'll stay and watch, if I won't be in the way," he said. "I like watching craftsmen at work."

It didn't take them long. They unshipped lengths of batten, cut pieces to size and nailed them on. The horses were brought up and backed into the shafts. The wagons began to move. The sound of the battens cracking was audible ten yards away.

"Oh well," Valens said. "We tried."

The carpenters explained that they'd been pretty sure it wasn't going to work. However, they would give it some thought and try to come up with something else.

Some junior officer he didn't know brought him the inventory he'd asked for. Over a third of the column were bow-waisted or half-lock. He gave up the idea of abandoning them and trying to distribute their loads among the rest of the carts. He thanked the officer and went back to the coach.

"Have you solved the problem?" she asked.

"No."

She nodded. "How many . . . ?"

"About a third."

The interruption didn't seem to have bothered her. "In that case, you have only one option. You must remove the armor from the affected vehicles. Of course, this will seriously compromise your plan for using the carts as a mobile fortress. You can, of course, put some of the undefended carts in the middle of the formation and so shield them from attack, but —"

"Not all of them," Valens said. "Which means there'll be a great big weak patch somewhere in the wall, which we'll have to defend some other way. We could concentrate the cavalry and men-at-arms —"

"To some extent." In other words, forget it. He wondered if she was enjoying his failure, but it didn't seem likely. Any sort of pleasure seemed beyond her completely. "You would be better advised to move out as quickly as possible, and head directly for my people's territory. At least you can be sure that the Mezentines won't follow you into the desert."

"We aren't going anywhere near the desert."

"You have no choice."

He left without replying. Outside, he stood for a moment and looked at the line of halted wagons. People were standing about in groups, talking quietly or not at all. Horsemen rode up and down the line, carrying messages, inspecting, relaying orders. They were worried, but it was all under control; they knew he could be trusted to sort things out. To be trusted, relied on, even loved; he felt the pain of it deep inside, the way a man with an arrowhead buried too deep inside to be extracted feels it every time he moves. I've killed them, he thought, just like Orsea killed the Eremians: for duty, for love.

"Is there anything I can do?"

He turned his head, and just then, in his mind, it was like looking into a mirror. "Orsea," he said. "I'm sorry, I was miles away."

"I gather there's some problem with the carts," Orsea said. He had that stupid, sad look on his face, that preemptive admission of guilt that made Valens want to say, *It's all right, this time it's not your fault.* That would be a lie, of course, since it *was* Orsea's fault they were here; Orsea's sense of duty, compounded by Valens' love. "Can't Vaatzes suggest anything? It should be right up his street, this sort of thing."

"Vaatzes isn't here." Valens didn't want to snap, but he couldn't help it. Orsea had been born to be shouted at. He was wearing the fashionable long-toed riding boots that were useless for walking in; they made him look like some rare breed of marshland bird. "He's disappeared, and so's his assistant. But we're working on it." He scowled. "You don't happen to know anything about woodwork, do you?"

"No."

"Of course not. Me neither. Useless, aren't we?" He laughed. "Oh, we know lots of stuff: how to train hawks, how to run a council meeting, the correct way to address an ambassador, how to use archers to cover an infantry advance. Pity that a few bits of broken wood can screw us up completely. I don't know." He turned away; the sight of Orsea's face made him want to lash out. "Maybe we should just jump on our horses and ride away, leave the rest of them to sort it all out for themselves. They couldn't be worse off without us than they are already."

"That's not true," Orsea said; he sounded bewildered, like a child who sees his parents arguing. "You're good at this. You can deal with it."

If it had come from anybody else, he might have tried to believe it. "My wife thinks we should dump the armor and make a run for it, head for her territory, the Cure Hardy." He stopped, as though there was something wrong with his mouth. "She thinks we'd be safe there. A lot of us would die trying to cross the desert, but not nearly as many as we'd lose if we carried on with the original plan." He turned sharply and looked Orsea in the eye. "What do you think? Is that what you'd do, in my place?"

Orsea seemed to shrink back, as though Valens had hit him. "I'm the last person —"

"Yes, but I'm asking you. What do you think?"

"I don't know."

Valens felt the energy seep out of himself. "Well of course you don't, you haven't got all the facts. I'm sorry. I just don't feel like making a decision like that."

"I can understand," Orsea said.

You more than anybody. "In fact," Valens said, "we're not going to do anything of the sort. Which is stupid, because I have an unpleasant feeling it's the right thing to do; but I'm too weak to make the decision, so we aren't going to do it." He looked past Orsea, at the line of carts. "I'm going to send on the carts that don't have the problem, and keep the damaged ones here until they can be fixed properly, by cutting out the broken bits and fitting in new ones. I'm told it could take a day or so to find suitable timber and as long again to do the job, but that can't be helped. We can't afford to abandon that many wagons, so they'll have to be fixed, and we'll have to try and protect them in the meantime." He breathed in, as though he was making a speech. "It'll mean dividing the army, and there's not enough to defend both units, so I'll split the archers and foot soldiers up between the two parts of the convoy, and send the cavalry out to look for the enemy. If they come for us, the cavalry can engage them in the open, try and stop them getting here. If we get away with it, we'll all meet up somewhere and carry on as before. How does that sound?"

"Excellent," Orsea said; and the sad thing was, he meant it. Just the sort of thing he'd have done himself, which was why the maps of Eremia weren't accurate anymore, showing a city that had ceased to exist. I've made the wrong choice, Valens told himself; I know it, and I don't seem to care. I think we've lost this war.

As soon as Valens let him go, Orsea hurried away to continue his search for a bush. Not an easy thing to find on a barren, rocky hillside; but his rank and his natural diffidence made it impossible for him to pee with the whole Vadani nation watching him.

No bushes, as far as the eye could see. A few stunted thorn trees, but their trunks were too thin to stand behind. In the end, he had to settle for a large rock, which only screened his lower half. His relief was spoiled by the fact that a sharp wind had got up while he was talking to Valens. It blew piss back onto his trouser leg. One of those days.

Alfresco urination was one of the things he hated most about traveling with a large number of people. It had bothered him when he led the Eremian army, casting a huge, disproportionate shadow over each day. He knew why: he was sure the men would laugh at him. Pathetic.

He'd finished, and was lacing up the front of his trousers, when he heard voices behind him. He panicked until he was quite sure it was nothing to do with him.

A small, two-wheeled cart — a chaise, he decided, mildly ashamed of his precision in trivia — was rolling down the slope, passing along the line of the halted convoy as though such sights were too commonplace to be worth noticing. A ridiculous, fussy little cart, with thin, spindly wheel-spokes like crane-fly legs, and a brightly colored parasol perched over the box; on which sat a huge man and a tiny blond woman in a red dress. Orsea stared for the best part of two minutes, the ends of his trouser-laces still in his hands. It wasn't just the incongruity that stunned him. Somehow, perhaps by the confident way she perched, with a large carpet bag clutched in her lap, she gave the impression that she was normal, and it was the Vadani nation who were making a spectacle of themselves. He couldn't begin to understand why the stupid little cart's wheels didn't crumple up and blow away in the wind like chaff every time they rolled into a pothole.

A cavalry officer in full armor, red campaign cloak, tall black boots gray with dust, shuffled forward to meet her. Too far away to see the look on his face, but Orsea could guess. The sort of look a twelve-year-old boy would wear if his mother showed up while he was playing with his friends. The woman in the red dress leaned down to ask him something. He looked round for a while, then suddenly pointed. It was a moment before Orsea realized the man was pointing at him.

He remembered, and dropped the laces. Probably too late. The woman was climbing down from her seat — the officer's arm was stretched out for her to steady herself by; you can't beat the cavalry for manners, no matter how bizarre or desperate the situation. Orsea watched as she came bustling straight at him; he looked over his shoulder, but there was nobody standing behind him.

"Are you Duke Orsea?" Her voice was high and sharp; someone who never needed to shout, even in a high wind.

"That's right. I'm sorry, I don't think I —"

She reached in her bag and pulled out a small linen pouch, about the size of an apple. "Your wife ordered some potpourri," she said, pointing the pouch at him as if it was some kind of weapon. "It's all right," she added, "it's paid for."

He stared at her for a count of five before saying, "You came all the way out here to deliver *that?*"

She laughed; a sound like a fox barking. "No, of course not. I'm on my way from Calva to the sheep-fair at White Cross. But they told me at the Unswerving Loyalty that the Vadani court was on a progress, or going camping or something. I guessed you'd be with them, so here I am."

Potpourri. Dried flowers and leaves and bits of lavender and stuff. As he dug in his pocket for money for a tip, he could hardly believe what he was hearing. Surely, when the world came to an end, and the Vadani were facing certain death, things like that simply ceased to exist. It wasn't possible for the world to contain war and potpourri at the same time.

"Thanks," he heard himself say. "She'll be really pleased."

"No trouble," she chirruped back. "Do you think they'll be able to spare me some hay and a bucket of oats for my horse? I've probably got enough to get me as far as the Modesty and Prudence, but better safe than sorry."

"Try the ostlers," he was saying, when the significance of what she'd told him hit him like a hammer. "Excuse me," he muttered, and broke into a run. She called out something, but he didn't catch what she was saying.

There are times when it's better to run frantically, headless-chicken fashion, than to arrive. When finally he found Valens' carriage — he felt like he'd run five miles, up and down the middle of the convoy — he pulled up and froze, realizing as he panted like a thirsty dog that he was in no fit state to tell anybody about anything, not if he expected to be taken seriously. He dragged air into his burning lungs and tried to find a form of words. Then he balled his left fist and rapped it against the carriage door.

No answer. His mind blanked. Clearly, the carriage was empty; in which case, Valens wasn't here; consequently, he could be any-where. Orsea felt his chest tighten again, this time with panic rather than fatigue. His discovery was obviously so important that it couldn't wait, but searching the entire convoy . . . Just in case, he knocked again, much harder. This time, the door opened.

"Who are you?"

He recognized her, of course; the only female Cure Hardy he'd ever seen. "I'm Orsea," he said, realizing as he said it how inad-equate his reply was. "I need to see Valens, urgently. Do you know where . . . ?"

"No." She was looking at him as though she'd just noticed him on the sole of a brand-new shoe. "What do you want?"

"It's very important," Orsea said. She made him feel about nine years old; but while he was standing there babbling, the

Mezentines could be moving into position, ready to attack. "Can you give me any idea where he's likely to be? The whole convoy's in danger."

She frowned. "Have you told the duty officer?"

Pop, like a bubble bursting. "No," Orsea admitted. "No, that's a good idea. I'll do that."

She closed the carriage door; not actually in his face, but close enough for him to feel the breeze on his cheek. Something told him he hadn't made a good impression. The least of his problems.

Even Orsea knew how to find the duty officer; dead center of the convoy, look for a tented wagon with plenty of staff officers coming and going. Mercifully, one of them was an Eremian, who escorted him, in the manner of a respectful child put in charge of an elderly, senile relative, up the foldaway steps into the wagon.

Orsea had nearly finished telling his story when he realized that the duty officer, a small, neat, bald Vadani, didn't believe him. It was the lack of expression on his face; not bewilderment or shock, but a face kept deliberately blank to conceal what he was thinking. "I see," he said, when Orsea had finished. "I'll make sure the Duke gets your message."

"Will you?"

"Of course." Orsea could see him getting tense, afraid there'd be a scene, that he'd be forced into being rude to the known idiot who technically ranked equal with Valens himself. "As soon as I see him."

"When's that likely to be?"

"Soon." Pause. The officer was trying to hold out behind his blank face, like a city under siege. "I expect he'll send for me at some point today, and when he does —"

"Don't you think you should send someone to find him?"

Orsea couldn't help being reminded of a fight he'd seen once, in the streets of Civitas Eremiae. A huge, broad-shouldered man was being trailed by a tiny, elderly drunk, who kept trying to hit him with a stick. Over and over again the big man swatted the stick away, like a fly, but eventually the drunk slipped a blow past his guard and hit him in the middle of the forehead. A lucky strike; the big man staggered, and while he was off guard, the drunk hit him again, three or four times on the side of the head. Realizing that he could be killed if he didn't do something, the big man tried to grab the stick, and got slashed across the knuckles and then beaten hard just above the ear. He swung his arm wildly but with force; the back of his hand hit the drunk in the mouth, dislocating his jaw and slamming him against a wall; he slid down and lay in a heap. With that picture in his mind's eye, Orsea looked down at the duty officer, sitting very upright in his straight-backed chair. If I goad this man again, he thought, he's going to have to strike back; but I've got no choice.

"I'm not sure that'd be appropriate," the duty officer said. "But I assure you, as soon as I see him —"

"Haven't you been listening to me?" Orsea could hear the shrill, petulant anger in his own voice; it revolted him. "As soon as you see him could be too late. If the innkeeper at Sharra knows we're here and there's a Mezentine patrol stationed there —"

"Assuming," the duty officer interrupted quietly, "that what this woman told you is true."

I must try and make him understand. "She found me, didn't she?" he said. "She heard we were here from someone; she told me it was the innkeeper who told her. I can't imagine why she'd want to lie about it. Think about it, can't you? There's this merchant with a delivery for my wife. Here, look." He thrust the little cloth sack at the officer's face, like a fencer testing the distance. "Now, if she wasn't told where I was likely to be, how do you think she found me? Just wandering around at random on the off chance she'd run into me?"

The officer leaned back a little, putting space between himself and the smell of the bag. "You may like to bear in mind that we're on a road," he said, voice flat and featureless. "People travel up and down roads, on their way to wherever they happen to be going. It seems more likely to me that she fortuitously came across this column while following the road than that she heard about us at Sharra and made her way here across country, in a ladies' chaise, just to deliver a bag of dried flowers."

Orsea pulled in a deep breath. "I don't agree," he said. "And I'm asking you to send someone to find Valens, right now. Are you going to do it?"

The officer's eyes were sad as well as hostile. "I'm afraid I can't," he said.

"Fine." Orsea swung round, traversing like a siege engine on its carriage, to face the Eremian officer who'd led him there. "All right," he said, "you do it."

The Eremian was only a young man, embarrassed and ashamed. "I'm sorry," he began to say.

"You heard what I just told him?"

The Eremian nodded wretchedly.

"Good. I'm telling you to find Duke Valens and pass the message on."

Such a reproachful look in the young man's eyes. "Actually, I'm supposed to be taking a note to —"

"Never mind about that." Orsea couldn't help thinking about the drunk with the stick. "It can wait. Do you understand what I want you to do?"

The young man was looking past him, at the duty officer. Orsea couldn't see what he saw, but the young man nodded slightly. "Of course," he said. "Straightaway." He left quickly, grateful to get away, leaving Orsea and the duty officer facing each other, like the big man and the little drunk. I won, Orsea thought, I got my way. Shouldn't that make me the big man, not the other way round?

The carpenters weren't happy. Valens found that hard to take, since he was merely telling them to do what they'd told him was the only way. But apparently there wasn't enough good seasoned timber to do the job; they could use green wood, but —

"I know," Valens snapped. "You told me."

Dignified silence. They were good at dignified silence. "Do the best you can," he growled at them, and left with what little remained of his temper.

Heading back to his coach, he met a sad-looking ensign; an Eremian, he noticed from his insignia. He looked weary and ground down, as though he'd been given an important job he didn't know how to do.

"I've got a message for you," the sad ensign said. "From Duke Orsea."

One damn thing after another. "Go on, I'm listening."

He listened, and when the ensign had finished, he said, "Orsea told you that? Himself?"

The ensign nodded. "He reported it to the duty officer —"

Valens wasn't interested in any of that. "All right," he said, "here's what I want you to do."

He fired off a list of instructions, detailed and in order of priority. He could see the ensign forcing himself to remember each step, his eyes terrified. Fear of failure; must be an Eremian characteristic. "Have you got that?"

"Yes."

"Repeat it all back to me and then get on with it."

It all came back at him like an echo; it sounded very impressive, as though Duke Valens was on top of the situation. It'd be nice if he was, since the lives of everybody in the column depended on him. If only the warning hadn't come from Orsea; anybody else, a soldier, a half-blind crippled shepherd, a twelve-year-old boy, and he'd be comfortable with it. But no, it had to be Orsea. Still, the risk was too great. If he ignored it, and the Mezentines came . . .

The ensign darted away, swift as a deer pursued by hounds, born to be hunted, inured to it. Valens stopped to take a deep breath and clear his mind, then went to find the duty officer.

21

His third visit to the Unswerving Loyalty; Miel Ducas was starting to feel at home there. Mind, he wasn't sure he liked what the
Mezentines had done with the place. Rows of hastily built sheds
crowded the paddock behind the original stable block, and the
yard was churned and rutted from extreme use. Stacks of crates
and barrels masked the frontage; it hadn't been a thing of beauty,
but the supply dumps hadn't improved it. Mezentine soldiers
everywhere, of course; definitely an eyesore. He wondered if he
ought to point out to someone in charge that the inn was, properly
speaking, his property, and he hadn't authorized the changes.

They let him out into the yard for half an hour, for exercise.
They were punctilious about it — probably because they were
cavalrymen, used to the need to exercise horses. The degree of
joy he felt at being allowed into the open air disturbed him. Something so trivial shouldn't matter, now that his life was rushing to
its end. He'd wanted to achieve a level of tranquility; how could it
possibly matter whether or not he saw the sun one last time before
he died? But the light nearly overwhelmed him, after a sleepless
night in a stone pigsty. Perhaps it wasn't the light so much as the
noise. Out here, people were talking to each other. Not a word
had been spoken in the dark; his fellow prisoners' silence had been
harder to bear than anything they could have said to him. As soon
as they'd left the pigsty, Framain and his daughter had walked

away from him, crossed to the other side of the yard. He could see them talking to each other, but he couldn't make out what they were saying. Probably just as well.

He watched a Mezentine groom leading a horse across the top of the yard, passing a man sharpening a bill-hook on a big wheel grindstone. The horse tried to shy as it passed the shower of orange sparks, but the groom twitched its headstall and it followed him, resigned rather than calm. Someone else was forking hay out of a cart into a hayloft. A sack of grain rose into the air on the end of a rope, as a winch creaked. A boy, not Mezentine, raked up horse dung into a barrow. Nobody seemed interested in Miel Ducas, apart from the two guards who watched him as though he was the only thing in the world. He felt mildly ashamed that he hadn't given any serious thought to trying to escape; properly speaking, it was his duty, but he simply couldn't be bothered. If he tried to get away, they'd only kill him. It was less effort to stay where he'd been put, and he was enjoying watching the people.

They brought in a cart — he was treating it as a show put on for his benefit — and took off one of the wheels. Enter a wheelwright, with tools and helpers; they struck off the iron tire with cold chisels and cut out a damaged spoke. Miel wondered how they were going to fit the replacement; would they have to dismantle the whole wheel, and if so, how were they going to get the rim off? They were bringing out strong wooden benches. Miel tried to remember; he'd seen wheels made and mended before but hadn't bothered to observe, assuming in his arrogance that it wasn't any of his business. Now, he realized, he urgently wanted to know how it was done. If they took him back inside, and he missed the exciting part, it'd be like listening to most of a story and being cheated of the ending. Felloes, he suddenly remembered; the rim of a wheel is made up of six curved sections, called felloes, dowelled together, held rigid by the spokes, restrained by the tire. Where had he learned that; or had he been born knowing it?

"Are you going to move?" one of his guards said.

That struck Miel as a very odd question. "I'm sorry?"

"You're supposed to be exercising," the guard explained. They'd put the wheel on its side on top of a large barrel. It had taken three men to lift it into place. "But you're just standing still."

Fair enough. "I was watching them mend the wheel," he explained. "Is that all right?"

The guard shrugged. "You're supposed to be walking about," he said.

"Have I got to?"

"You please yourself," the guard replied. Clearly he didn't approve. "It's just some men fixing a wheel."

"I know," Miel said.

The wheelwright was tapping carefully on the inside of the rim, easing the felloe off the dowels. Obviously you'd have to be careful doing that. Too much force and you'd snap off a dowel. How would you cope if that happened? Drill it out, presumably; not the end of the world, but a nuisance. "I wish I could do that," Miel said. The guard didn't reply. They'd got the felloe off; now the wheelwright was flexing the damaged spoke in its socket, the way you waggle a loose tooth. Were all the spokes on Mezentine carts interchangeable, so that you could simply take out a broken one and replace it with a brand-new spare from the stores? But perhaps it wasn't a Mezentine cart.

"That's enough," the guard said. "You've got to go back inside now."

Miel didn't argue, though he couldn't really see why a few minutes more would make such a difference. But it wouldn't do to get stroppy with the guard, who was only doing his duty. Miel realized that he felt sorry for him, because he still had duty to do.

She didn't look at him as they were herded back into the pigsty. Framain gave him a blank stare, then looked away. The door closed, shutting out all but a few splinters of light. Miel found the corner he'd sat in before. The wall he leaned his back on was damp and crusted with white powder, like fine salt. There was a strong smell of mold, wet and pig.

"I'm sorry," he said aloud.

He might as well have been alone. He could barely see them in the dark. Nevertheless, he felt he ought to apologize. He hadn't done so before, and it was an obligation, possibly the last one he'd ever have to discharge. He wasn't particularly bothered whether they accepted his apology or not. Still; if it was his last duty, he might as well do it properly.

"It was my fault," he said. "Obviously that Mezentine I rescued led them to us. I knew at the time it was a bloody silly thing to do. I guess it was self-indulgence, me wanting to do the right thing." He smiled, though of course they wouldn't see. "Really, I should've learned by now, as often as not doing the right thing makes matters worse. Mind you," he added, "you were just as bad as me in that respect. You should've left me in the bog where you found me, it wouldn't have made any real difference in the long run."

Silence. Perhaps they'd both fallen asleep — exhausted, maybe, by their exercise session.

"Anyway," he went on (now that he'd started talking, he found that he was afraid to stop, because of the silence that would follow), "I'm very sorry it turned out like this. I hope you can make a deal with the Mezentines and get away. Of course, all that work you did will be wasted, as far as you're concerned." He stopped himself. There was a fair chance they didn't need to be told that. "If it means anything, I really am sorry you got caught up in the bloody mess I've made of my life. I wish there was something I could do, but there isn't."

If they'd been asleep, he'd have heard them breathing. To stay that quiet, they had to be awake. There, he thought, duty done. The rest of my life's my own.

He breathed out and relaxed his back and neck, letting his head droop forward. Irony: at last he was free to do what he chose, except there wasn't anything to do. He wished they'd let him back out in the yard, so he could watch the wheelwright for a little longer. He contemplated crawling up next to the door, in case there was a crack or a knothole big enough for him to see through, but he dismissed the idea as requiring too much energy. Later, perhaps, when he started to feel bored. Instead, he considered the rapier-blades of light and the dust specks, like stars, that glittered in them for a while before floating away into the shadows. It turned out to be a pleasure, sitting still and letting his mind slip out of focus. That was all wrong, of course. A condemned man awaiting execution in a pigsty shouldn't be enjoying himself. That thought made him smile. He had a duty to feel miserable, but he was neglecting it. No more duty. Often in the past, when he'd heard that someone had killed himself, he wondered how anybody could possibly choose to die; such a strange choice to make, the prey failing in its obligation to evade the hounds for as long as possible. But sometimes the deer did just that; they stopped, not from exhaustion or injury or because there wasn't anywhere for them to go. Not often, but it happened; and Miel wondered if they came to this same place, the point where the obligations of instinct become weak enough to be put aside. An animal lives to serve a function, its duty to survive long enough to procreate and so maintain and propagate the species. Apart from that obligation, its life is mere tiresome necessity, the need to find enough to eat every day, the need to escape from predators. He thought about love, which was just a sophistication of that duty; something you were required to believe in, like a state religion, but only so that you'd do your otherwise unpalatable and irksome duty of acquiring and raising children. Of course, the deer has its duty to the wolves and hounds, who depend on it for their existence (obligation of the prey to the predator; obligation of the individual to society; of the beloved to the lover). In that case, the willing surrender after going through the obligatory motions of pursuit made perfect sense. The deer must run in order to keep the wolves fit, to give them a criterion by which to choose their pack leaders; the wolves must hunt in order to keep the numbers of deer in balance, so that they don't overpopulate their habitat and wipe themselves out through starvation and epidemic disease. Balance; as in the relationship between a great lord and his people. Miel wondered if this was the lesson he should've been learning — the hints dropped all round him had been heavy enough: that duty to friends and lovers is solemn enough, but no more valid than duty to enemies; quite possibly the most sacred duty of all. Or perhaps the distinctions were artificial and there was only one duty, and dependents, lovers and predators were really all the same thing.

He noticed that the blades of light had almost faded away, like the last melt of snow; so much for being bored, lying in the dark with no work to do. He felt no inclination at all to sleep, and his only regret was that his presence stopped Framain and his daughter from talking to each other. Something scuttled over his foot, but to his surprise he felt no shock of revulsion. Have I forgotten how to be afraid? he wondered. Normally I'd be halfway up the wall by now if a rat ran over me.

He found that as the light died away, his vision actually improved; he found it easier to make out shapes in the gloom without the distraction of the bright glare. His two fellow prisoners were slumped heaps in the opposite corner; there was also a barrel, four or five sacks and something that puzzled him for quite a while until he worked out that it was a small log-pile. Odd, because he'd always been disappointed with his poor night vision. The obvious conclusion was that he'd been trying too hard all these years. He let his mind drift through a range of reflections and sudden perceptions; he felt both relaxed and wonderfully sharp, as though he could solve any problem just by thinking it through from first principles. It's not supposed to be like this, he scolded himself. A man facing death should be wretched, sobbing, screaming with misery and fear, or frantically trying to divert his mind with pointless trivia. He'd heard of kind-hearted jailers who sat up with their prisoners through the last night, playing chess or cards, making a point of losing. He admired the principle, but what a wasted opportunity to be alone with the thoughts that really matter, all irrelevant distractions cleared away.

At some point, they must have fallen asleep. He heard the rhythm of their breathing change. He forgave them, since they were probably going to make a deal with the Mezentines and survive. He bore them no ill will on those grounds. It would have been nice to know if the experiment to make vermilion had worked, just as he'd have enjoyed watching the men repair the wheel. If they had the vermilion formula, they'd be better placed to bargain with the Mezentines. He hoped so. In the state they were in, death would be wasted on them.

In spite of himself, he began to wander, sliding into the debatable region between asleep and awake. He was writing poetry and composing music. He had the verse and half the refrain of a wonderful song — he wasn't sure what it was about but he knew it was there, as though he had it on his lap wrapped in a sack. He knew it would evaporate as soon as he woke up. It always did. Perhaps life slips away like that at the moment of death, and the few fragments he'd manage to catch as it faded would turn out to be garbled nonsense, a dreamer's false impression of poetry and music, incomprehensible in the context of being awake again.

In his dream, something was tapping at the door. At first it was an old woman in a shawl, wanting to come in out of the cold; it was the Ducas' duty to provide hospitality, and he considered getting up to let her in. Then it was just the guard bringing them something to eat. Then he heard the unmistakable sound of a nail being wrenched out of wood.

He opened his eyes. Needless to say, that fine night vision was blurry and thick, and for several seconds he couldn't make out anything. A board creaked under great stress. It sounded strangely like one of the slats of the door being prized off with a crowbar, but that made no sense at all.

"Hello," he called out in a muffled, croaky voice (not at his best when he first woke up, the Ducas). "Who's there?"

Somebody made a shushing noise. He felt properly remorseful. Maybe the guards had come to fetch him, but they didn't want to wake up Framain and his daughter. No, that didn't make sense either.

Another sort of creak; a hinge-hoop turning around a rusty, undersized pintle. In which case, someone was coming through the door, trying to be stealthy and quiet, but failing. That was completely beyond him, because why would the guards . . .

"Framain?"

Not a voice he knew, but whoever it was sounded painfully tense. It was the sort of whisper that comes out louder than a normal tone of voice. "Framain, are you there?"

Long silence. Miel was about to point out that Framain was asleep when he realized that the regular breathing had stopped. Framain must be awake, but he wasn't answering. The door creaked a little more, and Miel could see a rectangle of the dark blue of the night sky. Whoever it was had opened the door.

If the door was open, maybe he could get out.

Immediately, he felt that he didn't want to. It was dangerous (yes, but not nearly as dangerous as staying put). It was inconvenient. It was the middle of the night. He felt the shameful resentment that comes with getting an unwanted present. He wanted to stay where he was.

"Daurenja?"

Framain's voice; and he couldn't interpret the tone of it at all.

"Come on, for crying out loud," the unknown man in the doorway growled back. Daurenja; not a name he knew, but clearly it meant a lot to Framain, because Miel saw his shape move; he was standing up; they both were. They were leaving. In which case . . .

"Don't just sit there, you idiot." Framain's voice, addressing him. They wanted him to leave with them. But . . .

But he'd got to his feet anyway; instinct, or simply that he didn't want to give offense by declining the invitation. He wondered if the enigmatic Daurenja would mind him coming too. Shocking bad manners to gatecrash somebody else's jailbreak.

"Who the hell . . . ?" Daurenja started to say. Framain muttered, "Later." Nothing more said by either of them. Presumably that constituted a formal invitation. Hell of a time to discover that he'd got cramp in his leg.

From sitting still for so long, presumably. He wanted to laugh, mostly because Framain and this Daurenja sounded so *serious;* as if they thought they stood a chance of getting away with it — somehow evading the guards, crossing the inn yard without being seen, retrieving or stealing horses, mounting up, riding away (and where to? He knew for a stone-cold-certain fact that the Loyalty was the only habitable dwelling within feasible reach, unless you counted Framain's house). All that, and an unscheduled, hobbling freeloader. He decided to go with them simply to see how far they managed to get.

It was like an arrowhead stuck in his calf muscle, but he made it as far as the doorway. The other three were already outside, standing perfectly still, waiting for him. Any moment now, and the guards . . .

He saw the guards. One lay on his face, the other on his side. Lamplight from somewhere twinkled a reflection in a dark pool that probably wasn't water. Not one but both of them; and done so quietly that he'd dozed through it. If that was Daurenja's un-aided work, he must be a talented man. He tried to feel pity for the guards, but couldn't quite do it. Perhaps they really were going to escape, after all.

Stepping out of the pigsty into the yard was a bit like jumping into water without knowing how deep it is. He wasn't sure he could have done it, if he'd cared about staying alive. As it was, he felt his stomach muscles tighten into a knot as painful as his cramped leg. He wished he knew what the plan was, assuming there was one.

They were heading for the stables — the original block, not the new ones the Mezentines had built. It occurred to him that, since Daurenja hadn't known about him, he couldn't have provided a horse for him to ride. Was he supposed to run alongside them, like a dog, or were they proposing to turn him loose at the court-yard gate and leave him to fend for himself? If it hadn't been for the two dead guards, he'd have stopped by the mounting block and waited for the Mezentines to find him and take him back to the pigsty. He thought about them again, and about the two scav-engers he'd killed with the hunting sword, when he escaped from their camp; and, for good measure, about the desperate flight of Ziani Vaatzes, who'd also killed two men in order to get out of prison.

Daurenja had stopped. A moment later, someone started to say something, but didn't get far enough for Miel to make out what he was saying. He saw Daurenja move; he seemed to have pulled a black shape out of the shadows, a man, and they were fighting. No, that was overstating the case. Daurenja had caught hold of him round the neck and was forcing him down on his knees, smoothly and effortlessly, like a man wrestling with a child. It was a remarkable display of physical strength, and Miel wished he could admire it. Daurenja's opponent must have done something to loosen that appalling grip on his neck; he wriggled and got loose for a moment. Then Miel saw Daurenja's arm outlined against the dark blue sky. It curled round the side of the man's head; it was like watching twenty years' growth of ivy in less than a second. Then there was a loud, sharp crack; the shape in Daurenja's embrace jerked and wriggled for a very short moment and was let fall, flopping on the ground like grain from a split sack.

Miel had seen so many men killed in his life — some by others, some by himself — that the sight had gradually lost its meaning, to the extent that he could no longer remember the first one he'd seen, though he'd been sure at the time he'd see it in his mind every time he shut his eyes for the rest of his life. Now it was just a process, like threshing wheat or dressing game. But the sound — a crack like a thick dry branch breaking, carrying implications of such a terrible strength exerted with such purpose — shocked him so much that he felt his guts spasm; he'd have been sick if the Mezentines had bothered to feed him, but his stomach was empty. Instead, he felt acid fluxing in his throat and into his mouth, so that he nearly choked. He couldn't have moved if someone (not Daurenja, obviously; not Framain) hadn't grabbed a handful of his shirt and tugged him so hard he overbalanced, and had to take a step forward to keep from falling. Once he was moving, he kept going, except that he shied like a horse when his toe thudded into a soft heap on the ground, and he had to be dragged again, standing on something that yielded at first to his weight and then resisted; springy, like green branches, or ribs. "What's the matter with you?" her voice hissed accusingly in the darkness. Fortunately, he could safely assume she didn't want a reply.

Daurenja was pulling the stable door open. There was light inside; it gushed out and stained the yard yellow for a moment, so Miel could see a tall, thin man who must be Daurenja slipping inside. A muffled voice, cut off short, as Framain followed him in.

Three horses stood saddled and bridled, feeding placidly from a long manger of barley and oats. They didn't seem bothered about the man's body slumped on the ground in front of them, like a drunk's clothes on the floor. In the pale lamplight, Miel could see a bizarre creature, long and thin and bony, more of an insect than a man apart from the absurd ponytail of black hair dangling down his back. He was in the act of lifting a saddle off its peg.

"Bridle," he said, and Miel realized he was being spoken to. "There, look. You do know how to bridle a horse, don't you?"

Strange voice; educated, you'd begin to say it was cultured but then think better of it. Hardly the voice you'd expect to hear from the long, thin insect. Hardly the voice of the man who'd just killed four strangers with his bare hands for the crime of getting in the way. Miel looked round for the bridle, and saw her holding it, looping the reins over her forearm. Daurenja had lowered the saddle onto the back of a nondescript bay gelding. In the middle of a desperate and bloody escape, for some reason they were stopping to tack up a horse.

For me, Miel realized. But I don't want help from the likes of him . . .

The horse lifted its head to avoid the bridle; he saw Daurenja's arm snake out, just like the last time, and for a moment he firmly expected to see the horse strangled. Instead, Daurenja took the bridle and gently eased the bit into the horse's mouth. As soon as he touched it, the horse became completely calm and lowered its head to the optimum height for fitting a bridle. Miel had seen grooms who could do that. A rare gift, apparently, vouchsafed to only a few.

Daurenja was handing him the reins. He took them and watched the other three mount up. Daurenja mounted like water poured from a bottle, seen in reverse. It was, Miel couldn't help thinking, the way you'd imagine the hero of the story would do it — assured, graceful, quick, and once he was mounted he seemed to merge with the horse, controlling it with the same thoughtless ease you use when moving your own leg or arm. He'd be the perfect hero, if only he wasn't a monster.

"Come *on*," she said, as if chiding him for using up all the hot water. He grabbed the reins and the cantle of the saddle, and made a complete botch of mounting, losing both stirrups and flopping forward onto the horse's neck.

Back in the yard again; there were men with lanterns; somebody shouted at them as they rode past. Miel's horse broke into a canter before he was ready, and the saddle hammered the base of his spine. Twenty years of riding; he couldn't remember what to do. It was just as well that the horse was inclined to follow the tail in front.

Only a complete idiot or a hero gallops in the dark. After a few strides, Miel lost his nerve completely. Instead of standing to the pace, he sat and flumped painfully, gripping the pommel of the saddle like a scared child. Escaping from the Mezentines was washed completely from his mind. All he could think was, *I'm going to fall off, help.* He could feel the horse extending its stride to keep up. All the fear he'd so skillfully reasoned away in the pigsty flooded back, drowning his mind. He was going to be killed, and he didn't want to be.

How long the ride lasted he had no idea, but after a lifetime the gallop decayed into a trot, then a walk; they were climbing, but he had no strength left in his knees or back to lean forward. He heard the horse wheeze, and apologized to it under his breath. Every movement it made jarred his pulled muscles. He just wanted the journey to end; a little pain was all it took, apparently, to shake him out of his high-minded resolve. Not even proper torture; discomfort. He was pathetic.

The first smear of lighter blue in the sky took him by surprise. It must've got there while his attention was distracted. Daylight, though; they'd have to stop when the sun came up. Hunted fugitives lay up during the day to avoid being seen, it was the rule.

They didn't stop. The sun came up, a red mess on the horizon. They were climbing a heather-covered moor, pimpled with white stones about the size you'd use for wall-building. The outline of Sharra directly behind him told him all he needed to know about where he was. In the middle of nowhere, precision is a waste of effort.

"We'll stop here." Daurenja's voice, so unexpected as to be arbitrary. Actually, the choice was good. They were high enough up to have a good view all round, but hidden by a little saucer of dead ground under the top of the ridge. With the bulk of the rise behind them, they could sneak out unobtrusively as soon as they saw pursuers approaching, and the direction of their escape would be masked by the gradient. Clever, resourceful Daurenja; a proper old-fashioned sort of hero, not like the tortured, ineffective types you got in all the modern romances.

"Get off," he went on, "we'll rest the horses for an hour."

Miel realized he'd forgotten how to get off a horse. He kicked his feet out of the stirrups and tried swinging his leg over the animal's back. He must have done something wrong, because he slithered and ended up breaking his fall with his kneecap.

"Would somebody mind telling me who the hell that is?" Daurenja said.

"He's nobody." Her voice. "You *bastard*."

"Don't start," Daurenja snapped. "This really isn't the time."

Miel lifted his head, mostly to see if Daurenja looked as weird in daylight as he had under the lamp. He saw him facing her, a let's-all-be-reasonable look on his extraordinary face. Behind him, Framain was coming up slowly; the exaggerated strides of someone who's not used to it trying to move without making a noise. He had a rock in his hands.

"How dare you . . ." she was saying; then she caught sight of her father. There was a split second before she realized she had to keep Daurenja's attention distracted; he must have picked up on it, because he swung round, reached out his ludicrously long arm and punched Framain on the side of the head. Framain collapsed like a shoddily built rick. Daurenja turned back as though he'd just swatted a fly. She sprang past him and threw herself on top of Framain; clearly she was afraid Daurenja had killed him, but he groaned and pushed her away.

"Excuse me," Miel said.

Framain looked up and saw him. His expression showed that he'd forgotten about Miel. He wiped a dribble of blood off his chin.

"I'd like you to meet my business partner," Framain said. "Daurenja, this is Miel Ducas. He's going to hold your arms while I smash your head in."

Daurenja glanced quickly at Miel; he was judging distances, doing mental geometry. He took two long strides, sideways and back, placing himself out of distance of all three of them.

"You," he said, looking at Miel for the briefest time required to make eye contact, then returning the focus of his attention to Framain, "get lost. Nothing to do with you. Get on your horse and go away."

It would've been very easy to obey. Daurenja had a foreman's voice, the kind that makes you do as you're told without stopping to think. Besides, he was right: none of the Ducas' business, therefore no obligation to intervene. Since it seemed pretty evident that the three of them together would be no game at all for Daurenja in a fight, there didn't seem to be anything Miel could usefully do.

"If it's all the same to you," he said, "I'll hang around for a bit. I mean, I haven't got a clue where we are, for a start, and —"

"Do what he says," Framain growled at him. "I don't need you."

"I know. I just —"

"Go *away.*" So she didn't want him there either. It was just as well, Miel decided, that he wasn't a democrat.

"Fine." Miel stood up. "Can I keep the horse?"

No reply; he no longer existed. He gathered the reins and led the horse away. It didn't want to move, so he twitched its head sideways; at least that still worked. "I'll head this way," he called back without looking round. "And thank you for rescuing me."

Once he was over the lip of the saucer, he stopped and glanced back; then he found the heaviest rock he could lift, put the reins under it to keep the horse there, and walked as quietly as he could manage back the way he'd just come. Just under the cover of the lip he stopped, crouched down and listened.

He could hear Framain's voice, shouting, but couldn't make out the words. After a while she joined in, shrill, practically hysterical. Framain interrupted briefly, and then she resumed. He'd never heard so much anger, so much passion in any voice, male or female. Then there was a sound like a handclap, but extremely loud, and her voice stopped abruptly. Framain roared, and then he heard Daurenja say, "No" — not shouting, just speaking extremely clearly. At some point while he was eavesdropping, a stone had found its way into his hand. It fitted just right into his palm and nestled there comfortably, like a dog curled up at your feet. He crawled up to the top of the lip and looked down.

She was lying on her face. Framain was kneeling beside her, hugging his ribs, finding it hard to breathe. Daurenja stood a long stride away from him — long distance, in fencing terms. He had his arms folded too; he looked impatient and mildly annoyed. The knuckles of his right hand, gripping his left elbow, were scuffed and bleeding slightly.

Absolutely none of my business, Miel thought, taking aim.

The stone hit Daurenja just above the ear; not hard enough to knock him down but sufficient to make him stagger. Not the right time for sophistication, Miel decided. He ran down the lip, just managing to keep his balance, and crashed into him. The two of them fell together, and before they hit the ground, Miel could feel fingernails digging into his neck.

His weight helped. Landing on Daurenja was like falling into the brash of a fallen tree; his ribs, like branches, gave and then flexed. The grip on Miel's neck didn't slacken and he felt panic surging through him. The palm of his hand was on Daurenja's face, he was pushing away as hard as he could, but all that achieved was to tighten the grip. At that moment, death lost all its serenity and grace. He was the prey in the predator's jaws, wriggling and kicking a futile protest against the natural order of things. In his mind, dispassionately, like a neutral observer, he realized that he was losing the fight — not over yet, but he certainly wouldn't bet money on himself. It was, he decided, a pity but no tragedy. Mostly he felt resentful, because in the final analysis this thin freak was beating him, which inevitably made him the better man.

He didn't hear anything, but Daurenja's grip suddenly loosened and he stopped moving; then his body was hauled out of the way and Miel saw Framain looking down, though not at him. He realized that he was exhausted, too physically weary to move. Death, he decided, simply didn't want him, like the fat boy who never gets asked to join the gang.

"My business partner," Framain said. "It's all right, he's not dead. We need him, unfortunately. He's going to take us to join the Vadani duke. It's his way of making it up to us." Framain stopped, made a sucking noise and spat, very carefully, on Daurenja's upturned face. "I suppose I ought to thank you, but you should've done as you were told. This is a family matter, nothing to do with you."

"Would you help me up, please?" Miel said.

Framain frowned, as if he didn't understand, then reached out, caught hold of Miel's wrist and hauled him upright. He nearly fell down again, but managed to find his feet.

"Are you all right?" Framain didn't sound particularly interested.

"I think so. Just winded."

"We need some rope, or something we can tie his hands with," Framain said. "Got to be careful with him, it's like tying up a snake." That made it sound like he'd done it before; regularly, even. "He hit my daughter, you know," he added. "Punched her face. She's all right, but . . ." He sighed. "We need him, at least until we reach the Vadani. It'll be awkward killing him there, but you know what they say. Nothing worthwhile is ever easy."

No rope on the horses' saddles; they had to take Daurenja's shirt off and plait strips of it. Framain was fussy and impatient at the job, fretting in case Daurenja came round before they were ready. She helped at the end. Her mouth was swollen and purple, and her left eye was closed. Daurenja was in scarcely better shape. Whatever Framain had hit him with had left a long gash on his bald scalp. It had bled copiously, as scalp wounds do, so that his neck and ponytail were caked in blood. They propped him against the slope and Framain tied his hands and feet together, working edgily, at arm's length. "I'm surprised we managed it, actually," Framain observed casually, as they stood up and looked at him. "Just the three of us. Of course, it helped that he was taking care not to damage us. In some respects he's quite predictable."

"You should kill him now." She was using the tone of voice in which she chided him about details of mixing the colors. "Forget about joining up with the Vadani. That was his idea, presumably. Anyway, we don't need them. They're losers, or they wouldn't be running."

Framain scowled at her. "We haven't got anywhere else to go."

"Thanks to *him*." A different *him* this time.

"Be that as it may. Besides, what he said makes sense. The Vadani can't mine silver anymore; they need money. They'll be glad to help us, if we tell them we can make them a fortune."

"But the clay —"

"It's the Vadani, or going back home and waiting for the Mezentines to arrest us for killing those soldiers, or wandering aimlessly till we run out of food or a patrol gets us. Use your common sense for once."

The same argument, just a different topic. Presumably it would last as long as they did. Framain turned to Miel like a man looking for an escape route. "I suppose you're curious to find out why we're planning to kill the man who just rescued us all," he said.

"I was wondering, yes," Miel said mildly. "I'd got the impression you hadn't parted on good terms."

"Don't tell him," she interrupted, a hint of panic in her voice. "He's nothing to do with us. And we don't need the Vadani, let's do it now and get it over with, before the bastard escapes."

Framain raised his hand. Remarkably, this had the effect of silencing her. She turned her back on them both, though Miel was prepared to bet she was watching Daurenja, like a terrier on a leash at the mouth of a rat-hole. "My daughter's quite right, actually," he said, in a strangely calm, almost pleasant voice. "But from what I know about you, I get the feeling that if I don't tell you, it's quite likely you'll carry on interfering. The easiest way to get rid of you is to tell you. Of course, I'll need your assurance that you won't ever tell anybody what you're about to hear. On your word of honor," he added, with a faintly mocking smile, "as the Ducas."

Miel shrugged. "If you like," he said.

"In that case . . ." Framain sighed, and sat down on the ground, gesturing for Miel to do the same. "It's a long story," he said.

You already know about me (Framain said). We used to be a fairly dull, respectable family, nobility of the middling sort, in Eremia. We were tenants-in-chief of the Bardanes, with just short of a thousand acres of low-grade pasture on either side of East Reach. When all our land and money was gone, I promised myself I'd get it back, somehow or other; for her sake as much as mine, because I loved her and I felt it was my duty. With hindsight it'd have been kinder to cut her throat, but it didn't seem that way at the time.

Now, Daurenja here; he's quite a character. Most of what I know about him is what he told me himself, so I can't vouch for the truth of it. I'd be inclined to assume anything he ever said was a lie, but bits of information I picked up over the years from more reliable sources bear some of it out, so I've had to give him the benefit of the doubt, at least in part. You'll have to judge for yourself, I think.

Gace Daurenja was born about forty years ago in a large manor house at Combe Vellein; it's a smallish place just across the border from Tollin. That's right; by birth he's Cure Doce, though he'll tell you his mother was Eremian, of good family. He mentioned her name once, but it's slipped my mind. Not a family I'd ever heard of, but I'm hardly an authority.

He says he left home when he was fourteen to go to the university at Lonazep. That's partly true, from what I gather. He was fourteen when he left, and he did go to the university. That wasn't his main reason for leaving, though. The details are a bit hazy, understandably. It was something to do with an attack, one of his family's tenants. I haven't been able to find out if it was a girl or a boy he attacked, or whether it was rape or just his normal vicious temper. I don't think the child died, but it was a wretched business; anyway, he was packed off to Lonazep with books and money. I imagine the intention was that he'd stay away for good.

I've got no problem with conceding that Daurenja's a brilliant man, in his way. He can learn anything, in a fraction of the time it'd take a normal man. He's exceptionally intelligent, an outstanding craftsman, remarkably strong and agile, and I've never seen him get tired. When he first came to live with us, we didn't have any water; we had to carry it half a mile from the nearest stream. Daurenja dug a well; his own idea, we didn't ask him to do it. To be honest, the thought hadn't even occurred to me. I came out into the yard one morning and there he was; or at least, there was his head, sticking up out of a hole in the ground. He had to go down over seventy feet before he struck water, and he only stopped working when it got too dark to see. I wish I could show you that well. It's faced inside with stone — not mortared, just shaped and fitted together. He picked the stones out of the river and carted them back all by himself, and the winch he made for drawing up the bucket is a wonderful piece of work. You can lift a ten-gallon bucket with your little finger. So you see, he had the potential to do anything he wanted. His appearance was always against him, of course, but he made up for it with charm; he could lay it on when he wanted to, but perfectly judged, not too heavy-handed with it. His main problem, I believe, has always been his temper; or rather, his lack of self-restraint.

At first, he was a model student at Lonazep. He studied everything they were prepared to teach him, four or five courses simultaneously, which was unheard of, needless to say. He had plenty of friends, and when he wasn't studying he was a little on the rowdy side, but certainly no worse than most. Students at Lonazep are supposed to be a little bit boisterous, it's their tradition. But something happened. Again, I don't know the facts, but this time there definitely was a death; either a fellow student or an innkeeper's daughter. Luckily for him, the university has jurisdiction over its students, and they couldn't bring themselves to do anything too much to someone with such a brilliant mind. The story was that he transferred to Corlona to continue his researches there.

The name doesn't ring a bell, I take it. Corlona's on the other side of the sea; I believe it's one of the places where the Mezentines recruit their mercenaries. In any event, it was held to be far enough away, and by all accounts it's a very fine university, far better than Lonazep for mathematics and the sciences. When he got into trouble there, he moved on to another university a long way inland, and I believe he managed to stay there for several years. When he had to leave there, however, he was pretty much at the end of his resources. It was simply too far away for money to reach him from home, and his reputation was starting to precede him. Understandable: he was probably the only white face on the continent, outside of the coastal towns, so he was somewhat conspicuous. Really, he had no choice but to risk it and come back over here. Not that home had much to offer him. He didn't want to be recognized in Lonazep or the Cure Doce country; he was cut off from his family's money, because of course all the bankers and commercial agents were on notice to look out for him. If he came back he'd be on his own, no money, ill-advised to stay in any one place for very long. I imagine it took a certain degree of courage to make the decision; but courage is a quality he's never lacked.

As luck would have it, he wound up in Eremia just about the time I discovered the clay deposits, which I recognized as being suitable for making porcelain. My problem at that time was that I had no money at all. I needed to pay the premium for a lease on the land itself, not to mention buying all the equipment. The irony was that the man who owned the head lease only wanted a stupid little bit of money for it; my father would cheerfully have spent that much on a good hawk, or a book. But at the time I was making my living as a copyist; oddly enough, that was where I came across the book that helped me recognize the clay for what it was. You know the sort of money a copyist gets. I was cursing my bad luck and thinking I might as well forget all about it, when Daurenja came in to our shop to sell a book.

When I say sell, what I mean is, he'd lend us the book to copy, and we'd pay him a few thalers. It was the usual arrangement. Apparently, Daurenja had hung on to a few of his books from his university days. The book we borrowed from him was an artist's color-book, of all things. Come to think of it, you've seen it often enough. Of course, as soon as I saw it I was fascinated. I knew that if I was going to make porcelain I'd have to learn how to make the colors to decorate it with; so I made a secret copy of it for myself. Unfortunately, I didn't stop there. I assumed that anybody who owned a book like that must know a thing or two about the subject. That's how I got to know Daurenja.

I told him about my plans for making porcelain. At first I didn't let on about the clay, but it was stupid to think that someone like that wouldn't put two and two together. He quickly figured out that I must have found a supply of suitable material, and one evening he asked me straight where my clay deposit was.

Well, I'd more or less given up hope of being able to get my hands on that clay seam, so I reckoned I had nothing to lose. I told him, yes, I knew where to find the right clay, but I didn't have the money to buy the land. He went all thoughtful for a while, then said that money shouldn't be a problem, if I was interested in forming a partnership.

I console myself with the thought that it's not just stupid people who do stupid things. I agreed; he said he'd go away and raise the money. I imagined that'd be the last I saw of him. What he did, though, was go home, all the way back to the Cure Doce. It was a terrible risk, in the circumstances. Things had changed since he went away. Rumors of his various adventures had filtered through, and nobody was willing to cover up for him or risk themselves to keep him out of trouble. But he got home somehow, and persuaded his family to give him at least part of his inheritance. I think it was done through land exchanges and letters of credit; basically, they bought him an estate in either Eremia or the Vadani country, all done in the names of secret trustees, with cunning ways of routing the income through to him without anybody finding out. A lot of merchants were involved at various stages, so I imagine a fair proportion of the money got used up in commissions and expenses. Even so, all the time I knew him he had more than enough for his needs — books, tools, materials, and all the funding I required for my work. He never spent more than he could possibly avoid on food or clothes or anything like that. As far as I can tell, that sort of thing's never mattered to him. Everybody's idea of the unworldly scholar, in fact.

He stopped and looked round. Daurenja, trussed like a bull calf for castration, was stirring. His eyes were closed but his lips were moving around the gag, and his throat quivered slightly.

"Dreaming," Framain said. "If it wasn't for the gag, he'd be talking in his sleep. He does that. I'm told it's quite normal — talking in your sleep, I mean. Loads of people do it. My son did, and my father, too." He frowned, as though annoyed with himself. "When I was a kid, it used to scare me. Most nights he'd fall asleep in his chair, and after a while he'd start talking — quite normal tone of voice, like he was having a pleasant conversation, but none of it made sense. It wasn't gibberish. It came out as real words, proper sentences, but completely meaningless. *He's* not like that, though," he added, and the frown tightened into a scowl. "He always says the same thing. Probably he's saying it now. It's all the sort of stuff you'd say to your girl when you're seventeen and in love. Soppy, that's the only word for it. *You mean all the world to me, I'll always love you, you're the meaning of my life, you're my sun and moon and stars;* it's enough to make you want to throw up. Then after a bit he starts calling out a name; *Majeria, Majeria,* over and over again. Then he either stops and sleeps peacefully or else he sits bolt upright and screams. High-pitched screaming like a girl, you wouldn't think he was capable of making a noise like that. Anyway, he screams three or four times and wakes up. But by then, of course if you've got any sense you're not there to see it, because when he wakes up from a screaming fit, he starts lashing out. He'll still have his eyes shut, and he punches and kicks like a maniac for about a minute; then his eyes open, and he sits there, blinking, mouth wide open. Oh, he's a charmer, Daurenja."

"What was that name again?" Miel asked. "The one he shouts out."

"Majeria. And no, I haven't got a clue who she's supposed to be. I've asked him a couple of times, during the day, when he's awake. He reckons he's never heard of anybody called that."

Anyhow (Framain went on), that's how we came to be partners. His money paid for everything: the clay beds, the house and buildings, equipment and supplies. His trustees opened a line of credit for us, in both our names, so I could buy things without having to ask him first. That's another of his good points. He's really very generous with money.

To start with, we all worked very well together. It was me, him, my son Framea and my daughter there. We got off to an excellent start. He was the one who figured out how to fire the clay to make the porcelain without cracking or distortion. He built the kilns practically single-handed; hell of a job, and you've seen them for yourself, it's beautiful work. I've got to say, all the success we had in the early stages was basically him, not me.

Anyhow; once we'd got the mix and the firing right, we thought we were on the home stretch. All we had left to do was work out how to do the colors for decorating the finished pieces. Nothing to it, we thought. We'd got his book, and there're pages and pages in it about making and applying different colors. We were impatient to get the last details sorted out and go into production.

(Framain was silent for a long time, as though he'd forgotten Miel was there. He was frowning, like someone trying to remember something that's on the tip of his tongue; a name or a date or exactly the right word. Miel cleared his throat a couple of times, but Framain didn't seem to have noticed. Then he looked up sharply . . .)

All through the early stages (Framain continued), Daurenja had led the way. The truth is, I'm not much good at alchemy, or what-ever the word is. I haven't got the mind for it. I can follow instruc-tions, verbal or in a book; I can do as I'm told, better than most. But — well, it's like music. Some people can compose tunes, oth-ers can't. I'm a musician who can play someone else's tune on a flute or a harp, but I can't make them up for myself. Daurenja's the creative one. He looks at a problem an ordinary man can't begin to understand, and it's as though he can see things that the rest of us can't. When we were trying to get the consistency of the clay, for example; I was all for working away at it gradually, trial and error. He thought about it for a while, and suddenly came up with the answer. It made sense to him, he'd figured out how it worked. He tried to explain it to me, but I couldn't follow it at all. Not that I minded in the least. On the contrary, I was delighted.

But when we came to the colors, I started to get the feeling that his mind wasn't on it in quite the same way. It started, I think, after an accident. He'd been mixing some things over a fire and there was a bang like thunder and a great spurt of flame — nobody was hurt, luckily, no real harm done, though obviously we were all shaken. At first I thought it was preying on his mind, which was why he seemed so preoccupied all the time. But it wasn't that. If he was worrying about the same thing happening again, afraid he'd get hurt, you'd have expected him to have lost his enthusiasm. But it was the other way about. If anything, he was keener — dedicated, single-minded, almost obsessive — but not in the same way. He went quiet. There were days he'd hardly speak to us, which was pretty unusual. He'd be all day mixing things and boiling things up in big iron kettles, but nothing ever seemed to come of it, and when I asked him how he was getting on, he'd be evasive, guilty almost, like he was doing something wrong. All I could think of was that he'd figured out how to do the colors but didn't want to share with us — which didn't make sense, because even if he'd got the colors, they were no good to him without the clay, and I owned that, it was my name in the lease, so he couldn't go behind my back or anything like that. Even so, it made me suspicious and edgy. My son picked up on the changed atmosphere, and the fact that we weren't making any progress. Pretty soon we were all snapping at each other, quarreling over stupid little things, taking offense and getting on each other's nerves. It was pretty miserable for a week or so; and it didn't help that we were all living on top of each other. It was winter, desperately cold outside. We always get snow earlier than most places, and that year it was particularly bad. You didn't go outside unless you had to, and you tried to stay close to the fire. But Daurenja always had something heating or simmering; he yelled at us if we got close to his stuff, we'd yell back that we were cold, he'd fly into a temper — I suppose I should've been trying to keep the peace, but I was cold and fed up too, so I didn't make the effort. What made it so bad was the feeling that we were so close to finishing. I kept telling myself it wouldn't be for very long, and then somehow we'd be rid of him. We'd start production, there'd be money rolling in, and either he'd move on or we would. I made myself put up

with the anger and bad feeling, because I was sure it was only for
a little while longer. Also, by then I was sure Daurenja had given
up working on the colors, and I knew that without him I wouldn't
be able to solve the problem on my own. I needed him but he
wasn't trying. That just made me angry. But I didn't say anything
or ask him straight out. I went on my own slow, painstaking, futile
way — following the book, trial and error, getting nowhere at all.
My son and daughter had precious little to do except sit around
shivering in the cold, because Daurenja wouldn't let them get near
the fire. I don't suppose that helped, exactly.

It was the end of one of those days. Because it was so cold, we'd
taken to sleeping in the workshop, so we wouldn't have to cross
the yard to the house. I had my pillow and blankets at the far end,
next to a little charcoal stove that Daurenja used for his work. He
slept the other end, by the fire. My son and daughter usually went
up into the old hayloft, but it was getting colder, so they'd come
down to be closer to the fire. Anyway, that night I was worn out,
I'd been splitting and stacking logs for most of the afternoon; I lay
down and went straight to sleep.

I was woken up by a scream. I was on my feet before I was
awake, if you see what I mean; I think I'd assumed the roof had
caught fire, or something like that. It was dark, of course, apart
from the glow from the fire. I couldn't see anything unusual; I
think I called out, asked what the matter was, but nobody answered me. I started forward, walked into the corner of the bench;
and then someone charged into me and knocked me off my feet.
I went down, got my hand trodden on; I yelled, and then I heard
the door-latch clatter.

I couldn't make out what was happening. I started calling out
names, but nobody replied; so I fumbled around till I found the
lamp and the tinderbox. Obviously, lighting a lamp by feel in the
dark takes a fair bit of time, and while I was doing it I was calling
out, wondering why the hell nobody was answering. The stupid
tinder wouldn't catch, damp or something. In the end I gave up
and followed the edge of the bench up toward the fire, where there

was light to see by. About halfway — I put my hand on the bench vise, which told me where I was — I tripped on something that shouldn't have been there and went sprawling again. It felt like something in a sack. I got up and carried on to the fire, where I saw Mahaud.

She was lying by the hearth; on her back, but wide awake, both eyes open, with her dress up around her waist. I shouted to her but she didn't move at all. I thought she was dead for a moment, but then she blinked. I yelled for Framea, but I guess I'd already figured out what had happened; without putting it into words or anything, just the shape of an idea in my mind.

I got a taper lit and then a couple of lamps. I knew as I was doing it that I was taking my time, as though I was putting off the moment when I'd be able to see and my guess would be proved right. Framea, my son, was lying face down. When I turned him over, I found the little hook-bladed knife. I think it was Daurenja's originally, but we all used it for all kinds of things. He'd been slashed from the collarbone diagonally up to his right ear. Everything was sodden with blood; he'd been lying in a black sticky pool of it, and his shirt and hair were soaked. There was blood on the surface of his eyes, would you believe; actually on the whites of them. I suppose that meant he died immediately, without even a chance to close his eyes instinctively. That sort of thing's supposed to be a comfort — it was so quick he can't have felt anything. I can't say it's ever made me feel better.

I'm ashamed to say I dropped him; he flumped down like a sack, I heard the thump as his head hit the floorboards. The feel of his blood all over my hands was disgusting; I stood there with my hands in the air so I wouldn't touch anything, get blood everywhere. I couldn't think at all. It was as though what I was seeing was too big to fit inside my head. I'd clean forgotten about Mahaud, Daurenja, anything that might have happened. I wasn't even looking at Framea; all I could see was death, in all its revolting enormity. I wasn't angry or afraid or horrified or grief-stricken — I'd not really grasped the fact that the dead thing on the ground there was my son. Could've been a stranger, and I think I'd have reacted the same way. It was as though death was some kind of religious faith that I'd always been skeptical about, and suddenly I believed in it, for the first time. Death existed, it was real, and that realization was so big it forced everything else out of me.

I can't remember snapping out of it, but obviously I must've done. I can remember standing there, trying to decide what to do next: go to my daughter, or run outside and try and catch Daurenja before he got away. I simply couldn't make up my mind. I stood there like an idiot, jammed like a bit of seized machinery. In the end, I made my decision. It was like I heard a little voice in my head, infuriatingly calm, telling me it was dark and freezing cold outside, so it'd be more sensible to do the indoor job. Ridiculous reason for making a choice like that, but there had to be something to break the jam, start my mechanism going again.

I tried to wake her up, but of course she wasn't asleep. I shouted, I tried shaking her, but it didn't make any difference. Her body moved when I shook her, but her eyes stayed wide open and fixed. Even when I stared directly into them, I knew she wasn't looking at me. It was as though I was invisible, like a ghost. But I kept trying to make her hear me or see me, over and over again. I was still trying when the dawn came. I only noticed because the fire had burned out and it was starting to get cold; that made me realize there was daylight coming in through the open door, because I could see even though the fire and the lamps had gone out.

Around the middle of the afternoon I couldn't bear it anymore. I went outside — I was shaking all over from the cold, but putting a coat on was just too much trouble. Snow was falling, so his tracks were nearly covered. All the horses were still there. As far as I could tell, he hadn't taken anything at all. I told myself he'd surely freeze to death, in that weather, on foot without a coat or a blanket. I knew I was supposed to want justice or revenge or whatever you like to call it, but the fact is, I couldn't make myself feel even slightly interested in Daurenja, not right then.

I lit a fire that evening, mostly because I realized she'd die of cold if I didn't. I sat up all night just looking at her. I know I didn't sleep at all. I wanted to look away, but I simply couldn't take my eyes off her face. I got all the blankets and coats and sheets and piled them up on top of her. I was so cold I couldn't feel my hands or feet, even with the fire banked right up, but that didn't seem even remotely important. The next morning I carried Framea out to the woodshed. I put him over my shoulder — the blood was drying but still tacky — and when I got him there I laid him down on the ground, like he was some piece of cargo, and shut the door. I had no feelings about his body other than what was left of that initial disgust. When I got back I took off the shirt I was wearing, so I wouldn't have to feel the blood soaking through it. I sat there bare-chested in the freezing cold, and couldn't be bothered to put any clothes on.

The next day I realized I had to make some sort of effort to feed her. I made porridge in a big old iron pot, and stuffed it down her throat with a wooden spoon. Several times I was sure she was going to choke rather than swallow. It was three days before she moved, even; she was lying in her own piss and shit, dried porridge crusted all over her face, and her hair on the left side singed from the heat of the fire. All I'd done was keep her alive, just about. I was so weak I kept falling over, but it was a while before I realized it'd be a good idea if I ate something too. I hadn't noticed feeling hungry. I think I drank some water, but I don't remember doing it.

Well, it got better eventually. One day she got up off the floor, crawled to the wall and slumped against it. A day or so later, I came back from getting in logs to find her sweeping the floor. That's all she did for a long time: cleaning, tidying, housework. Ridiculous; but I just left her to it. I didn't even try talking to her. She got down on her hands and knees and scrubbed all the blood-stains away with a bucket of water and a bit of rag.

The food ran out. I didn't want to leave her, but I had to go. I took the cart and went out to the nearest farm; I knew I could get there and back in a day. It was dark when I got home, and when

I came through the door she asked me where I'd been. I told her. We didn't talk anymore that night. She's never said what happened; at least, not to me. But I found a piece of paper; she wrote it all down, about four sentences. Just the facts.

I know what she wrote is true, by the way. It was the cut that proved it; the fact that it ran from right to left. Framea and my daughter are right-handed, like me; we all are, in our family. But Daurenja's left-handed — at least, he favors the left hand, though he's practically ambidextrous. They say it's a sign of great intelligence, don't they?

22

"Quite right," a voice said behind them. "Or that's what I've always told myself."

Daurenja was awake. He'd tried to wriggle himself into a tolerable sitting position, but instead had flopped over on his side, so that he seemed as though he was talking to the ground. The gag, which he'd somehow contrived to work loose, hung round his neck like a stockman's muffler, and he looked like a clown; but Miel had to grab hold of Framain's arm to stop him charging over and beating him unconscious.

"My father didn't like me being left-handed," Daurenja went on conversationally. "He thought it was some kind of defect. I got tired of getting bashed every time I picked up a spoon, so I learned how to use my right hand too. I think he did me a favor. Having to do everything cack-handed all those years taught me dexterity."

Miel couldn't look at him; he was too busy restraining Framain. "Is it true?" he asked. "What he just . . . ?"

"Every word." Nothing in his tone of voice except whole-hearted corroboration. "The boy caught me raping his sister. I was holding the knife to her throat so she'd stay quiet; it was bad luck he woke up when he did. I jumped up and swiped at him; like a fool, I'd forgotten I still had the knife in my hand. But that's not an excuse. If I hadn't been holding it, I expect I'd have killed him bare-handed."

Miel hesitated, then asked, "Why?"

"Why kill him? To shorten the odds." An explanation of the obvious to a slow-witted person. "I had to escape. I knew I could handle either of the men on his own, but both together might've been a problem. One from two leaves one. A great strength of mine is the ability to see straight to the crux of the problem."

Miel could feel Framain's grip tighten on his arm, but now he was holding him up rather than back.

"If you meant to ask, why did I rape the girl . . ." A laugh, dry as sand. "Story of my life, really. Just when I think I've found the right place to be, the right work to do, my heart lets me down. Always the same. Love has always been my undoing."

Miel glanced over his shoulder. She wasn't there.

Framain caught his eye and shook his head. "She'll be all right," he said. "Just leave her alone."

It occurred to Miel that this probably wasn't true, but he made a conscious decision not to do anything about it.

"We need him to get us to the Vadani," Framain said quietly. Miel assumed he was talking to himself.

"That's right," Daurenja said. "You need me. For which," he added, "I'm grateful. I've got no illusions about myself, there's an unpleasant side to my nature and I can't help it. But I always find a way to put things right. It's my rule that I live by. Mostly, all I can do is send money; which is fine when you're dealing with peasants and innkeepers, but this time I wanted to go that extra step further. That's why it's taken me so long, in your case. It's taken me a while to find something valuable enough to give you." He sounded like an indulgent uncle. "As soon as I got it, I came here as fast as I could. You being captured by the Mezentines was sheer luck; it meant I could save you; added bonus. I went to the house, you see, and as soon as I got there and saw the place had been turned over I figured out what'd happened. It was obvious they'd bring you to the Loyalty. Anyway, it'll be a weight off my mind. All this time it's been bothering me to death. Really, I had no choice about killing the boy; it had to be done, but I'm sorry. Soon we'll be all square again, and I can move on."

Miel had closed his eyes for a moment. He opened them again. "We've got to take him to Duke Valens," he told Framain. "We can't just kill him, out here in the wilderness. He should be tried and executed. Killing him ourselves would be no better than murder, it's what he'd do. You do see that, don't you?"

"If they were going to kill me, they'd have done it by now." Daurenja sounded weary, almost bored. "But if you take me to the Vadani, I can put things right. That's all I ask."

"I'll gag him," Miel said.

"Wait a moment." Framain sounded different. "What do you mean, you've found something valuable?"

"Just that." A pleasant voice. "Surely you've grasped by now, the porcelain idea's no good anymore, it's been overtaken by events. Even if we cracked the colors problem tomorrow, we couldn't use it. You can't run a successful factory in the middle of a war, in occupied territory, with the enemy promising to kill every Eremian they can find. No, what I've got is bigger than porcelain, and it couldn't have come at a better time. Valens will give every last thaler he's got for it; and if that's not enough, we can sell it to the Mezentines. It's a weapon, you see. It'll make all their scorpions and mangonels and onagers and siege engines obsolete overnight. There's just one step more I need to fix and I'm ready. We'll be partners again, just like before. Finally, we'll both get what we wanted when we started out. Come on, Framain, you know me. I do a lot of very bad things from time to time, but I'm not a liar. I needn't have come for you at all. I could've left you there. But you know I always pay my debts." Daurenja paused for a moment, and Miel couldn't help marveling at the spectacle: a man bound and hobbled like a colt for gelding, talking to the ground, but sounding like a kind-hearted lord cajoling a proud, stubborn tenant into accepting charity. He could see now how a weak man like Framain wouldn't have the audacity to kill him. "Or you could cut my throat right now," Daurenja went on, "and for all I know you might make it safely into Vadani territory; you might find Valens' column, and he might take you in. He might even let you earn your keep as a clerk; you can write legibly, after all, and where there's an army there's always bookkeepers. Or you could join the Vadani court as my honored guest. Did I mention I'm the second most important man in the duchy these days? Well, maybe third most important right now. But I'm expecting a promotion very soon." He sighed. "You owe it to her, you know," he said. "She deserves some kind of a life, and what's she got to look forward to, now the porcelain idea's fallen through? She's too old to marry, no dowry, no family. Wasn't the whole point of the exercise to give her the kind of future she deserves? I know you by now, Framain, you're a dreamer and a realist at the same time. Nothing's going to bring your son back, but quite unexpectedly you've got a real chance to get what you wanted all along. Or you could kill me in a fit of pique and carry on fending for yourself. But that's never been your strongest suit, has it?"

Framain was silent for a long time. When he eventually spoke, he said, "Tell me about this weapon."

Daurenja laughed. "With pleasure. It'll be a simple thing, like an iron log with a hole down the middle, but it'll smash down walls and kill men by the thousand; oh, and an idiot or a cripple could work it just as well as the strongest man alive. I'm an engineer; I'm the best there is, it's a gift I was born with. I'm a genius maker-of-things who's spent his life looking for something worth making. When I've finished, it'll be *perfect*. Everybody in the world will want it, more than anything else; more than love. And I risked my life to find you and beg you to accept a half-share in it, as a gift. Just for once, Framain, do something intelligent."

Before Miel could react, Framain had jumped to his feet. As he marched across the hollow he stooped to pick something up — a stone, presumably, there wasn't anything else it could be. He crouched, swung his arm and bashed the side of Daurenja's head; there was a solid noise, like a maul striking an oak wedge.

"I hate the sound of his voice," Framain said distantly. "Could you possibly find me a bit of rag? I'm going to gag him properly this time."

Miel looked but couldn't find anything. Framain got impatient; he tore another strip off Daurenja's shirt and used that.

"What are you going to do?" Miel asked quietly.

Framain sagged, like a man who's just put down a load that was too heavy for him to carry. "He'll take us to the Vadani," he said.

"Do you believe what he said? About this weapon?"

"Yes." Slowly, Framain sat down again. "Yes, it makes a lot of sense, actually. I think I told you how preoccupied he was, for a while before it happened. I had an idea his mind was on something else. Presumably, this weapon of his."

"And you think he'll share it with you?"

Framain nodded. "I believe the offer's genuine. That's quite in character. He thinks people are like machines. If they break down, they can be fixed." He sighed. "If he's taught me one thing, it's that there's no such thing as evil." He laughed. "Doesn't that seem like an odd conclusion to draw, from my dealings with something like *that?* But it's true, I'm sure of it. What I mean is, it's possible for someone to do the sort of things he's done and still regard himself as a more or less normal human being; he thinks to himself, I've done something wrong, but it's fine, I can put it right. If there really was such a thing as evil, he couldn't think like that. No, it's not that easy — some people are monsters, they're evil through and through; you tell yourself that so you can make sense of the world. It's like believing in a religion, a god and a devil, all good on one side, all bad on the other. But that's not how it is. Instead, you've got people who are capable of doing things that you can't even bear to think about; for bloody certain you can't ever forgive them. But they can still feel guilt and shame, they can still fall in love, try and do the right thing, appreciate what the right thing is — and then they cheerfully go and do the next unbelievably bad thing, and it all goes round again. So you tell yourself, it's because they're not right in the head, it's an illness, they aren't in control of what they do. That's another easy way round it, and of course it isn't true. And then you get people like me; and people like you, as well. It should be up to us to kill men like him on sight, like wolves, but we don't. We talk ourselves into believing that it'd be wrong, which is just that same old belief again, an excuse for not facing something we can't understand. I don't know," he added, slumping forward. "You heard what he said? My heart lets me down, love's always been my undoing. I knew he was in love with her — you can call it obsessed or besotted if you like, but that's just flavors of words. I'd been aware of it for some time. I knew she'd never have anything to do with him, because of how he looks, because he's a freak. I thought sooner or later he'd say something and she'd bite his head off; I was worried his work would suffer, or he'd up and leave, and I needed him to mix the colors for the porcelain. I didn't realize I was supposed to kill him, murder him in his sleep or put mercury in his beer, because if I let him live something terrible would happen." He was crouched forward, his head in his hands. "And when you came, it was just the same. When you came back with the sulfur, because of her; I should've smashed your head in with a hammer, instead of pulling you out of the bog. You've done almost as much harm as he did, and all for love. What am I supposed to do, sit up on the roof with a bow and arrow and shoot everybody who comes within bowshot? All I ever wanted was to have some money, like I was born to."

Miel thought for a long time. "Seems like you might get it after all."

Framain laughed again; practically a sob. "That's why I maintain there's no evil," he said. "Because I'm not an evil monster, am I? But I'm no different to him. I'm going to take his offer, because — well, like he said, my son's dead, that can't be helped now, and I do want the money."

In order to earn his commission in the Duke's household cavalry, Nennius Nennianus had mortgaged the sixty-seven acres of apple and pear orchards his dead uncle had left him, spent nine years as a garrison lieutenant in the coldest, remotest station on the frontier and done nothing while his childhood sweetheart despaired of waiting for him and married a middle-aged lumber contractor. Three months after achieving his lifelong ambition, he found himself in charge of, responsible for and to blame for a scene from any officer's nightmare: a column of wagons with their wheels off and their guts hanging out, stranded in plain view on a hillside with the enemy expected any moment.

The problem was his training. Nine years on the frontier had taught him how to deploy soldiers as easily as he moved his own fingers, but nothing he'd learned in theory or from bitter experience had prepared him for dealing with carpenters. Plead with them; they assume you're weak. Yell at them; they look shocked and walk away. Can't bribe them; you've got nothing they want. They reminded him of the old gray sow on his uncle's farm; lure it with apples, drag on it with a rope, break sticks across its back, and all you'd do was make it more stubborn.

The chief carpenter (not that they had a coherent hierarchy or chain of command; each time he tried to talk to them, he found himself facing someone new) was explaining it to him. They'd done as the Duke ordered and cut and shaped new timbers for the knackered carts out of green wood. As they'd predicted all along, green wood simply wouldn't take the load; it splintered, or it split, or the heads of the nails pulled through. They'd wasted their time, and the carts were just as busted as they'd been when they started, if not more so. Suggestions? The carpenter paused for thought and internal debate. It might be possible to cut timbers out of half the carts and use them to bodge up the other half, but he was fairly sure it wouldn't work. He'd try it, if so ordered, but he didn't hold out much hope; and by then, of course, half the carts would be fucked up beyond all possibility of salvage. Other than that, he had nothing constructive to offer.

There must be something you can do. Nennius considered saying it, but decided to save his breath. Instead, he thanked the carpenter with the stately politeness peculiar to soldiers talking to thoroughly obnoxious civilians, and walked away before he lost his temper completely.

Sitting on a stone, staring up at the crest of the mountain ridge where the enemy would be most likely to come from, he tried to figure out where he'd gone wrong and was forced to the conclusion that he hadn't. He found the thought profoundly disturbing. An error on his part could probably be put right — if not by him, by someone cleverer and more capable. An impossible situation, on the other hand, was beyond fixing, therefore desperate and quite likely fatal. The infuriating thing was that on the frontier, he'd have known exactly what to do next. Fall the men in, load as much as they could carry on their backs and start walking to wherever it was they were supposed to go to. The only sensible course; but that wasn't what he'd been told to do. His orders were simple and clear; as soon as the wagons have been mended, bring them on and catch us up. It was like being thrown in the sea with weights tied to your feet, with orders to save yourself but on no account to swim.

Below in the valley, he could just make out a group of deer, coming down out of a small copse to drink in the river. Eight hundred yards? Nine? Not so easy to judge distance in this terrain. Visibility, on the other hand, wasn't a problem. He could see, and be seen, for miles. He felt an obligation to be busy with something military; he should be scanning the slopes above him, figuring out the route the attacking enemy would be most likely to take, planning the details of his hopeless, pointless final defense. Manhandle the derelict wagons into the shuttered-square formation he'd been told about in the briefing, to force the enemy to storm an iron-plated fortress under withering volleys from the archers. He could do that. If he fought the defense with determination, ingenuity and passion, he could probably hold out for two days, by which time the water would run out and make his efforts irrelevant. There was a riverful of water in the valley, but he only had a finite quantity of barrels. Then again, a skillful negotiator could wrangle favorable terms of surrender, if he wasn't facing an enemy you couldn't trust as far as you could spit. On the frontier he'd have made the effort. Here, he simply couldn't see the point.

Suddenly, he realized that four dots he'd been staring at for the last five minutes were, in fact, moving. They were coming down the slope — not following his projected optimum route, but maybe they weren't as good at tactics as he was — eleven or maybe twelve hundred yards away. Deer; no, because deer saunter. Only horses plod.

Having perceived the enemy approach, proceed immediately to place your command in a posture of defense. He stood up (his back twinged from careless sitting) and looked around. A few of the men had seen the specks already; they were motionless and staring, as though they'd heard tales about horses but never imagined they'd actually get to see one. The rest of them were drifting slowly through the motions of their appointed futile tasks, resigned, bored and deep-down convinced that the enemy wouldn't come and they'd all get out of this mess in one piece. Maybe they aren't the enemy after all, Nennius told himself. They could just be travelers (in a war zone, in the middle of nowhere), or shepherds, or messengers from Valens come to tell him that the rest of the army had just won an overwhelming victory, and the war was over.

Maybe. He called over a sergeant and told him to take a dozen men and either bring the four mystery horsemen in or drive them away. The sergeant set off looking like a man who's just been ordered to jump into a volcano, and came back remarkably soon afterward, nervously escorting three men and a woman. They were riding horses with Mezentine-issue saddles, but they were pale-skinned and dressed in dirty civilian clothes. One of them was tied up so securely he could barely move, and Nennius realized, in a moment of agonizing hope, that he recognized him.

"For crying out loud get that man untied and over here," he shouted. One of the other prisoners was yelling something, but it couldn't be important. The sergeant hauled the trussed-up man off his horse and got busy with a knife.

"You're that engineer," Nennius said, before the gag was out of the man's mouth. "The Mezentine's sidekick."

The sergeant loosened the gag, and the strange-looking man flexed his jaw a few times before saying, "Gace Daurenja. And yes, I work for Ziani Vaatzes."

Hope is really just a variety of fear, all the more painful because it twitches a chance of escape in front of your nose as it slides by. "We've got a problem," Nennius said breathlessly, "with the carts. Can you fix it?"

Daurenja looked at him and blinked. "I can try," he said.

Nennius explained, the words tumbling out of his mouth. Then he said, "Well?"

Daurenja nodded. "Yes," he said, "I think I can fix that. We'll need a big, hot fire, something we can use for anvils, and five of the armor plates off the wagons. How soon . . . ?"

"Now," Nennius replied with feeling.

"All right." Daurenja seemed bizarrely calm, and for the first time it occurred to Nennius to wonder why he'd been tied up, in company with two men and a woman, in the middle of the wilderness. Wondering, however, was an inappropriate luxury, like satin cushions and goose-liver pâté. "Anvils," Daurenja prompted him.

"What? Yes, we've got anvils." Nennius looked round for someone to shout at; a sergeant, experienced in the ways of stressed-out officers, was already walking fast in the right direction. "And you want a fire."

"Charcoal," Daurenja said, stretching his fingers; cramp, presumably. "Find two large, flat stones; they'll do for a hearth." He wasn't talking to anyone in particular, but a couple of troopers set off to look for flat stones. I wish I could do that, Nennius thought; he can make people do things without rank or the chain of command, without even knowing he's doing it. A born foreman, which is just another word for officer. "I don't suppose there's such a thing as a double-action bellows anywhere."

Nennius had no idea what he was talking about, but someone else — one of the farriers, he remembered — had dropped into motion, like some mechanical component. Daurenja yawned and wriggled his back. "The first thing I'll need to do is make up the mandrels, so I'll want three strong men with sledgehammers to strike for me." (They materialized out of the crowd of soldiers, which had been clotting around him since he'd started to speak; he drew assistants to him like a magnet draws filings.) "What've we got in the way of wrought-iron stock?"

There's something wonderful about handing over a burden of worry; a glorious relief, like shedding chains. The process didn't take very long and it was delightfully smooth. Half an hour later, as the bellows blew tongues of flame up through the mounded charcoal and Daurenja touched a pair of calipers to a spare cart-axle and nodded his approval, Nennius realized that this strange man, this freak who'd just ridden in bound hand and foot, was now in complete command of the column, and he was overwhelmed with the sudden dissipation of anxiety. Relieved of command; exactly that.

"What I'm doing," Daurenja was telling the world in a calm, splendid voice, "is making an iron bar exactly the same size as the timber we've got to fix. Then we're going to cut strips off a sheet of the armor plate, get them good and hot so they'll work easily, and fold them round three sides of the bar to form a sort of jacket, if you see what I mean. That'll hold the timber together on three sides, and the armor plate'll brace the fourth side; then, even if the timber breaks, it can't go anywhere." He lifted his head and smiled. "A bit of a sledgehammer to crack a nut, but it'll get the job done. Once we've got going, assuming we keep at it nice and steady, we should be ready to move out this time tomorrow." He turned his head and looked at Nennius. "Will that be soon enough? What's the tactical position? I'm assuming the threat's coming from the garrison at the inn on Sharra."

"That's right," Nennius said.

Daurenja nodded. "In that case it's not so bad," he said. "I've just come from there. I didn't have a chance to count heads or anything, but there're not enough of them to mount a serious attack in force. If they want to take us, they'll have to get help from the next post down the line. Mind you," he added with a slight frown, "there's a good chance they'll have scouts out; looking for me, actually, sorry about that. But, all things being equal, we should be well out of here by the time they're in any position to bother us."

Which reminded him. "Those people you came in with," Nennius started to say.

"My guests," Daurenja said firmly, and his authority was beyond question as the glowing charcoal flared to the bellows. "Please make sure they're looked after properly; they've had a pretty rough time. I'd appreciate it if you'd see to it yourself."

(But they had you all tied up, like a dangerous criminal.) "Of course," Nennius said.

"I imagine they'll be staying with us," Daurenja went on, scrutinizing the fire, "but if they want to move on, perhaps you could let them have fresh horses and supplies, anything they want. They're my friends," he added with quiet emphasis, "so I'd be grateful if you could . . ."

"Right away." Nennius had to make a conscious effort not to salute. "Is there anything else you need here?"

Pointless question, like telling a man in his own house to make himself at home. "No thank you," Daurenja replied gravely. "I think I can manage for now. I'll let you know how we get on."

In other words, dismissed. Nennius dipped his head in the approved manner, and turned his back. As he walked briskly away, the first blows of a hammer chimed behind him like a wedding bell.

They'd put the three of them (only now he had to think of them as the honored guests) in a tent; sat on the ground, with a guard outside. Nennius winced: time for diplomacy. "It's all right," he snapped at the guard, who made himself scarce. At least they hadn't been tied up. He shouldered through the tent flap and smiled.

"Have you had anything to eat?" he said.

All three of them looked at him as if he was mad. Then the older of the two men said, "We want to see the officer in charge."

Nennius broadened his smile. It felt uncomfortable on his face, like an ill-fitting boot galling his heel. "That's me," he said. "Can I get you anything?"

"That man, the one we brought in —"

"Daurenja," Nennius said. It seemed important to show that he knew the name.

"He's a murderer," the man said. "You've got to put him under arrest until we can get him before a court."

On balance, Nennius would have preferred it if the man had punched him in the face. The dazed, wretched feeling would've been the same, and it'd have been over quickly. "I'm sorry," he heard himself say. "I don't —"

"He murdered my son," the man went on. "He's admitted it, in front of a witness. Presumably you can deal with it yourself, if you're the commanding officer. I'm not quite sure about how the jurisdictions would work out, but in the circumstances —"

"I'm sorry." An understatement. "I can't do that. You see —"

The older man tried to jump up; the younger one grabbed his arm and yanked him back, not gently. "Don't give me that," the older man said. "He's —"

"It's all right," the younger one interrupted. Clearly the wrong thing to say.

"He killed my son and raped my daughter." A loud, clear voice; probably they could hear him right across the camp, even in spite of the hammering. "He's admitted it. I want him tried and hanged."

"That's not possible."

"Don't be ridiculous. Look, if you don't believe me —"

"It's true," the other man said. The woman had her head turned away, fastidiously, as though ignoring a couple of drunks. "My name's Miel Ducas. I heard him confess."

Miel Ducas; wasn't he a guerrilla leader? Unimportant. Nennius couldn't spare any mental capacity for heroes of the Eremian resistance; he'd just thought of something. "Daurenja's one of the Duke's engineers, he answers directly to Valens. I haven't got any authority."

For a moment, the older man's anger seemed to hover in the air like a falcon; then it slumped into the most ferocious resentment

Nennius could ever remember witnessing. "Where is the Duke?" he asked quietly. "We'll have to take Daurenja to him."

Which meant the moment had passed. "We'll be joining up with him," Nennius said, "as soon as this column is mobile again. We've had to stop to repair the carts." He took a deep breath. "I'll make sure Daurenja doesn't leave the column until we meet up with Valens' party. I'm afraid that's all I can do."

"We understand." Ducas, trying to keep the peace, the way well-meaning idiots do. "Thank you. But it really is very important." Now he's going to try and change the subject. "Can you tell us what's going on here, please?"

Nennius explained as succinctly as he could manage while being silently hated to death by the other man; then he summoned a young ensign who had the misfortune to be too close, left him in charge of looking after the guests, and escaped. Outside, he stood for a moment and listened to the ringing of hammers. So simple; wrap a bit of iron round it; so obvious. Of course, it would never have occurred to the carpenters, and it definitely hadn't occurred to him, or anybody else for that matter. As for Daurenja being a rapist and a murderer; well, Nennius had no problem at all believing that. The appalling thing was, he really couldn't care less, so long as the carts got fixed. That, he decided, was why countries had to have dukes and kings and governments; someone who could pin a medal on a man like that for saving the column, and then string him up as a criminal.

In spite of the hammering from the night shift, he slept well, and an ensign had to shake him awake in the morning, to tell him that the work had been finished well ahead of schedule, and the carters were backing the horses into the shafts, ready to start. Meanwhile, the three guests who'd come in with the engineer had apparently found a notary and sworn out depositions about something or other. They'd insisted that he should have them as soon as he woke up, and since he'd given orders that they should have anything they wanted . . .

Well. He could read them later, at some point.

The column was under way by mid-morning. Nennius sent outriders on ahead to see if they could pick up Valens' trail, or find anybody who knew which way he'd gone. *Catch us up* had been all very well when he was convinced he'd never get the carts going again; now he had a whole new set of problems to fret over. Water; food; fodder for the horses; finding the right road; making up time; fending off Mezentine sorties. It's a rule of human life that when a soldier successfully deals with an apparently insuperable difficulty, he gets rewarded with something twice as bad. The new concerns kept him happily occupied for the rest of the morning, and at noon he halted the column to see how the repairs were holding up.

"Fine," Daurenja announced, crawling out from under a cart. His back and sleeves were white with dust, but he made no effort to brush himself off. "Don't look as though they've shifted at all. Provided we take it reasonably steady, we shouldn't have any bother."

Not quite what he wanted to hear. "When you say reasonably steady . . ."

Daurenja thought for a moment. "Brisk walking pace," he said. "You don't want to go any faster than that on these roads, even if the carts were new from the workshop." He pulled a face. "I know you want to make up time and join up with the Duke, but we've got to be realistic. Leave it to the outriders to catch him up and tell him to wait for us. If you push the pace and bust up the carts, we'll never get there." He looked away, and added: "How are my friends getting along? I haven't seen them."

"Fine," Nennius replied awkwardly. "I shifted some people around so they could have a wagon to themselves, and I've seen to it they've all got fresh clothes and plenty to eat." He hesitated. Did Daurenja know about the sworn depositions? Probably. Since he'd mended the wagons, he had become the hero of the column, the man who'd saved the day. Whoever gave the order to place him under arrest wouldn't be popular with the troops. As for his accusers, they weren't even Vadani. Miel Ducas he'd heard of, vaguely; the other two — had he been told their names? If so, he'd forgotten them. He'd assumed they were telling the truth, mostly because of Daurenja's unfortunate appearance; he looked like someone who was capable of rape and murder, but that was sheer unfounded prejudice. For all Nennius knew, they were compulsive liars, delusional; Mezentine agents paid to discredit the miracle-working engineer. Anybody could swear an affidavit, but what about corroborative proof? (And would he be entertaining these high-minded doubts if Daurenja hadn't just saved the column?)

"That's fine," Daurenja said. "Thanks, I'm obliged to you." He smiled reassuringly. "I expect it all seems pretty odd to you, but I want you to trust me. I know who my friends are, even if they don't. It'll all smooth out, and everything'll be fine. There's nothing in it for you to worry about."

Again; *dismissed*. Nennius nodded. After all, said the quiet voice of logic in his mind, if there really was anything in their wild claims, would Daurenja be acting like this toward them, when he could have them tied up and dumped by the roadside if he wanted to? Serves me right, Nennius decided, for judging by appearances. And as soon as we meet up with the Duke, it won't be my problem anymore.

The next day and night were delightfully uneventful: no problems with the carts, no dust-cloud behind them marking the approach of a Mezentine army, and the river shown on the map was exactly where it was supposed to be, so they could fill up with enough water to last them at least three days. Food and fodder for the horses weren't yet a matter of desperate urgency, so if they could only make contact with Valens' contingent in the next forty-eight hours . . .

Which they did.

The crows had found them, and begun the long, patient work of rendering them down into raw materials. They flew off angrily as the column came over the rise, reluctantly abandoning their quarry to the superior claims of a better class of scavenger.

A quick inspection showed that the crows hadn't been the only ones who'd come there to feed. The bodies had been stripped of their clothes, weapons, boots and possessions, then stacked up in neat piles like cordwood. At first glance, the ratio of Mezentines to Vadani seemed to be something in the order of three to one. The stacks lined the road verge at intervals of roughly fifteen yards, up to the brow of the next rise and presumably over it.

Daurenja was the first to break the silence. "I'm guessing they were going to come back and bury them," he said. "It's what they usually do. Looks like something drove them off before they could get around to it."

Nennius had seen dead bodies before, of course: on the frontier, and when he'd ridden with Duke Valens to the relief of Civitas Eremiae. He was no expert, but he knew a bit about the subject: the waxy look of the skin, the degree to which the flesh had shrunk, the beginnings of a stench. A lot depended on how hot it had been, whether it had rained or not, how heavy the dew had been. An informed guess: no more than three days.

"No carts," said one of the junior officers. "But they'd have taken them along with the clothes and armor and stuff, so that's nothing to go on."

A long silence; then someone else asked, "So, do you think we won?"

"Took some of the bastards with them, at any rate," the junior officer replied. "Some of them," he repeated.

The ratio of men to women and children among the Vadani dead: maybe four to one. So far, nobody had recognized anybody they knew among the log-piles. Their faces, Nennius noticed, looked rather like apples that had been stored in the barn a little bit too long.

"I gather it's something of an industry these days, looting the dead," someone else said. "Well organized, a lot of people involved. Makes you wonder where they're planning on selling the stuff, though. I wouldn't have thought there's any customers left."

The man at Nennius' feet had a grave, wise expression on his face, spoiled rather by the damage a crow had done to his left eye. Mezentine. Cause of death a puncture wound in the chest, too big for an arrow. A horseman's lance, possibly a boar-spear with a crossbar, by the way it had caved in the ribs on its way through. "Have any of the outriders come back yet?" he asked, well aware that the answer would be no; not in the five minutes since he'd last asked the question. For all he knew, his scouts were right there, in one of the neat stacks. "Send out another dozen; and I want the looters found, they may know what happened." He paused, then added: "Bring in half a dozen. If you find any more, I don't need to know what's become of them."

Someone dismounted close by. "It carries on quite a way," he reported. "It's like this for a good half-mile up ahead, and that's as far as I went."

"Suggesting a running battle rather than an ambush," someone commented. "Which is more or less how the Duke had got it planned, isn't it?" Nobody said, *That could have been us; I'm so glad we weren't there.* No need.

Someone else joined the discussion. "Hoofprints and cart tracks," he said. "Of course they're all scraped up, and there's no way of knowing which are the looters. A lot of horses, though."

"Do you think it was the garrison from the inn?" someone asked.

"Too many for that. We were told there was only one squadron."

"That's what I saw," Daurenja said. "In which case, this must be a different unit. It'd be helpful to know which direction they came from, but I expect that's too much to ask."

"Makes you wonder how they found us," someone said. All very calm and reasonable; like men contemplating the root harvest, or the outcome of a race meeting. "Mind you, if their scouts saw us, it wouldn't take a giant leap of imagination to figure out we'd been left behind for some reason and the main body was up ahead. They'd go after the Duke first, and then come back for us."

"Assuming they've won," someone else pointed out. "We don't even know that for sure."

In the pile was a Vadani man with blood caked under his fingernails, lying on top of a Mezentine with both arms missing. *Both* arms. An arm's a bitch to cut through at the best of times, tough as dry wood and springy as willow brash. The angle needs to be just right, and even then it takes a lot of strength and an uncluttered swing. Both arms . . .

"The looters won't have gone far," the junior officer was saying. "It'll have taken them a good while to strip all this lot, then stacking the bodies; and they won't be moving too fast with so much stuff to carry. If we had any idea of which direction they went in . . ."

Intelligent questions; good, helpful, intelligent observations. We are, above all, professionals. "We can't stop to bury them," Nennius said. "I don't know whether to press on or go back. If they've won . . ."

If they've won, then it follows that we're all that's left. Suddenly, we're the sum total of the Vadani people, under the command of Captain (acting duke) Nennius Nennianus. He swung round, looking for somewhere to hide. Pointless, of course. What if the Mezentines were coming, and they really were all that was left? Would anybody survive to tell future generations that it had all been Captain Nennius' fault?

"We'd better keep going," Daurenja said quietly beside him. "If the Mezentines are on their way back to get us, they'll find us easily enough even if we turn round. If Valens is still out there, we need to join up with him as quickly as possible. We'd better get ready for a fight, though. No point in making it easy for them."

They were waiting for him to say something. "Yes," he said, "we'll do that. And I want those looters found. The sooner we find out what's happened, the sooner we'll know what we've got to do."

That seemed to be enough. Suddenly, everybody seemed to know what they were supposed to be doing (apart from himself, of course). He envied them. His life so far had hardly been easy, but its lines had been straight and its signposts legible. Apparently, a few naked dead men piled up in orderly ricks beside a road had been enough to change all that. The implication was unwelcome but perfectly clear. Up to now, he'd been missing the point entirely.

Walking back to find his horse, he ran into the Eremian: Miel Ducas, the resistance leader. His instinct was to quicken his pace and turn his head, to avoid pointless conversation. Instead, he slowed down, long enough for the Eremian to catch his eye.

"Excuse me," Ducas said. "Can you tell me what's going on?"

"There's been a battle." Not, when he thought about it, the best way of saying it. "We've found bodies; ours and theirs. It's not clear who won. We're pressing on, same plan as before."

"Oh." Ducas nodded. "Thank you," he added; reflexive politeness of the nobility, meaningless. "Is there anything I can do to help?"

"No. Thank you," Nennius added quickly. "All under control."

"Thanks to Daurenja." Ducas was looking at him as though pleading for something. "I gather he's pretty well saved you from disaster."

"Yes." Damn all monosyllables. "Yes, we'd have been sunk without him." Nennius hesitated, then made himself go on. "Is it true? What the other man said."

"I don't know," Miel replied. "But I heard him admit it. And I don't see any reason why they'd lie about something like that." Hesitation. "I can see what a difficult position it puts you in."

For some reason, Nennius found the sympathy infuriating; his own reaction surprised him. "Not at all," he said. "Like I told you before, it's not my jurisdiction. I'm not even sure the Duke's got any authority in the case, since it's crimes committed by an Eremian against Eremians in Eremia."

"He's not even Eremian," Ducas said. "Daurenja, I mean. He's Cure Doce by birth, apparently." He frowned. "So who would be the competent authority?"

"Don't ask me, I'm not a lawyer. Your own duke, I suppose. He's with the Vadani, last I heard. But it'd be complicated by the fact that Daurenja's an officer in Vadani service; you'd have to get Valens' permission to proceed against him, even if you could find the proper Eremian official to hear the case; and that's unlikely, since —"

"Since so many of the Eremians are dead now." Ducas nodded reasonably. "But in this case, I suppose the proper authority would be me. Theoretically, I mean. All that side of Eremia used to be my land, and strictly speaking Framain and his household were my tenants." Suddenly he smiled, a nervous, frightened expression. "Which makes me judge and chief prosecution witness. As though it wasn't complicated enough already. I don't suppose you're the slightest bit interested, are you?"

Nennius looked away. "I've got rather a lot to do right now," he said. "And I need Daurenja, at least until we meet up with Valens' party, assuming they're still alive. I can take formal notice of what you've just told me, but that's about it, I'm afraid. And I'd be obliged if you wouldn't make an issue out of it. At least, not till things have sorted themselves out."

"When the Mezentines have been wiped out to the last man, you mean." Ducas nodded again. "Of course. Thank you for your time. I'm sorry for wasting it." He started to walk away.

"I'll make sure Daurenja doesn't leave the column until we meet up with the others," Nennius said.

"Of course; he's a very useful man, and we owe him our lives." Ducas grinned; not the sad smile of a moment ago. "Pity, that. If he could just desert and go away, it'd make life so much easier. I'll do what I can to keep Framain from cutting his throat in the night."

Nennius' horse wasn't where he'd left it. Someone had moved it, no doubt trying to be helpful. He stood completely still for several minutes, entirely unable to decide what to do. Then they found him again.

There had been, they told him, a development. Come with us, we'll show you.

It turned out to be just another stack of dead people, naked and cut about. "Pure fluke," some excitable young officer was saying.

"Someone happened to barge into this pile with a cart, and I was at the wedding, I saw her quite close up, so I recognized her. And then I saw him, too." He was standing over two bodies that had been separated from the others; he looked like a dog standing over a toy it wants you to play with. Such cheerful enthusiasm.

Nennius looked at the bodies. A man he recognized; a strange-looking young woman. She'd been hit with a spear through the ribs; her head had been half split, like a stringy log with a knot in it.

"That's General Mezentius," Nennius said. "Who's she?"

Don't you know? the young officer's face was shouting. "That's the Duchess," he said. "Valens' wife."

23

And again.

As his fingers took the strain of the bowstring, he realized from the pain that something was wrong with them. He glanced down and saw that the skin on either side of the middle joints of his first two fingers had been blistered and rasped away. He pushed the bow away from him with his left arm, hauled the string back with his right until his thumb knuckle brushed the corner of his mouth. The bow was fighting him now, like a panicked animal on a tether. Down the shaft, on the point of the arrowhead, he saw his target (impossible to think of it as a living thing, let alone a human being. His instructor had told him that, years ago: shoot at a deer and you'll miss; shoot at the sweet spot behind the shoulder, size of a man's hand, and you'll have no problem). As the string began to pull through his fingers, he raised his left arm a little for elevation and windage. At just the right moment, the arrow broke free, lifted as the air took the vanes of the fletchings, peaked and swooped like a hawk. He watched it into the target, heard the strike. A straightforward heart-and-lungs placement; he was still moving, but already dead. Valens pinched the nock of another arrow between thumb and forefinger and drew it from the quiver. And again.

Only three arrows left in the quiver now. A minute or so since he'd refilled it, frantically scrabbling arrows out of the open barrel while keeping his eye fixed on the next target. Good archers only count the misses; he'd missed four times today. The stupid, stupid thing was that he liked archery, it was one of the few things he actually enjoyed doing (and so, of course, never had time for). Every stage of it soothed and pleased him; the smooth softness of putting the doeskin glove on his right hand, the expression of strength in the draw, the instinctive precision of the aim, the complete concentration, the fine judgment of tremendous forces poised in a moment of stillness, the visceral joy of the loose, the beauty of the arrow's parabola, the solid pride of a well-placed hit. Using this precious, delightful skill to kill people was obscene. Using it to defend himself and his people from extinction was simply ridiculous, like dancing or flirting for your life.

And again. A Mezentine had managed to scramble up the side of one of the iron plates; he'd lost his momentum and was hanging from the top edge by his fingertips, his feet scrabbling wildly for an impossible foothold on the smooth, flat surface. Valens watched him for a moment; he was trying so hard, he'd done so well to get that far when all the others had failed; he wanted him to succeed, simply out of admiration for his courage and agility. The Mezentine got the sole of his foot flat on the plate and boosted himself up, an astonishing effort; he'd got his upper body up onto the edge and was using his weight to balance. He'd made it; so Valens shot him. He slithered back down the way he'd come and pitched in a slovenly heap of limbs on the ground. The cartwheel rolled over his head, crushing it into a mash.

As Valens nocked the next arrow, he spared a moment to glance into the barrel. Empty.

He hesitated. Vaatzes' wonderful strategy of moving fortresses was posited on the assumption that the arrows wouldn't run out. But they'd been shooting for two days and a night, and their splendid supply of ammunition was strewn out behind them like litter on the road; no chance to go back and pull arrows out of the dead. Two more shots and that was that.

Where the hell were all these Mezentines coming from? It was like rooks or pigeons over decoys, on a really good day, when they never stop coming in. He'd had days like that; they seemed to materialize in midair, as if they generated spontaneously somewhere in the distance. It wasn't supposed to be like this. Vaatzes had been thinking in terms of occasional running battles with maybe two or three squadrons at a time, not a whole division, or two divisions; hundreds, not thousands. He realized he was drawing and aiming at a Mezentine riding parallel to his wagon. Only two shots left; he made his arms relax.

Out of the corner of his eye, he noticed that the cart that had been there all morning had disappeared, at some point, when he wasn't watching. Another one; he'd tried to keep a count at first but he'd lost track. A dozen, maybe, that the enemy had managed to stop and overwhelm (a dozen that he could see from where he was). The losses hadn't registered with him any more than the kills had done. Quite simply, he was worn out, like the deer that stops because it can't run anymore.

Well: if they were out of arrows, two shots wouldn't make any difference one way or another. He nocked, found a target and loosed. At ten yards, you'd be hard put to it to miss. One left, and then the Mezentines could swarm all over the carts like flies on cowshit for all he could do about it. Relieved of duty on grounds of exhaustion.

He scanned for a target. A Mezentine captain, standing up in his stirrups and shouting orders; a sitter, too easy if this was pleasure rather than business. Since it was the last shot, he allowed himself a little indulgence, and shot him through his open mouth.

And that was that. He unstrung his bow before putting it down, since keeping a bow strung when not in use ruins it. He'd die and be discarded as perishable and useless, but the bow was a very good one, valuable. It'd bring the looters a good price and serve its next owner well, if properly looked after. Then, wearily (let's go through the motions and get it over with), he dragged his sword out of the scabbard. It was the hanger he'd been given by the grateful trader, in commemoration of that skirmish whose name he'd forgotten. If there was any poetic justice in the world, he'd bear it to victory through extraordinary feats of courage and slaughter. Unlikely.

He stood up, wavered a little until he found his balance, and looked around. He wasn't the only one who'd run out of arrows. The carts all around him were heaving with Mezentines, like maggots in spoiled meat. Without the arrows to keep them off, they were having no trouble blocking and stopping the wagons, pulling down the drivers and fighters. He turned his head, and realized with a spurt of cold terror that the cart had stopped and he was alone on it — a moment ago there'd been a driver and two other archers, but either they'd been killed or they'd jumped down and run away. He felt disappointed. Somehow he'd never imagined himself dying alone, among strangers.

There was a hand on the top edge of the iron plate; four fingers, like worms or grubs. The instinct that moved him to slash at them was disgust, something like a fear of spiders or slugs. He chopped the fingers off, and felt his blade jar on the iron plate. There goes the cutting edge, he thought; oh well. Next came a head and shoulders. He saw a pair of wide-open eyes staring at him in horror; he misjudged the swing a little and sliced off just the scalp, like taking the top off a boiled egg. Enough to make whoever it was lose his grip on the iron plate, at any rate. As good as a kill, in context. While he was doing that, another one had his upper body and one knee on the top of the plate. That one he hit in the face, cutting into the bridge of the nose, and the cheeks on either side. The next one was over and into the cart before he'd finished with the last one, but he just had time for a short jab before the Mezentine found his balance. Sloppy; the point went in through the hollow between collarbone and shoulder, and it was lucky he had the presence of mind to follow up with a kick in the groin, which doubled the Mezentine up and made him stagger, trip against the edge of the plate and fall backward off the cart. The next one hit him on the knee before he was even ready.

He wasn't aware of falling, or moving at all, but he was kneeling, and a Mezentine was standing over him, swinging a sword with both hands. He gave up, then noticed the opening and remembered he was still holding the hanger. His fencing instructor would have said it served the Mezentine right for taking too long over his stroke (you don't need to cut hard, just hard *enough*). The stab in the pit of the stomach was really just a prod, rushed and half-hearted, but it got the job done; a pass, but no medal.

Valens remembered that he'd been hit; then he remembered that it didn't matter, because he was wearing his leg armor. He stood up and looked down at his knee. The cop was creased but not cut through, not bent enough to jam the hinge. A Mezentine reared up in front of him but he killed him easily; so much so that, a moment later, he couldn't remember a thing about him, what it had taken to dispose of him or how he'd fallen.

He looked again. Another hand was tightening its grip on the edge of the plate. Then he thought: there's no point to this. Let them have the stupid cart; time to leave. He glanced over his shoulder, to where the other cart had been but was no longer. If there was nothing left to fight for, why fight?

The jump down was further than he'd remembered. He landed awkwardly, yelped stupidly as his ankle buckled under him; painful, but it still worked in spite of his clumsiness. The Mezentine on the cart was looking down at him, apparently unaware how lucky he was that he still had all his fingers. Valens grinned at him and ran.

Not very far; too cluttered. He could see no moving carts, just still ones crawling with the enemy. There were dead people everywhere he wanted to put his feet (so much *mess;* how would anybody ever get it all cleared up?). He stumbled and hopped, trying to get across the track and up the steep slope on the other side, where horses couldn't follow him. The enemy didn't seem to notice him; since he wasn't a cart, he wasn't important. No other Vadani running away; apparently they'd all held their ground and died where they stood. Well, good for them. A Mezentine on a cart tried to reach out and swipe at him, but his cut fell a good six inches short; an afterthought, not a serious attempt on his life. He ignored it and kept going, not stopping until he'd pawed and crawled halfway up the slope; at which point he suddenly discovered that he was too exhausted to go any further.

From where he was he had a splendid view, as from a grandstand; best seat in the house, fitting for a Duke. He could see maybe two dozen carts, stationary, some with horses still in the shafts, some empty, some garnished with bodies, two overturned. If there were any Vadani still alive down there he couldn't see them, and where had all those Mezentines got to, the unlimited supply of targets there'd been a moment or so ago? Four, five dozen, no more; they were standing up on the carts, or slowly, wearily climbing down, like farmhands getting off the haywains at the end of a very long day. They looked tired and wretched; he remembered that feeling, the miserable emptiness after another routine victory, another difficult hunt with nothing edible to show for it. Nobody was bothering to look up. They plodded as though every muscle and joint in their bodies ached. He almost felt sorry for them.

Fifty yards away, directly below him, an officer was shouting: fall in, regroup, form into columns. They obeyed sullenly, clearly wishing he'd shut up, or at least stop yelling at them when they were tired out. The officer started counting heads, then gave up. They were having trouble catching some of the horses; he knew that too-tired-to-play-games feeling, when you'd rather lose the horse than take another step.

It was a very strange feeling, to still be alive after the defeat. It wasn't a possibility he'd considered; naturally he'd assumed that if they lost, he'd be killed in the fighting. The thought of being left over at the end had never occurred to him. Now even the enemy were turning their backs on him; he wasn't valuable enough to them to be worth climbing a bit of a slope for.

Somehow, he figured that the esteem of the Perpetual Republic was something he could learn to live without. Other things — other people — might be harder to dispense with. Just suppose he was the only survivor (the only coward who ran away). The last Vadani duke. The last Vadani.

That wasn't a concept he was prepared to hold still for. He scrambled to his feet — one of the Mezentines saw or heard him, looked up, shouted, pointed, but his friends didn't seem interested — and scuttled along the side of the slope, using his hands as much as his feet, grabbing at tufts of heather and couch grass to stop himself from sliding and losing his balance. From the top of the slope, he'd have a better view.

Noise below him; thudding and voices, shouts. He paused, nearly lost his foothold, took a moment to steady himself before looking down. By then, the picture had changed. The road was flooded with horsemen; not Mezentines, because the few of them still on their feet were trying to scramble back onto the carts, out of the reach of the swords and lances. His old friend the Mezentine officer was yelling again, urgent, angry and terrified. His voice stopped dead in midsentence. From where Valens stood it was just a confused scuffle. He was a good hundred yards up; all he could see was horses, the tops of heads, too much movement to make sense of. No good at all. The shale under his foot gave way and he let himself slither on his back, until a chunk of rock against the sole of his boot stole his momentum. He jumped up, overbalanced, caught himself and looked down.

He'd missed it; all over, while he'd been fooling about in the dirt. No Mezentines to be seen; not live ones, anyway. Most of the Vadani had gone as well; he caught sight of a dozen or so disappearing over the lip of the slight rise that cut off his view. More shouting from that direction; the counterattack was still going on, but moving at a rate he couldn't catch up with. He struggled down the rest of the slope to the road. A cavalry trooper, dismounted, looked up sharply as he slid and crashed into view; stared at him for a moment as though he had two heads.

"What the hell's going on?" Valens shouted. "Yes, it's me," he added, as the trooper's mouth fell open. "What's happening?"

But the trooper didn't seem able to speak, even backed away

a step or two, as if facing a ghost. For crying out loud, Valens thought. "Who's in command? I need to talk to him, now."

The trooper lifted his arm and pointed, back down the road, to where the noise was coming from. Another man stepped up beside him. He didn't seem able to speak, either. What was wrong with them?

"Fine," he snapped, "I'll go and look for myself."

There were horses standing nearby, but he'd seen the Mezentines try to catch them and fail; he really wasn't in the mood for recalcitrant animals. His knee was starting to ache where it had been clouted by the Mezentine, and the bottom edge of the greave was galling his instep. On the other hand, he thought, I could sit down on this rock and wait for whoever's in charge to come to me.

He wasn't kept waiting long. Over the lip came a column of riders; dusty, bloody but unmistakably Vadani. They rode with the same utter weariness as the victorious Mezentines had done, not so long ago. He recognized the officer riding at the front, though offhand he couldn't remember his name.

"What happened?" he asked again.

This time he got a reply. "I think we got them all," the officer said. "Near as makes no odds." He stopped his horse and flopped out of the saddle, landing heavily and wincing at the stiffness in his knees. "Strangest thing. Who'd have thought mercenaries would've held their ground like that?"

For a moment, Valens couldn't make any sense of what he'd just heard. "You mean we won?"

The officer's turn to look blank. "Well, yes," he said. "It took us a while and it got a bit grisly at the end, when we thought they were going to run for it but they didn't. But I don't think there was ever any doubt about it, not since that Eremian lunatic lost his rag and started laying into them."

"What Eremian?"

The officer shrugged. "I don't actually know his name." Someone next to him leaned down from the saddle and muttered something. "That's right," the officer said, "Jarnac Ducas. Great big bloke, never talks about anything except hunting." At that point it must have occurred to him that Valens had missed something important; he stood a little straighter and became a trifle more soldierly. "It was when the Mezentines stopped Duke Orsea's coach," he went on. "At least, they blocked it and cut the reins, but they didn't try and board it. But then this Ducas turns up — defending his duke, I guess, he seems that sort of man. Anyway, he went at it like you wouldn't believe. He'd got hold of one of those poleaxe things; not much finesse about it, but a lot of energy. I saw it myself; hell of a thing. He was pretty much cut to ribbons by the time they brought him down, and by then the tide had more or less turned. Colonel Brennianus rallied best part of a squadron of the household division, and we sort of snowballed from there. He didn't make it, unfortunately; neither did the Eremian. Otherwise, we came out of it pretty well. It was only here, in the middle, that things got out of hand."

Orsea: something he'd forgotten, which he was sure he'd never forget. "Duke Orsea's party," Valens said quickly. "Are they all right?"

"Thanks to that Ducas fellow, not a scratch. Well, the Duke himself got a tap on the head quite early on; got cut off trying to lead from the front, I imagine. Then Ducas went in after him, and that's when it got going."

The clot that had formed in Valens' throat eased a little, and he breathed in deeply. "What about General Mezentius? And the Cure Hardy?"

(He'd tried to say, *and my wife,* but for some reason he felt embarrassed about using the word, as though it was somehow an admission of weakness.)

The officer didn't answer. After two, maybe three seconds, Valens asked, "All of them?"

"I can't say for sure," the officer replied. "But I saw them stop and board the coach; and Mezentius was riding with them at the time. That was two days ago, and nobody's told me . . ."

"It's all right," Valens heard himself say, as a gate closed in his mind, shutting some things out and some things in. "You've done well." (Was that really him speaking? It seemed so improbable, somehow.) "For a while there, I thought we'd had it." *I ran away,* was what he wanted to say. "Just my luck to have missed the good bit." He took a deep breath. "We need to get moving again," he said. "What about horses for the carts?" And after that he was back to business, the kind of thing he was competent to deal with. Others joined him, clotting around him like blood in a wound. He could feel the Vadani beginning to heal about him. Soon he was giving orders, pulling out of his mind the important details that other people tended to overlook but which he always remembered. They were giving him back his place in the machine — the axle, spindle, driveshaft, from which the other components drew their power. He had no trouble performing the function, but he felt like an imposter — the man who turned and ran, masquerading as the Duke. If only he'd known, he kept telling himself; if he'd known the battle was going their way and his bit of it was an unimportant aberration, he would never have even considered running; he'd have held his place on the deserted cart, kept fighting, almost certainly been killed. Instead, while he was crouched down halfway up the hillside, an Eremian and a cavalry colonel whose name was only vaguely familiar to him had checked the enemy advance, driven them back, wiped them out and died in the process. Stupid guilt, irrational, pointless and far too strong to beat.

Apart from the fact that they were alive and had won a stunning victory, everything was about as bad as it could be. Horses: half of the wagon teams had been run off or killed, and the mounts of dead cavalrymen — plenty of those — weren't trained to drive, needless to say. More than a quarter of the carts themselves were damaged to the point where they couldn't move. This problem was, to some extent, mitigated by the number of dead civilians, who wouldn't be needing transport anymore. On that score, the best that could be said was that there were still plenty of them left; sobbing, shrieking, refusing to obey orders, demanding to speak to someone in authority, rushing about searching for lost relatives, fussing about the burial of their dead, needing to be fed and watered and listened to. Valens could probably have coped with them better if they'd been angry with him, or blamed him. Instead, they took to cheering him whenever he broke cover; women grabbed at him as he scurried past, blessing him for saving them. They were firmly convinced that he'd led the counterattack and wiped out the Mezentines. He overheard men swearing blind that they'd seen him at the front of the cavalry charge, in shining armor, sword in hand, swiping off heads like a boy with a stick topping nettles. He wanted to feel proud, honored, choked with emotion; instead, he found it irritating and desperately inconvenient. He gave them permission to bury their dead, mostly to give them something to do and keep them from getting under his feet. The column was stuck, after all. Food was running out (they should have reached the first of the supply dumps by now), there was plenty of water in the river down in the valley but a shortage of casks and barrels to carry and keep it in. Just when he needed him, Mezentius was thoughtlessly, selfishly dead, and the civilians had taken an instant dislike to Major Tullio, the officer who'd led the vital counterattack and done most of the work since. For some reason they blamed him for the deaths and losses, saying he'd hung back, waited too long, stood by while women and children were butchered. A whole long day of that sort of thing; and then the other column arrived.

If Valens had spared them a thought since the battle, it was only a vaguely guilty relief that they hadn't been there to be slaughtered with the rest. The first he knew about their return was when some young fool whose face he vaguely remembered from somewhere came charging up to him while he was busy with a map, and told him his name was Captain Nennius, and he needed seven tons of flour as a matter of urgency.

When Nennius had recovered sufficiently from Valens' reaction to explain himself coherently, they managed to sort out everything that needed to be done straightaway, and Nennius went away to let his people know they'd found the Duke, but there wasn't going to be any food. They rode in with their carts loaded down with dead people, which didn't really improve the situation. Valens did his best to make Nennius into a substitute hero, but since he hadn't actually fought anybody or mended any carts with his own hands, it didn't work terribly well. There weren't nearly enough picks, mattocks, buckets, spades and shovels for the burial details, the ground was rock hard, and soldiers kept drifting away to help with gravedigging when they should've been doing something useful. And as if that wasn't enough . . .

He knew Miel Ducas, vaguely; they were distant cousins, after all, and he'd met him during the peace negotiations to end the Eremian-Vadani war. Back then, as he remembered, the Ducas had been tall, handsome, bouncy and insufferable. Now he was just tall, and a nuisance Valens could have done without. He fended him off for a while with commiserations on the death of his cousin. That didn't work too well, since it was the first the Ducas had heard of it.

"Jarnac?"

"Yes. He died very bravely. In fact, if it hadn't been for him, I don't —"

"Jarnac's dead?"

"Yes."

The Ducas frowned, as if he'd just been told that his cousin had been elected king of the elves. Then he shook himself like a dog and said, "I need to talk to you about this man Daurenja."

Talk about changing the subject. "What about him? I haven't seen him for days, not since we left the city."

The Ducas explained, and when he'd finished, the headache that Valens had been warding off all day was suddenly there, fully formed and perfect as a hen's egg in a nest of straw. "He's with your lot now, then?" he said.

"Yes. Captain Nennius has placed him under informal arrest, whatever that means."

Precisely nothing. Valens suspected it was something the young officer had made up on the spur of the moment, to keep the Ducas quiet. Officer-level thinking; he was impressed. "I'm not quite sure what you want me to do," Valens said. "I'd have thought it's a matter for Duke Orsea rather than me."

"That's what Nennius said," the Ducas replied. "Though, properly speaking, under Eremian law the proper court of first instance would be the district assize for the place where the crimes were committed. Meaning me," he added mournfully. "Orsea would only be involved if Daurenja was convicted and lodged an appeal. But there's a problem with that, since I'm the chief witness. I'm the only outside party who heard the confession, you see."

As well as the headache, Valens had a sort of prickly feeling at the nape of his neck, something halfway between a tickle and an itch. Eremians, he thought.

"I'm afraid you're going to have to sort it out yourselves," he said, "and then there'd have to be extradition proceedings, if Daurenja decided he doesn't want to come quietly; I can't just hand him over to you neatly wrapped in straw and twine. More to the point, right now he's my chief engineer, until that bloody Mezentine turns up again. You say he was the one who fixed all those broken carts?"

"Yes, but he's a murderer. And a rapist, and I don't know what else. You can't just let him prowl around as though nothing's happened. You've got to do something about it."

There; that was all it took, to turn Valens the model duke into a tyrant who didn't give a damn about justice. "Come to think of it," Valens said quietly, "I seem to remember you're a bit of a fugitive from justice yourself. Weren't you under arrest for treason when Civitas Eremiae fell?"

Clearly the Ducas hadn't been expecting that. Long pause, then, "Strictly speaking, yes. But that was —"

"In which case," Valens said, "I'm afraid I'm going to have to place you under informal arrest," wonderful phrase, that; he'd have to promote Nennius to full colonel for it, "until things have calmed down a bit and I've got the time and the energy to be bothered with the fine points of Eremian jurisprudence. Talking of which: if you're an indicted traitor, would that debar you from sitting in judgment on Daurenja? I don't know how you used to do things in Eremia, but I imagine a clever lawyer could have some fun with it. I guess we'd have to try you for treason first." He smiled savagely. "I know," he went on. "Why don't you go and talk it over with Orsea, right now? I'm sure he'd be delighted to see you after all this time. Now, if you'll excuse me, I've got a war to fight."

He started to walk away; then the Ducas said: "Fine. You could join us. Maybe you'd care to explain to Orsea why you were writing letters to his wife."

No, I mustn't, Valens thought; and then, Well, why not? He turned round, using the pivoting motion to back up the punch. He caught the Ducas unprepared on the point of the chin; he staggered and sat down in the dirt, looking completely bewildered.

That should have been that, except that a couple of soldiers who'd seen their duke forced to defend himself against the Eremian (it had to have been self-defense, because Valens would never hit someone unprovoked) ran up looking concerned. "He's under arrest," Valens snapped. "Stick him in one of the empty carts until I can be bothered to deal with him, and make sure he doesn't get away. He's got a history of breaking arrest."

It was because of the Ducas that she came.

Orsea came first; that night, when he'd finished the day's work and finally managed to get rid of everybody. He'd closed the tent flaps, thrown a scoop of charcoal on the brazier and taken off his shirt; and suddenly, there was Orsea's stupid face at the opening, letting the cold air in.

"I need to talk to you," he said. "About Miel Ducas."

Valens shivered. It was cold, and he was tired. "Who? Oh yes, I remember. I think I've done you a favor."

"I'm sorry?"

Valens sighed. "Come in, if you're coming." Orsea had to stoop to get in the tent; unfair, that someone so useless should be taller than him. "What I meant was, I've caught your traitor for you. He's yours. Do what you like with him."

Orsea looked at him. "I don't think it's quite as simple as that," he said. "Bearing in mind what it was he actually did."

"It was some business with a letter, wasn't it?"

It had been too easy; the temptation too great. Orsea gazed at him with the sullen resentment of the man who's been hit and knows he can't hit back. "Miel Ducas hasn't done you any harm," he said quietly. "You might as well let him go."

"Does that constitute an acquittal?" Valens replied. He had no idea what he was fighting with Orsea about, but the urge to fight him was irresistible; he was so weak, so easy to hurt. "If so, I'll release him into your custody. Would that suit you?"

Orsea, of course, said nothing.

"Fine," Valens snapped. "Or maybe I'll keep him. I gather he's a useful man. They say he made a pretty good job of defending Civitas Eremiae, before you had him jailed."

Orsea sighed wearily. "Look," he said, "I don't know what I've done to upset you. I know I haven't been much use to anybody since — well, since I came here. But there's no point taking it out on someone else. Obviously, what Miel did doesn't really matter anymore, except to me."

"I see. So you're dropping the charges?"

"I suppose so, yes."

"I can turn him loose, then. Not a stain on his character."

"Yes."

Valens nodded briskly. "I'll do that, then," he said. "Provided he lays off my engineer. For all I know, this Daurenja's a murderer and a rapist, and probably a cannibal and a demon-worshipper and all sorts of other interesting things, but he's also the sort of man who can fix busted carts; and I happen to be fighting a war. Nasty business needs nasty people. The pure in heart only fuck things up and get people killed." He smiled pleasantly. "I'm sure you know that better than anybody."

"Yes," Orsea said. "I'd sort of arrived at that conclusion for myself."

"Splendid. In that case, there's the deal. Your Ducas can go free provided he leaves me and my officers in peace. I'll give him a horse and a feed-sack full of money, and he can go off into the wide world to seek his fortune. Agreed?"

Orsea breathed out slowly; the man who'd rather get beaten up than fight, because victory would make things worse for him than defeat. "Knowing Miel, I don't think he'll agree to that."

"It's not up to him," Valens snapped. "In fact, what your friend the Ducas thinks about anything is probably the most unimportant thing in the world right now. Anyway," he added, trying to restrain his temper, "what the hell do you care about what Daurenja may have done?"

"Actually, quite a lot. You may have forgotten, but he saved my wife's life, when the Mezentines ambushed your hunting party."

Rather like being stabbed by a small child with a sharp knife. Suddenly Valens didn't know what to say.

"I know," Orsea went on. "Being under an obligation to someone like that; it throws everything out of true. It's a bit like owing your life to a man who's been trying to seduce your wife. It beats me, I must admit. What would you do, in a situation like that?"

If you were half a man, Valens thought; if you were only very slightly less pathetic, I'd take her away from you tomorrow, even if it meant hiring murderers to cut your throat in the dark. I know: what about Daurenja? He would seem to have a knack for that sort of thing. Instead, he said: "That's an interesting one. I think what I'd do, if I was in your shoes, would be to get out of this tent while you're still capable of walking. Do you think you could manage that, or shall I get someone to help you?"

Orsea smiled blandly at him, and he thought: sore losers are bad enough, but a sore winner's insufferable. I don't think I'll ever be able to forgive him for that; for being completely at my mercy, and in the right. "So what about Miel Ducas?" Orsea said. "Are you going to let him go?"

"Only on the conditions stated," Valens replied. "Otherwise he can stay where he is until the Mezentines come and slaughter the lot of us."

"I see." Orsea turned to leave. "Thank you so much for your time."

"My pleasure. Please give my regards to your wife."

Which was, he reflected later, as he lay in the dark staring up, a bit like killing yourself to frame your enemy for murdering you; a sort of bleak satisfaction; looked at objectively, though, not terribly clever.

The right thing to do. He could see it clearly in his mind; it was practically blinding him as it glowed in the dark. Arrest Daurenja, let Ducas go, apologize to Orsea, never see or write to her again. The virtues and immediate reward of always doing the right thing, as exemplified by Orsea Orseoli, Duke of the Eremians, that nearly extinct nation.

(My father would have Daurenja in here like a rat up a conduit; he'd give him his own knife for the job, probably sharpen it himself, so as to be sure it was done properly. My father would have lost this war by now; except that he'd never have let himself get involved in it.)

He yawned. He felt tired, but in no way able to sleep. Let's just be grateful we've got the Mezentines, he thought. If I can play for time just a little bit longer, they'll exterminate us all and I won't have to do anything, right or wrong.

He turned over onto his side, and it occurred to him to remember that his wife was dead; killed by the Mezentines, because he'd been too stubborn and too proud to take her advice (which would have resulted in the deaths of about a fifth of his people; slightly more than the Mezentines had killed in the battle, but there was still plenty of time and scope to make up the difference). He knew he should be appalled by how little he cared about that. He thought: she couldn't possibly love me now, love what I've become because of all this. I've lost her as conclusively as though she'd been the one killed out there on the road, instead of that poor, overeducated savage woman, who only wanted what was best for all of us.

(Wonderful epitaph for a wasted life, but a little bit too long to fit on a tombstone.)

Well: her death had made one significant difference. With her dead, the alliance with the Cure Hardy was certainly gone for good; with it, the chance of escaping across the desert. No allies, no place to go; like Orsea, she'd been unbearable, hard done by and right. And, like Orsea, he'd destroyed his people. The realization hit him like an arrow; not just routine early-hours-of-the-morning depression, but a straight, clear look at the truth. They were finished. The clever idea hadn't worked, and they were screwed. And his biggest mistake: turning back on the hillside, instead of carrying on running away. It had been an easy mistake to make: looking at heaps of the slaughtered enemy, his own forces in possession of the field, and mistaking it for victory.

He flipped over onto his back and stretched out his arms. His father used to have a saying — something he'd heard somewhere, it was too clever for him to have made it up himself: giving up is a privilege only granted to the weak. Sometimes he assumed it was just garbage, like most of the old fool's pet maxims. At other times, like this one, it was the only truth that mattered. Ah, but he had so many things to give up on, spoiled for choice, wallowing in opportunities. I could give up on myself, he thought; then he realized, I've already done that. But I won't give up on the Vadani, and I won't give up on her. (Another thing the old man had said: screw doing your very best; *succeed . . .*)

He was still awake when the first spikes of light poked through the seams of the tent flap. He yawned, stretched and covered his face with both hands, running the tips of his fingers down the length of his nose. Another long day to look forward to.

"Are you awake?"

He started, lost his balance and slid off the bed onto his knee. "I'm sorry," she said quickly, "I didn't mean to —"

"That's all right," he mumbled, "that's fine. What are you doing here?"

He scrambled into a sitting position, his back to the bed, and looked up at her. She was wrapped in an old blanket, so all he could see was her head and her feet. "I wanted to talk to you," she said. "If it's not a good time . . ."

"No, it's fine." Without turning his back on her, he slithered up against the bed until he was sitting on it. "There's a chair behind you. Sit down."

She already had. "I hope it's all right," she said. "Only . . ."

"Orsea sent you."

He didn't know why he'd said it, because obviously he'd done no such thing. "No, of course not," she said. "But he came back to our tent last night looking like death on legs. He wouldn't tell me where he'd been until I lost my temper with him." She was looking straight at him. "What did you say to him? He's practically suicidal."

Valens sighed. "I was as unpleasant to him as I could possibly be. False modesty aside, when it comes to being thoroughly obnoxious, I'm pretty much the state of the art. Oh, and I hit him. No, I tell a lie. It was the other one I hit, that Ducas fellow. They're pretty much interchangeable, anyhow."

"That's not true." Her voice was very calm. "Orsea said it was Miel you fell out over."

Valens laughed. "You could say that," he replied. "But it was just an excuse, as far as I was concerned. You don't need me to tell you why your husband and I don't get on well."

She nodded precisely; a small, sharp movement. "It was Miel I wanted to talk to you about."

"Really?" He shrugged. "Fire away."

"I want you to let him go."

"Fine. He can go."

"Without that ridiculous condition you wanted Orsea to agree to."

"Sure." He made a vague gesture of submission. "He's free to go and do whatever he likes. Hold on a moment and I'll put it in writing." He leaned across and drew the writing desk toward himself. "You can take it with you if you like."

"You're giving in, then? You've changed your mind?"

"Yes. What does it look like?"

"Why?"

He gave her a what-a-stupid-question smile. "Because you asked me to, of course."

She frowned. "Would you do anything I asked you to?"

"Yes." He said it without thinking. "Yes," he repeated firmly, "I'm pretty sure I would."

"If I asked you to leave me alone and never talk or write to me again?"

"Definitely." He looked at her. "Are you? Asking me that, I mean."

"No."

"Good." He looked past her. "So why are you so concerned about the Ducas' welfare?"

She shrugged. "I've known him for a long time; all my life, really. If my father hadn't died so suddenly, I'd almost certainly have married Miel Ducas instead of Orsea."

"I see. Would you have liked that?"

She nodded. "It'd have been very comfortable," she said. "A bit like leaving home and moving into the house next door. I don't love him, of course."

"No," Valens said, "I don't suppose you do. So, if not him . . ."

"Orsea." She looked down at her feet. "You know that."

"Yes. Just Orsea?"

"No. But enough."

"How much is enough?"

"As much as it takes."

Valens nodded. "All right," he said. "Though I must confess, it beats me how anybody could love someone like him; not excluding his mother, his old nurse and his dog. He's an idiot."

"No." There wasn't any anger in her voice. "He isn't, actually."

"Oh really." Valens jumped up. "Here's a man who wakes up one morning. What'm I going to do today? he says. Here's an idea: why not invade the Perpetual Republic for no perceptible reason and start a war that fucks up the entire world?" He waved his hands, an exaggerated gesture. "If you say he's not an idiot, he's not one. Now all we've got to do is call in all the dictionaries in the world and change the definition of idiot to mean somebody with a fucking clue."

Now she was standing up as well. Her front foot was pointed toward the tent doorway, implying that she was about to leave. "Does that mean you've changed your mind about Miel Ducas?"

"No, of course not," he snapped. "And sit down, for crying out loud. I'm sorry," he added quietly. "All that was just showing off."

"I know." She sat down. "And you know you're wrong about Orsea. He's not stupid, just weak; and unbelievably unlucky. Though I've always tended to assume the two go together somehow."

Valens leaned forward, cupped his chin in his hands. "I think he makes his own bad luck."

"No." She was correcting him, like a teacher. "Not all the time. Besides, all his mistakes and his errors of judgment stem from one piece of really bad luck that simply wasn't his fault."

"Really? What was that?"

She smiled weakly. "Marrying me." She shifted her head slightly, asking him not to interrupt. "If he hadn't married me, he wouldn't have become the duke. It's only because of me that he's been in a position to make the mistakes. If he'd married anybody else in the world, he'd have gone through life perfectly happy as a minor nobleman, getting things more or less right, and there'd never have been a war or anything. Besides," she added, "I should never have married him; only I didn't know him well enough at the time to realize what a mistake I was making."

Valens frowned. "I thought you said —"

"I love him? Yes, I do. Practically at first sight. But he's never really loved me; or at least, he loves me because I'm there, if you see what I mean. Because I'm his wife, and he knows that loving your wife is the right thing to do." She grinned. "What I mean is, if he was married to someone else, he wouldn't leave her and run off with me. He wouldn't — what's the quotation? You're the one who knows these things. He wouldn't count the world well lost for my sake."

Valens looked at her. "Actually," he said, "I don't know quotations. I have to look them up."

"Oh. I assumed . . ." She shrugged. "Anyway, you see what I mean. If it was a choice between me and doing the right thing, I wouldn't stand a chance."

"I see." He frowned. "And that's your definition of true love?"

"I suppose so. Like, for example . . ." She was looking over his shoulder. "Like doing something really bad and terrible, because you realize you simply don't have a choice: leaving your husband, for instance. Or starting a war. Sorry," she added. "Did I just make a joke or something?"

Valens shook his head. "I was just reminded of something I read recently. Actually it was that bloody stupid deposition the Ducas made me look at; you heard about that? It's something that Daurenja's supposed to have said, in his confession. He said: love has always been my undoing."

She looked at him. "He's supposed to be a murderer, isn't he?"

"I'm sure he is," Valens replied. "And a very useful engineer. I'm just picturing him standing up in court and saying: I did something really bad and terrible, but I realized I simply didn't have a choice. So: fine, I say, case dismissed. Is that how it should be?"

"I don't know," she replied. "I've never done anything like that."

He breathed out slowly. "Really?" he said. "What about writing to me? Wasn't that bad enough, considering how it ended?"

"No." Her eyes were cold and bright. "I can't be blamed

because somebody turned me into a weapon." She studied him for a moment, then said: "You can't blame me for the war."

Valens winced, as though she'd hit him. "Well, no," he said. "Personally, I tend to think the Mezentines —"

"You know what I mean."

"So I should just have sat quietly at home and let them kill you?" He shook his head, as though conceding that he was deliberately dodging the point. "That's what Orsea would have done, of course."

"Yes," she said. "Because Orsea would never be in love with someone else's wife."

He shook his head again. "Come on," he said, "you can do better than that. What did you say just now? The world well lost for love? Actually," he added, "I do know that one. Pasier, the fifth Eclogue. But only because they made me read it when I was a kid."

"You don't like Pasier?"

"Too soppy. His heroines sit around waiting to be rescued, you can practically see them tapping their feet impatiently, wondering where the hero's got to. And then the hero dies tragically, and they're all upset and miserable. Anybody with half a brain could've seen it'd all end in tears; and all the heroine need have done was pack a few things in a bag, wait till dark and slip out through the back door, instead of making some poor fool of a hero come and fetch her. Besides, how could a hero give a damn about somebody so completely insipid?"

She looked at him. "You don't like Pasier."

"No. I think his heroines are bitches and his heroes deserve everything they get. Which explains," he added, "why I don't go in much for self-pity, either. I have no sympathy for stupid people."

What was she thinking? The writer of the letters whose words he knew by heart had told him everything about herself. He had explored her mind like a scholar, like a pilgrim. The girl he'd spoken to once when he was seventeen was so well known to him that he could have told you without having to think what she would be likely to do or say in any possible circumstance. The woman sitting in front of him was different. He hardly knew her.

"You're wrong," she said. "It's from the seventh Eclogue, and the line is *the world well lost for her sake.* Your version couldn't possibly be right, it wouldn't scan. Whatever you think about Pasier's heroes and heroines, his scansion's always impeccable."

He scowled. "Agreed. He obeys all the rules. I think that's why he's a bit dull for my liking. He always does the right thing; makes him sort of predictable. Same with his characters; they always do the right thing. It means you can always figure out well in advance what's going to happen in the end. They always die horribly, but with their honor intact, leaving the world a better place. Which is pretty much true to life, if you think about it. I mean, the world can't help but be a better place if there's one less dick-headed idealist cluttering it up."

She took a deep breath. "I know I haven't said this before," she said, "but what you did — saving Orsea and me when the city fell — it was the most wonderful —"

"Mistake," he interrupted. "Stupidest thing I ever did. It was a Pasier moment; exactly the sort of thing one of his boneheads in shining armor would've done. Probably, subconsciously, that's what I was thinking of when I made the decision. Self-image, I think that's the expression I'm looking for. I got this mental picture of myself as a romance hero, and it appealed to me. The world well lost for love. No, I should've stayed at home and read a good book."

"But you didn't."

"No. I didn't have that option. And if I could've foreseen what was going to happen . . . If I'd had a vision of this moment, so I could've seen exactly what a complete and utter fuck-up I was going to make, with dead civilians heaped up like cords for the winter log-pile and basically no chance at all of getting out of this in one piece, I'd still have done it. I'd do it again tomorrow." He closed his eyes for a moment. "Would you care to hazard a guess why? And you sit there, cold as last night's roast mutton, and tell me you love Orsea, final, nonnegotiable."

"I do."

"Well, fine." Valens jumped up and turned his back on her. "That's your privilege. I take it you're like me, don't suffer fools gladly. And since we're both agreed that I'm the biggest idiot still living, I quite understand your choice. Orsea may be a clown and a source of trouble and sorrow for everybody in the known world, but he's a harmless genius compared to me. You haven't got a spare copy of Pasier with you, by any chance? I feel in the mood for reading him again, but I left my copy back in the city, along with everything else I used to own."

"I'm sorry." He couldn't see the expression on her face, and her tone of voice was flat, almost dead. "You were the only real friend I ever had. I used to live for your letters. I think you're the only person I've ever known who's tried to understand me."

"But you love Orsea."

"Yes."

"There you are, then. Tell you what, why not get him to write to you? *Dear Veatriz: how are you? The weather has been nice again today, though tomorrow it might rain.* He could probably manage that, if he stuck at it for a while."

"I really am very sorry," she said, and, for the first time since his father died, Valens allowed himself to admit defeat; to recognize it, as if it was some foreign government whose existence he could no longer credibly ignore. "It's all right," he said. "Funny, really. I used to think you brought out the best in me, and now it turns out you have the opposite effect. Shows how much I really know you. After all, it's different in letters: you can be who you wish you were, instead of who you actually are."

"That's not true," she said. "I know who you really are. It's — well, it's a waste, really."

"Did you know my wife's dead?" he asked suddenly, almost spitting the information out. "The Mezentines killed her. I really wish I could feel heartbroken about it, or sorry, or even angry. Instead — you know how I feel? Like when I was a kid, and my father had arranged a big hunt, and then it pissed down with rain and we couldn't go out. But when he died, I felt so bad about that. He loved it so much, and I hated it. I started going out with the hounds again to punish myself, I guess. Now, when I go out, it's the only time I feel at peace with myself. Even reading your letters never made me feel that way. You know what I used to do? As soon as I got a letter from you, I'd cancel all my appointments, I'd read it over and over again — taking notes, for crying out loud — and then I'd spend a whole day, two or three sometimes, writing the reply. You can't begin to imagine how hard I worked, how I *concentrated;* there'd be books heaped up everywhere so I could chase up obscure facts and apposite quotations. First I'd write a general outline, in note form, with headings; then a separate sheet of paper for each heading, little diagrams to help me figure out the structure. Then I'd copy out a first draft, leaving plenty of space between the lines so I could write bits in over the top; then a second and third draft, often a fourth. If I'd have worked a tenth as hard on politics, I'd have conquered the Mezentines by now and be getting ready to invade the Cure Hardy." He laughed. "Bet you thought I just scribbled down the first thing that came into my head. I wrote them so that's what you'd think — like we were talking, and everything came spontaneously from my vast erudition and sparkling, quicksilver mind. I spent a whole day on one sentence once. I couldn't decide whether it'd sound more natural and impromptu if the relative clause came at the beginning or the end. Actually, it was a bloody masterpiece of precision engineering, though I do say so myself. And the irony is, you never realized. If you'd realized, it'd have meant I'd failed."

He stopped talking and turned round sharply; he'd heard the tent flap rustle. A sergeant was hovering in the doorway, looking worried and trying to apologize for interrupting.

"It's all right," she said, "I was just going."

He couldn't bear to see her go, so he looked down at the ground until he saw her shadow pass out into the light and break up. Then he turned on the sergeant like a boar rounding on the pack.

"What the fuck do you want?" he said.

The sergeant looked terrified. "It's Vaatzes, sir," he said. "That Mezentine. He's come back."

24

Until he left the city, Ziani had never thought much about food. Like all Mezentines, he'd taken it for granted. He'd had a vague idea that vegetables somehow came up out of the ground, and meat was the bodies of dead animals; anyhow, it was crude, primitive and mildly distasteful, and he really wasn't interested. The Republic's attitude to eating was that it was just another bodily function, to be performed as quickly and efficiently as possible, in private. A long time ago there had been grain mills in the city, but now their races and wheels were more profitably employed powering the driveshafts of machine shops. Mezentia bought its flour from the savages ready-ground and handed it over to the Bakers' Guild, to be converted into manufactured wares as swiftly as possible. The bakers produced three types of loaf (small, medium, large); each loaf identical to others in its category, its weight and dimensions strictly in accordance with the prescribed specification.

Because nobody in the city ever went hungry, it was hard for Ziani to grasp the idea of there being no food; a whole population with nothing to eat. It was impossible, because in the city the bakers had a carefully agreed rota system that governed their opening hours, making sure there was always a bakery open for business at any hour of the day or night. Trust the savages to be different. Their food came from farms; it traveled from the farms to markets — big open spaces crammed with heaps and bins of raw, untreated, inchoate food, which people bought and took away to process themselves. And that was when the system was functioning perfectly. When something went wrong — in a war, for example — even that pathetic excuse for organization broke down, and there was a very real danger of people not having anything to eat. Extraordinary, but that's how some people manage to live; like cottages perched on the rim of a volcano.

Not that he objected; quite the reverse, since it had given him the opportunity to make a hero's entrance when he arrived in Valens' camp at the head of a short column of carts laden with flour, root vegetables, salted and preserved meat, cheese and a load of other stuff he didn't even recognize, but which the general manager of the miners' camp at Boatta assured him was both edible and wholesome.

The food had actually been an afterthought, a by-product of his detour to Boatta, which in turn had been nothing but camouflage, to explain away his long absence. The fact that it meant that everybody in Valens' column was pleased to see him was an unexpected but very welcome bonus.

"Before we left, we thought it'd be a good idea to empty out the stores and bring the stuff on with us," he explained truthfully. "To stop the Mezentines getting hold of it, as much as anything. It was only when the manager went through the inventory that we realized just how much food they'd got stockpiled there. My guess is that there was a standing order for so much flour and whatever each month, which was more than the miners needed, but nobody ever thought to reduce the amount; so the unused supplies were just squirreled away in the stores."

Valens shrugged. "Three cheers for inefficiency and waste, in that case," he said. "They've just saved all our lives."

They were unloading the flour barrels, rolling them down improvised ramps from the tailgates of the miners' carts. Crowds of civilians were watching, with the wary but rapt attention of dogs watching their owners eat. It's just flour, Ziani thought; even if they're starving hungry, it's just an inert white powder with no moving parts.

"Nobody told me what you were doing," Valens was saying, "or where you'd got to. I don't remember telling you to go and bring in the miners from Boatta."

"Don't you?" Ziani looked at him blankly. "I thought we discussed it; or maybe it was Carausius who gave me the order, I can't remember offhand. Anyway, it seemed logical enough; I had to go over there anyway to make sure they'd made a proper job of sabotaging the silver workings, so while I was there, why not get the evacuation organized at the same time? I'm just glad it worked out so well."

Valens nodded. "It's just as well you were able to find us," he said pleasantly. "I hadn't actually decided on the itinerary when we left the city, so you can't have known we were headed this way. I hate to think what might have happened if you'd missed us."

"Oh." Ziani raised his eyebrows. "I'm surprised to hear you say that. I knew you'd be on this road, because the first supply dump's at Choris Andrope — you showed me the list of depots, or I saw it somewhere, and I knew you'd be following the mountain roads, but obviously keeping as much distance as you could between yourself and the Eremian border. So, this was the only possible road you could've taken."

"I see," Valens said. "You figured it out from first principles."

"Well, it's hardly applied trigonometry." Ziani shrugged. "Besides, we were able to confirm your position when we picked up a couple of Mezentine stragglers on the way. Which reminds me," he added, looking away for a moment, "there's something I need to talk to you about, when you can spare a moment."

"Now?"

"It'll keep," Ziani replied, slightly awkwardly. "It's a delicate matter for discussing in the open like this."

"That sounds a bit dramatic."

"Does it? I'm sorry. Oh, I nearly forgot. I gather you had some trouble with some of the carts, but Daurenja managed a temporary fix. I'd better have a word with him about that. Do you happen to know where he is?"

Before he went looking for Daurenja, Ziani returned to the cart he'd ridden in on and opened the lid of the link box. Inside was a weatherbeaten canvas satchel. He looped the strap round his neck and shut the lid.

Daurenja was where Valens had said he'd be. They'd set up a makeshift forge, and half a dozen smiths were beating nails out of scraps of cart-armor offcut; Daurenja was drilling holes in a rectangular piece, to make up a heading plate. The drill-bit was getting hot and binding, so he paused every now and then to spit into the hole. Ziani waited until he'd finished before interrupting.

"You're back." Daurenja seemed overjoyed to see him. "Nobody knew where you were, I was worried."

"Never mind about me. Where were you?"

Daurenja frowned. "Absent without leave, I'm sorry to say. There was a bit of private business I wanted to clear up; I thought it'd only take a day, at most, and it was pretty urgent, it wouldn't wait. You've probably heard, I jeopardized the whole column by not being on hand when I was needed. I'm sorry: error of judgment on my part."

Ziani grinned. "I heard about it," he said. "And I gather Miel Ducas is under guard somewhere as a result. Is that right?"

Daurenja nodded. "Not that I'm worried, he won't do anything while I'm —"

"That's not the point." Ziani scowled. "I'm just anxious not to run into him unexpectedly, that's all. He and I don't get on."

"I see. Well, you're all right for the moment." Daurenja smiled. "They brought in a bunch of the scavengers; you know, the gang that's been stripping all the dead bodies. Apparently he knows one of them, I'm not sure of the details. Anyhow, he's in with them at the moment, so he'll be out of your way and mine for a while." He wrinkled his forehead. "I didn't know you and —"

"Nothing to do with you. What's all this about the plate mountings on the small carts?"

When he'd finished with Daurenja, he wandered about for a while until he was fairly sure he wouldn't be interrupted, then found an empty cart on the edge of the camp. There he opened his satchel and took out a dog-eared, much-folded piece of parchment. It was a map. He looked at it for a while, then took a pair of dog-leg calipers from his pocket and measured some distances, muttering calculations under his breath. When he'd finished, he folded the map carefully and put it away again before climbing down out of the cart.

It took him a minute or so to find a Vadani officer with nothing to do.

"Go and find Duke Orsea," he said, "and then come and tell me where he is."

The officer looked at him. "On whose authority?"

"Mine. Oh, and round up half a platoon for guard duty."

The officer didn't know what to make of that; still, he decided, better orders from a Mezentine civilian of dubious status than no orders at all. "Where will I find you?"

"Either around here somewhere or with Duke Valens."

The officer nodded. "How long will you be needing the men for?"

"Indefinitely."

So much to do, Ziani thought, as the officer hurried away, so little time and no help. It was so much easier back at the ordnance factory. Better organized, and reliable, civilized people to deal with. Never mind, he consoled himself. Getting there. Halfway there, at least, and most of the hard work done already.

(Briefly he considered the clerk, Psellus. He'd been a stroke of luck, though whether the luck was good or bad he wasn't quite sure yet. And something else to think about, as if he hadn't got enough on his mind already.)

There were a few other documents in the satchel; he checked they were still there, but didn't bother getting them out or reading them. Then the mine superintendent from Boatta found him, with a query about billeting arrangements. Vexing; but he'd taken a lot of trouble to make sure that the Boatta contingent answered directly to him. A small private army, just in case he needed it.

"Oh, and that other business." The superintendent looked round as he spoke, deplorably conspicuous, as many straightforward people are when they're trying to act furtive. "My boys found her all right; they've just got back."

Ziani nodded calmly. "They brought the body?"

"It's in the small chaise," the superintendent replied, "under a pile of sacks. I told one of the lads to keep an eye on it, make sure nobody goes poking about."

"Fine, thanks." Ziani yawned, a feigned gesture that became genuine as his weariness asserted itself. He hated having to concentrate when he was tired. "I'll need you in a little while," he said. "Where will you be?"

The superintendent shrugged. "I've got duty rosters to fill out," he said. "I was going back to our wagons."

"All right, just so long as I know where you are."

"You're sure this is all . . . ?"

"Don't worry about it."

When he was alone again, he made a conscious effort and emptied his mind of everything except the map. The other business could all fall through and no real harm done, if the worst came to the worst. The map — especially now that the Cure Hardy princess was dead. More luck (good or bad).

He could hear hammers: Daurenja's blacksmiths, doggedly making nails to mend the damaged carts with. It seemed like a lifetime ago, when he'd spent his days quietly, efficiently making things, while wise men, properly qualified in such matters, shaped policy far away in the Guildhall. Now, though, he knew that the policy-makers were men like Psellus the clerk; his inferior in every conceivable respect, an implement. Too late now to settle down somewhere and get a job. Still, the sound of hammers hurt him, like birdsong heard in the early morning, on the way to the gallows. A day's useful work and a quiet evening at home was all he'd ever asked for. And love, which had spoiled everything.

(The Cure Hardy, he thought. How much had that stupid woman in the ridiculous red outfit really known about the Cure

Hardy? The map; his ludicrous venture into the salt trade. The map. And having to rely for so much on the detailed cooperation of the enemy . . .)

He glanced up and noted the position of the sun. Time to go and find Duke Valens.

He found him sitting on the ground, his back to a cartwheel, making notes on a wad of scrap paper and doing calculations one-handed on a portable counting-board. He looked up, squinting into the sun, then said, "There was something you wanted to talk to me about?"

"If you've got a moment. I can see you're busy."

Valens laughed. "Wasting my time," he said. "I'm trying to work out how long we've got, even with what you brought in, before we starve to death. I figure we might just make it to the supply dump, provided the Mezentines haven't found it already. And assuming you can fix up the carts."

Ziani shook his head. "You don't need me for that, it's just basic joinery. Besides, Daurenja's appointed himself chief engineer; I saw him at that forge he's rigged up, making nails. I'd only be in the way."

"If you say so." Valens picked up one of the casting counters and fiddled with it. "But you can see why I said it's a waste of time doing all these stupid calculations. I'm afraid we aren't going to get there. The margin's too tight." He flipped the counter like a coin and caught it backhanded, without even looking. "Oh, I've thought it through. I've considered sending the fast wagons ahead to get the supplies and fetch them back here, but that's just begging the Mezentines to have another go at us. They're bound to have scouts out watching every move we make. I might as well draw them a map, with the depot marked on it in red ink."

Talking of maps . . . "This may sound stupid," Ziani said, "but do we have to go to Choris Andrope? Yes, I know that's where the depot is; but even if we make it and the food's still there, it won't have solved anything, just postponed it. Excuse me if I'm speaking out of turn, but I get the impression you haven't got any-where in particular in mind as a destination; you're just planning to wander about until the Mezentines go away."

"That's right." A slight frown on Valens' face. He opened his hand and stared at the counter, then glanced away, as if he'd been looking into the sun. "Just like you told me to."

Ziani shrugged. "If I said that, I can't have been expressing myself clearly; in which case, I apologize. But anyway, things have changed since then. I don't think wandering about is a viable option."

"Agreed." Valens winced. "But what choice is there?"

"Withdrawal to a place of safety."

"No such thing."

"Yes there is." Ziani dropped down on his knees beside Valens and lowered his voice. "With the Cure Hardy; the Aram Chantat. You remember, they suggested it themselves."

Valens pulled a face. "So did my dear wife," he said. "She told me I should take my people across the desert. Acceptable losses, she said. With hindsight, we'd have been better off doing that. But we can't do it now. We've lost too many people already."

"We can cross the desert," Ziani said.

Valens scowled at him. "That's it, is it? Your brilliant idea?"

"We can cross the desert," Ziani repeated evenly, "because there's a way. A string of oases, each of them no more than two days on from the last one." He pulled the map out of his satchel and laid it flat on the ground, weighing the corners down with small stones. "I learned about it from a merchant, the widow of a man who used to trade salt. You can cross the desert in three days."

Valens smiled. "She sold you this map."

"It wasn't like that." Ziani heard fear in his own voice. "We were going to go into partnership, to revive her husband's old salt run. This was our secret weapon, if you like."

"I see. And you were going to put up the money. Did she try and sell you any public buildings while she was at it?"

Just at the last minute, when you've built a machine, there's one crucial component, and it won't fit; or it binds and the wheel won't turn or the key jams halfway down the keyway. You tell yourself it only needs a few moments of fettling with files and stones. The essential thing is not to try and force it. "I know it's there," he said.

"You've been there? Tried it out for yourself?"

Ziani shook his head. "I read the dead husband's journals," he said. "Logs and daybooks, schedules of expenses. He used the route for seven years."

"Really. And then he just stopped."

"Yes. But for a very good reason. He died."

Valens flipped the counter again. This time he dropped it. "How sad. So, why didn't his widow sell the secret to someone else, if she didn't like running the route herself?"

Ziani grinned. "Nobody would've bought it. Not safe, you see."

"Not safe. You're doing a wonderful job of persuading me."

"Not safe," Ziani said doggedly, "because one of his contacts had given away the secret to a Cure Hardy bandit chief. That's how the husband died; the Cure Hardy ambushed him. Once they'd started infesting the route, who'd want to buy it?"

Valens sighed. "Sorry if I'm being unreasonably skeptical," he said, "but if the Cure Hardy knew about a short cut across the desert, why did my dear wife and her party come the long way round, with half of them dropping dead along the way?"

But when the component finally fits, there's a soft, firm click and the wheel begins to run. "I believe the secret was lost when the bandit chief and his raiding party got themselves wiped out. They'd kept it to themselves, for obvious reasons. Nobody else knew about it, apart from my merchant's husband."

"You're speculating."

"Not really," Ziani said. "The bandit's name was Skeddanlothi, and you killed him."

Valens picked another counter off the board, gripping its rim between thumb and forefinger. "The name rings a bell," he said.

"Skeddanlothi and his gang were raiding quite deep in Vadani territory; near here, in fact. Just over those mountains, and —"

"Thank you, yes, I remember." Valens frowned. "It's true, I couldn't for the life of me figure out how they'd managed to get this deep into our space without being picked up on the border; come to that, why it was worth their while coming all the way out here, across the desert, just to steal a few goats." He switched the counter from his left hand to his right. "Have you got all these papers; the journals, and all that stuff?"

Ziani shook his head. "But I did see them. I read them, every word. They bear out the map. I can describe each of the oases for you, if you like. At the first one, there's a row of wooden sheds, where the merchant's husband kept a stockpile of salt. There's a pen for the horses, and a stone silo for grain and forage. The roof blew off it in a sandstorm, so it's patched up in places. He had to take two mules loaded with slates to make good the damage. There's probably still some grain left in the bins, though it'll be six years old at the very least. I don't know if grain keeps that long."

"If it's dry and dark," Valens said absently, "and the rats haven't got in. But of course I can't check any of this unless I actually go there."

Ziani shrugged. "It was in the journals."

"Presumably this merchant of yours had employees," Valens went on. "They'd have known the route. Why haven't any of them tried to use the secret? Can you produce one of them to back up your claim?"

"No, of course not." Ziani scowled. "There were four of them. Two died in the ambush. One died about six months later. The other one borrowed money from the widow to set up a grain mill at Gannae Flevis. He was still making payments, the last time I spoke to the widow."

Valens nodded. "What about her?" he said. "If she was living in the city, she ought to be somewhere in the convoy."

Ziani shook his head. "She didn't like the idea," he said. "She told me she was going to join her niece's mule-train, trading fabrics with the Cure Doce. I'm sorry, I didn't ask for any details, so I've got no idea where she's likely to be."

"That's a nuisance," Valens said. He yawned. "Sorry, I'm a bit weary. It's been a long day. And you'll have to excuse my skepticism," he went on. "But — well, let's suppose somebody wanted to hand me over to the Mezentines, on a silver dish with an apple in my mouth. It'd help enormously if I could be persuaded to take a specified route, so they'd know exactly where to wait for me."

"There is that." Ziani had caught his breath. "Assuming you think I'd want to do such a thing. And that the Republic would negotiate with me. But I guess you don't think that."

Valens snuggled his back against the hub of the wheel, as though scratching an itch. "Anything's possible," he said. "I could build up a fairly convincing case if I wanted to. For a start, where did you get to when the rest of us left the city? Yes, I know you went to Boatta and picked up the miners. But maybe you didn't go straight there. Maybe you took a detour to meet someone; a Mezentine, maybe, with an interesting offer to put to you. Help us end the war and you can come home, no hard feelings. Maybe even your old job back, in the weapons factory. A man could be tempted."

"You think so?"

"I would be, for sure." Valens shrugged. "Assuming I could believe they really meant it. It can be a real bitch sometimes, can't it, knowing who you can believe in."

"If you say so."

"For example," Valens said, "there's this Miel Ducas, and his cousin; the one who got killed just now. They were convinced, both of them, that you were up to no good. The Ducas was sure that you were responsible for him getting arrested for treason. He even went as far as to tell his cousin you'd admitted it, to his face. And Jarnac Ducas told one of his senior officers, who told someone else . . . Maybe the story got stretched a bit in the retelling, I don't know. It all strikes me as a little bit far-fetched."

"Actually," Ziani said, "it's perfectly true. I found out about — well, the letter. I thought I could do myself some good with Duke

Orsea by telling him. I wanted to get sole command of the defense of Civitas Eremiae."

"Really? Why?"

"Because my scorpions *were* the defense, mostly," Ziani replied with a shrug. "I didn't want some amateur nobleman interfering. Also, I wanted Miel Ducas' job. And his land, and his money. Didn't do me much good in the end, of course. But he was guilty, remember. It's not like I forged the letter."

Valens smiled. "That's true," he said. "You didn't write the letter, I did. You just carried out your duty as a loyal subject. Not that you *were* one, of course." He yawned again, though this time it was forced. "My father had a saying," he continued. "I love treachery, he used to say, but I can't stand traitors. He was full of stuff like that. Other people's lines, mostly, but he passed them off as his own. Never fooled anybody. Credibility, you see. He told so many lies, people tended not to believe him even when he was telling the truth. Personally, I've always tried to be the opposite: tell the truth, and people know where they stand with you." He frowned, then said, "Let me have a look at that map."

Ziani handed it to him. Valens glanced at it.

"There has been a traitor working for the Mezentines," he went on. "That's how come there was a full regiment of Mezentine cavalry waiting for us at Cor Evenis, down on the main east road. For all I know they're still there, wondering why we haven't shown up yet. I told the traitor that's where we were headed, just before we left the city; then I sent some fast scouts, to see if there was an ambush laid for us. They reported back just before the attack on the column here; too late for me to do anything about it, because the traitor got killed in the battle. You may have come across him; General Mezentius."

"He was a —"

Valens nodded. "Rather a shock to me. Still, I suppose he figured we didn't stand a chance in the war, and wanted to get in with the winning side. Can't blame him. Loyalty's a wonderful thing, but any virtue taken to excess turns into stupidity in the end. The silly part of it is, it was a Mezentine who told me about him; inadvertently, of course. Anyway, that's beside the point. The question is, do I believe in you and your map? And if I believe in you, do I also believe there really is a road across the desert?" He sighed. "It'd be lovely if I could," he said. "Even if the Mezentines managed to follow us, I don't suppose they'd want to risk upsetting the Cure Hardy. I get the impression that they're the only force on earth your lot are genuinely scared of; not that it's ever lost them any sleep, because there's that wonderful desert in the way, keeping them penned in like a bull in a paddock. If ever they got the idea that the desert could be crossed after all, I reckon they might make some serious changes to their entire foreign policy." He closed his eyes. "I'm not entirely sure how the Aram Chantat will react if I turn up without their crown princess. They're likely to be upset, but whether with me or the Perpetual Republic I couldn't safely predict. There's also the fact that I've sent out a lot of scouts — good men, my own personal intelligence corps — and they assure me there aren't any Mezentine forces I don't already know about lurking behind rocks this side of the city. If you really were leading me into an ambush, they'd probably have found the assault party by now. A regiment of heavy cavalry's not an easy thing to hide in open country."

Ziani reminded himself to breathe. "And the map?" he said.

"Oh heavens, the map." Valens nodded. "Well now, let's see. Take away your motive for lying, and we're more or less forced to accept that you're telling the truth. In which case, you sincerely believe in the map. I don't think you're the sort of man who buys treasure maps from people you meet in the street. In which case, it's likely that the salt woman — her name's Henida Zeuxis, and she used to live next door to the Temperance and Tolerance in the Horsefair, right? See? I know all sorts of things about people, including where they go on their days off — most likely the salt woman believes in the map as well. So the gamble is, was her husband lying to her, or exaggerating? I don't know. You've met her, I haven't. What do you think?"

Easy as that, apparently; at the end, after all the filing and shaping and fettling and fitting. "I don't think she'd got the imagination to lie, or the skill to forge the journals. And if her old man was as half-witted as her, he must've hit on something really good, or he'd have gone out of business. He strikes me as a plodder, your ideal employee. I had men just like him working for me at the ordnance factory. If he'd been a horse, you could've stuck him on a treadmill and forgotten about him till his next feed was due. Yes, I believe in her, and the map, and the short cut across the desert. For what my opinion's worth."

Valens breathed out, like a man putting down a heavy sack. "That's what it comes to," he said. "Little scraps of trivia about unremarkable people swaying the fate of the whole Vadani nation. My father'd be livid if he could see me now. He always reckoned that making history was strictly the preserve of the upper classes." He shook his head. "You'd never have thought it to look at him, especially when he'd been drinking, but he was an idealist. There was an old boy on the council who used to say to him, you act like we're living in the upstairs rooms when in fact we're camping out on the midden. My father could never figure out what he meant by that, but he was right." Ziani watched him pull himself together. "All right, then, we'll give it a try. Oh, and thanks." He grinned wearily. "Consider yourself provisionally awarded the rank of Hero of the Vadani People and public benefactor, first class. There's no salary, but if we end up anywhere half civilized, I'll get a medal struck or something."

"Thank you," Ziani said gravely. "That makes it all worthwhile."

Which left only one chore to be got out of the way. It could wait a little longer.

Meanwhile, there was plenty to do. Fixing up the carts was the priority. The arrival of the miners helped; the armor plates could be cannibalized off the worst-damaged wagons and fitted onto the miners' carts; the rejects could then be stripped for parts to fix up the salvageable vehicles. Once the armor had been moved over, he let Daurenja take charge of bullying and cajoling the Vadani carpenters, while he concentrated on fabricating and fitting parts that had to be specially made: braces, brackets, reinforcing plates and the inevitable infinity of nails. Anything requiring even a little skill he did himself; partly because experience had greatly increased his contempt for Vadani metalwork, partly because it was a sweet pleasure to be bashing and filing metal again; as though he was back in the factory; as though nothing had happened. Working with iron and steel was a holiday after so long spent forging and shaping human beings; unlike people, rods and billets responded predictably to fire and hammer, and when you cut into them you got filings, not blood.

Valens' scouts started coming back with thoughtful looks on their faces. They hadn't seen an army, or outriders, or any trace that a large body of soldiers had been on the move. Instead, they muttered about finding abandoned farmhouses, barns that were empty when they should have been packed with hay; a merchant convoy glimpsed in the distance that left the road as soon as it saw them; a newly built bridge across a small river in the middle of nowhere.

No interference from the Duke, at any rate. Instead of being everywhere all the time, nosing about, asking maddeningly good questions, he'd become increasingly hard to find. The consensus of opinion was that he was lying low in order to avoid Duke Orsea, who was on his case because of the Eremian nobleman, Ducas, who was still being held confined in a small, stinking corral with the other prisoners.

There were other excitements, eagerly discussed in raised voices over the incessant thump of hammers. A large party of the scavengers who'd done so well out of trotting along at the heels of the running battle, like a sausage-maker's dog, had been rounded up and brought in. They were penned up in a hollow square of empty lamp-oil jars and vinegar barrels, tied up, ignored by everyone except their guards, grudgingly and sporadically fed, mostly on soup made out of slightly spoiled barley which the horses were too picky to touch. What Valens wanted them for was a complete and perfect mystery. Better to wring their necks straightaway and save their food, even if it was just condemned horse-fodder.

Predictably, the weather took a turn for the worse. It started as fine, light rain, the kind that saturates your clothes before you realize you're getting wet. Then it poured. The dust turned instantly into thick, sticky mud, weighing down boots and gumming up hands, messing up tools, swallowing a dropped nail or pin, spoiling tolerances, souring tempers. It's hard to cut to the thickness of a nail-scribed line when your eyes are full of water, and every time you shift your feet, the ground under them tries to suck off your footwear. Forced into the cramped shelter of the wagons, the civilians suffered noisily, wringing hearts and wasting time. Rainwater seeped into sloppily sealed flour barrels, dripped through tears in wagon canopies, swelled timbers and coated bolts and spindles with a sheen of tacky orange rust. Soon there were no dry clothes to change into, and men's boots squelched in the morning when they crammed their feet into them. Valens sat under an awning and gazed wretchedly at the road, wondering if it was impassable yet. A rill off the side of the mountain swelled into a river in spate and washed two carts (two fully refurbished, perfectly roadworthy carts) off the road and down the slope, where they rolled onto the rocks and were scrunched into kindling. The forge fires bogged down into black sooty ooze and couldn't be relit. The work, nearly complete, was now clearly doomed to take forever. If the Mezentines didn't get them first, they were all going to drown; swallowed in their sleep by the mud.

The end of the work took Ziani by surprise. Quite suddenly (late one afternoon, an hour before the lamps were due to be lit), in spite of the rain and the mud, the spoiled food and the sodden timber, they finished off the last of the smashed-up carts, and the column was officially ready to set off. Someone found Valens and told him; he ruled that they might as well stay where they were until morning and get everything ready for an early start. In the meantime, they could deal with the leftovers of unfinished business — shoeing horses, making an inventory of supplies and munitions, drawing up watch rotas and executing the prisoners.

It was a long, wretched and tedious job. Originally the idea was to hang them in a civilized fashion, but it didn't take long for Major Nennius, officer in charge, to realize that that wasn't going to work. There were no trees sturdy enough to serve as makeshift gallows, and he was only able to scrounge up enough four-inch-square-section long timbers to build two sets of scaffolds. Even hurrying things along at maximum speed, he could only turn off two men every fifteen minutes; eight an hour, and he had sixty-seven to deal with, or sixty-eight if the Ducas was going to join them (apparently that hadn't been decided yet). In addition to which, the rain had soaked into the ropes, which meant the knots didn't slide properly. Someone suggested waxing them with beeswax, a smart-sounding idea that turned out to be useless in practice. Two hours into the job, after five of the first eight executions had gone unpleasantly wrong, Nennius decided that hanging was a refinement he couldn't afford. They were already working by torchlight, and his men had spent the day working on the carts; they were tired, wet, hungry and miserable, and he had the impression that their patience wasn't unlimited.

Unwilling to take the decision himself, he balloted his junior officers. Three of them were ardently in favor of beheading and argued their case with a fervor he found more than a little disturbing. The other four voted for strangling. Hooray, Nennius told himself, for democracy.

Once the decision had been taken, however, it turned out that nobody could be found with a good working knowledge of practical strangulation. It was simple, someone said, you just put a bit of rope round a chap's neck and pull it tight until — well, until it's all over. Nennius, however, wasn't convinced. He'd never seen a man strangled to death but he had an idea that there was rather more to it than that. Someone suggested having a prisoner in and doing a trial run. Nennius shuddered and sent out for chopping blocks and axes.

Not, he had to concede, that he'd ever seen a man decapitated in cold blood before, either. But he felt rather more confident about it than about strangling. Provided they could find a way to make the prisoner keep still, how hard could it be? A bit like chopping through tree-roots, he told himself. He gave orders for the axes to be carefully sharpened.

Perhaps it was because it was late and wet and dark; it didn't go well. The first prisoner presented himself with admirable resignation, as if he could sense that everybody was fairly close to the end of their rope, and he didn't want to make things any more fraught than they already were. But the headsman muffed the stroke, cutting into the poor man's shoulder blade instead of his neck. The prisoner jumped in the air and squirmed about uncontrollably — not his fault, Nennius had to concede, it was pure instinct and muscle spasm — and finally had to be put out of his misery with spear-thrusts and a heavy rock to the back of the head. The spectacle had a very bad effect on the rest of the prisoners, who turned uncooperative; the next victim needed four men to hold him down, and the headsman refused to swing for fear of hitting one of the helpers. Further delay, while some men botched up a sort of a crush — a heavy oak beam with a strong leather strap to secure the head, and a thick, wide plank to lay over the body, on which three men could sit. The arrangement worked, more or less, although the headsman's nerves were shot and he needed three cuts to clear his third victim, who yelled like a bullock being dehorned throughout. The next six went through all right, and then the headsman's hands slipped on the wet axe-handle, so that the blade glanced off the back of the victim's skull and sank two inches into the headsman's left foot.

After that, nobody seemed to want the job, until a smarmy young ensign who Nennius particularly disliked volunteered and, in default of other applicants, was appointed. He'd been one of the fervent pro-decapitators in the debate earlier, and he went at it with three parts enthusiasm to one part skill. It'd have been all right if he'd been a big, brawny man with plenty of upper body strength; instead, he was short and scrawny, too weak to control his swing, and he was quickly demoted on appeal from the helpers, who feared for their lives. At this point it dawned on Nennius that if he wanted to have any credibility left come morning, he was going to have to do the filthy job himself.

It wasn't like chopping tree-roots, or splitting logs. It wasn't like anything else he'd ever done before. It was exhausting, difficult, disgusting and very, very precise. But if you concentrated furiously all the time and held the axe at just the right angle and hit very hard indeed, you could sort of chip the head off the neck with one cut; whereupon it slid through the restraining strap and flipped up in the air, while the trunk jerked and spasmed, upsetting the men perched grimly on the board into the sticky red mud. An eighth of an inch either way and you'd screwed it, and that meant fifteen seconds or so of frantic hacking, which more often than not broke the neck rather than cutting it. All in all, Nennius decided, this wasn't what he'd joined the service for. In fact, it was a thoroughly unsatisfactory way of doing things, and there was still a very long way to go.

Midnight came and went. There were complaints from the rest of the camp, particularly from civilians, about the noise, which was disturbing people's sleep. There was also a message from Duke Valens, reprieving Miel Ducas, who shouldn't have been included in the general warrant in the first place.

It was understandable, perhaps, that nobody told Miel Ducas that he'd been spared; the execution party had plenty of other things to do, and it was easy for details to get overlooked. Accordingly, Miel spent the night huddled in a corner of the biscuit-barrel stockade. He'd wormed himself against the barrels as if he was trying to squeeze himself through the tiny crack that separated them, and if anybody came within two feet of him he lashed out with his hands and feet.

In spite of everything, there was still a part of his mind that was perfectly, cruelly clear; and it very much wanted to know where the sudden panic, the overpowering fear of death, had come from. He wasn't sure. The best explanation he could come up with was that he was well aware that he'd been included in the warrant by mistake — *kill the prisoners,* they'd said, meaning the captured scavengers; but the sergeant in charge of the guard had assumed the order referred to everybody currently under restraint. Miel had tried to explain; first quietly and reasonably, then at the top of his voice, so everybody in the camp could hear him. While he was yelling and screaming, he was bitterly ashamed of himself, and he knew perfectly well, deep inside his mind's sound core, that he was only objecting because it was a mistake, because it was *unfair.* Childish reasoning, giving rise to childish behavior; the Ducas doesn't throw tantrums, particularly in the hearing of seventy-odd poor unfortunates who are doing their best to compose themselves as they wait for the end. Lack of consideration for others had always been the greatest sin, after disloyalty. Every time he paused for breath, he could hear them muttering and swearing at him telling him to shut up, put a sock in it, get a grip. He realized that at the end he'd lost everything, and he tried to use that to pull himself together. But each time he heard the axe fall — the clean shearing hiss, the soft thump followed by a shriek that marked a botched cut, the deep bite of the edge going through into the oak of the block — the panic surged up and spurted into his brain, overruling all his objections and setting him off again, like a baby woken up in the night.

Each time the guards came and grabbed someone, he thought, I wish they'd take me, and then it'd be over with; then, as the hurdles that served the pen as a makeshift gate were slammed and chained, he snuggled harder still against the barrels, shivering like a man with a high fever, desperate with relief because they'd taken someone else, not him. Then the pause; then the axe-fall, and off he'd go again, explaining in a yell that slurred the words together about the mistake in the warrant; then the hurdle-chain would rattle and he'd think, They'll take me next, just to stop me making this horrible disgusting noise; and so back to the beginning, top dead center of the flywheel, and the wish that they'd take him next.

He counted, of course: fifty left, forty-five, forty, thirty-five, thirty, twenty-five, twenty, nineteen. At times he was sure the terror would kill him before they finally condescended to come for him; then he'd slump, just as scared but too exhausted to move at all. His trousers were wet with piss and he'd skinned his throat with shouting, and he hated the scavengers for sitting still and quiet in the dark, while he made such a pathetic exhibition of himself. He realized he'd been yelling for Orsea, for Veatriz, for Jarnac (but he was dead already; thoughtless shit, to be dead when he was needed for a typical swashbuckling Ducas rescue); for Valens, for the sergeant of the guard, for the adjutant-general, for Daurenja, whose worthless life he'd saved from the just fury of Framain. Apparently, none of these was minded to help him; embarrassed, probably, by the appalling fuss he was making. Little wonder nobody wanted to know him, at the end.

Nine. He could hear someone crying; a feeble, bubbling noise. He realized he was listening to himself.

Eight; and the guards had paused in the gateway, looking round. When they left, the I-wish-they'd-taken-me-instead feeling made a feeble surge before drowning in terror.

Someone else was talking, but the hammering in his ears blotted out the words. He knew he was waiting for the fall of the axe; a voice in his head was saying, *When they come for me I'll fight, I know how to fight, I'm good at fighting, I'll kill them all and escape.* He wished the voice would shut up; but instead it changed. It was someone else, talking to him. He discovered that his eyes were tight shut, and he didn't seem able to open them again.

Something touched him, and he felt his leg kick out. Impact, and a shout; pain and anger. *There, you see, I'm fighting them, I've got one already, that just leaves —*

"Keep still, for crying out loud, I want to talk to you."

Strangely enough, the voice was familiar. In another time and place, it had belonged to a woman; the woman at the scavengers' camp, who'd tried to teach him to sew. With a jolt, he remembered who the other prisoners were.

"I'm sorry," he heard himself say. "Did I hurt you?"

"Yes. Stupid question, of course you did. Now listen." She lowered her voice. "There's not a lot of time left. We need to get out of here before it's our turn and they come and get us. Do you understand me?"

"You mean . . . ?" Was she really talking about escaping? Didn't she realize the guards would be back any moment, as soon as the axe fell? She made it sound as though they had to hurry and get down to the market before all the fresh coriander had been sold. "We can't," he said. "They'll stop us."

"Be quiet and listen. I've been watching them." She was talking so quietly he could barely hear; quick, businesslike. "When they come in to fetch the next one, they leave the gate open, in case they've got their hands full with someone struggling. There's a moment when the gate's open and their backs are turned. They're worn out, you can tell just by looking at them. We'd have to be quick, but we could slip past and they wouldn't see us. If we got just outside the gate and waited till they came out again, we could get away. Really," she added furiously. "I've watched the last four times, and it's always the same. If we got away, we could head for Eremia. They wouldn't follow, they're about to move out, I've heard them talking about it. We could find your friends in the resistance, or even the Mezentines; they'd be interested in knowing what's been going on here. Well?"

Well, he thought. Absolutely nothing to lose; so how was he going to explain to her that he was too scared to move? It would sound ridiculous, but he knew he wouldn't be able to make it. "You go," he said.

"On my own? I can't. I don't know how to saddle a horse, or which direction to go in. Listen: my husband was the third one they took. I tried to get my uncle to go with me, but he's wrenched his knee, he couldn't walk. I've tried everyone I could think of, but they were too scared or they'd given up. If I can't find someone to go with me, I'll die. I know about you now; you're good with horses and finding your way about, they say you're a great war hero and everything. You've got to help me, there's nobody else left. *Please*."

It was really only because he was too tired to make the effort to refuse; and because he couldn't keep still anymore, and anything was better than being kept waiting until all the others had been used up. Besides, it wouldn't work, and they'd be caught and killed on the spot, so at least there was a chance he wouldn't be led out there to the chopping block. But mostly it was because he felt so weak, and doing what you're told is always easier than fighting. If he refused she'd probably get angry with him, and he hadn't got the strength to face a scene.

The sound of the axe falling; someone swearing in exasperation; a shout, three parts weariness to one part fury. She was standing up, grabbing his arm and yanking on it. He had to get up, or she'd have dislocated his shoulder.

His legs buckled twice on the way to the gate. As they passed, someone said, "Where are you going?"; his heart froze, but she dragged him past and into what he supposed was position for the maneuver they were about to attempt. He'd forgotten the details of the plan already.

The gate opened. The guard's shoulder brushed his face, but the guard didn't stop or look round. They'd passed him, and she was hauling at his sleeve. The gate had been left open.

He wasn't aware of taking the six or seven steps; the thunder in his head was too loud, and he couldn't feel his legs. But they were on the other side of the gate, and the guards came bustling past, hauling a man by his wrists; his back was arched and he was digging his heels in, so that they plowed ruts in the mud as he was dragged past; his head was as far back as it would go. All told, he was in a bad way, but he made tolerable cover. Perhaps, if he'd known what a service he was performing for the Ducas, it would've made it easier for him to bear. Perhaps not.

She was pulling at him again, like a lazy horse. He followed, ambling. It was, of course, ridiculous; they wouldn't get twenty yards. In between waves of terror, he occupied his mind with wondering why she'd taken him with her. She seemed so efficient, so self-possessed; not the sort who needed a man to look after her. The most he'd be able to achieve would be to get them both caught. The thought crossed his mind that she fancied him. He managed not to laugh out loud.

Well, they'd made twenty yards. Perhaps she was telling the truth, and she really couldn't tack up a horse on her own. Some women were afraid of horses, the way some big, strong men were scared of spiders. Perhaps she thought that as soon as they were across the border, the Ducas' loyal retainers would come scuttling out of their hidey-holes in among the rocks to fight over the privilege of sheltering them. Perhaps she'd seen how very, very frightened he was, and had taken pity on him. (Well, quite. Nothing like looting the dead for a living for honing the delicate sensibilities.) In any event, they were in the open. Behind them, the biscuit-barrel stockade was a vague, looming shape, lit by a fuzzy yellow glow from the hurricane lanterns. Ahead of them, pale shadows that had to be tents. She steered him away from them — for someone who needed him along because only he knew the way, she had a superb sense of direction — toward a dark open space on their right. Closer; he could make out the dark gray outline of rails. The horse-fold, surrounded by a ring of gate hurdles. Was she really thinking of stealing a horse? Not a good idea, in his professional opinion as the duty big, strong man. Highly unlikely that the Vadani kept their tack in a neat pile in the corner of the fold. Bareback and without a bridle, a horse would be a liability rather than an asset. Not his place to argue, though. She led; he followed.

Up to the hurdle fence; over it (the middle rail was brittle and snapped under his weight with a noise like a tournament), through the fold — horses raised their heads and stared sleepily at them as they passed — and over the other side. Now that *was* smart: a short cut, to avoid going through the middle of the camp. Suddenly it occurred to Miel that they might get away with it, after all. But it seemed so pathetic . . . why hold still and be killed, when you can just walk away with only a little luck and determination? Could you really opt out of death so easily, like skipping a tiresome social engagement by pretending you had a cold?

She was talking to him.

". . . All we've got to do is get across this flat bit of ground and we're on the uphill slope. They won't even —"

She stopped dead. A shape was thickening out of the darkness; a man, blocking their way. Oh well, Miel thought; and then, The hell with giving in. We've got this far.

"Hold it," the man was saying. "No civilians past this point without authority, so unless you've got a pass . . ."

She was talking to him: "Oh, I'm terribly sorry. We were just taking a walk, we hadn't realized we'd come so far. We'll head straight back."

"That's all right," the sentry was saying, when Miel hit him with a rock. He wasn't sure how it had got into his hand. He must have stooped and felt for it, but it had come to him like a properly trained dog; he could just get his fingers around it comfortably. The sentry's head was turned toward her — had he even noticed she wasn't alone? — and he wasn't wearing a helmet.

The trick was to throw the stone without actually letting go of it. Judge it just right and you can crack a man's head like a nutshell. Miel saw him drop; he let go of the stone and jumped on him, his knees landing on his chest and forcing the air out like a blast from a bellows. *What the hell are you doing?* she was saying somewhere above him, as he scrabbled about looking for the sentry's sidearm — he was half lying on it, which made it horribly awkward to get it out of the scabbard; lucky the poor fool was either already dead or thoroughly stunned. After two or three massive tugs he got it free; she was nagging, *Come on, leave it, we don't need it, you'll ruin everything.*

Women, he thought, as he carefully located the hanger-tip over the hollow between the sentry's collarbones, and leaned on the handle. Miel felt the sentry's legs kick out and his back squirm, but that was usual, like a chicken beating its wings after its neck's been broken. The humane dispatch of game is the first duty of the honorable predator.

"What the *hell*," she was hissing at him, "do you think you're doing?"

"Killing the prisoners," he replied.

"Leave it." (Like he was a dog with a dead bird he'd picked up; the spaniel, the brachet and the lymer are bred soft-mouthed, to release retrieved game without spoiling it.) "Come on. Now."

He ignored her, drew the hanger from the wound and placed its tip delicately in the dead man's ear. There would be a crunching sound as he put his weight on it.

She was pulling at him again; reluctantly, he allowed himself to be dragged to his feet. He left the hanger and stumbled after her, clumsy as a drunk.

She didn't say anything to him until sunrise, by which time they'd been trudging uphill for hours. He'd quickly lost track of time. In his mind, over and over again, he was running through the killing of the sentry (the rock, the hanger, the two penetrations; the sounds, the feel. They were moments that he was comfortable living in; they nourished him, like supplies sensibly rationed, and he savored them).

"Where are we?" she said.

Good point. He stopped and looked round to get his bearings.

Easy enough. There was Sharra, too far away for them to see smoke rising from the chimneys of the Unswerving Loyalty, but he knew it was there, just below the horizon on the other side. Falling away from it, the long combe in which Framain's house lay hidden like an embarrassing secret. He considered the merit of heading for it; they might just get there before collapsing from hunger and fatigue, or they might not. There'd be water and shelter there, but probably no food — had the Mezentines set fire to the place when they rounded them up? He couldn't remember that far back. "I know where we are," he said.

She nodded. He looked at her, properly, for the first time. She was dirty, ragged, painfully thin; there was caked blood on her forehead and in her fringe, probably from one of those scalp wounds that bleed like a fountain. "All right," she said, "which way?"

That was just a little more than he could take. He sat down awkwardly on the rocks and burst out laughing. When she began swearing at him, he explained (quite patiently, he thought, in the circumstances) that there wasn't a way, because there was nowhere for them to go.

25

It was, ran the general consensus, one mystery too many. Why the Ducas, magnanimously reprieved by special order of the Duke himself (the messenger had been questioned and had vowed repeatedly that he'd delivered the reprieve to the Ducas personally), had seen fit to break out of the stockade, murdering a sentry in the process, nobody could say for sure. It stood to reason, however, that it must be something to do with the treason for which he had originally been condemned. It was remembered that, on the fall of Civitas Eremiae, he hadn't immediately joined his duke in exile, as was his duty, but had used the resistance as an excuse to stay away, safely out of the reach of justice. It could hardly be a coincidence that he had shown up immediately after the failed Mezentine attack, particularly since, by his own admission, he'd been with the Mezentine garrison at Sharra shortly before the raid took place. There was also the bizarre way in which he'd tried to have Daurenja, the savior of the rear echelon, arrested and condemned for some mysterious crime he was supposed to have committed years earlier. Duke Orsea's refusal to comment was simply aristocratic rank-closing. It did him credit, to a degree, that he was prepared to cover up for his friend, even though that friend had already betrayed him at least once (and wasn't there supposed to be something going on between the Ducas and Orsea's wife? Some business with a letter); in the circumstances, however, his attitude came across as a stubborn attempt to obstruct Valens' quite legitimate inquiries, and won Orsea no friends among the Vadani. The details were irrelevant, in any case. The Ducas had murdered a Vadani soldier in cold blood. Complex issues of jurisdiction no longer mattered. He was a criminal in the eyes of Vadani law, and would pay the penalty if and when he was caught — though that seemed unlikely if, as was generally believed, he'd returned to the safety of his Mezentine friends at Sharra. Meanwhile, the Vadani had other, more pressing concerns, and delaying the march on account of one fugitive renegade was, naturally, out of the question.

Four days after the change of course, he found the courage to talk to her.

They'd stopped for the night in a little combe, not much more than a dent in the hillside. He assumed it had been chosen because of the stand of tall, spindly birch trees, which masked them from sight. It was a dark, cold place; he was sure nothing lived there. She had climbed down from the coach, pleading cramp after a long day. Of course, they couldn't have a fire, for fear that the smoke would give away their position. She was sitting on the trunk of a fallen tree, squinting at her embroidery in the thin red light of sunset.

"Are you still doing that?" he asked.

She looked up. "Of course," she said. "It's nearly finished. I've put so much work into it, I couldn't bear the thought of leaving it behind."

He looked at it: a baldrick, the sort you hang a hunting horn from. A goshawk and a heron; the hawking livery of the Orseoli. She was making it for him, of course.

"It's very good," he said awkwardly. "Can I see?"

She held it up. "You've seen it before," she said. "I've been working on it for three months."

Implication: he should've recognized it. But one piece of cloth with patterns stitched on it looked very much like all the others; apart from their wedding day, he couldn't remember seeing her without some rag or other on her knees. It was, after all, what women did.

"Of course," he said, "I remember it now. It's coming on really well."

She sighed. "I've run out of green silk," she said. "So I can't finish the background — here, look, the patch of reeds the heron's supposed to be flying up out of. I've got some other green, but it's the wrong shade."

He frowned. "Couldn't you turn that bit into a bush or something?"

"I suppose so. But then it wouldn't look right."

"I won't mind."

She looked up at him, and he realized she wasn't making it for him. He was the pretext, at best; she had to embroider, and decency required that the fruit of her needle should be some useful object for her husband. Now, because of the Mezentines and the war, she couldn't finish the work, and it wouldn't be fitting for her to start something new until the baldrick was completed. Accordingly, here she sat, the workbasket on her knees, the baldrick spread out, but no needle in her hand; like a cow in a crush, waiting patiently because it had nowhere it could go.

"It'd look wrong," she said. "I'd have to put something else in the opposite corner to balance it, and that'd mean unpicking what's there already. Besides, I haven't got enough brown left."

He wanted to say: so fucking what? I'll never go hunting again, so I'll never use it. Put the stupid thing away and talk to me instead. What he said was, "Perhaps we'll run into one of those merchant women on the road. They sell embroidery silks. I remember, we met one a few days ago." (No; longer ago than that. But each day seemed to fuse with the others, like a good fire-weld.) "If I'd known, I could have asked her."

She shrugged. "I don't suppose she'd have had the right green," she said. "It's not a particularly common one. I got what I've been using from that woman who used to call at the palace, back in

Civitas Eremiae. I don't know what the chances are of running into her again."

Orsea couldn't think of anything safe to say. He knew the merchant she was talking about. She must've been the one who delivered the letters — the letters Valens had written her, and her replies. Presumably the price of her couriership had been substantial sales of overpriced haberdashery. But there wouldn't be any more letters, just as there'd be no more cold, bright autumn days after partridges with the falcons. It occurred to him that everything he'd known all his life was gone forever, apart from her; and the irony was, he didn't know her at all.

In which case, he might as well say it.

"I need to talk to you," he said.

"Talk away." She sighed, turned the embroidery over and took a small blue-bladed knife with an ivory handle out of her basket. "You know, I think I will unpick this corner after all. I've still got plenty of light blue and white. I could do the sky reflected in a pool or something."

She was nicking the tiny loops of the stitches, like a giant cutting the throats of dwarves.

"I need to ask you . . ." He stopped. He'd never been particularly good with words anyway. Ideas that were sharp and clear in his mind disintegrated like sodden paper when he tried to express them. The only person he'd ever really been able to talk to was Miel Ducas.

"Sorry," she said, "I missed that. What did you want to speak to me about?"

"I need to know, Veatriz," he said, and stopped again. It sounded too pompous and melodramatic for words. "You and Valens. The letters."

She looked at him so blankly that for a moment it crossed his mind that the whole thing was a mistake; he'd completely misunderstood, and there never were any letters. "What about them?" she asked.

"Are you in love with him?"

"No." She was concentrating on the tip of the knife; a small, dainty thing, presumably Mezentine.

"Then why did you write to him?"

She shrugged. It wasn't an answer. He waited, but she didn't say anything.

"Can't you see how it looked?" he said. "You must have realized."

"I suppose so," she said, and between them there was a wall of iron, like the defenses bolted to the sides of the carts.

"Then why did you do it?"

"Does it matter anymore?" She lifted her head and looked at him.

"Do you still love me?"

"Yes," she said. "Do you still love me?"

"Yes, of course I do." He said the words like a mother answering a child's annoying question.

"Well, then." She sighed. "What do you think's happened to Miel?"

"Don't change the subject," he said, but he knew she hadn't done any such thing. That Miel Ducas should have taken away their sins, like some sacrificial animal, was somehow inevitable: the Ducas lives only to serve the state, and the state is the Duke. That, at least, had never been more true. Orsea had seen to that. He was all that was left of Eremia now; an irrelevant survival. Once, years ago, someone digging in the palace grounds had unearthed a big, crude-looking gold cup. He'd brought it, quite properly, to the Duke, who'd rewarded him suitably with twice its value by weight. Orsea could remember sitting holding it: an ugly thing, badly made, bent and slightly crumpled, valuable only as a curiosity, and because of the material it was made from. Presumably it was very old, made by someone who'd lived there a long time ago, for a rich patron whose name had been forgotten centuries before. There had been a city, with a ruler who employed craftsmen; probably he had a suitable household, faithful courtiers who lived only to serve, a code of honor. Presumably he'd tried to be a good duke, always do the right thing. Inevitably, he would have made mistakes. Now, all that was left of all that was one awkward, stupid-looking gold thing, precious only because of the universal convention by which gold is valuable. If the duke who commissioned the cup had had a wife who loved him once, that was irrelevant now as well. Orsea had given orders for the cup to be put in a safe place where he wouldn't have to look at it. He imagined the Mezentines had it now, or the fire had melted it.

The cup had survived, but that wasn't enough. So with love; even if it survives, it's not enough, shorn of context.

"I do love you," she said. An accusation; a reproach. He believed her. If he hadn't; if she'd said she loved Valens, he'd have given her up without a moment's hesitation (because he loved her; it would've been the right thing to do). He'd been prepared for that, even hoping for it, as a condemned man looks forward to execution as a final end to his misery. No such luck. Love still held them in their places, like the traces that bind the donkey to the treadmill. Love is duty. Miel Ducas could have confirmed that, if only he'd still been there.

As it was; she could say that to him, and all it did was brace the iron plate between them, tighter than Daurenja's three-quarter bolts. The fact was that he didn't deserve her. Valens, swooping down with his cavalry into the ruins of Civitas Eremiae, had snatched her away to safety, like the hawk striking the heron, and it was wrong, against nature, to deny the supremacy of the stronger, the absolute right of conquest. Keeping her (being allowed to keep her) was therefore an abomination; his fault and hers, for which they must inevitably pay a price.

I could explain all this so clearly, Orsea thought, if there was anybody in the world I could talk to.

"I love you too," he said, casually as a sleepy monk making his responses in the middle of the night. "I'm sorry I mentioned —"

"It's all right," she said. "Just, don't talk about it again. It's all my fault, all of this."

No, he couldn't have that. "Oh, right," he said. "It's your fault we're both here, alive, instead of being killed when they took the city. Well, that's what would've happened, if Valens hadn't rescued us, because of the letters." He smiled, cold as breath condensing on steel. "I really wish there was some way I could thank him, given I owe him my life, but I can't; how could I? You know what? I should've stayed in the city and been killed; I'd have been out of the way then. You and Valens —"

"Please don't." She was right, of course. Just melodrama, a big speech, with no audience. Even a duke can't make speeches if there's nobody left to listen to them. "I'm sorry," he said, and pulled a face that was almost comic in its intensity. "I shouldn't —"

He stopped short; someone was coming. An officer and two soldiers, walking briskly, on their way somewhere, with important business to see to. He stepped aside to let them go past, but they stopped. Apparently they had something to say to him.

"Duke Orsea." A statement rather than an inquiry.

"That's right."

"My name is Major Nennius. I have to tell you that you're under arrest."

While they waited, they talked about silver; better and more efficient ways of mining it, smelting the ore, refining the bloom to leach out traces of copper and other impurities. The Mezentines, he said, were capable of producing silver that was ninety-five parts in a hundred pure, although the specification allowed an additional margin of three parts for export work, five for domestic consumption. When the war was over and they opened the mines up again, he'd teach the superintendents how to improve purity and increase production by means of a few simple procedures, which could be incorporated into the mines' established working practices without the need for significant investment or extensive retraining. Valens replied that he would appreciate any help that Ziani could give them; once the war was over, the cost of reconstruction and making good would inevitably be high, and a quick, efficient recommencement of silver production would make all the difference. Fortuitously, given that nearly all the mine-owners and representatives of the major cartels had been killed, either in the wedding-day raid or the recent battle, obstruction from vested interests ought not to be as much of a problem as it would have been before the war.

The tent flap opened. Ziani recognized the newcomer, though he couldn't recall his name; a busy young man who'd been doing rather well during the emergency. He made a mental note to find out more about him, in case he could be made useful.

"Duke Orsea," the young officer said.

He stood back to let the escort bring Orsea in. Ziani made himself keep perfectly still, and it was probably just as well that Orsea didn't look at him as he came into the tent.

"Valens?" he asked mildly. The two soldiers weren't touching him, but they flanked him on either side, with the officer blocking the doorway to cut off his escape. "What's going on?"

There wasn't the faintest trace of expression on Valens' face; but he said, "Oh, I think you can probably guess. Sit down, please."

But there wasn't a chair; so the officer (Nennius, Ziani remembered. Recently promoted) had to fetch a folding chair from the back of the tent and set it up. "I'm sorry," Orsea was saying, "but I really don't have a clue. Is this something to do with Miel Ducas? I've been meaning to talk to you about that, but you've been so busy."

Valens was scowling. "Fine," he said. "I'm all for proper procedure. That way, everybody knows where they stand."

"You're sounding very official. Is something wrong?" Orsea glanced over his shoulder; he seemed surprised to find that Nennius and the two guards were still there.

"I have reason to believe . . ." Valens hesitated, then went on: "I have reason to believe that you've been in contact with the enemy. I'd like to hear what you've got to say about that."

Orsea looked so utterly bewildered that for a moment Ziani held his breath. Then Orsea said: "Contact with the enemy? You mean, in the battle?"

"Before the battle," Valens said quietly. "That's rather the point." He opened the wooden box that stood on the folding table in front of him, and took out a small square of folded parchment. "I'm afraid I've been reading your mail," he said.

Orsea frowned. "That's a letter, is it? For me?"

"Yes." His hand was resting on it. "I can't let you have it, I'm afraid; evidence and all that. Major Nennius, would you please read the letter out loud? Admirably clear handwriting," he added. "I hate it when people scrawl."

Nennius stepped forward, and Valens handed him the letter. Nennius opened it and cleared his throat; that made Valens smile, just briefly.

Lucao Psellus to Orsea Orseoli, greetings.

Everything's been arranged as we agreed. The only change of plan is that we can't send a whole division; there simply isn't enough time. I'm sure it won't make any difference, since we'll have an overwhelming advantage of surprise.

Concerning your own personal safety. Naturally, it's got to look right. I've briefed the expedition commander, and he'll see to it that all his officers will know what to expect. To begin with, stay in your coach. As soon as the fighting reaches you, come straight out and give yourself up. Say, in a loud, clear voice, "I am Duke Orsea, I surrender." You have my solemn undertaking that you will not be harmed. You'll be taken straight to a Mezentine officer. Give him this letter. He'll recognize the seal. I'll be there at the Unswerving Loyalty to meet you after the battle and escort you back to Mezentia; from there you'll go directly to your new estate at Lonazep, where you can start your new life. Unfortunately, it won't be possible for your wife to accompany you; but rest assured that our men will have strict instructions not to harm her; she'll be separated out from the rest of the prisoners and sent to join you as quickly as possible. I know this may sound unduly haphazard, but I assure you that you can rely on us; I've arranged for a substantial bounty to be paid to the men who secure your wife and yourself, alive and unharmed. That's the joy of mercenaries; motivating them is never a problem if you've got the money.

I appreciate that this has all been very difficult for you, and I may say that your misgivings do you credit. It can't have been an easy decision to take. However, believe me when I tell you that you're doing precisely the right thing. The only hope, for your people and yourself, is to end the war before the Vadani contrive to inflict serious losses on the Republic. As for Duke Valens: by seducing your wife he has betrayed you in a manner that is beyond all forgiveness. A man like that can have no claim on your loyalties; and, by your own admission, your duty to your people overrides all personal obligations.

I look forward to meeting you in person at last, when all this is over.

During the long silence that followed, Ziani forced himself to keep his eyes fixed on the patch of ground directly in front of him. The last thing he wanted was to catch Valens' eye, or Orsea's. It had all been beautifully clear in his mind when he was giving Psellus his instructions back in the deserted city; he'd seen it in his mind's eye as a splendid piece of geometry, a work of clear lines and simple design — a tumbler under pressure from a spring, retained by a sear tripped by a lever. This close, all he could see was tool-marks and burred edges.

"The letter was found," Valens said eventually, in a perfectly flat voice, "on the body of a merchant woman. Pure chance, as far as I can tell; by the looks of it, she was thrown by her horse and broke her neck tumbling down a rocky slope. Fortuitously, she was discovered by the miners coming up to meet us from Boatta. Ziani Vaatzes searched the body and found the letter, and showed it to me. He's identified the seal. Apparently it's rather special. Ziani, what was it again?"

His cue. "The Republic's defense committee," he said. "Commonly known as Necessary Evil. My understanding is that they're the ones running the war. I vaguely remember there was a Lucao Psellus on the committee, though I never had anything to do with anybody that high up the hierarchy."

Another long silence; then Orsea said, "You don't actually believe any of this, do you?" He sounded so bewildered, it was almost endearing.

"You were seen meeting with a merchant," Valens went on, "shortly after the expedition left the city. You were seen taking delivery of something from her: a basket, or a package. You spoke to her briefly. She had asked for you earlier by name. The witnesses have identified the body as the woman you spoke to. I can have them brought here if you like, or we can wait for the formal hearing. Though I suppose I should tell you," Valens added with the unquiet ghost of a grin, "that the hearing'll be a formality, going briskly through the motions. The last thing I need right now is to get bogged down in jurisdictions and immunities and acts of state. So, if you've got anything to say, you'd better say it now."

A long silence. Orsea was peering at him with his face screwed up, as if it was too dark to see properly.

"This is all complete drivel," he said eventually. "For pity's sake, Valens. I haven't got the faintest idea what's going on — nobody ever tells me anything, and why should they? But if this is something to do with you and Veatriz —"

Valens broke eye contact for a moment. "You're not helping yourself," he said.

"But . . ." Orsea nodded, as if acknowledging that the rules had changed halfway through the game. "All right," he said. "Yes, I remember that merchant woman. She turned up in a stupid little chaise — with a red parasol, I think. Anyway, she handed me some potpourri, which Veatriz had ordered from her some time before we left Civitas —"

"Potpourri?" Valens interrupted.

"Yes. You know, bits of minced-up dried flowers, lavender and stuff. You put it in little saucers to make the room smell nice."

"You're saying she tracked you down in the wilderness, when nobody except me knew where we were headed, just to sell you dried flowers?"

"No, of course not." As close to anger as Valens had ever seen him. All the more likely, in that case, to be synthetic. "She was on her way from Calva to White Cross; she happened to stop off at the Loyalty, and heard we were nearby. She'd got this unfilled order for the potpourri stuff, must've had it with her, and I suppose she'd got a tidy mind or something. Look, there was a cavalry officer who saw her arrive. Maybe he overheard what she said to me."

Valens nodded. "Captain Vesanio. I've spoken to him. She asked for you by name, and quite by chance you were standing by, only a few yards away. He heard what you said to her, and he saw you take a package from her."

"Exactly," Orsea said. "The dried flowers. I took them, and I gave them to Veatriz. Call her here and ask her yourself. She'll tell you, she ordered it before we left. She probably knows the stupid woman's name and everything."

Valens smiled. "Was that meant to be a defense?" he said. "I guess my attention must've wandered, and I missed it. Seems to me you're just agreeing with what I've told you."

"But that's what happened." He could see Orsea starting to go red in the face; please don't let him cry, he thought. "That's all that happened. Really."

"Not quite." Valens' voice was getting softer. "You came looking for me, with a message. A warning, rather; you warned me that the Mezentines were at the inn and knew where we were. I believed you. We packed up and moved on, straight into the ambush. Yes, I remember that very well."

"But . . ." Orsea's eyes were wide. "The woman said she'd been told where we were by someone at the Loyalty. I thought you ought to know, because if they knew about us at the inn, and the

Mezentines were there too, then we were in danger. Which was true," he added desperately. "It must have been true, because the Mezentines found us, didn't they?"

"Quite. They knew exactly where we were; *after* I'd heard your message and acted on it." Valens shook his head. "As defenses go," he said, "this one's a pretty poor specimen. Disagree with me about *something*, for crying out loud, even if it's only the color of her hat."

Orsea didn't say anything. He was staring, his mouth slightly open, like a man who's just seen something he knows is impossible.

"There's the letter," Valens said wearily. "It pretty much speaks for itself. There's your own admission that you were seen talking to the bearer of the letter on at least one occasion; also, you admit that you and your wife had had previous dealings with her, before we left Civitas Vadanis. You also admit giving me the message that caused me to lead the expedition to the place where we were attacked." He frowned. "All right," he said, "you've heard the interpretation I'm putting on these facts we all agree are true. Maybe you could give me yours, and we'll see if it makes better sense."

Orsea looked round, as if he expected help to arrive. "I don't know, do I?" he said. "I suppose — well, I suppose somebody's trying to make it look like I'm a traitor, and I betrayed us all to the Mezentines. But —"

"But who would want to do that?" Valens interrupted. "Good question. Whoever it was, he was able to procure a letter from an authentic Mezentine official — a pretty high-ranking one at that; so the enemy were in on it as well. Are you going to argue that the Mezentines are plotting to discredit you?"

"I don't know." Orsea rubbed his face with the palms of his hands, as if he was trying to wake himself up. "I suppose it's possible, yes."

"I can't see it myself," Valens replied gently. "To be perfectly frank, why on earth would they bother? Well? Can you give me a reason? Can you tell me why you matter to them anymore?"

Silence. "No," Orsea said.

"Nor me," Valens replied. "Come to think of it, I can't come up with anybody who'd want to frame you for treason, or anything else, except for one person; the only man who's got any sort of motive for trying to get you into trouble, get rid of you."

Orsea looked at him. "You."

"That's right." Valens acknowledged him with a slight gesture of his left hand. "Me. I have a motive for getting you out of the way. What I don't have is the influence to get Commissioner Lucao Psellus of the defense committee to write an incriminating letter." He paused, then added: "And I don't really see me arranging for the Mezentines to ambush my own convoy, slaughter my people and near as damn it kill me in the process. I'm not the nicest man in the world, but I'm not the most stupid, either. I think I'd have found an easier way of getting shot of you — poison, an accident, all sorts of things spring readily to mind." A smile flashed across his face. "So, if it wasn't the Republic and it wasn't me; who else have you been pissing off, Orsea? You're such a mild, inoffensive fellow, always so anxious to do the right thing. Your friend Miel Ducas, maybe? The man you condemned for treason for hiding a letter? We haven't talked about him yet. Do you think the Ducas might be behind all this?"

Orsea breathed in, then out again. "No," he said.

"You don't? I'd have considered him myself, but if you say not, I'm happy to be guided by you. So, forget the Ducas; anybody else?" He spread his fingers on the top of the folding table. "You're really going to have to come up with somebody or something, if you want me to take your denials seriously. Come on, Orsea, help me out. I've been making all the running so far. Suggest *something*, if only for my sake. Otherwise . . ." He shrugged. "Well, what would you do, in my position?"

"I can't." Orsea was looking straight at him. "Do you want me to make something up? I can't think of any explanation, any reason. It's just not true, that's all."

Valens sighed, then shifted in his chair, leaning forward a little.

"The legal position," he said, in a rather forced tone of voice, "is complicated. A case could be made for saying that I have no jurisdiction over you, since you are the head of state of a foreign country — one that doesn't exist anymore, but the law can be funny about that sort of thing. If we were to have a proper trial, with lawyers and everything, I can see us getting well and truly laid up on that one. To be honest with you, I haven't got the time or the patience; and something like that, dragging on and on, isn't likely to do my people's morale any good, either. In fact, I'd prefer it if they didn't know that someone I'd trusted had sold us out to the Mezentines. I wouldn't particularly want them to know his motive for doing it — I'm quite satisfied in my mind what that motive was, by the way. I noticed that note of high moral indignation in your friend Psellus' letter — seducing another man's wife, completely unforgivable. For what it's worth, Orsea, I never did anything of the sort. We wrote letters to each other, that's all. Before I came and pulled you both out of Civitas Eremiae, the last time I set eyes on her I was seventeen. Now, maybe what I did was — well, bad manners, let's say, or worse than that, a breach of protocol and bad form generally. For that, I apologize. What you did . . ." He shrugged. "I've never seen the point of getting angry," he said. "Far better to deal with problems as efficiently as possible, which is much easier to do with a cool head. I'm sorry, but I know what's got to be done."

He paused, as if inviting Orsea to say something. Silence.

"Fine," Valens went on. "As I see it, there're two courses of action open to me. One of them — well, you can guess. The alternative is to send you over to your Mezentine friends, let them have the bother and expense of feeding and clothing you. The risk in that is what you could tell them, things they'd like to know about troop numbers, supplies, future movements. Now, I don't actually believe you know very much; quite likely you've already told them everything you can. Sending you to them wouldn't be too much of a risk, in my opinion. On the other hand, I'm not sure it's what I want to do. Have you got any strong feelings on the issue, one way or another?"

But Orsea shook his head. "I can't believe you really think I'd do something like that," he said. "So all I can think of is, you want me out of the way so —" He stopped, as though he didn't know the word for what he was trying to say. "If that's it," he said, "you're making a very bad mistake."

Valens frowned a little, like a parent rebuking a child's untimely frivolity.

"If you —" Again Orsea stopped short. "If anything happens to me because of you," he said, "she'll never speak to you again. You'll lose any chance you might've had —"

"I know." Valens' face was set, but his eyes were wide and bright. "That can't be helped," he said briskly. "And you aren't helping me make up my mind. Who's going to get you, the Mezentines or the crows?"

"You can't send me to the Mezentines. They'd kill me."

"Orsea." Exasperation; a patient man reaching the end of his tether. "Haven't you been *listening?* I'm sorry, but you've gone too far, and I don't have any choice." He turned his head to look at Nennius. "Change of plan," he said. "There won't be a formal hearing, I want this business settled straightaway. Please deal with it; now, as quickly as possible. I'll need a report — nothing long-winded, just a note with the date, time, names of three witnesses." He hesitated, then added, "Be reasonably discreet about it, will you? I don't want the whole camp knowing about it; not yet, anyway."

If Nennius hesitated, it was only for a fraction of a second; then he nodded to the two guards, who closed in around Orsea like the jaws of a pair of tongs. Orsea looked at them; he was still sitting in his chair, his hands on his knees.

"Orsea," Valens said. The tone of voice would have suited a man reprimanding a disobedient dog.

"No," Orsea said, and his voice was high and weak. "Valens, this is stupid. You can't honestly believe —"

"All right," Valens said (a gentle man pushed too far). "I wasn't going to mention it, because — believe it or not — I'm really not enjoying this. But so what; it wasn't the first time, was it?"

Orsea's mouth and throat moved several times before he managed to speak. "I don't understand."

"The first attack," Valens said wearily. "On my wedding day. Yes, I wondered about that; I gave it quite a lot of thought at the time, and then other stuff came along and got in the way. The Mezentine cavalry didn't just turn up out of the blue, on the off chance they'd catch us all out in the open. Someone told them where we were likely to be. It had to be someone who knew the plan for the day: which coverts we were going to draw, where the birds were, roughly how long we'd take over each drive. I've been trying to remember who I discussed the plan with; well, the falconers, obviously, but I ruled them out, they didn't have any way of passing on a message. I suppose they could have been reporting back to someone else, but I doubt it. I've known most of them all my life, and the rest are from families that've been in our service for generations. No, the only person I could remember going over the program with in detail was Jarnac Ducas; and for the life of me, I couldn't see him as a traitor, not under any circumstances. Then I found out my friend Mezentius had been spying for the Mezentines, so I assumed it was him; but he wasn't even there, he was away on the frontier. I know, because I wanted him to be at the wedding, but he couldn't make it back in time. Then it struck me, left me wondering how I could've been so dim. You got the details of the plan from Jarnac — you asked him, making out you were interested; he'd have assumed there was no harm in telling you. Then you scribbled a few lines to your friend Psellus —"

"You're out of your mind, Valens." Anger, but too weak with shock to rise above petulance. "I was nearly killed. That weird engineer, Daurenja, he rescued me. Ask him."

Valens tapped the letter on his desk with his forefinger. "Presumably you had an arrangement with Psellus to make it look convincing, just like in this letter here. I'm not going to discuss it with you, Orsea, this isn't a trial. I'd more or less figured out it was you before we left the city, but I was too weak and scared of — well, what you said just now. I forgave you; I reckoned you'd have learned your lesson, you wouldn't try anything so stupid again. Then, when this last lot happened, I tried to put you at the back of my mind, until Vaatzes' people found the woman's body and the letter. Even then, I wasn't going to do anything, because of her. I suppose I was fooling myself, thinking — well, no point in saying it, we both know what I'm talking about. But then she came to see me, about that fool Miel Ducas, and we talked about various things."

Orsea grinned at him, like a dying animal baring its teeth. "She turned you down."

Valens smiled; empty, like a flayed skin. "She made me realize I'd been acting like a bloody fool for quite long enough; that I should never have interfered at Civitas Eremiae, and that it was time I cut my losses and started behaving like a grown-up with responsibilities. I'm very sorry," he went on, looking away, "but I can't risk a third time, not even for you. Nennius, if you'd be so kind."

The guards caught hold of Orsea's wrists; they sort of flicked him up out of the chair and onto his feet; so accomplished at holding and controlling a man that it was impossible to tell whether Orsea was trying to struggle or not. They turned him round (no ostentatious use of force; small movements are the most efficient) and propelled him out of the tent. Nennius saluted formally and followed them. The tent flap fell back into place.

Ziani looked up, trying to see Valens' face without being too obvious about it, but his head was turned and in shadow. He waited for Valens to say something.

"Well," Valens said. "That's another rotten job I can cross off my list. My father always used to say, when you've got a load of shitty jobs to get done, do two or three a day for a week and it's not so bad." For a moment he let his chin sink onto his chest, and then he looked up again. "Silver mines," he said. "We were talking about air pumps for underground galleries."

"Were we?" Ziani shook his head. "I'm sorry," he said, "I can't remember."

Valens clicked his tongue. "You were saying that a big double-action bellows was all right for relatively shallow shafts, but for deeper work there's some way of using fires to suck air down into the tunnels. Sounded a bit dubious to me, but you're the engineer."

Ziani took a deep breath. "What's going to happen to him?"

"What do you think?" Valens laughed. "You Mezentines may be streets ahead of us in everything else, but when it comes to judicial murder, we've got you beat every time. You won't find any condemned traitors getting away from us by jumping out of windows or carving up sentries. Count yourself lucky on that score that you didn't have us to contend with. No, they'll probably take him round behind one of the big supply wagons and do it there. It's where the butchers go to slaughter chickens, out of sight of the horses so they don't spook. It's amazing, the way horses freak out if they see something getting killed; though not people, oddly enough, only other animals. Though we did have a few of the wagon horses go crazy during the battle; smashed up their traces and bolted, miserable bloody creatures. It makes you ask yourself: why can't anything in this world ever hold *still?*" He paused, then shrugged his shoulders. "It was justice, that's all. I can see why you probably don't like the look of it, you having had such a close call yourself. Can't blame you; but it's got to be done."

"What about the Duchess?" Ziani asked. "Will she understand?"

Valens scowled, then said: "No, of course not. I've screwed that up, for good. But that's no bad thing. It was a distraction; all very fine and splendid when there's nothing serious going on, but when you're facing the annihilation of your people, you need to keep a clear head. If we're going to get across the desert, I'll need to be able to concentrate. Hence the clearing up of odds and ends." He shifted suddenly in his seat, then became still again. "That Nennius is a competent man. Still a bit young, but he has the rare and valuable virtue of doing what he's told." He yawned; genuinely tired, as far as Ziani could judge. "Do you think I should've sent him back to the Mezentines?"

"No," Ziani said.

Valens nodded. "It did seem like a fair compromise," he said, "but I thought, what the hell, let's just for once do something properly, instead of fudging the issue just in case we've misjudged it. My father always used to say, never ever give anybody a second chance. I always used to think he was a vicious bastard. Well, he was, but I'm beginning to understand why. Didn't somebody say once that the tragedy of mankind is that as they get older, sons gradually turn into their fathers? Probably a young man, the one who said that. I wish I'd had the chance to know my father when I was a bit older. He died when I was at that rebellious stage, and so I've always been torn between hating and despising everything he stood for, and trying to be his deputy, so to speak, doing the things he'd have done if he'd lived. Of course, he'd never have gone to Civitas Eremiae; which rather puts me in my place, don't you think?"

Ziani stood up. "If that's everything you wanted to see me about . . ." he said.

Outside, nothing seemed out of the ordinary. They were carrying hay on pitchforks to feed the horses, or rolling barrels, or searching for strayed children, or arguing with the sentries about some camp regulation or other. Obviously Nennius had done a properly discreet job; not a good idea to spook the rest of the flock by slaughtering a duke where people could see. Well; the news would circulate quickly enough. Built into Ziani's calculations was the assumption that Orsea's death would be a popular move among the Vadani; they'd all sleep better at night knowing that the traitor who'd brought the Mezentines down on them was dead, and Valens would be respected for not allowing the malefactor's exalted rank to save him. He paused to remember Orsea as he'd first encountered him — wounded in the disastrous battle, confused, tearing himself apart with guilt, still able to find a little compassion for the misfortunes of a stranger. Well; like a true nobleman, he'd lived to serve. In death he'd been useful. By now, he was just a carcass, inedible meat. One more, among so very many.

"There you are." He looked round and saw Daurenja loping toward him like a big, friendly dog. "I've been looking for you, but nobody seemed to know where you'd got to."

Not now, Ziani thought. "I've been busy," he said. "The Duke . . ."

"Won't take a moment." Daurenja fell in beside him, matching his pace exactly. "I've been thinking," he said. "You remember I talked to you a while back, about this pet project of mine. The exploding sulfur compound, and making a tube to use it in."

"Oh, that." Ziani frowned. "I haven't given it any thought, I'm afraid."

"That's all right," Daurenja said magnanimously. "You've had other things on your mind. But I've been thinking about it — what you said, about forging the tube rather than casting it. Great idea, and I can see the sense in it, but there's a few small details I'd like your opinion on. For a start —"

"Not now," Ziani said.

"Oh, just while we're walking," Daurenja replied cheerfully. "I'm sure it's me being thick, and you can explain what I've been missing in just a few words. Let's see, now. You were talking about staves, like making a barrel; presumably you're thinking about butt-welding them around a mandrel. But —"

"You don't want to take any of that too seriously," Ziani said irritably. "I was just thinking aloud. On reflection, I'm fairly sure it wouldn't work."

"Oh, I don't agree. I think you've cracked it. But were you thinking about welding all the staves in turn, a separate heat for each one, or trying to do the whole lot in one heat? Only there's distortion to think about if you're doing them piecemeal, but if you're going for simultaneous, you'd need to rotate the mandrel, which'd mean —"

Ziani stopped. "Why don't you listen?" he said. "I'm not interested in helping you with this ridiculous idea of yours. I've heard about what happened to your last business partner." Daurenja pulled what he guessed was supposed to be an appeasing face, but he ignored it. "If I were you," he went on, "I'd clear out now, while you still can. Piss off back to the Cure Doce, or Lonazep. Or the Mezentines, if you really admire them so much — if you're Cure Doce by birth, that makes you a neutral, they've got no quarrel with your people. Go away, and leave me alone."

"I don't think so." Daurenja looked faintly disappointed, maybe a little hurt. "Thanks to you, I've made myself very useful here. They need me. I'm afraid you can't just chuck me out if and when you feel like it, I'm working directly for the Duke these days. Besides," he added, "things have changed rather a lot in the last half-hour, haven't they?"

"What do you mean?"

Daurenja sighed. "I happened to see my friend Major Nennius just now," he said. "I don't think he saw me; he was preoccupied, a job he was doing. Not," he added quickly, "that I blame you. Had to be done, I can see that quite clearly; you had no choice. But I don't think Duke Valens would be very happy if he knew about how it had come about, if you get my meaning."

It was that kind of fear that chills you to the bone; not the heart-stopping kind that forces all the breath out of you, or the immediate physical danger that loosens the bowels and the bladder. In spite of it, Ziani found he could keep quite calm. "I don't understand," he said.

"Of course you do," Daurenja said indulgently. "And I appreciate it's not something you feel like discussing, especially out here in the open where people might be eavesdropping. We'll have a nice long chat about it some time, when we're both of us not quite so busy. I will say this, though: you're a clever man. False modesty aside, I've always reckoned I'm quite smart, a cut above everybody else I've ever come across — you've got to believe that, haven't you, or how can you justify doing the difficult, nasty stuff? But I can see, compared to you I'm crude and ignorant. You could say, I am to you as the Vadani are to the Mezentines. Uncouth, you could call it. Unsophisticated." He smiled warmly. "I knew you were the right man for me to tag along with; I knew it when I first heard about you. A man after my own heart, I thought. I mean, look at what you've achieved, and practically nothing to work with. And look at you now. Leading the Vadani to join up with the Cure Hardy and change the entire world; and all so you can go home. Quite apart from the skill of it, the sheer scope of your vision is magnificent." He shook his head. "I know this sounds corny as hell, but I'm really proud to know you, Ziani Vaatzes. Today of all days; when it all started to come together, I mean." He shrugged. "Look," he went on, "I can tell you're not really in the mood for talking about lap-welds and expansion coefficients; we'll leave it for another time. I hope you don't mind me saying my piece, by the way. Only, my principle's always been, be open with people, tell them what you think. That's got to be the right way, hasn't it?"

He smiled again and walked away.

26

Eight days of blundering through potholes and ruts. Intermittent rain; the carts bogged down twice, once in a mudslide, once in the bed of a shallow river that wasn't on the map and hadn't been mentioned by any of the guides. Food running low; rations had to be reduced by a third; fodder for the horses a worse problem. A mild outbreak of some kind of fever, which killed a dozen or so civilians. Ahead of them, the mountain range; beyond that, the edge of the desert. No sign, yet, of the Mezentines.

A village, Limes Vitae; Valens had heard about it, mostly because it was proverbially the last place on earth, the very edge of the world. According to family legend, one of his father's uncles had been there once, though why or what he thought of it wasn't recorded. It had sent a dozen light infantry to fight in the first war against the Eremians, and had last paid taxes seventy-four years ago. If there was still a settlement there, and if they had food and hay, getting over the mountain was possible. If not; well.

A few thin cattle on the stony plain bore witness to some level of habitation, as the carts ground up the road through the foothills. A boy, who stopped to stare and was scooped up by outriders, confirmed that the village was still where it had always been. There was food there; just enough to see the villagers through the winter, since it had been a poor year generally, and the merchants who traded root vegetables and salt fish for hides and wool hadn't arrived; there was some rumor about a war somewhere. Hay? Enough for all the horses in the column? The boy didn't want to commit himself on that, but the grown-ups had been saying that hay would be short that winter.

Valens left the boy in the custody of a grim-faced woman who cooked for the soldiers, and summoned his general staff. Limes Vitae, he told them, was unlikely to welcome them with open arms, and even less likely to offer to share its reserves. Accordingly, since they couldn't rely on being given, they were going to have to take.

Tactically, not very much of a challenge. Two wings of light cavalry moved into position on the far side of the village shortly before dusk, taking great care not to be seen. At dawn, a double squadron of heavy cavalry advanced at a gentle pace along the main road into the village. A shepherd raised the alarm; by the time Valens' heavy dragoons reached the village square, the place was deserted and the barns, cattle-pens, poultry runs and root cellars were empty. They made themselves at home as best they could, eventually turning up a few barrels of wheat beer that had been too heavy to load in the hurried evacuation. Nobly, they left half of the foul-tasting stuff for their colleagues in the light division, who rode in halfway through the afternoon, escorting the villagers and the carts laden with the missing supplies, which they'd ambushed as planned on the narrow road that led to the hidden valley the boy had told Valens about. Neat, flawless, bloodless, as a good operation should be.

Valens sent Nennius to give the villagers a choice; they could leave their homes and join the column, or stay where they were and starve through the winter. It didn't surprise Valens very much to learn that they preferred, unanimously, to stay. He couldn't blame them. Their only contact with the central government within living memory was a callous act of theft, carried out with all the precision and élan of the better class of professional brigand. So much for Valens the Good Duke.

A quick inventory of the supplies told him that the entire

resources of Limes Vitae would supply the column, on half-rations, for ten days. Two days to the edge of the desert; eight days across it, if the dead merchant's diary could be relied on and they managed to find the short cut. No need for a decision, now that turning back was no longer an option. Just to be sure, he told Nennius to ask the villagers if they'd seen any Mezentines; black-faced men in armor on big horses. By their reaction, the villagers must have assumed he was making fun of them.

Climbing the mountain proved to be far harder than anybody had anticipated. Valens had assumed it would be slightly but not much more difficult than slogging up the slopes and scarps they'd tackled already; slow, painful climbing with occasional halts to fill in and rebuild crumbled road ledges or bridge storm-streams running down the hillsides. The dead merchant had managed it, with his team of mules. It had taken him two days.

Halfway through the first day, Valens realized why the merchant had used mules rather than a cart. Quite possibly there had been a road there, once upon a time when the world was new. Now, however, there was a thin scratch that zigzagged across the face of the mountain, the sort of line Vaatzes the engineer might have scribed on a piece of metal, rubbing in blue dye to make it visible. No earthly chance of taking a cart further than the first mile.

At a hastily convened meeting of the engineering department, Valens asked urgently for suggestions.

"It's a question of time," Vaatzes said, and for the first time since he'd met him, Valens saw that he was worried. "Yes, we could widen the road by cutting into the mountain; to a limited extent, we could bank up the other side with rocks. At a rough guess, working flat out we could reach the top in under a month. In two days . . ." He shrugged. "Either we turn back now, or we ditch the wagons, load what we can onto the horses' backs and walk. I don't suppose it'll take us that much longer on foot than it would've done if we could've taken the wagons, if that's any consolation."

"Your bloody trader —" Valens interrupted.

"If he could do it, I don't see why we can't," Vaatzes replied. "I didn't get the impression from reading the journals that he was any sort of adventurer, blessed with superhuman strength and endurance. He regarded crossing the mountains as a chore and a pain in the bum, but no worse than that."

"Just suppose we do make it over the mountains," someone said. "What then? I thought the idea was that the carts were going to be our mobile fortress. And there's shelter to think about."

"The carts won't go up the mountain," Daurenja said. "That's a plain fact, like something in mathematics you can demonstrate by doing a calculation. If we go back down the mountain, we've got eight days and then we starve. No disrespect, but I can't see what there is to talk about."

They left the carts. It wasn't the most popular order Valens had ever given. The sight of the Vadani people struggling up the road with enormous loads strapped to their backs, like city people out for a country picnic, would've been comic in a different context. As a gesture of solidarity, Valens made the cavalry dismount and load supplies on their horses, an initiative which at least had the merit of wiping the smirks off their faces. Cavalrymen dislike walking. Even then, it was a full-time job to stop the civilians from dumping their packs as soon as the gradient started to get tiresome; they seemed to be under the impression that there was more than enough food and forage piled up on the horses, and the Duke was making them carry stuff up a steep hill as part of a monstrously inappropriate practical joke. On the first day there were ninety-seven casualties — twelve deaths, sixteen broken legs, six non-fatal heart attacks and sixty-three debilitating sprains, falls and similar injuries — and they lost the use of fourteen horses.

The second day was no improvement; the worst part of it being the realization that there was going to have to be a third day, and quite possibly a fourth. This meant a further rations cut, which in turn led to a spate of nocturnal food looting, only just short of a full-scale riot, which cost another seven lives. By noon on the third day, the death toll had passed fifty, with three times that number of sick and injured incapable of walking. The soldiers were demanding to be allowed to jettison their armor; a fair number hadn't waited for permission, and the sun sparkled on a trail of abandoned metalwork marking the column's ascent, like the track of a snail. To check this before it got out of hand, Valens dressed in full armor to lead the way, a gesture he bitterly regretted after the first half-hour as the arches of his greaves chafed his ankles into mince.

Just before dusk, someone told him that there was smoke in the valley below them. Since the only inflammable material on the whole mountain was the carts they'd left behind two days before, the implications were disturbing enough to take his mind off his aching feet for the last hour of daylight.

"It's possible," someone conceded at that night's staff meeting. "We've brought horses up here, so I guess they could too. Or maybe they've dismounted like we did; though in that case, I don't see them catching us up in a hurry."

"They won't try and attack us on the mountain," someone else asserted confidently. "They'll wait till we're over the top and down on the plain. If they're dismounted and leading their horses, they won't have to try and catch us up; they can do that as soon as they're back on level ground again."

"There's no guarantee it's the Mezentines at all," someone else put in. "Could be scavengers, like the ones we ran into earlier."

"Unlikely," Nennius murmured. "We killed them all, remember? Besides, why bother to burn our carts?"

"No use to them without horses."

"True, but why let everybody between here and Sharra know where they are?"

"The Mezentines would have a reason to burn them," Nennius argued. "To stop us circling round behind them and going back to them. They'll want to be sure they've seen the last of those armor plates."

"If the Mezentines want to attack us on the plain, I say let 'em," someone else said. "The rate we're getting through the food and hay, we'll be able to afford to remount the cavalry by then, so we can give them a fight. By the time we get down there, they'll be in no better condition than us. Worse, probably; they've had further to come without fresh supplies; they won't have found anything at Limes Vitae, that's for sure."

Midafternoon on the fourth day, and the view from the top was obscured by low cloud and mist. Below, a long way away, there was supposed to be a desert, with the Cure Hardy on the other side of it, and Valens was taking his people there because he had no choice. Squinting into the mist and seeing nothing, he retraced the workings of the mechanism that had brought him here. It had started with Orsea — no, to be fair, it had started with the peace settlement between the Vadani and the Eremians, which his father had arranged with her father, the Count Sirupat. While the Eremians and the Vadani had been at each other's throats, the Perpetual Republic had ignored them both, since they posed her no threat. Then there was peace, which spawned Orsea's original crass mistake; then Ziani Vaatzes — he'd played some part in all this — gave the Republic a pretext for disinfecting its border of undesirable savages; but instead of crumpling up like a leaf in a fire, the Eremians had fought too well, forcing the war to grow like a clever gardener growing early crops in a hotbed. That was when he'd been drawn in, for the sake of a woman he'd fallen in love with because (he knew the mechanism operated in a loop) of the peace negotiations, which had brought her to Civitas Vadanis as a hostage. For her sake he'd thrown the Vadani into the war; now, for the war's sake, he'd lost her forever, while still having her on his hands like someone else's precious possession left in his unwilling care; and he was here, on top of a mountain looking down at a desert which led to the wilderness of the barbarian nomads, his last and only hope of survival. Wonderful.

Going down the mountain was much, much harder than getting up it. For some reason Valens couldn't begin to imagine, someone had gone to the trouble of making the pathetic little track they'd followed up the mountain. Maybe there'd been a village there once, or a frontier station or a signal post, or a temple to some obsolete god. Nothing had gone down the mountain in a long, long time except water (and, presumably, Vaatzes' dead merchant and his mules). There was no track. To start with, they tried following the course of a broad stream, but it quickly fell away into a series of waterfalls plunging off sheer edges. No wild animals were stupid enough to come up here, so there weren't any deer or goat trails to follow. Valens realized quickly enough that there wasn't a right way to go; the entire expedition would have to make its own way down as best it could, a slow, disorganized shambles, a human mudslide. Giving the order to halve the rations yet again (impossible to enforce, of course, with everybody spread out on the mountainside like butter on bread), he tried very hard indeed not to think about who might have set light to the abandoned wagons, or where the happy arsonists might be now.

The worst problem proved to be the horses. By noon on the second day (the low cloud hadn't lifted; if anything, it was thickening), he'd almost reached the point where he'd be prepared to give the order to turn them loose and leave them there, in the hope that some of them might find their own way down. Leading them was very nearly impossible, and the amount of time they were wasting trying to coax the wretched animals along was heartbreaking. Unhappy-looking officers reported to him every hour or so to tell him the latest casualty figures, animal and human; the number of injured civilians who couldn't walk and so had to be carried was swelling at a terrifying rate, and Nennius had already urged him several times to leave at least some of them behind. So far, he hadn't given in, but the only strength he could draw on to maintain his resolve was the thought that it was precisely the sort of thing Orsea would've done (reluctantly, blaming himself to death, doing the right thing). The hell with it, he told himself, over and over again; I'm stubborn and pig-headed, I won't leave the injured and I won't turn the horses loose. It's just a matter of holding on a little longer, and then facing the decision again, once every hundred yards or so.

Dawn on the third day of the descent. The low cloud had lifted during the night, and they could see: where they were, and where they were going. The good part of it was that they were at least three-quarters of the way down, and the gradient was easing up. Other than that, Valens was sorry to have lost the mist. The sight of the desert depressed him more than anything he could remember.

There was a fringe of scrub — little stunted clumps of thorn bush, like an unshaved face — and then there was nothing but sand. He'd expected it to be gray, like the stuff washed down by rivers, the only sand he'd ever seen; instead, it was almost white, a glowing ocean like steel at welding heat. The rises and troughs looked so much like waves at this distance that he couldn't help imagining that it was a vast lake — the idea of trying to walk on its surface seemed ludicrous; you'd wade in, and then you'd sink, and the sand would close over your head as you drowned. It wasn't even flat; the sad little joke that had sustained them all, going up and down the mountain, was that the desert had to be better than all this bloody climbing. Apparently not. He realized, as he stared at it until his eyes hurt in the glare, that for a moment or so he'd forgotten the entire Vadani nation strung out all around him. He'd been thinking, how the hell am *I* going to get across that; I, not we. A fine time to be thinking about grammar (my decision, my mistake, our slow and painful death). One question, however, lodged in his head as he scrambled among the rocks: did I have Orsea killed not because he was a traitor but because I'd reached the conclusion that he was an idiot, too stupid to be allowed to live? The more the question preyed on his mind (the further down the slope they went, the hotter it became; his clothes and even his boots were saturated with sweat), the more he was afraid that that was exactly what he'd done; the fool's stupidity had offended him beyond endurance, and he'd taken the excuse to get rid of him. In which case, sooner or later, he was going to have to admit to what he'd done, and apologize to somebody.

Evening staff meeting on the flat sand; bitterly cold, hardly warmed at all by crackling bonfires of dry thorn twigs, which flared up ferociously and went out almost straightaway. The main subject on the agenda . . .

"According to the map, it's there," Vaatzes repeated for the third or fourth time. "We can't see it because it's over the horizon. But if we keep going due east from the double-pronged spur — which is exactly where it should be according to the map, by the way — we should reach the first oasis in about nine hours' time. That's what the map says; you can look for yourselves. And it's no good scowling at me. I didn't draw the bloody thing, and I've never been here before in my life. Either we trust the map, or we give up and die."

"Are we sure that's the right double-pronged spur?" someone asked nervously; he was sitting just outside the ring of firelight, and Valens didn't recognize the voice. "For all we know, there could be two or three more or less similar. And if we set off on the wrong line, we're screwed; we'll never find the oasis just by roaming about — assuming there's an oasis to find, which is by no means —"

"What are you proposing?" Valens interrupted quietly. "Do you think we should stay here while the scouts ride up and down the foothills looking for more double-pronged spurs? It's a good idea," he added. "Actually, it's the right thing to do, simple common sense. Unfortunately, we can't. No time. As it is, I predict we'll run out of food before we're halfway there, even if we hit the right course and everything's where the map says it is. Sorry," he went on, with a slight shake of his head, "but we're just going to have to assume it's the right two-pronged spur and press on regardless. Unfortunate, but there it is." He grinned suddenly. "My only hope is that the Mezentines really are on our heels with a huge army, and that they follow us out there and starve to death a day or so after we do. Not that I'm vindictive or anything. I just feel that fatal errors of judgment are things you should share with your enemies as well as your friends."

Short, embarrassed silence; then someone said: "If they really are following us, we should see them tomorrow, coming down the slope. At least then we'll know what's going on, whether we've got them to contend with as well as everything else."

"I should say they're the least of our worries," Valens said confidently. "Which is rather splendid, don't you think, to be able to dismiss the threat of the most powerful nation in the world in one trite phrase? I like to think I've contrived to screw things up on so magnificent a scale that getting slaughtered by the Mezentines is probably the second-best thing that could happen to us."

They didn't like him talking like that, of course, but he couldn't really motivate himself to stop it and behave properly. All through that part of his life that separated his first sight of her from that night in the slaughter before Civitas Eremiae (the realization ambushed him like a squadron of Mezentine dragoons, unexpected here among the ruins of everything), at every turn he'd faced a choice, between giving up and forcing a way through, and always he'd chosen to press on; stumbling forward instead of running away, because he'd known where he was supposed to be going. The route was marked for him in the map by success; everything he'd done had turned out right, and so he'd known he was doing the right thing. Then had come the second phase, between rescuing her from the Mezentines and forfeiting her when he ordered Orsea's death, during which everything he'd done had gone wrong, and the signposts along the way had brought him here, to the desert's edge. Here began the third phase, finding him without purpose or direction, no choices left; a rare kind of freedom.

Walking on the sand was like treading in deep mud; even on the flat, every step was an effort, draining strength from his knees and calves. Honor required him to carry a heavier pack than anybody else, to walk in front, to set a smart pace and only stop out of compassion, to let the weaklings catch their breath. Years of trudging up the steep sides of combes to approach upwind of grazing deer and wading through marshes to reach the deep pools where the ducks flocked up had given him the strength and stamina of a peasant, but after a couple of hours of treading sand, only shame and the last flare of arrogance kept him on his feet and moving. If they kept going, they had a chance of reaching the first oasis (if it existed) before nightfall. Something told him that if they failed to reach it by the time darkness fell, they'd never reach it at all. It wasn't, of course, a line of reasoning he could justify to anybody else; so, if he wanted to get them there before it was too late, the only way he could do it was to walk on ahead of them and thereby force them to follow him. Crude but simple.

As if making fun of his self-induced melodrama, the oasis appeared suddenly out of nowhere about two hours before dusk. It had been hiding from them in a little saucer of dead ground, and the first Valens knew of it was when he hauled himself up the scarp of a dune and realized he was looking straight at the top of a tall tree. He was too tired to run toward it, or even to yell for joy; *good*, he thought, and carried on plodding. As he approached, the oasis rose politely out of the saucer to greet him. A stand of spindly trees, about a quarter of an acre, surrounded by a neat lawn of wiry green grass, fringed with hunched-up thorn bushes; beyond question the most beautiful thing he'd ever seen in his life. He kept going until he was a hundred yards from the edge of the lawn, just in case it turned out not to be real; but when the sun sparkled on something in the middle of the stand of trees, he realized that he hadn't got the strength to cover the last stage of the journey. He sat down awkwardly in the sand and started to cry.

Presumably someone came along and helped him the rest of the way, because at some point he found himself standing on the edge of a pan of rusty brown water. It appeared to be full of Vadani, who'd waded in up to their shoulders and necks. Some of them were swimming in it; others were conscientiously watering their horses on the edge, their clothes dripping wet, their hair plastered down on their foreheads. They'd brought no barrels or water-bottles with them down the mountain, because water weighs ten pounds a gallon.

"There, you see?" Vaatzes' voice buzzing in his ear. "Just like I said it'd be. Piece of cake."

Brown, gritty water, more than they could possibly drink; but you can't eat water. They were talking about slaughtering the horses while there was still some meat on their bones.

"Or," suggested Ziani Vaatzes, "we could send a message to your in-laws and ask them for some food. It'd only be polite to let them know we're here."

The rest of the general staff looked at him as though he was mad. Valens thought for a moment.

"Not a bad idea," he said. "Assuming I can find volunteers. And assuming horses can go faster than men in this shit."

"I believe so," Vaatzes replied. "At least, that's the impression I got from the journals. According to the merchant, once you've crossed the desert, if you keep going straight on you come to the big salt pan, and there's always people there, even when the rest of the tribe's moved on. They keep a good stock of food and forage — not sure it'll be enough to last all of us very long, but anything we can get must be better than nothing. The main assumption will be that they've heard of you. I don't know how closely the ordinary Aram Chantat follows current affairs. I'd have thought the marriage of the crown princess would've counted as big news, but you never know. The danger is that if they don't know who we are, they'll swoop down and cut us to pieces for being foreign."

(The journals had been right about the sheds that the merchant had built here; the pen for the mules, the cover and even the grain bins. They turned out to be empty, of course.)

"I'm prepared to risk that," Valens replied confidently. "If I was bothered about that side of things, I'd be more worried about showing up without my dear wife. They'd only have my word for it that the Mezentines killed her; besides, even if they believed me, letting your wife get killed suggests a degree of carelessness that they might be reluctant to forgive. I wish now I'd taken the trouble to find out a bit more about the way they think."

Eventually, after a painfully embarrassing silence, Major Nennius volunteered. He set off with an escort of twelve very unenthusiastic troopers, leading a change of horses loaded with supplies. In his saddlebag was a carefully traced copy of the map, and a letter of credentials addressed to the Aram Chantat. The look on his face as he rode away reminded Valens unsettlingly of Orsea on his way to execution.

A full two days to reach the second oasis. No longer even any pretense that the food crisis was under control. Civilians couldn't be trusted to carry what little was left, and the soldiers were having trouble coping with the begging and screaming of mothers with hungry children; their friends, neighbors, relatives. At least a dozen horses were killed during the night; the carcasses were stripped bare in minutes, and fights broke out over the marrow in the bones. It didn't make it easier to handle to realize that it was panic, the fear of hunger rather than hunger itself. The worst side effect was exhaustion. Men and women who'd been rioting and scuffling all night had trouble keeping up during the day. Valens could no longer be induced to listen to the reports. He'd become obsessed with the idea that he could see a dust-cloud closing in rapidly on them from behind, the occasional flash of light. The fact that nobody else could see anything had no effect on his conviction. There was no point talking to him, the officers said, he wasn't listening. With Nennius gone, generally presumed dead, it was anybody's guess who was in charge. The officers went through their routines, more to occupy their minds than out of duty or hope. Nobody knew who had the map, or who was navigating, or who was in the lead. Reaching the second oasis inspired no celebrations, and nobody waded in up to the neck in the water this time.

Early the next day, Valens left his tent (for the last time; he'd given orders for it to be jettisoned as surplus weight). He washed quickly in the brown water of the oasis, then sat down under a tree to comb his hair. It was a last flicker of vanity, which had never been a particular fault of his at the best of times — his clothes were torn and caked in sand, all the work that had gone into them wasted, and he'd never cared about how he looked, provided that he looked like a duke; today, however, he took the trouble, because it really didn't matter anymore. His reflection in the water was thin and indistinct, so he combed more or less by feel. It wasn't a face he particularly wanted to see, in any case.

But there was another face looking down into the water beside his. He jumped up, slipping in the sandy mud and catching his balance just in time.

"I'm sorry," she said. "I startled you."

Valens, lost for words. "That's all right," he said.

Of course he hadn't seen her since Orsea died. He hadn't even asked after her, sent anybody to see how she was. The fact that she was here told him she'd managed to get over the mountains and across the desert. She looked terrible, in fact: her hair tangled, her face red in patches from the sun, the hem of her dress filthy, her shoes (stupid little satin sandals, believe it or not) wrecked like a barn blown down in a storm. She walked slowly over to him — she was limping — and sat down, her heels in the mud like a little girl.

"I wanted to tell you," she said. "I don't blame you."

If there was anything about himself that Valens was proud of, it was his ability to know if someone was lying to him. He tried not to exercise it.

"I'm absolutely furious with Orsea." She made it sound like he'd come home drunk and been sick in the wardrobe. "It was such a stupid thing to do. And so typical. If only he'd told me, I'd have talked him out of it, I know. It'll have been his idea of doing the right thing. I imagine they told him I'd be safe if he —"

"That's right," Valens heard himself say. "It's pretty clear from the letter we found that that's what the deal was."

"Letters!" She laughed. "Who'd have thought squiggles on a bit of dried sheepskin could cause so much trouble in the world. Letters and good intentions; and the other thing."

No need to ask what the other thing was.

"I had to do it," Valens ground on; he felt like he was wading in mud, and each time he dragged his boot out, his other foot sank in even deeper. "I couldn't have covered it up; if people had found out, I wouldn't have been able to lead them anymore, and they needed someone to get them —"

He was about to say, *get them here*. Not, he conceded, the most compelling of arguments.

"Oh, I know." She shook her head. "I know he'd have done exactly the same thing." Suddenly she giggled, at the same time as a tear broke out from the corner of her eye. "That doesn't really make you feel any better, does it?"

"No."

"He was an idiot." She smiled. "Always the right thing, no matter how much damage it caused. The tragedy was, it always *was* the right thing to do; it was just that either he did it the wrong way — oh, he had a wonderful talent for missing by a hair — or else something unexpected would happen that only a clever man — a reasonably clever man — could've foreseen. He was a good, decent, ordinary human being, which is what I loved so much about him . . ."

(*And why I could never love you;* unspoken.)

"And that's why he treated me so badly, I guess," she went on, dabbing at her eye with her filthy sleeve and leaving urchin-like streaks of grime on her cheek. "He felt he didn't deserve me, and he resented it; somehow it turned into my fault, and it was because he loved me so much. He couldn't talk to me for months before the end; we just sort of grunted at each other, like an old miserable couple waiting to see who'll be the first to die." She looked up at him. "I don't blame you," she said. "You're no more to blame than a tree-branch that falls on someone's head."

Again he was reluctant to look at her, because that'd tell him if she meant it. "I don't know," he said, looking at the brown water. "You can't help blaming the weapon, even though it's stupid and pointless. You know, there are times when I think that's all I am: a weapon, being used by someone else. At least, I like to think that way. It'd mean none of this was really my fault." He sighed. "My father used to collect fancy weapons; there was a room full of them, back at the palace. He'd buy them and prance about with them for a few minutes — he was a lousy fencer, I guess that's why he made me learn — and then they'd be put away and never looked at again. I did the same thing, I have no idea why. The difference is, he liked the things because they were pretty and he reckoned they were the sort of thing a duke ought to have. I bought them because I hate fighting, and I've had to do rather a lot of it." He frowned. "There's my tragedy, if you like. I've always been so very good at the things I don't like doing, and being good at them makes me do them, until I forget I hate them. The things I wanted to do, or wanted to be, for that matter — well; if you love drawing but can't draw, you don't bother with it. No point being reminded of your shortcomings. Always play to your strengths, my father told me."

"I remember him," she said quietly. "I didn't like him very much."

"Neither did I. It's a shame I've turned into him over the years. But you don't need to like someone in order to love them."

She laughed. "I always liked Orsea," she said. "I suppose I've got a soft spot for weak people."

(*Which is why you and I were friends, once;* he could have written that in a letter, but he couldn't say it out loud.)

"Can't say I ever did," Valens replied stiffly. "I couldn't get past the ineptitude. I don't like people who can't do things well."

"He liked you." She was looking away now. "He thought you were everything he ought to be; admired you and liked you as well, which I think is probably a rare combination. But he knew he bothered you, so he tried to keep his distance. He didn't want to be a nuisance."

Valens smiled. "He was just like me, then," he said. "We've both got the knack of being the opposite of what we want to be. I feel so sorry for him now . . ." He waved his arm in a vague encircling gesture. "Now that I've brought us here, I mean. Now that I know what it feels like. You know what? If I'd been him, in this situation, I'd have done what he did. The only difference is, I wouldn't have been found out."

She stood up. "I'd better let you get on," she said. "I expect you're very busy."

"Me?" He shrugged. "I ought to be, but I'm not. They keep trying to make me take an interest, but the truth is, I've more or less given up. Which disappoints me; I'd always assumed I'd keep going to the bitter end, just in case there was a way out I hadn't noticed yet. But this is the first time I've really screwed up, and it's shown me just how feeble I really am. You know what? In the battle, when the Mezentine cavalry were cutting up the column, I very nearly ran away — I was halfway up the hill, and I only stopped because I was worn out; and then it turned out we'd won after all, so there wasn't anything to run away from. I haven't been able to get over that. I just couldn't see why I should hang around and get killed when it wouldn't do anybody any good."

"Well," she said. "It wouldn't have."

He shook his head. "I'd have lasted about half an hour," he replied. "About as long as it took me to find a tree and a bit of rope. I think the Mezentines killed me that day, and ever since I've just been wandering about wondering how come I can still breathe."

She looked at him. "Orsea would never have done that," she said. "When the city fell, he went rushing out trying to get himself killed. He made a mess of it, of course."

Valens nodded. "Would you have wanted him to have succeeded?"

"No. There's never any excuse for dying. It's such a selfish thing to do, if there are people who love you."

(Which was the difference, she didn't say; the condition that didn't apply in Valens' case. So he didn't ask: what about me; if I'd been in Orsea's place that day, should I have stood my ground and fallen nobly? He didn't want to make her tell a deliberate lie.)

"You're right." He vaulted to his feet — showing off, like a teenager — and straightened his back. "I really should be attending to business, rather than lounging around like a gentleman of leisure. How are your feet, by the way?"

"My feet?"

"Blisters. You were limping earlier."

She shrugged. "I turned my ankle over in the sand. I expect it'll wear off."

Valens smiled. "I'd better find you a horse to ride."

"No thanks. It'd look bad, and I'm unpopular enough as it is. Being the widow of a condemned traitor . . . It's all right," she added, "I'll manage. I'll admit that walking isn't my idea of fun, but I'm getting the hang of it."

"You're being brave."

"If you like. Really, it's a matter of having other things to think about."

"If you change your mind . . ." He clicked his tongue. "I've got no idea how all this is going to end," he said. "Badly, I imagine."

"As far as I'm concerned, it already has. Go on, I'm holding you up."

He turned and walked away, not looking round.

The morning of the seventh day in the desert, and he was suffering from nerves.

The way he felt reminded him of the first time he'd seen her. All he knew about her was that she was the foreman's daughter; as such, she represented advancement, promotion, a means of rising in his trade without needing to rely on other people being able to recognize his true merits. In his mind's eye, therefore, he'd seen her as a vital component in a mechanism, beautiful in the simplicity and economy of its design. He'd been kept waiting in the porch of her father's house. She won't be out till she's good and ready, her father had said with a wry grin; she'll be doing her face, puts more effort into it than any of you buggers making bits for scorpions. That remark had caught his imagination as he stood, half in and half out of the street, watching his breath cloud in the cold air. He'd perceived her then as an artifact, something manufactured, her face engineered with skill and dedication; and he was delighted to think that his prized component was being engineered to exacting tolerances and the tightest possible specification. Of course, the old man went on, I don't suppose any son-in-law of mine's going to stay on the fitting bench very long, and old Phylactus'll be retiring before the year's out. He remembered how he'd fixed his eyes on the door, not looking at the old man, ready to catch his first glimpse of her as soon as the latch lifted and she came out. The excitement; the nerves.

(Of course, he'd spoiled it all by falling in love with her.)

That same excitement, as he watched the glowing, indistinct line that separated the sand from the sky. They were coming; when they came, that was where he'd see them first, and know that everything he'd built was finally fitting together; the active and passive assemblies engaging, the male and female components matching up, every gear-tooth meshing, every key moving in its keyway.

(It was a pity there had to be a battle and so many people killed, but you can't have everything.)

To occupy his mind, he ran calculations. Assuming a constant for the speed of a horseman in the desert, assuming that everybody was in the right place, making allowances for human inefficiencies; he glanced up at the sun, that imperfectly calibrated timepiece. There was still time. Besides, if he'd been right in his assessment of the properties of his materials, they wouldn't show up till they were good and ready. Doing their faces, as it were. All allowed for in his tolerances.

The nerves annoyed him, but there wasn't anything he could do about them. He made himself relax; leaned back against the thin tree trunk, spread his arms wide, exaggerated a yawn. At least the nervousness kept his mind off how hungry he was (and if his calculations were out, of course, he'd starve to death, along with everybody else; his life depended on the precision of the mechanism, but he couldn't bring himself to be afraid of death, only of failure).

Could horses gallop in the sand? Come to that, how long could a horse gallop for, even under ideal conditions, without having to stop for a rest? He'd used some figure he'd heard somewhere for the maximum sustainable speed of heavy cavalry, added fifteen percent tolerance, and based his workings on that. Was fifteen percent enough to allow for sand? Filthy stuff, he hated it. They didn't have it in Mezentia, except as a packaged material for making foundry molds; they didn't have it lying about all over the floor, making it well-nigh impossible for people to move and go about their business. The untidiness of these miserable places revolted him. Why couldn't the rest of the world be decently paved and cobbled, like it was back home?

A thought occurred to him and he hurriedly looked round. Daurenja had been trailing round after him for days now, like a dog sniffing round the fuller's cart, and he really didn't want to talk to him; now or ever. It would be so sweetly convenient if he got himself killed in the battle . . . But that'd be too much like good luck. There'd be time and scope to get rid of him later.

Falling in love with her had been a mistake; but it had also been the beginning of his life, the moment when things began to matter. That moment, when the door opened and she'd come nervously out into the porch, had given birth to this one, and all the moments in between; this had all started then, because without her, none of this would have been necessary. Suppose he hadn't fallen in love with her; he'd be foreman of the ordnance factory, presumably married to someone or other — happy enough, in all probability, but he wouldn't have been Ziani Vaatzes. That complex, unsatisfactory component only existed in relation to her. Remove her, and there was nothing, no point. It'd be like eating an orange simply to produce orange peel. The machine exists for a purpose, and every part, every assembly follows on from that purpose; without it, you're left with nothing but scrap metal, no matter how marvelously engineered.

He couldn't help smiling. Love had been his downfall, sure enough, but without it, he'd never have existed in the first place.

There'd be a man doing his job, wearing his clothes and answering to his name, but he'd be a complete and irrelevant stranger.

"Vaatzes." Someone calling for him. He pressed his back to the tree trunk and slid up it to his feet. "Over here," he called out.

He recognized the face, but couldn't put a name to it. "You're wanted," the face said. "Staff meeting."

"What, another one?" Ziani scowled. "What's the point? There's nothing to talk about."

Whoever-it-was shrugged. "He wants to see you. Over there, by that big rock at the edge of the water."

Ziani nodded, and started to walk. Valens probably just wanted someone to bully (are you *sure* the map's accurate? Can you be *certain* that's what the journal said, and was the merchant telling the truth? To which he'd reply, no, of course not; and the Duke would scowl horribly at him. Presumably it had some therapeutic value; in which case, he was happy to oblige. Like Miel Ducas, he lived only to serve).

"I know you can't vouch for the accuracy of the map" (well; nearly right), "but maybe you can cast your mind back and remember if there was anything in the journals . . ." Ziani nodded, allowing his mind to disengage, while saying the right things to keep Valens reasonably happy. Would it matter terribly much if he made up a few spurious diary entries? On balance, better not to.

"The food position's fairly straightforward," Valens was saying to somebody else. "Tomorrow we start eating the horses. Ever since I realized how much time we'd lost getting over that fucking mountain, I've been banking on the horses to get us across this desert. In which capacity they do it, as transport or as provisions, doesn't really matter at this stage. We've got nothing left for them to pull or carry, and if we do get to the other side, we won't need them desperately. Either the Cure Hardy'll take us in and look after us, or they'll slaughter us. Besides, if we don't kill the horses, they'll starve anyway. The fodder's completely gone, and they won't get far on a bellyful of oasis grass. It's that coarse, wiry stuff mostly, they won't eat it even when they're famished. It'd be good if we could keep a few of the thoroughbreds as presents for our hosts. They were quite keen on a few to improve their bloodlines. We'll start with the scraggiest specimens and leave the best till last. Common sense. Next on the agenda, casualties. Anybody interested in the figures, or shall we skip and go on?"

They skipped. Someone started talking earnestly about watch rotations. Ziani tried to concentrate on what he was saying, to keep his mind from dwelling on what ought to be about to happen. Apparently, they were presently working to a six-shift rotation, but wouldn't it be much better to go to seven shifts, thereby allowing each duty officer an extra half-hour's sleep, even though it would mean using more officers? The benefit of this approach . . .

Ziani never got to find out what the benefit was likely to be. The first thing he noticed was a head turning; then another, then four or five more, and the watch rotation enthusiast shut up in the middle of a sentence and tried to peer over Valens' shoulder to see what everybody was looking at.

What's the matter? Ziani thought. Never seen a running man before? Whoever he was, he was going flat out, veering precariously to avoid people in his way, or jumping over their legs if they didn't shift quickly enough. When he reached the rock and the general staff, he only just managed to keep from toppling over into the water. He looked round for Valens, and gasped, "Dust-cloud."

No further explanation needed. "Where?" Valens snapped, jumping up like a roe deer startled out of a clump of bracken. The runner was too breathless to speak; he pointed.

(Well, now, Ziani thought; and in his mind's eye the porch door opened.)

An orderly defense, according to the big brown book Valens had grown up with (Precepts of War, *in which is included all manner of stratagems and directions for the management of war, at all times and in all places, distilled from the best authorities and newly illustrated with twenty-seven woodcuts*), must be comprised of five elements: a strong position well prepared, proper provision of food and water, good supply of arms, a sufficient and determined garrison and a disciplined and single-minded command. *Precepts of War* had been three times a week, usually sandwiched in between rhetoric and the lute, and had consisted of copying out from the book into a notebook. The five elements of an orderly defense were as much a part of him as being right-handed.

As they watched the dust-cloud swelling, he ran through them one more time in his mind. Position: open on all sides. Provisions: none. Arms: all those barrels of carefully reclaimed arrows they'd left behind with the carts. Garrison: a mess. Command . . .

So much for his education. The cloud was rolling in, a strange and beautiful thing, sparkling, swirling, indistinct. Faintly he could hear the jingling of metal, like bells or wind-chimes. He had seen and heard approaching armies before, but this time everything felt different, strangely new and unknown.

"We've done everything we can," someone was reassuring him. "The men are in position."

He wanted to laugh. There was a thin curtain of cavalry, little more than a skirmish line; behind that, the infantry and dismounted dragoons were drawn up in front of the stand of spindly trees that fringed the oasis. Behind them, the civilians. He knew what the Mezentines would do. Light cavalry to engage and draw off the horsemen. Heavy cavalry to punch through the foot soldiers and send them scrambling back as far as they could go, themselves forming the clamp that would crush the civilians back to the edge of the water. From there it would be a simple matter of surrounding the oasis and pressing in, slowly and efficiently killing until there was nobody left. There were other ways in which it could be played out; he could abandon the oasis and run, in which case the Mezentines with their superior mobility would surround them in the open, or he could attack and be shredded on their lance-points, with a brief flurry of slaughter afterward.

They were trying to tell him things, details of the defense, who was commanding which sector, how many cavalry they'd managed to scrape together for him. He pretended to listen.

Visible now; he could make out individual horses and riders, although there was precious little to distinguish one from another. He was impressed; the Mezentines had managed to cross the mountain and the desert in remarkably good shape, and they held their formations as precisely as a passing-out parade. Clearly they'd found a way of coping with the difficulties that had defeated him, and he could think of no terribly good reason why he should add to their problems by trying to kill or injure a handful of them before the inevitable took its course. It was obvious that they were superior creatures, therefore deserving victory; even so, it did occur to him to wonder how they'd contrived to get this far in such astonishingly good order — as if they'd known, rather better than he had, where they were going and what they were likely to have to face. But that was impossible . . .

"They'll offer a parley," someone was telling him. "They won't just attack without trying to arrange a surrender first. You never know, they might offer terms . . ."

Valens grinned. "I don't think so," he said. "Unless my eyesight's so poor I can't see the wagons full of food they'd need to get us back across the desert alive. No, they've come to finish us off, simple as that."

"We'll let them know they've been in a fight," someone else asserted. Valens couldn't be bothered to reply.

He'd chosen a point in the sand, a dune with its edge ground away by the wind. When they reached that point, he'd give the order for his cavalry screen to advance. It'd be automatic, like a sear tripping a tumbler, and then the rest of the process would follow without the need of any further direction. He'd considered the possibility of telling the cavalry to clear out — get away, head off for the next oasis, in the hope that the Mezentines would be too busy with the massacre to follow them. There was a lot to be said for it: several hundred of his men would have a chance of escaping, instead of being slaughtered with the rest. He wasn't sure why he'd rejected it, but he had. Maybe it was just that it'd be too much trouble to arrange — giving the new orders, dealing with the indignant protests of the cavalry, imposing his will on them. If they had any sense, they'd break and run of their own accord. If they didn't, they had only themselves to blame.

He hadn't been paying attention. The Mezentine front line had already passed his ground-down dune, and he hadn't noticed. He shouted the order, and someone relayed it with a flag. The skirmish line separated itself and moved diffidently forward; a slow amble, like a farmer riding to market. In reply the front eight lines of Mezentines broke into movement, swiftly gathering speed. He wasn't able to see the collision from where he was standing, but he didn't need to.

A lot of silly noise behind him. From what he could hear of it, people were panicking. He assumed they had a better view than he did. The first Mezentine heavy cavalry appeared in front of him; they'd broken through the skirmish line, no surprise there, and they were charging the infantry screen. He sighed and stood up. It was time to go and fight, but he really didn't want to shift from where he was. His knees ached. He felt stiff and old. Even so . . .

He frowned. Men were walking past him, trudging to their deaths like laborers off to work in the early morning. He let them pass him; some of them shouted to him or at him, but he took no notice. The one good thing was, it didn't matter anymore what anybody thought of him. He was discharged from duty, and the rest of his life was his own.

(In which case, he thought, I'd like to see her again before I die. A mild preference; it'd be nice to die in the company of the one person he'd ever felt affection for, who for a short while had felt affection for him. He frowned, trying to figure out where she was likely to be.)

"What's happening," an old woman asked her. "Can you see?"

"No," she lied. "There's too much going on, I'm sorry."

"But we're winning," the old woman said. "Aren't we?"

"I think so."

Not that she understood this sort of thing. She knew it was very technical, like chess or some similarly complicated game. You had to know what you were looking at to make sense of it. But unless the Vadani had some devastating ruse up their sleeves (and that was entirely possible), it wasn't looking good. Too much like the last time, except that it was happening in the open rather than in among crowded buildings. The line of horsemen she'd seen riding out to meet the enemy (the celebrated Vadani cavalry, generally acknowledged as the best in the world) simply wasn't there anymore; it had been absorbed like water into a sponge; evaporated; gone. There were more soldiers out on the edge of the oasis, she knew, but it seemed unlikely that they'd make any difference. Of course, she wasn't a soldier, and there wasn't anybody knowledgeable around to ask.

"The infantry'll hold them," an old man was saying. "It's a known fact, horses won't charge a line of spear-points. They shy away, it's their nature. And then our archers'll pick 'em off. They'll be sorry they ever messed with us, you'll see."

Behind her, nothing but still, brown water. Would it hurt less to swim out and drown, or stay and be slashed or stabbed? It was a ludicrous choice, of course, not the sort of thing that could ever happen. To be sitting here, calmly weighing up the merits of different kinds of violent deaths; drowning, probably, because she'd swim until she was exhausted and then the water would pull her down, and the actual drowning wouldn't take long. She considered pain for a moment: the small, intolerable spasm of a burn, the dull, bewildering ache of a fall, the anguish of toothache, the sheer panic of a cut. She knew about the pain of trivial injuries, but something drastic enough to extinguish life must bring pain on a scale she simply couldn't begin to imagine. She'd seen the deaths of men and animals, the enormous convulsions, the gasping for breath that simply wouldn't come. She knew she wasn't ready for that; she never would be, because there could be no rapprochement with pain and death. She felt herself swell with fear, and knew there was nothing she could do to make it better.

She looked round instinctively for an escape route, and saw the old man and the old woman. They weren't looking at her; they were staring at a man walking quickly toward them.

("Isn't that the Duke? What's he doing here? He's supposed to be —"

"Shh. He'll hear you.")

Valens; of all people. It was a purely involuntary reaction; all the breath left her body, her mouth clogged and her eyes filled, because Valens had come to save her. At that moment (she hadn't forgotten Orsea, or the fact that she didn't love him, or that the sight of him made her flesh crawl and she didn't know why), she knew, she had faith, that she wasn't going to die after all. Valens would save her, even if he had to cut a steaming road through the bodies of the Mezentines like a man clearing a ride through a bramble thicket. She knew, of course, how little one man could do on his own, how hopeless the situation was, how even if they escaped from the Mezentines they had no chance of crossing the desert on their own. Those were unassailable facts; but so was his presence — her savior, her guarantee, her personal angel of death to be unleashed on the enemy. She tried to stand up, but her legs didn't seem to have any joints in them.

"We should try and get over to the left side," he was saying. "I've been watching, and their left wing's trailing behind a bit." He stopped and frowned at her. "Well? You do want to get out of this, don't you?"

"Yes, of course."

"Fine." He nodded. "I've left a couple of horses. Can't go quite yet; if they see us making a break for it, they'll send riders to cut us off. But when the attack's gone in, they won't be so fussy about stragglers." Suddenly he grinned at her. "I'm running away," he said. "No bloody point hanging around here. The trick's going to be choosing exactly the right moment to make the break."

The old woman was staring at him; she'd heard every word, and her face showed that her world had just caved in.

"Well?" he said. "Are you coming or aren't you?"

The infantry screen lasted longer than expected; longer than it takes to eat an apple, not quite as long as the time you need to bridle a horse. A quick glimpse out of the corner of his eye as they rode for the little gap on the left flank told him that the Vadani were fighting like heroes. He scowled; the timings were precise, and if they held the Mezentines up for too long, they could screw up everything.

"We'd better go now," he shouted, not turning his head, hoping she could hear him.

He kicked the horse on. It was a big, sullen gelding, civilian rather than military but all he'd been able to find. It sidestepped, pulling hard on the reins. He slapped its rump with the flat of the hanger, and it bustled angrily forward. He felt the hanger slip out of his hand; his only weapon. Oh well.

"Come on," he yelled, and gave the horse a savage kick in the ribs. He saw its neck rise up to smack his face, felt his balance shift and his left foot lose its stirrup. He hung for a moment, then knew he was falling backward over the horse's rump. As he fell, he saw her fly past; then his shoulder hit the ground and his body filled with pain. He felt it take him over, driving every thought out of his head. Hoofs were landing all around him — his horse, the enemy, he neither knew nor cared. He opened his mouth to scream, but nothing came out.

He heard a scream, assumed it was his own, realized it wasn't. He opened his eyes and tried to move.

It didn't hurt at first; he'd managed to prop himself up on one elbow before he made one slight movement too many and the pain flooded back. It took seven or eight heartbeats to subside.

Next to him, he could see now, lay a Mezentine. There was an arrow lodged in his temple; it had driven through the steel of his helmet but hadn't managed to get much further, since Valens could see the tips of the barbs. Not deep enough, evidently, to kill outright; the man's lips were moving, and his eyes were huge with enormous strain. For good measure his left leg was bent at the knee almost at right angles, the wrong way. That'll have been the fall, Valens decided. Falling off horses can be bad for you.

It occurred to him to wonder who'd been here shooting arrows at the Mezentines.

Then he felt the thump of hoofs, jarring up through his elbow into the complicated mess of pain. Instinct made him turn his head a little, and though his shoulder punished him for it, he shifted a little further to get a better view.

A horseman. He was rising elegantly to the trot, an eight-foot lance couched in the crook of his elbow. He wore glossy brown scale armor — leather, not steel — from collar to ankles, and under a high, pointed conical helmet his face was as pale as milk. A bow and quiver lolled beside his right thigh, and his horse's legs were short and thick. He came to a halt, stood up in his stirrups to look round, then slid into an easy, loping canter. Unmistakably, he was Cure Hardy.

27

The trial of Lucao Psellus before the Security Commission was a strangely muted affair. Given the nature and quality of the material, it should have been the showpiece of the autumn term. In the event, it was generally held to have been a botched, unsatisfactory affair which would have solved nothing, had it not been for the melodrama that followed it.

Partly, of course, the problem lay in the almost indecent haste with which it was conducted. None of the up-and-coming prosecutors had time to lobby for the brief, which was awarded to an elderly time-server by the name of Basano Philargyrus, who had previously specialized in minor default cases and undefended adulteries. Inevitably, the hearing was restricted; members of Necessary Evil and the Security Commission only. Even so, a few previews of some of the more sensational evidence would normally have been released through the usual channels. As it was, the only hard data to seep through was the charge itself, and that was so nebulously phrased as to be meaningless: neglect and dereliction of duty, unauthorized contact, failure to apprehend a fugitive. To a public desperate for some kind of reassurance after the disaster, it was too little, too grudgingly supplied. Worse, instead of making capital out of the general resentment, none of the opposition factions seemed prepared to take up the matter or even acknowledge that there was an issue.

The charge actually recited before the hearing (held, for reasons nobody could quite understand, in the cloister garden where Necessary Evil held their regular alfresco meetings) was somewhat more detailed:

That the accused, Lucao Psellus, had exceeded his authority in negotiation with the abominator Ziani Vaatzes; that in doing so, he had knowingly or inadvertently allowed Vaatzes to use him as his agent in designs against the Guilds and the Republic; that he had exercised insufficient care and diligence; that he had failed to report relevant information to the proper officers of the Commission . . .

"Which are grave enough charges, fellow Guildsmen, even when stated so plainly. The facts that underlie these charges, however, are infinitely more serious. For the avoidance of doubt, allow me to summarize as follows."

Prosecutor Philargyrus hesitated for a moment, to wipe his forehead on the back of his hand and shift his weight to his other foot. Someone at the back of the group whispered to his neighbor that, if anything, the prosecutor looked more nervous than the accused.

"Under direct instructions from Commissioner Boioannes himself — which instructions are freely admitted; we shall be entering a full transcript into evidence at the discovery stage — Commissioner Psellus traveled to the Vadani border in an attempt to open negotiations with the abominator. The extent of his authority was clearly defined; essentially, he was to offer such inducements as were necessary to deceive Vaatzes into returning of his own free will into territory under the control of the Republic. Any promises made to him would not be considered binding. Any information helpful to the Republic which Psellus could obtain from Vaatzes would be welcome, but was not of the essence of the mission. Commissioner Psellus has at no time claimed that he did not perfectly understand these instructions, and therefore they may be deemed to be undisputed evidence."

On the back row, someone had started to fidget. This sort of solid, pedestrian opening summary might be all very well at defaulters' sessions, but political juries had a right to expect daintier fare. It was almost as though someone was deliberately trying to make what should have been a thrilling occasion as dreary as possible. But who would do such a thing?

"Arriving at the border, Commissioner Psellus quickly established contact with Vaatzes and a face-to-face meeting was arranged. Note that, although having the resources to do so, Psellus neglected to inform your Commission of this development before the meeting took place. Having traveled to Civitas Vadanis, Commissioner Psellus found the city deserted. Again, note that he did not immediately retrace his steps and communicate this momentous fact to the military authorities, but proceeded to attend the meeting."

Frowns in the second and third rows. These minor derelictions should have been left to the end, where they wouldn't have cluttered up the flow.

"Now," Philargyrus went on, his voice flat and only just audible, "we come to the meeting itself. For what took place we have only Commissioner Psellus' own account; but that account, even if it represents a full and fair summary of what was said and done, constitutes in our view a clear admission of guilt as far as the charges are concerned. In brief, Commissioner Psellus and the convicted abominator Ziani Vaatzes together concocted a scheme to discredit the fugitive and war criminal Orsea Orseoli, former Duke of Eremia, in the eyes of the Vadani government. It was an elaborate, rather fanciful business, involving the fabrication of compromising documents, the suborning of a Vadani merchant venturer and her cold-blooded murder. As matters have turned out, it would appear to have been successful; and you may be tempted to credit Commissioner Psellus for exacting some kind of crude justice on an acknowledged and declared enemy of the Republic. Before doing so, however, we invite you to consider the real cost of the bargain."

(He keeps looking at somebody, someone in the third row observed to his neighbor, but I can't quite see who. It's like he's taking a cue, or looking for approval.)

"Note, in passing, the malignant subtlety of the abominator Vaatzes; and, by the same token, the culpable simple-mindedness of your colleague, Commissioner Psellus. As an inducement to persuade us to allow him to return home, Vaatzes offered Psellus information about the likely itinerary of the Vadani convoy. It was in his power, Vaatzes claimed, to persuade Duke Valens to change course and head across the desert, making for the home territory of the Cure Hardy. He was aware of a safe route, made passable by a string of oases. He gave Commissioner Psellus a copy of a map showing the route, together with further notes and commentaries that would allow a substantial force of cavalry to cross the mountains at the edge of the desert with relative ease while avoiding observation by the Vadani. Meanwhile, he would lead Duke Valens and the convoy over the mountain by another, harder route, thereby forcing them to abandon their armored wagons and much other essential equipment, and reduce their food supplies to an inadequate level. Softened up by these privations and taken unaware in the middle of the desert by our forces — who would have been realistically provisioned and adequately briefed on matters of geography and topography — the Vadani would prove easy prey, and could be eliminated once and for all."

Pause; or was it hesitation?

"Commissioner Psellus," he went on eventually, "would seem not to be familiar with the expression, *too good to be true*. Arguably, it was not his fault that Vaatzes had already arranged through other contacts for our forces to ambush the convoy at an earlier stage; as we all know, the ambush was beaten off with heavy losses, as Vaatzes fully intended it should be. The fact remains that, had Commissioner Psellus reported his deal with Vaatzes promptly and to the right quarters, the first ambush could have been countermanded and valuable lives saved. What is both indisputable and unforgivable, however, is the Commissioner's simple stupidity — you may care to regard it as willful blindness — in not appreciating the quite appalling implications of Vaatzes' proposal — namely, that a safe and practical route across the desert exists, and that, should the Cure Hardy become aware of it, the security of the Republic would be hopelessly compromised forever."

Even Philargyrus, with his dreary delivery and unfortunate style, couldn't fail to get a frisson of horror out of his audience with that. It was, of course, the only point that mattered, and the only thing on anybody's mind, ever since the news broke. It was what Psellus had been brought here to be condemned to death for; the question was . . .

"You may argue," Philargyrus went on, perhaps a shade too quickly, "that since Vaatzes had come across this terrible information, it was inevitable that he should convey it to Duke Valens in the hope that he would pass it on to the Cure Hardy, to use against us; that Psellus' part in this debacle was not wholly instrumental in bringing this disaster down on us. I beg to differ. As a result of Psellus' criminal stupidity, we have sent an army into the desert, demonstrated to the Cure Hardy — a vicious and irrational race — that we too know the secret passage across the supposedly impassable barrier; we have sent an army that has engaged and been completely destroyed by Cure Hardy forces. It is highly likely, given the paranoid mentality of the barbarians and bearing in mind their reaction to our forces' incursion, that they will choose to view what has occurred as an act of war. In short; even if it was done innocently and without malice, Commissioner Psellus has left us at the mercy of the only power on earth with the capability and the will to inflict serious damage on the Republic, perhaps even — it has to be said — to destroy it. There can only be one possible response on the part of your Commission; you must find Commissioner Psellus guilty as charged and impose the severest penalty available in law."

"Well," said one commissioner to another during the recess, "he got there in the end."

His friend looked round before replying. "If you care to tell me what that performance was in aid of, I'll be very greatly obliged to you. Who was sitting at the end of the fourth row? I couldn't see; that stupid fountain was in the way."

"I couldn't see either. But you're right, he did keep looking up and glancing in that direction." A deep frown and another glance round. "You didn't happen to notice where Boioannes was sitting? I can't remember seeing him."

Before his friend could reply, the bell rang for the votes to be cast. That didn't take very long; and, after the sentence had been passed and the prisoner led away, the usher called them back into the cloister for an announcement.

This time everybody knew where Boioannes was; he was standing right in the middle, holding a crumpled piece of paper. His eyes were very wide, and he spoke entirely without expression.

"I have just been informed by the Chief of Staff," he said, "that the council of delegates representing the officers of our mercenary forces have unilaterally canceled the contract of employment between themselves and the Republic. Their grounds . . ." He had to repeat the words several times before he could make himself heard again. "Their grounds for so doing are that they were engaged to fight the Eremians and the Vadani, not the Cure Hardy; and the arrival at our newly established frontier station at Limes Vitae of an emissary from the Aram Chantat bringing a formal declaration of war —"

It took the ushers several minutes to restore some sort of order.

"We have pointed out to the council of delegates that, under the penalty clause in the contract, a unilateral breach of this kind entitles us to withhold any and all further payments, in money or kind, including all arrears and agreed bonuses. I have to inform you that the council of delegates accepts that the contract has been forfeited and that they will receive nothing from us, but refuse to change their minds. In short, at noon tomorrow the Republic will no longer have an army, and must look for its defense to its own citizens, at least until some alternative source of manpower can be —"

*   *   *

They could hear the shouting down in the cells.

"I can see why he was reprieved," the tall, thin commissioner said to his short, stout colleague. "And reinstated, come to that. Though if you ask me, he shouldn't have been convicted in the first place. After all, what'd he done, except follow orders? It was all there in writing . . ."

"Ah yes." The short, stout commissioner nodded wisely and helped himself to cinnamon and grated cheese. "It was all there in the copy in the minute book they found in Boioannes' office when they searched it. What we got shown at the hearing was something quite other. Besides, I don't seem to remember you voting for acquittal. It was unanimous."

"Well of course." The tall man shrugged. "But that's by the bye. The thing is, the only point at which Psellus exceeded his authority was once he'd found out about the existence of this confounded secret way across the desert; and of course, he does the only possible thing he can do in the circumstances. He tries to have the Vadani column wiped out to the last man before they can reach the savages and tell them about it. Didn't work, as we know. In all probability, he was set up by Vaatzes, just as they say he was. Doesn't matter. Simple fact is, the only thing that could possibly have saved us was wiping out that column before they met up with the Cure Hardy; he tried to do it, gave it his best shot; give him his due, it nearly worked, only a day or so in it. At least he tried."

The short man smiled as he stirred his cup. "So you'll be supporting him in the ballot, then?"

"Not sure I'm prepared to go that far," the tall man replied thoughtfully. "To be honest with you, I'm not really sure what to do. No precedent; I mean, a ballot for chairmanship of Necessary Evil . . ."

"I don't see how we have any choice, frankly," the short man replied. "With the mess we're in, it's like the whole structure of politics in this town's melted away like ice in springtime. Boioannes gone, the Guilds actually talking to each other — actually listening to each other, which is more disturbing still, if you ask me. Nobody knows where the hell they are or who's running anything. Why not have a ballot? The state we're in, what harm could it actually do?"

The tall man sipped his drink, but it was still a little too hot for comfort. "Well, quite," he said. "And by the same token, why not Psellus? One thing you can say for him, he's guaranteed a hundred percent clean. Poor fellow was so obviously out of the loop at all times, stands to reason he can't have been in with one faction or the other. If it's compromise and conciliation we're after, we could do a lot worse. It's just a shame he's an idiot."

The short man sighed. "I don't think anyone's come out of this looking particularly smart," he said. "For a start, when it all came out about how Boioannes had been manipulating the war, and none of us had a clue what he'd really been up to —"

"Speak for yourself." The tall man smiled. "There were a few of us who had our suspicions, believe me."

"Easy to say after the event."

"True. Guaranteed bloody fatal to say *before* the event. Though whether it's better to be clever and a coward is a moot point, I suppose. Doesn't matter. Boioannes is out of the picture — did you hear, by the way, the Foundrymen've issued a formal notice of expulsion from the Guild?"

The short man (who was a Fuller and Dyer) chuckled. "I'm sure he'll be cut to the quick if he ever hears of it, wherever the hell he's gone. Last rumor I heard said he was back in the old country."

"Unlikely." The tall man shook his head. "Too many widows and orphans over there who'd like to discuss the conduct of the war with him. Personally, I think he's in Lonazep. In which case," he added, "let's hope Compliance live up to the standard they've set themselves recently and fail to find him. Last thing we need is Boioannes on trial and making trouble for everybody."

"Agreed."

Cool enough to drink by now; there was a brief pause. Then the short man said, "Do you really think we've had it this time, like everybody's saying?" As the tall man started to scowl, he added quickly, "I know, I wouldn't have raised the subject, except I happened to overhear them talking at the finance meeting this morning; they're offering the Jazyges five times the basic rate, but so far they've shown no interest at all."

"Is that right?"

The short man shrugged. "It's what they were saying."

"But the Jazyges are — well, if you ask me, they're no better than the Cure Hardy. In fact, we might as well be sending recruiters out there, try and get some of the other tribes to come in with us against the Aram Chantat. It'd make as much sense as —"

"I've heard they're considering that," the short man said.

That shut the tall man up for a long time.

"Well in that case," he said eventually, "yes, I think we're probably screwed. In fact, the only hope I can see for us is if we all vote for Psellus and he manages to persuade his friend Vaatzes to lead the entire Aram Chantat out into the desert and lose them there. Other than that . . ."

"Don't go saying things like that where anybody's likely to hear you," the short man replied grimly. "Otherwise, there's a real risk they might try it."

Both of them seemed to have lost their appetite for mead mulled with spices. They put their cups down on the little brass table and avoided each other's eye.

"It's a thought," the tall man said at last.

"Don't joke about it."

"I think we've reached the stage where black comedy's our likeliest source of inspiration," the tall man said. "There's a joke doing the rounds, don't know if you've heard it: what've common sense and Ziani Vaatzes got in common? Answer: they've both gone out the window. Puts it rather well, if you ask me. So yes; why the hell not? After all, Boioannes was prepared to negotiate with the man. If he can get us out of this . . ."

The short man pulled a sour face. "Everywhere I go," he said, "people are talking about Vaatzes as though he's some sort of supernatural entity, instead of a foreman who got caught playing with things he shouldn't have. What earthly reason do you have for supposing he could make the Aram Chantat suddenly disappear in a puff of smoke, even if he wanted to?"

"He made our army disappear."

The short man seemed unwilling to pursue that argument. "If I vote for Lucao Psellus," he said after a while, "and I'm not saying I'm going to; but if I do, it's because he's the man least likely to trust that arsehole Vaatzes ever again." He made a violent gesture, rocking the table and almost upsetting the cups. "I still find it impossible to believe that one individual could have such an effect on the safety of the Republic," he said. "In one of the savage countries maybe; they have kings and dukes, they positively invite that sort of thing. But one man — a foreman, for pity's sake. I just can't see it."

"Most of it must've been luck," the tall man replied soothingly. "Finding out about the way across the desert; sheer luck. Even we can't legislate for that sort of fluke." He stood up. "I'd better be making tracks," he said. "I don't want to be late for my afternoon meeting. Something tells me that the dear old leisurely ways of doing things may well prove to be yet more casualties of the massacre in the desert."

Hardly the most important meeting of the year; no more than the monthly review of performance and production at the ordnance factory. As always the manager, deputy manager, department heads, supervisory managers and their staffs were there waiting for him; the man he was rather looking forward to meeting again, however, was the new foreman — new; Falier had already taken over the job by the time he'd first met him, but everybody still called him the new foreman; as though time had somehow stopped running; as though everybody was subconsciously waiting for Ziani Vaatzes to come back. It was Vaatzes, of course, he wanted to discuss with Falier, in the light of his discussion at lunch . . .

*   *   *

His footsteps in the porch; the scrape as he dragged his boots off without bothering to untie the laces. It was a silly, childish habit, and bound to spoil good, expensive boots in the long run.

"I'm home," he called out. That annoyed her too. She knew he was home as soon as she heard the area gate creak. From there to the front door, always exactly nine seconds; precise as a machine.

She didn't bother to answer, as she scraped burned milk off the bottom of the pan with the back of a wooden spoon. "I said I'm home," he called out. "Where are you?"

"In the kitchen."

He bustled through, grimy-handed, brushing against the doorframe. "Hell of a flap at work today," he said. "You know that government bloke who kept on dragging you in to talk about — well, you know. Apparently, he's been put on trial, for treason or something."

If she'd been a cat, she'd have given herself away by putting her ears back. "Serves him right," she mumbled. "Sit down, dinner's nearly ready."

"It gets better," he continued — she had her back to him and didn't know if he was looking at her or not. "Apparently he was convicted, and then they let him off."

"Pity."

"And now," he went on, "they're talking about making him something high up in the Guilds; and you'll never guess why."

"Because he's horrible?"

"Because while he was doing some secret mission or other, he actually met Ziani. Right there in the heart of enemy territory. Met him and talked to him."

The pan handle was too hot, but she couldn't seem to let go of it. "So he's still alive, then. The last I heard, he was meant to be dead."

"Honey." He sounded upset about something.

"Well, that's what I heard. They sent a cavalry army or something specially to get him. Don't say they made a mess of that too."

"Apparently." She could feel him willing her to turn round.

Instead she rested the pan carefully on the stove top and let go. "Honey, you aren't worried about anything, are you?"

"Of course I'm worried, if that horrible man Psellus is going to be running the Guilds," she snapped. "He's strange, I don't like him. He wants something from me and I don't know what it is."

"Fine." Now he was going to lose his temper. "So what am I supposed to do about it? Challenge him to a duel or something?" He paused; when he spoke again, his voice was colder. "Are you thinking, *that's what Ziani would've done, if someone was bothering me like that?* Well, maybe you're right. As we both know, he was crazy in the head."

"I really don't want to talk about him," she said, loud and quick. She scooped the beans out of the pan, added them to his plate and stabbed the fire with the poker as if it had been Lucao Psellus.

"All right," he said. "I just thought you'd be interested."

"Well I'm not."

That night, when he'd gone to bed, she opened the triangular cupboard in the corner of the kitchen and took out a packet of cardamom seeds, which she emptied into a bowl. Then, with a small peeling knife, she carefully slit the edges of the packet and smoothed the coarse parchment out into a sheet. It was a bit too shiny, so she took a minute or so to smooth it down with the kitchen pumice, until the surface was dull. From his study she took the brass inkwell and a new goose quill — he'd miss it, but that couldn't be helped; he was always losing things, so it wouldn't be too much of a problem. She sharpened the quill with her peeling knife, taking care to scoop up all the shavings and put them on the fire. As a final precaution, she wedged the door with the kitchen chair.

It was a while before she could nerve herself to start. She hadn't written anything for years now. Did he know she even could? The question had never arisen. Probably he assumed she couldn't; it wasn't a highly valued accomplishment among women of their class. She smiled, remembering Ziani's stupid book, which he'd left lying about in his study because he had no idea she could read it. Not that it had been worth reading.

Slowly and carefully she wrote the address. Important not to get ink on her fingers; you had to pumice them to the bone before you could get rid of the stain, and he wouldn't believe her if she said it was soot. She winced at the unfamiliar pressure of the quill against the side of her knuckle. People who did a lot of writing got used to it, presumably, but it had always struck her as an uncomfortable tool to use.

My husband says . . .

A clumsy way to start; still, she'd written it now.

My husband says Psellus is going to be the new head of necessary evil . . .

(Should that have been capital N and capital E? Not that it mattered.)

. . . and I'm worried. Is it true? If he starts asking questions again, what should I tell him? If he's going to be in charge of everything, sooner or later he's going to find out something bad. You promised at the start nothing bad was going to happen to me. You never come and see me anymore . . .

She lifted her hand away so she could read the last few words. Shouldn't have written that. It was what they all said, sooner or later; the women she'd always pitied, promising herself she'd never be one of them. She thought for a moment; inspiration struck.

. . . so I can't ask you face to face what's going on. It scares me, not knowing, I'm afraid I'll get something wrong. I don't want to make things bad for either of us. I know you can't come and see me any time soon, because of what's happened, but you must have friends who could bring a message. I . . .

She stopped just in time. She'd been about to write *I miss you* or *I want you*. That was the trouble with writing; so easy to get carried away and put down something without thinking.

I know what a difficult time this must be for you and how hard it'll be to find someone to bring me a letter, but please try. For both our sakes. You know I wouldn't pester you like this if I wasn't really scared.

Best to leave it at that. She laid the quill carefully on the side of the table, the nib hanging over the edge so as not to stain the wood, then put the lid back on the inkwell. She didn't have any sand to blot with, and she wasn't sure if you could use flour instead; better to leave it to dry off in its own time. That, of course, meant waiting around, since she couldn't very well leave it lying there while she put the inkwell back in his study. She considered replacing the quill as well as the inkwell, since they cost good money, but it wasn't worth the risk. She picked it up carefully, just in case there was still ink on it, and flipped it into the fire, her nose crawling at the foul smell of burning feather. While the ink was drying she put some beans in water to soak overnight and scrubbed out tonight's pan with a thorn twig.

Once she was sure the letter wouldn't smudge, she folded it; once lengthways in the middle, then three times sideways. A drop of tallow from the candle was all she had to seal it with; and while the tallow blob was still soft, she pressed the letter A into it with her fingernail. Then she got the long-necked stone bottle she collected the beer in and wedged it in the top, with just a corner sticking out. To be on the safe side, she put the bottle away in the cupboard and closed the door. The last chore was finding a jar to store the cardamoms whose packet she'd cut up.

He was asleep when she climbed the ladder to the upstairs room; lying on his side. She sighed quietly. When he slept on his back he snored, so he made an effort to lie sideways, but clearly he hadn't got the hang of it yet; his left arm was trapped under his body, which meant he'd wake up with pins and needles in the morning and make a fuss. As she climbed in next to him, he grunted and twitched away. It wasn't like she hated him or anything, but there were times she wished she hadn't had to marry him. It had made sense at the time, of course, when he'd explained it to her.

For various reasons she didn't sleep well; and, as is so often the case, when she finally did fall asleep, it was only an hour or so before dawn, which meant she woke up late, after he'd already left for work. Infuriating; she had to dress in a hurry (she hated leaving the house with her hair in a mess) and dash down to the market with the beer bottle so as to hand the letter over in time. The courier (she didn't even know his name) leered at her annoyingly as he stooped to pick up the scrap of paper she'd apparently let fall from her pocket. His hand brushed hers as he mimed handing the paper back, which made her feel slightly sick. It wasn't a deliberate try-on, she knew that; probably he wasn't even aware he was doing it. She hated men, sometimes.

Once he was safely out of sight, she sat down on one of the stone ledges beside the market-house wall. Her hands were aching, and when she looked down she realized the knuckles were white. Deliberately she relaxed; hands, then arms and shoulders, then her back and legs. It made her wonder how people who lied for a living managed it. Presumably they got used to it, like slaughtermen or butchers, or soldiers after their first few battles.

With a click of her tongue she got up again. She hated running late. She'd have to rush to get Moritsa to school (was today the spinning test, or was it tomorrow?), and after that, all the usual chores to cram in before he came home again. Some days she had no idea where the time went.

The door was open when she got back. She was cursing herself for not shutting it properly on her way out when she realized there was someone in the house: two men in military uniform, light armor but no weapons. She felt all the energy drain out of her.

"Ariessa Falier?"

She nodded. "You didn't have to bash the door down," she said. "You could've waited outside till I got home. I was only gone a few minutes."

The soldier looked past her at the door, which wasn't the least bit bashed in (they had little wire hooks, she remembered, for lifting latches from the outside). "Very sorry," he said, "orders. While we're on the subject, where have you been? You don't usually leave the house till it's time for the kid to go to school."

If she hadn't had so much practice with people like him, that would've thrown her. Instead, there was no perceptible delay before she answered, "I went to get the beer for this evening. There's a special sort Falier likes, but you've got to get there early or it's all sold."

The soldier nodded very slightly, as if complimenting her on her facility. It helped, of course, that it was true about the beer. Did the soldier know about Falier's exacting taste? She wouldn't be at all surprised.

"The bottle's empty," he said quietly.

"I didn't get there early enough."

This time he smiled. "Wasted trip, then."

"Yes. Looks like it's going to be one of those days."

He stared at her face for a second or two, then said: "It'd be appreciated if you could spare the time to come up to the Guildhall. There's a few questions . . ."

"I can't. I've got to take Moritsa to school."

"Already been done." The smile sharpened into a slight grin. "We'll collect her as well, if you're not back in time. She can come and wait at the guard lodge until you've finished."

For a moment she wished she was a man. She'd have liked to have been Ziani, killing the two guards in the stable, the day he escaped from the Guildhall. Instead she had to stay still and quiet and wait to hear what was coming next.

"Of course," the soldier continued smoothly, "you don't have to come if you don't want to. But I'm sure you do really. Your civic duty, and all that."

She lowered her head slightly. "So, is it true, then, what they were saying? Psellus has got Boioannes' old job."

She'd managed to surprise him there, at least. "You're pretty well up in current affairs, aren't you?"

"My husband was talking about it last night."

He nodded. "Most women wouldn't even have heard of Commissioner Boioannes. Commissioner as was, of course. He's a wanted man now."

"And Psellus is the new boss?"

He shrugged. "They don't bother telling me stuff like that. They just tell me to go and pick up women." Leer; all men do it. "I prefer it that way," he said. "Never did understand politics."

It was a pity, she decided as she drove through the streets on the way to the Guildhall, that the only times she got to ride in a carriage were when she was under arrest. Under other circumstances there'd be a great deal of pleasure in looking down on the tops of the heads of people she passed, watching familiar landmarks whirl by at an unnatural pace. As it was, she couldn't enjoy it. Everything good gets spoiled, sooner or later.

Round the side of the Guildhall rather than in through the front door this time; none of the usual waiting on benches in corridors, but straight through into the sort of room she hadn't believed existed. The walls were paneled with dark wood, almost black, deeply and rather crudely carved with leaves, flowers, birds and vines tumbling with fruit. The floors were tiled; not the austere black and white checkerboard you'd expect to find, but red clay tiles glazed in warm, bright colors. Everything was old and ornate; and the plaster ceiling was painted with an extraordinary scene which she simply couldn't make out. For a start, all the people were naked, but it wasn't that kind of painting at all. The men were excessively muscular, the women were rounded and plump, and — no two ways about it — their skins were pink, like the savages. The obvious conclusion was that this wasn't the work of the Painters' and Sculptors' Guild. The pink skins, together with the feeling of extreme age, meant that all this stuff dated back to before the Mezentines came here from the old country, and the painting, the carving and the floor tiles were all the work of the savages, the ancestors of the Eremians and the Vadani, who'd lived here before the Republic was founded.

She wasn't the least bit interested in history, let alone art; but since she had nothing else to occupy her mind with except fear, she wondered about it. Why hadn't all this stuff been torn down years ago, and replaced with proper decorations, neatly done, in accordance with the appropriate specification? Right here, in the Guildhall itself, you'd think they'd know better. It couldn't be because they liked this primitive stuff better than genuine Guild work. Maybe it was there to remind them of how close they were to the savages, in both space and time. Or maybe they meant to get rid of it but hadn't got around to it yet. From what she knew of the Guilds, that was the likeliest explanation. Somewhere there must be a Redecoration Committee, still striving to iron out a compromise between the agendas of the different factions: the conservatives, who favored plain beech panels and whitewash, versus the radicals, hell-bent on sweet chestnut flooring and hessian wall-hangings.

The door opened, and someone she didn't know came in. The fact that it wasn't Psellus disconcerted her, but the man himself looked harmless enough; a short, round, balding pudding of a man in his early thirties, with little fat fingers tipped with almost circular nails. He sat down on one side of a long, thick-topped black table, and waved her to a chair on the other side. At least her chair was recognizably Mezentine: the Pattern 56, straight-backed with plain turned legs and no armrest. Her cousin Lano made the seats for them at the furniture factory down by the river.

"My name is Dandilo Zeuxis," the human pudding said, in exactly the sort of high voice she'd have expected from him. "I'm Commissioner Psellus' deputy private secretary. The Commissioner can't be here himself, unfortunately."

"Is it true?" she interrupted. "Is he the new boss now?"

Maybe he was deaf. "The Commissioner has instructed me to ask you if you can shed any light on the whereabouts of your previous husband's toolbox. Apparently, although it was listed in the inventory of house contents compiled by the original investigating officers, there's no record that it was ever impounded for evidence or removed from the premises at the time of his arrest. Curiously, there's no mention of it in the later inventory taken before the trial itself. Since the box appears to have gone missing at some point between Foreman Vaatzes' arrest and his trial — during which time, of course, Foreman Vaatzes himself wouldn't have had access to it — we were wondering if you or a member of your family removed it."

She glanced at him for a moment, but it was like looking into a mirror. "Have you checked the factory?" she said.

He glanced down at some papers on the table in front of him; the way he leaned forward suggested he was a bit short-sighted. "Yes," he said. "All areas of the factory to which Foreman Vaatzes had access have been thoroughly searched."

"Oh." She shrugged. "I thought maybe one of the people he worked with might've borrowed it. Needed a special tool for a job or something."

He seemed to be thinking for a few seconds; then he checked his papers again. "Unlikely," he said. "I have here the list of items contained in the box at the time of the original search. Would you care to see it?"

She gave him a big smile. "Sorry," she said, "I can't read. Also, it wouldn't make any sense to me even if I could. I don't know anything about tools and stuff."

He nodded. "Well," he said, "looking at this list it all seems to be fairly straightforward, ordinary hand tools, nothing that wouldn't be on the open racks at the factory. It would appear that Foreman Vaatzes kept all his specialist tools at work. On the list there's just a hand-drill, various files, a hacksaw and an assortment of blades, that sort of thing. Nothing you'd expect anyone to go out of his way to borrow."

"I see," she said. "So, if it's all just ordinary stuff, why are you so interested in it?"

He laughed; and then the shape of his face reverted straight-away to its previous setting. "You can't remember anything about it, then?" he said. "Can you tell me where it was usually kept?"

"Of course. Under the bench in his study."

"You don't remember if you happened to move it anywhere? When you were cleaning, perhaps, or tidying up."

She shook her head. "He didn't like me going in there," she said.

"Yes, but after he'd gone. Maybe you took the opportunity to give the study a thorough tidying."

"I don't think so," she said firmly. "I had other things on my mind apart from spring-cleaning."

He seemed to play with that thought for a moment, like a dog chewing on an old shoe. "Many women would use housework as a way of taking their mind off something like that," he said. "Familiar routine work is quite therapeutic under such circumstances, so I'm given to understand."

He was like one of those burrs you catch on your sleeve and can't seem to get rid of. "Not me," she said. "Maybe I'd be able to help better if I knew what it was you're looking for."

Gone deaf again. "When your husband was making things at home," he went on, "did he stay in the study or did he use other parts of the house? The kitchen table, maybe."

"No. He was very considerate like that."

"Indeed." She must have said something that puzzled him, or else failed to say something he'd been expecting to hear. He rubbed the tip of his small, round nose against the heel of his hand. "Apart from the toolbox and the rack on the study wall, was there anywhere else in the house where he regularly stored tools?"

"No. At least, not that I knew about."

"Do you know if he was in the habit of bringing tools home with him and then taking them back when he'd finished with them?"

She shook her head. "Wouldn't have thought so," she said. "There weren't any pockets big enough in his work clothes to carry anything much."

"What about friends, neighbors? Did he borrow tools from them?"

"Usually it was more the other way round. People would borrow his things and then forget to give them back." She scowled at him. "You still haven't told me what all this has got to do with defending the city from the savages."

"Was there anybody you can think of who borrowed something shortly before he was arrested?"

"No."

"You can't remember who it was, or there wasn't anybody?"

"Both."

"Your husband, Falier. Did he borrow tools from Foreman Vaatzes?"

She thought for a moment. "Yes," she said, "now and again. Not very often."

"Does he bring tools home from work?"

"No. He doesn't work at home like Ziani used to."

He narrowed his eyes into a frown; then a fit of coughing (which reminded her of a small dog barking) monopolized him for quite a while. Shaking like a building in an earthquake, he groped for the water jug and a plain earthenware beaker, but the fit was so ferocious that he couldn't keep steady enough to pour. She thought about doing it for him, but decided not to. When he'd finally stopped trying to tear himself apart from the inside, and had drunk three cupfuls of water in quick succession, he blinked at her like a fish out of water, and nodded. "Thank you," he whispered. "You've been very helpful."

"Is that it? Can I go?"

He frowned. "If you wouldn't mind sparing us a little more of your time. Please wait here." He stood up, one chubby paw pressed to his chest. "Someone will be along to see you very soon."

He left, and the paneled, heavily molded and studded door closed behind him with the softest and firmest of clicks. She sat still and quiet for a minute or so; five, ten, and then she lost track. The windows were behind her, and for some reason she felt reluctant to get out of her chair and move, even for something as innocuous as looking out of the window to see where the sun was in the sky. After what felt like an hour, her back started to hurt. She wriggled, but it didn't help. She turned round as far as she could without actually getting up, but the window was just beyond the edge of her vision.

They must know something, she thought. But they can't know about the letter. They were at the house when I came back from handing it over. They couldn't have known I was going to write it, because I didn't know I was going to until Falier told me about . . . She shivered. There was still plenty of time before Moritsa needed to be fetched from school, but she couldn't help worrying. She told herself to calm down. She'd been in worse situations before, and without the letter there wasn't anything they could prove.

Had that man's coughing fit been genuine? Hard to believe it wasn't; in which case, maybe the delay was simply because he'd gone somewhere to lie down and drink honey and hot water until he felt better. As for all that stuff about a toolbox, she couldn't make head or tail of it. They must've known she wouldn't know anything about tools, so why had they asked her?

Didn't matter. No need to understand, so long as she kept up a solid defense, kept her head and didn't contradict herself. The good thing about the toolbox questions was that she could tell the truth; so much less effort than making things up.

The door opened, and a soldier (armor but no weapons) came in. He glowered at her as though she was making the place look untidy, and said, "If you'll follow me." Her legs were stiff and wobbly from sitting still for so long.

He led her up a huge, wide stone staircase, along a broad, high-ceilinged corridor that seemed to go on forever, up another staircase, along some smaller corridors to a dead end with a small door in it. He knocked and waited before opening it and beckoning her in. Once she was inside, he shut it behind her. She listened, but couldn't hear the sound of his boot-heels clumping away across the tiles.

This room was much smaller, about the size of her kitchen. There was a plain board table, and one four-square Type 19 chair, which she sat on. Nothing else. The light came in through a skylight, what there was of it. No fireplace; she felt cold. The man who'd designed the room had done his job well. You couldn't sit in it on your own for more than a minute or so without realizing that you were in a lot of trouble, which presumably was the intention. She'd heard somewhere that architects design buildings with all sorts of mathematical calculations; ratios of height to width, that sort of thing. Was there a special sum you could do to figure out the most depressing possible dimensions for a room? If so, there'd be a specification somewhere in the Guilds' books, like there was for everything else. All in all, this place made it very hard to believe in the existence of a concept such as love, even though almost certainly that was what had got her here. A room like this could kill love, like the clever jars the silk-makers use for killing silkworms; seal love in the jar and it quickly, painlessly suffocates, leaving the valuable remains undamaged.

When the door opened again, it startled her. She sat up, and saw a tall, slim, rather beautiful young man, her own age or maybe a year younger. He smiled at her and said, "If you'd care to follow me."

"What's going on?" she asked, but he didn't seem to have heard her. He was holding the door open for her, the smile still completely incongruous on his face, like a scorpion in the salad bowl. She got up, and he led the way; along different corridors, down different stairs, through an enormous, deserted hall, out into a cloister surrounding a garden.

"We'll take the short cut," the young man said, with a conspiratorial smile, and led her across the lawn, past a fountain and a small arbor of flowering cherries to a little, low door in a massive wall, so high she couldn't see the top of it. The young man searched in his pocket and found a key; it was stiff in the lock and he had to have several goes at it before he got it open.

"Thank you for your time," he said.

On the other side of the gate she could see a street. In fact, she recognized it: Drapers' Way, leading to the long row of warehouses beside the mill-leet for the brass foundry. She hesitated.

"Can I go?" she said.

He smiled again. "Of course."

There was something scary about the gate; she could feel herself shying at it, like a nervous horse. The nice young man simply stood there, no trace of impatience, as though he was some kind of mechanical door-opening device cunningly made in the shape of a human being. If I close my eyes, she thought; if I close my eyes and run . . .

"Excuse me," the nice young man said.

"Yes?"

He looked more than a little shy. "I know I shouldn't ask this," he said, "but is it true? Are you really the ex-wife of Vaatzes the abominator?"

"Yes. Didn't you know that?"

He looked at her for a long time; like an engineer who sees a rival's secret prototype, and tries to memorize every detail of it, so he can go away and build a copy. "Thank you for your time," he said.

Later, she picked Moritsa up from school. She was in a sulk because she hadn't done well in her spinning test.

"Your own fault. You should've practiced, like I told you to."

"I hate practicing. It's boring."

She made Falier's dinner. There was the leftover mutton in the meat safe; she'd been saving it for the end of the week, but it didn't look like it'd keep till then. Leeks, barley and a few beans to go with it. The bread wasn't quite stale yet. When he got home, she asked him if anything had happened at work. He looked at her and said, "No, should it have?" He was in one of his moods.

When he'd gone to bed, she sat in front of the fire, watching it burn down.

28

At least the Aram Chantat weren't vegetarians, as the late Duke Orsea had believed. On the contrary, if it moved (but not fast enough to escape) they ate it. Sand-grouse and quail weren't too bad, but the funny little birds they served up spit-roasted on arrow shafts just tasted of gristle and grit. She reckoned they were thrushes, but he inclined to the view that they were too small for that. Some kind of starling, was his guess.

And a wonderful improvement on nothing at all, no question about that. To begin with, the gratitude was so thick in the air, walking through the camp was like swimming in mud. There was so much to be grateful for: the Aram Chantat had saved them from the Mezentines, fed them, given them warm blankets for the freezing-cold nights, brought up ox-carts for them to ride in so they wouldn't have to walk the rest of the way across the desert; they'd bound up and dressed their wounds, cured their heatstroke and dysentery with revolting little drinks in tiny clay beakers, even buried the dead in an efficient and respectful manner. The one thing they didn't do was talk, if it could possibly be avoided; but nobody seemed to mind that, at least to start with.

They made an exception in Valens' case. When the convoy reached the edge of the desert (at least, they assumed that was what it was, because of the arrow-straight, deeply rutted road they came to, and the fact that the stunted thorn bushes were slightly closer together), they were met by a coach; an extraordinarily, breathtakingly ornate coach, that looked as though it was on fire until you got close enough to see that every square inch of it was covered in gold leaf. Looking at it hurt the eyes, so instead you gazed at the eight immaculately perfect milk-white horses, or the twenty escort riders, covered like their horses from head to foot in gilded scale armor, apparently unaware of the murderous heat. Out of the burning carriage came a prodigiously tall young man in a pure white robe and gold slippers. He approached the head of the column and snapped at the captain of the Aram Chantat escort, who murmured something back in a voice so soft that none of the Vadani could make out what he'd said. But the vision in white must've understood enough, because he walked slowly and directly to Valens, ignoring the existence of everybody else, and dipped his head in the slightest of bows.

"Duke Valens," he said, in a perfect received-Mezentine accent. "Perhaps you would care to come with me."

It would have been a monstrous sin to deny this perfect creature anything. For some reason, none of the Vadani showed any inclination to go with him. Painfully aware of his filthy clothes and unshaven face, Valens nodded and followed, heading toward the glowing, blinding coach. When he was five yards away from it, two little girls in white smocks scuttled forward from the shadow of the wheels and unrolled a magnificent purple carpet, which the godlike man in white stepped on without looking down. A folding step evolved out of the side of the carriage; simultaneously, a cloth-of-gold awning leaned silently out over the coach door.

Well, Valens thought, I've seen worse. He put his foot on the step and climbed out of the penumbra of the gold fire into total darkness. He heard the door click precisely behind him.

"We have the honor of greeting our son-in-law," said a tiny voice.

Not pitch dark after all; a faint gleam of light leaked out through a gold gauze lampshade surrounding a single small oil lamp. By its meager glow Valens could see a tiny, shriveled little man, completely bald, smooth forehead, cheeks gaunt as a corpse, thin lips, no more than seven teeth, wrapped up like a baby in a massive swathe of heavy white wool blankets. There were figures on either side of the little man, but all he could see of them were dim, bulging shapes.

The little man was waiting for a reply, but Valens couldn't think of anything to say. Someone cleared his throat, a short, clipped sound.

"I take it I have the privilege of addressing Duke Valens Valentinianus," the little man said, in the most perfectly correct Mezentine accent Valens had ever heard. "Allow me to offer my heartiest greetings, despite the tragic circumstances of this meeting."

Son-in-law, he remembered. This exquisite maggot must be her father. He realized with a dull ache of horror that he couldn't remember her name.

"Pleased to meet you," he mumbled. "And thank you. I . . ."

Whatever he'd been intending to say, it didn't seem to want to clot into words. The little man raised a claw about an eighth of an inch. More would have been mere vulgar display.

"When your Major Nennius contacted our frontier patrol, they quite properly sent a messenger to inform us. He rode at top speed until his horse died under him; fortuitously, he was able to requisition another horse within a matter of minutes. He too died shortly after reaching us, but not before delivering his message. We came at once, not stopping to change our clothes or provision ourselves for the journey. We have driven without pause, stopping only to change horses. We are greatly relieved to have arrived here in time to greet you ourselves, instead of delegating such a momentous privilege to others. We are pleased that you have come, and await with trepidation your confirmation that our soldiers have served you adequately."

Valens blinked. He had no idea what the little man was trying to say.

"They saved our lives," he said. "I'm very grateful."

The claws came together in a silent clap. "Excellent," said the little man. "Words cannot express my delight. And now we must have some tea."

Something tinkled faintly, and from somewhere in the darkness a small gold tray appeared, held steady as a rock by two tiny pale hands. On it rested a little gold bowl, from which steam rose.

"For me?" Valens asked stupidly.

"If you would care for it," the little man said.

It burned his mouth and tasted of slightly stale water. As soon as he put the cup back on the tray, it disappeared completely.

"Please sit." Valens had forgotten he was standing. Pale hands, not the same ones that had produced the tea, put down a plain low white stool. It was made of bleached ivory, and proved to be as uncomfortable as it looked.

Deep breath. "I'm very sorry," Valens said, "about your daughter."

"My great-granddaughter." The voice was small and precise as the point of a needle. "All my children and grandchildren are dead. Your wife was, indeed, the last of my family. Accordingly, her loss is more than usually unfortunate." He could have said *inconvenient* just as easily. "I must confess that when I heard the news of her death, I was greatly distressed. However, the circumstances under which the news reached me have done much to reconcile me to her loss." The pitch of the voice changed very slightly, but enough to make Valens' flesh crawl. "Is it really true? Did you cross the desert in nine days?"

Valens nodded.

For a moment, the little man's eyes seemed to flare, like embers blasted by the bellows. "You must tell me all about it," he said. "The circumstances of her death, and your remarkable journey."

For the next hour, Valens did just that; and if the little man found his imprecision and woeful carelessness in observing details annoying, he masked it behind a tiny fixed smile, except when he was asking one of his innumerable, razor-sharp questions. Every few minutes, someone he couldn't see would mutter something; each interruption must have registered with the little man, because he would acknowledge it with a flicker of his little finger; a full crook of the top joint apparently showing approval, a waggle indicating irrelevance or stupidity. All the time, his eyes stayed fixed on Valens' face, and if he blinked once, Valens must have missed it.

"Thank you," he said, when Valens had answered his last question. "It comforts me to know the truth." A tiny sniff. "Now you must be very tired." (An order more than an observation.) "A suitable coach will be at your disposal very soon. We will convey you and your followers" — an infinity of contempt in that word — "to our camp, where you can rest and recover your strength before we speak again. I am most grateful to you for talking to me. If there is anything at all that you or your people require, please tell one of my officers, and the matter will be dealt with immediately."

Behind him, the coach door opened, flooding the world with painful scorching light. Someone covered the little man's head with a lace cloth. A finger, pressed very gently on Valens' shoulder, told him it was time for him to leave.

Outside, the sun was unbelievably bright. The immaculate young man in white led him to another coach, just as blinding but silvered rather than gilded. The carpet, step and awning appeared by the same magic. Valens followed the man in white like a sheep being led into a crush. There was one seat in the coach, and the blinds were drawn. As soon as the door clicked behind him, the coach started to move.

He could have lifted the blind, of course, but he knew he wasn't meant to; so he sat in the dark for an indeterminate period, somewhere between hours and days. The coach stopped twice; each time, the door opened just enough to admit a little silver tray (one silver cup of the hot dishwater and three tiny, rock-hard cakes) and a spotlessly clean silver chamber-pot, exquisitely decorated with scroll-and-foliage engraving. The coach's suspension was so perfect that pissing in the chamber-pot at the gallop was simplicity itself. Curiously, it wasn't removed at the second stop; but not a drop had been spilled, so that was presumably all right.

He was asleep when the coach stopped for the third time, and ferocious light woke him up out of a half-dream in which he was talking to the little man but couldn't hear a word either of them was saying. The door was open, and a different tall young man in white was beckoning to him. His back and legs ached unbearably, and the light was like nails driven into both sides of his head at once.

The first thing he noticed was tents; an ocean of them, all brilliant white, like a bumper crop of absurdly large mushrooms. Then he realized that there weren't any other coaches apart from his and the little man's golden miracle.

"Where are . . . ?" he started to say. The young man smiled.

"They are being taken care of," he said. "Please follow me."

He had to walk a whole ten yards, five of them on the dusty, gravelly soil rather than carpet. He could feel the young man's embarrassment, but obviously there was nothing he could do about that. The tent he was led into was about the size of an average farm barn, brilliant white on the outside, dark as a bag inside. These people, he decided, must regard light the way the Vadani felt about mud; there's a lot of it about, but the better sort of people take reasonable steps to avoid getting covered in it. He sat down on a heap of cushions, which were the only visible artifacts in the tent, apart from a solid gold chamber-pot the size of a rain bucket. He was alone again.

Presumably he must have fallen asleep when the tent flap opened and yet another tall young man in white brought him a tray of food. This time, it wasn't a sparse little snack of cakes; in fact, he was amazed that someone so slight-looking could carry that much weight, let alone put it down so effortlessly, without grunting. It was all, needless to say, lean roast meat. He guzzled as much of it as he could bear, and washed it down with the thimbleful and a half of water that came with it, in a dear little silver bottle.

Nobody could stay awake for very long after that. He woke up some time later, tortured with indigestion and dry as parchment, in the dark. No trace of light seeped through the heavy fabric of the tent, which suggested it was night. He lay on his back, too uncomfortable to sleep. The likeliest explanation was that at some point he'd died without noticing it, and this was the afterlife they promised you in the old stories; whether it was one reserved for the very good or the very bad he wasn't quite sure.

Dawn came painfully slowly, gradually building up a glow in the tent walls. He couldn't hear anything at all — he had to prove to himself that he hadn't gone deaf by dropping the silver bottle onto the tray. While he was doing that, he noticed that his filthy clothes had somehow turned into spotlessly clean white robes, like the ones worn by the tall young men, and his boots had evolved into ridiculous little silver-thread slippers with pointy toes and no backs. It was that which helped him clarify his newly found religious faith. This had to be the very bad people's place.

After a thousand years or so, the tent flap opened again. Not a tall, slim young man in white this time; an older man, in a plain robe of sort-of-gray woolen cloth, wearing sensible boots that Valens would have traded his duchy for. The man looked at him for a moment as if he was something regrettable that couldn't reasonably be avoided, and said, "This way."

This way proved to be the five yards or so to the tent next door, across a red, blue and purple carpet. Inside, the tent was pitch black; a clue, he decided, to the identity of his host.

"You have rested." Not a question. "Please sit down. You must try the orange and cinnamon tea; it's stronger, but one needs a little stimulation in the morning."

Stimulation; the little man sounded so frail that Valens reckoned anything more stimulating than slow, shallow breathing would probably kill him. "Thank you," he said.

The cup was put into his hand.

"I must apologize," the little man's voice went on, "about the rather dim light. I'm afraid that my eyes are rather sensitive. Direct sunlight gives me a headache."

"That's quite all right," Valens mumbled.

"In fact," the voice continued, quite matter-of-fact, "practically everything in my life hurts me these days — breathing, eating, drinking, sleeping, waking up, moving, keeping still, every kind and description of bodily function brings with it a different and complementary pain. I had hoped," he added wistfully, "to have died earlier this year, but regrettably I realized that I could not permit myself to do so. My last surviving son, you see; quite suddenly, my doctors tell me it was his heart. With only my great-granddaughter left — you can appreciate the problem, I feel sure. At the best of times, a line of succession is such a slender thing, a single strand of spider's web, and our enemies are so strong, so unrelenting." A short pause, no doubt to gather strength. "The Rosinholet and the Bela Razo made a joint attack on us earlier this year; not just a cattle raid, but a concerted attempt to wipe us out. My son undertook the defense, but he had turned into an old man; too weak to ride a horse, too confused to manage all the intricacies of a serious war. I had to relieve him of command in the end. We saw them off, eventually, but I knew then that something had to be done. They will return, I feel certain of it; with them, I expect, they will bring the Aram no Vei and the Luzir Soleth. The simple fact is, there are too many of us; the Cure Hardy, I mean. We have bred too many cattle and too many children, and the pasture will not support us all. Some nations have tried sitting down — staying in one place all the time, I mean, as you do — but we simply can't live like that. The only logical solution is for one of the nations of the confederacy to go away, or else be wiped out."

Silence; not expecting a reply or a comment, just a pause for breath and reflection. Nevertheless, Valens said, "You want to cross the desert and settle there?"

"Precisely." The little man sounded pleased that he wasn't going to have to explain. "We heard about the annihilation of the Eremian people by the Perpetual Republic of Mezentia. Most regrettable, of course; but it stands to reason that if a nation is wiped out, their lands fall empty."

"But Eremia's not big enough, surely," Valens said without thinking.

"No, of course not," the old man sighed. "We should need the entire territory between the mountains and the sea. But if the Eremians have disappeared, and we allied ourselves with you, that would only leave the Mezentines to be disposed of — assuming," he added, with the ghost of a chuckle, "that we could get across the desert without losing more than half our number of effective fighting men. That was the question that remained unanswered when my great-granddaughter left here to marry you." He sighed again, a long, thin noise like the last exhalation of a dying animal. "And now you have brought us a safe, quick path across the desert; now, I need only live long enough to see Mezentia got rid of, and my duty will at last be done. My people will have a safe home, I will have my successor, and you . . ." A laugh like dry twigs snapping. "I assume you would like to be revenged on the murderers of your wife. Personally, I've never been able to see the merit in revenge, except as a deterrent to further offense, but my people think very highly of it. My great-granddaughter's death will be all the pretext they need, without the prospect of a new home." Pause. "I take it you would wish to see the Mezentines destroyed?"

One thing you couldn't do to the voice was lie to it. "Yes," Valens said. "I'd like to see them butchered to the last man, woman and child. I'd like to stand and watch, when I get too tired to take part myself. But not if it means risking the lives of what's left of my people. I'd rather let the Mezentines get away with what they've done completely unscathed."

Two hands too weak to clap patted each other. "Splendid answer," the voice said. "Exactly what my successor should have said; and I have no doubts at all about your sincerity, let me stress that. Everything I have heard of you leads me to believe that you are a good king, like your father before you. Which is why," he went on, "I shall have to live long enough to do the taking of revenge myself. I told you I don't believe in it; I don't believe in our gods, either, but my people do. On balance, it seems far more likely that they are right than I am. We will wipe out the Mezentines for you; you won't have to make that choice. If you prefer, you are welcome to stay here and wait until the job is done and our army returns. You may regard it as a belated wedding present, if you wish. As reciprocation for the wonderful gift you've given us — the safe way across the desert — it is, I fear, wholly inadequate. Tell me," and the voice quickened just a little, "how did you find out about it? There have been rumors, of course. Many of my people have claimed there was such a thing, over the years. Only recently a foolish young man called Skeddanlothi — a cousin of mine, unfortunately too distant to be able to succeed me — declared that he had found it and would prove his assertion by going there himself. Of course, he never came back, so presumably he was misinformed."

"A merchant," Valens heard himself say. "A trader from my country found it, apparently. He came here several times to buy salt; when he died, he left a diary, and a map. One of my . . ." He couldn't think of a word to describe Vaatzes. "One of my people found the map, and when the Mezentines were closing in on us, we took a chance and followed it; and here we are."

The noise that greeted these words didn't sound at all like laughter, but what else could it be? "Remarkable," the voice said eventually. "And salt, of all things. Well; I don't suppose it matters how the way was found, so long as it really exists. Tell me about the oases; will they water an army of two hundred thousand, do you think? Of course, I have sent surveyors, men who know about that sort of thing; I shall know for sure soon enough. But I'm impatient. What do you think? Will there be enough water?"

Valens heard a voice saying, "Yes," and realized it was his own. "And water won't be a problem once you reach the mountains on the other side; it's how to transport the quantities of food you'll need . . ."

"Oh, don't worry about that." The voice sounded almost cheerfully dismissive. "We have vastly more experience in that sort of thing than you do, by all accounts."

Despite the dark, Valens' eyes felt tired. He rubbed them before saying: "Can you really field an army of two hundred thousand?"

The strange sound again, equivalent to laughter. "An *expeditionary* force of two hundred thousand light cavalry and lancers, followed by the heavy cavalry and dragoons — say three hundred and fifty thousand — would probably be adequate for the task and still leave a sufficient reserve here in case of further attacks from our enemies." Short pause. "I should, of course, be asking your opinion, not purporting to state a fact. Do you think five hundred and fifty thousand cavalry would be enough to deal with the Mezentines? I understand that their field army is made up entirely of foreigners serving for money; a mixed blessing, at best, I should imagine. We could send a larger force, but my experience is that once you pass a certain point, a large army is more of a hindrance than a help."

This time it was Valens who paused before speaking. "How many of you are there?" he said.

Laughter again; a different sound, like the barking of a very small dog. "How delightful, that you feel sufficiently at ease already to ask such a direct question!" Then the pitch of the voice changed again; lower, quite businesslike. "I regret to say that I don't have an up-to-date census to hand; five months ago, however, when we held the usual muster and games to celebrate my birthday, on the fifth day all the men of military age fit for active service paraded on the plain beside the Swallow River. As each regiment marched past its commander-in-chief, each man placed an arrow on a pile. When the parade was over, the arrows were gathered up into barrels, each holding one thousand. We filled seven hundred barrels, with a few hundred arrows left over. If you ask me what proportion of our people are fit for military service, I would estimate somewhere between an eighth and a tenth. Does that answer your question?"

"Yes." Valens thought for a moment, then said, "As far as I know, the total population of Mezentia is something around eight hundred thousand; it could be less, I'm pretty sure it's not much more. So yes, I think half a million men would probably be enough."

"You think so? I wonder." The voice was very faint. "Allow me to confess my ignorance. I have never seen a city. Come to that, I have never seen a stone-built house. Only a tiny handful of my people have seen anything of the kind. I admit to finding the whole concept both repellent and strangely fascinating; to live your entire life in a box, to see the same view every morning when you wake up; remarkable. But I understand that Mezentia has the highest, thickest walls in the world, with massive gates and high towers, and extraordinary machines that hurl rocks and spears to defend them. I am told that when an enemy shuts himself up in such a very strong box, the only way to deal with him is to keep him there until he starves, and either comes out or dies." A click of the tongue, faint but perfectly clear. "I assume that this process takes time, and I think I have explained why I am in something of a hurry. Yes, I believe that five hundred thousand cavalry could shut the Mezentines up in their box, for a little while, until they themselves began to feel hungry and so were obliged to move on. Do you think the Mezentines' city can be taken? I really don't know enough about these things to form a sensible opinion."

Valens thought: I wonder who made the decision to start the war. I wonder what passed through his mind, just before the scales tipped slightly more one way than the other. He said: "I think it's possible. You see, I have a man . . ."

"Ziani Vaatzes."

"Yes, him. He nearly managed to defend Civitas Eremiae against them. I've come to know him, a little. I think, give him a long enough crowbar and he can pull apart any box on earth."

"I know a little about him," the voice said softly. "And I would tend to agree." Another pause, and Valens wished there was enough light to show him the little man's face. "I must confess, I'm given rather to flights of fancy. I picture things in my mind that I have never seen; picture them the way they should be, if you follow me, rather than how they are. I have a very clear picture in my mind of Ziani Vaatzes. At some point, I suppose, I shall see him in the flesh, and be vastly disappointed. Of course, I have never seen a Mezentine. I understand that their skins are brown. I shall ask my soldiers to bring me some dead bodies from the oasis. Did you know that the Rosinholet are experts at curing and preserving dead bodies? When a particularly famous and valuable man dies, they cure his skin and stuff it with wool bound tight on a wooden frame, to simulate the bones. Sometimes they mount their illustrious dead on horses, or sit them on the boxes of their wagons. I shall see if we have any Rosinholet embalmers among our slaves, who could manufacture a dozen or so Mezentines for me. It would be appropriate, don't you think? The Mezentines are wonderful makers of things, so I don't see why they shouldn't be made into things themselves. Perhaps, given his rather special skills, Ziani Vaatzes could build appropriate mechanisms to go inside them, so that they can do more or less everything they could do when they were alive. Who knows, maybe we could improve on the design a little in some respects, unless Foreman Vaatzes considers that would constitute an abomination." A soft, dry sound, like a dusty carpet being beaten. "Forgive me, I wander off sometimes. Here's an idea. Let's send for Foreman Vaatzes and ask him for his professional opinion. What do you think of that?"

"There you are," Daurenja said, materializing suddenly in the doorway of the tent.

Ziani looked up and scowled. "Not now," he said. "I'm busy."

"Are you?" Daurenja ducked, his ridiculously long neck bending like a drawn bow, and stepped inside the tent, blotting out the light for a moment or so as he came. "Doing what?"

"Resting. Go away."

Daurenja folded his legs and back and sat down on the ground next to him. "Really," he said cheerfully. "That's no way to talk to your business partner."

"I haven't got one."

"Yes you have." He was sitting unpleasantly close, his back to the tent's center pole. His hair was wet and hung loose down his back in rat-tails. He was wearing a pristine white robe, like the ones the Aram Chantat nobles wore, and on his feet were a pair of curly-toed red velvet slippers. "That's one of the things I wanted to talk to you about. Not the main thing, though. Mostly, I wanted a few quiet minutes to tell you how brilliant you are."

Ziani sighed and started to get up. A hand with a grip like a bench-vise grabbed his shoulder and pulled him down, so fast and so smooth that he had no chance to resist. "Please stay and listen," Daurenja said. "Surely you can spare a few moments to hear a few nice things about yourself."

Ziani picked the hand off his shoulder; touching it was like drawing the guts out of dead poultry after it's hung for a week. "If they're nice," he said, "they probably aren't true. I've never gone much on fiction."

"Don't worry on that score," Daurenja said with a mild giggle. "Everything I'm about to say is perfectly true. Well, you can be the judge of that."

Ziani tried to get up again, but his knees were too weak. "I don't want to talk to you," he said.

"In a minute you will." Daurenja yawned. "Where's the best place to start? Shall we begin with the Duke's wedding day, when you betrayed the hunting party to the Mezentines?"

Ziani felt cold, and all his joints appeared to have seized. "That's bullshit," he said. "And you know as well as I do, it was Duke Orsea who —"

"Ah. Poor Duke Orsea. But I think we'll come to him later. Actually, on reflection, I think we ought to start at the beginning, or as close to it as makes no odds. Tell me; after you ran away from the city, were you actually heading for the Eremian camp, or was running into them a fat slice of sheer good luck?"

This time, Ziani lashed out. He was aiming for Daurenja's chin, but when his fist reached the place where the target should have been, it met nothing but air. Almost simultaneously, something very hard and fast hit Ziani just above the right ear. More surprised than anything else, he folded his arms and legs, like a spider killed suddenly on its web, and dropped to the floor.

"As I was saying." Daurenja's voice, blurred and distant, reached him through the pain like a far-off light glimpsed through mist. "Did you deliberately set out to find Orsea from the start? I suppose what I'm asking is, was the plan already more or less complete in your mind at that early stage, or were you still making it up as you went along?"

Ziani felt sick and dizzy; it was like being very drunk and having the hangover at the same time. He tried to gauge the distance between Daurenja's legs and himself, but it was too much effort.

"I don't know what you're talking about," he mumbled.

"By all means lie if you want to," Daurenja said pleasantly. "It doesn't matter to me, because I know the truth. And yes, I know it's true. The plan's there for anybody to see, if he's got the wit to know what he's looking at. I've been studying it for months now, piecing it together. It's been an education, and an honor. I was only able to figure it out because we're so very much alike, you and me." He shifted a little, moving slightly sideways, slightly back. There was some fencing move or other where you did that. "Ever since I saw it for what it is, I've been trying to take it apart, bit by bit, to figure out how it works. You know, you really are a clever man, Ziani. It's the combination of imaginative flair and scrupulous attention to detail that does it. It's odd, really; I mean, the Mezentine tradition hardly encourages innovative design, does it? There's a set specification, you copy it exactly or they string you up. Really, when you think of a talent like yours being neglected like that, it's a crying shame."

Ziani saw movement out of the corner of his eye, then felt the impact of a powerful blow; a kick in the ribs, which squeezed all the air out of his body.

"Now I'm pretty clear in my mind about what happened up to the fall of Eremia," Daurenja went on. "By arming the Eremians with scorpions, you made sure that the war escalated out of control, making the Republic commit itself far more deeply than it wanted to. The sideshow with Duke Valens and Orsea's wife; clearly you didn't set any of that up, but you did ensure that Orsea found out about it; that suggests you were planning a long way ahead by that point, so I'm assuming that most of the main elements were already clearly established in your mind." He paused, as though waiting for a reply or some sort of comment. There was disappointment in his voice when he resumed. "Now I'm going to have to press you for an answer here," he said, "because obviously the next bit is crucial to a clear understanding of the mechanism. Was it you who opened the gates and let the Mezentines in to Civitas Eremiae?"

"No."

He could see Daurenja frowning. "I think you did," he said. "It's the sort of bold, radical approach that hallmarks your work; also the way you make one process further several different functions. For example: you needed to draw the Vadani into the war. I'm guessing you assumed that Orsea and Veatriz would seek asylum with Valens; I don't imagine you actually predicted Valens' big, romantic gesture, that was really just a massive bonus. Still, no shame in being lucky; and a beautiful design like yours sort of encourages luck to happen; you attract it, like decoying geese." He stopped, then said, "Anything you'd like to add before we move on? No? Oh, I wish you'd share with me. I'd love to know how you went about figuring it all out, it'd be a master class in design. Oh well." He waited hopefully a little longer, then went on: "The other function was controlling Valens himself, through his thwarted love for Orsea's wife. Very clever. What Valens secretly wants more than anything is to snatch Veatriz out of the jaws of death and have her fall into his arms; but just when he thinks he's getting there, he finds himself lumbered with Orsea as well. Obviously, that's an intolerable position to be in — which is exactly what you want, since you need to break Valens down — gradually, at a carefully controlled rate of decay — to the point where he's weak enough for you to manipulate him directly. The love-triangle thing does that perfectly, and I'm guessing that that's the real reason Civitas

Eremiae had to fall. You'd never get Orsea away from his city unless it was burned to the ground, and you'd never get Veatriz to
Valens' court without Orsea. On reflection, I bet you were expecting the rescue or something like it; not banking on it, of course,
but quietly confident it'd happen. There, you see; decoying luck,
like I said a moment ago."

Ziani tried to speak, but he hadn't got enough breath back yet.

"Talking of luck," Daurenja went on, "I'm going to stick my neck
out and say that the hidden way across the desert was the major
breakthrough. Sorry, but there's no way you could have known
about that until you reached Civitas Vadanis. On the other hand,
I'm pretty sure you'd already resolved on bringing about the marriage alliance with the Cure Hardy. That must've come at a very
early stage, because of course that's what everything's been about:
bringing the Cure Hardy into the war, since they're the only power
on earth that could beat the Republic. You must've decided to involve them, I'm assuming through the marriage-alliance mechanism, right back in the very early stages, probably before you first
met Orsea. In which case, I insist on you answering this one, you
must've just left a gap in the design — a big hole marked *Find a way
of getting Valens to marry a Cure Hardy princess* — and worked round
it until you heard about Skeddanlothi's raid — was that before or
after you arrived in Civitas Vadanis? — and realized there must
be a secret way across the desert out there somewhere, waiting to
be rediscovered. Am I right?"

"No," Ziani said. Daurenja kicked him again. He retched violently, but nothing came out.

"I think I'm right," Daurenja went on. "I have to say, it's a privilege to study a mind like yours in action. All right, there was that
crucial slice of luck; just like the thing between Valens and Veatriz
was a slice of luck. What matters is how you used it; and that's
where this fantastic attention to detail comes in. As soon as you've
realized the significance of Skeddanlothi, you ferret around until
you find the trader's widow and the map. Not just more luck; you
found it because you had a pretty good idea of where to look.

What, you asked yourself, could the Vadani possibly want from the Cure Hardy that'd make it worth someone's while finding out about the oasis route? Answer: salt, of course. Once you've got salt, you can target salt traders past and present, and sooner or later you'll find what you're after. I always think luck's a bit like splitting a log. You're much more likely to succeed if you read the grain and look for flaw-lines."

Ziani made a monstrous effort and spasmed his back into a sharp contraction, enough to get him onto his hands and knees. It took time; and when he'd finally made it, Daurenja kicked him hard, just under the left nipple, and landed him back more or less where he'd started.

"The way you made use of the marriage alliance," Daurenja went on. "You know what I think? I believe you were the one who put the idea in Chancellor Carausius' head to start with. Did you?"

"No, of course not."

"I think you did. And the way you handled Carausius after that; leading him along, step by patient step, and I'll bet he never even realized he was being guided. And of course, you had to be so careful; even the slightest hint that you were playing games with Valens and he'd have shied and ruined the whole thing. Very risky, of course, since you were already working Valens over on two other fronts at the same time: the armored wagon idea, which you needed so as to get him out of the city and into the open, where you could manipulate him pretty much at will; and also the business with the mines — quite brilliant, by the way, as a little self-contained mechanism serving two functions: you get Valens' confidence and a reputation as an engineering miracle worker, which you need in order to build your ascendancy over him, and at the same time you're in a perfect position to give the silver mines practically intact to the Mezentines at the critical moment, to make sure they've got enough money to keep them in the war. The economy and efficiency of that arrangement — well, purely in engineering terms, in my opinion it's actually one of the best things you've ever done; either that, or the way you set up Orsea, at the end. Though," Daurenja went on after a brief pause for reflection, "the Orsea thing runs it fairly close, in terms of two birds and one stone — you get rid of a minor but appreciable threat to yourself, you use Orsea to build up your credibility and bargaining position with the Republic, and of course you finally destroy Valens by making him murder Veatriz's husband, thereby ruining his chances of getting the girl forever. You leave him more or less pulped, just when you need to have him at his most docile and suggestible — so you can get him to change course and head across the desert." Daurenja shook his head and smiled. "I really wish you'd let me in on the technical details; like, for example, at what stage you finalized each part of the design. For instance, was getting rid of Orsea a major component right from the beginning? I'd be inclined to believe it must have been, because it's such a beautiful little assembly for achieving so many key objectives at just the right time. But if it wasn't, and it just sort of came to you on the fly; and I do wish you'd put your hostility aside for a moment and take me through the way you got Carausius hooked on a Cure Hardy alliance . . . Well," he added, more in disappointment than resentment, "I guess I can't expect a Mezentine to betray Guild secrets, can I? Maybe later you'll tell me. I'd really like that, if you could possibly see your way to it."

Ziani rolled onto one elbow. His ribs ached so much he could hardly breathe. "What do you want?" he asked.

"You know perfectly well what I want," Daurenja replied. "I've told you often enough. I want to be your student, your apprentice, your assistant, your partner and your friend. Thanks to you, I've established myself here with the Vadani. I'm rock-solid, as that tiresome affair with my former partner Framain demonstrated. It's been so frustrating for me in the past; just when I'm getting somewhere, making progress, building an environment where I can work and start achieving something, some peccadillo or other comes home to roost and I have to clear out in a hurry. I've left enough notebooks and folios of drawings behind me to furnish a library; the distilled results of years of work, abandoned, while I run for my life. Now at last — thanks to you — I'm valuable enough to the Duke that he's prepared to overlook my little ways. On its own, that'd justify all the hard work I've put in since I first met you."

"Glad to have been of service," Ziani grunted.

"You aren't now," Daurenja replied pleasantly, "but you will be, when the time comes. And that's another thing. I'm more or less certain that your wonderful grand design really will work; it'll all come out the way you want it to, you'll get to be the conqueror of Mezentia, you'll ride in triumph through the shattered gates and set up your throne room in the Guildhall, as the Cure Hardy's trusted governor and commander of the army of occupation. At which point," Daurenja went on cheerfully, "there'll be a vacancy for the job of chief military engineer to the Aram Chantat empire, and no prizes for guessing who'll take over. As soon as you get what you want, I'll get what I want; what I *deserve*. Then, with the resources of the new empire to back me up, and no more infuriating rules and restrictions to interfere with how I choose to live my life, I'll finally be able to fulfill my true potential. Thanks to you."

Ziani glanced away. He found Daurenja uncomfortable to look at; like a reflection in a curved sheet of polished steel, a distorting mirror.

"Now you're thinking," Daurenja went on, "that I must be a prize idiot, letting you know how much I've figured out about you. You're thinking, I can't allow this fool to live, I've got to get him out of the way as soon as possible. Knowing you, I expect you've already thought of a way; several ways, and all of them mechanically perfect. But you won't do it, and you know why? Because you need me. Honestly, you do; and why? Because there's another great big hole in your schematic, and this one's marked *Find a way of breaking through the defenses of Mezentia*. Correct me if I'm wrong, but you haven't really given it any thought. You know that the Aram Chantat don't know spit about siege warfare; the Vadani aren't much better. You know the city's got the highest, thickest walls in the world, laid out so as to give the artillery on the walls the optimum fields of fire. You know that unless you come up with a stunning innovation, the Mezentines will slaughter the Aram Chantat in much the same way as you slaughtered the Mezentines at Civitas Eremiae. Well," Daurenja said, and the smugness in his voice was as thick and waxy as goose dripping, "I can fill that hole for you, if you'll help me build my explosive-powder machine; my life's work, the one thing I want more than anything else. Plain and simple: we need each other so much. We're like the ideal married couple; so much in common, and such differences as we have make us complement each other perfectly. My strengths balance out your weaknesses, and vice versa. We depend on each other absolutely, like the two parts of a dovetail joint. Or," he added with a smile, "like lovers. Or like lovers should be, but so rarely are, in my wide and varied experience. But then, it's always love that drives us, isn't it? Men like you and me." He sighed, like a man waking up out of a beautiful dream. "One of the things I value most in our relationship is the affinity of minds. I think you're probably the only man I've ever met who's got the intelligence and the depth of character to understand me. As we get closer, I think you will come to understand me, eventually. I hope you'll make the effort; you'll find it worth your while if you do. Isn't it perfect? I can give you what you want, you can give me what I want, and the same operation will fulfill both our desires. Just like lovers, really. How are you feeling, by the way? Not in any pain, I trust."

"I think you've broken one of my ribs."

"I doubt it," Daurenja replied. "I think you'll find I know my own strength to within a pretty tight margin of error. I studied anatomy in Lonazep, you know. A good working knowledge of anatomy is very useful if you're going to have to beat people up now and again. After all, the human body's just a machine. If you're going to use it — yours or someone else's — it helps if you know how it works, and what kind of stresses and strains it'll take." He paused, as if considering what he'd just said. "Actually," he went on, "that wasn't meant as a threat, but since it makes quite a good one, feel free to interpret it as such. Of course, going whining to Valens won't do you any good. The most he'll do is lecture us on playing rough games and tell us to make friends and be nice to each other. And I know so much about you that Valens doesn't need to hear. I really do need your help, to build the tube for turning my explosive powder into a weapon; but if the worst comes to the worst and you make more trouble than you're worth to me and I have to sacrifice you for the good of the project, I suppose I'll have to muddle through on my own. Or maybe we can capture another red-hot Mezentine engineer, and I can persuade him to help me. You see, I've got options; you — well, let's not dwell on it. I'd far, far rather work with you. I like you; and that counts for a lot in any partnership. I never liked Framain; not my sort of person." Suddenly he laughed. "This is a bit of fun though, isn't it? You've come all this way, achieved so much, fitted so many other people into your design; and now you're the key component in mine. Isn't it a relief, when all's said and done, to know that now, at last, you're finally not alone anymore?"

They woke him up in the middle of the night and bundled him politely into a carriage; not the shiny silver one, just a plain old wooden thing with a hide canopy and a bench seat. The windows were covered, and he'd lost track of time completely. It came as a surprise, therefore, when the coach stopped and they opened the door and it was daylight outside.

He was back at the frontier post. He was unsteady on his feet as he scrambled down out of the coach. The Vadani, what was left of them, were sprawled across an open plain, littered untidily, like things spilled out of a box. Beautiful white tents were scattered about; people were sitting outside them, cooking over fires from which thin white smoke rose straight up into the still air. Heads turned to stare at him, but nobody moved at first. An Aram Chantat soldier nodded toward a tent.

"Mine?" Valens asked stupidly. The soldier turned and walked back to the coach, which rattled away as soon as he was inside.

In the tent was a plain camp bed, with a frame of willow branches mortised and dowelled together, and split withes stretched across it for suspension. It was comfortable, almost luxurious. He lay down and closed his eyes. In the disputed territory between awake and asleep, he heard her voice, and opened his eyes.

For once, she was actually there.

"You've come back, then. We were worried."

He thought for a moment; then replied: "I think I just met their king. My father-in-law. Actually, he's something like my great-grandfather-in-law, not that it matters. All his family predeceased him, which just goes to show, if you live long enough, eventually you get lucky. Do you happen to know where Ziani Vaatzes is? I need to talk to him."

She shook her head. "Are you all right?"

"Depends." He made an effort and sat up. "For savages, they're pretty damned sophisticated. It takes us about a million dead geese to make a bed this comfortable."

"They fold away, too," she said. "I imagine everything here's got to be portable and collapsible."

He yawned. "I had a long talk with their head man," he said. "Apparently they're going to wipe the Mezentines off the face of the earth for me. I said not to bother on my account, but they reckoned it was no trouble." He tried to stand up, but his knees weren't prepared to take responsibility for his weight. "To be honest, I haven't got the faintest idea what's going to happen next, or how we fit in, or how much of it's going to be my fault. I just wish I'd died out there in the desert."

She looked at him. "You've got to learn," she said. "There's things you could have put in a letter that you can't say face to face. Not unless you mean them."

"I wish I'd died in the desert," he said. "The only good thing about still being here is knowing you're safe. I don't really care about anything else anymore."

She looked away. "Define safe," she replied.

"No thank you." He yawned again. "Sorry," he added. "I guess the last few weeks are catching up with me. Oh, I forgot. The king of the savages is extremely old, and when he dies, I'm supposed to succeed him."

She frowned. "Do you want to?"

"No."

"Have you got a choice?"

"Not really." He shook his head like a wet dog. "Do you know what I really want most of all right now, more than anything else in the whole wide world?"

"No. Tell me."

He grinned. "I want a pack of dogs and a bloody great big spear, and I want to find something edible with four legs and kill it."

It was in the place he'd told her it would be; in the top of the broken crock where the poultryman left the eggs, under the cracked roof tile. It was a little square packet of parchment. Any of her neighbors would have assumed it was a dose of powdered willowbark from the woman who sold medicines.

She'd noticed it early in the morning, when she collected the eggs; but he was there, so she didn't dare pick it up. She left it, hoping he'd go out, but for some reason he didn't go in to work. Instead he sat in the study all day, staring at a big sheaf of drawings. When she came in to ask if he wanted anything, he tried to hide them with his sleeve.

All day she waited. Three or four times she almost managed to persuade herself that it'd be safe to get the letter and read it, but she resisted the temptation. As it happened, she would've been quite safe. Falier only left the study once all morning, to go to the outhouse . . .

Of course. How stupid of her.

As she hurried toward the front door, he came out of the study. "Where are you off to?" he asked her.

"To put the money out for the egg man," she replied.

He frowned. "What money? You haven't asked me for any money."

Stupid; careless. "No," she replied.

He sighed. "How much?"

"Three turners."

He fumbled in his pocket. "Three turners for a dozen eggs," he said. "Couldn't you get them cheaper in the market?"

"His eggs are always fresh."

He gave her three small coins. "There's a man at work whose mother keeps hens," he said. "I'll ask him if there's ever any spare. We're not made of money, you know."

"That's a good idea," she said meekly. "Can I get you anything?"

"What? No. Have you seen my small penknife? The little one with the black handle?"

She nodded. "In the kitchen," she said. "I used it to dress the fish."

"Oh for —" She could see him making an effort not to be annoyed. "Next time, couldn't you use something else? That's my special knife for sharpening pens."

"All the kitchen knives are blunt. You said you'd sharpen them."

"Yes, all right, when I've got five minutes."

You said that last week, she didn't reply. "It's in the drawer," she said. "I washed it up carefully."

"Right, yes, thanks." He stomped out into the kitchen; she bolted through the front door and shut it behind her.

First, she put the money in the bottom of the crock. Only then did she look to see if it was still there. Seeing it was like a miracle. She palmed it quickly, squeezing her hand around it without closing her fingers. Then she crossed the yard, opened the outhouse door, sat down on the edge of the earthenware pot, shut the door and bolted it. Today, the bolt had to be stiff (he'd promised he'd see to that, too). She broke a nail working it into its keeper.

My darling . . .

She shut her eyes as the muscles of her stomach tightened.

My darling,

I know you must be very worried and upset. It hurts me terribly to think of you, not knowing what's going on, or whether you're in danger. I think about you all the time.

I'm safe. That's all I can tell you for now. I'll come for you as soon as I can, but that may not be for a while. The people I'm with are going to look after me, but . . .

She skipped a couple of lines.

I'm sorry I can't tell you any more, but I've got to be so careful. Trust me, my darling. I promise you, everything's under control. I'll be coming home, and it'll be soon. I don't care what it takes or what I have to do. The only thing that matters to me is being with you.

I love you.

She folded the parchment up again, putting him back into his little packet.

"What the hell happened to you?" Valens hissed, as they brushed through the tent flap together into the darkness. "You look like you've been in a fight or something."

"Doesn't matter," Ziani muttered back. "What's . . . ?"

"Ziani Vaatzes." The thin, fragile voice startled him. He couldn't see where it was coming from. "I am delighted and honored to meet you. The hero of Civitas Eremiae; and the armored wagons. Such a simple yet ingenious idea, but of course it was overtaken by circumstances. And a Mezentine; I think I shall indulge my curiosity and have some light."

Only a brief flicker, lasting hardly longer than a flash of lightning; a very old man, completely bald.

"Thank you," said the voice. "So it really is true; there are men in the world with brown faces. Remarkable. My apologies for staring at you so blatantly; but at my age, to see something new is such a rare thing. And the man who discovered the way across the desert. What a long way you've come, Foreman Vaatzes."

"Thank you," Ziani said, for want of anything else to say.

He could hear Valens breathing beside him; fast, nervous, like a man waiting for his bride's veil to be lifted. As for himself, he could almost have wished that this moment would last forever. Almost.

"Duke Valens thinks most highly of you," the voice went on. "He believes that you might be able to find a way to bring down the walls of Mezentia. With the very greatest respect; do you really think you could do that?"

(And Daurenja's hand on his shoulder, forcing him to his knees . . .)

"Yes," Ziani said.

extras

orbit

meet the author

K. J. PARKER is a pseudonym. Find more about the author at
www.kjparker.com.

introducing

**If you enjoyed
EVIL FOR EVIL,
look out for**

THE ESCAPEMENT

Book Three of the Engineer Trilogy

by K. J. Parker

The Cure Doce ambassador was a small, wiry man with short white hair, enormous hands and a nose like a wedge. As soon as Psellus walked into the room he jumped up, as though the door was a sear that tripped the catch that held him in his seat. He spoke in snips, like a man cutting foil.

"Thank you for seeing me on such short notice," he said. "Time, obviously —"

Psellus nodded vaguely. "Quite," he said. "They tell me — please, sit down — they tell me the savages are nine days' ride from here. Time is therefore very much on my mind at the moment." He sat down and wondered, as he always did when he had to conduct a meeting with important people, what the hell he was supposed to do with his hands. He could fold them in front of him on the table, but that implied a level of briskness that he didn't really feel capable of. And the only alternative was just to let them hang from his wrists, like coats in a cupboard. "If you have any suggestions to make, I'd be delighted to hear them."

The ambassador nodded, and folded his hands on the table. "My understanding," he said, "is that at the moment you have no effective field army. Is that correct?"

Psellus smiled. "Yes."

Perhaps the ambassador hadn't been expecting a one-word answer. He flinched, as though Psellus had just said a rude word. "We can offer you twelve thousand archers, eight thousand men-at-arms and eleven hundred heavy cavalry," he said. "We've already taken the precaution of mustering them at Liancor —"

"Where's that?"

Another rude word, apparently. The ambassador took a moment to recover, then said, "It's the closest point on our side to the road the savages are likely to take. We've mobilized simply as a precaution, to discourage them from trespassing on our territory." He smiled. "We have no quarrel of our own with either the Vadani or the savages. However —" He snatched a little breath, and Psellus thought: Ah. He's about to lie to me. "However, we feel that it would be impossible, ethically speaking, for us to stand idly by and watch while the savages overrun and destroy a great city crammed with helpless civilians, women and children. We are prepared to help you —"

"Thank you."

The ambassador looked like a man trying to wrestle with an opponent made entirely out of water; there was nothing to get hold of, and it kept slipping away unexpectedly. "Provided," he went on, "that you in turn recognize the nature of the commitment we're making to you, and undertake to bear it in mind when the post-war balance of power comes to be reassessed. For a long time now, we've been actively seeking a closer relationship with the Republic, a relationship which you have hitherto seemed less than eager to pursue. We feel —"

"Excuse me." Psellus held up his hand (nice to find a use for it at last). "I'm very new at this, and I'm afraid I don't speak the language very well. You've probably heard I didn't want the job, I'm really not capable of doing it, by any stretch of the imagination, and I still don't quite understand how I came to be given it. One minute they were going to execute me, the next — well, here I am." He shook his head sadly. "But there we are, it's done and can't be helped, and now it's all on my shoulders, whether I like it or not." He looked up. "You don't mind me telling you all that, do you?"

The ambassador was staring at him. "No, of course not. Your frankness is —"

"The thing is," Psellus went on, looking over the ambassador's shoulder at a mark on the wall, "I really do have to find a way of saving the City, because nobody else is willing or able, and so if I don't do it — well, it's not something that bears thinking about. So, I've got to manage it somehow, but I don't know the first thing about diplomacy, so I'm not even going to try. I'm going to ask you to bear with me while I do the best I can. Is that all right?"

The ambassador nodded. He seemed to be having trouble finding any words.

"Thank you," Psellus said. "This is how I think matters stand, and perhaps you'll be kind enough to tell me if I've got it all disastrously wrong. Now, then. Like me, you can't really bring yourself to believe that the savages will be able to take the City, even though there's a quite ridiculously huge number of them, and they've got the abominator Vaatzes helping them, which means if they haven't already built siege engines as good as the ones we make, they'll do so pretty soon. No, you look at our walls and the city gates, and you think — just as I used to do — there's no power on earth that could ever crack that particular nut, engines or no engines." He paused to draw breath, then went on. "But you know that we haven't got any proper soldiers anymore; we have no army of our own, and so many mercenaries got killed fighting the Eremians and the Vadani that they simply don't want to work for us anymore, especially now the savages have found a way of crossing the desert and have joined up with our enemies. You believe — quite rightly, of course — that we're terrified, feeling helpless, we don't know what to do, and so we'd be willing to pay anything and make any concessions you'd care to name in return for the loan of your army, just to make us feel a little bit safer until we've had a chance to pull ourselves together and figure out how we're going to defend our city." He paused again, smiled meekly and asked, "Is that about right, or have I misunderstood you entirely?"

"That's about right," the ambassador said.

"Splendid, I'm glad about that. It's so important that people tell me when I make mistakes, or how will I ever learn better? Anyway, I'm sure you know much more about fighting wars than any of us do, so you must've assessed the position and decided that the advantages — the concessions you can screw out of us while we're on our knees like this — outweigh the rather dreadful risk you're running, picking a fight with a million savages. Oh, did you know that, by the way? Actually, it's closer to eight hundred thousand soldiers, when you leave out the carters and drovers and all the people in the army who don't actually fight, but that's still an awful lot. You do know; excellent. Well, of course you do, now I come to think of it; I imagine you're who gave us the figures in the first place, because we haven't got any scouts, and who else would be out there counting?" Psellus smiled again, and continued. "Now I'm the last person to tell you that you've made a bad decision, and it's very encouraging to know you've got so much faith in us, since you know so much more about these things than we do. I still can't help thinking that in your shoes, the last thing I'd want to do is let myself get dragged into a war that's none of my business, fighting against a vast army of savages who'll wipe me off the face of the earth if they win. Still, if that's a risk you're happy to take, far be it from me to argue with you. We need you desperately and in return you can have anything you want."

There was a long, dead silence. "Anything?"

Psellus nodded vigorously. "You name it. Money, land — you can have Eremia if we win, it's no use to us, or the Vadani silver mines if you'd prefer, it's entirely up to you. Just say what you want and I'll have a treaty drawn up. And in return, you'll lend us your army. Well?"

The ambassador took a moment to clear his throat. "Agreed," he said.

"Splendid." Psellus beamed at him. "There, we've made an alliance, and it was so much easier than I thought it'd be. When Boioannes was in charge, it used to take weeks to hammer out a treaty, and he knew a lot about diplomacy, unlike me. Now, how soon can your soldiers get here? Or —" Psellus frowned. "Here's where it gets difficult again. I don't know whether we need them here at the City, or whether they'd be more useful hindering the savages and making it hard for them to reach us. You're the expert. What do you think?"

Nothing in the ambassador's long and varied experience had prepared him for a question like that. "It's a complicated decision," he said. "On the one hand —"

"The way I see it," Psellus went on, "an army of a million people is obviously a great advantage in a battle, no doubt about it, but until you actually get to the battlefield, it's also a tremendous problem. Must be. Food and so forth, hay for the horses, clean water. Now, we've done a little research — dreadful, really, it's taken something like this to make us realize just how woefully ignorant we are about everything other than making things and selling them — and we can't see how the enemy can keep themselves fed and watered just from what they can find in the fields and villages, which means they must be having to bring in their food and so on from somewhere else. God only knows where," Psellus added with a grin. "I mean to say, you increase the population of the mountain duchies by a million, the Eremians and the Vadani could only just about feed themselves at the best of times, so it's not like there can be any huge granaries bursting at the seams with stockpiled sacks of flour. Probably some of your merchants have been trading with them — it's perfectly all right, I quite understand — but from what little I know about your people, I don't suppose that can have made much difference. No, the only source of supply I can think of is the savages' own herds of cattle — they're nomads, as I'm sure you know, that's how they live, and they must have managed to bring their cattle with them across the desert when they came. Which is fine, of course, from their point of view, except that there can't be all that much pasture in the mountains for all those hundreds of thousands of animals; and when the grass has all been eaten, and any hay that our men overlooked while they were there, they'll have to slaughter most of them before they starve. And yes, they can salt down the carcasses, but even that won't last forever. Time, you see. They're almost as short of it as we are." Psellus stopped talking for a moment, as if thinking about something, then added, "Of course, all this stuff is just what's occurred to me while I've been thinking about it, and like I've told you already, I'm hopelessly ignorant about military matters, so I may have got it all completely wrong. But if I'm right — and if I'm not, do please say so — it seems to me that the best use we can make of your army is messing about with their lines of supply. Would you agree?"

The ambassador hesitated, as though trying to translate what he'd heard into a language he could understand. "Of course," he said. "It's the only logical —"

"Though of course," Psellus went on, "there's a bit more to it than that. The last thing we want to do is make them come here before we've done what we can to get ready for them. If your soldiers were to drive off all their cattle, it could force them to attack us straightaway, simply because the only reserve of food large enough to feed them and close enough to be any use is what we've got here — though I think you ought to know, we're not exactly well provided for in that department ourselves. Of course, I've made arrangements for every ship we can buy or hire to bring in as much food as possible from across the sea — the old country won't send us soldiers anymore, but they're still happy to sell us wheat, thank goodness — but it's all got to come in through Lonazep, and I understand it's absolute chaos there at the moment. Still, they probably don't know that, and if they do, it's not as though they'd have a choice, if we somehow contrived to run off all their livestock. So, we don't want to leave them starving. We just want to slow them right down, so we've got time to build up our walls and get in as much food as we can for a long siege. That's our best chance, I reckon. If it's a matter of who starves first, I think we can win. If it comes to fighting, we might as well not bother." Psellus breathed out (he still wasn't used to talking uninterrupted for so long), then added, "Do you think I'm on the right lines here, or have I got it all wrong? Really, I'd value your opinion. It's been such a worry, trying to learn all this very difficult stuff in such a tearing hurry. It'd be such a relief if an expert like yourself can reassure me I haven't made a dreadful mess of it all."

The ambassador looked at him warily for a while, then said, "Can I ask you what you did before all this?"

"I was a clerk."

"A —"

Psellus nodded. "I was a records clerk for nine years, after I'd finished my apprenticeship. Then I got my transfer from the executive to the administrative grade. I was a junior secretary in the Compliance directorate for six years, and then general secretary for five years after that. And then," he added sadly, "Ziani Vaatzes came along, and now look at me. Lord of all I survey. I met him once, did you know that? Vaatzes. He's the key to it all, of course." Psellus shook his head. "I'm terribly sorry, I'm rambling, and you're a busy man. Now then, about this army of yours."

Later, in the ten minutes or so between appointments (he had his beautiful clock to thank for such an indecent degree of precision; he still loved it for its beauty, but it nagged him like a wife), he wrote down the minutes of his meeting with the ambassador and compared them with the plan he'd prepared beforehand. Well, he thought, now at least we have a few soldiers, thanks to the incredible stupidity of the Cure Doce. He still couldn't quite believe it. But then, they'd been brought up to believe the Republic was invincible — invincible and gullible. Two mistakes, and they'd probably cost the Cure Doce their existence. Not that it mattered, if they could buy him time to turn the City into one of those extraordinary star shapes he'd seen in the book.

He put the sheet of minutes on the pile of papers to be filed and spent his last two minutes of solitary peace going over his plan for the meeting with the architects. He would never be able to understand the book, but they might.

Suddenly, he smiled. Wouldn't it be a superb piece of irony, he thought, if we actually contrived to get away with it? A million enemies, and we beat them because there's too many of them to take the city. The sheer perversity of it appealed to him enormously. They lose, because they sent a million men to do the job of fifty thousand; I beat a million men by fighting just one.

Which reminded him. He pulled a fresh sheet of paper from the pile, inked his pen and wrote, wastefully, in the middle of the page:

His wife

VISIT THE ORBIT BLOG AT

www.orbitbooks.net

FEATURING

BREAKING NEWS
FORTHCOMING RELEASES
LINKS TO AUTHOR SITES
EXCLUSIVE INTERVIEWS
EARLY EXTRACTS

AND COMMENTARY FROM OUR EDITORS

WITH REGULAR UPDATES FROM OUR TEAM,
ORBITBOOKS.NET IS YOUR SOURCE
FOR ALL THINGS ORBITAL.

WHILE YOU'RE THERE, JOIN OUR EMAIL LIST
TO RECEIVE INFORMATION ON SPECIAL OFFERS,
GIVEAWAYS, AND MORE.

imagine. explore. engage.